The Mammoth Encyclopedia of
SCIENCE FICTION

The Mammoth Encyclopedia of
SCIENCE FICTION

by
George Mann

ROBINSON
London

Constable Publishers
3 The Lanchesters
162 Fulham Palace Road
London W6 9ER
www.constablerobinson.com

First published in the UK by Robinson,
an imprint of Constable & Robinson Ltd, 2001

First published in the USA by St. Martin's Press 1999

A copy of the British Library Cataloguing in
Publication Data is available from the British Library.

ISBN 1–84119–177–9

Printed and bound in the EU

10 9 8 7 6 5 4 3 2 1

To Scott, because he wasn't there when the cup smashed . . .

And to Keith, for the Sunday-afternoon lessons in 'Word Alchemy'. I haven't forgotten . . .

Contents

Acknowledgments

There are many people who have helped me find my way to producing this book – most know who they are. I would particularly like to mention my family in its many varied forms, Steve Robinson, Jon Howells and all at Ottakar's, Steve Baxter, Peter F. Hamilton and William Palmer for making me realize it was possible, Michael Boshier for the beer and the friendship, Chris Smith because I promised I would, Murphy for getting in the way, Krystyna Green for making it all happen, and my partner Fiona for her undying patience, love and support.

I am grateful to you all.

The author would like to add that any mistakes or omissions are his own.

Foreword

The Mammoth Encyclopedia of Science Fiction is a book written for fans, by a fan. It is a book for anyone who has ever enjoyed science fiction or who wishes to know more about the genre.

My original aim was simple – to provide you, the reader, with an up-to-date guide to the science fiction genre. So inside this book you will find entries on both classic and up-and-coming writers, on movies and television series, as well as the important themes and devices of the genre. Obviously I have had to limit my remit – some authors only just missed out on an entry. The same can be said about the entries for science fiction movies – I have limited myself to the one hundred most influential pieces of genre film, or those that have a direct link to a classic novel. I have also provided entries on the twenty most important or popular television series from both America and the UK.

Within the author entries are links to various other sections of the book, as well as lists of recommended further reading that suggest authors who explore similar themes or who have written novels in similar styles. I hope you find these useful. I have also included an appendix at the back of the book that gives all the listed titles in alphabetical order, referenced by author. As far as I know this is the first time this has been done and it should enable you to find quickly the name of the author who wrote a particular novel, and then to locate the entry on that author within the book.

Most importantly, I hope that this reference work will allow you to discover new authors and thus broaden your literary horizons. Science fiction is a genre of limitless possibilities and ideas, and there is something within it for everyone. I hope that this book helps you with your search.

George Mann
October 2000

The History and Origins
of Science Fiction

Science Fiction begins in prehistory.

Or, perhaps, if you listen to some critics, with Thomas More, with Voltaire, with MARY SHELLEY's *Frankenstein* (1818), with the stories of EDGAR ALLAN POE, with JULES VERNE or H. G. WELLS or, indeed, with HUGO GERNSBACK and his AMAZING STORIES magazine of the 1920s.

If taken on its most basic level, as a form of fantastic fiction, science fiction (from now on referred to as SF) is as old as storytelling itself. But surely this is not the case? Shouldn't SF, by its very name, include at least some allusion to science and scientific theory?

The origins of the SF genre are as hotly debated as those of any other established branch of literature, and the disagreement that surrounds the topic is almost as complex as the questions themselves. What is the first novel that can truly be called SF? And do we take this as our starting point, or was there a crucible or melting pot of ideas from which it was formed? Indeed, what is it that actually makes an SF novel SF?

In other words, to find the origins of our genre, we must first go in search of definition.

What is SF?

Most people feel that they can recognize SF when they come across it in their daily lives, whether it is a novel or an episode in a television drama. Indeed, when used as a marketing tool SF is defined in broad and inclusive terms, taking in everything from space vessels and laser guns to kooky aliens and vampires. This is not necessarily helpful.

For SF to be recognized as a distinct genre, there have to be some boundaries, rules or ideal parameters that define what constitutes science fiction and exclude what doesn't.

Let us take two examples from literature and see where they lead us. First, the classic novel *Titus Groan* (1946) by Mervyn Peake. In this work the author portrays the lives of a group of people who exist within the confines of an enormous castle, Gormenghast. This castle is effectively a city unto itself, so huge and labyrinthine that much of it remains unexplored by its current inhabitants who go about their lives according to a set of obsessively detailed scriptures and ancient regulations that give the place a real sense of oppressively looming history. Peake explores in great depth the bizarre environment of these people and examines in telling detail the effect it has on the inhabitants themselves. He does not concern himself with how the castle of Gormenghast came to exist originally nor with where it is to be found, neither does he establish the means by which this particular cross-section of humanity has come to be there. It simply *is*.

Now set this alongside FRANK HERBERT's comparably epic *Dune* (1965).

In *Dune*, Herbert sets out, in much the same manner as Peake, to describe in painstaking detail an imaginary world, the PLANET Arrakis, and the way of life that its ecology imposes upon its necessarily hardy inhabitants. However, what sets *Dune* apart from *Titus Groan* is the manner in which its author establishes his invented world. Herbert goes to great lengths to place the distant planet in a recognizable, if unavoidably remote human context – an interstellar Empire that has arisen and developed over many years, discovering in the process other habitable worlds upon which to settle colonies. He describes in true ECOLOGICAL terms the physical geography of the planet, even to the consistency of its soil, and the various forms of life that may have evolved in this environment over time. He does not make it easy for his human characters to get by, forcing them to live strictly according to the description he has given of his world – for example, by having them wear rubber 'stillsuits' that enable them to recycle their body fluids: Arrakis is a vast parched desert with no water supply of its own. Some of the characters have technological implements to aid them in their quest for survival, others do not. Some of the author's extrapolations are credible, others are not.

At one point Herbert even explains the characters' dreams of making the planet more hospitable to human life, and the TERRAFORMING process by which they plan to do it. But what is most important about *Dune* is its intrinsic attempt at realism, as the lives of the characters are shaped by the scientifically defined landscape of their environment.

This comparison between two classic works of imaginative fiction, one fantasy, the other science fiction is by no means the final word on the subject, and is at best an over-generalization. But it can be seen as representative of the relationship between much fantasy and SF. Science fiction is a literature concerned with the *process* by which a depicted environment has become different from our own, or with the *means* by which humanity finds itself there. This does not rule out narrative elements of intrigue, adventure and so forth, far from it, but it does imply that SF will attempt to examine the wider picture, for example by questioning how aliens might have developed on Mars and exploring the effects that their existence could have upon the way in which human beings view themselves and the wider universe. One of the best ways to envisage a time different from our own, to devise a temporal 'laboratory' within which to test new ideas, is to look forward to the future. SF emphasizes its difference from fantasy by attempting to construct a rational framework for anything that it describes.

This, however, is not to say that the genres cannot usefully interact with each other. SCIENCE FANTASY or SPACE OPERA will use devices derived from SF to describe new and exciting environments, but in many ways both subcategories remain more true to the pulp-fiction genres of the 1920s and 1930s. This is because they do not bother to make plausible their invented futures, being more concerned with the adventure components of their storylines and more willing to go beyond the realms of scientific plausibility to create spectacular effects. This is another factor that can make it more difficult for us to reach a satisfactory definition of 'real' SF.

There is also the question of actual science.

Most true SF stories will, in their attempt to render credible their particular vision of the future, draw upon some scientific theory or device to strengthen its plausibility. However, there is also a school of thought that argues that 'softer' disciplines like psychology and sociology should also be considered as sciences. This has interesting implications for SF.

ALFRED BESTER's *The Demolished Man* (1953) is a good example of this. The novel depicts a society within which the majority of people have telepathic powers – hardly a scientifically plausible notion. However, in his exploration of the theme, Bester clearly considers the rational arguments for and against telepathy, and attempts to extrapolate as clearly and as realistically as he can the effects that the introduction of psychic powers would have on society. He describes an America that has evolved very differently than it would have under 'normal' circumstances, a UTOPIA of sorts, in which crime is rarely heard of and can usually be detected before it even takes place. However, Bester also examines the other side of the coin, and shows how this type of environment could be seen as oppressive and even dangerous. What Bester does in *The Demolished Man*, and what makes it a genuine SF novel, is to devise one (admittedly implausible) change to society and then extrapolate coherently the repercussions that the introduction of this change would have on the development of civilization. His book is a triumph of sociological speculation and in its method, if not in its use of conventional science, it exemplifies true science fiction.

The same can be said of much ALTERNATE WORLD fiction.

Gloriana, or the Unfulfill'd Queen (1978) by MICHAEL MOORCOCK examines the possibilities of a British Elizabethan Empire that differs completely from the historical records but whose ambience is often fantastical and in keeping with period fantasias such as William Shakespeare's *A Midsummer Night's Dream* (first performed c. 1596, published 1600) and Edmund Spenser's *The Faerie Queene* (1590–1596). KEITH ROBERTS's *Pavane* (1968), on the other hand, is realistic and hard-hitting, attempting to extrapolate realistically how society might have developed if the Spanish Armada had defeated Drake's navy and the British Isles had remained a Papal dominion. *Pavane* is SF not so much in its content as in its telling. It is meticulous and thoroughly worked out.

So SF, by necessity, is an open and wide-ranging genre whose definition can have as much to do with the way in which a book is written as with its content. It also incorporates the more fantastical Space Opera, which, although it has its proponents who insist on claiming a 'scientific' foundation for the intergalactic conflicts and militaristic alien invasions, for the most part prefers to concentrate on the end result – spectacular action – rather than the means – convincing extrapolation. This inclusiveness makes any binding definition hazardous, but it is fairly safe to assume that most 'real' SF is covered by the following loose description:

SF is a form of fantastic literature that attempts to portray, in rational and realistic terms, future times and environments that are different from our own. It will nevertheless show an awareness of the concerns of the times in which it is written and provide implicit commentary on contemporary society, exploring the effects, material and psychological, that any new technologies may have upon it. Any further changes that take place in this society, as well as any extrapolated future events or occurrences, will have their basis in measured and considered theory, scientific or otherwise. SF authors will use their strange and imaginative environments as a testing ground for new ideas, considering in full the implications of any notion they propose.

Obviously, many SF novels and stories fail to achieve what they set out initially to do, and many of the more space-opera-type stories are written as sheer entertainment. But it is the way in which they are written and their attempts to adhere to rational, recognizable frameworks that make them truly science fiction.

So, with these guidelines in mind, let us consider the origins of the genre and attempt to locate the first true example of an SF novel.

The Origins of SF

The foundations of SF were laid many thousands of years ago, with such wonderful works of mythology as *The Epic of Gilgamesh* and *The Egyptian Book of the Dead*. There is no way in which these ancient texts can be meaningfully interpreted as science fiction, but they do offer us a starting point for a more general form of fantastic literature that points the way to the eventual emergence of the genre. But, of course, it was not until much, much later that SF would actually develop as a distinct branch of literature.

It is important to remember that, for as long as human beings have been able to communicate ideas to one another, allegorical tales have existed as a useful testing ground for new ideas. However, it is only during the last two or three centuries that a recognizably modern scientific viewpoint has formed and begun to pervade both society and literature. Until this point, most fantastical writing had been of a RELIGIOUS nature and, as such, was intent upon perpetuating the pious myths upon which it was based, as well as these myths' underlying lessons and philosophies. For the most part, it is unhelpful and often harmful to the credibility of the genre to attempt retrospectively to classify this sort of material as SF.

In 1516 Thomas More published, in Latin, his famous political work *Utopia*, which displays a particularly resonant awareness of its time and extrapolates contemporary political thought to create its setting. An English translation appeared in 1551. It describes, in great detail, an unknown island (clearly modelled on the recently discovered America) where a 'perfect' society has been established – the first depiction of a Utopian state. The book is fundamentally satirical, as More intends it to be known that he does not believe that such a profound social equilibrium as he depicts could ever be reached. His book triggered an explosion of Utopian fictions: they continue to appear today, but are ultimately more correctly considered as political rather than science fictional writings.

Utopia does, however, indicate the direction that fantastical literature was beginning to take.

There followed a succession of fantastical works over the next few centuries, as writers began to make use of devices that would later become intimately associated with the SF genre. *Gulliver's Travels* (1726: rev. 1735) by Jonathan Swift is one fine example, as is Voltaire's lesser-known *Micromégas* (1752). Both are satirical and use devices such as ALIENS and strange new worlds as a means of commenting on the society of their contemporaries. These are not the alien races that would come to appear much later in episodes of STAR TREK, but metaphorical humans with no previous experience of our culture. Their ignorance is used to satirical and often ingenious effect. Nevertheless, these stories remain, ultimately, fantasies.

So what is the first true SF novel – and when did it appear?

BRIAN ALDISS proposes in his excellent history of the genre, *Billion Year Spree* (1973), that we should view the classic Gothic Romance by MARY SHELLEY, *Frankenstein, or the Modern Prometheus* (1818), as the first novel to be truly recognizable as SF. There are many grounds for agreeing with him.

Frankenstein shows a keen awareness of the technological and scientific knowledge of its time, and develops this to form the basis of the novel. From some perspectives, *Frankenstein* shows clearly the beginnings of the development of SF as a form distinct from other fantastical literature. In a similar way to much other fiction of the time, *Frankenstein* draws on images taken from philosophy, poetry and mythology but adds the extra dimension of science. It is essentially a Gothic Romance in which Shelley, bravely, used current scientific thought to render her demon credible. The monster is no longer a devilish entity that simply exists – it is created, bit by bit, by a human being, and literally shocked into existence with electricity. Magic or mystical invocations are nowhere in sight and although religious analogies are drawn, they remain purely metaphysical. Science, not religion, has become the key to unlocking life.

Shelley's novel represents a bold step forward into a new way of thinking, and shines a light ahead of itself, making further exploration possible. In *Frankenstein*, Shelley opened up a Pandora's box of notions and ideas that had been bubbling away under the surface of society for years. She gave them voice and form, and proved herself to be years ahead of her time.

It is fair to say that *Frankenstein* represents the first true SF novel to appear, according to our previous definition. However, there are reasons to believe that the novel had an even more significant bearing on the

Gothic Romance, and it is also important to mention that, until the middle of the twentieth century, *Frankenstein* did not have a big influence on the development of the SF genre. It stands alone as a testament to the foresight of one young woman, and it was not until many years later, when the genre was already established, that it would be recognized as the classic piece of SF that it is.

It took a few years more and the work of a number of other writers before the genre began to emerge in its current and recognizable form.

It is important to mention here the work of the nineteenth-century American writer EDGAR ALLAN POE who has been lauded by a number of critics, nowhere more memorably than in THOMAS DISCH's study of the SF genre *The Dreams Our Stuff is Made Of* (1998), as the first writer of what today's reader might accept as genre fiction. While it remains undeniable that Poe has had a more direct and profound influence on the modern HORROR story, exemplified in the work of such writers as Stephen King and Clive Barker, it is nonetheless notable that a number of his stories make use of ideas that would later become associated with SF. In the works of Poe we encounter alien races existing out in the ether of space, we witness balloon flights to the moon, and we peruse the travel journals of a twenty-ninth-century woman. The power of these stories is undeniable and they represent the seeds that would eventually flower into the modern genre, yet they remain, like the fantstical tales that had preceded them, allegorical fantasies.

The 'fantastic journey' and the utopian/anti-utopian story developed into a more recognizably modern form of SF with the publication of the first SCIENTIFIC ROMANCE, the French author Jules Verne's *Journey to the Centre of the Earth* (1863).

Scientific Romance

The 'Scientific Romance' represents the first real step on the road towards the consolidation of the central ideas and themes of SF into one dominant form, the first version of science fiction in a recognizably 'modern' manifestation. The term did not actually come into use until about thirty years after Verne's *Journey to the Centre of the Earth*, with the publication of H. G. Wells's *The Time Machine* (1895), but it is legitimate as well as convenient to consider Verne in the same context.

Journey to the Centre of the Earth achieves much. Its precision of detail is certainly inspired by the works of Poe (whom Verne admired greatly, to the extent that he later wrote a sequel to Poe's *The Narrative of Arthur Gordon*

Pym (1837)), but it shows a more clear and ready grasp of science and the scientific method. It describes the descent of Professor Von Hardwigg and his spirited nephew Harry into the mouth of an Icelandic volcano, from which they go on to discover a subterranean world inhabited by prehistoric monsters. The author approaches the scenario itself with judicious logic, explaining how these dinosaurs could have survived for so long in isolation, but it is the manner in which the character of Von Hardwigg, a chemist and mineralogist, approaches his discovery that is most enlightening. The novel is full of the scientific speculation of the day. It casts a scientist in the lead role, and shows very clearly how he uses the scientific method to aid him in his quest to discover how this subterranean world has come about. It is also an adventure, and – this is important to remember – it was widely read and therefore had an important and far-reaching influence on other writers of the day.

If *Journey to the Centre of the Earth* marks the beginning of SF as a definite genre, then Verne's later works *From the Earth to the Moon* (1865), *Twenty Thousand Leagues under the Sea* (1870) and *The Mysterious Island* (1874) represent its continued growth, as he toys with new ideas and continues to develop imaginative scenarios that can nonetheless be explained logically in terms of cause and effect. Verne did not create mere fantasy lands. He wanted to know from whence they came.

It is this insistence on a fundamental realism that has caused Verne's novels to be retrospectively seen as of key importance in the development of SF. It is also significant that they were translated and read all over the world – people in droves came to the books looking for adventure and got it, but with an edge of scientific inquiry that left them with a new, very different SENSE OF WONDER. The magic of the realms of fantasy had been superseded by the fascination of speculation rooted in reality.

These 'extraordinary voyages', as they were then known, had an exceptional influence on the work of many writers, including that of EDWIN A. ABBOTT and ROBERT LOUIS STEVENSON. But their most profound effect was on the British writer H. G. Wells, whose *The Time Machine* (1895) represents the definitive moment at which science fiction came of age.

Wells's *The Time Machine* is the epitome of a science fiction novel, marking the important leap from Verne's adventurous 'extraordinary voyages' to fully fledged SF.

It achieves this in a number of ways.

Firstly, it postulates a device, based on a scientific theory, that will see its character transported forward through time to various stages in the existence of man. It extrapolates from current EVOLUTIONARY theory to justify its portrayal of future humanity as two distinct species. Perhaps most importantly, it also uses scientific speculation to comment critically on the Victorian society of Wells's own time.

Wells wanted to stir up the complacent Victorians and provide them with what he thought could be an accurate vision of their future. He saw the gentle yet docile Eloi race as symbolic of the effete upper classes, whilst the Morlocks represented the descendants of the uneducated but more evolutionarily successful worker underclass. His fictional future was a satire on Victorian society, but it was also scientifically plausible according to the speculation about evolution that was current at the time.

The Time Machine pioneered the use of many SF concepts that have now become genre clichés, so often have they been recycled by other writers over the years. Indeed, the story culminates in what has become one of the most enduring images of the genre, the terminal beach, as the Time Traveller watches the final, dying moments of the Earth before the Sun expands to swallow the planet. Wells was not optimistic about the future, and in *The Time Machine* he attempted to show his Victorian readers one possible means by which they might eventually bring about their own downfall.

Everything about *The Time Machine* was fresh and original. Wells had given readers an ostensibly 'scientific' method for traversing the time streams: he posited a device created through the application of advanced science that would allow its inventor to actually visit times to come. The book was revolutionary, and in a similar way to the works of Verne it put scientific thought at the forefront of modern literature. Science had opened the door to the future.

Wells did not stop there, and in the heady years that followed he produced some of the finest writing that the genre has ever seen. Who can forget the end of *The War of the Worlds* (1898), in which malignant Martian invaders are destroyed not by human resistance, but by a simple strain of the common cold? In this and the books that followed, including such titles as *The Invisible Man* (1897), *The First Men in the Moon* (1901) and *The Island of Dr Moreau* (1896), Wells set out a template for the development of the genre that would eventually come to be known not by its original name of 'Scientific Romance' but as Science Fiction.

Dawn of the Magazines

Whilst the themes and concerns of Scientific Romance continued to attract a large readership and to be explored by many authors in Britain and Europe in the years after the First World War (the works of OLAF STAPLEDON are a notable example), a rather different development was under way in the United States.

'Pulp' magazines and 'Dime' novels began to featrure SF stories and found that their sales soared. This helped to popularize the emerging genre, generating a dedicated fan base that would later develop into both a readership and, ultimately, a good source of new authors.

However, the founding of *Amazing Stories* magazine in 1926 by editor Hugo Gernsback represented the first real attempt to put SF before the reading public as a distinct genre in its own right.

Gernsback was perfect for the job. He had previously worked as an editor on popular science magazines such as *Modern Electrics* and *Science and Invention*. Alongside scientific articles in these early magazines, Gernsback had regularly published examples of what he called 'Scientifiction' – fiction with a grounding in scientific fact. Most of it was stylistically stiff and rather too conventional, lacking the narrative drive and sense of adventure of the Scientific Romance of the day, in many cases simply acting as a text showcase for new technological ideas or gadgets. Indeed, Gernsback's sole novel, *Ralph 124C41+* (1925), written along these lines, is generally regarded as unreadable today.

But with the founding of *Amazing Stories*, things changed. Gernsback obtained the rights to republish and serialize the works of Poe, Wells and Verne, and encouraged readers to submit stories with a distinctive technological edge. This in turn gave US writers an outlet for their work, and fostered a trend for technophilia in their fiction. The advent of science fiction as a mass-appeal genre was just around the corner.

Amazing Stories was an immediate success, and although many of its early stories had the same faults that had plagued the tales that had appeared previously in *Modern Electrics* and *Science and Invention*, the magazine did see the first publication of writers such as E.E. 'DOC' SMITH and Jack Williamson. Much of this newer work was an early form of Space Opera, but it drew on existing genre ideas and adhered to the rules of Gernsback's 'Scientifiction'.

It was not long before the unwieldy 'Scientifiction' became known as 'Science Fiction'. The genre as we know it today had received its name.

Gernsback's reign at *Amazing Stories* was beset by financial difficulties and in 1929 he lost control of the magazine. It was sold on to other owners and continued to publish a range of stories, maintaining Gernsback's standards but serializing too a number of good pulp novels that kept it operating as a buoyant concern.

Gernsback himself went on to found other SF magazines such as *Scientific Detective Stories* and *Air Wonder Stories*, but never managed to repeat the success he had achieved with his former magazine, the possible exception being *Wonder Stories* (an amalgamation of *Air Wonder Stories* and *Science Wonder Stories*), which ran for a healthy number of issues during the early 1930s.

Amazing Stories itself has been sporadically relaunched ever since, with its latest incarnation under the ownership of the games company Wizards of the Coasts ceasing publication as recently as the year 2000. It now looks set to make a return as an Internet-based concern.

However, where *Amazing Stories* had experienced financial problems during the early 1930s, a new magazine named *Astounding Stories* had thrived. *Astounding Stories* had started publishing just four years after *Amazing Stories* and, offering better rates of pay, had attracted many of the other magazine's best writers.

Initially, *Astounding*'s stories had a more adventurous slant than those that appeared in *Amazing Stories*, and many writers were keen to join in with the sense of pulp fun that was prevalent in the magazine at the time. Scientific speculation was a constant feature but only when it helped the writer tell the story; essentially, *Astounding Stories* was a melodramatic pulp.

But, things were soon to change. When JOHN W. CAMPBELL took over as chief editor of *Astounding Stories* in 1937, the GOLDEN AGE of science fiction was about to dawn.

John W. Campbell and the Golden Age of SF

The original Golden Age of SF is believed by many to have occurred during the war years of 1939–43. It was arguably the most important period in SF history, and saw the emergence of many of the classic writers, as well as the establishment of a more sober and serious tone for the genre. There is little doubt that this maturing of the genre was partly due to the Second World War and the effect that it was having on the mood of the time, but much of it can also be put down to the constant and attentive work of editor John W. Campbell.

A little more than a year after Campbell had taken over as editor of *Astounding Stories*, he had already changed the name. *Astounding Science Fiction* was the new legend that was printed on the front of each issue, and with this change in title came an important and revolutionary change in content.

The year 1939 saw the debuts of a number of important SF authors – ROBERT A. HEINLEIN, THEODORE STURGEON, A. E. VAN VOGT – as well as good work from established writers such as ISAAC ASIMOV and E. E. 'Doc' Smith. Campbell nurtured these authors, insisting that they worked through fully and logically any ideas they proposed and asking them to consider the sociological and psychological effects of their notions and to translate them into stories of greater maturity and depth. The authors responded enthusiastically and although it alienated some readers who had grown to admire the more pulp-orientated theme of the magazine, it turned *Astounding Science Fiction* into the true mouthpiece of the genre.

The Golden Age period saw the development of many of the key concepts of SF that would later come to define the field. The authors took ideas from the pages of the early pulps, and then subverted them, turning them into something new and even more exciting. Science became an integral part of many of the stories, as authors developed aspects of current scientific theories or ideas. Indeed, some of these writers were scientists in their own right.

It was from this heady brew that the important sub-genre of HARD SF was to be distilled, a form of powerfully science-loaded SF that would later, in a further incarnation, come to dominate the magazine.

During the years from 1939 to 1943 *Astounding Science Fiction* featured some of the most wonderful short stories and serializations ever to be written. Heinlein developed his FUTURE HISTORY in its pages, Asimov his *Robot* and *Foundation* sequences, Van Vogt published *Slan* and Smith his entire *Lensman* saga. Campbell encouraged them all, and when L. RON HUBBARD proposed his pseudo-science, 'Dianetics', Campbell encouraged him too. Campbell devoted himself to the ideal of raising the standards of SF and providing readers with steadfast adventure stories that were nevertheless fully thought out and expertly realized. It is hard to quantify the overall effect that Campbell had on genre fiction; many authors credit him with having provided not just the impetus to write intelligent and coherent science fiction, but the actual ideas on which they were to base their stories and novels. The Golden Age period is a testament to his editorial skills.

Campbell remained in the editorial seat of *Astounding Science Fiction* until his death in 1971, overseeing a further change of name – to ANALOG – and a later reassessment of the magazine's contents. It continues to be published under the latter name today.

After the war years, there was an inevitable change in the way in which

SF was both published and perceived. Magazines continued to thrive, and if *Astounding Science Fiction* was seen to be growing a little stale, a little too emphatic about the 'hard' sciences such as physics, chemistry and biology, then newer magazines such as THE MAGAZINE OF FANTASY AND SCIENCE FICTION and GALAXY were just beginning. These magazines saw a shift towards the 'softer' sciences such as psychology and sociology, and demanded a higher level of literary ability from their writers. Authors such as PHILIP K. DICK and ALFRED BESTER were writing their own particular brands of SF, more experimental stories that would never have found a market in Campbell's *Astounding Science Fiction*. Over in Britain, NEW WORLDS was making an impact with similar material and during the 1950s its editor, John Carnell, would reprint many of the excellent stories that appeared in the American magazines of this time.

The 1930s and 1940s also saw a number of mainstream authors such as ALDOUS HUXLEY in *Brave New World* (1932) and GEORGE ORWELL in *Nineteen Eighty-Four* (1949) make use of SF ideas and concepts. In some ways this highlights the shift in the public's perception of the genre that was beginning to take place. Science fiction was becoming respectable.

The 'Cosy Catastrophe' and the Reader as Hero

The 1950s brought with it a boom in paperback publishing, in which SF shared. In the US Ace Books began running a series of back-to-back novels, *Ace Doubles*, featuring two different authors presented in one paperback. Philip K. Dick, amongst others, made this his home territory.

Science fiction was beginning to move away from a magazine-dominated market and into the world of books, and this meant that full-length novels had to be written quickly and efficiently. Dick fuelled his vast output with amphetamines, but most other authors kept to more reliable methods.

In some ways this lengthening of the basic SF format meant a partial return to the pulp disciplines of the genre: writers' word-outputs had to increase significantly. In other ways, however, it provided greater scope for characterization and the detailed exploration of psychological and sociological themes. This in turn led gradually to a general darkening of tone and a less optimistic outlook on the future.

The end of the Second World War had been a triumphant time for the Allied forces, and there were inevitable celebrations as the soldiers returned home. But as time passed people began to realize the startling effect that the war had had on their lives and to understand more fully the devastation it had wrought across the globe. The 1950s was a time of consolidation and recuperation as the world took stock of the damage and families came to terms with their losses of loved ones. No one wanted to read about heroic superhumans saving the world or about ambitious space missions. Public perceptions were changing, and with them the protagonists who inhabited the pages of SF.

The self-reliant hero was gone, and in his place stood the average man (women's liberation by the 1960s feminist movement lay some years in the future), much like the typical SF reader who, far from being a daredevil who knew how to react in any given situation, stood bemused and baffled by the changing world around him. If aliens invaded, they preyed on small towns with no impregnable protection, or took over the minds of ordinary individuals so that nobody would notice until it was too late.

This is typified nowhere better than in the work of the British writer JOHN WYNDHAM.

Wyndam's writing shifted up a gear after the war; whereas before he had mainly written pseudonymous pulp fiction, he now began publishing disaster novels that mirrored people's fear of foreign invasion and the political paranoia caused by the advent of the Cold War. His most famous novel, *The Day of the Triffids* (1951), has a pervasive sense of unease about it, exactly the type of 'man against the world' scenario that was typical of the SF of the day. The chief protagonist's sight is saved because he is blindfolded (following hospital treatment) when orbital flares scorch the vision of most of the world's population. Genetically modified mobile plants, 'Triffids', with lethal whiplike stings attempt to take over, capitalizing on the fact that nearly everyone is blind. They soon gain a hold and eventually the bewildered protagonist, his female partner and their child retreat to a secure area – the Isle of Wight – where they can try to live out a 'normal' existence. The critical point is this: he does not attempt to save the world (though he is determined, at the end of the novel, to devote his life to eradicating the triffid menace) and he is not a 'typical' hero. He is a man trying to protect his family from the horrors of a world in decline and wants nothing more than to survive – something every reader can relate to. There is no room for wish-fulfilment in the stories of this period, no time for high adventure or monster-bashing. People only wanted to make sense of the changing world around them.

Typically, in Wyndham's novel middle-class virtues prevail and survival, of a kind, is secured for the main characters. A comfortable compromise solution for those who had just faced the terrors of a world war and emerged as victors. Brian Aldiss coined a phrase to describe this kind of resolution – the 'Cosy Catastrophe' – a disaster story in which traditional values are the main bulwark against cataclysm.

This ethos did not significantly outlast the decade. The 1960s saw yet another change of pace, and whilst the hippies of the time got down and made love, the science fiction writers were growing ever more pessimistic.

The Loss of Optimism and the Advent of the New Wave

As pessimism about the future took an ever stronger hold within the ranks of SF writers, they turned away from the outside world and began to question the very nature of reality itself. This shift of focus was coupled with a philosophical search for the essence of human existence. Writers were beginning to view the human mind as the next frontier to be explored – we'd already done the Solar System – and the increased use of psychedelic drugs was having a big effect. The barriers between inner and outer realities had become blurred.

Philip K. Dick in particular explored this theme, along with his quirkily metaphysical examination of religion and the religious impulse. This resulted in some wondrous, if surreal novels like *The Three Stigmata of Palmer Eldritch* (1965) and *Do Androids Dream of Electric Sheep?* (1968). These novels represent Dick's urge to explain the world around him in terms of the people who inhabited it. In a world gone mad, how do we tell what reality is, and if we cannot define reality, then how do we define ourselves? Similarly, his classic *The Man in the High Castle* (1962) questions the events of history and asks what would have become of us had the Germans won the war? Science fiction was becoming philosophical, and with this philosophizing came a stronger desire to view SF as a valid form of literature, a medium in which it was legitimate to search for the answers to the major questions of human existence.

In Britain, this best manifested itself in the NEW WAVE movement, which was centred around *New Worlds* magazine and its new editor, the young MICHAEL MOORCOCK.

Moorcock was interested in experimentalism and the urge of a new generation of authors to redefine the genre. In his own way, he is as important and relevant to any history of the genre as John W. Campbell, in that the work that he chose to publish in *New Worlds* revolutionized the genre and in such a way that SF would never be the same again.

It is hard to put a finger on what the New Wave movement came to represent, so open were its boundaries and so intangible was its effect.

Moorcock encouraged authors like J. G. BALLARD and Brian Aldiss, among many others, to deconstruct the typical form of the SF short story and rebuild it as something new. Aldiss remained content to subvert the typical genre ideas and toy with the effects; Ballard began writing what he called 'condensed novels' – short stories with an emphasis on non-linearity and the depiction of desolate landscapes; Moorcock himself developed his surreal and apathetic *Jerry Cornelius* character, who remains, perhaps, his most enduring creation. The key to the New Wave was the manner in which it viewed its subject – cynically, but as a form of literature, as ready to be exploited as any other genre.

The result was phenomenal. Moorcock encouraged his writers to adopt more mainstream concerns such as unconventional narrative structure and characterization. This cross-fertilization meant that the science would often be subsumed by the style and form of the story; to the people who were writing it, it was the story that counted. The authors became more concerned with the sociological impact of their ideas, or with the psychological effects that they might have. Much of what they wrote was satire, and much of it remained cynical and pessimistic. Indeed, one thing that was very prominent in much of the writing of this time was the obsession with the notions of entropy and dissolution that arose. Ballard particularly viewed the world as a crumbling landscape, a planet on the slippery slide to oblivion along with its dominant species. One of his best works, the short story *The Terminal Beach*, is chillingly effective in its description of the ultimate need for humanity to surround itself with devastation.

It was not long before New Wave sensibilities had crossed the Atlantic and begun to affect the American SF authors' way of thinking. Thomas M. Disch first published his wonderful *Camp Concentration* (as a novel, 1968) in Moorcock's magazine, whilst SAMUEL R. DELANY sold him the engaging *Time Considered as a Helix of Semi-Precious Stones*.

HARLAN ELLISON, one of the great American SF stylists, edited perhaps the most representative anthology sequences of the time, *Dangerous Visions* (1967) and its sequel *Again, Dangerous Visions* (1972), did the same thing for the US market that *New Worlds* was doing in Britain. The future, for SF authors, was becoming a dark and miserable place, an Earth that none of us would want very much to inhabit. Unlike the disaster novels of the 1950s, the dystopias of the 1960s were here to stay.

Indeed, this pessimism saw SF right through the 1960s and into the early 1970s, a decade that would at first see its fiction concerning itself with large-scale disaster and the terrors of Vietnam. But then, with the advent of the movie STAR WARS in 1977, came a surge of optimism. This was also inspired by the Moon landings at the end of the 1960s and a growing and renewed confidence in the possibilities of technology.

Disaster Averted

The beginning of the 1970s in SF resembled the 1960s as far as the main preoccupations of the genre's authors went. Environmental disaster and fears about OVERPOPULATION lay heavy on their hearts. John Brunner was halfway through his seminal quartet of ecological novels, *Stand On Zanzibar* (1968), *The Jagged Orbit* (1969), *The Sheep Look Up* (1972) and *The Shockwave Rider* (1975) when the decade began, and they remained representative of New Wave concerns.

Vietnam had also inspired a rash of antiwar SF novels, as well as a number of books examining the psychological effects of MILITARY life. JOE HALDEMAN's *The Forever War* (1975) is a touching and brutal exploration of these themes.

But, with a gradually increasing confidence in technology came a different line of reasoning: could science not provide us with the means of avoiding these disasters? SF had come full circle, and although it would never return to the happy naivety of its youth, the genre began once again to see science as a possible salvation of the species.

LARRY NIVEN, in his extraordinary novel *Ringworld* (1970), sought to put an end to many fears of overpopulation. A space arcology could be built around the sun to provide enough living space for all of humanity. If maintained with the proper skill and attention, there would be no need ever to worry about the increasing population again – anything was possible if we would only put our minds to it. *Ringworld* is a dramatic and inspiring novel, and is written with exceptional speculative scientific skill.

Other writers saw the key to the overpopulation problem as the terraforming of Mars or other nearby planets, using science to make them capable of supporting human life. Their atmospheres could be adapted to make them breathable, while their soils could be fed nutrients that would allow plant life and crops to grow. Soon the pages of SF were filled with stories of an inhabited Moon and a verdant Mars. This was not the Mars of the early pulp romances, but a realistically conceived human colony that would use technological know-how as a tool for survival.

There were other means available, too. If the planet could not be changed to suit us, the new science of GENETIC engineering might mean that we could change to suit the planet. The human form could become malleable, and we would be masters of our own destiny. FREDERIK POHL describes in convincing and humane detail the trials of a man adapted to exist on the hostile surface of Mars in *Man Plus* (1976).

Indeed, *Astounding Science Fiction* magazine, which had continued to publish fairly standard Campbellian SF throughout the 1950s and 1960s, had already reinvented itself during 1960 as *Analog: Science Fact and Fiction*. It became known as the definitive magazine for Hard SF and remains so today.

The pessimistic bubble had burst, and it seemed that optimism was once again on the increase.

This was compounded by the release of two important movies in 1977. Both *Star Wars* and CLOSE ENCOUNTERS OF THE THIRD KIND saw humanity TRANSCENDING its roots as an Earthbound species and spreading out to the stars. The two movies are very different from each other – *Star Wars* is a Science Fantasy that aimed to provide the modern viewer with a new myth (it partially succeeded) whilst *Close Encounters* saw friendly aliens arriving to show us the delights of the universe. Both viewed humanity as corruptible, but inherently good.

The 1970s also saw a rise in the number of female authors associated with the genre, thanks to the feminist revolution. URSULA K. LE GUIN saw the genre as the perfect proving ground for her ideas, and set about deconstructing the Utopian state in her seminal novel *The Dispossessed: An Ambiguous Utopia* (1974). She had previously used the genre as a means of tackling complex GENDER issues in *The Left Hand of Darkness* (1969). OCTAVIA BUTLER followed suit, and her fiction tackled issues of race as well as of gender. Both these writers were enabled, through the genre, to tackle important issues through the use of allusion and metaphor that would have perhaps become too complex in any other form of literature.

SF was becoming cosmopolitan and beginning to look towards a brighter, inclusive future.

But, with talk of developing technologies and advancements in science came questions about the role of machines in human society. Some saw the increasing role of computer technology as a threat, both to their livelihoods and to their humanity. Others came to see computers as the ultimate tool, the means by which the human race could progress to the next level of its existence. Computers were fast and efficient, and it was not long before authors had worked out how to incorporate them into human biology. Man met machine, and attempted to assimilate it. CYBER-PUNK was born.

Man Meets Machine

The early 1980s saw a downturn in the amount of SF being published. Perhaps this was partly due to the new cosmopolitan feel of the genre: more than at any previous time SF was heading in several directions at once, reassessing its values and boundaries and, as a genre aware of its own fragility, lacking a certain confidence. But SF *was* growing more and more inclusive. Science too was beginning to catch up with SF and it was becoming increasingly difficult for writers to keep pace with the original source of their inspiration. It was not that these writers wished to predict the future – true SF has never been about that – it was simply that real science was having all the good ideas first.

There had also been an increase in the amount of escapist Quest Fantasy being published and read, most of it derived from J. R. R. Tolkien and *The Lord of the Rings* (1954–5). Some authors had had a measure of success during the 1970s with similar sequences of novels, and the lure of a quick buck had turned many a head over the intervening years.

However, the SF that *was* appearing was more diverse than ever.

GENE WOLFE began the decade with the publication of the first instalment of *The Book of the New Sun* (1980–83), an elaborate and literary multi-volume novel that masqueraded as a fantasy but was actually an acute and healthy piece of FAR FUTURE SF. It remains the best treatment of the Dying Earth theme to date.

In Britain, IAIN M. BANKS was having fun producing satirical Space Opera of a kind not seen for years. *Consider Phlebas* (1987) began his long sequence of Culture novels, describing an immense interstellar society of humans and aliens who are often at odds with each other and the universe around them. Importantly, Banks was drawing not only on the early pulp roots of the genre but on everything that had come to pass since. In essence, his SF is Space Opera that is both lyrical and adventurous, philosophical and fun.

GREG BEAR would also make headway during the 1980s with the publication of *Blood Music* (1985), a detailed and expressive piece of Hard SF that saw humanity tinkering with its own microbiology, programming their bodily fluids to rather dramatic and astounding effect. This represented the first step on the road to a new and radical Hard SF movement that would come about in the early years of the 1990s. There was a lot going on.

However, there remains one important development above all others from the early 1980s that has gone on to inform nearly all of the SF that has followed it over the last fifteen years: Cyberpunk, the sub-genre concerned with the melding of man and machine into an exotic and often highly volatile amalgam.

The relationship between humanity and the machines of its own creation was not a new field of exploration for SF, but with the increasing intrusion of science into everyday life, as well as the incredible progress being made in computer science specifically, it was ripe for examination.

Cyberpunk touches on many things. On the surface it is a sub-genre obsessed with the *noir*, a seedy, gritty realism that has as much to do with style as content. Scratch the surface and you come to the crux of the matter – cyberpunk is about the struggle for dominance between mankind and machines and the way in which developing technology will come to influence our lives.

Another important aspect of cyberpunk is the people it chooses to represent, the people who fill its pages and throng its mean streets or plug themselves into their computers to communicate with the world. Like the disaster novels of the 1950s, the books that were appearing during the early to mid-1980s had predominantly 'normal' people as their subjects, the typical man or woman in the street, and were showing the reader how new and developing technology had impacted on their lives.

The sub-genre itself draws its name from a short story, *Cyberpunk* (1983) by BRUCE BETHKE. (The story was later revised as a novel and – appropriately – is available in electronic form for download over the Internet). Indeed, there are many fine examples of the early Cyberpunk novel (BRUCE STERLING's *Islands in the Net* (1987) being one) and as a sub-genre it reinvented itself with each new breath.

However, as a mode of writing it is best typified by the now-classic novel, *Neuromancer* (1984) by WILLIAM GIBSON.

Neuromancer was strange and new. It described the exotic realms of 'Cyberspace', a kind of VIRTUAL REALITY Internet into which people could become completely absorbed, using IMPLANTED technology to interface directly with their computers. This is not virtual reality in the sense that we know it, this is a reality wholly different from our own. The computer has learned to control the functions of the human brain, and any experiences that take place in CYBERSPACE are as valid as those that do not. A new DIMENSION has been born.

Almost as if by necessity, as a means of making cyberspace more attractive, the near-future 'real' world described in *Neuromancer* is sliding head first into dystopia. Crime, drugs and poverty rule the streets, and the big corporations are as corrupt as any government. The story itself follows the progress of a cyberspace hacker who has tried to rip off his bosses and as a result has had his nervous system sabotaged so that he cannot return to the digital realm. It becomes a search for identity in a world of blossoming multiple realities, as well as a rich and influential examination of humanity. The book asks if it is only our biology that makes us human, if only our genes set us apart from the ARTIFICIAL INTELLIGENCE (AI) we create? When we plug into a machine, and the machine talks back, is it still just a tool for human use, or has it become something more? Are computer programmers dehumanizing the world with their creations, like latter-day Frankensteins caught up in the tide of progress?

Artificial Intelligence had been a concern of the genre for a number of years; indeed, the ANDROID theme had been explored to great effect by such writers as ROBERT SILVERBERG in *Tower of Glass* (1970) and Philip K. Dick in *Do Androids Dream of Electric Sheep?* RIDLEY SCOTT had explored it on the screen in BLADE RUNNER (1982), which tackled the themes of Dick's book – on which it was loosely based – whilst at the same time attempting to depict visually the cynical angst of the Cyberpunk movement.

However, this was a new type of intelligence, an electronic construct that was just around the corner and that would inhabit the invisible data banks between realities.

In 1968 cinema audiences had seen the computer Hal turn on its colleagues in 2001: A SPACE ODYSSEY. But what cyberpunk was positing was the birth of a new virtual species, a species that did not necessarily want to be affiliated with humanity.

There followed a flood of novels and stories about the awakening of this new electronic species. Not all of them were confident of the human race's ability to control these machines, showing them bringing about the destruction of Earth. Others were more optimistic, portraying AI as the next step in human evolution, the first point at which transcendence of the flesh would be achieved. Gone were the days of religious heavens or hells; humans and machines together could construct their own other-worldly realms and computer technology was the new religion.

The possibilities for these electronic entities were endless; not bound by physical form, they could exist in any other guise they wanted. Not only that, they could program their own realities around them to fulfil their every desire. If machines were going to have this much fun, then human beings wanted a piece of the action.

It was not long before SF authors were portraying humanity down-loading itself into its machines so to that it could cohabit with the new breed of electronic entities. Many writers saw this as giving their characters a form of immortality, a haven to retreat to instead of old-fashioned death. In this way they could later communicate with the living, or, alternatively, become something even greater, 'beyond human'. This was to become one of the key concerns of SF in the 1990s: the quest for the means of transcendence through science and technology rather than through spirituality. Allusions would no longer do, however, and writers wanted to know exactly how their characters would make this leap into the next life.

New theories of quantum physics also meant the serious possibility of space travel. SF was beginning to return to the dreams of its youth. This time, though, there was one fundamental difference. Real science.

The new radical Hard SF movement had begun.

The New Wave of Radical Hard SF and the Rebirth of Space Opera

As the 1990s began, British SF was having a renaissance of its own. The 1980s had seen the launch of a new SF magazine, INTERZONE, that had plugged the hole left by the passing of *New Worlds* in the 1970s. *Interzone* did much to encourage the emerging British writers who were developing on their own terms the notions of the American Cyberpunk movement. The Australian writer GREG EGAN contributed much to the magazine, and his second novel, *Permutation City* (1994) was a very 'hard' and very scientific exploration of the Artificial Intelligence issue and of the possible transcendence of the human form. It set out in confident and plausible detail the means by which a digital virtual reality realm could be constructed and opened up to the 'real' world. When Egan wrote about computer programming, the readers believed him.

There was more. STEPHEN BAXTER had begun writing his massive *Xeelee* sequence, which posited a Future History for the human species and used detailed, accurate physics to describe everything from space travel to the inner workings of stars. PAUL J. McAULEY was tinkering in his SF with human biology, showing how computers and NANOTECHNOLOGY – molecule-size machines – could be used to manipulate human genes to develop new strains of life.

A similar thing was happening in America. Greg Bear had already reinvented our blood supply during the mid-1980s and now he was tackling space travel and AI in *Queen of Angels* (1990). KIM STANLEY ROBINSON had worked out the best way to approach Mars – with science and politics in harmony with human needs. His *Mars* trilogy, *Red Mars* (1992), *Green Mars* (1993) and *Blue Mars* (1996), charts the progressive terraforming of the Red Planet in wonderful, intricate detail.

Hard SF was on the increase, and it was aiming for absolute accuracy.

However, there was almost a counter-movement going on in reaction. Space Opera had returned with a vengeance.

In Britain, Iain M. Banks continued his drive to produce quality space fiction, while PETER F. HAMILTON provided us with his gargantuan *Night's Dawn* trilogy: *The Reality Dysfunction* (1996), *The Neutronium Alchemist* (1997) and *The Naked God* (1999), an epic tale that combined elements from SF's entire range of ideas and effects.

In America various series of Military SF novels were beginning to appear. DAVID FEINTUCH'S *Seafort Saga* and ELIZABETH MOON's *Serrano Legacy* are two of the finest 'Hornbloweresque' sequences that follow the progress of their respective characters as they work their way up through different military hierarchies.

However, this new Space Opera was not simply naive adventure. There were serious issues to be dealt with, and at the same time the writers sought to explain the inner workings of their worlds. There was science here, as always, but it was kept underneath the layers of adventure and fun.

In many respects, the resurgence in Space Opera was a reaction to the still overzealous production of generic fantasy. These fantasies often appeared in large series or enormous tomes, offering the reader a sense of perceived value. The new Space Operas that were appearing worked in much the same way, with regularly published additions to the series, or physically large multi-volume works. This had the effect of getting SF back onto the bookshop shelves, thereby re-establishing its commercial credentials.

'Literary' SF was also enjoying modest success. New writers like JEFF NOON and PAUL DI FILIPPO were pushing the boundaries of the genre ever further out into the ether. Both apply a skewed Dickian logic to their imagined worlds, and both appear to view the world through increasingly bizarre eyes. It is as if, by portraying the world through surrealist, non linear fiction, they get closer to the strange reality that is modern existence. It is too early to tell if they are right.

As the 1990s drew to a close, the genre was in a healthy state.

Speculation about its future was positive in tone, and if many of the really big ideas in the genre had been explored before, the writers now had the science to enable them to look at the details. As science focused increasingly on nano-level matters, the details of SF got finer and finer, while its scope continued to be as big as the imagination of its writers. Science fiction was alive and well, and looked set to carry its readers forward into the twenty-first century.

Where Do We Go From Here?

It is perhaps too soon to be able to identify the main themes that emerged in SF during the 1990s. There was a definite attempt to develop the themes of the 1980s, an effort to apply real scientific thinking to ideas about Artificial Intelligence and the uses to which it might be put. There was also a shift towards genetic concerns and a search for an alternative 'biological' transcendence. Speculation about nanotechnology informed much of the later fiction of the decade, filling its pages with wonder and surprise. Technology is becoming the new magic, able to conjure up electronic spectres or define for us a new reality.

It seems inevitable that humanity is eventually going to step forward into the next stage of its evolution, and whilst many people are prepared to wait for the natural process to run its course, many others are not. CLONING is now a real possibility; Mars has been visited again by robot probes in recent years and there are more unmanned missions to come; the International Space Station is under way and scientists have built an 'engine' the size of a grain of sand. Science fiction helps us to prepare for the effects on human society of these things, both through careful analysis of their possible impact and through reasoned warnings about the haste with which we adopt new technologies. As the future looms larger, the SF genre becomes ever more relevant to our understanding of the life we live now.

Suggested Further Reading

Undoubtedly the best history of the genre is Brian Aldiss and David Wingrove's *Trillion Year Spree* (1986, the revised edition of Aldiss's earlier (1973) *Billion Year Spree*). For a more American perspective, Thomas M. Disch's *The Dreams Our Stuff is Made Of* (1998) is a first-rate combination of analysis and memoir.

Science Fiction
on the Page

ABBOTT, EDWIN (1839–1926), Great Britain

Edwin Abbott, clergyman, teacher and scholar, published the novel *Flatland: A Romance of Many Dimensions* in 1884, originally under the pseudonym of its chief protagonist, Mr A. Square.

This is a seminal work that can be seen as a precursor to HARD SF, as it is based upon a highly plausible mathematical theory that it uses as a metaphor to explore the world. There is also an inherent SENSE OF WONDER in *Flatland* characteristic of the SF genre.

The novel follows the progress of Mr A. Square as he finds himself transported between DIMENSIONS and learns to come to terms with his altered perception of the universe. The story is ingenious and ahead of its time, a direct forerunner of many later novels that explore ALTERNATIVE REALITIES and altered states. It can also be viewed as a social satire, commenting on the very distinct class structure that existed in Abbott's time.

With *Flatland*, Abbott successfully employs elements of the fantastic as a way of expressing a mathematical theory. Writers such as STEPHEN BAXTER and GREGORY BENFORD have also made much use of mathematical physics as an aid to describe the nature of the universe.

See also
ALTERNATIVE REALITY; DIMENSIONS; HARD SF; SENSE OF WONDER

Recommended Further Reading
The Three Stigmata of Palmer Eldritch (1964) by PHILIP K. DICK; *Vurt* (1993) by JEFF NOON; *Raft* (1991) by STEPHEN BAXTER

Bibliography
Flatland: A Romance of Many Dimensions (1884)

ADAMS, DOUGLAS (1952–2001), Great Britain

Douglas Adams began his career in SF in the seventies as a scriptwriter for various television and radio series for the BBC, including some now-classic episodes of DR WHO.

It was the success of his comic radio series, *The Hitchhiker's Guide to the Galaxy* (originally broadcast in 1978) that prompted Adams to rework the script into a novelization that retained the same title and was published in 1979.

Dark and caustic, but nevertheless brimming with satirical humour, the novel has become a classic of modern COMIC SF.

The book opens with its chief protagonist, Arthur Dent, narrowly escaping the destruction of the Earth. He is smuggled aboard an alien craft that has arrived to aid the demolition of the planet to make way for a 'bypass' in space. Once aboard, we follow Arthur's progress as he goes on to encounter many strange and surreal people and situations.

The Hitchhiker's Guide to the Galaxy spawned a number of sequels that, although often hilarious, are less consistent in quality than their predecessor. They are *The Restaurant at the End of the Universe* (1980), *Life, the Universe and Everything* (1982), *So Long, and Thanks for All the Fish* (1984) and *Mostly Harmless* (1992). Together they comprise Adams's 'trilogy in five parts'.

Throughout the series Adams's humour darkens, and by *Mostly Harmless* it is clear that he views the human condition through particularly uncharitable eyes. However, this sharpens the overall tone of the series; the books are enhanced by Adams's keen observations.

It is easy to see from where many later works, including the comic television series RED DWARF, have drawn their inspiration.

A second and less well-known sequence of novels by Adams follows the activities of Dirk Gently, a private eye whose adventures contain elements of the fantastic cross-fertilized with pulp crime. The books in this series are *Dirk Gently's Holistic Detective Agency* (1987), *The Long Dark Teatime of the Soul* (1988) and the projected *Salmon of Doubt*. Before his death on 11 May, 2001 Adams was rumoured to be working on a new instalment in the *Dirk Gently* sequence. This was perhaps one of the most anticipated of genre novels – it now remains to be seen whether it will ever see publication.

In the meantime, the other incarnations of *The Hitchhiker's Guide to the Galaxy* (it has also been filmed by the BBC) and its sequels continue to entertain the many fans of COMIC SF.

See Also
COMIC SF

Recommended Further Reading
The Stainless Steel Rat (1961) or *Bill, the Galactic Hero* (1965) by HARRY HARRISON; *Strata* (1981) by TERRY PRATCHETT; *Untouched by Human Hands* (1954) by ROBERT SHECKLEY

Bibliography
The Hitchhiker's Guide to the Galaxy (1979)
The Restaurant at the End of the Universe (1980)
Life, the Universe and Everything (1982)
So Long, and Thanks for All the Fish (1984)
Dirk Gently's Holistic Detective Agency (1987)
The Long Dark Teatime of the Soul (1988)
Mostly Harmless (1992)

ALBEDO ONE
Albedo One Productions
Occasional (two or three times a year)
Subscription address: Albedo One, 2 Post Road, Lusk, Co. Dublin, IRELAND
Website address: http://homepages.iol.ie/~bobn
Albedo One is the premier Irish magazine of SF, Fantasy and Horror.

Recent issues have boasted a printed cover, but the magazine still contains a black-and-white photocopied interior. However, the editorial and literary quality of the contents more than makes up for this.

A typical issue will contain four or five stories, an interview and a worthwhile collection of book reviews. Regular contributors include BRIAN STABLEFORD, Hugh Cook and David Murphy.

Albedo One manages to blend successfully good-quality fiction with some excellent non-fiction, offering a balanced magazine that could, from the purely aesthetic point of view, benefit from some enhanced production values.

ALDISS, BRIAN (1925–), Great Britain
Brian Aldiss is one of the grand masters of British SF, but is also renowned as a critic, poet and mainstream novelist. His name has a strong association

with NEW WORLDS magazine and the NEW WAVE, although Aldiss was writing long before the advent of this movement and his work was already concerned with many of the issues that would later identify it.

His first novel, *Non-Stop* (1958), took as its setting a vast GENERATION STARSHIP, the inhabitants having, over many years, lost track of their surroundings and forgotten altogether that they were on a starship. When curiosity gets the better of Roy Complain, the chief protagonist, he sets out to explore uncharted territory and he goes on to discover the truth about their environment. It is a classic of the genre and one of the most satisfying examinations of the generation-starship concept.

Hothouse (1962) was Aldiss's next major work, winning the HUGO AWARD for its year. It remains one of his most intriguing novels to date.

Set in a dark FAR FUTURE at a point when the sun is about to go nova, it describes how the remnants of the human race struggle to survive in the branches of an enormous banyan tree that has grown to cover an entire face of the Earth. These little green people find themselves pitted against highly evolved and dangerous insect and plant life. Aldiss succeeds in creating a vision of the distant future that is entirely alien to our current perceptions of the world and our place within it.

Other excellent work by Aldiss includes the short-story collection *Space, Time and Nathaniel* (1957), the evocatively ALIEN *Helliconia Trilogy* (1982–85) and the psychedelic *Barefoot in the Head* (1969), cited as one of the most important books of the New Wave movement.

Barefoot in the Head is a difficult book in which, after the 'Acid Head War' has taken place and the entire culture has been subjected to hallucinogenic drugs, a new MESSIANIC figure is created. However, when he finds himself on the cusp of believing in his own ability to perform miracles, he casts the role away. It is not Aldiss's best book, but it does encapsulate much of what the New Wave was trying to say and is very much a product of its time. Similar themes are explored in MICHAEL MOORCOCK's *Behold the Man* (1969).

Aldiss is also the author of the controversial *Billion Year Spree* (1973) (greatly revised and expanded in 1986 as *Trillion Year Spree*, with David Wingrove), a detailed history of the SF genre that was the first book to herald MARY SHELLEY's *Frankenstein* (1818) as the first true SF novel. This is an argument much more accepted by the SF establishment today; originally Aldiss was ridiculed and his book failed to meet with reviews. The later edition, however, went on to win a HUGO AWARD, and, along with THOMAS DISCH'S *The Dreams Our Stuff is Made Of* (1998), remains one of the best historical studies of the genre.

Aldiss also put this theory into fictionalized form in his excellent novel *Frankenstein Unbound* (1973), which sees a scientist from the twentieth century journeying back in time to the early nineteenth century where he encounters both Mary Shelley and avatars of her literary creations.

After an engaging autobiography, *The Twinkling of An Eye* (1998), and a moving tribute to his late wife, *When the Feast is Finished* (1999), Aldiss returned to SF, in collaboration with scientist and writer Roger Penrose, with *White Mars* (1999). Subtitled 'A Modern Utopia', the book deals with the colonization of the Red Planet and the socio-political considerations that such a move would entail. It stutters, however, falling over itself with dry passages and lacking the sheer inventiveness of some of Aldiss's earlier work. It is not a bad book – it is simply that Aldiss has shown us in the past the dizzying heights that he is capable of reaching.

As a critic, Aldiss has made an enormous contribution to the genre. As a novelist, his work is quintessential.

See Also
FAR FUTURE; GENERATION STARSHIP; LITERARY SF; MESSIAH; NEW WAVE; SPACE OPERA; TIME

Recommended Further Reading
Behold the Man (1969) by Michael Moorcock; *Camp Concentration* (1968) by THOMAS M. DISCH; *Universe* (1951) by ROBERT HEINLEIN; *The Book of the Long Sun* by GENE WOLFE (1993–6)

Bibliography (Selected)
Space, Time and Nathaniel (short stories, 1957)
Non-Stop (1958)
The Canopy of Time (short stories, 1959)
Vanguard from Alpha (1959)
Bow Down to Nul (1960)
The Primal Urge (1961)
The Male Response (1961)
Hothouse (1962)
The Airs of Earth (short stories, 1963)
Greybeard (1964)
The Dark Light Years (1964)
The Best Science Fiction Stories of Brian W. Aldiss (short stories, 1965)
Earthworks (1965)
The Saliva Tree and Other Strange Growths (short stories, 1966)

An Age (1967)
Report on Probability A (1968)
Intangibles Inc., and Other Stories (short stories, 1969)
Barefoot in the Head (1969)
The Moment of Eclipse (short stories, 1970)
The Hand-Reared Boy (1970)
A Soldier Erect (1971)
The Book of Brian Aldiss (short stories, 1972)
Frankenstein Unbound (1973)
The Eighty-Minute Hour (1974)
The Malacia Tapestry (1976)
Brothers of the Head (1977)
Enemies of the System (1978)
A Rude Awakening (1978)
New Arrivals, Old Encounters (short stories, 1979)
Moreau's Other Island (1980)
Life in the West (1980)
Foreign Bodies (short stories, 1981)
Helliconia Spring (1982)
Helliconia Summer (1983)
Seasons in Flight (short stories, 1984)
Helliconia Winter (1985)
Ruins (1987)
The Year Before Yesterday (1987)
Best Science Fiction Stories of Brian W. Aldiss (short stories, 1988)
Forgotten Life (1988)
A Romance of the Equator (short stories, 1989)
Dracula Unbound (1991)
Bodily Functions (short stories, 1991)
Remembrance Day (1992)
A Tupolev Too Far (short stories, 1993)
Somewhere East of Life (1994)
The Secret of This Book (short stories, 1995)
White Mars (1999, with Roger Penrose)

AMAZING STORIES

Historically, *Amazing Stories* is perhaps the most important SF magazine ever to be published. This is not because of any particular aspect of the magazine's format, or indeed any of the stories that it contained, but simply because it was the first in a long line of magazines to concentrate solely on SF, and gave the genre both a home and a name.

Amazing Stories was founded by HUGO GERNSBACK in 1926 and lasted under his editorship for only three brief years before being sold on because of bankruptcy. Nevertheless, the impact that it had on the reading public was phenomenal.

Gernsback had had previous success with a number of early popular-science magazines such as *Science and Invention*, for which he had produced a selection of pedagogic stories of 'scientifiction' to publish alongside the more mundane non-fiction articles. Their immediate popularity prompted him to launch *Amazing Stories*, a magazine intended to focus solely on this 'scientifiction', a genre of pulp fiction that soon became known as 'science fiction'.

Amazing Stories was in many respects a pulp magazine, but Gernsback did place a very definite emphasis on scientific speculation and the demonstration of scientific ideas. It reprinted stories by H. G. WELLS, JULES VERNE and EDGAR ALLEN POE, and early pulp SPACE OPERA originated in its pages with stories by authors like of E. E. 'DOC' SMITH.

But after Gernsback lost control of the magazine in 1929 and *Amazing* was sold on to various other publishing houses, it tended to take a back seat while the newer, fresher ASTOUNDING SCIENCE FICTION took its place as market leader. *Amazing* continued to publish for many years under a succession of different owners, the most recent being the role-playing-games company Wizards of the Coast. This more recent incarnation of the magazine featured a large proportion of media tie-in fiction alongside its more typical SF, and finally ceased publication in August 2000. The future of the magazine seems uncertain.

However, the legacy of *Amazing Stories* is an important one to the SF genre. Gernsback was the first editor to realize that the emerging genre was in need of a dedicated home, and in providing one he helped bring about the genre as we know it. Without *Amazing Stories*, other SF magazines might not have appeared on the market and SF authors would have been left without a means of publishing their work. Indeed, the proliferation of the SF genre today can largely be put down to Gernsback's early attempts to publicize his magazine and involve young American readers in the quest to develop a new mode of speculative writing. Some critics believe that Gernsback's rigidity stifled the imagination of writers who would otherwise have provided him with more exciting and daring space adventures, but it remains a fact that without *Amazing Stories* the genre would have never had the popular kick-start that it needed.

ANALOG

Editor: Stanley Schmidt

Monthly

Subscription address: PO Box 54625, Boulder CO 80323-4625

Website address: http://www.sfsite.com

Analog is consecutively the longest-running SF magazine in existence.

The magazine began life in 1930 as *Astounding Stories*, and under the editorship of Harry Bates provided an early challenger to AMAZING STORIES. With higher rates of pay, and therefore a better calibre of author, it was not long before *Astounding Stories* snatched the first-place position from its competitor. The magazine successfully operated as a quality pulp until 1937, at which point the now legendary JOHN W. CAMPBELL assumed the editor's chair and changed the name of the magazine to the more appropriate *Astounding Science Fiction*. A year later he instigated a new editorial policy that eventually gave rise to the GOLDEN AGE of SF, as he discovered and encouraged a number of key writers to produce thoughtful, character-based stories with logical, scientific premises. Important authors who produced work during this period include ROBERT HEINLEIN, ISAAC ASIMOV, THEODORE STURGEON, A. E. VAN VOGT and E. E. 'DOC' SMITH. The Golden Age period is seen as lasting during the war period from about 1938 to 1943. In essence, true SF was born and consolidated in the pages of *Astounding Science Fiction* during this time.

Campbell continued in his editor's role until he died in 1971. It is reported that he became increasingly difficult to deal with during his later years, and it is certainly true that the magazine failed to change with the times. Campbell maintained his rigid editorial policy, and although good fiction continued to appear in the pages of *Astounding Science Fiction*, the real revolutions were happening elsewhere. In 1960 the magazine changed its name to the present *Analog*, in recognition of the fact that the market had diversified, and *Astounding Science Fiction* had become known as the last magazine home of proper HARD SF.

Author BEN BOVA took over the editor's position after Campbell and relaxed the editorial policy a little, allowing a greater variety of stories to be published in *Analog*. This had the effect of broadening the readership and encouraging a wider selection of new authors to publish their work in the magazine. Bova resigned from his editorial post in 1978 to be succeeded by Stanley Schmidt who still occuies the position today.

The current *Analog* remains the true bastion of American Hard SF. It is now published as a monthly digest and a sister magazine to ASIMOV'S

SCIENCE FICTION, and frequently features stories by leading names in the Hard SF field. There are also regular popular-science articles and non-fiction departments, including book reviews and recommendations. The magazine, like many of the more recently established periodicals, tends not to serialize novels any longer, but it does feature a high proportion of novellas and novelettes alongside its shorter stories.

Its reputation and history alone make *Analog* worth reading. It continues to publish quality Hard SF, and while its sister magazine *Asimov's Science Fiction* may have a more relaxed and broader-based editorial policy, it is still heartening to see a magazine that maintains its appeal for a smaller, dedicated readership. After over seventy years of continuous publication, *Analog* has become an institution in itself.

Analog has also been nominated for and awarded a huge number of genre awards over the years.

ANDERSON, KEVIN J. (1962–   ), USA

Kevin J. Anderson is an author who seems to work best in collaboration with other authors, or within the previously defined boundaries of a SHARED WORLD setting. This is not meant to play down his skill as a writer of genre fiction but to highlight his own particular strengths.

The latter point is best typified by Anderson's work for the STAR WARS and X-FILES franchises, within which he has made his name with novels such as *Darksaber* (1995) and *Antibodies* (1997). It is Anderson's ability to breathe life into these franchises, making their worlds his own, that has led to him being labelled as one of the most proficient shared-world authors of recent years.

This success has also led to his collaboration with BRIAN HERBERT, son of FRANK HERBERT, on a trilogy of authorized preludes to the famous *Dune* sequence. Beginning with *House Atreides* (1999), and continuing with *House Harkonnen* (2000) and *House Corrino* (projected, 2001), the series is a consistent addition to the *Dune* canon. Although lacking the epic scope of Herbert's original novel, these books do offer an interesting account of the early lives of some of the characters that 'later' appear in the classic. Indeed, it is fair to say that even Frank Herbert's original sequence began to narrow in scope with each extra book that was published.

Anderson's best work to date, however, has been in collaboration with American writer Doug Beason. The excellent *Lifeline* (1990) is a HARD SF tale that tells of the survival of four space habitats after a nuclear holocaust has taken place on Earth, effectively cutting them off from the planet.

This was followed by a number of other successful collaborations with Beason, including *Assemblers of Infinity* (1993), in which an ALIEN virus, based on NANOTECHNOLOGY, begins infecting human colonists on the Moon, and *Ignition* (1996), a techno–thriller that deals with a terrorist threat against a space mission to Mir. There has also been a number of novels that feature the exploits of two FBI agents, beginning with *Virtual Destruction* (1996), but so far these have been rather predictable and a little too polished.

Of Anderson's solo work, the most successful has been *Resurrection Inc.* (1988), a DYSTOPIC tale in which corpses are reanimated into a zombie-like underclass for the purposes of slavery. Other titles of note include *Blindfold* (1995) and *Hopscotch* (1997).

See Also
ALIEN; DYSTOPIA; HARD SF; NANOTECHNOLOGY; SCIENCE FANTASY; SHARED WORLD

Recommended Further Reading
Dune (1965) by FRANK HERBERT; *Queen City Jazz* (1994) by KATHLEEN ANN GOONAN; *Necroville* (1995) by Ian McDonald

Bibliography
Resurrection, Inc. (1988)
Gamearth (1989)
Gameplay (1989)
Game's End (1990)
Lifeline (1990, with Doug Beason)
The Trinity Paradox (1991, with Doug Beason)
Afterimage (1992, with Kristine Kathryn Rusch)
Assemblers of Infinity (1993, with Doug Beason)
Climbing Olympus (1994)
Star Wars: Jedi Search (1994)
Star Wars: Dark Apprentice (1994)
Star Wars: Champions of the Force (1994)
Blindfold (1995)
X-Files: Ground Zero (1995)
Star Wars: Darksaber (1995)
Born of Elven Blood (1995, with John G. Betancourt)
Ill Wind (1995, with Doug Beason)

X-Files: Ruins (1996)
Ignition (1996, with Doug Beason)
Virtual Destruction (1996, with Doug Beason)
X-Files: Antibodies (1997)
Hopscotch (1997)
Fallout (1997, with Doug Beason)
Ai! Pedrito! When Intelligence Goes Wrong (1997, from the story by L. RON HUBBARD)
Lethal Exposure (1998, with Doug Beason)
Prelude to Dune: House Atreides (1999, with BRIAN HERBERT)
Prelude to Dune: House Harkonnen (2000, with BRIAN HERBERT)
Prelude to Dune: House Corrino (Projected, 2001, with BRIAN HERBERT)

ANDERSON, POUL (1926–   ), USA

Poul Anderson is one of America's most prolific authors of science fiction, and the quality of his work is none the worse for it.

Born of Scandinavian parents in 1926, Anderson has had a long-term interest in Scandinavian lore and language, and this comes across in much of his writing, perhaps most evidently in *Tau Zero* (1970).

It is a grand novel of HARD SF, in which the Swedes have been appointed governors of the Earth, keeping a watchful eye over a vast Romanesque empire. The story follows the progress of the starship *Leonora Christine* as it sails out into space in search of a new colony planet. However, problems arise with the interstellar drive, meaning that the ship is unable to decelerate, and the crew are flung to the far reaches of the universe. The novel brims with big scientific ideas, but at times the text does struggle under the weight of slightly wooden characters.

Anderson's first novel, *Brain Wave* (1954) explores the consequences of humans and animals suddenly acquiring vastly improved intellects, and their difficulties in trying to comprehend such TRANSCEN-DENCE. It remains one of his most satisfying books.

Much of Anderson's best work is set within a loosely structured FUTURE HISTORY known as the *Technic History* sequence. Briefly, this large series of novels and stories follows two independent threads, one detailing the exploits of spacefaring merchant prince Nicholas Van Rijn, the other following the adventures of Terran agent Dominic Flandry. The pick of the series as a whole includes *Mirkheim* (1977),

Ensign Flandry (1966) and *A Knight of Ghosts and Shadows* (1974). Nearly all, however, are worthy of note.

To his credit, Anderson continues to produce startling and well-informed science fiction. *Genesis* (1999) speculates that machine intelligence will before long supersede the human variety, leading to the gradual extinction of humanity and human history. In the deep FAR FUTURE, an enormously intelligent construct seeks to view its experiments through a uniquely human perspective. This leads to the 'virtual emulation' of two human beings. The story is at once moving and imaginative.

Anderson's shorter fiction has appeared frequently in magazines and anthologies. The best of it is collected in *Alight in the Void* (1991) and *The Queen of Air and Darkness* (1973).

See Also
ALIEN; ARTIFICIAL INTELLIGENCE; FUTURE HISTORY; HARD SF; TRANSCENDENCE; FAR FUTURE; SPACE TRAVEL; PLANETS

Recommended Further Reading
The *Tales of Known Space* sequence by LARRY NIVEN; *The Galactic Centre* sequence by GREGORY BENFORD; *The Patternmaster* sequence by OCTAVIA BUTLER; *Revelation Space* (2000) by ALASTAIR REYNOLDS

Bibliography
Brain Wave (1954)
The Broken Sword (1954)
No World of Their Own (1955)
Planet of No Return (1956)
Star Ways (1956)
The Snows of Ganymede (1958)
War of the Wing-Men (1958)
The Enemy Stars (1959)
Perish by the Sword (1959)
Virgin Planet (1959)
War of Two Worlds (1959)
We Claim These Stars (1959)
Guardians of Time (short stories, 1960)
Earthman, Go Home! (1960)

The Golden Slave (1960)
The High Crusade (1960)
Murder in Black Letter (1960)
Rogue Sword (1960)
Strangers from Earth (short stories, 1961)
Orbit Unlimited (short stories, 1961)
Mayday Orbit (1961)
Twilight World (1961)
After Doomsday (1962)
The Makeshift Rocket (1962)
Let the Spacemen Beware (1963)
Shield (1963)
Time and Stars (short stories, 1964)
Trader to the Stars (short stories, 1964)
Three Worlds to Conquer (1964)
The Corridors of Time (1965)
Agent of Terra (1965)
Flandry of Terra (1965)
The Star Fox (1965)
The Trouble Twisters (short stories, 1966)
The Fox, the Dog and the Griffin (1966)
Ensign Flandry (1966)
World Without Stars (1967)
Beyond the Beyond (short stories, 1969)
The Rebel Worlds (1969)
Satan's World (1969)
Tales of the Flying Mountains (short stories, 1970)
A Circus of Hells (1970)
Tau Zero (1970)
The Byworlder (1971)
The Dancer from Atlantis (1971)
Operation Chaos (1971)
There Will Be Time (1972)
The Queen of Air and Darkness (short stories, 1973)
Hrolf Kraki's Saga (1973)
The People of the Wind (1973)
The Many Worlds of Poul Anderson (short stories, 1974)
A Knight of Ghosts and Shadows (1974)
The Day of Their Return (1974)
Fire Time (1974)

Inheritors of Earth (1974, with Gordon Eklund)
Star Prince Charlie (1975, with Gordon Dickson)
The Winter of the World (1975)
Homeworld and Beyond (short stories, 1976)
The Best of Poul Anderson (short stories, 1976)
Mirkheim (1977)
The Avatar (1978)
The Earth Book of Stormgate (short stories, 1978)
The Demon of Scattery (1979, with Mildred Downey Broxon)
The Merman's Children (1979)
A Stone in Heaven (1979)
The Devil's Game (1980)
Conan the Rebel (1980)
Explorations (short stories, 1981)
Fantasy (short stories, 1981)
Winners (short stories, 1981)
Cold Victory (short stories, 1982)
The Gods Laughed (short stories, 1982)
Maurai and Kith (short stories, 1982)
New America (short stories, 1982)
Conflict (short stories, 1983)
The Long Night (short stories, 1983)
The Unicorn Trade (short stories, 1983, with Karen Anderson)
Orion Shall Rise (1983)
Time Patrolman (1983)
Past Times (short stories, 1984)
Dialogue with Darkness (short stories, 1985)
The Game of Empire (1985)
The Year of Ransom (1988)
Space Folk (short stories, 1989)
The Saturn Game (1989)
The Boat of a Million Years (1989)
Alight in the Void (short stories, 1991)
Kinship with the Stars (short stories, 1991)
The Armies of Elfland (short stories, 1992)
Harvest of Stars (1993)
Game of Empire (1994)
The Stars Are Also Fire (1994)
All One Universe (1996)
Starfarers (1998)

Operation Luna (1999)
Genesis (1999)
Hokas, Hokas, Hokas (2000, with Gordon Dickson)

ANSIBLE

Ansible is a HUGO AWARD-winning fanzine/column, edited by science fiction author and critic DAVID LANGFORD. It is available online (at www.ansible.demon.co.uk) or via Birmingham Science Fiction Association (UK). There is also a related *Ansible Link* column published monthly in INTERZONE.

Typically *Ansible* will include comical anecdotes, obituaries and news relating to the SF world, as well as the often hilarious 'Thog's Masterclass' where Langford showcases mistakes or bad literary form excerpted from novels and stories.

It is to his credit that Langford manages to find enough material to sustain *Ansible* and to maintain the level of quality and accuracy that his readers have come to expect.

ANTHONY, PATRICIA (1947–   ), USA

Texan author Patricia Anthony has, during the second half of the 1990s, made a significant impression on American LITERARY SF.

Her work usually has its basis in stories of ALIEN intrusion or interference, but often finds itself more concerned with the human condition, or with human reactions to extraordinary situations. It might even be fair to say that the alien presence in much of her fiction is almost incidental to the overall tone, that it is used as a device to develop her unique perspective on human nature.

This is perhaps seen best in *God's Fires* (1998), a remarkable novel that discusses the reaction of the Inquisition in sixteenth-century Portugal to a 'star' that falls from the sky and is found to contain three miraculous beings. Although the plot is driven by the incidents surrounding these strange visitors, the novel itself has more to do with the impression they make on the humans affected by their arrival.

Other novels include *Brother Termite* (1993), which successfully parodies the political thriller, featuring aliens in the White House, and *Cold Allies* (1993), a tale of a mighty world war in which aliens are quietly, insidiously, lurking in the background.

During the later years of the decade, Anthony produced the heart-wrenching Great War novel *Flanders* (1998). It is perhaps her best work to date, but nearly all its SF elements are overshadowed by her constant analysis of the human condition and her intense focus on characterization. The novel has more in common with supernatural fantasy and allegory than with science fiction.

The author maintains a website at http://www.patricia-anthony.com

See Also
ALIEN; ALTERNATE WORLD; LITERARY SF

Recommended Further Reading
Pavane (1968) by KEITH ROBERTS; *The Left Hand of Darkness* (1969) by URSULA K. LE GUIN; *The Sparrow* (1997) by MARY DORIA RUSSELL

Bibliography
Cold Allies (1993)
Brother Termite (1993)
Happy Policeman (1994)
Conscience of the Beagle (1995)
Cradle of Splendor (1997)
Eating Memories (short stories, 1998)
Flanders (1998)
God's Fires (1998)

ASIMOV, ISAAC (1920–92), USA

Born in Russia but for most of his life resident in America, Isaac Asimov has had an enormous impact on the genre as a whole. His depiction of ROBOTS paved the way for many later works, although it is generally accepted that the Czech author Karel Capek was responsible for adding the word 'robot' to the English language.

Asimov first made his mark during the GOLDEN AGE of science fiction, and his best work has become synonymous with that period. It was in the pages of JOHN W. CAMPBELL's ASTOUNDING SCIENCE FICTION magazine that many of the episodes that make up Asimov's most famous trilogy of novels first appeared.

The *Foundation* trilogy, comprising *Foundation* (1951), *Foundation and Empire* (1952) and *Second Foundation* (1953), is an intelligent story of the collapse of a vast interstellar empire and the subsequent preservation and eventual rebirth of civilization through the work of a lone genius.

Hari Seldon, Asimov's hero, has developed a predictive science based on psychology and entitled 'psychohistory'; with it he predicts the Roman Empire-style fall of the Galactic Empire and takes steps to lessen the impact by creating two 'Foundations', one based on the physical sciences, one on 'psychohistory'. These 'Foundations' work to preserve human knowledge and understanding, and during the course of the trilogy come under threat from various unknown elements such as the 'Mule', a mutant warlord.

The *Foundation* saga is SPACE OPERA on a grand scale, thought-provoking and exciting, even if it does fall a little short in its literary craftsmanship.

Asimov is perhaps equally well remembered for his excellent series of *Robot* stories, which span much of his career and, full-lengh novels excepted, are collected in *The Complete Robot* (1982). They are masterful explorations of ARTIFICIAL INTELLIGENCE – logical stories that examine the relationships that may evolve between humans and intelligent machines. In them, Asimov proposed the 'Three Laws of Robotics', a set of programmed instructions that would provide the robots with logical directives to which they must comply. They are: (1) A robot may not injure a human being or, through inaction, allow a human being to come to harm. (2) A robot must obey the orders given it by human beings except where such orders would conflict with the First Law. (3) A robot must protect its own existence as long as such protection does not conflict with the First or Second Law.

Most of Asimov's *Robot* stories revolve around various interpretations of these laws, and the consequences of conflicts between them. His two novels of this period, *The Caves of Steel* (1954) and *The Naked Sun* (1957) follow similar patterns, and feature a human private eye and his robot assistant.

After a hiatus of many years, in which Asimov wrote nothing but nonfiction, he returned to science fiction with a number of novels that, surprisingly, tied together his *Foundation* and *Robot* series into one vast sequence. Perhaps a little long-winded, but at the same time of interest to fans of the original series, the newer novels (in internal chronological sequence) are *The Robots of Dawn* (1983), *Robots and Empire* (1985), *Forward the Foundation* (1993), *Prelude to Foundation* (1988), *Foundation's Edge* (1982) and *Foundation and Earth* (1986). Within this framework fit the earlier series mentioned above.

A later addition to the sequence is the *Second Foundation Trilogy*, which begins with *Foundation's Fear* (1997) by GREGORY BENFORD, and continues with *Foundation and Chaos* (1998) by GREG BEAR and *Foundation's Triumph* (1999) by DAVID BRIN. Although consistent, none of these sequels live up to the sheer scale of the original work.

Outside of this epic FUTURE HISTORY, Asimov's best single novel is, possibly, *The End of Eternity* (1955). It is concerned with TIME TRAVEL and complex paradoxes, and follows the progress of Andrew Harlan, a recruit of the organization Eternity, who must go backward and forward through time to enforce changes on human history. The plot thickens when Harlan falls in love with an agent from another organization that wishes to see the end of Eternity so that human history can be saved from stagnation. Again, like Asimov's earlier *Foundation* trilogy, the book contains some excellent ideas, but is not as well crafted as many of his *Robot* stories.

Asimov remains one of the best-known authors of American SF and although his work never really progressed much beyond the conceptual limits of the Golden Age it remains much loved, as does its author's memory.

A monthly publication, ASIMOV'S SCIENCE FICTION MAGAZINE, began publishing during his lifetime. Although it was named after him, Asimov only ever wrote brief editorials for it, leaving much of the actual commissioning editorial work to others.

See Also
ARTIFICIAL INTELLIGENCE; CRIME; FUTURE HISTORY; GOLDEN AGE; HARD SF; PLANETS; ROBOT; SPACE OPERA; SPACE TRAVEL; TIME

Recommended Further Reading
The *Future History* sequence by ROBERT HEINLEIN; The *Technic History* sequence by POUL ANDERSON; The *Xeelee* sequence by STEPHEN BAXTER; The *Greg Mandel Trilogy* by PETER F. HAMILTON; *Tik-Tok* (1983) by John Sladek

Bibliography
I, Robot (short stories, 1950)
Pebble in the Sky (1950)
The Stars, Like Dust (1951)
Foundation (1951)

The Currents of Space (1952)
Foundation and Empire (1952)
David Starr, Space Ranger (juvenile, 1952)
Second Foundation (1953)
Lucky Starr and the Oceans of Venus (juvenile, 1954)
The Caves of Steel (1954)
The End of Eternity (1955)
The Naked Sun (1956)
Lucky Starr and the Big Sun of Mercury (juvenile, 1956)
Earth is Room Enough (short stories, 1957)
Lucky Starr and the Moons of Jupiter (juvenile, 1957)
Lucky Starr and the Rings of Saturn (juvenile, 1958)
Nine Tomorrows (short stories, 1959)
Fantastic Voyage (1966)
Nightfall and Other Stories (short stories, 1969)
The Early Asimov (short stories, 1972)
The Gods Themselves (1972)
Buy Jupiter (short stories, 1975)
The Bicentennial Man (short stories, 1976)
The Complete Robot (short stories, 1982)
Foundation's Edge (1982)
The Robots of Dawn (1983)
Norby, the Mixed-up Robot (juvenile, 1983, with Janet Asimov)
Norby's Other Secret (juvenile, 1984, with Janet Asimov)
Robots and Empire (1985)
Norby, Robot for Hire (juvenile, 1985, with Janet Asimov)
Norby and the Invaders (juvenile, 1985, with Janet Asimov)
The Winds of Change (short stories, 1986)
Robot Dreams (short stories, 1986)
Foundation and Earth (1986)
Norby and the Queen's Necklace (juvenile, 1987, with Janet Asimov)
Fantastic Voyage Two: Destination Brain (1987)
Norby Finds a Villain (juvenile, 1987, with Janet Asimov)
Azazel (1988)
Prelude to Foundation (1988)
Nemesis (1989)
Norby and Yobo's Great Adventure (juvenile, 1989, with Janet Asimov)
Norby Down to Earth (juvenile, 1989, with Janet Asimov)
Robot Visions (short stories, 1990)
The Complete Stories: Volume One (short stories, 1990)

Nightfall (1990, with ROBERT SILVERBERG)
Norby and the Oldest Dragon (juvenile, 1990, with Janet Asimov)
Norby and the Court Jester (juvenile, 1991, with Janet Asimov)
Child of Time (1991, with ROBERT SILVERBERG)
The Complete Stories: Volume Two (short stories, 1992)
The Positronic Man (1992, with ROBERT SILVERBERG)
Forward the Foundation (1993)
Gold (short stories, 1995)
Magic (short stories, 1995)

ASIMOV'S SCIENCE FICTION MAGAZINE

Editor: Gardner Dozois
Monthly
Subscription address: PO Box 54625, Boulder, CO 80323-4625
Website address: http://sfsite.com

Launched in 1977 as a quarterly magazine, and from then on developing into a monthly digest, *Asimov's Science Fiction* has in recent years become the most successful SF periodical on the market.

Originally, the magazine was named after ISAAC ASIMOV purely to take advantage of his popular name – he contributed the occasional editorial article, but the actual commissioning editorial work was left first to George Scithers and then to a succession of other editors. The magazine immediately flourished, and attracted a number of big-name writers – ROBERT SILVERBERG, JOHN VARLEY, KIM STANLEY ROBINSON and JOE HALDEMAN, among others. Ever since, authors have seemed to flock to its pages, and its various editors and stories have garnered themselves numerous HUGO AWARDS over the years.

Asimov's Science Fiction is currently published as a sister magazine to ANALOG, which is now owned by the same publishing company. Its present editor Gardner Dozois is one of the most respected magazine editors working in the genre and as well as commissioning excellent stories by well-known writers, he continues to edit a yearly 'Best of' anthology of short SF. This annual anthology is invaluable to the casual reader who wishes to save time by not having to leaf through entire issues of the various magazines to find stories that they know they will enjoy.

The magazine also features regular SF poetry alongside its mix of novellas, novelettes and short stories. Robert Silverberg appears frequently with a non-fiction column called 'Reflections' and genre author

PAUL DI FILIPPO provides readers with his excellent insight into the world of books.

Asimov's Science Fiction continues to publish groundbreaking stories by a wide range of writers and Dozois appears to have fairly liberal editorial guidelines for authors. This results in an eclectic variety of stories that does much to maintain the magazine's appeal.

Asimov's Science Fiction is essential for any SF reader's library.

ASTOUNDING SCIENCE FICTION
See ANALOG

ATWOOD, MARGARET (1939–   ), Canada
A Canadian novelist of literary mainstream and slipstream fiction whose most popular novel, *The Handmaid's Tale* (1985), is of genre interest.

It is a DYSTOPIC novel of the NEAR FUTURE in which, due to a sudden decrease in the fertility of women, the government has taken control of the conception process. The heroine, Offred, has been lined up to bear a child; the novel is the story of her flight and eventual escape, a salvation of sorts, from the authorities.

The book has a particularly feminist outlook, making it an excellent example of GENDER SF in the vein of ANGELA CARTER or DORIS LESSING. The novel also bears some superficial resemblance to *Nineteen Eighty-Four* (1949) by GEORGE ORWELL in its dystopic vision of a possible future.

See Also
DYSTOPIA; GENDER; NEAR FUTURE

Recommended Further Reading
The Left Hand of Darkness (1969) by URSULA K. LE GUIN; The *Canopus in Argos* sequence by DORIS LESSING; *Heroes and Villains* (1969) by ANGELA CARTER; *The Gate to Women's Country* (1988) by SHERI S. TEPPER

Bibliography (Selected)
The Handmaid's Tale (1985)

BALLARD, J. G. (1930–   ), Great Britain

Born in Shanghai in 1930, J. G. Ballard spent much of his childhood among the horrors and ruination of war, the bleak images of which pervade much of his fiction and inspired his autobiographical mainstream novel, *Empire of the Sun* (1984).

After a spell in a Japanese civilian prisoner-of-war camp, Ballard's parents moved him to England at the age of sixteen. He began publishing short fiction in NEW WORLDS magazine in the late 1950s and early 1960s after studying at Cambridge and service in the Royal Air Force.

His first four novels, *The Wind from Nowhere* (1962), *The Drowned World* (1962), *The Burning World* (1964) (UK title: *The Drought* (1965)) and *The Crystal World* (1966) all adopt a similar theme – the apocalyptic devastation of the Earth via natural disaster – to form a loose thematic sequence.

Of these four, *The Drowned World* stands out, and established Ballard as a force to be reckoned with in the SF world. It describes a world in which solar flares have melted the ice caps, causing sea levels to rise and cover much of the planet. The ecology is regressing to a Triassic stage, and an expedition goes out into the swamps of a flooded London to catalogue the changing fauna and flora.

The other books in the sequence concern worlds devastated by other natural forces gone bizarrely awry.

It is devastated landscapes such as these, blighted environments in which his characters stand either helpless or triumphant, that define much of Ballard's work. Indeed, this pessimistic streak caused much controversy during the early years of Ballard's career, and his preoccupation with entropy and dissolution linked him closely with the British NEW WAVE movement.

The publication of *Crash* (1973) was to mark another development in Ballard's career, as well as a spell of fresh controversy. It is a surreal book that examines man's fetishistic obsession with technology and machines – in this case the automobile. Ballard has his characters fulfil their erotic fantasies by crashing cars in a strange melding of blood and sex. The novel caused widespread debate, as did DAVID CRONENBERG'S movie version in 1997, but consolidated for Ballard the direction he wished to take with his fiction.

Ballard is also renowned as a short-story writer, such collections as *The Terminal Beach* (1964) and *Vermilion Sands* (1971) showcasing his skill as a literary craftsman. The stories in the latter collection all take place within a surreally decadent holiday resort known as Vermilion Sands; the book set the standard for various collections of thematically linked stories still to come, as well as for the depiction of closed communities, a theme Ballard was later to return to in *Running Wild* (1988) and *Super-Cannes* (2000).

With the publication of *Empire of the Sun*, which provided Ballard with a massive increase in his readership, he began moving away from the SF genre, reworking his vision to incorporate the mass media and a more mainstream market. Much of his writing, such as the recent novel *Super-Cannes*, still smacks of LITERARY SF, but is perhaps more sensibly considered as the work of a mainstream novelist with a subversively surrealist outlook. This is not to say that Ballard has consciously turned his back on the genre, simply that, in a similar way to M. JOHN HARRISON (who was directly influenced by the work of Ballard), he has found the mainstream more suitable for the exploration of his later concerns.

See Also
DYSTOPIA; ECOLOGY; LITERARY SF; NEW WAVE; UTOPIA

Recommended Further Reading
The Sheep Look Up (1972) or *The Jagged Orbit* (1969) by JOHN BRUNNER; *The Dispossessed* (1974) by URSULA K. LE GUIN; *The Sirens of Titan* (1959) or *Slaughterhouse Five* (1969) by KURT VONNEGUT; *The Committed Men* (1971) by M. John Harrison

Bibliography
Billenium (short stories, 1962)
The Wind from Nowhere (1962)
The Drowned World (1962)
The Voices of Time (short stories, 1962)
The Burning World (1964)
The Terminal Beach (short stories, 1964)
The Impossible Man (short stories, 1966)
The Crystal World (1966)
The Day of Forever (short stories, 1967)
The Disaster Area (short stories, 1967)
The Overloaded Man (short stories, 1967)
The Atrocity Exhibition (Short Stories, 1970)
Vermilion Sands (short stories, 1971)
Chronopolis and Other Stories (short stories, 1971)
Crash (1973)

Concrete Island (1974)
High-Rise (1975)
Low-Flying Aircraft and Other Stories (short stories, 1976)
The Best of J.G. Ballard (short stories, 1977)
The Best Short Stories of J. G. Ballard (short stories, 1978)
The Unlimited Dream Company (1979)
The Venus Hunters (short stories, 1980)
Hello America (1981)
Myths of the Near Future (short stories, 1982)
Empire of the Sun (1984)
The Day of Creation (1987)
Running Wild (1988)
Memories of the Space Age (short stories, 1988)
War Fever (short stories, 1990)
The Kindness of Women (1991)
Rushing to Paradise (1995)
Cocaine Nights (1996)
Super-Cannes (2000)

BANKS, IAIN M. (1954–   ), Great Britain

Scottish writer Iain M. Banks has, in recent years, developed a reputation as one of the most revered authors of SPACE OPERA in Britain. Perhaps his successful double life as an author – he also writes mainstream literary fiction without using his middle initial 'M' – is a mark of his literary skill: he first came to prominence with *The Wasp Factory* (1984), a dark, surreal tale of mental and physical weirdness, before going on to write *Consider Phlebas* (1987), the first of his 'Culture' SF novels.

Consider Phlebas is a superb novel of war, set against the backdrop of a so-called UTOPIA. The culture is a vast civilization that has long since TRANSCENDED the political and economical concerns of humanity and believes itself to be utopian in nature. The bulk of the population live in enormous 'Orbitals' or ARTIFICIAL ENVIRONMENTS which are maintained by ARTIFICIAL INTELLIGENCES. Indeed, these 'Minds' are the pinnacle of the Culture's supposedly non-existent class system; they feel a sense of responsibility towards the biological life forms that they guard and entertain.

However, the inherent ethos of this powerful culture leads it to the conclusion that it must interfere with other races in an attempt to help them achieve enlightenment. In the first novel, this has provoked a war.

Banks, Iain M. 53

The book follows the progress of Horza, a shape-shifter who is attempting to track down a missing Mind before the Idirans, the ALIEN enemy, can find it themselves. The book is well plotted and written, if a little too long, and set the scene for a number of other Culture novels to come. *Consider Phlebas* also introduced Banks's penchant for comical ship names, such as *Clear Air Turbulence* and *Shoot Them Later*, a device that has been adopted by a number of other genre authors.

Other books in the sequence include *The Player of Games* (1988), *Use of Weapons* (1990), *Excession* (1996), *Inversions* (1998) and *Look To Windward* (2000). Of these, *Use of Weapons* and *Excession* are perhaps most worthy of note.

Use of Weapons is a multi-layered book that questions the bonds of family on a world gone mad, and successfully turns on their head the reader's perceptions of the chief protagonist, while *Excession* is the story of an alien artefact that appears on the edge of the Culture's sphere of influence and refuses to give up its secrets. Both are extremely well written and evocative, and both have particularly moving scenes towards their conclusions. Indeed, Banks has developed his own distinctive style of twist and turn that leaves the reader awaiting the realization that will inevitably come in the last few pages. Rarely does it fail to affect.

There is also a profound sense of irony in all of Bank's Culture work – the Utopia that is decidedly anti-Utopian, the persistence of biological life simply because the machines feel a duty to protect it. It is this self-deprecating pessimism that really characterizes Bank's work.

Outside of the Culture sequence, Banks has produced two further SF novels, and although they lack the fully realized framework of his other books, both *Against a Dark Background* (1993) and *Feersum Endjinn* (1994) are successful in their own right.

Banks continues to produce quality SF in tandem with his career as a literary novelist. His many fans greet each of his new books with glee.

See Also
ALIEN; ARTIFICIAL ENVIRONMENTS; ARTIFICIAL INTELLIGENCE; SPACE OPERA; SPACE TRAVEL; TRANSCENDENCE; UTOPIA

Recommended Further Reading
The *Night's Dawn Trilogy* by PETER F. HAMILTON; The *Gap* sequence by STEPHEN DONALDSON; *The Star Fraction* (1995) by KEN MACLEOD

Bibliography (Selected)

Consider Phlebas (1987)
The Player of Games (1988)
Use of Weapons (1990)
The State of the Art (short stories, 1991)
Against a Dark Background (1993)
Feersum Endjinn (1994)
Excession (1996)
Inversions (1998)
Look to Windward (2000)

BARNES, JOHN (1957–   ), USA

Over recent years, John Barnes has proved himself to be one of the more underrated authors of American SF.

His first novel, *The Man Who Pulled Down the Sky* (1987) is a successful examination of interplanetary POLITICS, in which Earth has been repressed by a free market that spans the entire Solar system and a spy from one of the outer PLANETS journeys to the home world in an attempt to foment an uprising.

Barnes's best book to date, however, and the novel that truly established him as a writer to be watched, is *A Million Open Doors* (1993). It takes as its setting a universe populated by 'The Thousand Cultures', a myriad human colonies that have scattered themselves amongst the stars. When a method of instantaneous matter-transmission or TELEPORTATION is developed, the colonies once again begin to communicate with each other. The story follows the progress of an ambassador for The Thousand Cultures who is sent to a distant planet to tentatively re-establish contact.

A later sequel, *Earth Made of Glass* (1998), is set against the same background.

In 1996 Barnes teamed up with Apollo 11 astronaut Buzz Aldrin to produce *Encounter with Tiber*, a rather drawn-out novel of an ALIEN encounter that nevertheless effectively manages to encapsulate Aldrin's take on the reality of space travel. In it, a new space race is begun when a signal is received from the distant planet Tiber. The novel recounts the attempts of two men and their descendants to make sense of the signals and eventually contact the alien Tiberians.

More recently, Barnes produced the excellent *Finity* (1999) that, in a similar way to both PHILIP K. DICK'S *The Man in the High Castle*

(1962) and Robert Harris's *Fatherland* (1992), discusses the ALTER-NATE WORLD that might have come about had Germany defeated the Allies during World War Two. However, things are more complicated than they seem. The protagonist, Lyle Peripart, begins to dig around in an attempt to find out what really happened to the United States of America and why they seem to have simply disappeared from the pages of history. The secrets he uncovers eventually lead to an exploration of VIRTUAL REALITY and ARTIFICIAL INTELLIGENCE.

Other Barnes books worthy of note include *Mother of Storms* (1995), an ECOLOGICAL tale of global warming, and *Apostrophes and Apocalypses* (1999), a strong collection of his best short fiction.

See Also
ALIEN; ALTERNATIVE REALITY; ALTERNATE WORLD; ARTIFICIAL INTELLIGENCE; ECOLOGY; PLANETS; POLITICS; TELEPORTATION; VIRTUAL REALITY

Recommended Further Reading
The Stars My Destination (1956) by ALFRED BESTER; *The Man in the High Castle* (1962) by PHILIP K. DICK; *The Sheep Look Up* (1972) by JOHN BRUNNER

Bibliography
The Man Who Pulled Down the Sky (1987)
Sin of Origin (1988)
Orbital Resonance (1991)
A Million Open Doors (1993)
Mother of Storms (1995)
Kaleidoscope Century (1995)
Encounter with Tiber (1996, with Buzz Aldrin)
One for the Morning Glory (1996)
Washington's Dirigible (1997)
Patton's Spaceship (1997)
Caesar's Bicycle (1997)
Earth Made of Glass (1998)
Apostrophes and Apocalypses (short stories, 1999)
Finity (1999)
Candle (2000)

BAXTER, STEPHEN (1957–   ), Great Britain

Stephen Baxter began his writing career in 1987 with the publication of his first short story, 'The Xeelee Flower', in INTERZONE magazine. This was the beginning of a long association with the magazine, and went on to form the basis of his excellent *Xeelee* sequence.

This sequence is a detailed FUTURE HISTORY of the Earth and the human race, taking place on a grand scale that runs from the NEAR FUTURE occupation of Earth by ALIENS to the eventual destruction of our universe at the hands of the enigmatic Xeelee. The sequence as a whole contains some of Baxter's most successful writing to date.

The *Xeelee* stories were collected together, with amendments, in *Vacuum Diagrams* (1997), and the novels associated with the sequence are *Raft* (1991), *Timelike Infinity* (1992), *Flux* (1993), *Ring* (1994) and *Reality Dust* (2000). These novels contain detailed extrapolations of modern scientific thought and for this reason Baxter has become generally recognized as one of the key forces behind the new wave of radical HARD SF writers, which also includes such authors as PAUL J. McAULEY and GREG EGAN. Indeed, this insistence on including genuine scientific speculation in his work has led to Baxter inheriting the title of 'heir-apparent' to ARTHUR C. CLARKE.

Baxter and Clarke have worked together on a number of projects, including the recent *The Light of Other Days* (2000), a speculative novel that discusses the ramifications of a communications revolution in the not-too-distant future. It is not altogether as successful as many solo Baxter and Clarke novels, although its concern with media intrusion and the invasion of personal space is very relevant to the current media debate.

Baxter himself is perhaps best known for his 1995 novel *The Time Ships*, an authorized sequel to H. G. WELLS's masterwork, *The Time Machine* (1895). The book deals with TIME TRAVEL in a sophisticated manner, basing its premise on modern scientific thought, but still managing to retain the unparalleled SENSE OF WONDER manifest in Wells's original.

The novel was critically acclaimed and was awarded the PHILIP K. DICK AWARD for its year.

After the success of *The Time Ships*, Baxter produced a slew of more contemporary hard-SF novels. *Voyage* (1996) casts an analytical, unforgiving eye over the American space programme, having its characters cannibalize old Apollo technology in an attempt to send people to Mars. Indeed, this reassessment of modern space travel appears to have become a staple of Baxter's later work, with *Titan* (1997) sending humans to the eponymous moon of Saturn, and his *Manifold* trilogy, beginning with *Time: Manifold One* (1999) describing the rekindling of the space programme via a privately funded operation.

Baxter is an author unafraid to explore new possibilities, both with his characters and with his form. His less successful *Mammoth* series, which begins with the rather juvenile *Mammoth* (1999) and is followed by the more mature *Longtusk* (2000), is an anthropomorphic fantasy that still smacks of Baxter's uncompromising passion for detail and research. (Indeed, one American critic has already labelled the series 'Hard Fantasy'.)

Also worthy of note are Baxter's numerous short stories, a selection of which are collected in *Traces* (1998). His name continues to feature frequently in the pages of many genre magazines, and his output shows no sign of slackening.

Baxter is one of the most productive authors of the genre and his profile increases with each new book. With time, he looks set to become one of the SF 'greats.'

See Also
ALIENS; FUTURE HISTORY; HARD SF; NEAR FUTURE; SENSE OF WONDER; SPACE; SPACE TRAVEL; TIME

Recommended Further Reading
The Seedling Stars (1957) by JAMES BLISH; *The Collected Stories of Arthur C. Clarke* (2000) by Arthur C. Clarke; the *Foundation* sequence by ISAAC ASIMOV; the *Technic History* sequence by POUL ANDERSON; the *Heechee* sequence by FREDERIK POHL

Bibliography
Raft (1991)
Timelike Infinity (1992)
Flux (1993)
Anti-Ice (1993)
Ring (1994)
The Time Ships (1995)
Voyage (1996)
Vacuum Diagrams (short stories, 1997)
Titan (1997)
Gulliverzone (juvenile, 1997)
Moonseed (1998)
Traces (short stories, 1998)

Webcrash (juvenile, 1998)
Mammoth (1999)
Time (1999)
Longtusk (2000)
The Light of Other Days (2000, with ARTHUR C. CLARKE)
Space (2000)
Reality Dust (2000)
Icebones (2001)
Origin (projected, 2001)

BEAR, GREG (1951–   ), USA

One of the three 'killer Bs' of American HARD SF – the others being GREGORY BENFORD and DAVID BRIN – Greg Bear has become one of science fiction's greatest assets. At times his books can reach dizzying heights of scientific speculation, with an inherent SENSE OF WONDER that is missing from so much modern SF, but he never fails to keep in touch with the human aspects of his story.

It was not always this way.

Bear's earliest books were unremarkable – not unsatisfactory, but not outstanding either. Of this early-period output perhaps the most worthwhile novel is *Hegira* (1979), which tells of a trio of humans who set out to learn more about the strange planet on which they were born. What the book lacks in narrative drive it makes up for in vision and scope, but it still does not prepare one for the quality of later books such as *Blood Music* (1985) and *Eon* (1985).

Blood Music is an evocative novel of BIOLOGY and TRANSCEN-DENCE in which a scientist instils sentient life into a colony of DNA molecules, creating a series of microscopic biological computers. He injects these into himself, triggering a rapid reproductive process that eventually leads to the birth of a new entity that assimilates a number of human beings before ascending to another plane of reality. It is hard SF with an almost HUMANIST outlook, and is all the better for it.

The same year also saw *Eon* from Bear, another excellent novel that tells the story of an enormous artificial hollow asteroid that enters the Solar System. Human explorers venture out to the artefact, only to find an even more confusing interior; the DIMENSIONS of the hollow space are apparently infinite and the object has been created by humans from an alternative reality. It was followed by the equally superb sequels, *Eternity* (1988) and *Legacy* (1995).

The Forge of God (1987) is a SPACE OPERA that depicts the destruction of the Earth by ALIENS, whilst its sequel, *Anvil of Stars* (1992), describes the terrible revenge inflicted on them by the surviving humans.

Perhaps Bear's best work, however, is that which takes place within the context of his FUTURE HISTORY, beginning with *Queen of Angels* (1990) and continuing with *Heads* (1990), *Moving Mars* (1993) and *Slant* (1997).

Queen of Angels is a tale of NANOTECHNOLOGY and the revolution that such a technology could bring about. It follows an adapted policewoman on the trail of a poet turned murderer, whilst at the same time detailing the transcendence of an ARTIFICIAL INTELLIGENCE into sentience; it succeeds not only as a hard SF novel but also as a CRIME story and an exploration of artificial life. It is not the easiest of Bear's books to read, but it does repay careful attention.

Set within the same future history, *Heads* is a tale of CRYONICS and the search for absolute zero, whilst *Slant* returns to two of the characters from *Queen of Angels* to find them battling against a plague of mental illness. Both are narrower in scope than their predecessor, but both are worthy as sequels. *Moving Mars*, however, is set further along the timeline, and details a new technology that allows dissatisfied Martian colonists to literally move the planet into a new orbit, away from Earth interference. Grand in scale, the plot is nevertheless a little unrealistic.

More recently, after producing *Foundation and Chaos* (1998), part of a trilogy of authorized sequels to ISAAC ASIMOV's *Foundation* sequence, Bear returned to the theme of human biology and EVOLUTION with *Darwin's Radio* (1999). It is a NEAR FUTURE technothriller in which apparently junk DNA in the human genome suddenly becomes active, reawakening an ancient, inherent disease that affects expectant mothers, destroying both them and their children.

The book is fast-paced and well written, yet lacks the sheer appeal of Bear's earlier *Queen of Angels*.

A selection of Bear's better shorter work can be found in *Tangents* (1989).

See Also
ARTIFICIAL INTELLIGENCE; BIOLOGY; CRIME; CRYONICS; DIMENSIONS; EVOLUTION; FUTURE HISTORY; HUMANIST SF; NANOTECHNOLOGY; NEAR FUTURE; SPACE OPERA

Recommended Further Reading
The *Uplift* sequence by DAVID BRIN; the *Galactic Centre* sequence by
GREGORY BENFORD; the *Foundation* sequence by ISAAC ASIMOV;
the *Xeelee* sequence by STEPHEN BAXTER; *Queen City Jazz* (1994) by
KATHLEEN ANN GOONAN

Bibliography
Hegira (1979)
Psychlone (1979)
Beyond Heaven's Mirror (1980)
Strength of Stones (1981)
The Wind from a Burning Woman (short stories, 1984)
Corona (1984, STAR TREK novel)
The Infinity Concerto (1984)
Blood Music (1985)
Eon (1985)
The Forge of God (1987)
Eternity (1988)
Tangents (Short Stories, 1989)
Queen of Angels (1990)
Heads (1990)
Anvil of Stars (1992)
Moving Mars (1993)
Legacy (1995)
Slant (1997)
Foundation and Chaos (1998)
Dinosaur Summer (1998)
Darwin's Radio (1999)
Rogue Planet (2000, STAR WARS novel)
Darwin's Children (2000)

BENFORD, GREGORY (1941–), USA
Another of the 'killer Bs' of American HARD SF, along with GREG
BEAR and DAVID BRIN, Gregory Benford has produced a number of
excellent novels over the last two decades.

Like Bear, Benford's early work shows signs of a writer still learning his
craft; collaborations such as *If The Stars Are Gods* (1977, with Gordon
Eklund) and *Shiva Descending* (1980, with William Rotsler) are unspectacular at best.

It was with *Timescape* (1980), however, that Benford first produced a novel truly worthy of note.

Himself a scientist on the cutting edge of research, Benford drew upon his own experiences to depict what is still regarded as the best portrayal in SF of scientists at work. The novel concerns itself with a young researcher in the 1960s who finds his experiments spoiled by a strange interference. He eventually realizes that this interference is actually a series of messages sent back in time by scientists at the end of the twentieth century who wish to make their predecessors aware of an impending ECOLOGICAL disaster in the hope that it can be averted. It remains his best book to date.

Benford later returned to the research laboratory in *Cosm* (1998), a startling NEAR FUTURE novel that describes an experiment gone wrong in which a tiny universe the size of a basketball is accidentally created. The upheaval created by such an amazing discovery sends reverberations throughout the entire scientific world, and puts both the experiment and its deviser in danger.

Benford has also produced a massive and disturbing FUTURE HISTORY, the *Galactic Centre* sequence, that depicts a universe overrun by ARTIFICIAL INTELLIGENCE and in which machines are the dominant form of life. Indeed, the machines later become hostile and human colonies must fight or flee to survive their expansion across the galaxy. The novels associated with the sequence include *In the Ocean of the Night* (1977), *Across the Sea of Suns* (1984), *Great Sky River* (1987), *Tides of Light* (1989), *Furious Gulf* (1994) and *Sailing Bright Eternity* (1995). They are detailed and LITERARY, although still retaining an edge of true scientific speculation that keeps them just within the confines of hard SF.

In 1986 Benford teamed up with David Brin on *Heart of the Comet*, in which a group of scientists burrow into Halley's Comet as it passes by the Earth, inhabiting its core until it returns to the Solar System on its next transit seventy-six years later. The researchers emerge somewhat different to how they were when they originally set off on their expedition. It is an interesting collaboration between the two writers, but unfortunately the whole fails to live up to the sum of its parts.

Recent novels from Benford include his sequel to ISAAC ASIMOV's *Foundation* sequence, *Foundation's Fear* (1997), which is the first of a trilogy written in collaboration with Brin and Bear, and *Eater* (2000), which explores the possibilities of a sentient BLACK HOLE that arrives at the edge of the Solar System wishing to incorporate the human race into its symbiotic intelligence.

See Also
ARTIFICIAL INTELLIGENCE; BLACK HOLE; ECOLOGY; FUTURE HISTORY; HARD SF; NEAR FUTURE; LITERARY SF; ROBOT

Recommended Further Reading
The Forge of God (1987) by GREG BEAR; the *Uplift* sequence by DAVID BRIN; the *Foundation* sequence by ISAAC ASIMOV

Bibliography
Deeper than the Darkness (1970)
In the Ocean of Night (1977)
If the Stars are Gods (1977, with Gordon Eklund)
Find the Changeling (1980, with Gordon Eklund)
Shiva Descending (1980, with William Rotsler)
Timescape (1980)
Against Infinity (1983)
Across the Sea of Suns (1984)
Artefact (1985)
Heart of the Comet (1986, with DAVID BRIN)
In Alien Flesh (short stories, 1986)
Great Sky River (1987)
Tides of Light (1989)
Beyond the Fall of Night (1990)
Furious Gulf (1994)
Sailing Bright Eternity (1995)
Matter's End (short stories, 1996)
Foundation's Fear (1997)
Cosm (1998)
The Martian Race (1999)
Eater (2000)
Worlds Vast and Various (short stories, 2000)

BERRY, RICK (1953–   ), USA
Rick Berry is an American artist and illustrator whose work is of elaborate depth and surreality. His images frequently combine elements of oil painting and pencil or chalk sketches with digital coloration and effects.

Berry spent many years travelling through the US, trying his hand at various pursuits before settling down for a career as an illustrator. He has no formal training and professes to paint from his own inspiration, developing each piece as he works without any preconceptions about how it will finally look. It is usual for a Berry piece to focus on people, or more often one person – an abstract figure displaying themself and their environment to the viewer. There is a dark and Gothic tone to much of Berry's work, a bruised examination of humanity and its place in the world, as well as a sophisticated portrayal of the human interface with technology; more often than not, Berry's characters are implanted with various machines or augmented with cybernetic components. In essence, Berry's work captures explicitly the detail of the latter-day post-CYBERPUNK movement.

Famous book illustrations by Berry include WILLIAM GIBSON's *Neuromancer* (1984), MICHAEL MOORCOCK's omnibus collection *Sailing to Utopia* and, more recently, various jackets for STAR WARS media tie-in novels.

BESHER, ALEXANDER, Japan / USA

A minor author of CYBERPUNK whose work is reminiscent of both WILLIAM GIBSON's and JON COURTENAY GRIMWOOD's, but not as good as that of either author.

Besher's first novel, *Rim* (1994), is set against the backdrop of a NEAR-FUTURE Japan and details the exploits of Professor Frank Gobi as he enters a VIRTUAL REALITY city in an attempt to find and rescue his son. The book suffers from its rather unoriginal take on virtual reality, yet it still has some redeeming features, picking up pace and character about a third of the way through. It was followed by *Mir* (1997) and *Chi* (1999), which together with *Rim* form a loose trilogy.

See Also
CYBERPUNK

Recommended Further Reading
Neuromancer (1984) by WILLIAM GIBSON; *Islands in the Net* (1988) by BRUCE STERLING; *reMix* (1999) by JON COURTENAY GRIMWOOD; *To Hold Infinity* (1998) by JOHN MEANEY

Bibliography
Rim (1994)
Mir (1997)

Chi (1999)
Hanging Butoh (2001)

BESTER, ALFRED (1913–1987), USA

Alfred Bester first made his mark in SF during the GOLDEN AGE, with a string of highly intelligent and well-plotted short stories for the popular magazines of the time.

It was not until later, though, during the 1950s, that Bester truly showed his hand. After a number of years working as a scriptwriter for various television shows and comic books, he returned his attention to SF.

His first genre novel, *The Demolished Man* (1953), is one of the true classics of science fiction, a masterpiece of LITERARY SF that is so tightly plotted and energetically presented that it remains unequalled today. Bester exudes style and panache.

The story concerns itself with a media businessman, Ben Reich, who commits murder in a society in which crime is almost unheard of because it is full of telepaths. He almost gets away with it, until he is caught by police inspector Lincoln Powell and taken in for corrective brainwashing, or 'demolition'. The strength of the book, however, lies not in the plot but in the presentation: Bester excels in literary style and description and plays with the form of the text to depict textually telepathic 'conversations'. The book was to go on to win the very first HUGO AWARD for Best Novel of the year.

The Stars My Destination (1956), which is also known by the far superior title *Tiger! Tiger!* (in reference to William Blake), was Bester's next novel. It follows the progress of Gully Foyle, a space pilot who is left to die in the void when his vessel is wrecked but instead develops mysterious powers, including the ability to 'jaunt' or TELEPORT. He returns to the planet with a grudge against his former boss; indeed, it is this desire for revenge that leads to Foyle inheriting his new powers and surpassing his roots as an unpromising space pilot. Together with *The Demolished Man*, *The Stars My Destination* established Bester as one of the finest writers ever to grace the SF genre.

However, after a long hiatus during which Bester became literary editor of *Holiday* magazine, his next return to SF was to pale by comparison with his former exuberance.

The Computer Connection (1975) is not an unsatisfactory work, but neither does it achieve the sheer excellence of Bester's previous two genre novels. It describes the struggle of a group of immortals who attempt to take over Extro, the supercomputer that governs the Earth, in a move to rid the planet of political oppression. Unfortunately things go awry and the computer instead takes over one of the immortals – the rest of the group must then try to work out how to destroy their supposedly immortal friend.

Bester next produced *Golem 100* (1980) and *The Deceivers* (1981), two average novels that are perhaps a little misdirected after the achievements of his earlier work. *The Deceivers* was to be the last of his books published during Bester's lifetime.

He died in 1987, aged 74.

But in 1998 a novel entitled *Psychoshop* appeared, supposedly a collaboration between Bester and ROGER ZELAZNY. In fact, it was the novel Bester had been working on when he died; Zelazny finished it and prepared it for publication. Although reminiscent of Bester's later work, the book is not as good as one would expect from a collaboration between these two outstanding authors.

Bester's short fiction is collected in the superb *Virtual Unrealities* (1997), a posthumous retrospective of his career.

Bester was to have a major influence on many other genre writers, both during his lifetime and after it. He remains one of the most widely respected authors of American science fiction, and his two classic novels, *The Demolished Man* and *The Stars My Destination* are revered by many as two of the best ever written.

See Also
CRIME; GOLDEN AGE; LITERARY SF; TELEPORTATION

Recommended Further Reading
A Million Open Doors (1993) by JOHN BARNES; *Hothouse* (1962) or *Non-Stop* (1958) by BRIAN ALDISS; *The Fifth Head of Cerberus* (1972) by GENE WOLFE

Bibliography
Who He? (1953)
The Demolished Man (1953)
The Stars My Destination (1956)
Starburst (short stories, 1958)
The Dark Side of the Earth (short stories, 1964)
The Computer Connection (1975)
The Light Fantastic (short stories, 1976)

Star Light, Star Bright (short stories, 1976)
Starlight: The Great Short Fiction of Alfred Bester (short stories, 1976)
Golem 100 (1980)
The Deceivers (1981)
Tender Loving Rage (1991)
Virtual Unrealities (short stories, 1997)
Psychoshop (1998, with ROGER ZELAZNY)

BETHKE, BRUCE (1955–), USA

A fairly minor genre author who has nevertheless had an impact on the CYBERPUNK movement with his eponymous 1980 short story, 'Cyberpunk'. Detailing the exploits of a group of teenage computer hackers, it encapsulated much of what the movement was to become – indeed, inspiring critics to adopt its title as the name of the newly formed subgenre.

The story was revised and expanded to novel length, and is available to download from http://www1.fatbrain.com/asp/bookinfo/bookinfo.asp?theisbn=EB00002364 for a fee of $4.

Bethke's only other novel of note is *Headcrash* (1995). A NEAR FUTURE example of COMIC SF that follows the adventures of a jilted computer programmer who uses VIRTUAL REALITY as a means of wreaking revenge on his previous employers. Humorous and light, the novel is a good remedy to the many cyberpunk novels that take themselves a little too seriously.

Bethke is reportedly working on a sequel, *Headcrash 2.0*.

See Also
COMIC SF; CYBERPUNK; NEAR FUTURE; VIRTUAL REALITY

Recommended Further Reading
Neuromancer (1984) by WILLIAM GIBSON; *Islands in the Net* (1988) by BRUCE STERLING

Bibliography (Selected)
Cyberpunk (1980)
Headcrash (1995)

BLISH, JAMES (1921–1975), USA

One of the most respected writers of thoughtful, LITERARY SF, James Blish created some of the best genre writing to come out of the 1950s.

Many of his early stories appeared in magazines such as ASTOUNDING SCIENCE FICTION and formed the backbone to a large SPACE OPERA sequence known as the 'Okie' stories. These stories tell of ANTI-GRAVITY devices, or 'Spindizzies', that are used to lift entire cities into orbit. Throughout the sequence, these cities wander the stars as the Earth grows old and stagnates, their near-immortal inhabitants going on to form a huge Galactic Empire. It is a vast and enjoyable space opera, which nevertheless shows its more serious side in its portrayal of history as a cyclical process; the 'flying' New York City eventually encounters the end of the universe, but then, during the ensuing TRANSCENDENCE, plays a major role in the birth of the next one. Originally the stories were collected in four volumes, *Earthman, Come Home* (1955), *They Shall Have Stars* (1956), *The Triumph of Time* (1958) and *A Life for the Stars* (1962), but were eventually collected together in one huge volume as *Cities in Flight* (1970).

Regarded as Blish's best full-length novel, and certainly his most thought-provoking, *A Case of Conscience* (1958) sees him at the peak of his form, and the book is one of the earliest and most profound attempts to discuss RELIGION in SF. It follows Jesuit biologist-priest Ramon Ruiz-Sanchez on his journey to the ALIEN planet Lithia, which resembles Earth during the epoch of the dinosaurs. He finds there a race of intelligent reptiles who live in an apparent UTOPIA, but without any concept of God. Ruiz-Sanchez is tortured by this dichotomy, and is forced to decide whether these creatures who know nothing of Original Sin are in fact creations of the Devil.

The book is startling and intellectual, and is one of the finest examples of American SF, justly winning the HUGO AWARD for Best Novel in 1959.

Also during this period, Blish produced another of his best works in the form of the thematically linked collection, *The Seedling Stars* (1957). A trained microbiologist, Blish introduced BIOLOGY into SF with this sequence of stories that concerns the scattering of human beings throughout space like spores. These human colonists have all been GENETICALLY engineered and manipulated to allow them to better survive in their new and often hostile environments. The best known of these stories is 'Surface Tension', which details the trial of a group of tiny colonists who live inside a pool of water and are attempting to break the surface so as to transcend their situation. Their success invokes an almost unparalleled SENSE OF WONDER, and the story was to have a major influence on many writers, including STEPHEN BAXTER, who went on to write a number of HARD SF stories that follow a similar pattern and clearly owe some of their inspiration to Blish.

Of Blish's other work, his collaboration with Norman L. Knight on *A Torrent of Faces* (1967) is worthy of note. It describes an Earth ravaged by OVERPOPULATION but nevertheless managing to maintain some sort of uneasy stability.

It is fair to say that Blish wrote much of his best work during the late 1940s and 1950s, some of it among the most successful SF to come out of that period. He later went on to produce a huge number of STAR TREK novelizations, as well as the first original *Star Trek* novel (*Spock Must Die*). But these were obviously written primarily for money and do no display the literary and intellectual skill evident in his earlier work.

See Also

ANTI-GRAVITY; BIOLOGY; GENETICS; HARD SF; LITERARY SF; OVERPOPULATION; RELIGION; SPACE OPERA; TRANS-CENDENCE

Recommended Further Reading

Traces (1998) by STEPHEN BAXTER; *The Secret of Life* (2000) by PAUL J. McAULEY; *Logan's Run* (1967) by William F. Nolan and George Clayton Johnson; *Man Plus* (1976) by FREDERIK POHL

Bibliography

Jack of Eagles (1952)
The Warriors of Day (1953)
Earthman, Come Home (1955)
They Shall Have Stars (1956)
The Seedling Stars (short stories, 1957)
Fallen Star (1957)
The Triumph of Time (1958)
Vor (1958)
A Case of Conscience (1958)
Galactic Cluster (short stories, 1959)
The Duplicated Man (1959, with R.A.W. Lowndes)
So Close to Home (short stories, 1961)
The Star Dwellers (1961)

Titan's Daughter (1961)
The Night Shapes (1962)
A Life for the Stars (1962)
Doctor Mirabilis (1964)
Best Science Fiction Stories of James Blish (short stories, 1965)
A Torrent of Faces (1967, with Norman L. Knight)
Black Easter (1968)
Anywhen (short stories, 1970)
Cities in Flight (1970)
The Day After Judgement (1971)
. . . And All the Stars a Stage (1971)
Midsummer Century (1972)
The Quincunx of Time (1973)
The Best of James Blish (short stories, 1979)

BOULLE, PIERRE (1912–   ), France

Pierre Boulle is a French writer most famous for his classic World War Two novel *The Bridge on the River Kwai* (1954).

However, it is for his later (1963) *Monkey Planet* (UK title) that he is included here.

In it, space explorers travel to the distant planet Soror, which is known to have a breathable atmosphere and is thought to support life. Indeed, upon arrival the travellers find a planet similar to Earth in many ways. However, they soon come to learn that instead of humans, apes have become the dominant, intelligent species: *Homo sapiens* is merely an animalistic slave race. After a year of imprisonment, the explorers escape and return to Earth but, relativistically, seven hundred years have passed in their absence. To their dismay they find the Earth too is now overrun with apes.

Monkey Planet is an excellent piece of satirical LITERARY SF and was filmed successfully, although none too faithfully, as PLANET OF THE APES (1968, starring Charlton Heston). The film was followed by four less successful sequels, as well as a television series. A remake of the movie is currently in production with Tim Burton as director.

See Also
FAR FUTURE; LITERARY SF; POST-APOCALYPTIC

Bibliography (Selected)

La Planète des Singes (1963: translated as *Monkey Planet* (UK) and *Planet of the Apes* (US))

BOVA, BEN (1932–   ), USA

It was as an editor that US writer Ben Bova made his first major impact on the SF field.

Bova was a science writer for a research laboratory when the offer came in for him to assume the editorship of ANALOG magazine after the death of JOHN W. CAMPBELL in 1971. The magazine had begun to stagnate during the last year's of Campbell's long editorship, and Bova, tentatively at first, and then with gusto, began widening the scope of the fiction he published to bring the magazine more in line with the modern genre climate. He maintained Campbell's penchant for the more hard-edged and scientifically rational story, and if anything helped to foster the magazine's reputation as the first port of call for HARD SF readers – and writers. *Analog* flourished under his editorship, and it is fair to say that he probably saved the magazine from an inevitable decline. He was awarded numerous HUGO AWARDS for his editorial skill and judgement during this period.

Bova stayed with *Analog* until 1978, and then, after a brief stint as an editor of *Omni* magazine, settled down to become a full-time writer.

Bova had been writing successfully for a number of years before he took the post at *Analog*. His first published novel was a juvenile, *The Star Conquerors* (1959).

The Kinsman Saga (1987) probably represents the best-known of his early post-*Analog* work, and comprises the two novels *Kinsman* (a fix-up of earlier stories, 1979) and *Millennium* (1976). *Colony* (1978) is an appendage to the main *Kinsman* sequence.

These novels tackle many of the themes that would later come to dominate Bova's writing – for example, the POLITICAL wrangling over funding of the space programmes, and the need for humanity to branch out to the stars. In fact, the stories themselves are rather dry, a little too weighty with philosophizing and scientific speculation and with insufficient human interest to keep the reader engaged. *Kinsman* follows the progress of left-wing astronaut Chet Kinsman, who is forced to compromise his politics if he wishes to get to the Moon, whilst *Millennium* explores the ramifications of a 'Star Wars' policy of the type that would later become such a key part of President Reagan's time in office. The later *Colony* concerns the running of an orbital colony station as a NEAR-FUTURE Earth goes to pieces beneath it.

In each of these novels, Bova ably demonstrates his Hard SF rationale but the stories themselves are rather devoid of character.

However, later works by Bova are more ambitious. *The Voyagers* sequence, beginning with *Voyagers* (1981) and continuing with *Voyagers II: The Alien Within* (1982) and *Voyagers III: Star Brothers* (1990), sets its Hard SF premise within a SPACE OPERA framework that sees a more human and adventurous approach to the story's subject. An ALIEN vessel enters the Solar System and the US and the USSR mount a joint expedition to investigate. Eventually, working together, humanity is able to learn from the alien visitors and begin its expansion to the stars.

Mars (1992) and its sequel *Return to Mars* (1999) are perhaps Bova's best novels. In them the first manned missions to the Red Planet are depicted in full and intricate detail. An international team of astronauts is sent to Mars to establish whether life exists in the harsh conditions there.

However, a meteor shower punctures their sealed-environment tent, and a number of them fall mysteriously ill. American Jamie Waterman, after battling with the mission's Earthbound bureaucrats, assumes unofficial control and goes on to find a form of primitive lichen living on the floor of the enormous Martian canyon Vallis Marineris. The sequel sees Waterman heading back to the planet to continue his research, at the same time attempting to fight off the predatory corporate sponsors of the mission who want to see Mars become a tourist attraction.

Indeed, this is one of Bova's most frequently addressed issues – he envisions the space programme being privatized and swallowed up by rapacious corporate investors.

The *Mars* books, although they expound the traditional virtues of Hard SF, have a human edge that is missing from much of Bova's earlier work.

Also worthy of note are Bova's 'Moon' novels *Moonrise* (1996) and *Moonwar* (1997), which describe the establishment of a human settlement on the Moon and the ensuing political nightmare when the NANO-TECHNOLOGY it relies on to survive is banned by the governments of the Earth.

Bova has recently also been considering other PLANETS in the Solar System and the eventual means by which we may visit them or harness their resources. *Venus* (1999) concerns a mission to the lethal planet by a man who is attempting to recover the body of his brother, lost on a previous attempt to land on its hostile surface.

Ben Bova is one of the leading proponents of American Hard SF, and his writing raises real issues that have to be addressed if the human race is ever going to make its way to the other planets of the Solar System, let alone to the stars. What is more, Bova goes on to consider the ways in which humanity might make this giant leap, and the resources that will be needed for any such mission to succeed. He is an optimist and a true writer of the future.

A website is maintained, with the help of the author, at http://www.benbova.net

See Also
HARD SF; NANOTECHNOLOGY; PLANETS; SPACE; SPACE TRAVEL

Recommended Further Reading
The *Mars Trilogy* by KIM STANLEY ROBINSON; *Bios* (1999) by ROBERT CHARLES WILSON; *The Secret of Life* (2000) by PAUL J. McAULEY; *Voyage* (1996) or *Titan* (1997) by STEPHEN BAXTER

Bibliography
The Star Conquerors (1959)
Star Watchman (1964)
The Weathermakers (1967)
Out of the Sun (1968)
The Dueling Machine (1969)
Escape! (1970)
Exiled from Earth (1971)
THX 1138 (1971, movie novelization)
Flight of Exiles (1972)
Forward in Time (short stories, 1973)
When the Sky Burned (1973)
The Winds of Altair (1973)
Gremlins, Go Home! (1974, with Gordon Dickson)
End of Exile (1975)
The Starcrossed (1975)
City of Darkness (1976)
Millennium (1976)
The Multiple Man (1976)
Viewpoint (short stories, 1977)
Colony (1978)

Maxwell's Demons (short stories, 1978)
Kinsman (1979)
Voyagers (1981)
Voyagers II: The Alien Within (1982)
Test of Fire (1982)
Escape Plus (short stories, 1983)
Orion (1984)
The Astral Mirror (short stories, 1985)
Privateers (1985)
Prometheans (short stories, 1986)
Battle Station (short stories, 1987)
Peacekeepers (1988)
Vengeance of Orion (1988)
Cyberbooks (1989)
Future Crime (short stories, 1990)
Orion in the Dying Time (1990)
Voyagers III: Star Brothers (1990)
Mars (1992)
Sam Gunn, Unlimited (1992)
To Save the Sun (1992)
The Trikon Deception (1992, with Bill Pogue)
Challenges (short stories, 1993)
Empire Builders (1993)
Triumph (1993)
Death Dream (1994)
Orion and the Conqueror (1994)
The Watchmen (1994)
Brothers (1995)
Orion Among the Stars (1995)
Moonrise (1996)
Moonwar (1997)
Storm Fury (1997)
Twice Seven (short stories, 1998)
Immortality (1998)
Sam Gunn Forever (1998)
Return to Mars (1999)
Venus (2000)
Jupiter (2000)

BRADBURY, RAY (1920–   ), USA

Primarily a writer of short stories, most of Ray Bradbury's fiction is fantasy and horror rather than SF. He has no use for science except as an allegorical device. However, some of his fiction, although not SF by definition, can certainly be classified as SCIENCE FANTASY.

In *The Martian Chronicles* (1950), Bradbury writes of the experiences of a group of Martian colonists in a loose but thematically linked series of tales that span twenty-seven years at the end of the twentieth century and the beginning of the twenty-first. Poetic and insightful, the stories concern themselves with the changing human dynamics and the relationship between the colonists and the shape-shifting ALIEN natives. In many respects the tales are LITERARY and HUMANIST, and although Bradbury's images of the Martian colony are long since outdated, this hardly matters; the stories themselves are haunting exercises in narrative style and are more truly about emotion and character, not about the (likely) reality of Mars. Originally published in various genre magazines, the collected *Martian Chronicles* remain Bradbury's best work to date.

The collection justly received widespread mainstream success upon publication, helping to establish Bradbury as a serious literary player. The stories were adapted, not too successfully, as a television series in the 1970s.

Bradbury's best novel-length work is *Fahrenheit 451* (1953), a dark, DYSTOPIC story set in a future society in which literacy and print are outlawed. The chief protagonist is Montag, a 'Fireman' – a man trained to seek out and burn books – who comes to realize the importance of reading and literature. Like the 'criminals' he tracks down at the beginning of the novel, by its end he is memorizing an entire book to preserve it for future generations. The novel was filmed in 1966 by François Truffaut under the same title.

The only other book by Bradbury to feature much in the way of SF themes and devices is *The Illustrated Man* (1951), another collection of short stories linked by an overall framework. The 'illustrated man' of the title is covered by tattoos – each of these tattoos represents a different story. The best of these include 'The Long Rain' and 'Zero Hour'.

Of Bradbury's other short-story collections, the most worthy of note are *The October Country* (1955), *The Machineries of Joy* (1964) and the more recent *Quicker Than the Eye* (1996).

See Also
DYSTOPIA; LITERARY SF; SCIENCE FANTASY

Recommended Further Reading
Desolation Road (1988) by Ian McDonald; *Nineteen Eighty-Four* (1949) by
GEORGE ORWELL; *Brave New World* (1932) by ALDOUS HUXLEY

Bibliography (Selected)
Dark Carnival (short stories, 1947)
The Martian Chronicles (short stories, 1950)
The Illustrated Man (short stories, 1951)
The Golden Apples of the Sun (short stories, 1953)
Fahrenheit 451 (1953)
The October Country (short stories, 1955)
Dandelion Wine (1957)
The Day it Rained Forever (short stories, 1959)
R is for Rocket (short stories 1962)
Something Wicked This Way Comes (1962)
The Machineries of Joy (short stories, 1964)
The Vintage Bradbury (short stories, 1965)
S is for Space (short stories, 1966)
I Sing the Body Electric! (short stories, 1969)
Long After Midnight (short stories, 1976)
To Sing Strange Songs (short stories, 1979)
The Stories of Ray Bradbury (short stories, 1980)
Dinosaur Tales (short stories, 1983)
The Toynbee Convector (short stories, 1988)
Quicker Than The Eye (short stories, 1996)
Driving Blind (short stories, 1997)
Ahmed and the Oblivion Machine: A Fable (1998)

BRIN, DAVID (1950–   ), USA

The third of the 'killer Bs' of American HARD SF – after GREG BEAR
and GREGORY BENFORD – David Brin made his mark on the genre in
1980 with the publication of *Sundiver*, the first in his huge SPACE
OPERA *Uplift* sequence.

The book is more space opera than hard SF, although the two are not
mutually exclusive and Brin does make use of his training is astronomy
and physics when describing his universe. The story follows a group of
humans and 'uplifted' animals – dolphins and chimpanzees that have
been GENETICALLY enhanced by the humans to provide them with
full sentience – into the Sun, where they meet some members of an

ancient ALIEN race who pass on to them knowledge of the origins of life in the galaxy. The book won both the HUGO and NEBULA AWARDS for Best Novel of its year. The series continued with the sequels *Startide Rising* (1983), *The Uplift War* (1987), *Brightness Reef* (1995), *Infinity's Shore* (1996) and *Heaven's Reach* (1998), which follow the progress of the human and animal races as they slowly uncover the secrets of the Progenitors, the father race that seeded our galaxy and others with life before disappearing. Well realized and bursting with sheer exuberance, the *Uplift* sequence is reminiscent of GOLDEN AGE space opera in its scope and sense of adventure.

The Postman (1985) saw a change of pace and style for Brin, as he portrayed a POST-APOCALYPTIC environment in which the protagonist adopts the role of a postman, ferrying information and news among secluded groups of survivors after a nuclear holocaust has devastated America. He eventually finds himself involved in the slow rebuilding of civilization. The novel received mixed reviews upon initial publication, and a dire movie version in 1997 did not enhance its popularity. Nevertheless, its images persist, and it is one of the best-known, if not best-respected, post-apocalyptic tales.

Another ambitious project for Brin, along similar lines, was *Earth* (1990), a massive novel of ECOLOGY and OVERPOPULATION in which the Earth teeters on the brink of extinction because of a mistake in a physics laboratory involving a BLACK HOLE. More satisfying than *The Postman*, *Earth* succeeds in blending adventurous plotting with big hard-SF ideas.

More recently Brin has written *Foundation's Triumph* (1999), the final volume in a set of authorized sequels to ISAAC ASIMOV'S classic *Foundation* sequence. Earlier volumes were written by Benford and Bear respectively.

Brin has also collaborated with Benford on *Heart of the Comet* (1986), a disappointing novel about the exploration of Halley's Comet. The ideas are there but the commingling of the two different authors' styles does not live up to expectations.

Brin's best shorter work is collected in *The River of Time* (1986), which includes his famed novella *The Crystal Spheres*.

See Also

ALIEN; GENETICS; HARD SF; ECOLOGY; OVERPOPULATION; POST-APOCALYPTIC; SPACE OPERA

Recommended Further Reading
The *Xeelee* sequence by STEPHEN BAXTER; *The Sheep Look Up* (1972) by JOHN BRUNNER; the *Night's Dawn Trilogy* by PETER F. HAMILTON

Bibliography
Sundiver (1980)
Startide Rising (1983)
The Practice Effect (1984)
The Postman (1985)
The River of Time (short stories, 1986)
The Heart of the Comet (1986, with GREGORY BENFORD)
The Uplift War (1987)
Earth (1990)
Glory Season (1993)
Otherness (short stories, 1994)
Brightness Reef (1995)
Infinity's Shore (1996)
Heaven's Reach (1998)
Foundation's Triumph (1999)

BROOKE, KEITH (1966–   ), Great Britain
A writer of the INTERZONE generation and editor of the superb INFINITY PLUS website, Keith Brooke has produced four novels to date.

His first, *Keepers of the Peace* (1990) is a NEAR-FUTURE tale that camouflages anti-militaristic sentiments under the guise of a MILITARISTIC SF novel. It follows the progress of a group of soldiers who are given the task of holding the tentative peace in a USA that is falling apart at the seams.

Expatria (1991) and its sequel *Expatria Incorporated* (1992) are set within a FUTURE HISTORY that also includes many of Brooke's shorter works. They take place on the technologically backwards colony world Expatria, which over long periods of time has lost touch with the rest of humanity. The first novel revolves around a young protagonist who is under investigation for murder, whilst the second details the re-establishment of contact between Expatria and a vessel from Earth.

Lord of Stone (1998) is a fantasy novel set during the aftermath of a war. It was self-published on the Internet, and is available from http://www.iplus.zetnet.co.uk/kbrooke/stone/ to download as care-ware.

Brooke has also written a number of excellent short stories in collaboration with fellow Interzone author ERIC BROWN. They are collected together in *Parallax View* (2000).

See Also
FUTURE HISTORY; MILITARISTIC SF; NEAR FUTURE; PLANETS

Recommended Further Reading
Bill, the Galactic Hero (1965) by HARRY HARRISON; *The Time- Lapsed Man and Other Stories* (1990) by ERIC BROWN

Bibliography
Keepers of the Peace (1990)
Expatria (1991)
Expatria Incorporated (1992)
Lord of Stone (1998)
Parallax View (short stories, 2000, with ERIC BROWN)
Head Shots (projected, short stories, 2001)

BROWN, ERIC (1960–   ), Great Britain
Renowned for many years among readers of INTERZONE magazine for such inventive and insightful short stories as 'The Time-Lapsed Man' and 'Vulpheous' (uncollected), it is fair to say that Eric Brown writes LITERARY SF with panache and style. As a literary craftsman he excels and his observations are astute and effective.

However, until the publication of *Penumbra* (1999), Brown, although respected by his peers, had gone virtually unnoticed by the mainstream market.

Penumbra is about the adventures of police lieutenant Rana Rao as she stalks a serial killer in twenty-second-century Calcutta, as well as those of a tug pilot who is sent out to a distant planet where he goes on to encounter a mysterious alien race. Written with verve, *Penumbra* still sadly lacks the sheer individuality of Brown's shorter fiction.

This is best showcased in the two collections, *The Time-Lapsed Man and Other Stories* (1990) and *Blue Shifting* (1995) that illustrate Brown's painstaking use of language as well as his ability to take a strong idea to its logical conclusion.

Brown has also recently produced a number of excellent shorter works that, although still uncollected, are known as the *Fall of Tartarus* sequence. These stories all have the common setting of the planet Tartarus, which orbits a distant star that is about to nova. The stories deal with the effect the imminent destruction of the planet is having on the people who inhabit it, and include some of Brown's most thoughtful writing to date.

With *New York Nights* (2000), the first in his projected *Virex* trilogy, Brown produced a novel that manages to sustain the clarity and style of his shorter work. Essentially it deals with VIRTUAL REALITY and ARTIFICIAL INTELLIGENCE while relating the adventures of two missing-persons investigators in a DYSTOPIC New York City. When a woman employs the agents to track down her missing lover, the two of them become embroiled in a plot to destroy a malignant machine intelligence that is invading people's neural implants via virtual reality. This is perhaps Brown's most ambitious work to date and his characters are portrayed with vitality and depth; he makes good use of science fiction as a tool to deliver his personal perspective on the world.

Brown has also produced, in collaboration with fellow author KEITH BROOKE, a collection of stories entitled *Parallax View* (2000).

See Also
ARTIFICIAL INTELLIGENCE; CRIME; DYSTOPIA; LITERARY SF; PLANET; SPACE TRAVEL; VIRTUAL REALITY

Recommended Further Reading
The Naked Sun (1957) or *The Caves of Steel* (1954) by ISAAC ASIMOV; *The Demolished Man* (1953) by ALFRED BESTER; *Traces* (1998) by STEPHEN BAXTER

Bibliography
The Time-Lapsed Man and Other Stories (short stories, 1990)
Meridian Days (1992)
Engineman (1994)
Blue Shifting (short stories, 1995)
Untouchable (juvenile, 1997)
Walkabout (juvenile, 1999)
Penumbra (1999)

New York Nights (2000)
Parallax View (short stories, 2000, with KEITH BROOKE)
New York Blues (projected, 2001)
Deep Future (projected, short stories, 2001)

BRUNNER, JOHN (1934–1995), Great Britain

John Brunner began his career in SF at a remarkably young age, publishing his first novel, *Galactic Storm* (1951), at the age of seventeen. After this he spent many years in literary apprenticeship, producing dozens of SPACE OPERAS for the American Ace Doubles series.

The novels published during this period are nearly all eloquent and rich, the best of their kind – space operas full of intrigue and adventure but at the same time having about them a certain literary quality that was lacking from much of the other pulp fiction of the time. It is fair to say that in the early part of his career Brunner made an indelible impression on the predominantly American readers of the Ace Doubles paperbacks.

During the 1960s Brunner was also to become associated with the British NEW WAVE, a movement that expounded the use of more LITERARY, mainstream devices in SF, as well as fostering a preoccupation with entropy and dissolution.

Novels such as *Telepathist* (1965) and *The Squares of the City* (1965) from this period show Brunner in a new light, as the space-opera feel of his earlier work gives way to a more sure and developed form and he begins to reveal his true talents.

Telepathist concerns the TRANSCENDENCE of a deformed and crippled protagonist, Howson, who becomes accepted by society again when he is found to have inherent telepathic powers. It is an evocative and sometimes moving portrait of a man at first ostracized by society, then suddenly accepted by it, and the psychological burden that he must learn to bear.

The Squares of the City is only partly successful as a literary representation of the game of chess. A huge city takes the place of the board, and the characters are the players. However, while the novel does not wholly succeed, it does indicate the direction in which Brunner was heading, and the literary heights that his work would later reach.

Indeed, with the publication of *Stand On Zanzibar* (1968), Brunner's most ambitious novel, and at the time the longest work of SF to be published, he showed his true skill as a writer.

Stand On Zanzibar features a superbly drawn DYSTOPIA in which pollution and OVERPOPULATION are about to lead to a massive environmental collapse. In it, Brunner plays with narrative form and style to create an innovative and creative book that won the 1968 HUGO AWARD for Best Novel.

The plot weaves together a number of different narratives that, taken together, produce an image of a slowly disintegrating world in which there are too many people, too many machines and not enough resources. It is bleak and startling, but still stands as Brunner's most inventive book.

Three other novels followed over the next few years, thematically roughly similar, to form a loose quartet with *Stand on Zanzibar*. They are *The Jagged Orbit* (1969), *The Sheep Look Up* (1972) and *The Shockwave Rider* (1975). Together they comprise Brunner's most notable body of work, and represent some of the most prophetic writing of the 1960s and 1970s.

The Jagged Orbit describes a USA buckling under the pressure of a racial war while society at large suffers from oppression by the state, which feels free to institutionalize people on a whim, and the depredations of arms merchants and drug dealers who are growing rich on immoral trade.

The Sheep Look Up is perhaps Brunner's darkest book, and depicts a North America which is facing extinction due to incredibly high levels of pollution. An ecologist 'hero' attempts to stir people into action, but to no avail – the country is doomed to die. The novel is a depressing warning of the foolishness of inaction.

Finally, *The Shockwave Rider* draws its images from the world of computers, portraying a society oppressed by overexposure to machines and technology. This dystopia is more a warning against the excesses of technology than against environmental collapse.

Brunner's later work never managed to reclaim the glory of these four masterpieces, although many of the books concerned are still substantial, some even returning to the space-opera genre that he had once abandoned.

Sadly, Brunner died at the World Science Fiction Convention in 1995. He never gained the recognition he truly deserved, first as a writer of fluent, adventurous space opera, then as an author who produced some of the best literary work of the British New Wave.

See Also
DYSTOPIA; ECOLOGY; LITERARY; NEW WAVE; OVERPOPULATION; SPACE OPERA; TRANSCENDENCE

Recommended Further Reading
Logan's Run (1967) by William F. Nolan and George Clayton Johnson; *Earth* (1990) by DAVID BRIN; *Fahrenheit 451* (1953) by RAY BRAD-BURY; *The Demolished Man* (1953) by ALFRED BESTER

Bibliography (Selected)
Galactic Storm (1951)
The Brink (1959)
Echo in the Skull (1959)
The World Swappers (1959)
Threshold of Eternity (1959)
The Hundredth Millennium (1959)
The Atlantic Abomination (1960)
The Skynappers (1960)
Sanctuary in the Sky (1960)
Slavers of Space (1960)
Meeting at Infinity (1961)
I Speak for Earth (1961, as Keith Woodcott)
No Future in It (short stories, 1962)
The Super Barbarians (1962)
Times Without Number (1962)
Secret Agent of Terra (1962)
The Ladder in the Sky (1962, as Keith Woodcott)
Castaways' World (1963)
The Rites of Ohe (1963)
The Astronauts Must Not Land (1963)
The Dreaming Earth (1963)
Listen! The Stars! (1963)
The Space-Time Juggler (1963)
The Psionic Menace (1963, as Keith Woodcott)
Endless Shadow (1964)
To Conquer Chaos (1964)
The Crutch of Memory (1964)
Now Then (short stories, 1965)
The Repairmen of Cyclops (1965)
Day of the Star Cities (1965)
Telepathist (1965)
The Squares of the City (1965)
Enigma from Tantalus (1965)
The Long Result (1965)

The Altar on Asconel (1965)
The Martian Sphinx (1965, as Keith Woodcott)
No Other Gods but Me (short stories, 1966)
A Planet of Your Own (1966)
Born Under Mars (1967)
The Productions of Time (1967)
Quicksand (1967)
Out of My Mind (short stories, 1967)
Not Before Time (short stories, 1968)
Bedlam Planet (1968)
Father of Lies (1968)
Stand On Zanzibar (1968)
Double, Double (1969)
Timescoop (1969)
The Jagged Orbit (1969)
The Traveler in Black (short stories, 1971)
The Wrong End of Time (1971)
From This Day Forward (short stories, 1972)
The Dramaturges of Yan (1972)
The Sheep Look Up (1972)
Time-Jump (short stories, 1973)
The Stone that Never Came Down (1973)
Web of Everywhere (1974)
Total Eclipse (1974)
The Shockwave Rider (1975)
The Book of John Brunner (short stories, 1976)
Foreign Constellations (short stories, 1980)
Players at the Game of People (1980)
The Crucible of Time (1983)
The Tides of Time (1984)
The Shift Key (1987)
The Best of John Brunner (short stories, 1988)
Children of the Thunder (1989)

BUJOLD, LOIS McMASTER (1949–   ), USA

American writer Lois McMaster Bujold has been constantly and steadily producing quality SPACE OPERA for a number of years.

Her *Vorkosigan* saga is set within a universe peppered with human-colony PLANETS and interconnected by WORMHOLES. Most of the stories focus on the exploits of various members of the Vorkosigan family, feudal nobles of the planet Barrayar that was lost to the colonial network many years ago and has only recently been rediscovered.

The stories themselves are intelligent, witty adventures that are often laced with POLITICAL intrigue, as the governments of the various planets attempt to settle their feuds with rather underhand methods or blatant MILITARY force.

Miles Vorkosigan, the hero of many of the *Vorkosigan* novels, is the result of one such intrigue, a handicapped, brittle-boned young man who was born malformed due to attempts to poison his parents.

Bujold deals with this character in an affectionate and humane way, and sees Miles rise above his disabilities to become a soldier in the Barrayarian Navy as well as the leader of a small Mercenary movement. It is to Bujold's credit that her characterization of Miles is both humorous and touching.

The best novels of the sequence to date are *Falling Free* (1988), *The Vor Game* (1990), *Barrayar* (1991), *Memory* (1996) and *Komarr* (1998). *The Vor Game* having won a HUGO AWARD and *Falling Free* a NEBULA.

The *Vorkosigan* series is generic but enjoyable, funny and satisfying, and represents some of the best American Space Opera of its kind.

See Also
MILITARY SF; SPACE OPERA

Recommended Further Reading
The *Seafort Saga* by DAVID FEINTUCH; the *Serrano Legacy* by ELIZ-ABETH MOON; the *Honor Harrington* sequence by DAVID WEBER

Bibliography
Shards of Honor (1986)
The Warrior's Apprentice (1986)
Ethan of Athos (1986)
Falling Free (1988)
Borders of Infinity (short stories, 1989)
Brothers in Arms (1989)
The Vor Game (1990)
Barrayar (1991)
The Spirit Ring (1992)
Mirror Dance (1994)
Memory (1996)

Cetaganda (1996)
Cordelia's Honor (1996)
Dreamweaver's Dilemma (1997)
Young Miles (1997)
Komarr (1998)
A Civil Campaign (1999)

BURGESS, ANTHONY (1917–1993), Great Britain

Anthony Burgess is remembered best for his disturbing and outstanding novel *A Clockwork Orange* (1962), which became a cult classic and was very controversially filmed by STANLEY KUBRICK. However, Burgess should also be remembered as a critic, composer and mainstream novelist of some distinction. He was diagnosed in the late 1950s as having a brain tumour, at which point he became a full-time writer. He nevertheless lived a productive life until his death in 1993.

A Clockwork Orange is a bizarre, yet strangely moving and compelling LITERARY DYSTOPIA. It takes as its setting a NEAR-FUTURE England and its narrator is the fifteen-year-old Alex, a social miscreant who sets out with his gang of friends to rape, pillage and murder in reaction against the social control being imposed by the State. What follows is a disturbing, violent odyssey in which Alex is finally caught and 'cured', his mind reprogrammed by State psychologists to make him passively compliant. Touchingly, he also loses his soul. This is best exemplified by his inability any longer to enjoy the music of Beethoven, his favourite composer, once he has been through the psychological torture of his 'correction'. The novel is SOFT SF of the highest order – it studies both the psychological and sociological aspects of Alex's position, and the dystopia it describes is one in which State control has, possibly, gone too far and inadvertently created its own monster.

What sets Burgess's *A Clockwork Orange* apart from the other dystopias of its time is the author's bravura use of language – the entire novel is narrated by Alex in 'nadsat', a fictional argot derived from both Russian and English but vividly expressive and easily comprehensible. This is Burgess's most accomplished achievement – a near-future novel narrated in a near-future language. The book is original and influential, its images and language influencing not just the SF genre but world literature in general.

Burgess's other SF exists on the borders of the genre.

1985 (1978) is an answer to GEORGE ORWELL's *Nineteen Eighty-*

Four (1949), or at least an attempt to draw inspiration from it. It describes a dystopia similar to Orwell's but without its verisimilitude and with a very different POLITICAL perspective – in Burgess's novel Britain has been overrun by an Arab Empire.

The End of the World News (1983) is a book split into three separate parts, the first two being biographical studies of two twentieth-century figures, the third being set aboard a space vessel that is escaping the destruction of Earth. The characters on this vessel have been watching two historical programmes, the first about Freud, the second about Trotsky. The reader has been watching these programmes alongside them.

Much of Burgess's other work remains outside the SF genre. It seems that he was never entirely comfortable inside it. However, the SF that he did produce, particularly his greatest achievement, *A Clockwork Orange*, is intelligent, stylish and worthy of our attention.

See Also
DYSTOPIA; NEAR FUTURE; POLITICS; SOFT SF

Recommended Further Reading
Nineteen Eighty-Four (1949) by GEORGE ORWELL

Bibliography (Selected)
A Clockwork Orange (1962)
The Wanting Seed (1962)
1985 (1978)
The End of the World News (1983)

BURNS, JIM (1948–   ), Great Britain

Welsh artist Jim Burns has, since the 1980s, become recognized as one of the Grand Masters of the SF art world. His images are characterized by a strong sense of realism and wonderfully stylized environments, whilst at the same time they display a true understanding of their source material. His preferred medium is usually acrylic, although recently he has made great use of digital imaging technology to powerful effect.

Burns trained as an artist in both Wales and London and began his career as an SF illustrator in the early 1970s. This early period, during which Burns worked primarily for British publishers, saw him develop his now familiar style of ultra-realistic character depiction, juxtaposing this realism with backdrops that were both fantastic and exotic. He soon earned a dedicated following among SF fans for his bold and thoughtful representations of characters and their worlds. Indeed, much of this enthusiasm for his work can be put down to the fact that Burns's paintings show very obviously that he actually reads the work he has been commissioned to illustrate first, then selects a relevant and powerful image to paint. His affinity with SF literature is unparalleled amongst genre artists.

The 1980s saw a shift in the cover-art markets, and Burns begin to 'export' much of his work to the US. This has given an important international dimension to his appeal. He is now one of the most frequently commissioned SF artists in the field, with his work regularly appearing on both sides of the Atlantic and a HUGO AWARD for Best Professional Artist to his name.

Burns's classic dust-jacket illustrations are too numerous even to begin listing here, but of his most recent work the cover paintings for PETER F. HAMILTON's *Night's Dawn Trilogy*, GENE WOLFE's *Book of the Short Sun* series and PAUL J. McAULEY's *Red Dust* (1993) are all worthy of praise.

Jim Burns's work, along with that of his contemporary CHRIS MOORE, has come to be considered as the epitome of modern science fiction art.

BURROUGHS, EDGAR RICE (1875–1950), USA

Edgar Rice Burroughs is one of the most fondly remembered authors from the early pulp days of the SF genre. His enduring creations – *Tarzan of the Apes*, the lost subterranean world of *Pellucidar*, the strange and verdant PLANET of *Barsoom* – are a constant reminder of the sheer *fun* that could be had with the emerging genre in those early, heady days.

It is all too easy to mock the simplicity of Burroughs's stories and the stereotypical nature of his standard hero – the brave, bold warrior who will overcome all manner of strange and wonderful beasts to rescue the ineffectual princess – but at the heart of these tales lies an important and deliberate aim by the author: to give the reader a sense of adventure and enjoyment, to whisk them off to a distant world or unfamiliar land where they can forget about mundane reality and immerse themselves in the new and exotic. It is an aim that is missing from the work of many modern SF authors, which goes some way towards explaining the success of the more escapist fantasy genre over the last couple of decades.

Burroughs's best work of SCIENCE FANTASY remains *The Land*

that Time Forgot (1924), a tale of exploration and adventure in which he describes the discovery of a mysterious island near the South Pole upon which dinosaurs and other primitive species have survived. EVOLUTION has shaped these creatures in strange and enigmatic ways, and the heroes, stranded on the island, must find a way to escape if they wish to survive. It is a lively and entertaining story and even if the scientific speculation is rather contrived the novel is still enjoyable. Portions of the book were filmed in 1975 as the classic feature film THE LAND THAT TIME FORGOT.

The *Tarzan* books aside – although they have considerable crossover appeal they remain fundamentally fantasy – most of Burroughs's Science Fantasy work falls into three distinct sequences.

The *Barsoom* books are set upon a verdant Mars (Barsoom) inhabited by all manner of humanoid ALIENS. John Carter, the hero of many of the books, is transported to Barsoom by magical means beyond his control, and goes on to have a number of colourful adventures, eventually culminating in his winning the hand of Princess Thoris. The sequence begins with *A Princess of Mars* (1917), and continues for another eleven books, the best of which are *The Chessmen of Mars* (1922), *Swords of Mars* (1936) and *Synthetic Men of Mars* (1940).

The *Pellucidar* sequence is set within a hollow Earth, a locale where dinosaurs and primitive men live side by side and adventures are had by all. In the first volume, *At the Earth's Core* (1922), a group of scientists use their drilling machine to tunnel down into the hollow space at the centre of the planet. Once there, they find a subterranean landscape inhabited by many forms of prehistoric life that have survived there untouched for millions of years. They explore, and get caught up in a number of rather sticky situations. The series ran for a further six books, the best being the direct sequel *Pellucidar* (1923) and the cross over novel *Tarzan at the Earth's Core* (1930). *At the Earth's Core* was filmed in 1976 and retained the same title.

Burroughs's third series of Science Fantasies is made up of the four *Venus* books and is essentially a planetary romance in the same vein as the Barsoom novels – but not as good. The sequence comprises *Pirates of Venus* (1934), *Lost on Venus* (1935), *Carson on Venus* (1939) and *Escape on Venus* (1946). As in the other series, the scientific speculation lacks consistency and real thought.

Edgar Rice Burroughs remains one of the most popular figures from the genre's early history, and as such should be awarded the respect he deserves. The majority of his stories are now dated and fantastical, but they nevertheless remain greatly enjoyable. His *Pellucidar* novels are perfect stories to lose oneself in on a lazy Sunday afternoon.

See Also
EVOLUTION; SCIENCE FANTASY; SCIENTIFIC ROMANCE

Recommended Further Reading
Journey to the Centre of the Earth (1864) by JULES VERNE; *The Narrative of Arthur Gordon Pym* (1837) by EDGAR ALLAN POE; *Jurassic Park* (1990) by MICHAEL CRICHTON

Bibliography
Tarzan of the Apes (1914)
The Return of Tarzan (1915)
The Beasts of Tarzan (1916)
The Son of Tarzan (1917)
A Princess of Mars (1917)
Tarzan and the Jewels of Opar (1918)
The Gods of Mars (1918)
Jungle Tales of Tarzan (short stories, 1919)
The Warlord of Mars (1919)
Tarzan the Untamed (short stories, 1920)
Thuvia, Maid of Mars (1920)
Tarzan the Terrible (1921)
At the Earth's Core (1922)
The Chessmen of Mars (1922)
Pellucidar (1923)
Tarzan and the Golden Lion (1923)
The Land that Time Forgot (1924)
Tarzan and the Ant Men (1924)
The Cave Girl (1925)
The Eternal Lover (1925)
The Moon Maid (1926)
The Tarzan Twins (1927)
Tarzan, Lord of the Jungle (1928)
The Master Mind of Mars (1928)
Tarzan and the Lost Empire (1929)
The Monster Men (1929)
Tarzan at the Earth's Core (1930)
Tanar of Pellucidar (1930)

Tarzan the Invincible (1931)
A Fighting Man of Mars (1931)
Tarzan Triumphant (1932)
Jungle Girl (1932)
Tarzan and the City of Gold (1933)
Tarzan and the Lion Man (1934)
Pirates of Venus (1934)
Tarzan and the Leopard Men (1935)
Lost on Venus (1935)
Tarzan and the Tarzan Twins with Jad-Bal-Ja, the Golden Lion (1936)
Swords of Mars (1936)
Back to the Stone Age (1937)
Tarzan and the Forbidden City (1938)
The Lad and the Lion (1938)
Tarzan the Magnificent (1939)
Carson of Venus (1939)
Synthetic Men of Mars (1940)
Land of Terror (1944)
Escape on Venus (1946)
Tarzan and the Foreign Legion (1947)
Llana of Gathol (1948)
The Man Eater (1955)
Savage Pellucidar (1963)
Tarzan and the Madman (1964)
John Carter of Mars (short stories, 1964)
Beyond the Farthest Star (short stories, 1965)
Tarzan and the Castaways (1965)

BURROUGHS, WILLIAM (1914–1997), USA

Not strictly a writer of genre SF, American author and journalist William Burroughs has been adopted by avant-garde elements of the SF community for his use of SF devices and themes. His work has an undeniable cult status and its insight into the human condition *in extremis* remains unrivalled in its imaginative intensity.

Much of Burroughs's early work was controversial and remained unpublished until his later life when restraints on the publication of experimental literature were relaxed. Nevertheless, Burroughs had a profound influence on fellow members of the Beat Generation of American writers and commentators during the 1940s and 1950s.

Junky (1953), later revised and reissued as *Junkie* (1977), and *Queer* (1985) remain his most moving works, fictionalized accounts of his life as a heroin addict and a homosexual, written with an unblinking honesty and blending moments of realistic clarity with spells of drug-induced fabulation.

The Naked Lunch (1959) is perhaps his best single novel, cutting surreally between scenes that revel in their stark boldness and literary originality. A number of these scenes take place in two DYSTOPIC cities, one of which, 'Interzone', gave its name to a popular British genre magazine (INTERZONE). The book is at once moving, tragic and funny.

Nova Express (1964) is another of Burroughs's books featuring themes and devices that would qualify it as SF, and much of his other writing makes use of fantastical imagery. Similar in many ways to *The Naked Lunch*, it is, like the earlier book, more truly a novel about drug addiction, but it does feature a hallucinatory 'Nova Mob' who are attempting to take over the Earth.

The Naked Lunch was filmed (as *Naked Lunch*) by David Cronenberg in 1991.

William Burroughs died in 1997, aged 83.

Bibliography (Selected)
The Naked Lunch (1959)
Nova Express (1964)
Junkie (1977)
Queer (1985)

BUTLER, OCTAVIA E. (1947–   ), USA

Octavia Butler is a writer who has taken the standard concepts of SF and turned them on their heads. Her novels are filled with subversive commentary on the nature of the human race, and, ultimately, on the future that we will leave for our children to inherit. Almost uniquely in SF, Octavia Butler writes from the perspective of a black female American, and her characters are infused with her own wise and worthy sensibilities.

Her first novel, *Patternmaster* (1976), marks the beginning of her *Patternist* sequence, and concerns an aeons-long debate between two ALIEN immortals who are planning to shape the human race to a form that best suits their needs. Later books in the series – *Mind of My Mind* (1977), *Survivor* (1978), *Wild Seed* (1980) and *Clay's Ark* (1984) –

complete a cyclical tale that begins in history and ends in the FAR
FUTURE. Human beings are shaped through a breeding programme –
some inherit telepathic abilities, others do not. Others encounter an alien
race and contract a virus that causes them to mutate. A constant tension
can be felt bubbling underneath the surface of the story, as these variations on the basic human form eventually come into conflict.

Butler's strength lies in the impressive manner in with which she subtly
weaves her racial and GENDER-based concerns into the structure of the
novels without letting them overtly dominate the sequence. SF is the
perfect form for tackling these issues subtly because devices such as
GENETIC engineering and EVOLUTION allow the creation of allegorical situations in which real issues can be tackled in a sophisticated and
intelligent way.

Butler's second sequence, *Xenogenesis*, develops a similar theme but is
perhaps even bleaker than her previous work. The trilogy comprises
Dawn (1987), *Adulthood Rites* (1987) and *Imago* (1989) and concerns the
arrival of an alien species on an Earth that has been devastated by human
conflict. Within this POST-APOCALYPTIC nightmare, a tiny cluster of
humanity survives in suspended animation. The aliens awaken these
sleepers so that they may breed with them and make use of any worthwhile genes that our species has retained. Eventually a new, stable society
is formed, but it represents a stage at which the human race would never
have arrived without outside interference.

Also worthy of note – and perhaps the one of Butler's novels to deal
most explicitly with the racial issue – is the moving *Kindred* (1979), in
which a black woman suffers a TIME slip and finds herself stranded in
nineteenth-century America. To her horror she finds herself confronted
with the horror of slavery and various other kinds of brutality. Although
more properly described as a fantasy, *Kindred* is emotionally powerful and
serious, and easily deserves to be considered alongside Butler's main body
of work.

Octavia Butler's voice of reason resounds through the genre. Her issues
are our issues, and before the human race can step forward into the next
stage of its evolution they need to be resolved. Butler has a torch that
lights the way – it is up to us to follow her.

See Also
ALIEN; EVOLUTION; FAR FUTURE; GENDER; GENETIC;
TIME

Recommended Further Reading

The Left Hand of Darkness (1969) by URSULA K. LE GUIN; *The Handmaid's Tale* (1985) by MARGARET ATWOOD; The *Canopus in Argos* sequence by DORIS LESSING

Bibliography

Patternmaster (1976)
Mind of My Mind (1977)
Survivor (1978)
Kindred (1979)
Wild Seed (1980)
Clay's Ark (1984)
Dawn (1987)
Adulthood Rites (1987)
Imago (1989)
Parable of the Sower (1993)
Parable of the Talents (1998)
Lilith's Blood (2000)

BYRNE, EUGENE (1959–   ), Great Britain

An accomplished satirist, Eugene Byrne has only in recent years begun to make a mark on the SF genre, with a number of stories in INTERZONE magazine as well as the novel *ThiGMOO* (1999).

His first book, *Back in the USSA* (1997), is a collection of ALTER-NATE WORLD stories written in collaboration with KIM NEWMAN. Each of the stories is set in the United Socialist States of America, a hypothetical version of the USA that is governed by a revolutionary socialist regime and finds itself at odds with Capitalist Tsarist Russia. The stories all take place within the period starting in 1912 and ending in post-socialist 1998; they chart the decline and fall of the socialist state.

Brimming with humour and anecdotal commentary on celebrity, the authors nevertheless take a serious look at socialism and democracy in a world that never was.

ThiGMOO, Byrne's first solo outing, again showcases his wry commentary, this time exploring the theme of ARTIFICIAL INTELLIGENCE. Two university associates have spent years creating a 'Museum of the Mind', a database of fictional characters from history who are all programmed with artificial intelligence. However, when the university authorities attempt to delete the database, some of the characters escape into the World Wide Web where the protagonists must attempt to track them down. The book has an interesting take on the theme of artificial intelligence, but it occasionally lapses into sheer slapstick that lacks the witty insight of some of Byrne's previous work.

It remains to be seen what Byrne's rather wacky intellect will produce for readers next.

See Also
ALTERNATE WORLD; ARTIFICIAL INTELLIGENCE; VIRTUAL REALITY

Recommended Further Reading
The Man in the High Castle (1962) by PHILIP K. DICK; *Resurrection Inc.* (1988) by KEVIN J. ANDERSON; *Necroville* (1995) by Ian McDonald

Bibliography
Back in the USSA (short stories, 1997, with Kim Newman)
ThigMOO (1999)
Things Unborn (projected, 2001)

CADIGAN, PAT (1953–　), USA

Over the last decade and a half, American writer Pat Cadigan has earned herself a reputation as the First Lady of CYBERPUNK. This reputation could very well be deserved.

Her first novel, *Mindplayers* (1987), took as its setting a NEAR-FUTURE society in which mental illness is illegal, though desirable: street dealers sell neuroses like drugs, so that people can escape the monotony of everyday existence. When chief protagonist Allie Maas accepts a backstreet 'madcap' that induces a permanent psychosis, she finds herself in a hospital under the watchful eyes of the Brain Police. After being 'cured', she is given an ultimatum: go to prison, or train to become a 'mindplayer', a therapist who enters into other people's psychoses in an attempt to induce a recovery. The novel becomes an exploration of the preoccupations of the modern mind.

Although the novel as a whole is successful, the second half of the book flounders due to a lack of plotting, becoming a series of interlinking mood pieces that attempts to define the psychological pitfalls of modern life.

Far superior is Cadigan's second novel, *Synners* (1991). The book is more obviously cyberpunk, but it is also an excellent, detailed examination of ARTIFICIAL INTELLIGENCE in which human/computer interfaces have become infected with a virus that imitates an AI and is causing the deaths of many users. The novel is gritty and realistic, and is surpassed only by Cadigan's next work of fiction, *Fools* (1992).

Again set in a dirty near-future America, *Fools* is a startling multi-layered novel that established Cadigan as a force to be reckoned with. Portraying a world of VIRTUAL REALITY and CYBERSPACE, it raises questions about personality and our very notion of self when the main protagonist, an actress, begins to discover that she may not be who she thought she was. It is left for the reader to make sense of the action, as it is witnessed through the eyes of narrators who may or may not be trustworthy. *Fools* finds its author at the peak of her powers.

However, the second half of the 1990s was a quiet time for Cadigan, with her only output being *Tea From an Empty Cup* (1998), a disappointing novel that again explored the seedy world of virtual reality, this time in New York City, but failed to live up to the standard of her previous work. The novel was expanded from an earlier, shorter story, and perhaps this is where it failed – the plot does not sustain the size of the book.

It remains to be seen whether Cadigan's long-awaited next novel, *Dervish is Digital* (projected, 2000) can restore her to her former glory.

See Also
ARTIFICIAL INTELLIGENCE; CYBERPUNK; CYBERSPACE; NEAR FUTURE; VIRTUAL REALITY

Recommended Further Reading
Neuromancer (1984) by WILLIAM GIBSON; *Schismatrix* (1985) by BRUCE STERLING; *reMix* (1998) by JON COURTENAY GRIMWOOD

Bibliography
Mindplayers (1987)
Patterns (short stories, 1989)
Synners (1991)
Fools (1992)
Dirty Work (short stories, 1993)
Tea From an Empty Cup (1998)
Dervish is Digital (projected, 2000)

CALDER, RICHARD (1956–   ), Great Britain

British by birth, but resident in both Thailand and the Philippines for a number of years, Richard Calder's prose is full of a lyricism and sense of landscape that could only be conjured up by someone so well steeped in other cultures.

Calder's first novel, *Dead Girls* (1993), begins a trilogy of post-CYBERPUNK extravaganzas that continues with the similarly titled *Dead Boys* (1995) and *Dead Things* (1996). The books are surreal and strange, but there is no denying the Gothic beauty and precision of their telling. In a future Thailand that has become obsessed with the lures of capitalism, decadent men hire the services of artificial, ROBOTIC prostitutes. However, a NANOTECHNOLOGY virus is spreading during these sexual encounters, and eventually leads to the birth of a curious hybrid species, half human, half robot. The sexual plague spreads, and a GENDER war ensues – the second and third parts of the trilogy cover the aftermath of this and the manner in which it is dealt with. Calder's writing has similarities with that of WILLIAM GIBSON but with something else mixed in, a kind of fascination with the sexual relationship between men and machines that is reminiscent of J.G. BALLARD'S seminal novel *Crash* (1973). Calder is both adventurous and philosophical, blurring the boundary between the flesh and the construct.

More recently, after two further novels that again adopt a similar post-cyberpunk theme, Calder produced *The Twist* (1999), a conscious blend of SF with the Western. The novel is original and strong, and portrays a pseudo-Gothic town of Tombstone that has been overrun with Venusians who are attempting to steal the souls of its human inhabitants. There is not much of a plot, but that does not matter – this is a giddy, baroque journey into something new and exciting, and what the novel lacks in pace it makes up for in style. Calder's characters are well drawn and his environments well realized. *The Twist* constructs a detailed and fascinating setting for an innovative SCIENCE FANTASY of a type that rarely appears.

The Twist was followed by yet another Science Fantasy, this time set in a Moorcockian FAR FUTURE. *Malignos* (2000) depicts a technologically retrograde fifty-third century where slippage between parallel universes has perverted the natural order, and demon-like creatures, Malignos, have been spawned as a GENETIC offshoot of the human race. Fundamentally the story of a love affair between a human protagonist and a member of this new race, the novel adds a new spin to the portrayal of the far future. Here the Earth is not necessarily dying but is nonetheless surreally modified and strange, producing an image of a wholly alien time. Indeed, Calder appears to have made the far future his current domain: his output of short stories in magazines such as INTERZONE has picked up considerably and they all have a similar setting. This is a welcome development.

Richard Calder is an author of great ability. His prose stands out as expressive and LITERARY, while his constant reinvention of the subgenres he chooses to adopt identify him as a man of ideas. That occasionally Calder has stumbled when exploring difficult territories is to his credit; he refuses to step back and take the easy route, preferring to open up new imaginative highways with his own interpretations of human, ALIEN or machine experiences.

See Also
CYBERPUNK; GENDER; GENETICS; HORROR; FAR FUTURE; NANOTECHNOLOGY; SCIENCE FANTASY

Recommended Further Reading
Crash (1973) by J. G. BALLARD; *The Dancers at the End of Time* sequence by MICHAEL MOORCOCK; *Tea From an Empty Cup* (1998) by PAT CADIGAN

Bibliography
Dead Girls (1993)
Dead Boys (1995)
Dead Things (1996)
Cythera (1997)
Frenzetta (1998)
The Twist (1999)
Malignos (2000)
Impakto (projected, 2001)

CAMPBELL, JOHN W. (1910–1971), USA
John W. Campbell's effect on the SF genre is extremely hard to quantify. As a writer, his fiction is fairly unassuming and very much of its time – with the possible exception of *Who Goes There?*, the short story that inspired both movie versions of THE THING (1951 and 1982) – but as an editor he helped define and create the genre we know today.

Campbell began his career in SF as a writer for various pulp magazines such as AMAZING STORIES and *Astounding Stories*, with a number of SPACE OPERAS that were very fashionable at the time. He quickly became recognized as a writer of quality, and under various pseudonyms penned a good deal of serial fiction, primarily for *Astounding*.

However, the real turning point in Campbell's career was his acceptance of the editorial post for *Astounding Stories* in 1937.

The next year, he changed the magazine's name to ASTOUNDING SCIENCE FICTION, and began searching out new authors whose work would meet his expectations of what a 'good' SF story should be. This was the inception of the GOLDEN AGE period of SF history, and Campbell became its primary driving force.

It was not long before Campbell began to make his discoveries. In 1939 he published stories by authors like ROBERT HEINLEIN, THEODORE STURGEON, A. E. VAN VOGT and ISAAC ASIMOV. He also maintained his grip on E. E. 'DOC' SMITH, whose Space Opera he continued to publish for a number of years.

In part, the success of Campbell's magazine can be put down to the calibre of the authors he was working with. But it was Campbell himself who fostered these young writers and encouraged them to produce this new brand of speculative fiction that dealt with more mature issues and had its basis in speculation rooted in real science. Indeed, Campbell strove to make his writers consider the full implications of their ideas and to question the motives of their protagonists. In this way he helped bring about the dawn of a new age in SF and mould the intelligent, adult genre that we know today.

SF's Golden Age is reckoned to have taken place between 1939 and 1943, the time when Heinlein began his FUTURE HISTORY, Asimov his *Robot* and *Foundation* sequences, Van Vogt published *Slan* and Smith his *Lensman* saga. Many of the basic motifs and devices of the emerging genre would be explored first in this era, and a large number of the novels and stories that would later become recognized as classics would be published first in the pages of *Astounding*.

It is to Campbell's credit that many of the authors of this time have spoken forthrightly about his overall influence on their work and the ideas that he gave them. It is difficult to know how many classics were actually inspired by Campbell's original ideas – it is claimed that he frequently challenged his authors to produce stories based around his concepts. Campbell himself produced almost no fiction after he took over the editor's chair in 1937, but his fertile imagination, it seems, did not go to waste.

Campbell remained at the editor's post of *Astounding* until his death in 1971, whereupon he was succeeded by BEN BOVA. The magazine had by then begun to stagnate a little, as Campbell refused to relax his proud notions of what a good SF story should be and therefore editorial policy failed to change with the times. He did, however, see *Astounding Science Fiction* through yet another name change to ANALOG in 1960. He was one of the first real proponents of radical HARD SF.

Campbell's legacy lives on in the work of the writers he brought to prominence during the Golden Age period. His overall influence on the history of the genre is harder to ascertain but suffice it to say that without his work the genre would not exist in the form it does today – and SF readers would be all the poorer for it.

Bibliography (Selected)
The Mightiest Machine (1947)
The Incredible Planet (1949)
The Moon Is Hell! (short stories, 1951)
Cloak of Aesir (short stories, 1952)
The Black Star Passes (1953)
Islands of Space (1957)
Invaders from the Infinite (1961)
The Best of John W. Campbell (short stories, 1973)
The Best of John W. Campbell (short stories, 1976)

CARD, ORSON SCOTT (1951–   ), USA
Orson Scott Card is an author with a fabulous talent for storytelling. His works are often informed by the Mormonism into which he was born, and this provides him with a unique and unusual angle within the genre. He uses it to full effect.

Card's first novels of the late 1970s and early 1980s are unspectacular at best, although his short fiction of this time is outstanding: his first published story in 1977 was nominated for a HUGO AWARD. It was with the publication of the excellent *Ender's Game* (1985), however, that Card truly came into his own as a novelist.

Ender's Game follows the life of the young Ender Wiggin, a child prodigy who is removed from his family by the military and raised so that he is able to solve what he believes to be complex mind games. He goes on to crack each of these increasingly difficult puzzles, one after another, only to discover that they are not games at all but strategic military operations – and he has unwittingly caused the genocide of an intelligent ALIEN species. *Ender's Game* was awarded both the Hugo and the NEBULA Awards for its year.

The volumes that followed examined Ender's psychological trauma a number of years after this disturbing revelation, and explored his attempt to justify his actions to himself and his family. *Speaker for the Dead* (1986) is poignantly revealing about Ender's need for a family grouping and sees him visiting another alien world in an attempt to help them grieve for the death of their loved ones, at the same time attempting to redeem himself in the eyes of himself and his sister. It too won both the Hugo and Nebula awards for its year. *Xenocide* (1991) and *Children of the Mind* (1996) continue Ender's story, and to Card's credit adopt a wholly different form to the previous books. It is this disparity and diversity that maintains the series throughout. A later pendant to the *Ender* books, *Ender's Shadow* (1999), views the events that transpire in *Ender's Game* through the eyes of another of the children, Bean. It both illuminates and develops the plot of the original book.

Card's other sequence of note is the ALTERNATE WORLD saga, the *Alvin Maker* sequence.

The Alvin Maker books, which comprise *Seventh Son* (1987), *Red Prophet* (1988), *Prentice Alvin* (1989), *Alvin Journeyman* (1996) and *Heartfire* (1998), depict an early-nineteenth-century America that has never experienced a Revolution in its recent past. The Native American Indians have taken over the western half of the continent, while the settlers live in the east.

The portrayal of this alternative USA is intriguing and detailed – although the story itself is perhaps better considered a fantasy since Card makes use of devices such as folk magic and mythology. The novels also draw heavily on the RELIGIOUS teachings of the Mormons and in many ways work to perpetuate this cult's folklore. But at least Card's work is not preoccupied with 'scientific' triumphalism or technophilia, aiming simply to tell a story in the most accessibly literate way it can.

Orson Scott Card is a writer of ability and merit, and his perspective on the genre is original and forthright. His sometimes controversial stories have elevated him to a position of great standing in the modern SF world, and his success looks set to continue for many years to come.

See Also
ALIEN; ALTERNATE WORLD; MILITARISTIC SF; RELIGION; SPACE OPERA

Recommended Further Reading
Starship Troopers (1959) by ROBERT HEINLEIN; The *Night's Dawn Trilogy* by PETER F. HAMILTON

Bibliography
Capitol (short stories, 1979)
Hot Sleep (1979)
A Planet Called Treason (1979)
Songmaster (1980)
Unaccompanied Sonata and Other Stories (1981)
Hart's Hope (1983)
A Woman of Destiny (1984)
Ender's Game (1985)
Speaker for the Dead (1986)
Cardography (short stories, 1987)
Seventh Son (1987)
Wyrms (1987)
Red Prophet (1988)
The Folk of the Fringe (short stories, 1989)
The Abyss (1989)
Prentice Alvin (1989)
Xenocide (1991)
The Changed Man (short stories, 1992)
Monkey Sonatas (short stories, 1992)
Cruel Miracles (short stories, 1992)
Flux (short stories, 1992)
The Lost Boys (1992)
The Memory of Earth (1992)
The Call of Earth (1993)
Lovelock (1994, with Kathryn H. Kidd)
The Ships of Earth (1994)
Earthfall (1995)
Earthborn (1995)
Alvin Journeyman (1996)
Children of the Mind (1996)
Treasure Box (1996)
Homebody (1998)
Stone Tables (1998)
Heartfire (1998)
Enchantment (1999)

Ender's Shadow (1999)
Shadow of the Hegemon (projected, 2001)

CARTER, ANGELA (1940–1992), Great Britain

A mainstream, LITERARY writer whose work in the genre is more associational than explicit.

Heroes and Villains (1969) is the closest Carter comes to writing pure SF. It is set during the aftermath of a nuclear holocaust in a POST-APOCALYPTIC Gothic landscape among the remains of a blighted England.

Professors and scientists live within the remnants of the cities, their perimeters guarded closely by bands of loyal soldiers. Outside, in the mutated forests, live tribes of Barbarians. Marianne, a daughter of the city, escapes into the wilds and goes through a TRANSCENDENCE of sorts – her spiritual and sexual nature is awoken when she is adopted by a Barbarian tribe. Apparent throughout the novel is Carter's use of this transcendence as a metaphor for freedom of spirit and the recapturing of this quality by her female protagonist – the book can be read as a feminist statement. Indeed, much of Carter's work centres around the exploration of GENDER roles, particularly that of the female. Much of her writing makes use of the fantastical as a means of exploring personal identity.

Other novels by Angela Carter that have come to be associated with the genre include *The Infernal Desire Machines of Doctor Hoffman* (1972) and *The Passion of New Eve* (1977).

Angela Carter died in 1992 at the age of fifty-two.

See Also
GENDER; POST-APOCALYPTIC

Recommended Further Reading
The Dispossessed (1974) by URSULA K. LE GUIN; *The Handmaid's Tale* (1985) by MARGARET ATWOOD; The *Canopus in Argos* sequence by DORIS LESSING

Bibliography (Selected)
Heroes and Villains (1969)
The Infernal Desire Machines of Doctor Hoffman (1972)
The Passion of New Eve (1977)

CHERRYH, C. J. (1942–   ), USA

American novelist C. J. Cherryh has been one of the most prolific genre authors during the last twenty years, producing a vast array of novels at a rate unrivalled since MICHAEL MOORCOCK's phenomenally productive period during the 1960s. However, this has done nothing to compromise the quality of Cherryh's output, all of which is of an incredibly high standard.

Cherryh writes both fantasy and SF. Her most important SF sequence, and the one that encompasses nearly all of her work in this genre, is the *Union-Alliance* series, a vast SPACE OPERA that forms a FUTURE HISTORY of the next two thousand years and takes place within a sphere of space containing colony PLANETS and ALIEN worlds.

Earth has become immensely powerful, but is kept in check by the Union, a confederation of governments formed by the human-colony planets to ensure that the balance of power does not become unstable. This in turn has led to a loose Alliance of traders and merchants who wish to maintain their own neutral ground, to enable them to trade efficiently with all parties involved.

Into this set-up Cherryh feeds a steady stream of alien species, all depicted with a keen understanding of what it must be like to exist outside a human frame of reference – indeed, perhaps Cherryh's greatest strength is her convincing portrayal of alien races and their various customs and ways. However, many of these aliens have not been contacted by humanity because of a stated law that prevents humans from affecting the progress of alien species less evolved than themselves (in a similar manner to the Prime Directive that appears in STAR TREK: The Next Generation).

Cherryh makes ingenious use of this concept – a number of her stories take place within alien civilizations that at first seem to bear no relation to the sequence as a whole. That is, until it becomes explicit later that these aliens exist in the same universe as the Union-Alliance, but have had no contact with other species because of the human law.

It is difficult to pinpoint the best novels from the sequence, so diverse and all-encompassing is it. *Downbelow Station* (1981) describes the founding of the Alliance as a war between Earth and the Union draws to a close; *Cyteen* (1988) explores the impact of GENETIC engineering on the population of the Union by describing a whole society based around the production of human analogues or ANDROIDS; *Rimrunners* (1989) follows a stranded female soldier who manages to stow away on one of the enemy's vessels. Both *Downbelow Station* and *Cyteen* won HUGO AWARDS for their year.

Cherryh's work is outstanding. Her overarching Union-Alliance framework is complex and clearly thought out, her characterization is insightful and convincingly human (or alien, as the case may be), and above all her novels are exciting and ambitious. With POUL ANDERSON's *Technic History*, series as its more serious competitor, Cherryh's ambitious epic could still become the most long-lived and exuberant Space Opera of the twentieth century.

See Also
ALIEN; FUTURE HISTORY; GENETICS; PLANET; SPACE OPERA

Recommended Further Reading
The *Hooded Swan* sequence by BRIAN STABLEFORD; *A Fire Upon the Deep* (1992) by VERNOR VINGE

Bibliography
Brothers of Earth (1976)
Gate of Ivrel (1976)
Hunter of Worlds (1977)
The Faded Sun: Kesrith (1978)
The Faded Sun: Shon'Jir (1978)
Fires of Azeroth (1979)
Hestia (1979)
The Faded Sun: Kutath (1979)
Serpent's Reach (1980)
Ealdwood (1981)
Sunfall (short stories, 1981)
Downbelow Station (1981)
Wave Without a Shore (1981)
Merchanter's Luck (1982)
Port Eternity (1982)
The Pride of Chanur (1982)
Forty Thousand in Gehenna (1983)
The Tree of Swords and Jewels (1983)
Chanur's Venture (1984)
Voyager in Night (1984)
Angel with the Sword (1985)
Cuckoo's Egg (1985)
The Kif Strike Back (1985)

Visible Light (short stories, 1986)
The Gates of Hell (1986, with Janet Morris)
Chanur's Homecoming (1986)
Glass and Amber (short stories, 1987)
Legions of Hell (1987)
Kings of Hell (1987, with Janet Morris)
Exile's Gate (1988)
The Paladin (1988)
Cyteen (1988)
A Dirge for Sabis (1989, with Leslie Fish)
Wizard Spawn (1989, with Nancy Asire)
Reap the Whirlwind (1989, with Mercedes Lackey)
Rimrunners (1989)
Rusalka (1989)
Heavy Time (1991)
Chernevog (1991)
Yvgenie (1991)
The Goblin Mirror (1992)
Hellburner (1992)
Chanur's Legacy (1992)
Faery in Shadow (1993)
Foreigner (1994)
Tripoint (1994)
Fortress in the Eye of Time (1995)
Invader (1995)
Rider at the Gate (1995)
Cloud's Rider (1996)
Inheritor (1996)
Finity's End (1997)
Fortress of Eagles (1998)
Fortress of Owls (1999)
Precursor (1999)
Fortress of Dragons (2000)
The Hanan Rebellion (2000)

CLARKE, ARTHUR C. (1917–), Great Britain

Arthur C. Clarke is one of the truly great British writers. His career in SF has already spanned over fifty years, and looks set to continue into the new millennium.

Clarke did not begin publishing professionally until 1946, after World War Two had ended and he had finished his five-year stint as a radar instructor with the Royal Air Force. Like many other writers of the time, he began with a series of short stories, the first of which he managed to sell to JOHN W. CAMPBELL at ASTOUNDING SCIENCE FICTION magazine. Clarke's blend of scientific and technological know-how with his sense of optimism about the future of human development perfectly suited the emerging HARD SF ethos of Campbell's magazine as it emerged slowly from the GOLDEN AGE.

It was not long before Clarke published his first novel. *Prelude to Space* (1951) was a rather wooden attempt to envisage the first human mission to the Moon. Nevertheless, it demonstrated Clarke's powers of prediction (he had already described how communication satellites would eventually be developed in a non-fiction piece published in October 1945) and helped build his reputation in the science fiction world.

Clarke continued to produce an eclectic range of short stories and novels, but it is with *Childhood's End* (1953) that we really see evidence of the grand master of SF that he had become.

Childhood's End describes in beautiful, haunting prose the eventual TRANSCENDENCE of the human race and its metamorphosis into something strange, new and wondrous.

A fleet of ALIEN ships reaches Earth and the aliens swiftly set about taking control of the planet. The aliens themselves remain unseen for a while and communicate with humanity through a small number of human intermediaries. The story follows the progress of one such man.

It eventually transpires that the aliens, who turn out to look like the devils of human mythology, have come to Earth to help guide the human race into the next stage of its EVOLUTION. It seems that humanity is destined for greater things, and the aliens, who must remain stuck in an evolutionary cul-de-sac, are envious of its future. Soon, strange children are being born, beings incomprehensible to the average human. They have advanced powers of perception and appear to have a spiritual connection to the rest of the universe. Humanity divides into two distinct groups, 'ordinary' and 'advanced', and the alien 'Overlords' return to their home world. However, Jan, one of the original human contacts of the aliens, sneaks aboard an alien ship, stowing away so that he may see their home world. Relativity means, though, that many thousands of years pass during the journey so that when the creatures finally notice Jan's presence and return him to Earth, there is nothing there for him to recognize. He witnesses the ultimate moment of transcendence when the descendants of humanity are whisked away to meet the makers of the universe.

The book is an outstanding achievement and remains one of Clarke's best. Indeed, it prefigures much of his later work in that it confirms his inherent optimism about the future of humanity and the role that technology will come to play in its development. Far from adopting the pessimistic Cold War mentality of many of his contemporaries, Clarke was looking out to the stars and attempting to understand their secrets.

Other books followed, including *A Fall of Moondust* (1961) and the short-story collection *The Nine Billion Names of God* (1967), the title piece of which remains one of the most widely acclaimed short stories of all time. However, Clarke's SF reputation seemd to be marking time until, in 1968, he was recognized, together with Stanley Kubrick, as the creative force behind what was to become one of the most profound and famous movies of all time. 2001: A SPACE ODYSSEY was based on an earlier Clarke short story, 'The Sentinel', and had a script co-written by Kubrick and Clarke. He also novelized the script and this book version was released to tie in with the film.

The movie, which remains one of the most talked-about films of all time, was to have an amazing effect on Clarke's career. It catapulted him into a league of his own where he remains, unrivalled, to this day.

Clarke followed *2001: A Space Odyssey* with *Rendezvous with Rama* (1973). (He would later return to the universe of *2001* for a series of sequels: *2010: Odyssey Two* (1982), *2061: Odyssey Three* (1988) and *3001: The Final Odyssey* (1998).) *Rendezvous with Rama* is an intelligent and detailed novel about the human reaction to an enigmatic alien spaceship that enters the Solar System without warning. A small mission is dispatched to investigate, and the novel becomes a wonderful exercise in the exploration of the unknown as the vessel, Rama, begins to reveal its secrets.

Rendezvous with Rama won Clarke both the HUGO and the NEBULA AWARDS for its year, and was followed by three sequels, all co-written with Gentry Lee, which unfortunately get progressively worse as they go on. They are *Rama II* (1989), *The Garden of Rama* (1991) and *Rama Revealed* (1993). Indeed, collaboration with other authors would become feature of Clarke's later writing life as he began to suffer from increasing ill health. Most of the results are disappointing, with the possible exception of the recent *The Light of Other Days* (2000), co-written with fellow maestro of Hard SF, STEPHEN BAXTER.

The Light of Other Days concerns the advent of a new technology,

Wormcams, that enables people to spy on the events of the past. Humanity goes through a revolution, of sorts, as every moment from history becomes available for viewing and truth in public and private life becomes the norm. There are small rebellions against the new order but, for the most part, this novel is a further example of Clarke's steadfast optimism for the future. Humanity, he maintains, is gradually heading for transcendence, and any conceptual breakthroughs will only strengthen our resolve and teach us to live as a unified race instead of as warring factions. The Wormcam brings humanity closer together as a species, as honesty becomes the only viable way of life.

Arthur C. Clarke has had a profound impact and influence upon the SF genre, and his particular brand of optimistic Hard SF has inspired many writers the world over. It continues to inspire readers to this day.

Arthur C. Clarke's short fiction is collected together in the mammoth *The Collected Stories* (2000).

See Also
ALIENS; EVOLUTION; HARD SF; PLANETS; SPACE TRAVEL TRANSCENDENCE

Recommended Further Reading
Mission of Gravity (1952) by HAL CLEMENT; *Traces* (1998) by STEPHEN BAXTER; *Ringworld* (1970) by LARRY NIVEN; *Tau Zero* (1970) by POUL ANDERSON

Bibliography (Selected)
Prelude to Space (1951)
The Sands of Mars (1951)
Islands in the Sky (1952)
Expedition to Earth (short stories, 1953)
Childhood's End (1953)
Against the Fall of Night (1953, heavily revised as *The City and the Stars*, 1956)
Earthlight (1955)
Reach for Tomorrow (short stories, 1956)
Tales from the White Hart (short stories, 1957)
The Deep Range (1957)
The Other Side of the Sky (short stories, 1958)
A Fall of Moondust (1961)
Tales of Ten Worlds (short stories, 1962)

Dolphin Island (juvenile, 1963)
The Lion of Comarre and Against the Fall of Night (1968)
2001: A Space Odyssey (1968)
Of Time and Stars (short stories, 1972)
The Wind from the Sun (short stories, 1972)
The Best of Arthur C. Clarke (short stories, 1973)
Rendezvous with Rama (1973)
Imperial Earth (1975)
The Fountains of Paradise (1979)
2010: Odyssey Two (1982)
The Sentinel (short stories, 1983)
The Songs of Distant Earth (1986)
2061: Odyssey Three (1988)
Cradle (1988, with Gentry Lee)
Rama II (1989, with Gentry Lee)
The Ghost from the Grand Banks (1990)
The Garden of Rama (1991, with Gentry Lee)
The Hammer of God (1993)
Rama Revealed (1993, with Gentry Lee)
Richter 10 (1996, with Mike McQuay)
3001: The Final Odyssey (1998)
The Trigger (1999, with Michael Kube McDowell)
The Light of Other Days (2000, with STEPHEN BAXTER)
The Collected Stories (short stories, 2000)

CLEMENT, HAL (1922–   ), USA

Scientist and former teacher Hal Clement began his career in SF during the GOLDEN AGE, with a number of stories for editor JOHN W. CAMPBELL and his ASTOUNDING SCIENCE FICTION magazine. In these stories, Clement established himself as one of the first and greatest of all true HARD SF writers; these tales had little time for character development or lyrical prose, or even high adventure – but they were, and still are, stories full of science and ideas.

The best of the stories from this period are collected in *Natives of Space* (1965) and *Small Changes* (1969).

Clement's first novel, *Needle* (1950), shows an author still struggling to define his style, attempting to inject his plot with typical genre concerns while at the same time trying not to downplay his hard SF sensibilities. It is essentially a tale of ALIEN possession, in which a young boy enlists the help of one extraterrestrial in an attempt to free his father from possession by another. It was followed by an unsuccessful sequel, *Through the Eye of a Needle*, in 1978.

However, it is with Clement's loose sequence of novels about the alien PLANET Mesklin that we really see him come into his own.

Mission of Gravity (1954) is undoubtedly Clement's masterpiece, and is perhaps the most often cited example of a hard SF novel in the genre. It is set on a strange disc-shaped planet that is inhospitable to the human form, with gravity varying greatly across its surface, reaching a maximum of nearly seven hundred times that of Earth. A space probe has crashed near one of the poles, and the human protagonists must enlist the aid of the native centipedal aliens to help them recover it. The manner in which Clement describes the ECOLOGY of this strange world and the way in which the environment has shaped the EVOLUTION of the Meskilintes is both startling and bold. Indeed, the book has inspired much SENSE OF WONDER among readers and has become a true genre classic. The characters are perhaps a little wooden, but that is true of much of Clement's work – he leaves characterization to the writers of LITERARY SF while savouring the opportunity to propose strange, yet scientifically plausible environments and situations.

Mission of Gravity was followed by two further novels, *Close to Critical* (1964) and *Star Light* (1971). Both are worth seeking out and work well as sequels.

More recently, Clement has produced *Half-Life* (1999), an odd yet daring novel that sees its characters sent out to Titan, third moon of Saturn. The Earth has become overrun with various deadly plagues, and it is thought that the key to solving the crisis may be found in the pre-life environment of the moon. But once there the protagonists discover a form of living gel that interacts with their equipment and leads them to a conclusion about what is happening on the mother planet.

Half-Life is the epitome of a Hal Clement novel: because of the contagious plagues the characters are all quarantined from one another and there is absolutely no physical contact between them throughout the novel. All of the interaction takes place over a communications system and obeys a bizarre scientific convention that is set out at the beginning of the book. Due to this, most of the novel consists of dialogue; what action there is takes place on Titan's surface via remote control.

However, *Half-Life* is a brave attempt to create a new narrative style, a true hard SF novel that does not falter in its attempts to inspire wonder and provoke thought within its reader. It is not an easy book – but then, it is not intended to be. Whether it would be better with more human inter-action can only be decided by the reader.

Whatever the case, over the years Clement has provided the hard SF sub-genre with a body of informed writing that has scarcely deviated from its intended path. Occasionally he has missed the target, but one thing is certain: when Clement writes about science, the reader should pay atten-tion.

See Also
ALIEN; ECOLOGY; EVOLUTION; GOLDEN AGE; HARD SF; PLANET; SENSE OF WONDER

Recommended Further Reading
2001: A Space Odyssey (1968) by ARTHUR C. CLARKE; *Titan* (1997) by STEPHEN BAXTER

Bibliography
Needle (1950)
Iceworld (1953)
Mission of Gravity (1954)
Ranger Boys in Space (1956)
Cycle of Fire (1957)
Close to Critical (1964)
Natives of Space (short stories, 1965)
Small Changes (short stories, 1969)
Star Light (1971)
Ocean On Top (1973)
Through the Eye of a Needle (1978)
The Best of Hal Clement (short stories, 1979)
The Nitrogen Fix (1980)
Intuit (short stories, 1987)
Still River (1987)
Isaac's Universe: Fossil (1993)
Half-Life (1999)

CLUTE, JOHN (1940–   ), Canada
Born in Canada but for many years resident in Great Britain, John Clute is the premier critic of both the SF and fantasy genres.

Clute began his career as an SF commentator in the pages of NEW

WORLDS during the 1960s, making an immediate impact with his opinionated and stylish essays and reviews. He also produced a number of short stories during this period, but no collection has been issued to date.

Clute went on to become one of the founding members of INTERZONE magazine, and for many years remained their primary fiction reviewer. He now writes a controversial and insightful review column for the Internet-based periodical SCIENCE FICTION WEEKLY (http://www.scifi.com/sfw). His reviews are of great use: Clute is a man to be trusted, and he knows the genre like no other person alive. His articles are artful and well versed, and his insight brings meaning to the most complex of genre issues.

Two collections of Clute's articles and reviews have been published to date. They are *Strokes: Essays and Reviews 1966–1986* (1988) and *Look at the Evidence: Essays and Reviews* (1996).

However, Clute's greatest contribution to the genre remains the enormous *The Encyclopedia of Science Fiction* (Editor, second edition, with Peter Nicholls, 1993), which constitutes the most comprehensive and impressive piece of SF commentary and criticism ever to be produced. It won the HUGO AWARD for its year, and although now – unavoidably – a little out of date, the book is nevertheless a useful tool for both writers and readers alike.

Clute followed *The Encyclopedia of Science Fiction* with *Science Fiction: The Illustrated Encyclopedia* (1995), which drew on the previous volume and offered a sumptuously illustrated, concise guide to the genre.

Clute also produced, with John Grant, *The Encyclopedia of Fantasy* (1997), a companion volume to *The Encyclopedia of Science Fiction* . This, too, is unbeatably thorough and was similarly well received.

Clute's criticism is important to the genre and continues to enlighten its many fans. He has provided a running commentary on the genre for over thirty years – a major feat in itself – and for this he deserves every SF reader's gratitude.

A projected novel, *Appleseed*, has also been announced, although its publication date remains a mystery. It will be interesting to see whether Clute's inimitable writing style carries over successfully into his fiction.

Bibliography

Strokes: Essays and Reviews 1966–1986 (1988)
The Encyclopedia of Science Fiction (1993, with Peter Nicholls)
Science Fiction: The Illustrated Encyclopedia (1995)
Look at the Evidence: Essays and Reviews (1996)

The Encyclopedia of Fantasy (1997, with John Grant)
Appleseed (projected)

CRICHTON, MICHAEL (1942–   ), USA

A trained doctor, Michael Crichton has SF themes in many of his best-selling novels. He brings a genuine scientist's sensibilities to his work. Although a fair amount of his writing, particularly his more recent material, can be read as sensationalist, perhaps even anti-science in its tone, careful examination of his narratives reveals subtler underpinnings.

Crichton first came to prominence with *The Andromeda Strain* (1969), a thriller that describes the disaster that results when a spacecraft returns to a NEAR-FUTURE Earth bearing an ALIEN plague. As with much of Crichton's later work, it was filmed successfully in 1971, retaining the same title.

After writing and directing the excellent SF movie WESTWORLD (1973), there was a noticeable change in Crichton's output. A large number of novels and scripts followed, a fair amount of them SF, and although most are good, many read like treatments for movies. Indeed, in the selected bibliography below only *Timeline* (1999), Crichton's latest novel, has not yet made it to the movie screen – although it has already been adapted as a computer game.

In both its novel and screen forms, *The Terminal Man* (1972) explores the techniques and accompanying moral issues of implanting electronic central devices in people's brains; *Sphere* (1987) sees an ancient spacecraft discovered deep in the Atlantic Ocean; *Jurassic Park* (1990) and its sequel *The Lost World* (1995) find GENETICALLY recreated dinosaurs rampaging on a Costa Rican island. Yet Crichton's books are both popular and well thought out. *Jurassic Park*, more famous now for the Steven Spielberg blockbuster movie that turned into one of the biggest marketing phenomena of all time, is a scientifically plausible story of genetics and its application to the resurrection of extinct species. The book is full of action sequences and is written like a thriller, but Crichton manages to make his central idea credible. The novel's portrayal of the characters who develop the cloning techniques is perhaps questionable, but the processes themselves are lovingly and attentively described.

Crichton's most recent novel, *Timeline*, sees a group of historians sent back to the Middle Ages via a high-tech TIME machine, in an attempt to retrieve artefacts for a museum-cum-theme-park. However, after Crichton's initial attempt to rationalize his use of time travel by discourses on 'quantum foam' and 'time paradox', the novel turns into a medieval adventure from which the historians must attempt to escape with their lives.

Crichton is a writer who, because of his mainstream – not to say mass-market – popularity, tends not to be associated with the SF genre. Many of his novels do, however, use SF themes and ideas, and although to the purist they may seem a little sensationalist at times, they certainly succeed magnificently as entertainment.

See Also
GENETICS; NEAR FUTURE; ROBOTS

Recommended Further Reading
The Seedling Stars (1957) by JAMES BLISH; *Man Plus* (1976) by FREDERIK POHL; *Journey to the Centre of the Earth* (1864) by JULES VERNE

Bibliography (Selected)
The Andromeda Strain (1969)
The Terminal Man (1972)
Westworld (1974)
Congo (1980)
Sphere (1987)
Jurassic Park (1990)
The Lost World (1995)
Timeline (1999)

CROWLEY, JOHN (1942–   ), USA

An author now primarily known for his seminal work of fantasy, *Little, Big* (1981), John Crowley has nevertheless had a strong and lasting impact on the field of SF.

His first novel, *The Deep* (1975), explores in telling detail the lives of a group of humans who have been deposited on a strange, disc-shaped world by a possibly malign entity after having been rescued from their own endangered PLANET. Their new home appears to rest on an immense pillar that extends down into the unseen 'deep' of the title. Told by a sometimes unreliable ANDROID, as well as by a number of other narrators, the story is a delight, a bold LITERARY debut that marked Crowley out as an author of great integrity.

His next novel, *Beasts* (1976,) develops a theme that would later come to dominate much of Crowley's published SF: DYSTOPIA and its sociological consequences.

Not as successful as its predecessor, but still worthwhile, *Beasts* presents the reader with an America that has fractured into smaller nation states that bicker constantly with each other. Against this backdrop is placed Painter, a GENETIC-experiment hybrid of man and lion. Painter's emotional situation is portrayed with both empathy and dismay – he is hunted down by his creators, considered a 'failure', an experiment that has gone wrong. The book successfully tackles the enduring theme of MARY SHELLEY'S *Frankenstein* (1818) in a modern way and in doing so develops something that was not there before in the same degree – a deeper understanding of humanity and the detestable manner in which it can treat its own creations.

Beasts was followed by *Engine Summer* (1979), a book that stands out as Crowley's most remarkable piece of SF and should be treasured for its detailed and unforgiving depiction of humanity. It is the story of Rush That Speaks who lives in a commune that has been built up after a ruinous global collapse. This simple existence, subtly depicted against the back-drop of a POST-APOCALYPTIC America, is moving in itself. But when it is discovered that Rush That Speaks is in fact a simple VIRTUAL REALITY representation of his former self, switched on and off at the whim of its 'owner', it becomes all the more poignant. Elegaic and insightful, *Engine Summer*, from its title to its very last page, is a wonderful, evocative classic, and deserves to be better known.

Various shorter works that explore similar dystopic themes can be found in *Novelty* (1989) and *Antiquities* (1993), which also include samples of Crowley's fine fantasy. His *Aegypt* fantasy sequence, which is as yet incomplete and has dominated Crowley's writing over the last decade, begins with *Aegypt* (1987) and continues with *Love and Sleep* (1994) and *Daemonomania* (2000).

See Also

ANDROID; DYSTOPIA; GENETICS; LITERARY SF; POST-APOCALYPTIC

Recommended Further Reading

Earth Abides (1949) by GEORGE R. STEWART; *The Realms of Tartarus* (1977) by BRIAN STABLEFORD; *Man Plus* (1976) by FREDERIK POHL

Bibliography
The Deep (1975)
Beasts (1976)
Engine Summer (1979)
Little, Big (1981)
Aegypt (1987)
Novelty (short stories, 1989)
Great Work of Time (1991)
Antiquities (short stories, 1993)
Love and Sleep (1994)
Daemonomania (2000)

DELANY, SAMUEL R. (1942–   ), USA

Samuel R. Delany was one of the truly 'literary' SF writers to emerge during the 1960s NEW WAVE movement and his writing does much to confirm the theory that SF is indeed a valid form of literature.

Delany has an interesting background. He is a black, bisexual, highly educated American whose parents raised the family in comfortable middle-class circumstances.

A child prodigy, Delany published his first novel, *The Jewels of Aptor* (1962), when he was just twenty years old. It is a wonderful walk through a POST-APOCALYPTIC FAR FUTURE in which a small group of people set out on a mythic quest to find a jewel. The language is highly developed and stylized, containing early clues to Delany's abilities and offering a taste of what was to come.

Delany followed *The Jewels of Aptor* with a fairly conventional trilogy of novels, collectively known as *The Fall of the Towers* (1963–65), as well as a couple of singletons that, although good, trod much the same ground as his first novel.

But with the publication of *Babel-17* (1966), Delany began to demonstrate his maturity as a writer. Fundamentally, the book is a SPACE OPERA about language and the ways it affects our perception of reality. A radio signal from the stars is received – it is apparently in an ALIEN tongue, and the quest to decipher the message begins. But, it turns out that the message is in fact a weapon, an artificial language that must be understood if the protagonists are to turn away an invasion.

The book is undeniably complex: though it renders its world in terms of the Space Opera genre, it is clearly a detailed and sophisticated work that, like much of Delany's work which followed, makes much use of poetry and mythology in its attempts to define its world.

It was with his next book, though, *The Einstein Intersection* (1967), that Delany made his most important mark on the genre.

The Einstein Intersection is an elusive, at times barely penetrable story that describes the consequences of a cosmic collision wherein our reality intersects with another. Aliens claim our world for their own, and the narrator, a telepath and modern-day version of Orpheus, sets out on a quest to retrieve his lost love.

The prose is lyrical and lilting, and the work has a bizarre dreamlike quality about it, as if Delany has rendered his imagination straight onto the page, without pause for thought or linearity. Nonetheless, the book is cleverly structured and worked out with a precision that defies its author's baroque language and cryptic allegory. *The Einstein Intersection* is certainly SF, but it is also poetry.

Other important work by Delany includes *Dhalgren* (1975), which although not his best work is certainly his most widely read, and 'Time Considered as a Helix of Semi-Precious Stones', a short story that first appeared in NEW WORLDS magazine and has since been anthologized many times.

Much of Delany's later work is fantasy, although it still retains the mythic quality and wonderful style of his SF.

Like the characters who must decode the strange language in *Babel-17*, the Delany reader is required to probe the complexities of his writing if they wish to understand his dreams. Sometimes his narratives are pretentious, but more often than not they are literary edifices both beautiful and imaginative.

See Also
ALTERNATIVE REALITY; DIMENSIONS; FAR FUTURE; HUMANIST SF; LITERARY SF; SCIENCE FANTASY

Recommended Further Reading
The Dreaming Jewels (1950) by THEODORE STURGEON; *Lord of Light* (1967) by ROGER ZELAZNY; *The Three Stigmata of Palmer Eldritch* (1965) by PHILIP K. DICK; *I Have No Mouth And I Must Scream* (1967) by HARLAN ELLISON

Bibliography (Selected)
The Jewels of Aptor (1962)

Captives of the Flame (1963)
The Towers of Toron (1964)
The Ballad of Beta-2 (1965)
City of a Thousand Suns (1965)
Empire Star (1966)
Babel-17 (1966)
The Einstein Intersection (1967)
Nova (1968)
Driftglass (short stories, 1971)
Equinox (1973)
Dhalgren (1975)
Triton (1976)
Tales of Nevèrÿon (short stories, 1979)
Distant Stars (short stories, 1981)
Nevèrÿona (1983)
Stars in My Pockets Like Grains of Sand (1984)
Flight from Nevèrÿon (short stories, 1985)
The Bridge of Lost Desire (short stories, 1987)
The Star Pit (1988)
We in Some Strange Power's Employ, Move on a Rigorous Line (1990)
They Fly at Ciron (1993)
The Mad Man (1994)

DICK, PHILIP K. (1928–1982), USA

Philip K(indred) Dick was one of the most complex, productive and outstanding science fiction writers of the twentieth century. His work has strongly influenced many aspects of contemporary culture, due partly – but only partly – to the filming of his classic 1968 novel *Do Androids Dream of Electric Sheep?* in 1982 as BLADE RUNNER.

Movies based on Dick's work aside (TOTAL RECALL is another high-profile example), he is best remembered for his expressive, introspective SF novels that deal with his core preoccupations: the structure of reality, the search for human identity and the nature of RELIGION and the religious experience.

Dick began his SF career in 1952 with the publication of short stories in various genre magazines. His first published novel, *Solar Lottery*, appeared in 1955. Set on an Earth of the twenty-third century, it depicts a society that is run by random selection – the results of the eponymous lottery decide what place people will occupy in the hierarchical culture to which they belong. But, as in much of Dick's fiction, everything is not as it seems and the lottery is eventually exposed as a front devised by the true rulers of the world.

Dick's early work, which includes novels such as *The Man Who Japed* (1956) and *Dr Futurity* (1959) as well as *Solar Lottery*, is more straightforward in its narrative and characterization than the complex explorations of the nature of reality that he was to write later.

It was, perhaps, with the HUGO AWARD-winning *The Man in the High Castle* (1962) that Dick truly came to maturity as a writer. Still regarded as one of the best ALTERNATE-WORLD novels to be written to date, this novel portrays an America occupied by victorious Nazis and Japanese. In this disrupted time stream, the Allies lost the Second World War and a disillusioned writer living in the hinterland of middle America has written an alternate-world novel about what would have happened if the Allies had *won* the war. The characterization is profound and intricate: the various people who populate this surreal landscape have their own recognizable dreams and desires. This is one of Dick's great strengths: his ability to explore the *human* implications of any situation, however strange, as his characters search for meaning and identity in worlds that are distinctly out of kilter. *The Man in the High Castle* shows brilliantly how fragile are the roots of our 'reality' and demonstrates vividly how history could have taken some drastically different paths.

This exploration of the nature of reality is central to some of Dick's most respected work. In *The Three Stigmata of Palmer Eldritch* (1965), a man returns from a distant galaxy with a gift for mankind: Chew-Z, a drug that allows people to slip into vast VIRTUAL-REALITY worlds of their own devising and live there for perceived years with only seconds passing in real time. However, when a colony of people on Mars begins adopting Chew-Z as a means of alleviating boredom and loneliness, things start to go wrong; Palmer Eldritch has included a clause with his gift that allows him to enter into everyone's private reality and become their own personal god.

The Three Stigmata of Palmer Eldritch, with its multiplying inner vistas of reality and its concept of a humanity able to enact the role of and eventually to *become* its own god, is one of Dick's key works. *Ubik* (1969) takes its characters along a similar path, to where the dead come back to invade the realities of the living. This novel is perhaps a little confusing, and is not as accomplished an achievement as *The Three Stigmata of Palmer Eldritch*, but it sheds additional light on Dick's philosophical preoccupations. Indeed, a case can be made for saying that Dick's work cannot be properly understood until it is considered in its entirety, as a single body of work, so complex is this author's vision.

Perhaps Dick's most successful novel of this period was *Martian Time-Slip* (1964), which concerns a Martian colony that is struggling to survive. Forgotten by Earth, splitting into factions because of internal political wrangling, the colonists carve out an existence of sorts, alongside the hated native ALIENS, the Bleekmen. The humour and the horror of the colonists' plight make *Martian Time-Slip* one of Dick's most enduring novels.

Dick used drugs heavily for many years, which resulted in a slightly variable quality in his output during the 1960s and 1970s. One of his most personal and revealing novels is *A Scanner Darkly* (1977), which follows the progress of a high-tech undercover agent and his decline into narcotics abuse. At the heart of the story is a highly volatile drug called Substance D – or Death – that causes a separation between the two hemispheres of the brain, eventually leading to actual death. The main protagonist, Bob Arctor, has gone undercover in an attempt to track down the drug's supplier, but to do so he has become involved with the drug himself. It is a humane, subtle and touching portrayal of a man spiralling into the abyss of abuse and is, disturbingly enough, pretty clearly rooted in the author's own experience.

Of all of Dick's novels written during the 1960s, his most popular, partly due to the 1982 movie, *Blade Runner*, that was made from it, is *Do Androids Dream of Electric Sheep?* The book and film were formative influences on the CYBERPUNK genre, and both versions are interesting explorations of ARTIFICIAL INTELLIGENCE.

The Earth has been blighted by 'World War Terminus', and most animal species are extinct. Many humans have left the planet for distant colonies, and those who remain attempt to alleviate their guilt by caring for artificially created animals. Rick Deckard, the chief protagonist, is a police bounty hunter who has been assigned the task of hunting down and eliminating a number of illegal 'simulants' or androids who have been imported to the planet from Mars. At the same time, Deckard participates in a bizarre MESSIANIC cult that has enraptured the surviving population of America.

The novel explores, once again, the multiply layered nature of reality, this time by juxtaposing androids with real humans. There is also irony: Deckard's chief wish is to be able to afford to purchase and care for an artificial sheep while at the same time he thinks nothing of slaughtering the illegal human-like androids. Deckard also learns that his society's new

Messiah may also be a fake, and Dick makes it clear that this is a symbolic reflection of Deckard's own life.

Dick's outlook here is bleak and unforgiving, and with *Do Androids Dream of Electric Sheep?* he certainly manages to touch a raw nerve. In a world of high technology and GENETIC engineering, how do we know what constitutes reality and true consciousness? And what place do notions of the supernatural and the divine have in a world in which humanity can control the processes of life and death?

This interest in theology came to dominate Dick's writing from the later 1960s until the end of his life. Dick believed he had undergone a transcendant religious experience in 1974 and spent years 'transcribing' notes that he believed had been sent to him by some otherworldly being. His last novel of any substance, *VALIS* (1981), is a fictionalized attempt to analyse and describe his encounter with this entity, the Vast Active Living Intelligence System. Later books would rework this theme from different perspectives.

During his writing career, Dick reached dizzying heights of imaginative power never previously achieved in the genre. Many of his novels rank as true SF classics and with the release of the film of *Do Androids Dream of Electric Sheep?* in 1982 his work belatedly received the wider recognition it had long deserved.

Dick died in 1982, aged 54. The PHILIP K. DICK AWARD was established to honour his memory.

Nearly two decades after his death, Philip K. Dick remains possibly the most important SF writer of the second half of the twentieth century.

See Also
ALTERNATE WORLD; ALTERNATIVE REALITY; ANDROID; ARTIFICIAL INTELLIGENCE; DYSTOPIA; MESSIAH; RELIGION

Recommended Further Reading
The Collected Short Stories of THEODORE STURGEON; *Vurt* (1993) by JEFF NOON; *Behold the Man* (1969) by MICHAEL MOORCOCK; *Fatherland* (1990) by Robert Harris; *Junky* (1977) by WILLIAM BURROUGHS

Bibliography (Selected)
Solar Lottery (1955)
A Handful of Darkness (short stories, 1955)

The World Jones Made (1956)
The Man Who Japed (1956)
The Variable Man (short stories, 1957)
The Cosmic Puppets (1957)
Eye in the Sky (1957)
Dr Futurity (1959)
Time Out of Joint (1959)
Vulcan's Hammer (1960)
The Man in the High Castle (1962)
The Game-Players of Titan (1963)
The Penultimate Truth (1964)
The Simulacra (1964)
Martian Time-Slip (1964)
Clans of the Alphane Moon (1964)
Dr Bloodmoney, or How We Got Along After the Bomb (1965)
The Three Stigmata of Palmer Eldritch (1965)
Now Wait for Last Year (1966)
The Crack in Space (1966)
The Ganymede Takeover (1967, with Ray F. Nelson)
The Zap Gun (1967)
Counter-Clock World (1967)
Do Androids Dream of Electric Sheep? (1968)
Galactic Pot-Healer (1969)
Ubik (1969)
Our Friends from Frolix 8 (1970)
A Maze of Death (1970)
We Can Build You (1972)
Flow My Tears, the Policeman Said (1974)
Confessions of a Crap Artist (1975)
Deus Irae (1976, with ROGER ZELAZNY)
The Turning Wheel (short stories, 1977)
A Scanner Darkly (1977)
The Divine Invasion (1981)
VALIS (1981)
The Transmigration of Timothy Archer (1982)
Lies, Inc. (1984)
The Man Whose Teeth Were All Exactly Alike (1984)
Puttering About in a Small Land (1985)
In Milton Lumky Territory (1985)
Radio Free Albemuth (1985)

Humpty Dumpty in Oakland (1986)
Mary and the Giant (1987)
Beyond Lies the Wub (short stories, 1987)
Second Variety (short stories, 1987)
The Father-Thing (short stories, 1987)
The Days of Perky Pat (short stories, 1987)
The Little Black Box (short stories, 1987)
The Broken Bubble (1988)

DISCH, THOMAS M. (1940–   ), USA

Thomas Michael Disch is one of the most interesting writers in American SF. He first came to prominence during the NEW WAVE, publishing a number of now-classic stories and serialized novels in magazines at the time, including the British NEW WORLDS.

Disch's first novel, *The Genocides* (1965), displayed the pessimism that would later become a regular feature of his work. It describes an ALIEN invasion of the Earth in which the interlopers are indifferent to humanity's presence; they simply ignore its attempts to make itself known and go about planting enormous alien plants that eventually dwarf mankind and turn it into a race of vermin, fit only for extermination. The novel is typical of the New Wave movement in the way it up ends genre concepts in an attempt to do something new, while at the same time giving a sobering portrayal of our place in the universe.

Disch's most successful novel, and the book for which he is best known within the genre, is *Camp Concentration* (1968). It is a mature and LITERARY work, and an interesting study of the human condition.

In a bleak NEAR FUTURE, the US Army runs an experiment on a group of political prisoners who are being held in a concentration camp. These prisoners are injected with Pallidine, a drug that increases their intelligence to genius level and makes them able to concentrate better on tasks – before driving them insane and killing them after only a few months. The story is told in the form of the diary of one of the inmates as he uses his new-found intelligence to plot a revolt.

The title is a particularly clever pun, referring to both the nature of the prisoners' captivity and the effects of the experiments upon them. The novel is impressive and intelligent, and is one of the most memorable books to come out of the New Wave movement.

Of Disch's other novels, *334* (1972) is perhaps the most notable. It is a near-future tale set in a twenty-first century New York City. It focuses on a number of different characters who are living on the fringe of society and is one of only a handful of SF novels to depict a group of social outcasts and, through them, and the underclass of society at large with any sympathy. Revolving around an apartment in Manhattan with the address 334 East 11th Street (the numbers recur throughout the text), the story describes the growing struggle of daily life as it is seen by the populace of the future.

After another novel, *On Wings of Song* (1979), and a number of short-story collections, Disch was to begin moving away from the genre, instead focusing his attention on his more mainstream horror. Of these, The *MD* (1989) comes closest to returning Disch to the SF genre, with its ravaged near-future American setting.

The Dreams Our Stuff is Made Of (1998) is Disch's history and opinionated study of SF. Rather than following the linear structure of BRIAN ALDISS'S classic *Billion Year Spree* (1973) it comprises instead a series of topical essays, which although often excellent are a little America-centric and fail to recognize the current renaissance in British SF while still managing to pay tribute to the great SCIENTIFIC ROMANCES of the past. At one point Disch announces 'The future represented by SF writers continues to be an American future.' While a little unfair as a generalization, this is perhaps a fair comment, as many authors see America as the superpower that will have the biggest hand in the future of our race and planet, and their posited future societies tend to reflect this.

The book is a fascinating read and shows that Disch still has a lot to say within the genre; readers can hope that this will result in a renewed output of fiction from him.

See Also
LITERARY SF; NEW WAVE; SOFT SF

Recommended Further Reading
The Collected Short Stories of HARLAN ELLISON; *The Man in the High Castle* (1962) by PHILIP K. DICK; *The Final Programme* (1968) by MICHAEL MOORCOCK

Bibliography (Selected)
The Genocides (1965)
One Hundred and Two H-Bombs (short stories, 1966)
The House That Fear Built (1966, with JOHN SLADEK, as 'Cassandra Knye')

Mankind Under the Leash (1966)
Echo Round His Bones (1967)
Under Compulsion (short stories, 1968)
Black Alice (1968, with JOHN SLADEK, as 'Thom Demijohn')
Camp Concentration (1968)
The Prisoner (1969)
334 (1972)
Getting into Death (short stories, 1973)
Clara Reeve (1975, as 'Leonie Hargrave')
The Early Science Fiction Stories of Thomas M. Disch (short stories, 1977)
On Wings of Song (1979)
Fundamental Disch (short stories, 1980)
The Man Who Had No Idea (short stories, 1982)
The Businessman: A Tale of Terror (1984)
Torturing Mr Amberwell (1985)
The Brave Little Toaster (juvenile, 1986)
The Silver Pillow: A Tale of Witchcraft (1988)
The Brave Little Toaster Goes to Mars (juvenile, 1988)
The MD: A Horror Story (1991)
The Priest: A Gothic Romance (1994)

DONALDSON, STEPHEN R. (1947–), USA

Stephen Donaldson is an author best known for his classic High Fantasy sequence, *The Chronicles of Thomas Covenant the Unbeliever*, which comprises six novels and tells the tale of an estranged leper who becomes an unlikely hero of the realm. However, Donaldson has also produced the dark and disconcerting SPACE OPERA series known as *The Gap*.

The sequence begins with *The Gap into Conflict: The Real Story* (1990) and continues with *The Gap into Vision: Forbidden Knowledge* (1991), *The Gap into Power: A Dark and Hungry God Arises* (1992), *The Gap into Madness: Chaos and Order* (1994) and *The Gap into Ruin: This Day All Gods Die* (1996). *The Real Story* is actually a preliminary novella that introduces the main players who will take part in the saga, and is best read as a prologue to the sequence as a whole. Indeed, from these relatively quiet beginnings, the action flares into an epic, galaxy-spanning saga that culminates in the final volume with an impressive, if predictable, finale. Donaldson excels in his portrayal of characters who conform to neither of the standard clichèd definitions of 'good' and 'evil' – indeed, the whole series can be read as an intense study of character and human nature, with each person being a rounded and developed whole. At times it can be difficult to tell which of the characters Donaldson intends to be the 'hero'.

The sequence also readily adopts the standard concepts of Space Opera, as well as making generous use of devices that feature more usually in CYBERPUNK – 'Gap Drives' power interstellar travel, IMPLANTS and biological augmentation, although outlawed, are frequently used and a technologically superior ALIEN race is hell-bent on dominating the human race by modifying and controlling its genes. Throw into this heady mix a corrupt interstellar police force and a weak political system and chaos is bound to break loose.

Engaging and dark, the *Gap* sequence is Space Opera of a high calibre, which has perhaps been a little overshadowed by the startling success of authors such as IAIN M. BANKS and PETER F. HAMILTON, as well as a move in recent years towards an increased output of HARD SF. In a similar manner to Donaldson's earlier sequence, *The Chronicles of Thomas Covenant*, the *Gap* books draw on his skill as an observer of the human condition and his ability to blur the conventional lines between what constitutes good and evil in fiction. The *Gap* sequence demands to be read.

Donaldson was awarded the JOHN W. CAMPBELL AWARD in 1979 for most promising new writer. He maintains a website at http://www.library.kent.edu/speccoll/literature/prose/donald.html

See Also
HUMANIST SF; SPACE OPERA; SPACE TRAVEL

Recommended Further Reading
The *Night's Dawn Trilogy* by PETER F. HAMILTON; the *Culture* sequence by IAIN M. BANKS

Bibliography
Lord Foul's Bane (1977)
The Illearth War (1977)
The Power that Preserves (1977)
The Wounded Land (1980)
Gilden-Fire (1981)
The One Tree (1982)
White Gold Wielder (1983)
Daughter of Regals and Other Tales (short stories, 1984)

The Mirror of Her Dreams (1986)
A Man Rides Through (1987)
The Real Story (1990)
Forbidden Knowledge (1991)
A Dark and Hungry God Arises (1992)
Chaos and Order (1994)
This Day All Gods Die (1996)
Reave the Just (short stories, 1999)

DOYLE, ARTHUR CONAN (1859–1930), Great Britain

Known to most readers as the creator of the world-famous detective Sherlock Holmes, the late Sir Arthur Conan Doyle was certainly prolific in the crime-fiction genre but was also active in several others. Of his various SCIENTIFIC ROMANCES, the 'Professor Challenger' stories are some of the best-loved adventures in the genre.

Beginning with *The Lost World* (1912) and continuing with *The Poison Belt* (1913) and *The Land of Mist* (1926), and including a number of shorter stories, the Professor Challenger tales all revolve around the exploits of the eponymous academic and his various companions. *The Lost World* is perhaps the most fondly remembered of these and is still the most satisfying. In it, the Professor leads a controversial expedition to an out-of-the-way plateau in South America where he finds that prehistoric life has survived; dinosaurs and cavemen live together in a state of uneasy stasis.

The novel was to inspire a spate of similar books about lost lands and races by writers such as EDGAR RICE BURROUGHS. But it remains the original – and the best.

The Poison Belt, a shorter and altogether less successful book, is a precursor to the ECOLOGICAL disaster stories that would become popular during the late 1950s and early 1960s. It describes the panic that ensues when the Earth moves into a huge cloud of poisonous gas, and the steps taken by Professor Challenger and his colleagues to minimize the damage caused. If not as exciting as *The Lost World*, the book is still interesting in its exploration of themes that would later become clichés within the genre because of overuse.

The Land of Mist is the weakest of all of Doyle's romances, written a number of years later and featuring a Challenger who has succumbed to the spiritualism that Doyle himself had by now adopted. A number of Challenger short stories followed *The Land of Mist*; all are sub-standard when compared with Doyle's previous work.

Doyle did much for the genre in its early stages, helping to create motifs and themes that would persist throughout much of the GOLDEN AGE. His early and more successful scientific romances all attempted to establish in their narratives a degree of scientific credibility that is missing from a lot of other fantastic fiction of the time.

The Lost World has been filmed twice, with varying degrees of success, in 1925 and again in 1960.

See Also
SCIENCE FANTASY; SCIENTIFIC ROMANCE

Recommended Further Reading
Journey to the Centre of the Earth (1864) by JULES VERNE; *The Time Machine* (1895) by H. G. WELLS; *The Land that Time Forgot* (1924) by EDGAR RICE BURROUGHS

Bibliography (Selected)
The Lost World (1912)
The Poison Belt (1913)
The Land of Mist (1926)
The Maracot Deep and Other Stories (1929)

DUNN, J. R., USA

Literate and bleak, the work of American author J. R. Dunn is SF with a very definite moral edge. This is not a bad thing. Dunn is one of a number of writers who insist that SF is a form of *literature*, and that all literature has an obligation to educate its readers.

His first novel, *This Side of Judgement* (1994), is a fairly standard post-CYBERPUNK SF thriller. Perhaps a little too caught up in the trappings of the CRIME novel, it follows detective Ross Bohlen as he investigates a number of gruesome deaths in which the prime suspects are 'chipheads' – CYBORGS with computer chips implanted in their heads. The novel is an interesting blend of the cyberpunk and crime genres but it is not outstanding – it failed to prepare readers for the excellent piece of LITERARY SF that would follow.

Days of Cain (1996) is a dark, disturbing novel of TIME paradoxes that explores the moral and psychological implications of a mind driven to change the past. It thrusts its protagonists directly into one of the most harrowing and heart-wrenching periods of human history – the

Holocaust. A rogue time traveller has disappeared from the time streams, smuggling herself into Auschwitz with the grand intention of changing the course of history and saving thousands of Jewish lives. Into this situation arrives Gaspar, the man charged with pulling her out in an attempt to preserve the integrity of human history. His struggle with the implications of his actions takes up much of the book and gives a stunning insight into the mind of a man with the weight of history balanced precariously on his shoulders.

Dunn is also a military historian, and his precise attention to detail informs much of his writing; his picture of life in a concentration camp is both gruesome and accurate.

Days of Cain is not a light-hearted book. But then, it is not intended to be: the author succeeds in creating an absorbing story from one of the most disturbing episodes of human history, a story that is also one of the most outstanding pieces of literary SF of the 1990s.

It is unfortunate that Dunn's next novel, *Full Tide of Night* (1998) did not live up to the standard set by his previous book. It is a rewriting of Webster's classic play *The Duchess of Malfi* in an SF environment, and although satisfactory fails to capture the sheer psychological tension of its predecessor.

With *Days of Cain*, Dunn proved himself to be one of the most capable and thoughtful American writers of SF to emerge for a long time. It remains to be seen whether his next work will continue to build on this reputation.

See Also
CYBERPUNK; HUMANIST SF; LITERARY SF; TIME

Recommended Further Reading
Camp Concentration (1968) by THOMAS M. DISCH

Bibliography
This Side of Judgement (1994)
Days of Cain (1996)
Full Tide of Night (1998)

EGAN, GREG (1961–   ), Australia
In a relatively short space of time, Greg Egan has become one of Australia's greatest SF 'properties'. His first novel, *An Unusual Angle* (1983), was a mediocre fantasy that failed to satisfy. However, in a swift

about-turn, Egan began producing a stunning selection of HARD SF stories that prompted *The Times* to label him 'one of the genre's great ideas men'. This is a fair assessment.

Egan's stories were collected in *Axiomatic* (1995), *Our Lady of Chernobyl* (Australia, 1995) and *Luminous* (1998).

His first novel, *Quarantine* (1992), describes an Earth cut off from the Solar System by an enormous encapsulating force shield. It successfully blends private-eye fiction with hard-edged scientific speculation.

Egan quickly followed up the success of *Quarantine* with *Permutation City* (1994), a novel that deals with the question of identity in a vast virtual-reality universe created by humans as a haven.

The exploration of identity is a theme running through nearly all of Egan's work, as his characters struggle to define themselves against the backgrounds of his meticulously constructed worlds. Egan deals with such difficult topics as microbiology and computer technology, but rarely at the expense of his effective characterization. This is why many view him as one of the most successful writers of HARD SF: he does not alienate the reader with high-tech jargon but instead puts the scientific aspects of his work in understandable terms and characters with whom it is easy to identify.

Perhaps Egan's most adventurous novel to date is *Diaspora* (1997), which discusses the fate of the human race at the turn of the thirtieth century. Technology by this time has reached such a level that human beings are beginning to abandon flesh in search of more sophisticated and adaptable forms. This is an example of Egan's FUTURE HISTORY and it offers the reader a convincing vision of a wholly alien time.

Teranesia, a startling exploration of EVOLUTION, followed *Diaspora* in 1999. It concerns the progress of Prabir, the son of two entomologists studying butterflies on an otherwise uninhabited island. Where *Diaspora* is Egan's most adventurous work, *Teranesia* is his most emotionally charged, yet it rewards the reader with more of the expert scientific speculation that we have come to expect from this important author.

See Also

ALTERNATIVE REALITY; BIOTECHNOLOGY; CRIME; EVOLUTION; HARD SF; TRANSCENDENCE; VIRTUAL REALITY

Recommended Further Reading
Fairyland (1994) by PAUL J. McAULEY; *Traces* (1998) by STEPHEN
BAXTER; The *Galactic Centre* sequence by GREGORY BENFORD

Bibliography
An Unusual Angle (1983)
Quarantine (1992)
Permutation City (1994)
Axiomatic (short stories, 1995)
Our Lady of Chernobyl (short stories,1995)
Distress (1995)
Diaspora (1997)
Luminous (short stories, 1998)
Teranesia (1999)
Schild's Ladder (Projected)

ELLISON, HARLAN (1934–), USA
Harlan Ellison is not just a writer of SF.

He is also a fantasist, a crime writer, an author of supernatural fiction.
He is a welcome visitor to many genres but an exclusive inhabitant of
none.

What he *is* is one of America's premier lyricists.

Harlan Ellison began his association with the SF genre in the 1950s
with the frequent publication of good short stories. He moved from Ohio
to New York and became a journalist, among other things, writing a
variety of pieces about contemporary urban life. He then moved on again,
joining the army and eventually settling in Los Angeles as a scriptwriter.
Not long after this Harlan Ellison began to emerge as a writer of inspired,
energetic short stories that pinpointed exactly the concerns of modern
life. They are distinguished by a gritty realism that makes their satirical
impact even more biting and cutting.

'"Repent, Harlequin!" Said the Ticktockman' appeared in 1965, *I
Have No Mouth And I Must Scream* (a collection of short stories) in 1967,
The Beast That Shouted Love at the Heart of the World (also a collection) in
1969. Here was a man at his writing prime. His titles caught the reader's
attention, and the stories themselves did the rest. Indeed, Ellison won
numerous HUGO and NEBULA AWARDS for his work during this
period, and he remains one of the most 'decorated' writers the genre has
ever known.

It seems odd that an author as prolific, talented and high-profile as Ellison should have had little commercial success with his SF novels, but they lack the visceral, cutting-edge effectiveness of his shorter pieces. He is a writer with incredible energy, and it is almost as if he needs to dash off his ideas quickly and efficiently to allow him to move on to the next one. Indeed, during the 1960s and 1970s Ellison's output was like a verbal roller coaster, and you were lucky if you could grab a seat for the ride.

Aside from his chequered writing career, Ellison has also had a great impact on the genre as an anthologist. Ellison's work as a writer was always in keeping with the tone and preoccupations of the NEW WAVE movement that was developing at the same time as his own fast-paced career. Ellison realized this and used his phenomenal energy and amazing range of contacts in the field to produce two of the most expressive and intelligent examples of the SF anthology to date. They also captured vividly the very essence of the American New Wave movement.

Dangerous Visions (1967) and *Again, Dangerous Visions* (1972) contained many wonderful stories by authors of the period, but it was Ellison's own annotations for these stories that really made the anthologies what they were. A third volume, *The Last Dangerous Visions*, was announced in the early 1970s but never materialized.

Ellison's fiction output began to slow during the later 1970s as he spent more time on other projects and produced a wide range of non-fiction work.

However, his short stories of the New Wave period remain some of the best examples of the form that have ever been seen, and this must be tribute enough. Ellison is, without doubt a peerless chronicler of the human condition.

The Essential Ellison (1987) is a showcase for the best of Ellison's short work.

See Also
HUMANIST SF; LITERARY SF; NEW WORLDS; POLITICS; SOFT SF

Recommended Further Reading
The Ultimate Egoist (1994) by THEODORE STURGEON; *Driftglass* (1971) by SAMUEL R. DELANY; *The Machine in Shaft Ten and Other Stories* (1975) by M. JOHN HARRISON

Bibliography (Selected)

The Deadly Streets (short stories, 1958)

Rumble (1958)

A Touch of Infinity (short stories, 1960)

Gentleman Junkie and Other Stories of the Hung-up Generation (short stories, 1961)

Ellison Wonderland (short stories, 1962)

Paingod and Other Delusions (short stories, 1965)

From the Land of Fear (short stories, 1967)

I Have No Mouth And I Must Scream (short stories, 1967)

Doomsman (1967)

Love Ain't Nothing but Sex Misspelled (short stories, 1968)

The Beast That Shouted Love at the Heart of the World (short stories, 1969)

Over the Edge (short stories, 1970)

Alone Against Tomorrow (1971)

Approaching Oblivion (short stories, 1974)

Deathbird Stories (short stories, 1975)

Phoenix Without Ashes (1975, with Edward Bryant)

The City at the Edge of Forever (1977, STAR TREK Novel)

The Illustrated Harlan Ellison (short stories, 1978)

Strange Wine (short stories, 1978)

Shatterday (short stories, 1980)

Stalking the Nightmare (short stories, 1982)

The Essential Ellison (short stories, 1987)

Angry Candy (short stories, 1988)

Dreams with Sharp Teeth (short stories, omnibus, 1991)

Mefisto in Onyx (1993)

Mind Fields (short stories, 1994)

FANTASY AND SCIENCE FICTION, THE MAGAZINE OF

Editor: Gordon Van Gelder

Monthly

Subscription address: 143 Cream Hill Rd, West Cornwall, CT 06796-9975, USA

Website address: http://www.fsfmag.com

The Magazine of Fantasy and Science Fiction (F&SF) has long been seen as the one American market for writers who wish to produce SF that is more LITERARY or not restricted by typical genre convention.

It began publishing in 1949, and under a succession of various editors proved extremely viable. The eclectic variety of stories that F&SF accepted for publication led to it becoming recognized as one of the magazines that blazed the trail for the NEW WAVE period, as authors began to shift the emphasis away from HARD SF and more towards characterization and narrative experiment. The magazine attracted a number of excellent authors who wrote along these lines, including ALFRED BESTER, THEODORE STURGEON, DANIEL KEYES, BRIAN ALDISS, ROGER ZELAZNY, HARLAN ELLISON and WALTER MILLER. It also serialized ROBERT HEINLEIN's *Starship Troopers*, rather an out-of-character story for it.

The Magazine of Fantasy and Science Fiction has been awarded numerous HUGO AWARDS over the years and continues to publish excellent fiction by a variety of authors, still maintaining its relaxed approach to genre conventions. It also regularly features non-fiction articles and some excellent review columns, and Gelder appears to sit very comfortably in the editor's chair. It is hoped that the magazine will continue in the same vein for many years to come.

FARMER, PHILIP JOSÉ (1918–   ), USA

Master of the risqué, subverter of pulp heroics, infinitely jocular and satirical, Philip José Farmer is a wonder.

Farmer published his first short stories during the 1940s, but it was not until 1952 with the appearance of his novella *The Lovers*, that his name really became known. And not only known, but synonymous with daring: he won the 1953 HUGO AWARD for Most Promising New Author.

The Lovers, which was expanded to novel length in 1961 and remains one of Farmer's most important books, describes the strange, misguided love affair between a human and an ALIEN. An Earthman is sent to a distant PLANET to rid it of its insectoid inhabitants. However, he soon finds that the creatures are able to take on human form and, after being seduced by a female member of the species, he falls in love with her. However, it is not long before he finds out the terrible truth of the situation: he has inseminated her and she will die giving birth to their half-breed children.

The original story, and later the novel, is a startling exploration of alien biology, that was highly controversial in its day. The story's publication helped to earn Farmer a reputation for literary fearlessness that, rather than trying to shake off, he gloried in.

Farmer's work indicates a belief in several kinds of liberation, and much of it is explicit in its depiction of sexual activity. Novels such as *Flesh* (1960) cheerfully make use of semi-pornographic imagery, while at the same time exploring one of the other issues that fascinates Farmer: RELIGION. (There is nothing 'semi' about the events and imagery of the three novels – *The Image of the Beast* (1968), *Blown* (1969) and *A Feast Unknown* (1969) – that Farmer wrote for the West Coast imprint Essex House. He was happy to embrace wholeheartedly its 'no-holds-barred' editorial guidelines.)

Farmer is intrigued by the human impulse to worship and the concept of faith in an otherwise meaningless universe. *Jesus On Mars* (1979) is open in its treatment of this. A group of astronauts journey to the Red Planet where they discover an alien who has taken on the form of Jesus Christ. They proceed to hail it as the new MESSIAH, due simply to its appearance and their desire for it to be true.

Farmer's most impressive series, the Riverworld sequence, also makes use of godlike aliens and the search by its protagonists for the ultimate Maker. The series begins with *To Your Scattered Bodies Go* (1971), and continues with *The Fabulous Riverboat* (1971), *The Dark Design* (1977), *The Magic Labyrinth* (1980) and *The Gods of Riverworld* (1983).

The entire human race is resurrected along the banks of an apparently infinite river on a new and distant planet. It seems that a race of superior aliens is involved and a group of intrepid explorers, led by Sir Richard Burton, sets off to discover the source of the river and learn the secret of their origins.

The premise is superb, but ultimately the sequence fails to live up to its promise. Instead, it prefers to mark time in parodic adventure and does not fully explore the issues it raises. Nevertheless, it remains of interest for its initial concept and the SENSE OF WONDER it inspires, if for nothing else.

Much of the humour of Farmer's work stems from the pulp origins of the genre, and Farmer himself recognizes this in a number of his works as he plunders heroes from the pulp classics and puts them to work for his own devices. Thus *Tarzan Alive* (1972), *Doc Savage: His Apocalyptic Life* (1973), *The Other Log of Phileas Fogg* (1973) and *Hadon of Ancient Opar* (1974) make use of characters from the works of EDGAR RICE BURROUGHS and JULES VERNE, among others. Indeed, it would be unfair to call these novels simple pastiches, as Farmer takes great care to subvert his original subject matter whilst still providing an enjoyable adventure. He even lets a little of his risqué side show in some of these stories.

Philip José Farmer has never been an author to let himself be bound by convention. The roots of his inspiration may lie partly in the SF genre, but his ideas and style are most definitely his own. Where Farmer goes, subversive humour follows, though often there will be a serious undercurrent bubbling away beneath the text. Then it becomes a matter of whether the reader can stop laughing long enough to hear it.

See Also
COMIC SF; RELIGION

Recommended Further Reading
The *Tarzan* Sequence by EDGAR RICE BURROUGHS; *Behold the Man* (1969) by MICHAEL MOORCOCK; *Venus Plus X* (1960) by THEODORE STURGEON

Bibliography
The Green Odyssey (1957)
Strange Relations (short stories, 1960)
Flesh (1960)
A Woman a Day (1960)
The Lovers (1961)
The Alley God (short stories, 1962)
The Celestial Blueprint (short stories, 1962)
Cache From Outer Space (1962)
Fire and the Night (1962)
Inside Outside (1964)
Tongues of the Moon (1964)
Dare (1965)
The Maker of Universes (1965)
The Gate of Time (1966)
The Gates of Creation (1966)
Night of Light (1966)
A Private Cosmos (1968)
The Image of the Beast (1968)
A Feast Unknown (1969)
Blown (1969)
Behind the Walls of Terra (1970)

Lord of the Trees (1970)
The Mad Goblin (1970)
Lord Tyger (1970)
Love Song (1970)
The Stone God Awakens (1970)
Down in the Black Gang, and Others (short stories, 1971)
The Wind Whales of Ishmael (1971)
To Your Scattered Bodies Go (1971)
The Fabulous Riverboat (1971)
Tarzan Alive (1972)
Time's Last Gift (1972)
The Book of Philip José Farmer (short stories, 1973)
Traitor to the Living (1973)
Doc Savage: His Apocalyptic Life (1973)
The Other Log of Phileas Fogg (1973)
The Adventure of the Peerless Peer (1974, as 'John H. Watson')
Hadon of Ancient Opar (1974)
Flight to Opar (1976)
Ironcastle (1976)
The Lavalite World (1977)
The Dark Design (1977)
Riverworld and Other Stories (short stories, 1979)
Dark is the Sun (1979)
Jesus on Mars (1979)
Riverworld War (short stories, 1980)
The Magic Labyrinth (1980)
Father to the Stars (short stories, 1981)
The Unreasoning Mask (1981)
A Barnstormer in Oz (1982)
Stations of the Nightmare (1982)
River of Eternity (1983)
The Gods of Riverworld (1983)
The Grand Adventure (short stories, 1984)
The Classic Philip José Farmer 1952–1964 (short stories, 1984)
The Classic Philip José Farmer 1964–1973 (short stories, 1984)
Dayworld (1985)
Dayworld Rebel (1987)
Dayworld Breakup (1990)
Doc Savage: Escape from Loki (1991)
Red Orc's Rage (1991)

The Caterpillar's Question (1995, with Piers Anthony)
Nothing Burns in Hell (1998)
The Dark Heart of Time (1999)

FEINTUCH, DAVID (1944–   ), USA

American author David Feintuch has been steadily producing what can only be described as hearty 'Naval SF' for a number of years now. He won the JOHN W. CAMPBELL AWARD in 1996 for Best New Writer, and has kept up the pace ever since.

His first novel *Midshipman's Hope* (1994) begins his engaging *Seafort Saga*, a MILITARY SF sequence that has been described by many critics as 'Hornblower in space', after the creation of British writer C. S. Forrester whose most famous novels chart the progress of one young man through the hierarchy of the Royal Navy at the time of the Napoleonic Wars. Feintuch has a self-declared interest in naval history and this is reflected in his detailed and well-realized settings. The novels follow the exploits of one Nicholas Seafort as he rises through the ranks of the UN spacefaring army, eventually, in the last book to date, reaching the position of UN General Secretary, the most powerful position on Earth.

The novels are full of gallant fun and adventure, yet at the same time Feintuch attempts to study the moral issues of military life, with Seafort struggling to live up to his own standards of honour and upright behaviour.

The *Seafort Saga* is not a grand LITERARY epic – although it places due emphasis on exploring the psychology of its main character – more a generic SPACE OPERA that nevertheless manages to stand out from the crowd.

With this sequence, Feintuch has provided a fine example of popular and consistent Military SF. His only novel outside of this sequence is a fantasy, *The Still* (1998).

The author maintains a website at http://www.cris.com/~writeman/

See Also
MILITARISTIC SF; SPACE OPERA

Recommended Further Reading
The *Serrano Legacy* by ELIZABETH MOON; *The Honor Harrington* sequence by DAVID WEBER; The *Vorkosigan* sequence by LOIS McMASTER BUJOLD

Bibliography

Midshipman's Hope (1994)
Prisoner's Hope (1995)
Challenger's Hope (1995)
Fisherman's Hope (1996)
Voices of Hope (1996)
The Still (1998)
Patriarch's Hope (1999)

FILIPPO, PAUL DI, USA

American author Paul Di Filippo is best known in the genre for his stylish, incisive and surreal short stories, many of which have appeared in various genre magazines as well as in a number of fine collections.

Di Filippo's first book, *The Steampunk Trilogy* (1995) is a fix-up of three themed novellas, which are all set within a twisted and bizarre ALTERNATE-WORLD version of the nineteenth century. One tale involves the search for a missing Queen Victoria, another a love affair (that never actually occurred) between two famous literary figures. To label these stories as STEAMPUNK would be to diminish their unique literary qualities. With *The Steampunk Trilogy* Di Filippo confirmed to his readers what they had suspected for a number of years – that he was a writer who refused to be bogged down by conformity to genre, and that his writing sits most comfortably in the 'slipstream' that exists between genre and mainstream fiction.

Of his various short-story collections, *Ribofunk* (1996) is Di Filippo's most explicitly SF venture. The stories in the volume constitute a loose FUTURE HISTORY that deals in biological terms, with the NEAR-FUTURE fate of the Earth. If there is a general theme to the book, it is the questioning of the effects that BIOTECHNOLOGY may have upon the day-to-day running of our lives when it becomes an integral part of our society. Di Filippo is not optimistic: his energetic and satirical tales are sad and telling, inhabited by characters who exist on the periphery of mainstream culture.

Other short-story collections like *Fractal Paisleys* (1997) and *Lost Pages* (1998) are deft, funny and enjoyable, with stories that span the entire genre, from its fringes to its core.

Di Filippo's first novel, *Ciphers* (1997), revels in extremes. The book is steeped in Rock 'n' Roll and the American counter-culture. Music, sex and science blend into an often hilarious, surreal take on the author's native country that presents a hidden history of America and the world, a send-up of conspiracy theory and an entertaining, if bizarre, reading experience.

Di Filippo's second novel, *Joe's Liver* (2000), sees him take a step further into surrealism and away from the SF genre. Instead, he creates an impressive structure of literary wit and incisive prose. This author knows how to write and likes to show us this in the strangest and most outrageous ways that he can.

Paul Di Filippo continues in his individual and inventive deconstruction of the SF genre. His stories offer the reader episodes of startling clarity as well as moments of pure puzzlement. He may never be recognized as one of SF's most significant writers since his work is simply beyond genre definition. His is truly a wild and valuable talent.

The author maintains a website at http://www.cambrianpubs.com/difilippo

See Also
ALTERNATE WORLD; BIOTECHNOLOGY; LITERARY SF; STEAMPUNK

Recommended Further Reading
The Difference Engine (1990) by WILLIAM GIBSON and BRUCE STERLING; *Vurt* (1993) by JEFF NOON

Bibliography
The Steampunk Trilogy (short stories, 1995)
Ribofunk (short stories, 1996)
Fractal Paisleys (short stories, 1997)
Ciphers (1997)
Lost Pages (short stories, 1998)
Joe's Liver (2000)
Spondulix (projected)

FINNEY, JACK (1911–1995), USA
American writer Jack Finney is best known inside and outside the genre for his powerful and terrifying tale of ALIEN invasion, *The Body Snatchers* (1955). This is no 'cosy catastrophe' in the style of some British authors of the same period but a dark and unsettling study of the loss of individuality and personality in modern society, as well as of the threat to our rights to our own bodies.

Spores from space insidiously invade a small town in America. Once there, they begin to 'assimilate' the inhabitants of the town, growing replica bodies and destroying the originals. These replicas are devoid of personality and humanity, becoming more or less walking biological dolls.

The book is paranoid and bleak, but successfully satirizes the conformist America of the time. It had been filmed three times, in 1956, 1978 and 1993, with two adaptations using the slightly altered title INVASION OF THE BODY SNATCHERS and one simply dropping the definite article. The novel was also republished under the longer title.

Other work by Finney tends to cross genre boundaries with almost careless abandon; he was a writer who cared little for convention, instead borrowing whatever techniques seemed most appropriate for the telling of each tale. Short-story collections *The Third Level* (1957) and *I Love Galesburg in the Springtime* (1963) both contain stories that make use of SF concepts, while the novel *Time and Again* (1970) is a time-slip fantasy. Much of Finney's other writing contains elements that would usually be associated with the genre but ultimately are not definable as either SF or fantasy.

See Also
ALIEN

Recommended Further Reading
The War of the Worlds (1898) by H. G. WELLS; *The Puppet Masters* (1951) by ROBERT HEINLEIN; *The Midwich Cuckoos* (1957) by JOHN WYNDHAM

Bibliography
5 Against the House (1954)
The Body Snatchers (1955)
The Third Level (short stories, 1957)
The House of Numbers (1957)
Assault on the Queen (1959)
I Love Galesburg in the Springtime (short stories, 1963)
Good Neighbor Sam (1963)
The Woodrow Wilson Dime (1968)
Time and Again (1970)
Marion's Wall (1973)
The Night People (1977)
From Time to Time (1995)

FOSS, CHRIS (1946–   ), Great Britain

Chris Foss was one of the most important figures in SF art during the 1970s, greatly influencing the appearance of genre paperback books and inspiring a legion of imitators. His illustrations are beautiful renditions of spacecraft and other machines, depicted as encrusted with aerials and other protuberances, often angular and blatantly asymmetrical, yet nevertheless a joy to behold. Humanity itself is often absent from Foss's paintings, but its creations fill the skies or pepper the vast landscapes; Foss uses his art to exalt the bold technological future, to blend the practical with the sublime. His machines are the stuff of legend, and their portraits stood proud among the ranks of other, duller paperback covers that once crowded the shelves of bookstores.

During the 1970s Foss was also well known for his work illustrating editions of Alex Comfort's *The Joy of Sex* where he demonstrated his considerable talent for detailed figure studies.

During the last decade or so Foss has been relatively quiet within the SF genre. Nevertheless, he remains one of the major genre artists from the post-NEW WAVE period and his work helped to set the standard for many of his contemporaries, as well as for the next generation of cover artists. His smooth, deft use of the airbrush appears to have been an important influence on the work of JIM BURNS, who picked up the flag after Foss had begun to concentrate on other things and took over his place as Britain's leading practising SF illustrator.

FREAS, FRANK KELLY (1922–   ), USA

Kelly Freas reigned supreme among SF artists during the 1950s, with marvellous cover paintings and interior black-and-white illustrations for the genre magazines of the time, most notably for ASTOUNDING SCIENCE FICTION but also for THE MAGAZINE OF FANTASY AND SCIENCE FICTION and others. He also produced a wide range of paperback cover art during and after this period.

Freas's artwork is easily identifiable – a perfectionist's touch means that his paintings and drawings are exquisitely rendered, full of detail, realism and energy, and flowing with vibrant movement. He uses the whole spectrum of artistic technique to ensure that his work is of a consistently high standard, although, since he has not produced new artwork with any regularity for a number of years, the use of CGI (computer-generated imagery) is not so far evident in his illustrations.

In his time, Freas was the best artist working in the field. He produced many of the now-classic magazine covers of the 1950s, and has won the HUGO AWARD for Best Professional Artist with understandable frequency. His record of ten Hugos has only been surpassed by fellow American MICHAEL WHELAN. Freas is rightly regarded as the artist who revitalized SF art after the Second World War. His influence on the book and magazine covers of today can still be seen.

GALAXY

Galaxy magazine began publishing in 1950 under the editorship of H. L. Gold, who until that point had had minor success as a genre short-story writer himself.

The magazine set out from the start to publish a broader-based range of material than ASTOUNDING SCIENCE FICTION, by now solidly identified with technology-orientated SF. *Galaxy* came straight in and offered authors a new and exciting outlet for their work. It was not long before many writers were taking their stories to the new magazine, and throughout the next three decades it would remain one of the three top SF magazines in America.

Galaxy under Gold's regime had a comparatively open attitude to the material it took on and although it was happy to publish authors such as ROBERT HEINLEIN and ISAAC ASIMOV, both of whom stuck with the successful formulas they had already made their own, the magazine encouraged very different writers, ALFRED BESTER and RAY BRAD-BURY among them, to submit stories. In some ways, this shift of emphasis can be seen as a forerunner of the NEW WAVE movement that would emerge a decade or so later. Gold, like the New Wave editors, prompted his authors to concentrate on the psychological and sociological issues that their stories raised, taking the focus away from hard science.

In 1961, author FREDERIK POHL took over the editorship of *Galaxy* and stayed there for eight years. The magazine shifted to a bigger format and a bimonthly publication schedule.

Pohl was even more open with his editorial remit than Gold had been, and soon there were examples of SCIENCE FANTASY by authors such as JACK VANCE appearing in *Galaxy*'s pages alongside the more LITERARY SF for which the magazine had become known. Pohl also concurrently edited *Galaxy*'s sister magazine *If* at the time, a period during which several authors won HUGO and NEBULA AWARDS for stories that first appeared in *Galaxy*.

Pohl left *Galaxy* in 1968 and was followed by a succession of editors.

Eventually the magazine absorbed *If* and continued for a while longer, sometimes published monthly, sometimes bimonthly. But then its publication schedule grew increasingly erratic, and it ceased publication in 1980 after a failed attempt to resurrect it under a new publisher and editor.

In its time, *Galaxy* saw the publication in serial form of a number of SF classics, including Heinlein's *The Puppet Masters*, THEODORE STURGEON'S *More Than Human*, Bester's *The Demolished Man*, ROBERT SILVERBERG'S *Tower of Glass* and Pohl's own Gateway.

For nearly thirty years, *Galaxy* remained one of the three most popular SF magazines in America, and was distributed and reprinted in various countries around the world. Indeed, had it not been for the existence of this particular magazine, we might well not have a number of the classic novels and stories that we still enjoy today.

GAMBINO, FRED, Great Britain

British artist Fred Gambino has, during the last few years, literally put his mark on the SF covers of a number of leading British publishers. His impressive digital artwork displays both style and substance.

Like many of his contemporaries, Gambino began his career in the 1970s illustrating paperback covers. From here he worked towards an exclusive contract with one of the major publishers. This enabled him to branch out into other fields, although his SF work remains his most frequent and recognizable.

Gambino has a particular style, rather like a hybrid of the hard-edge 'techno' of CHRIS FOSS and the immaculate airbrushed hyper-realism of JIM BURNS. For many years Gambino worked in acrylics, producing wonderful images of emblazoned space machines or exotic ALIEN landscapes. Today, although he continues to produce acrylic art, more and more of his book covers make use of digital techniques, giving clean and super-realistic textures to his creations. Indeed, the almost sterile appearance of much of his work adds greatly to their aesthetic appeal but at times it almost contradicts the implied functions of the machines he depicts. His human characters, meanwhile, are often derived from photo-imaging and so remain true to their natural form.

Gambino has yet to make a powerful impact in America: much of his work to date has been for British publishers, illustrating British originals and, more often, supplying new covers for novels and series bought from the USA. Recent fine examples of his cover art include illustrates for

ISAAC ASIMOV's *Foundation* sequence, DAVID BRIN's *Uplift* sequence and ELIZABETH MOON's *Serrano Legacy*.

GARNETT, DAVID (1947–   ), Great Britain

Author, editor and critic David Garnett has produced a great number of books over the years, many of them written under various pseudonyms. As an editor, he has had some success with original anthology series such as *Zenith* and *The Orbit Science Fiction Yearbook*, both of which were, sadly, cancelled before they hit their stride. Garnett has also resurrected, with the approval of MICHAEL MOORCOCK, the NEW WORLDS anthology sequence, editing five editions to date. Carefully avoiding the trap of attempting to recreate the atmosphere of the original magazine, Garnett has included fiction from various modern genre writers such as STEPHEN BAXTER, PETER F. HAMILTON and PAUL J. McAULEY. With different publishers handling the various editions and no secure funding, however, it is uncertain whether the series will continue.

As an author in his own right, Garnett published his first novel, *Mirror in the Sky*, in 1969. It is a grand SPACE OPERA, full of action and fast-paced adventure but with an underlying current of disdain for its form – an almost NEW WAVE disapproval of the traditional SF format, never-theless ironically using it.

Of Garnett's other fiction, Time in Eclipse (1974) and the recent Bikini Planet (2000) are most worthy of note.

Time in Eclipse describes a vast VIRTUAL REALITY that is controlled by an omnipresent ARTIFICIAL INTELLIGENCE in a Britain ravaged by the effects of war. *Bikini Planet*, on the other hand, is a pastiche, a subversive, anarchic example of COMIC SF, which again satirizes the space-opera form to which much of Garnett's work is linked.

As an editor David Garnett has made some important additions to the roll-call of original SF anthologies. As for his own writing, both his work and his readers would benefit from a steadier output.

See also
ARTIFICIAL INTELLIGENCE; COMIC SF; NEW WORLDS; SCIENCE FANTASY; SPACE OPERA; VIRTUAL REALITY

Recommended Further Reading
Take Back Plenty (1990) by COLIN GREENLAND, *The Space Eater* (1982) by DAVID LANGFORD; The *Jerry Cornelius* sequence by MICHAEL MOORCOCK

Bibliography (Selected)
Mirror in the Sky (1969)
The Starseekers (1971)
Time in Eclipse (1974)
The Forgotten Dimension (1975)
Phantom Universe (1975)
Cosmic Carousel (short stories, 1976)
Stargonaughts (1994)
Bikini Planet (1999)

GERNSBACK, HUGO (1884–1967)

Hugo Gernsback was born in Luxembourg but moved to America at the age of twenty. He had a profound interest in science and electricity, and it was not long after his arrival in the USA that Gernsback began producing his own magazine, which he named *Modern Electrics*.

Modern Electrics flourished for a number of years, although it underwent various title changes and after a 1920 reinvention into the auspicious *Science and Invention* Gernsback began to publish stories alongside the technical non-fiction articles. He called these stories 'scientifiction' because most of them were written to illustrate some scientific notion or idea.

In 1926, encouraged by the success of *Science and Invention*, Gernsback launched the now famous AMAZING STORIES, the first true SF-dedicated magazine to appear in the English language.

Amazing Stories was fundamentally a pulp, but Gernsback, rightly or wrongly, demanded that his writers should focus on the technological aspects of their stories or base their adventures on some scientific premise. It was a huge success, and it gave the struggling writers of early SF a market and a home.

However, control of *Amazing Stories* was wrested from Gernsback's control just three years later when bankruptcy was forced upon him, and the magazine was sold on to another publishing house. It continues to appear sporadically today.

Gernsback himself went on to found a new company and start up a number of new SF magazines – *Air Wonder Stories*, *Scientific Detective*

Monthly and *Science Wonder Stories* among others. None of them would have the same impact as *Amazing Stories*, however, and most of them soon folded.

It is difficult to assess the impact of Gernsback on the SF genre in general. His one novel, *Ralph 124C 41+* (1925) is barely readable today, but his establishment of a 'dedicated' market for SF was one of the key steps in bringing the genre to the forefront of contemporary popular literature. With *Amazing Stories*, SF now had a name (it was not long before the unwieldy 'scientifiction' was changed to 'Science Fiction') and a public face. Without Gernsback's initiative other seminal SF magazines such as ASTOUNDING SCIENCE FICTION might never have come into existence.

The *Science Fiction Achievement Awards*, or HUGO AWARDS, are affectionately named after Gernsback to honour his early work in the genre.

See Also
AMAZING STORIES; ASTOUNDING SCIENCE FICTION; JOHN W. CAMPBELL

Bibliography
Ralph 124C 41+ (1925)

GIBSON, WILLIAM (1948–), USA
Born in the USA but for many years resident in Canada, William Gibson has become – it can be seen with the benefit of hindsight – one of the most important literary figures of the closing decades of the last century.

His classic first novel *Neuromancer* (1984) is perhaps the book that best defines the CYBERPUNK sub-genre, although Gibson was by no means the first author to become associated with this SF movement.

The book is a startlingly inventive novel, describing an edgy, high-tech NEAR FUTURE in which mega-corporations dominate the world economy and BIOTECHNOLOGY is rife. Perhaps most importantly, the book was the first to use the term CYBERSPACE and then go on to attempt to define it.

The plot is, at first glance, fairly standard. Case, a data 'cowboy' who uses advanced technology to project his personality into a vast VIRTUAL REALITY network and then steal information, has been biologically maimed by his former employers. His nervous system has been so badly damaged by toxins that he is unable to regain access to cyberspace. When he is offered the chance to buy his rehabilitation with a hacking job that will involve breaching the defences of an ARTIFICIAL INTELLI-GENCE, he is forced to act. The rest of the complicated plot follows Case's progress as he moves off-planet to a large orbital station or ARTI-FICIAL ENVIRONMENT where he will confront the AI.

However, the impact is not so much in the telling of the tale as in the detailing of the DYSTOPIC America in which most of it takes place. Gibson's future is not a bright utopia brimming with helpful technology – it is as dirty and seedy as any underworld of today. People are attempting to escape from harsh reality by fleeing into the vast informa-tion networks that rule their existence; their flesh is a burden that stops their TRANSCENDENCE into electronic form. Human identity has been lost in the rising tide of high technology and information, and Gibson's characters struggle to define not only themselves but their very humanity.

Neuromancer is in many ways a modern novel that transcends genre: it is an important commentary on our times and the changing face of the world, an unflinching examination of the new psychology and sociology that will shape humanity's future. It won the prestigious 'golden triple' – the HUGO, NEBULA and PHILIP K. DICK AWARDS – and it deserved to.

Gibson followed *Neuromancer* with two novels set within the same near-future framework. *Count Zero* (1986) and *Mona Lisa Overdrive* (1988) are both successful in their own right, but fail to recapture the sheer bravura of their predecessor. In them the evolving AIs of the first book begin to become self-aware and move out into the realms of cyberspace where they represent themselves as gods. The various characters who populate the novels all mirror Case in various ways, and all share the same concerns – the need to change themselves into some-thing new and find ways to survive in a world utterly transformed by technology.

A number of short stories that share the same background as the novels are collected in *Burning Chrome* (1986).

Gibson's next novel was written in collaboration with fellow cyber-punk author BRUCE STERLING. *The Difference Engine* (1990) is a STEAMPUNK extravaganza that describes a Victorian dystopia which has developed due to the early invention and wide-scale introduction of Babbage's pre-electronic computer – the 'difference engine' of the title. The book is witty and well drawn, although it 'stutters' a little due to an ill-conceived plot. However, the superbly evoked environment of a high-tech nineteenth century England more than makes up for this.

More recently Gibson has returned to the near future for another loose trilogy of novels. *Virtual Light* (1993), *Idoru* (1996) and *All Tomorrow's Parties* (1999) update Gibson's cyberpunk *noir*, revelling in the excesses of virtual reality and the possibilities of artificial life and artificial realities. Although the books do not reclaim the conceptual heights of *Neuromancer*, they develop further Gibson's take on the future, examining humanity's relationship with technology and the impact that it will have on tomorrow's morality – and mortality.

William Gibson has had a profound effect on the SF genre over the last two decades. His writing has helped to blaze a trail for the cyberpunk movement and revitalize American SF as a whole. Authors, such as PAT CADIGAN and JON COURTENAY GRIMWOOD have followed suit, adding their own harsh visions to the general cyberpunk perception of the future.

For Gibson, the future is a different place. Long may his vision continue.

One of Gibson's short stories, 'Johnny Mnemonic', was filmed in 1995, but was only partially successful in capturing the atmosphere of this outstanding author's fiction.

See Also
ALTERNATIVE REALITY; ARTIFICIAL INTELLIGENCE; BIOTECHNOLOGY; CYBERPUNK; CYBERSPACE; VIRTUAL REALITY

Recommended Further Reading
Islands in the Net (1988) by BRUCE STERLING; *Synners* (1995) by PAT CADIGAN; *reMix* (1999) by JON COURTENAY GRIMWOOD

Bibliography
Neuromancer (1984)
Burning Chrome (short stories, 1986)
Count Zero (1986)
Mona Lisa Overdrive (1988)
The Difference Engine (1990, with BRUCE STERLING)
Virtual Light (1993)
Idoru (1996)
All Tomorrow's Parties (1999)

GIGER, H. R. (1940–   ), Switzerland

Giger is an artist who revels in the surreal and the erotic. His images are born from a fusion of the technological with the organic, and in this coalescence something different and new is created – an ALIEN technology, as it were.

The only *books* that Giger's artwork has adorned are his own. However, he is important to the SF field for the work that he has carried out as a designer for a number of movies, the most famous of these being ALIEN (1979).

Giger's alien creatures are ferocious and strange, and they exude an air of mechanical menace that perfectly suits their role as biological killing machines. Their technology is rooted in GENETIC engineering, and the set pieces that Giger designed to illustrate this were bold and original. They later spawned many imitations.

What is most important is Giger's designs, however, is the sheer sense of 'alienness' that they display. A bizarre surrealism informs his images and makes them genuinely inhuman. But while Giger shatters our preconceptions and makes his creatures look truly alien, at the same time he subverts our expectations still further by revealing unnerving similarities between the species – the aliens may be born to kill, but that doesn't change the fact that they are sexual beings who have feelings. Giger gives his monsters character yet still manages to maintain their enigma.

After *Alien*, Giger went on to design the genetically engineered shapeshifter that appears in the unfortunately weak *Species* (1995). His artwork continues to be of interest to genre fans.

GOONAN, KATHLEEN ANN, USA

American writer Kathleen Ann Goonan is one of a number of authors who have recently set out to evaluate the impact that NANOTECHNOLOGY will have on the human race, both physically and psychologically.

Her debut novel *Queen City Jazz* (1994) is the first in her *Nanotech Cycle*, and describes a POST-APOCALYPTIC America that has been devastated by a plague.

In this dark NEAR-FUTURE setting, nanotechnology has become the next stage of human EVOLUTION, taking the species to spectacular heights – but as the book opens a nanoplague is in full swing and has wiped out half the population. Verity, a young girl from a small religious community in Ohio, finds she is able to communicate with the 'enlivened' surroundings and journeys to the 'living' Queen City, Cincinnati, where nanos are enacting the bizarre fantasies of their creator. Verity vows to use her skills to gain control of the city. The book rivals both NEAL STEPHENSON'S *The Diamond Age* (1996) and GREG BEAR'S *Blood Music (1985)* in its portrayal of a society utterly transformed by a new technology, but perhaps surpasses them both in its characterization. Goonan's prose is LITERARY and precise and her characters are realistic and believable.

Queen City Jazz was followed by two sequels, *Mississippi Blues* (1997) and *Crescent City Rhapsody* (2000).

Mississippi Blues follows Verity as she guides a fragmented group of survivors on a journey across the altered landscape of Middle America, in search of both a refuge from the nanoplague and a semi-UTOPIA. It is not as successful as the previous book, but is well written and manages to sustain the superior standards of characterization that originally distinguished Goonan's work.

Crescent City Rhapsody examines the situation of an entirely different set of characters who are also struggling to come to terms with the amazing changes that are ravaging their environment. At the same time an astronomer makes a startling discovery – that a pulse of interstellar radiation from space, called 'The Silence' because it has caused a communications blackout – actually contains a message from an ALIEN race that may change the nature of humanity for ever. The novel is full of big ideas and successfully conveys a vision of TRANSCENDENCE for the human race.

Outside the *Nanotech Cycle*, Goonan has produced *The Bones of Time* (1996), a novel with a rather far-fetched premise that nevertheless managed to garner a lot of critical praise. It follows a young mathematician who discovers the secret of TIME in the bones of a long-dead Hawaiian king. Meanwhile, humanity's first GENERATION STARSHIP is preparing for launch under the supervision of a dubious company called Interspace.

The novel is successful in its own right, but it does not have the exuberance evident in Goonan's other work.

The author maintains a website at http://www.goonan.com

See Also
DYSTOPIA; EVOLUTION; NANOTECHNOLOGY; GENERATION STARSHIP; TRANSCENDENCE

Recommended Further Reading
The Diamond Age (1996) by NEAL STEPHENSON; *The Bohr Maker* (1995) by LINDA NAGATA

Bibliography
Queen City Jazz (1994)
The Bones of Time (1996)
Mississippi Blues (1997)
Crescent City Rhapsody (2000)

GREEN, SIMON R. (1955–), Great Britain

British writer Simon R. Green is known as much for his fantasy, the *Haven* saga, as he is for his SF. Perhaps even more so: his *Deathstalker* sequence is more like fantasy than the SPACE OPERA that it purports to be. It is really a SCIENCE FANTASY in the same vein as STAR WARS and its various spin-offs.

The sequence begins with *Deathstalker* (1995), and continues with *Deathstalker Rebellion* (1996), *Deathstalker War* (1997), *Twilight of Empire* (1997, renamed *Deathstalker Prelude* for the UK market), *Deathstalker Honour* (1998) and *Deathstalker Destiny* (1999), although *Twilight of Empire* actually consists of three earlier books fixed-up into one volume.

This epic saga charts the progress of Owen Deathstalker as he becomes the unlikely leader of a rebellious faction that is taking up arms against the tyrannical Empire of the Iron Bitch. The sequence is an epic quest fantasy that has been translated into a space-opera setting, with much use of fabulation and fantastical imagery. *Deathstalker* is clearly modelled on *Star Wars*: the similar plight of the rebels against the evil empire that rules with an iron fist, the gradual development of the central character as his confidence grows alongside his moral stature, the mythic connotations of the saga and so on. Owen Deathstalker begins the sequence as a relative nonentity and gradually becomes a hero.

The *Deathstalker* sequence is formulaic and far from original, yet it nevertheless remains entertaining and popular with fans. Green should be applauded for producing a simple, exciting space opera of a type rarely seen in the genre any more. Although it fails to tackle any of the serious issues at the heart of so much SF, it provides a hero of mythic dimensions who continues to enthral readers.

See Also
SCIENCE FANTASY; SPACE OPERA

Recommended Further Reading
The *Star Wars* novels by KEVIN J. ANDERSON; *Dune* (1965) by
FRANK HERBERT

Bibliography (Selected)
Deathstalker (1995)
Deathstalker Rebellion (1996)
Deathstalker War (1997)
Twilight of Empire (1997)
Deathstalker Honour (1998)
Deathstalker Destiny (1999)

GREENLAND, COLIN (1954–   ), Great Britain
A writer with a profound interest in the British NEW WAVE movement,
Colin Greenland's first published novel was the fantasy *Daybreak on a
Different Mountain* (1984), which was followed by two more novels set in
the same world. These were published in 1987 and 1988 respectively.
Greenland already had an SF-related non-fiction book and several critical
articles to his credit and had also played a part in the initial establishment
of INTERZONE magazine.

Then, with the publication of *Take Back Plenty* in 1990, Greenland
produced one of the most ambitious British SPACE OPERAS of recent
years.

The novel concerns the exploits of Tabitha Jute, a fesity female adventurer who at the start of the story is in trouble with the law and at the end
liberates a massive interstellar STARSHIP, the *Plenty*, from the grasp of
the Capellans, evil overlords *par excellence*. The book is full of humour
and action and has great narrative panache and style. Greenland knows
the genre and its many conventions – as is evident from the way in which
he chooses to play with these conventions and parody them affectionately.
The book is not intended as a serious exploration of any particular theme
or device – it is simply romping good fun. It won the ARTHUR C.
CLARKE and the BRITISH SCIENCE FICTION AWARDS for its
year.

Take Back Plenty was followed by two sequels, *Seasons of Plenty* (1995),
in which Tabitha takes *Plenty* on the first voyage by humans to another

solar system and must deal with a saboteur along the way, and *Mother of Plenty* (1998), which sees Tabitha ejected from *Plenty* and left to discover the secrets of the Cappellans, in whose dying star system she finds herself. The trilogy as a whole forms one of the most simple yet effective space operas of the 1990s. A number of stories connected to the trilogy are collected in *The Plenty Principle* (1997), alongside the best of Greenland's other short fiction.

Greenland's other space opera, *Harm's Way* (1993), is also worthy of note. It is an interesting blend of Victoriana with space opera – a Dickensian novel recast as a space adventure, with enormous sail-ships that glide across the void and a Britannia that rules the stars. Perhaps surprisingly, it succeeds on many levels – as an adventure, as a satire, as a planetary romance. Indeed, Greenland manages to capture the essence of the Victorian saga and transplant it into his inventive SCIENCE FANTASY that, were it not for its distinctly surreal features, could be labelled STEAMPUNK.

Greenland is reportedly working on a graphic novel with artist DAVE McKEAN.

See Also
LITERARY SF; NEW WAVE; SCIENCE FANTASY; SPACE OPERA; STEAMPUNK

Recommended Further Reading
The *Night's Dawn Trilogy* by PETER F. HAMILTON; The *Culture* sequence by IAIN M. BANKS; The *Honor Harrington* sequence by DAVID WEBER

Bibliography (Selected)
Daybreak on a Different Mountain (1984)
The Hour of the Thin Ox (1987)
Other Voices (1988)
Take Back Plenty (1990)
Harm's Way (1993)
Seasons of Plenty (1995)
The Plenty Principle (short stories, 1997)
Mother of Plenty (1998)
Spiritfeather (juvenile, 2000)

GRIMWOOD, JON COURTENAY (1953–   ), Great Britain

Born in Malta and raised in Britain, the Far East and Scandinavia, Jon Courtenay Grimwood worked as a publisher and journalist before becoming a full-time author.

His first novel, *neoAddix* (1997), introduced to a delighted readership his particular brand of gruesome CYBERPUNK. Set against the backdrop of an ALTERNATE WORLD in which France is an Imperial state under neo-Napoleonic rule, *neoAddix* is populated by an eclectic mix of misfits and criminals. It is a successful CRIME thriller that explores vividly drawn future-*noir* territory, managing to feel fresh and original. Grimwood's strength lies in his style and pace: the story brims with excitement and NEAR-FUTURE strangeness. Japanese technology also pervades much of the text, with Sony ROM readers and tiny electronic eyes; indeed, most of the characters have been augmented, cyborg-style, to some extent.

neoAddix was followed by *Lucifer's Dragon* (1998) that improved on the format and featured a number of characters from the first book. The 'Lucifer's Dragon' of the title is an advanced VIRTUAL REALITY game which that its players on a tour of an apocalypse – typical of Grimwood's ironic portrayal of a future bristling with high-tech media and leisure-orientated technology.

However, it is with *reMix* (1999) that Grimwood really makes his mark. Loosely related to the previous two novels, but surpassing both in panache, *reMix* follows the exploits of rich-bitch teenager LizAlec as she attempts to escape from a European empire crumbling under the strain of a NANOTECHNOLOGY virus to the supposed safety of a lunar colony. Unfortunately things do not go as planned and she becomes a kidnap victim. As various people attempt either to rescue or murder her, she escapes and teams up with a feral child whom she meets hiding in the dirty access tunnels underneath the lunar city.

The novel is a superb example of cyberpunk, although it falters slightly towards the end with the introduction of an almost supernatural solution to LizAlec's plight. However, even this climax is written with enough intensity to sustain it and Grimwood ends the story in his by now characterically explosive style.

reMix was followed by *redRobe* (2000), which took Grimwood's development of the cyberpunk genre even further, resulting in his most successful novel to date. Sharing a background with his previous books, but featuring an entirely new cast of characters, *redRobe* follows the progress of Axl Borja, a killer for hire who has stepped out of line with the

Vatican and is sent on a mission of whose real purpose he is unaware to recover the missing memories of the recently deceased pope. The action takes place upon an ARTIFICIAL ENVIRONMENT – a space habitat named *Samsara* – that has a controlling ARTIFICIAL INTELLI-GENCE with a penchant for Eastern mysticism. The book is vividly written and full of adventure, technology and gore; *redRobe* set Grimwood at the forefront of modern British SF, confirming him as one of he most original talents in the field.

Grimwood is reportedly working on an entirely new sequence of ALTERNATE-WORLD novels. His thousands of fans await them eagerly.

See Also
ALTERNATE WORLD; ARTIFICIAL ENVIRONMENT; ARTIFI-CIAL INTELLIGENCE; CYBERPUNK; NANOTECHNOLOGY; VIRTUAL REALITY

Recommended Further Reading
Neuromancer (1984) by WILLIAM GIBSON; *Islands in the Net* (1988) by BRUCE STERLING; *Synners* (1995) by PAT CADIGAN

Bibliography
neoAddix (1997)
Lucifer's Dragon (1998)
reMix (1999)
redRobe (2000)
Pashazade (2001)

HALDEMAN, JOE (1943–   ), USA
Joe Haldeman is a writer whose work tackles with compassionate insight the difficult themes of war and conflict. Himself a veteran of the Vietnam War, Haldeman is one of its most effective diagnosticians. Much of his writing is very clearly influenced by his experiences and his best and most popular books are startling explorations of the nature of war. Although much of his work has, unavoidable, a MILITARY flavour, it is nonethe-less sensitive and humane in its analysis of the human condition.

Haldeman's first SF novel, *The Forever War* (1974), is very clearly such a book. It details the plight of a small group of soldiers who are fighting an interstellar war against an elusive enemy. Due to the scale of the war zone, the soldiers suffer time–dilation distortions when travelling to distant fronts: to the main protagonist, William Mandella, the war that he fights lasts for ten long years. However, due to the effects of relativity, a thousand years have passed on Earth and Mandella returns there to find society utterly changed and incomprehensible to him.

The novel is wonderfully evocative, and illustrates only too well the dislocation and alienation experienced by soldiers returning home after the nightmare of Vietnam. It won both the HUGO and NEBULA AWARDS and is recognized as one of the most satisfactory depictions of the military experience in SF.

The Forever War was followed by a belated sequel, *Forever Free* (1999), which picks up the story of William Mandella and his family who at the start of the novel are living on a distant PLANET in a society of post-human entities. The family grow tired of their oppression by their descendants and, together with a group of other soldiers left over from the war, they plan to hijack a spacecraft that will allow them to travel back to a time nearer their own. The book is a successful follow-up to *The Forever War* but does not quite capture the sheer power of its predecessor.

Another and superior book, *Forever Peace* (1997), also explores similar concerns but from a slightly different perspective. This time the war is taking place on Earth in the NEAR FUTURE. Soldiers control armoured machines in the Third World via remote links, for which sensory interfaces have to be implanted in their skulls. The book is thematically akin to *The Forever War* in the way that it portrays the sense of detachment felt by the soldiers when they emerge from their VIRTUAL REALITY control booths and attempt to slide back into normal society. Remarkably, the book achieved the same double award as *The Forever War*, winning both the Hugo and Nebula.

Of Haldeman's other novels, *Mindbridge* (1976) is perhaps his most ingenious. It follows the progress of a group of explorers who set out to chart a distant PLANET. Once they arrive they find a mysterious creature that bestows on them the gift of telepathy, which eventually leads to them making contact with an awe-inspiring ALIEN species.

The novel is notable not so much for its plot or characterization, both of which are accomplished, as for its attempts to play with narrative form; the story is written as a mixture of straight narration, memos, reports, graphs, fragments of dialogue and so forth. This makes for an original and interesting structure, marking Haldeman out as a writer unafraid to stretch himself and experiment within the genre.

Also of note is Haldeman's *Worlds* trilogy, which begins with *Worlds*

(1981) and continues with *Worlds Apart* (1983) and *Worlds Enough and Time* (1992) and concerns a POST-APOCALYPTIC Earth and the surviving human–occupied ARTIFICIAL ENVIRONMENTS in orbit. The populations of these isolated habitats must learn to survive without the resources of Earth and have to reach out eventually for the stars.

Haldeman's insights into the plight of soldiers during the Vietnam War are well-nigh are almost unparalleled in science fiction. Perhaps by setting his deeply felt stories against the backdrop of interstellar space Haldeman is simply telling the reader that conflict is universal, eternal and frightful. Whatever the case, his writing is powerful, gripping and thought-provoking.

The author maintains a website at http://home.earthlink.net/~haldeman/

See Also
ALIEN; MILITARISTIC SF; PLANET; SPACE TRAVEL; VIRTUAL REALITY

Recommended Further Reading
Starship Troopers (1959) by ROBERT HEINLEIN; The *Night's Dawn* Trilogy by PETER F. HAMILTON; *Ender's Game* (1985) by ORSON SCOTT CARD

Bibliography
War Years (1972)
The Forever War (1974)
Mindbridge (1976)
All My Sins Remembered (1977)
Infinite Dreams (short stories, 1979)
Worlds (1981)
Worlds Apart (1983)
Dealing in Futures (short stories, 1985)
Tool of the Trade (1987)
The Long Habit of Living (1989)
The Hemingway Hoax (1990)
Worlds Enough and Time (1992)
1968 (1995)
None So Blind (short stories, 1996)
Forever Peace (1997)

Forever Free (1999)
The Coming (projected, 2000)

HAMILTON, PETER F. (1960–   ), Great Britain

Peter F. Hamilton published his first novel, *Mindstar Rising*, in 1993. It is set in and around his native Rutland and featuring Greg Mandel, an ex-captain of the 'Mindstar Brigade' turned private eye. This was the first book in the 'Greg Mandel Trilogy' and was followed by *A Quantum Murder* (1994) and *The Nano Flower* (1995). Together they make up one of the more underrated trilogies of recent years, a successful blend of SF-cum-detective story set, unusually, against a rural English backdrop.

It is possible, though, that the spectacular success of Hamilton's later 'Night's Dawn Trilogy' has simply overshadowed the 'Greg Mandel' books.

The Reality Dysfunction was published in 1996 and kicked off one of the most extravagant – and popular – SPACE OPERAS for many years. The novel takes as its main theme the struggle between two opposing political forces, UTOPIAN (Edenism) and DYSTOPIAN (Adamism), and their attempts to co-exist in a shared universe. ALIEN life forms feature prominently.

An alien entity has become trapped between DIMENSIONS on a distant human colony world, and in doing so has inadvertently opened a gateway between living human reality and an after-death limbo populated by spirit beings. This leads to a flood of human souls being unleashed upon the unwary colonists whose bodies are then possessed by these entities from beyond the grave. It is not long before the 'possessed' have gained control over the entire PLANET and are planning to hijack a spacecraft and escape into the rest of the populated universe.

There follows an epic of adventure as human characters from both Adamist and the Edenist factions battle to find a way to combat the onslaught of souls who are invading their bodies and taking over their minds.

Hamilton's chief protagonists face a series of ever greater challenges, which will of course only be overcome through a *détente* between the two opposing factions who must reconcile their respective philosophies and forge ahead together towards a brighter future. The book strongly favours a non-MILITARISTIC solution to the crisis – rather ingeniously Hamilton sets matters up so that any possessed bodies that are killed in armed combat only increase the number of dead people able to come back since the original owner of the host body is slain along with its 'occupier'.

The Reality Dysfunction was followed by *The Neutronium Alchemist* (1997) and *The Naked God* (1999), which continued to explore the way in which humanity copes with the ultimate crisis. Hamilton creates a universe and plot on an epic scale rarely seen in modern science fiction.

The Confederation Handbook was published in 2000 to provide readers with detailed notes about the trilogy and its universe.

See Also

ARTIFICIAL ENVIRONMENT; DYSTOPIA; GENETICS; NANO-TECHNOLOGY; PLANET; SPACE OPERA; SPACE TRAVEL; UTOPIA

Recommended Further Reading

The Forever War (1974) by JOE HALDEMAN; *Necroville* (1995) by Ian McDonald; the *Uplift* sequence by DAVID BRIN; the *Culture* sequence by IAIN M. BANKS

Bibliography

Mindstar Rising (1993)
A Quantum Murder (1994)
The Nano Flower (1995)
The Reality Dysfunction (1996)
The Neutronium Alchemist (1997)
A Second Chance at Eden (short stories, 1998)
Lightstorm (juvenile, 1998)
The Naked God (1999)
Watching Trees Grow (2000)
Fallen Dragon (projected, 2001)

HAND, ELIZABETH (1957–   ), USA

American writer Elizabeth Hand produced her first novel, *Winterlong*, in 1990. It is a heady, baroque evocation of the distant future, set within a framework reminiscent of GENE WOLFE'S wonderful *The Book of the New Sun* in that it draws on fantastical imagery to portray a future time that is wholly alien to twenty-first-century powers of comprehension. GENETIC engineering gives this future its identity: the remnants of the human race who inhabit the shattered remains of a once-great city are scarred by the use of BIOTECHNOLOGY. Stepping into this world the reader encounters two children who, once united, must undertake a journey while trying to ignore the siren call of an evil that could, if left unchecked, lead them to bring about the end of the human race. Beautiful, haunting and LITERARY, *Winterlong* represents Gothic SF of the highest calibre. The novel is a little too long, but the high quality of its prose and style more than make up for this. *Winterlong* is a triumph of creativity. It was followed by two novels set in the same universe, *Aestival Tide* (1992) and *Icarus Descending* (1993), that show Hand's abilities as a writer coming into flower. Her SF is dangerous and enigmatic.

Much of Hand's later work would be better defined as modern Dark Fantasy. *Waking the Moon* (1994) and *Black Light* (1999) deal with a sinister RELIGIOUS cult in contemporary America.

Glimmering (1997) is an SF manifestation of millennial angst: it describes a turn of the century that is not altogether pleasant. Scientists have attempted to fix the problems of the ozone layer with a man-made substance known as Brite, but a solar flare has caused the compound to react with gases in the outer atmosphere and practically destroy it. Now glimmering colours and lights are all that can be seen in the sky as the remains of the Brite dance in myriad patterns across it. The story takes place chiefly in Manhattan, and describes the chaos that follows the destruction of the upper atmosphere. Dangerous cults spring up all around, and many of the characters believe the end of the world to be nigh. They attempt to escape their various nightmares by indulging in an orgy of substance abuse.

What comes across most strongly in *Glimmering*, apart from the power of Hand's prose, is her uneasiness with technology and, as in her previous novels, a rather cynical view of humanity's relationship with science. Hand is not an optimist.

Hand's best short fiction is showcased in *Last Summer at Mars Hill* (1999). The excellent title story sets the high standard of the collection.

See Also
BIOTECHNOLOGY; GENETICS; LITERARY SF; RELIGION

Recommended Further Reading
The Book of the New Sun by GENE WOLFE; *God's Fires* (1998) by PATRICIA ANTHONY

Bibliography

Winterlong (1990)

Aestival Tide (1992)

Icarus Descending (1993)

Waking the Moon (1994)

12 Monkeys (1995, movie novelization)

Glimmering (1997)

Black Light (1999)

Last Summer at Mars Hill (short stories, 1999)

HARRISON, HARRY (1925–   ), USA

There are many sides to the eclectic talent of Harry Harrison.

Born in America, well travelled, and now settled in Ireland, Harrison is best known for his cutting satirical forays into COMIC SF but he is also a fine purveyor of ALTERNATE-WORLD SF.

Harrison began his SF writing career with short stories for *Worlds Beyond* in the early 1950s. His first novel, *Deathworld* (1960), is a taut adventure about the colonization of a distant PLANET where life is incredibly hostile to humans. It was followed by *Deathworld Two* (1964) and *Deathworld Three* (1968), the three being assembled at various times as *The Deathworld Trilogy*.

However, it is for his next book, and the series that it began, that Harrison is best known. *The Stainless Steel Rat* (1961) was a fixup from a number of short stories and recounts the exploits of ex-criminal turned policeman Slippery Jim DiGriz. It is a satirical romp whose humour is largely directed against the self-important bureaucrats who pervade every level of society. Although hilarious, its barbed comedy can sometimes be quite fierce, and the underlying message remains clear: Harrison is a supporter of self-determination in its many forms.

Many *Stainless Steel Rat* books followed. They are *The Stainless Steel Rat's Revenge* (1970), *The Stainless Steel Rat Saves the World* (1972), *The Stainless Steel Rat Wants You!* (1979), *The Stainless Steel Rat for President* (1982), *A Stainless Steel Rat is Born* (1985), *The Stainless Steel Rat Gets Drafted* (1987), *Stainless Steel Visions* (1993), *The Stainless Steel Rat Sings the Blues* (1994), *The Stainless Steel Rat Goes to Hell* (1996) and *The Stainless Steel Rat Joins the Circus* (1999). Unfortunately, as the sequence progresses, the stories seem to lose their impetus and direction rather and although many are undeniably funny they do not have the same bite as the earlier novels.

Harrison's other comic SF sequence concerns the (mis)adventures of *Bill, the Galactic Hero*, which began with the eponymous first novel in 1965. This series tackles MILITARY life and the regimented thought processes that it imposes on humanity. The first story is a classic, while the sequels, which appeared some years later and were mainly co-written with other authors, tend to descend into slapstick for effect. In a cosy way reminiscent of the early genre pulps, they are still occasionally fun to read.

As well as these and other significant series, Harrison has written a number of important 'singletons'. *Make Room! Make Room!* (1966) is possibly his most environmentally aware novel, and certainly his most bleak. It is set in a DYSTOPIC New York City of the NEAR FUTURE, which is burdened by massive OVERPOPULATION. The book was filmed, none too faithfully, as SOYLENT GREEN (1973).

Harrison has also produced a large number of alternate-world novels in his prolific career. *West of Eden* (1984) and its two sequels describe a world where the dinosaurs did not die out and evolved as an intelligent life form. *Tunnel Through the Deeps* (1972, later retitled *A Transatlantic Tunnel, Hurrah!*) sees a British Empire building an subterranean tunnel to its American colony, while the recent *Stars and Stripes Forever* (1998) and its sequel *Stars and Stripes in Peril* (2000) posits a dramatically different outcome for the American Civil War.

Harrison is a writer of many strengths. There is no doubt that his name has become synonymous with quality comic SF, but there are many other facets to his body of work that should not be forgotten. Harrison continues to produce intelligent, thoughtful SF, and it is hoped that he will do so for many more years to come.

See Also
ALTERNATE WORLD; COMIC SF; DYSTOPIA; NEAR FUTURE; OVERPOPULATION

Recommended Further Reading
Bios (1999) by ROBERT CHARLES WILSON; *A Torrent of Faces* (1967) by JAMES BLISH and Norman Knight; *Logan's Run* (1967) by William F. Nolan and George Clayton Johnson; *The Dark Side of the Sun* (1976) by TERRY PRATCHETT; *The Two Georges* (1997) by HARRY TURTLEDOVE and Richard Dreyfuss

Bibliography

Deathworld (1960)
The Stainless Steel Rat (1961)
Planet of the Damned (1962)
War with the Robots (short stories, 1962)
Deathworld Two (1964)
Bill, the Galactic Hero (1965)
Plague from Space (1965)
Make Room! Make Room! (1966)
The Technicolor Time Machine (1967)
Two Tales and Eight Tomorrows (short stories, 1968)
Deathworld Three (1968)
The Man from P.I.G. (1968)
Captive Universe (1969)
Spaceship Medic (1970)
Prime Number (short stories, 1970)
One Step from Earth (short stories, 1970)
In Our Hands, the Stars (1970)
The Stainless Steel Rat's Revenge (1970)
The Stainless Steel Rat Saves the World (1972)
Tunnel Though the Deeps (1972)
Stonehenge (1972)
Star Smashers of the Galaxy Rangers (1973)
The Best of Harry Harrison (short stories, 1976)
The Lifeship (1976, with Gordon Dickson)
Skyfall (1976)
The Stainless Steel Rat Wants You! (1979)
Planet Story (1979)
Homeworld (1980)
Starworld (1981)
Wheelworld (1981)
Planet of No Return (1981)
The Stainless Steel Rat for President (1982)
Invasion: Earth (1982)
A Rebel in Time (1983)
West of Eden (1984)
A Stainless Steel Rat is Born (1985)
Winter in Eden (1986)
The Stainless Steel Rat Gets Drafted (1987)
Return to Eden (1988)

Bill, the Galactic Hero on the Planet of Robot Slaves (1989)

Bill, the Galactic Hero on the Planet of Bottled Brains (1990, with ROBERT SHECKLEY)

Bill, the Galactic Hero on the Planet of Tasteless Pleasure (1991, with David Bischoff)

Bill, the Galactic Hero on the Planet of Ten Thousand Bars (1991, with David Bischoff)

Bill, the Galactic Hero on the Planet of the Zombie Vampires (1991, with Jack C. Haldeman II)

Bill, the Galactic Hero: The Final Incoherent Adventure (1992, with David Harris)

Stainless Steel Visions (short stories, 1993)

The Hammer and the Cross (1993)

Galactic Dreams (short stories, 1994)

The Stainless Steel Rat Sings the Blues (1994)

One King's Way (1996)

The Stainless Steel Rat Goes to Hell (1996)

King and Emperor (1997)

Stars and Stripes Forever (1998)

The Stainless Steel Rat Joins the Circus (1999)

Stars and Stripes in Peril (2000)

HARRISON, M. JOHN (1945–   ), Great Britain

Michael John Harrison is one of the most complex of all UK genre writers, and perhaps one of the most difficult to define. He began his career in the late 1960s with short stories published in NEW WORLDS magazine when it was edited by MICHAEL MOORCOCK, some of which used the SHARED WORLD setting of Moorcock's own *Jerry Cornelius* multiverse. Harrison went on to become literary editor of *New Worlds* and contributed book reviews and other criticism under various pseudonyms.

Harrison's first novel, *The Commited Men* (1971), describes a typically DYSTOPIAN future England and explores many of the NEW WAVE concerns of the time.

The Commited Men was followed by *The Pastel City* (1971), which was to begin the *Viriconium* sequence, a rich SCIENCE FANTASY set against the backdrop of a FAR-FUTURE Earth, a bleak and blighted world. Harrison makes use of images plundered from the pages of fantasy to define the slowly dissolving world which he has his characters inhabit.

Harrison's meticulously depicted landscapes are bleached by entropy to form a POST-HOLOCAUST nightmare background against which his characters struggle to define not only their own identities but also to articulate their desire to escape the degraded world around them. This discussion of identity and the urge to escape was to become a recurring theme in Harrison's work around which all other concerns would revolve.

The *Viriconium* sequence continued with *A Storm of Wings* (1980), *In Viriconium* (1982) and *Viriconium Nights* (1984). Of these, *In Viriconium* shows Harrison at his most mature; it is a powerful and involving book that is steeped in metaphor, a fine example of LITERARY SF that has been seamlessly interwoven with fantasy.

The *Viriconium* sequence was collected together as *Viriconium* (1988).

Other Harrison titles of note include *The Centauri Device* (1974), in which Captain John Truck is caught up in the middle of a war to gain control of a super-doomsday device, and *Signs of Life* (1997), a startling piece of literary SF that sits as comfortably in the contemporary mainstream as it does alongside Harrison's more SF-related work. This novel is perhaps Harrison's most important work to date, showing a very clear and definite development in his style.

Indeed, with the publication of his sixth novel, *Climbers* (1989), Harrison began to move away from the genre, finding perhaps that the mainstream was better suited to his preoccupations of the time. This is not to say that Harrison will not return to SF: he is reportedly working on a SPACE OPERA that will serve as a companion volume to *The Centauri Device* and many of the short stories collected in *Travel Arrangements* (2000) first appeared in genre magazines.

See Also
DYSTOPIA; FAR FUTURE; LITERARY SF; NEW WAVE; POST APOCALYPTIC; SCIENCE FANTASY

Recommended Further Reading
The Dying Earth (1950) by JACK VANCE; *The Book of the New Sun* by GENE WOLFE; *The Dancers at the End of Time* sequence by Michael Moorcock

Bibliography
The Commited Men (1971)
The Pastel City (1971)
The Centauri Device (1974)

The Machine in Shaft Ten (short stories, 1975)
A Storm of Wings (1980)
In Viriconium (1982)
The Ice Monkey (short stories, 1983)
Viriconium Nights (short stories, 1984)
Viriconium 1988)
Climbers (1989)
The Course of the Heart (1992)
Signs of Life (1997)
The Wild Road (1997, with Jane Johnson, as 'Gabriel King')
The Golden Cat (1998, with Jane Johnson, as 'Gabriel King')
Travel Arrangements (short stories, 2000)

HEINLEIN, ROBERT A. (1907–1988), USA

Robert Anson Heinlein was one of the most important American SF writers to come out of the GOLDEN AGE. He created the templates of many of the themes and devices that would later become fundamental to the genre, and much of his work still resonates with a startling originality and depth. Of all the classic American SF authors, Heinlein has had the most influence on the genre as a whole.

Unlike many of his contemporaries, Heinlein did not begin publishing SF until he was in his early thirties and already had a prematurely curtailed (because of ill-health) career in the US Navy behind him. He began with a series of stories and serialized novels for ASTOUNDING SCIENCE FICTION magazine, and it was clear to readers from the very beginning that Heinlein was a writer fully formed – his work was mature, innovative and adventurous.

Perhaps the most significant aspect of this early stage of Heinlein's writing career, is the conceptual framework he built for his major fiction, a FUTURE HISTORY unlike anything the genre had previously seen. Where OLAF STAPLEDON, in such novels as *Last and First Men* (1930) and *Star Maker* (1937), had suggested a curve of evolution that would see the human race reaching far into the future, Heinlein mapped out an entire history of future events, stage by stage, and then produced wonderful stories that slotted precisely into it at particular points. Readers were hooked, and the optimism implicit such a forward-looking scheme rubbed off on other authors of the time. These stories and serial-izations would not be published in book form for a number of years, but to regular readers of the genre magazines Heinlein was already a hero.

It is fair to say that, after *Astounding* editor JOHN W. CAMPBELL, Heinlein was the most important figure of the Golden Age period, and his work helped to shape the genre as we know it today.

However, by the end of 1941 the USA had entered the Second World War and, although *Astounding* continued producing classic fiction right throughout the conflict, Heinlein did not publish any more SF until 1946. He ceased writing to do his bit for the war effort as an engineer.

Heinlein's return to writing after the war was marked by a definite shift in emphasis. He began work on a long series of juvenile SF novels for an American publishing house and succeeded in selling his more adult short stories to a number of magazines that did not usually deal with genre literature. This not only widened the market for his own writing but helped prepare the way for the recognition of SF as a valid form of popular literature.

Heinlein's best juvenile writing can be seen in such novels as *Rocket Ship Galileo* (1947), which also formed the basis of the film DESTINA-TION MOON (1950), *Red Planet* (1949), *Starman Jones* (1953), *The Star Beast* (1954), *Time for the Stars* (1956) and *Have Space Suit – Will Travel* (1958).

This period also saw the first publication in book form of his earlier Future History work, with *Methuselah's Children* (1958) and *The Man Who Sold the Moon* (1950), among others, appearing between hard covers.

Heinlein was also putting original adult novels straight into book form, bypassing magazine serialization. *The Puppet Masters* (1951) is an alarming tale of ALIEN invasion, which sees slug-like creatures attaching themselves to human nervous systems and controlling their bodies like mindless puppets. Eventually, the leading protagonist is able to convince the US Government of the danger it faces, and the interstellar menace is conquered. It remains one of the truly great alien-invasion stories of the 1950s.

The Door into Summer (1957), meanwhile, is a TIME paradox story that sees a man spend decades in suspended animation, only to find when he wakes in the twenty-first century that someone else has spent the intervening years acting in his name. He travels back in time to investigate the strange occurrences, and in doing so sets history back on its proper tracks and meets up with his long-lost love.

It was during this period that Heinlein made great headway in the genre, in the way that he adopted typical genre concepts and subverted them, revealing their inherent contradictions and beginning to tease new ideas from them. Heinlein's stories were not populated by the same simple protagonists who were to be seen in the pulps or in the space operas of the early years of SF – these were real people in believable situations, rounded characters who could be identified with, whose joy or terror the reader could share. Heinlein at his best was a chronicler of emotions as well as of ideas and events.

However, the late 1950s saw yet another shift in Heinlein's career. The novel *Starship Troopers* (1959), intended originally as a juvenile, earned him in some quarters a new, unwelcome and undeserved reputation – as a fascist. The book is certainly a strong endorsement of the benefits of MILITARY life, to the extent that the young male protagonist is seen to TRANSCEND adolescence and assume adulthood only when he demonstrates his abilities as a soldier. The book can also be interpreted as supporting the very strict regimentation which its soldiers are educated, a form of brainwashing that beats out of the young recruits any thoughts of free will or self-expression – they become robotic fighting machines, and Heinlein appears to revel in the notion. It is as if he is arguing that regimented military life is in many ways superior to the everyday existence of ordinary human beings.

This kind of didacticism marred much of the rest of Heinlein's writing career. There are good books – such as *The Moon is a Harsh Mistress* (1966) and *Time Enough for Love* (1973), which returns to the tale of the Future History protagonist from *Methuselah's Children* – but many, such as *Stranger in a Strange Land* (1961) could not recapture the essence of his earlier work.

This last-mentioned novel did become something of a cult book among students of the 1960s, chiefly because of the mystical spin that it gives to what is essentially a SCIENCE FANTASY about sublimation and transcendence.

It is a shame that a writer who started out with such power and ability should decline so sadly in his later years. Heinlein went from being one of the most important authors in the SF field to being one of the most disdained and the reasons for this are apparent in much of his later work. Nevertheless, he remains one of the giants of American science fiction, and was one of the most influential authors the genre had seen since H. G. WELLS. His Future History sequence will be remembered for its vitality and originality, his juveniles for their exuberance and sense of adventure, and many of his 'singletons' for their complexity and depth. Heinlein was one of only a handful of truly great writers that the genre has so far seen, and the SF genre itself, to the extent that he helped to shape it, is his work's most abiding monument.

Robert Heinlein died in 1988, aged eighty-one.

See Also
ARTIFICIAL INTELLIGENCE; ASTOUNDING SCIENCE FICTION; JOHN W. CAMPBELL; CRYOGENICS; FUTURE HISTORY; GALAXY; GENERATION STARSHIP; GOLDEN AGE; TIME

Recommended Further Reading
The *Foundation* sequence by ISAAC ASIMOV; the *Seafort Saga* by DAVID FEINTUCH; the *Eight Worlds* sequence by JOHN VARLEY; *The Forever War* (1974) by JOE HALDEMAN

Bibliography (Selected)
Rocket Ship Galileo (1947)
Beyond This Horizon (1948)
Space Cadet (1948)
Red Planet (1949)
Sixth Column (1949)
Waldo and Magic Inc. (short stories, 1950)
The Man who Sold the Moon (short stories, 1950)
Farmer in the Sky (1950)
The Green Hills of Earth (short stories, 1951)
Between Planets (1951)
The Puppet Masters (1951)
Universe (1951)
The Rolling Stones (1952)
Revolt in 2100 (short stories, 1953)
Starman Jones (1953)
Assignment in Eternity (short stories, 1954)
The Star Beast (1954)
Tunnel in the Sky (1955)
Double Star (1956)
Citizen of the Galaxy (1957)
The Door Into Summer (1957)
Methuselah's Children (1958)
Have Space Suit – Will Travel (1958)
The Menace from Earth (short stories, 1959)
Starship Troopers (1959)
6 X H (short stories, 1961)
Stranger in a Strange Land (1961)
Glory Road (1963)

Podkayne of Mars (1963)
Farnham's Freehold (1964)
The Worlds of Robert Heinlein (short stories, 1966)
The Moon is a Harsh Mistress (1966)
I Will Fear No Evil (1970)
The Best of Robert Heinlein (short stories, 1973)
Time Enough for Love (1973)
Expanded Universe (short stories, 1980)
The Number of the Beast (1980)
Friday (1982)
Job (1984)
The Cat who Walks through Walls (1985)
To Sail Beyond the Sunset (1987)
Requiem (short stories, 1992)
The Notebooks of Lazarus Long (1995, with D. Vassallo)
The Fantasies of Robert Heinlein (short stories, 1999)

HERBERT, BRIAN (1947–   ), USA

The son of *Dune* author FRANK HERBERT, Brian Herbert began his career in the SF genre with the publication of his first novel, *Sidney's Comet*, in 1983. It is an example of COMIC SF, and concerns a vast cometary body composed of human garbage. It was followed by a sequel, *The Garbage Chronicles* (1985), and although both novels are worthy of interest, they rest rather uneasily between absurdity and satire.

The same can also be said of Herbert's next novel, *Sudanna, Sudanna* (1985) and his collaboration with his father, *Man of Two Worlds* (1986). Both feature insufficiently realized ALIEN cultures, with the collaborative work also attempting to explore the nature of reality – the alien protagonists 'dream' the human race into existence.

Herbert's later work, such as *Prisoners of Arionn* (1987), is perhaps more satisfactory, if a little overshadowed by his father's reputation. Indeed, it was not until he revisited the setting of his father's *Dune* (1965) for a trilogy of preludes to the original novel that he really started to get noticed in the genre.

House Atreides (1999), written in collaboration with author KEVIN J. ANDERSON, is an accurate and consistent addition to the *Dune* canon and examines in some detail the early lives of a number of the protagonists who feature later in the established classic series. Although lacking the epic scope of the original, it is well conceived and stands comparison with the later books in the original *Dune* sequence. It begins with a young Leto Atreides being primed as the next ruler of the family on the Atreides home planet, Caladan. House Harkonnen is still entrusted with the planet Arrakis, or Dune, and the novel follows the stirrings of the intrigue that will eventually lead to the Atreides family being made governors of Arrakis.

The novel was followed by the second in the 'Prelude' trilogy, *House Harkonnen* (2000), which continued the narrative of the first book and satisfactorily maintains the build-up towards the events that eventually take place in the original novel.

After the third book in the sequence, *House Corrino* (projected, 2001), Brian Herbert has hinted that he may produce a sequel to the last of the original *Dune* novels, *Chapter House Dune* (1985). Perhaps the experience gained in writing the 'Prelude' novels based on his father's work will help him develop the skills necessary to produce the well-rounded and sustained genre novel that his work has always hinted he is capable of. Readers can only wait and see.

See Also
COMIC SF; SCIENCE FANTASY

Recommended Further Reading
Dune (1965) by FRANK HERBERT

Bibliography
Sidney's Comet (1983)
The Garbage Chronicles (1985)
Sudanna, Sudanna (1985)
Man of Two Worlds (1986, with FRANK HERBERT)
Prisoners of Arionn (1987)
The Race for God (1990, with Marie Landis)
Memorymakers (1991, with Marie Landis)
Prelude to Dune: House Atreides (1999, with KEVIN J. ANDERSON)
Prelude to Dune: House Harkonnen (2000, with KEVIN J. ANDERSON)
Prelude to Dune: House Corrino (projected, 2001, with KEVIN J. ANDERSON)

HERBERT, FRANK (1920–1986), USA

Born and raised on the West Coast of America, Frank Herbert will forever be remembered in the SF genre for his monumental multi-novel *Dune* sequence.

Dune (1965), the first and best book in the series, was Herbert's second novel, following the earlier *The Dragon in the Sea* (1956), a one-off techno-thriller set aboard a twenty-first century submarine.

It is interesting that of the many newer American writers to make an impact in the SF field during the mid-1960s, Herbert was one of the few not to become associated with the LITERARY NEW WAVE movement, continuing instead to produce steadfast, traditional SF that has actually flourished during the intervening years and remains popular today. *Dune* reads like a trade-off between a fantasy saga and a HARD SF novel. It is explicitly SF, perhaps being best described as a SPACE OPERA, but the manner in which Herbert adopts a pseudo-medieval social structure for his interstellar Empire, filled with images of dukedoms and towering castles, reminds readers of earlier, fantastical epics. And epic *Dune* certainly is.

The story is that of the PLANET Arrakis, or Dune, a desert world upon which humanity maintains precarious existence alongside the enormous ALIEN Sandworms. What is perhaps most fundamental about *Dune* is the manner in which Herbert details the ECOLOGY and desolation of the entire planet – this is no planetary romance, but a fully fledged exercise in world-building, imaginative 'engineering' on a scale never before seen in the genre. Arrakis is as vividly detailed as a real place, and is more dangerous and inhospitable to human life than even the most terrifyingly extreme environments of Earth. Humanity there is forced to eke out a nomadic tribal existence, harvesting the spice-drug Melange (which greatly enhances longevity) and recycling all their bodily fluids in order to survive in the harsh deserts. Humanity has dreams of TERRAFORMING the planet, but first the iron grip of the Empire must be thrown off and the various elements of planetary society must be willing to work together to succeed in such a massive enterprise.

Dune is a highly complex novel. It is also the tale of Paul Atreides, the young man who becomes a MESSIAH of the people and who eventually, after a process that continues throughout the sequence, TRANSCENDS his human form and achieves a state of godhood. It is a multi-layered extravaganza and, although occasionally weighed down by prose heavy with the burden of Dune's exceptional history, it succeeds.

Later books in the sequence – *Dune Messiah* (1969), *Children of Dune*

(1976), *God Emperor of Dune* (1981), *Heretics of Dune* (1984) and *Chapter House Dune* (1985) – fail to recapture the balance of the first novel, at times becoming overlong explications of history and myth. However, the sequence as a whole has had a major influence on the genre and captured the imaginations of millions of readers worldwide.

Dune remains one of the most important SF novels of the 1960s, winning both the NEBULA and HUGO AWARDS for its year. It was filmed, rather unsuccessfully, by DAVID LYNCH in 1984 under the same title.

Recently a new trilogy of preludes to the original series has begun to appear, written by Herbert's son BRIAN HERBERT in cooperation with KEVIN J. ANDERSON and drawing on Herbert's original notes. The series comprises *House Atreides* (1999), *House Harkonnen* (2000) and *House Corrino* (projected, 2001). Although not as deserving of critical acclaim as the original novel they form a consistent and interesting addition to the *Dune* canon.

Of Herbert's non-*Dune* work, a number of other triumphs deserve mention.

The Green Brain (1966) takes an interesting and original look at the concept of an environmental disaster. A community of grotesque mutated insects, which together constitutes a hive mind, plots to punish humanity for the damage it has done to the Earth's ecology. Nightmare scenarios ensue.

Whipping Star (1970) and, more importantly its sequel *The Dosadi Experiment* (1977) describe various forms of alien intelligence that are appropriately different from our own. The Calebans communicate telepathically over great distances, and when one dies, the others suffer accordingly. *The Dosadi Experiment* also examines a disturbing experiment in OVERPOPULATION and the subsequent results.

Destination: Void (1966), a solo effort, and its various sequels – all co-written with Bill Ransom (*The Jesus Incident* (1979), *The Lazarus Effect* (1983) and *The Ascension Factor* (1988)) – explore the creation of an ARTIFICIAL INTELLIGENCE that ultimately comes to the conclusion that it is God and must be worshipped. A bargain is struck – the human members of the crew of the starship that the AI inhabits will worship it according to its wishes on condition that it protects them from the terrors outside their vessel. The sequence, known as the 'Pandora' quartet after the name of the colony planet on which the crew find themselves, is evocative and impressive.

Herbert wrote many other novels and stories, none of which quite reach the heights of *Dune*. Most are perfectly worthy studies of alien cultures or worlds, although too often they struggle to put their notions across with any degree of clarity. But, Herbert will be remembered above all for the significant and important creative edifice that is *Dune*, a work of genuine relevance and great intelligence.

Frank Herbert died in 1986, aged sixty-six.

See Also
ALIEN; ECOLOGY; MESSIAH; OVERPOPULATION; PLANET; RELIGION; SCIENCE FANTASY; SPACE OPERA; TERRA-FORMING

Recommended Further Reading
Big Planet (1957) by JACK VANCE; *Mission of Gravity* (1954) by HAL CLEMENT; *Stranger in a Strange Land* (1961) by ROBERT HEIN-LEIN; the *Mars Trilogy* by KIM STANLEY ROBINSON; *House Atreides* (1999) by BRIAN HERBERT and KEVIN J. ANDERSON

Bibliography
The Dragon in the Sea (1956)
Dune (1965)
The Eyes of Heisenberg (1966)
The Green Brain (1966)
Destination: Void (1966)
The Heaven Makers (1968)
The Santaroga Barrier (1968)
Dune Messiah (1969)
The Worlds of Frank Herbert (short stories, 1970)
Whipping Star (1970)
Soul Catcher (1972)
The Godmakers (1972)
The Book of Frank Herbert (short stories, 1973)
Hellstrom's Hive (1973)
The Best of Frank Herbert (short stories, 1975)
Children of Dune (1976)
The Dosadi Experiment (1977)
The Jesus Incident (1979, with Bill Ransom)
The Priests of Psi (short stories, 1980)
Direct Descent (1980)
God Emperor of Dune (1981)

The White Plague (1982)
The Lazarus Effect (1983, with Bill Ransom)
Heretics of Dune (1984)
Eye (short stories, 1985)
Chapter House Dune (1985)
Man of Two Worlds (1986, with BRIAN HERBERT)
The Ascension Factor (1988, with Bill Ransom)

HUBBARD, L. RON (1911–1986), USA

An author of largely pulp-orientated SF, as well as the founder of a twentieth-century RELIGION, Scientology, L. Ron Hubbard has a reputation disproportionate to his actual achievement in the world of SF.

Hubbard began his career writing stories for JOHN W. CAMPBELL's ASTOUNDING SCIENCE FICTION magazine during the GOLDEN AGE of SF, although his writing always seemed to fit more comfortably with its sister magazine, *Unknown*; Hubbard produced far better fantasy than SF. It is surprising, in retrospect, that Campbell included Hubbard amongst his clique of favourite authors – unlike many of the other writers of the time he was not concerned so much with reinventing the form, more with providing readers with pacy if far-fetched adventure stories.

Of his early novels, the most successful is *Final Blackout* (1948), in which a dictator takes control of the UK in an attempt to fend off the other players in a series of wars that have been raging across the planet. Perhaps the nature of the quasi-MESSIAH of the novel is an indication of Hubbard's longing to establish around himself a support system of power and worship. Whatever his motives may have been, he took a step back from the SF genre during the 1950s to concentrate on the theories of spiritual TRANSCENDENCE that he called 'Dianetics'. Later, after Hubbard had gained a substantial following within the SF community, Dianetics would evolve into the latter-day religion, Scientology, which continues to attract various high-profile celebrities as well as devotees from all walks of life and remains highly controversial.

After many years spent away from the SF genre, Hubbard returned with the overlong SPACE OPERA, *Battlefield Earth* (1982), which is not so much the military thriller that it claims to be, more a complex pondering on the logistics of ALIEN warfare. It was recently filmed with limited success as *Battlefield Earth* (2000).

Hubbard died in 1986, but his ten-book sequence, *Mission Earth*, continued to be published. The sub-standard prose and general shoddiness of these books, together with the fact that so many of them appeared posthumously, have led some critics to question their provenance. Hubbard's estate has always claimed that they were written by Hubbard before he died.

The *Mission Earth* sequence begins with *The Invaders Plan* (1985) and concerns a hostile alien race's plot to conquer the Earth. It is really not worth consideration here, and the sequels only get worse as the story is dragged out *ad nauseam*.

Hubbard remains a popular figure in some SF circles, perhaps because he is remembered fondly for his time as a Golden Age writer. Some of his early work is worth seeking out, although it is a little too representative of its time. Later fictions should be left to the judgement of posterity.

See Also
RELIGION; SPACE OPERA; TRANSCENDENCE

Bibliography (Selected)
Buckskin Brigades (1937)
Death's Deputy (1948)
Final Blackout (1948)
Slaves of Sleep (1948)
The Kingslayer (short stories, 1949)
Triton & Battle of Wizards (1949)
Typewriter in the Sky & Fear (1951)
Return to Tomorrow (1954)
The Ultimate Adventure (1970)
Battlefield Earth (1982)
The Invaders Plan (1985)
Black Genesis (1986)
An Alien Affair (1986)
The Enemy Within (1986)
Fortune of Fear (1986)
Death Quest (1987)
Villainy Victorious (1987)
Voyage of Vengeance (1987)
Disaster (1987)
The Doomed Planet (1987)

HUXLEY, ALDOUS (1894–1963), Great Britain

Aldous Huxley is one of a relatively small number of mainstream LITERARY writers to become associated with the SF genre.

Undoubtedly his most explicitly science-fictional novel, and also his best, is *Brave New World* (1932), one of the truly classic DYSTOPIAS of the twentieth century.

The novel describes a society in which 'soma', a tranquillizing drug, is used to control the populace, a strict hierarchical class system is imposed by the state and GENETIC engineering is used to modify babies in test tubes before they are 'decanted'. It depicts a society that is technologically advanced, but at the same time utterly, disturbingly abhorrent. Huxley's insights into the human condition are profound. His prose is fluid and witty throughout, moving between serious speculation and humour without missing a step. As a result, *Brave New World* is satirical SF at its best.

Huxley's dystopia has had an amazing impact on the way in which the human race views itself in relation to science and scientific progress. Its title and much of its terminology have entered the vocabulary of discourse and many commentators still cite the book as a relevant warning about humanity's possible future transgressions against itself.

Parallels are easily drawn between *Brave New World* and GEORGE ORWELL's *Nineteen Eighty-Four* (1949), a dystopian novel that was to appear in print seventeen years later. Both novels view the state as an oppressive, controlling force and both see the population forced into a compartmentalized hierarchy with predefined roles.

Huxley's book is an antidote to the blind optimism of much science fiction writing of the time, its belief that science and technology would hold the key to a perfect tomorrow. Huxley pointed out, quite bravely, that this was simply not the case. Thoughtful writers would never consider the future in the same way again.

Most of Huxley's other fiction is very different in style and content to *Brave New World*. But *Ape and Essence* (1948) is a bleak and horrifying story of a different type of grim future, set during the aftermath of a nuclear war. In this POST-HOLOCAUST environment, society has degenerated and humanity has begun to devolve – toxic radiation levels mean that women may only conceive for a very short period every year. They are looked on as 'vessels', simple breeding machines. However, for all its intensity, the novel cannot equal the cumulative power of *Brave New World*'s dystopian vision.

Island (1962) is Huxley's attempt to explore a more optimistic alternative. In it, humanity is redeemed. An island community in the Indian Ocean develops a form of harmonious UTOPIA, quite different from the author's earlier bleak visions of man-made hell. The society is rooted in spirituality and makes use of mild recreational drugs – it is unfortunate that it all simply does not ring true. With *Brave New World*, Huxley gazed unflinching into the human future and the human spirit and described courageously what he saw. In *Island* he tried to avert his eyes, and in doing so suffered a fatal failure of nerve that rendered the novel sterile.

Huxley's other novels of genre interest include *After Many a Summer Dies the Swan* (1939) and *Time Must Have a Stop* (1944).

Aldous Huxley died in 1963, aged sixty-nine.

See Also
ALTERNATIVE REALITY; DYSTOPIA; GENETICS; LITERARY SF; POST APOCALYPTIC; UTOPIA

Recommended Further Reading
Nineteen Eighty-Four (1949) by George Orwell; *The Three Stigmata of Palmer Eldritch* (1964) by PHILIP K. DICK

Bibliography (Selected)
Brave New World (1932)
After Many a Summer Dies the Swan (1939)
Time Must Have a Stop (1944)
Ape and Essence (1948)
Island (1962)

IMPULSE
See SCIENCE FANTASY MAGAZINE

INFINITY PLUS
Infinity Plus is a website that is operated by genre author KEITH BROOKE. It aims to 'reprint' classic SF short stories by a wide range of SF and fantasy writers.

At present the list of archived authors is predominantly British – STEPHEN BAXTER, ERIC BROWN and PETER F. HAMILTON, among others. But the advantage of an electronic magazine is that it is readily available to everyone and a number of US writers such as Michael Bishop have recently posted stories or extracts.

The site itself is well maintained and constantly updated, and as well as regular fiction it features a selection of non-fiction – such interviews, reviews and so forth. So, far from being a media-orientated site like so many of the other online SF-related services, *Infinity Plus* is very much akin to a traditional magazine, but simply in electronic form.

Infinity Plus has been operating for a number of years now and has amassed a very worthy selection of archived fiction. On-screen is not necessarily the best format for reading, but the text is as clear as can be expected and the site provides a wonderful service for readers and writers alike.

Infinity Plus can be found at http://www.infinityplus.co.uk

INGS, SIMON (1969–   ), Great Britain

Perhaps one of the more underrated British CYBERPUNK authors, Simon Ings is a writer who produces fiction that is lyrical and LITERARY without losing the hard edge so essential to this sub-genre.

His first novel, *Hothead* (1992), is a tightly plotted technological circus of a book, in which the chief protagonist, Malise, has to save the Earth from a wave of hungry machines that are descending upon the planet. These machines are actually ARTIFICIAL INTELLIGENCE units that were originally sent out to inhospitable PLANETS to mine them for precious ores – instead they began to breed and, having consumed all of the ore to be found in the outer reaches of the Solar System, they are returning to Earth to search for more. Malise is wired with an illegal piece of HARDWARE that will allow her to enter CYBERSPACE in an attempt to prevent the machines from reaching the planet. At the same time, in the background, Europe is teetering on the brink of ECOLOG-ICAL collapse. The novel is well structured and well written, if bleak in tone, and it marked the debut of a fine new genre author.

Ings's next book was a mediocre fantasy, *The City of the Iron Fish* (1994), but he returned to the universe of *Hothead* with *Hotwire* (1995).

Set some years further into the future, *Hotwire* explores what happens when a number of cities begin to become self-aware. When a young man is employed by Rio to find it a body so that it may become human, he becomes embroiled in a plot to steal some high technology from a bizarre post-human orbital unit.

The novel, while a little surreal, is still worthwhile. It plays successfully with the form of a typical cyberpunk novel, creating something rather different from the usual data thievery and cyborg hacking – Ings makes characters out of entire cities.

Headlong (1999), Ings's fourth novel, is different again. The story follows the progress of Christopher Yale, a man who finds his wife dead when he is awoken from a sensory-deprivation tank. Yale's search for the reasons behind his wife's death forms the crux of the book, a fine example of a cyberpunk novel that is also a CRIME thriller set in a convincingly seedy London.

Ings's most recent novel, *Painkillers* (2000), is a literary mainstream novel.

The author maintains a website at http://www.fisheye.demon.co.uk/home.html

See Also
ARTIFICIAL INTELLIGENCE; BIOTECHNOLOGY; CRIME; CYBERPUNK; CYBERSPACE; HARDWARE; VIRTUAL REALITY

Recommended Further Reading
Neuromancer (1984) by WILLIAM GIBSON; *Islands in the Net* (1988) by BRUCE STERLING; *reMix* (1999) by JON COURTENAY GRIMWOOD; *Tea from an Empty Cup* (1998) by PAT CADIGAN

Bibliography
Hothead (1992)
City of the Iron Fish (1994)
Hotwire (1995)
Headlong (1999)
Painkillers (2000)

INTERZONE
Editor: David Pringle
Founded: 1982
Monthly
Subscription Address: 217 Preston Drove, Brighton, BN1 6FL, United Kingdom
£34/$60 for one-year subscription (12 issues)
Website address: http://www.sfsite.com/interzone

Interzone is the premier UK magazine of science fiction, following in the long tradition of legendary publications like NEW WORLDS and SCIENCE FANTASY. Indeed, it is now the only UK magazine to publish science fiction every month.

Founded in 1982 by a collective consisting of JOHN CLUTE, Alan Dorey, Malcom Edwards, COLIN GREENLAND, Graham James, Roz Kaveney, Simon Ounsley and David Pringle, and drawing its name from an imaginary city featured in WILLIAM BURROUGHS's novels, the magazine has gone from strength to strength.

During Interzone's first few years, various members of the collective group fell away until, in 1988, David Pringle took on the role of sole editor and publisher. To date, he continues in this position.

Early issues of *Interzone* had certain similarities to NEW WAVE magazine *New Worlds*, but it soon developed a personality of its own, with Pringle doing much to develop a welcoming atmosphere for new writers. Indeed, the magazine has been the breeding ground for many of the current major genre names, including STEPHEN BAXTER, ERIC BROWN, GREG EGAN, PAUL J. McAULEY and, more recently, ALASTAIR REYNOLDS. Other important names to feature in its pages include J. G. BALLARD, IAIN M. BANKS, PETER F. HAMILTON, M. JOHN HARRISON and MICHAEL MOORCOCK.

The magazine frequently contains up to six new short stories, an excellent film review column by Nick Lowe, an ANSIBLE digest by DAVID LANGFORD and an array of reviews by regulars such as Tom Arden, John Clute, Chris Gilmore and Paul J. McAuley. The author interviews, though less frequent, are often invaluable.

Interzone has been the magazine home of UK science fiction for nearly two decades, helping to nurture the genre and its many aspiring writers. Without it, the British science fiction scene would be very much the poorer. Those interested in where the genre will head next would do well to study its pages.

An index of previous issues, compiled by Greg Egan, can be found at http://www.netspace.net.au/~gregegan/IZ/index.htm

JENSEN, JAN LARS, Canada

Having produced a number of short stories and novellas for various genre magazines, including the award-winning *The Secret History of the Ornithopter*, Jan Lars Jensen published his first novel, *Shiva 3000*, in 2000. It is an exquisitely rich SCIENCE FANTASY that echoes ROGER

ZELAZNY'S classic *Lord of Light* (1967) in its exploration of Indian RELIGION and mythology. Set in the distant future and portraying a world in which Hindu gods walk the planet and interact with humankind, the book traces the movements of Rakesh, an ordinary man who is given the task of seeking out and defeating the deadly Baboon Warrior. In the world of *Shiva 3000* religion is physically manifest, Hindus have their 'chakras' surgically IMPLANTED into their spines and the future has blended seamlessly with the ancient past.

Jensen's prose is evocative and fluent, and the SENSE OF WONDER that he manages to create throughout *Shiva 3000* is truly impressive.

As his stories begin to appear ever more frequently in the genre magazines, and with an excellent first novel already under his belt, Jan Lars Jensen is a name to be watched.

The author maintains a website at http://www.mypage.uniserve. ca/~janlarsj/janlarsj/contents.html

See Also
RELIGION; SCIENCE FANTASY

Recommended Further Reading
Lord of Light (1967) by ROGER ZELAZNY

Bibliography
Shiva 3000 (2000)

KERR, KATHERINE (1944–   ), USA

Katherine Kerr is an American author best known for her Celtic fantasy sequence, the *Deverry* series. She has also published two SF novels of note.

Polar City Blues (1990) concerning, among other things, a human republic that is scattered over a number of neighbouring PLANETS. In comparison to the vast ALIEN confederation that spans interstellar space, this republic is tiny and fragile. When an alien emissary is murdered on Hagar, one of the human colony planets, this fragility is highlighted. Mystery ensues, and the novel is perhaps best described as an SF CRIME novel, with its backdrop of interstellar and inter-species politics adding depth and flavour. The book has many CYBERPUNK elements, but is not hard-edged enough to be classified as part of that subgenre. It also features a telepathic character who, having been taken to the scene of the murder in the hope that their empathic skills can help trace the killer, is hit by a psychic backwash and spends much of the novel in amnesiac shock.

A belated sequel is *Polar City Nightmare* (2000, with Kate Daniel), which returns to the setting of Hagar and revisits much of the same ground. This time an alien artefact is missing, and unless it is found the autonomy of the human republic will be at risk. Nevertheless, the book is well written and well paced, and succeeds as a sequel, even if it is a little too similar to its predecessor.

Whether Katherine Kerr will continue the Polar City series any further remains to be seen. Her fantasy novels, in the meantime, remain extremely popular with her legions of fans.

See Also
ALIEN; CRIME; CYBERPUNK; PLANETS

Recommended Further Reading
New York Nights (2000) by ERIC BROWN; *Queen of Angels* (1990) by GREG BEAR

Bibliography (Selected)
Polar City Blues (1990)
Polar City Nightmare (2000, with Kate Daniel)

KEYES, DANIEL (1927–   ), USA

Daniel Keyes has had a profound effect on the SF genre, achieving this with just one novel.

Flowers for Algernon (1966) was originally published in THE MAGA-ZINE OF FANTASY AND SCIENCE FICTION in 1959 as a long short story, and won the HUGO AWARD for the appropriate category in its year. Keyes went on to expand the story into a novel, which doubled his awards haul by claiming the 1966 NEBULA.

The deceptively straightforward narrative concerns Charlie Gordon, a mentally retarded floor-sweeper who becomes the subject of an experiment in human intelligence. Through surgery, Gordon has his IQ raised from a lowly 68 to genius level. He reads Milton, learns to love music and revels in his TRANSCENDENCE to a higher plane of intellectual life. But then the inevitable happens: the laboratory mouse, Algernon, which was transformed first by the experimental operation, loses its faculties and dies, and Gordon must face the imminent reality of his own slow decline.

Flowers for Algernon is a harrowing and touching story, perhaps the most poignant of all genre novels. Its moving portrayal of Gordon's decline ranks as one of the most humane examples of twentieth-century American fiction.

Keyes's book touches on many issues, most obviously the ethics and morality of human experimentation and manipulation. At a time when biological and GENETIC engineering are the cause of great public anxiety, this classic novel remains highly relevant.

The book was filmed in 1968 as CHARLY, successfully capturing much of the feel of the original novel. Later attempts to rework the concept, such as THE LAWNMOWER MAN, pale by comparison.

Another novel by Keyes of only slight genre interest, *The Touch* (1968), followed *Flowers for Algernon*, but failed to recreate the emotional impact of its predecessor.

See Also
HUMANIST SF; LITERARY SF; TRANSCENDENCE

Recommended Further Reading
Camp Concentration (1968) by THOMAS DISCH; *Days of Cain* (1998) by J. R. DUNN

Bibliography
Flowers for Algernon (1966)
The Touch (1968)

LANGFORD, DAVID (1953–   ), Great Britain

David Langford is Britain's premier SF fan critic and commentator. His often hilarious ANSIBLE newsletter, as well as his columns for INTER-ZONE and SFX magazines, sparkle with wit, proving that he is one of the funniest and most knowledgeable practitioners of genre non-fiction. This is a statement well supported by the vast number of HUGO AWARDS he has accumulated over the years for his achievements as 'Best Fan Writer'.

Langford has also produced some fiction – *The Space Eater* (1982) is his one attempt at serious genre SF, and straddles rather uneasily his COMIC SF impulses and a sober exploration of genre themes. In this story, a form of matter transmission or TELEPORTATION is tearing holes in the fabric of the universe, threatening to destroy the Earth. Two protagonists, hardy veterans, are dispatched to try and curb the use of the device. The novel charts their progress.

Later fiction from Langford tends towards comic SF. *The Leaky Establishment* (1984), although not strictly SF, is probably his best-known novel and concerns the search for a number of missing nuclear warheads. *Earthdoom!* (1987) and *Guts* (projected, 2001) are spoof disaster novel and spoof horror novel respectively, and are co-written with John Grant.

Langford provides a superb service to the SF field with his satirical commentary and subversive insights. *Ansible* has become an essential part of the critical scene and Langford's many columns and reviews are of continuing interest. His profile as a novelist would benefit from a more frequent output of book-length fiction but this might impinge upon his work as a critic. Readers should be thankful for what they have.

The author maintains a website at http://www.ansible.co.uk

See Also
COMIC SF; TELEPORTATION

Recommended Further Reading
The Stainless Steel Rat (1961) by HARRY HARRISON

Bibliography (Selected)
An Account of a Meeting with Denizens of Another World (1979)
The Space Eater (1982)
The Leaky Establishment (1984)
Earthdoom! (1987, with John Grant)
The Dragonhiker's Guide to Battlefield Covenant at Dune's Edge: Odyssey Two (short stories, 1988)
Irrational Numbers (short stories, 1994)
Guts (projected, 2001, with John Grant)

LE GUIN, URSULA K. (1929–   ), USA

Deservedly acclaimed for the literary and intellectual quality of her work in the genre, Ursula Le Guin has produced some of the most thoughtful and humane science fiction ever written.

From the very start, Le Guin set out to write SF on her own terms. Her first novel, *Rocannon's World* (1966), is part of an impressive and far-reaching FUTURE HISTORY known as the *Hainish* sequence, and follows the progress of a male scientist stranded on a distant colony PLANET where he is attempting to save the natives from hostile ALIEN invasion. What distinguishes the book is Le Guin's adept characterization and the skill and sensitivity with which she depicts the scientist's attempts to understand the native population by learning to adapt to their telepathic language.

In the *Hainish* sequence, Le Guin develops a complex background that enables her to explore in depth different facets of human nature and interaction. The Hainish are an advanced race who have seeded our galaxy with human life. The human race on Earth is simply one offshoot from this original EVOLUTIONARY node, and as it gradually makes contact with life on other planets humanity comes to realize that, biologically, the various sentient races of the galaxy are all very similar, even if, psychologically and sociologically, they are particularly diverse.

Le Guin's most famous novel, the HUGO and NEBULA AWARD-winning *The Left Hand of Darkness* (1969), is the book that catapulted her into the top rank of contemporary SF writers. It too exists within the *Hainish* framework, and concerns a mission to the snowbound planet Gethen. The protagonist is an anthropologist who finds it difficult to stay detached in his study of the planet's native population. These people, humanoid in appearance, are androgynous. They are normally neuter and only develop genitalia, which can be male or female, at a certain point in their sexual cycle. Through shared hardships and a painfully achieved new awareness of the importance of mutual respect, the anthropologist eventuallycomes to understand the true nature of Gethenian society. Le Guin's prose has an absolute clarity that makes the message of the story – that GENDER ceases to be an issue when two people are drawn to each other by love – all the more moving.

The last book in the *Hainish* cycle, *The Dispossessed* (1974), is subtitled 'An Ambiguous Utopia.' Its hero finds he is not comfortable in his own anarchistic society, so he journeys to a neighbouring capitalist world in an attempt to find a supportive environment in which he can work on his new device, the ansible, that will enable instantaneous interstellar communication to take place throughout the galaxy. However, he finds that the culture of this new world is more alienating than that he left behind. He returns to his home world reconciled – or at any rate resigned – to the material simplicity of its way of life and its philosophy of social cohesion through individual reponsibility.

The Dispossessed too won both the Hugo and Nebula awards for its year. Of Le Guin's 'singletons', *The Lathe of Heaven* (1971) is her best. It explores various levels of reality through the eyes of a man whose imagination brings about changes in it when he dreams. The book is an interesting exploration of the nature of reality: in it Le Guin probes the way in which our perception of the world makes it what it is. Is 'reality' a construct of our over-fertile imaginations?

Some of Le Guin's later material does not manage to recapture the power and strength of her earlier writing. Her *Earthsea* fantasy saga is primarily for older children, but is still of great interest to adults interested in her work since it provides a mature, thoughtful explication of the themes that have informed much of her fiction over the years. Indeed, in the last volume of the sequence, *Tehanu* (1990), her feelings about the feminist movement are made quite explicit.

Le Guin's output of LITERARY, HUMANIST SF contains some of the most informed and powerful writing the genre has seen. It has a moving and humane quality that gives both intellectual flavour and emotional resonance. Le Guin is a writer who is bold enough to admit her bewilderment in the face of humanity's contradictions and is unafraid to use her fiction as a way of tackling the problem.

See Also
ALIEN; ALTERNATIVE REALITY; FUTURE HISTORY; GENDER; HUMANIST SF; LITERARY SF; PLANETS; SOFT SF

Recommended Further Reading
The *Canopus in Argos* sequence by DORIS LESSING; *The Three Stigmata of Palmer Eldritch* (1964) by PHILIP K. DICK; *The Handmaid's Tale* (1985) by MARGARET ATWOOD; *Heroes and Villains* (1969) by ANGELA CARTER

Bibliography (Selected)
Rocannon's World (1966)
Planet of Exile (1966)
City of Illusions (1967)
A Wizard of Earthsea (1968)
The Left Hand of Darkness (1969)
The Lathe of Heaven (1971)
The Tombs of Atuan (1971)
The Farthest Shore (1972)
The Dispossessed (1974)
The Wind's Twelve Quarters (short stories, 1975)

The Word for World is Forest (1976)
Orsinian Tales (short stories, 1976)
Malafrena (1979)
The Compass Rose (short stories, 1982)
The Eye of the Heron (1982)
Always Coming Home (1985)
Buffalo Gals and Other Animal Presences (short stories, 1987)
Tehanu: the Last Book of Earthsea (1990)
Searoad: The Chronicles of Klatsand (short stories, 1991)
A Fisherman of the Inland Sea (1994)
Four Ways to Forgiveness (1995)
Unlocking the Air and Other Stories (short stories, 1996)
The Telling (projected, 2000)
Tales from Earthsea (projected, short stories, 2001)

LEIBER, FRITZ (1910–1992), USA

Perhaps more famous for the wonderful stories of sword-and-sorcery that form the *Lankhmar* sequence, Fritz Leiber also contributed much to science fiction with his funny, touching and exciting stories and novels.

His first novel of genre interest was *Gather, Darkness!* (1950), a tale of rebellion against dictatorship in a future society dominated by a strict RELIGION. Scientists, forced to dissemble, have disguised their advanced technical knowledge as witchcraft. They succeed in overthrowing the oppressive regime and re-establishing the rule of reason.

The Big Time (1961) concerns a complex and far-ranging war fought between two rival factions, the Spiders and the Snakes, who use TIME and SPACE as their battlegrounds, slipping in and out of differing time streams and alternative realities. The story actually takes place in a single room, ('the Place'), removed from the action and existing in a kind of limbo somewhere outside the 'normal' continuum. *The Big Time* was awarded the HUGO AWARD upon its first publication in GALAXY magazine. Stories linked with the novel are collected in *The Mind Spider and Other Stories* (1961).

Leiber's most ambitious SF novel is probably *The Wanderer* (1964) in which a PLANET, actually a huge spacecraft inhabited by feline ALIENS, enters the Solar System to refuel. The appearance of this vessel creates unintended disaster for the inhabitants of Earth, causing enormous tidal waves and irreparable damage to the climate. As catastrophe strikes, a few survivors behold the wonders of the universe, as seen through the eyes of the aliens, although much of humanity perishes.

With *The Wanderer*, Leiber delivered his genre masterpiece. Pessimistic, yet at times uplifting, the book raises the possibility that alien life forms may be neither friendly nor malign, but simply ignorant of the human race and the effects that their appearance might have upon it. *The Wanderer* was to win Leiber another Hugo Award, taking its rightful place among the genre classics.

Other Leiber SF titles include *A Spectre is Haunting Texas* (1969) and *The Silver Eggheads* (1962), both of which are fine examples of COMIC SF.

His best short fiction (excluding his *Lankhmar* stories) is collected in *The Mind Spider and Other Stories* and *The Ghost Light* (1984).

Leiber died in 1992, aged eighty-two.

See Also
ALIEN; COMIC SF; RELIGION; SPACE; TIME

Recommended Further Reading
Slan (1946) by A. E. VAN VOGT; *A Fire Upon the Deep* (1992) by VERNOR VINGE; the *Conan Chronicles* by Robert E. Howard; the *Elric Saga* by MICHAEL MOORCOCK

Bibliography
Night's Black Agents (short stories, 1947)
Gather, Darkness! (1950)
Conjure Wife (1953)
The Sinful Ones (1953)
The Green Millennium (1953)
Two Sought Adventure (short stories, 1957)
Destiny Times Three (1957)
The Big Time (1961)
The Mind Spider and Other Stories (short stories, 1961)
Shadows With Eyes (short stories, 1962)
The Silver Eggheads (1962)
A Pail of Air (short stories, 1964)
Ships to the Stars (short stories, 1964)
The Wanderer (1964)
The Night of the Wolf (short stories, 1966)
Tarzan and the Valley of Gold (1966)

The Secret Songs (short stories, 1968)
Swords Against Wizardry (short stories, 1968)
Swords in the Mist (short stories, 1968)
The Swords of Lankhmar (1968)
Night Monsters (short stories, 1969)
A Spectre is Haunting Texas (1969)
Swords Against Death (short stories, 1970)
Swords and Deviltry (1970)
You're All Alone (short stories, 1972)
The Best of Fritz Leiber (short stories, 1974)
The Book of Fritz Leiber (short stories, 1974)
The Second Book of Fritz Leiber (short stories, 1975)
The Worlds of Fritz Leiber (short stories, 1976)
Swords and Ice Magic (short stories, 1977)
Our Lady of Darkness (1977)
Bazaar of the Bizarre (short stories, 1978)
The Change War (short stories, 1978)
Heroes and Horrors (short stories, 1978)
Ship of Shadows (short stories, 1979)
The Ghost Light (short stories, 1984)
The Knight and Knave of Swords (short stories, 1988)
The Leiber Chronicles (short stories, 1990)
The Dealings of Daniel Kesserich (1997)
Ill Met in Lankhmar (short stories, 1999)
Lean Times in Lankhmar (short stories, 1999)
Return to Lankhmar (short stories, 1999)
Farewell to Lankhmar (short stories, 2000)

LEM, STANISLAW (1921–   ), Poland

One of the real characters of the genre, Stanislaw Lem is perhaps the best-known SF author to write outside the English language. His scathing deconstruction of the genre has tended to dominate his work: he writes SF that deliberately pursues a different agenda from that of the Anglophone establishment and forswears the trappings of mere 'entertainment' so that it may better provide a commentary on humanity free of sentimentality and the slick accoutrements of adventure. Lem's work is learned and worthy.

His best known novel, *Solaris* (1961) was also the first to be published in translation (USA, 1970). It is a wonderfully evocative, LITERARY work that describes a form of first contact with an ALIEN entity. A group of scientists have travelled to a distant PLANET, Solaris, to study the immense ocean that covers its surface. Once there, the protagonists all begin to be plagued by disturbing recurring memories that they had previously repressed. They deduce that the ocean is actually one huge, sentient entity, and that for some reason it is revealing their innermost dreams. There is no way to work out why: the alien intelligence is utterly incomprehensible, 'alien' in the deepest sense of the word.

Lem makes no assumptions that life elsewhere in the universe will be understood by humans: there is no reason why it should be. And with this realization we see the central concept informing Lem's work, as well as the reason for his apparent distaste for the genre in which he writes so well: the universe is simply too big for human intelligence to grasp, too unimaginably ancient and beyond our reach, for us to even begin to believe that we may one day conquer it. Lem is not a pessimist, simply a realist struggling to come to terms with the vast maze of life and to provide an alternative to the blatant, uncritical optimism about humanity's destiny that pervades much of Western culture. When Lem looks at the world, he sees a floating island of tiny minds adrift in one very small corner of the universe, its population ignorant of its own place in the grand scale of time and space.

This bleak but well-reasoned realism is a trait that characterizes most of Lem's SF. *The Invincible* (1964, English translation 1973) is thematically akin to *Solaris*, as is *His Master's Voice* (1968, English translation 1983), in that they both confront their human protagonists with an impenetrable, incomprehensible situation.

Much of Lem's work has appeared in translation over the years; it is said that they read even better in their original Polish. Whatever the case, Lem's commentary on and contributions to the genre have been very important. His self-declared point of view is that of an outsider looking in, and we should be grateful for this valuable perspective.

Lem's best short fiction is collected in *One Human Minute* (English translation, 1986).

Solaris was filmed by Russian director Andrei Tarkovsky in 1971 under the same title. Although not strictly adhering to the events detailed in the book, it remains one of the most thoughtful pieces of SF cinema to date.

See Also
ALIEN; LITERARY SF; SOFT SF

Recommended Further Reading
Sirius (1944) by OLAF STAPLEDON; *2001: A Space Odyssey* (1968) by
ARTHUR C. CLARKE; *The Fifth Head of Cerberus* (1972) by GENE
WOLFE

Bibliography (Selected)
Eden (1959, trans. 1989)
Solaris (1961, trans. 1970)
Memoirs Found in a Bathtub (1961, trans. 1973)
The Invincible (1964, trans. 1983)
The Cyberiad (short stories, 1965, trans. 1974)
Tales of Pirx the Pilot (short stories, 1968, trans. in two vols. 1979 and 1982)
His Master's Voice (1968, trans. 1983)
A Perfect Vacuum (short stories, 1971, trans. 1978)
The Futurological Congress (1971, trans. 1974)
Imaginary Magnitude (1973, trans. 1984)
The Chain of Chance (1977, trans. 1978)
One Human Minute (short stories, trans. 1986)
Fiasco (1986, trans. 1987)

LESSING, DORIS (1919–   ), Zimbabwe/Great Britain

Primarily a mainstream novelist with a profound interest in feminism and
the sociological perspectives of womanhood, Doris Lessing has, at times,
adopted the SF genre as a means of delivering her very personal view of
the world.

Some of her novels from the early 1970s touch on typical SF themes.
Briefing for a Descent into Hell (1971) explores in detail the mindset of a
person who is 'mentally ill', and in the process asks questions about the
nature of reality. *Memoirs of a Survivor* (1974) describes the slow decline
of civilization into a bleak DYSTOPIA from the viewpoint of a woman
watching the process from her window.

But, it is with the *Canopus in Argos: Archives* sequence that Lessing
most decisively makes her move into the SF genre. The sequence begins
with *Re: Colonized Planet 5: Shikasta* (1979), and continues with *The
Marriage Between Zones Three, Four and Five* (1980), *The Sirian Experi-
ments* (1981), *The Making of the Representative for Planet 8* (1982) and
Documents Relating to the Sentimental Agents in the Volyen Empire (1983).
These fascinatingly titled novels are a sometimes uneasy blend of RELI-
GIOUS philosophy and SPACE OPERA and attracted a varied critical

response on first publication. They are certainly LITERARY works and, if uneven, are still conceptually bold and intellectually stimulating.

In them, the Earth has been colonized by the friendly Canopans but has fallen under the influence of their enemies, the Puttorians. It is now known as Shikasta, 'the Stricken', and in the view of the Canopans is rushing headlong to oblivion.

The first book follows a representative of the Canopan Empire on their visit to the planet, tracking their attempts to 'save' the human race from dystopic hell. Later books in the sequence attempt to place the actions of humanity in the context of this massive colonized universe, and, in typical Lessing fashion, emphasize the tiny scale of a single human life against the vast backdrop of the cosmos. The *Canopus* books are not without their shortcomings but their blend of philosophy and space opera is never less than thought-provoking.

Later books by Lessing have also utilized the genre themes and concepts. *Mara and Dann* (1999) describes a POST-APOCALYPTIC future in which the eponymous characters must struggle for their survival. The story is fundamentally that of a journey, both in physical terms as the characters strive to make their way across the plains of Ifrik (Africa) and also spiritually as they travel inwards to the centres of their souls. Lessing is an author of great literary ability and her insights into the human psyche are intriguing.

Lessing continues to produce fiction of some genre interest. Outside the SF field she is, quite properly, regarded as an important contemporary literary figure whose writing continues to explore central issues of modern existence. Her SF work to date is best considered as part of her general body of writing. Like her mainstream writing, it is both powerful and moving.

See Also

DYSTOPIA; FUTURE HISTORY; GENDER; LITERARY SF; POST-APOCALYPTIC; RELIGION

Recommended Further Reading

The Handmaid's Tale (1985) by MARGARET ATWOOD; The *Patternmaster* sequence by OCTAVIA E. BUTLER; The *Hainish* sequence by URSULA K. LE GUIN

Bibliography (Selected)
The Golden Notebook (1962)
Briefing for a Descent into Hell (1971)
The Summer Before the Dark (1973)
The Memoirs of a Survivor (1974)
Re: Colonized Planet 5: Shikasta (1979)
The Marriage Between Zones Three, Four and Five (1980)
The Sirian Experiments (1981)
The Making of the Representative for Planet 8 (1982)
Documents Relating to the Sentimental Agents in the Volyen Empire (1983)
The Fifth Child (1988)
Mara and Dann (1999)
Ben, in the World (2000)

LEVY, ROGER (1955–   ), Great Britain

A relatively new SF talent, Roger Levy made his genre debut with *Reckless Sleep* (2000). Although a little patchy in places, it is an interesting study of VIRTUAL REALITY and the uses that may be found for it as the associated technology evolves.

Set in an apocalyptic world where tectonic shifting brought about by nuclear explosions is causing the planet to collapse in on itself, it follows the intrigues of Far Warrior Jon Sciler, a mentally damaged soldier who is attempting to recover from the devastating effects of a failed colonization attempt on the ALIEN planet, Dirangesept. In a narrative that shares some points of reference with JOE HALDEMAN'S *Forever Peace* (1999), Levy describes how the Far Warriors use technological interfaces to direct and control combat machines from a 'safe' vantage. But the combat machines have all been destroyed and now the Far Warriors must cope with the humiliation of their defeat.

As the surviving population attempts to find solace in the happier realms of virtual reality, a serial killer is stalking the last of the Far Warriors who survived the expedition to Dirangesept, and a sinister company called Maze is trying to hire them to aid in the testing of their new virtual world.

Levy succeeds in bringing his high-level intrigue to a satisfactory conclusion and although his prose can be a little stiff in places, his novel is fundamentally successful.

Given time to develop his craft, Levy could become an important factor in the future development of British science fiction.

See Also
ALIEN; DYSTOPIA; VIRTUAL REALITY

Recommended Further Reading
The Three Stigmata of Palmer Eldritch (1964) by PHILIP K. DICK; *Forever Peace* (1999) by JOE HALDEMAN

Bibliography
Reckless Sleep (2000)

LEWIS, C. S. (1898–1963), Great Britain

Born in Belfast and a great friend of his fellow Oxford academic J.R.R. Tolkien, theologist and author Clive Staples Lewis is perhaps best known for his substantial output of RELIGIOUS and moralistic works, as well as for his much loved children's allegorical fantasy, *The Chronicles of Narnia*.

However, his *Cosmic Trilogy*, which begins with *Out of the Silent Planet* (1938), is without doubt a work of science fiction.

It follows the adventures of Dr Ransom, a Cambridge academic who, in the first novel in the trilogy, is kidnapped and transported to Mars, where his captors plan to sacrifice him to the ALIEN inhabitants. While on Mars, Ransom is informed that although each planet has its own innate, governing spirit, Earth's is 'fallen' and out of contact with most of the world's inhabitants – hence the 'silent planet' of the title. The religious allegory is clear and Lewis is here, as in most of his writing, chiefly concerned to put forward Christian apologetics.

But, *Out of the Silent Planet* is nevertheless a successful book that begins the sequence well. It is very clearly a story with more than its fair share of religious symbolism and imagery but it is also a fine SCIENTIFIC ROMANCE set upon a well-realized alien PLANET.

It was followed by *Perelandra* (1943), another symbol-rich other-worldly adventure that again pits Ransom against his mortal enemy Dr Weston. This time the action takes place on the water planet Venus, which Lewis portrays as an Edenic paradise where Ransom adopts the role of Adam. The female ruler of the planet, whom Ransom is attempting to rescue, is a new Eve. The literary skill evident in Lewis's descriptions of the alien world is undeniable but as in *Out of the Silent Planet* the scientific elements of the story are conveniently glossed over. Indeed, Lewis portrays science as the evil force that is attempting to ravage his new Eden.

With *That Hideous Strength* (1945) Lewis takes this hostility towards science and technology even further. The action takes place back on Earth, and Lewis describes an experimental project in which a group of scientists is attempting to develop new methods of controlling human responses. These scientists are portrayed as evil and ungodly, and Lewis's yearning for a quieter, more 'spiritual' life for society at large has become all too apparent.

Nevertheless, their excellent descriptions of alien landscapes and high adventure make the first two volumes of the *Cosmic Trilogy* worthwhile as scientific romance. *That Hideous Strength* may sit well with Lewis's general body of writing, but its ambience is more that of occult fiction than SF.

Lewis died in 1963, aged sixty-five.

See Also
ALIEN; MESSIAH; PLANET; RELIGION; SCIENTIFIC ROMANCE

Recommended Further Reading
A Canticle for Leibowitz (1959) by WALTER MILLER; *A Case of Conscience* (1958) by JAMES BLISH; *The Sparrow* (1997) by MARY DORIA RUSSELL

Bibliography (Selected)
Out of the Silent Planet (1938)
Perelandra (1943)
That Hideous Strength (1945)

LOCUS
Founded by editor Charles Brown in the late 1960s as an SF news fanzine, *Locus* has gone on to become the most highly regarded journal of news, comment and reviews in the entire SF field, winning the Best Fanzine or Best Semiprozine HUGO AWARD nearly every year since it started publication.

The format has changed significantly over the years. *Locus* began life in 1968 as a two-page flyer, in much the same format as DAVID LANGFORD's ANSIBLE, but soon developed into a 'semiprozine' (a semi-professional magazine) as Brown began to invest more and more energy into its production. In the 1970s *Locus* became a monthly magazine, and Brown gave up his other work to become its full-time editor in 1976. This commitment and dedication paid off: *Locus* is now the most widely circulated of all SF non-fiction journals.

The magazine regularly features full listings of American and British publications, news on rights and publishing sales, obituaries, interviews and a wide range of reviews. Since the small-press magazine *Tangent* appears to have disappeared, *Locus* is one of the only magazines to regularly review other genre periodicals.

Brown continues to edit *Locus* and to thousands of people in many countries it has become an indispensable guide to the movements taking place in this ever-changing genre.

An excellent and informative website can be found at http://www.locusmag.com

LOVEGROVE, JAMES (1966–   ), Great Britain

James Lovegrove's first book, *The Hope* (1990), was a literary mainstream novel with no genre content. Seven years later he produced the excellent *Days* (1997), which was nominated for the ARTHUR C. CLARKE AWARD and marked his debut into the genre.

Days is a bizarre, original work. Reminiscent of the urban DYSTOPIAS of J. G. BALLARD, the book takes place entirely within a single day, following the movements and developments of a group of characters who are all associated with the enormous eponymous department store. *Days* describes a NEAR-FUTURE culture that is at once abhorrent and fascinating, where everything is consumer-driven and everything has its price. Brimming with satire on the extremes of modern life, at the same time creating an impressive, disturbing extrapolation of where these extremes might be taking us next, it is a book to be cherished.

Lovegrove followed *Days* with two dark fantasies of only minor genre interest – *Escardy Gap* (1998, with Peter Crowther) and *How the Other Half Lives* (2000) (although the second book is a particularly good example of its kind), as well as two rather drab pseudonymous television novelizations for the Sci-Fi Channel. However, with the publication of *The Foreigners* (2000), Lovegrove showed that he still has something to offer the SF genre.

The Foreigners is a novel of ALIEN invasion, although not in the usual sense of the phrase. The 'Foreigners' have arrived on Earth unannounced, bringing with them gifts of high technology and prospects of UTOPIA. However, all is not as it seems; one of the Foreigners is found murdered and detective Jack Parry must attempt to deduce the reasons behind the crime before the Foreigners take it as their cue to leave. The sinister feeling that there is something more to these apparently friendly aliens than meets the eye pervades the book, implying that the aliens may in fact be taming the human race, insidiously instilling into it a psychological dependence greater than that of mere gratitude. Lovegrove's prose is LITERARY and fluent, and this novel confirms his abilities as a writer.

Lovegrove's juvenile novel, *Computopia* (1999), part of the long-running *Web* series aimed at the teenage market, is also worthy of note.

See Also
ALIEN; DYSTOPIA; LITERARY SF; NEAR FUTURE; UTOPIA

Recommended Further Reading
Spares (1996) by MICHAEL MARSHALL SMITH; *Scepticism Inc* (1998) by Bo Fowler

Bibliography
The Hope (1990)
Days (1997)
Escardy Gap (1998, with Peter Crowther)
Guardians: The Krilov Continuum (1998)
Guardians: Beserker (1999)
Computopia (juvenile, 1999)
How the Other Half Lives (2000)
The Foreigners (2000)

McAULEY, PAUL J. (1955–   ), Great Britain

One of the new wave of radical HARD SF writers to emerge in Britain, along with others such as STEPHEN BAXTER and ALASTAIR REYNOLDS, Paul J. McAuley cut his writing teeth with stories for INTERZONE magazine.

His training as a research biologist is evident in much of his work, and the exactitude with which he peppers his stories with scientific theories is admirable.

His first novel, *Four Hundred Billion Stars* (1988), is a grandiose SPACE OPERA that takes place against the backdrop of an interstellar war. Humanity is battling against the enigmatic 'Enemy', and the protagonist of the novel, Dorothy Yoshida, is sent to investigate a mysterious planet that appears to have been TERRAFORMED. However, the only evident sentient life is a race called the Herders, who possess only primitive intelligence. The telepathic Dorothy must attempt to find out whether the planet has anything at all to do with 'The Enemy'.

The novel was an instant success, winning the PHILIP K. DICK MEMORIAL AWARD, and although it is a little slow-moving in parts it is well thought out and well written.

Of the Fall (1989) (UK title: *Secret Harmonies*) and *Eternal Light* (1991) are sequels to *Four Hundred Billion Stars*, and although they are still space operas they show even more evidence of McAuley's hard SF inclinations. In *Eternal Light* Dorothy finds herself on a mission to the Galactic Centre to attempt to discover the secret behind a star that is making its way towards the Solar System. Full of big ideas and mounting tension as the characters approach realization of the implications behind the travelling star, *Eternal Light* in particular exemplifies British hard SF at its best. The novel makes use of many genre concepts, including GENETIC ENGINEERING, ARTIFICIAL INTELLIGENCE and ALIENS.

Short stories related to the novels are collected in *The King of the Hill and Other Stories* (1991).

Red Dust (1993) is another of McAuley's strong early novels. On a Mars that has been partly terraformed by the Chinese and where this attempt at planetary engineering is now beginning to go wrong, a young man named Wei Lee finds himself thrust into the unlikely role of saviour. The novel has a CYBERPUNK feel to it, but makes use of many different SF themes and devices, such as VIRTUAL REALITY and RELIGION.

McAuley's next novel, *Pasquale's Angel* (1994), is an excellent example of ALTERNATE WORLD SF, in which Leonardo daVinci gives the industrial age an early kick-start by actually manufacturing some of his inventions, devices that in reality stayed on the drawing board. However, it was with *Fairyland* (1995) that McAuley produced his best work to date.

Hip and edgy, *Fairyland* takes a step sideways from the cyberpunk genre. The novel is an eclectic blizzard of ideas, its plot complex and divided into three parts. Briefly, the story follows Alex Sharkey, a dubious but morally resilient drug designer who is enlisted by a strange young girl to instil awareness into a 'Doll' – a small, blue-skinned pygmy genetically bred for servitude. This he does, with catastrophic results. The rest of the novel charts the growth of the 'Fairies', a subculture of self-aware Dolls who hide themselves away from mainstream culture all across Europe and use NANOTECHNOLOGY and virtual reality to further the interest of their race.

The book is startling in its originality, at once bleak and uplifting. As an exploration of artificial life it stands out as one of the most thoughtful and topical novels of recent years, winning both the ARTHUR C. CLARKE and JOHN W. CAMPBELL AWARDS for 1995.

More recently McAuley has produced a sequence of books known as the *Confluence Trilogy*, a FAR-FUTURE series that has similarities to the work of GENE WOLFE in the way it borrows imagery from the fantasy genre as a way of portraying the eeriness of the distant future. Indeed, throughout the trilogy (which is better read as one long novel), deliberate echoes of Wolfe's *Book of the New Sun* and *Book of the Long Sun* are to be heard as McAuley pays explicit tribute to his outstanding forerunner.

Set on the world of Confluence, a huge man-made ARTIFICIAL ENVIRONMENT long ago abandoned by its creators, the sequence follows the progress of Yama, a child found floating in a river, who may or may not be the MESSIAH who has come to save the crumbling, ancient PLANET. McAuley makes use of a vast array of images, portraying the world's various sentient animal species as ALIENS – they are, in fact, creatures that were long ago genetically altered (to give them enhanced awareness) by the descendants of humanity.

The three-volume novel is exceptionally ambitious in its scope and, if not quite as dazzling as Gene Wolfe's ongoing epic, is still a superb achievement in its own right. The books that comprise the trilogy are *Child of the River* (1997), *Ancients of Days* (1998) and *Shrine of Stars* (1999).

McAuley is one of a handful of British authors who are steadily producing SF of the highest quality, and he is renowned on both sides of the Atlantic for his style and inventive exuberance.

See Also
ALIENS; ALTERNATE WORLD; ARTIFICIAL ENVIRONMENT; FAR FUTURE; GENETICS; HARD SF; NANOTECHNOLOGY; SPACE OPERA; TERRAFORMED

Recommended Further Reading
The Seedling Stars (1957) by JAMES BLISH; *Blood Music* (1985) by GREG BEAR; *Martian Time-Slip* (1964) by PHILIP K. DICK; the *Mars* trilogy by KIM STANLEY ROBINSON; *Teranesia* (1999) by Greg Egan; *The Book of the New Sun* by Gene Wolfe

Bibliography

Four Hundred Billion Stars (1988)

Of the Fall (1989, published as *Secret Harmonies* in the UK: the author's preferred title is the American one)

The King of the Hill (short stories, 1991)

Eternal Light (1991)

Red Dust (1993)

Pasquale's Angel (1994)

Fairyland (1995)

The Invisible Country (short stories, 1996)

Child of the River (1997)

Ancients of Days (1998)

Shrine of Stars (1999)

Making History (2000)

The Secret of Life (2001)

McCAFFREY, ANNE (1926–   ), USA

Born in America but for many years resident in Ireland, Anne McCaffrey has become recognized as one of the most popular writers in the field. Her novels are fundamentally romances, and although they nearly all have explicitly SF underpinnings they can read like a form of rationalized fantasy. Indeed, the *Pern* sequence, for which she is best known, makes use of many standard fantasy concepts and devices, albeit in an orthodoxly SF environment (an alien world), to often interesting effect.

The *Pern* sequence begins with *Dragonflight* (1968) and continues with *Dragonquest* (1971), *Dragonsong* (1976), *Dragonsinger* (1977), *The White Dragon* (1978), *Dragondrums* (1979), *Moreta: Dragonlady of Pern* (1983), *Nerilka's Story* (1986), *Dragonsdawn* (1988), *The Renegades of Pern* (1989), *All the Weyrs of Pern* (1991), *Chronicles of Pern* (1993), *The Girl Who Heard Dragons* (1994), *Dolphins of Pern* (1994), *Dragonseye* (1997) and *Masterharper of Pern* (1998).

The series itself is set upon a distant colony PLANET that has long been forgotten by the Earthlings who originally developed the human settlement there. Humans now enjoy a cooperative relationship with bio-engineered dragons that were developed by the earliest settlers to help combat the threat of deadly ALIEN spores – the dragons' fire has been designed specifically to incinerate them.

The stories themselves take the form of planetary romance, in that they are primarily straightforward adventure tales in other-wordly settings.

Nevertheless, the writing is intelligent and the sequence is extremely popular.

Other novels by McCaffrey make use of more explicitly SF devices. In perhaps her best novel, *The Ship Who Sang* (1969), a female musician is biologically amalgamated with a space vessel and must learn to come to terms with her new form. The novel is an interesting exploration of what it means to be human, and at the same time a look at an entirely different form of ARTIFICIAL INTELLIGENCE – the woman actually becomes the machine, and therefore surrenders her humanity. *Partner Ship* (1992, with Margaret Ball), *The Ship Who Searched* (1992, with Mercedes Lackey), *The City Who Fought* (1993, with S. M. Stirling) and *The Ship Who Won* (1994, with Jody Lynn Nye) are all sequels.

Other series include the *Pegasus* books, which are set on a NEAR-FUTURE Earth and examine the social impact of developing telepathy, the *Killshandra* books about a musician able to communicate across space with alien crystals, and the *Tower and Hive* books, which focus on the progress of one young telepath.

Anne McCaffrey writes planetary-romance novels that hark back in their high-spirited sense of adventure to the pulps of the 1930s and 1940s, although with an added sophistication and an underlying SF rationale that identifies them as unique in their field. Her prose is fluent and satisfying, and the stories themselves are enjoyable, if a little over sentimental at times. Her novels enjoy a large, dedicated and enthusiastic following that must surely be the envy of many another SF author.

See Also
BIOTECHNOLOGY; CYBORG; GENETICS; PLANETS; SCIENCE FANTASY

Recommended Further Reading
The Demolished Man (1953) and *The Stars My Destination* (1956) by ALFRED BESTER; *Telepathist* (1965) by JOHN BRUNNER; *Man Plus* (1976) by FREDERIK POHL; the *Spellsong* sequence by L. E. Modesitt (Fantasy)

Bibliography
Restoree (1967)
Dragonflight (1968)
Decision at Doona (1969)
The Ship Who Sang (1969)

Dragonquest (1971)
To Ride Pegasus (1973)
Dragonsong (1976)
Dragonsinger (1977)
The White Dragon (1978)
Dinosaur Planet (1978)
Dragondrums (1979)
The Crystal Singer (1982)
The Coelura (1983)
Moreta: Dragonlady of Pern (1983)
Dinosaur Planet Survivors (1984)
Killashandra (1985)
Nerilka's Story (1986)
Dragonsdawn (1988)
The Renegades of Pern (1989)
The Death of Sleep (1990, with Jody Lynn Nye)
Pegasus in Flight (1990)
Sassinak (1990, with ELIZABETH MOON)
The Rowan (1990)
All the Weyrs of Pern (1991)
Generation Warriors (1991, with ELIZABETH MOON)
Crisis on Doona (1992, wih Jody Lynn Nye)
Partnership (1992, with Margaret Ball)
Damia (1992)
Crystal Line (1992)
The Ship Who Searched (1992, with Mercedes Lackey)
Chronicles of Pern (short stories, 1993)
Power Lines (1993, with Elizabeth Ann Scarborough)
Powers That Be (1993, with Elizabeth Ann Scarborough)
The City Who Fought (1993, with S. M. Stirling)
Damia's Children (1993)
The Girl Who Heard Dragons (short stories, 1994)
Dolphins of Pern (1994)
The Ship Who Won (1994, with Jody Lynn Nye)
Treaty at Doona (1994, with Jody Lynn Nye)
Lyon's Pride (1994)
Power Play (1995, with Elizabeth Ann Scarborough)
Black Horses for the King (1996)
Dragonseye (1997)
Freedom's Choice (1997)

McCARTHY, WIL (1967–   ), USA

American author Wil McCarthy has, over recent years, shown himself to be an author of both steadfast SPACE OPERA and intelligent HARD SF.

His first novel, *Aggressor Six* (1994), is a space opera full of high adventure and space warfare. An ALIEN race, The Waisters, have set about destroying human-colony PLANETS, with what can only be assumed as genocidal intent. The chief protagonist, Kenneth Jonson, manages to survive the destruction of his world, and because of his first-hand experience of the aliens he is drafted into a psychological warfare unit in the hope that he can discover a means of fighting back. The novel is successful in that, although it retreads old ground, it subverts the typical space opera and portrays a humanity on its knees. Much SF of this kind is optimistic, looking forward to a bright future in which humans are powerful and mature – McCarthy provides no such reassurances.

The book was followed by a sequel, *The Fall of Sirius* (1996), in which a small group of survivors are awoken from a CRYOGENIC sleep. The Waisters are returning to a human colony whose members have all GENETICALLY altered themselves to take the shape of the aliens, and the only people who know why are the survivors from the previous war. A massive culture clash ensues, when the last of the humans find their descendants have taken alien form.

McCarthy's second novel, *Flies from Amber* (1995), is set upon a colony planet far from Earth. When the colonists discover a strange mineral underneath the soil of their new home, an expedition from the mother planet sets out to investigate. Upon arrival they find not only the mineral but an alien species so unique that its members have adapted to life within a BLACK HOLE. The novel confirms McCarthy's hard SF inclination, and successfully blends a well-thought-out scientific notion with a more traditional SF setting.

More recently, McCarthy has produced *Bloom* (1998), which describes a truly alien form of life that has occupied the Solar System. Humanity has been pushed away to the outer planets, and a number of human colonies survive underneath the surfaces of various moons. The alien life form is a form of biological NANOTECHNOLOGY – Mycora – spores that are toxic to human beings, but are fast at reproducing and can survive in a vacuum. However, when a group of people are sent into the heart of the Mycora colony in an attempt to discover its true nature, they realize that the structures that exist within the cloud of spores represent sentient constructs, and that human beings are being assimilated into the clouds in a form of glorious TRANSCENDENCE. The novel is wonderfully evocative, and although the book 'stutters' with an ill-conceived ending, it succeeds in portraying a new form of life that is truly alien to our linear, matter-based existence. This is no small feat. *Bloom* is one of the finest examples of recent American hard SF.

McCarthy's latest novel, *The Collapsium* (2000), is suitably different from his earlier work, and describes a human society of the FAR FUTURE. The people of this culture have grown decadent and artful – two new technologies shape their lives. Wellstone is a form of programmable matter that can be used to fashion any conceivable object, while Collapsium is a crystal composed of miniature black holes, used to transmit data and matter across the Solar System. However, when rivalry gets the better of two opposing scientists, Collapsium puts the Sun itself at risk and its creators must attempt to limit the damage it may cause.

The novel is LITERARY and lyrical, yet it still maintains its author's hard-SF ideal. McCarthy is indeed a name to be watched in the future – although, judging by his fictions, he is already there.

See Also
ALIEN; BIOTECHNOLOGY; BLACK HOLE; CRYONICS; FAR FUTURE; GENETICS; HARD SF; NANOTECHNOLOGY; PLANETS; TRANSCENDENCE

Recommended Further Reading
Bios (1999) ROBERT CHARLES WILSON; *Vast* (1998) by LINDA NAGATA; *Queen City Jazz* (1995) by KATHLEEN ANN GOONAN; the *Dancers at the End of Time* sequence by MICHAEL MOORCOCK

Bibliography
Aggressor Six (1994)
Flies from Amber (1995)
Murder in the Solid State (1996)
The Fall of Sirius (1996)
Bloom (1998)
The Collapsium (2000)

McDEVITT, JACK (1935–), USA

Jack McDevitt is an author intent upon chronicling the human condition. His work tends to confront its characters with ALIEN beings or landscapes, which act as mirrors, allowing them to look more closely at themselves.

His first novel, *The Hercules Text* (1986), does just that. It describes the situation that arises when a quasar pulse containing a stream of messages and instructions from an alien civilization is received by Earth. This enables the Americans to produce a vast array of technologically advanced weapons and armaments. The Russians are enraged at this, and the book then descends into a POLITICAL boxing match between the two nations. The story is satisfactory, but only just. McDevitt fails to explore the possibilities behind his main premise – that intelligent alien life exists and is contacting us – preferring rather to detail the political wrangling that ensues from this epoch-making discovery.

Far superior is his second novel, *A Talent for War* (1988), which follows a young man on a trail to discover the secrets of an old war hero in the uncharted territory between human and alien space. What he finds comes to change his faith and the beliefs of those he represents.

His next book, *Engines of God* (1994), was to begin a loose thematic sequence that would comprise three novels and focus on the theme of future archaelogy. The other books included in this loose trilogy are *Ancient Shores* (1996) and *Eternity Road* (1997). Of the three, *Engines of God* is by far the best.

It begins with the discovery of an alien artefact on a PLANET in the outer Solar System, and goes on to chronicle the various archaeological finds that lead the characters to the discovery that a great alien civilization once existed, spanning star systems, but that it has now crumbled. At the same time, the Earth is heading for an ECOLOGICAL catastrophe and the characters must decide whether to proceed with their research – which could hold the key to saving the planet – or to return to try and help. The book is exciting and brimming with ideas, imparting a traditional SENSE OF WONDER to the reader as the characters begin to realize what the recently discovered alien monuments mean and attempt to decipher their oblique inscriptions. A belated sequel is *Deepsix* (projected, 2001).

More recently, McDevitt produced *Infinity Beach* (2000), which is perhaps his finest novel to date. It concerns first contact between humans and an ancient alien species. The discovery is to have a profound effect on the mindset of the human race, which as been searching the skies for signs of life for nearly a thousand years to no avail and believes the universe to be devoid of other intelligence. The chief protagonist is the CLONE of a woman whose sister took part in an aborted mission twenty-seven years before the start of the story. It is her investigation into the results of that mission that sparks off a chain of events that eventually leads to contact with the alien race.

Infinity Beach is a grand, sweeping SPACE OPERA, and successfully captures McDevitt's ability to analyse the psychological implications of a given situation. It also makes use of many genre devices and themes, such as TERRAFORMING, cloning, and faster-than-light SPACE TRAVEL.

McDevitt's best short fiction is collected in *Standard Candles* (1996).

The author maintains a website at http://www.sfwa.org/members/McDevitt/

See Also
ALIEN; CLONE; ECOLOGY; POLITICAL; SPACE TRAVEL; SPACE OPERA; TERRAFORMING

Recommended Further Reading
Revelation Space (2000) by ALASTAIR REYNOLDS; the *Heechee* sequence by FREDERIK POHL; the *Xeelee* sequence by STEPHEN BAXTER

Bibliography
The Hercules Text (1986)
A Talent for War (1988)
Engines of God (1994)
Standard Candles (short stories, 1996)
Ancient Shores (1996)
Eternity Road (1997)

Moonfall (1998)
Infinity Beach (2000)
Deepsix (projected, 2001)

McHUGH, MAUREEN F. (1959–), USA

Maureen F. McHugh published her first novel, *China Mountain Zhang*, in 1992 to almost instant acclaim. Character-driven, LITERARY and HUMANIST, it won both the HUGO and TIPTREE AWARDS for its year, as well as being nominated for a NEBULA AWARD. It is an outstanding debut, and has already assured McHugh a place in the SF hall of fame.

The book follows the life of Zhang Zhong Shen, a young, gay man living in a twenty-second century America under a communist Chinese regime. Shen is a man searching for an identity. His sexuality is punishable by death, his heritage is scattered somewhere in a distant country and aspects of his biology suggest that he isn't quite who he is supposed to be. When he loses his position in the social labour system he moves to Shanghai in an attempt to find himself.

The novel is evocative and insightful, offering the reader a startling perspective on the human condition and a thoughtful exploration of a possible future China. McHugh's writing is reminiscent of that of URSULA K. LE GUIN, in that it is psychologically and socially aware and focuses on the personal context of its characters. Indeed, this is true of much of McHugh's writing to date: a search for identity and GENDER, her characters' need to define themselves among the fragmentary recollections of their pasts as well as in their often incongruous present surroundings are distinguishing features of her work.

These themes can clearly be seen in McHugh's second novel, *Half the Day is Night* (1994), which is set in an underwater city. A bodyguard has been hired by a banker to protect her from the threats of a criminal organization, and the enclosed environment and threat of impending violence lead this bodyguard into a confrontation with his previously repressed memory of his history as a violent mercenary. Again, the narrative of the novel is almost, but not quite, subsumed by McHugh's interest in her characters and their personal development throughout the book.

McHugh's third novel, *Mission Child* (1998), takes place on a distant colony PLANET that has been left for many years to establish itself. When an expedition of 'offworlders' return to the planet, it upsets the equilibrium of the emerging society of the colony. The story itself is more an exploration of gender and loss than anything else: the protagonist, Janna, cannot commit herself to anything for any length of time, and at one point disguises herself as a boy. Eventually she comes to think of herself as 'Jan', and her identity is lost in the evolving culture of the planet and its thronging population.

McHugh writes thoughtful, intelligent and emotive SF. Her work is resonant with a deep understanding of the human condition. Readers should be grateful for her insights.

The author maintains a website at http://www.en.com/users/mcq/

See Also
ARTIFICIAL ENVIRONMENT; GENDER; HUMANIST SF; LITERARY SF; PLANET

Recommended Further Reading
The Left Hand of Darkness (1972) by URSULA K. LE GUIN; *Red Dust* (1993) by PAUL J. McAULEY; *To Hold Infinity* (1998) by JOHN MEANEY

Bibliography
China Mountain Zhang (1992)
Half the Day is Night (1994)
Mission Child (1998)

MCKEAN, DAVE (1963–   ), Great Britain
Dave McKean has a style that is all his own. An original McKean image will stand out against nearly anything else beside which it is placed.

McKean began his career as an illustrator in the 1980s, and it was not long before he began working with Neil Gaiman on the project for which he is best known: the *Sandman* comics.

McKean provided artwork for every one of the covers for the massive hit that was *Sandman*, and then every illustration for the covers of the bound-up graphic albums. The success of the comics gave him the enormous exposure he deserved, and thrust his name up into the top rank of the world's illustrators.

McKean's style is expressive and surreal, manipulating nature to its own expressionist ends. He is a latter-day Picasso, an artist who reworks the world according to his own imagination and then turns the result on its head for even better effect.

McKean works in a variety of mediums, anything from pen and ink to acrylics, from digital photography to CGI manipulation. He always strives for the right effect, whatever materials may be necesary to achieve it.

McKean's book jackets, aside from those for the *Sandman* graphic albums, are few and far between. The best recent example is for M. JOHN HARRISON'S *Signs of Life* (1997), which beautifully captures the very core of Harrison's story.

McKean is a modern master of expressionism, and his artwork is unique. His work in the SF field may have been limited in quantity but what little has appeared deserves to be cherished.

MACLEOD, KEN (1954–   ), Great Britain

Until very recently Ken Macleod had a fairly low profile within the genre.

A Scottish computer programmer and trained zoologist, his first novel, *The Star Fraction* (1995), is a taut CYBERPUNK thriller that explores in detail the EVOLUTION of an ARTIFICIAL INTELLIGENCE in a NEAR-FUTURE British DYSTOPIA. Macleod also focuses his attention on POLITICS, and this informs much of his writing.

The setting of *The Star Fraction* is reminiscent of GEORGE ORWELL's *Nineteen Eighty-Four* (1949) in the way in which the US/UN has become an omnipresent force that maintains total control over the country. The chief protagonist, Moh Kohn, is a mercenary who is hired to protect a group of scientists who are working on a memory-enhancement program. In typical cyberpunk fashion, Kohn is an efficient computer hacker and has a semi-intelligent weapon as an aide. When he becomes involved in an uprising against the state, he must find a way to get his people to safety while spearheading the revolution and attempting to uncover the mystery behind the elusive 'Watchmaker', a super-evolved computer program that is beginning to become self-aware. The novel is bold and detailed: if it comes over as a little preoccupied with the political systems it describes, this doesn't affect the pace and flow of its narrative.

Macleod's second novel, *The Stone Canal* (1996), is related to the first book, but takes place in entirely different time frames. Partly set in the 1970s, partly in the distant future on Mars, it follows the CLONE of anarchist Jonathan Wilde as he is resurrected so that various entities can attempt to uncover his secrets. The book is as tightly plotted and well realized as its predecessor, and established Macleod as a serious genre writer.

The Cassini Division (1998) takes the story even further into the future, building the sequence into a more detailed FUTURE HISTORY. Artificial Intelligences have overtaken the human race and established themselves across the Solar System and are also attempting to build a vast WORMHOLE bridge into the distant future. The Cassini Division is an elite force, the first line of defence against the supposed 'post-human' threat. However, their socialist-anarchist union is crumbling under the pressure of maintaining this defensive front, and a woman is sent to locate a top physicist who may be able to reconcile the humans with the machines.

The Cassini Division was followed by *The Sky Road* (1999), the final book in the sequence that began with *The Star Fraction*. Humanity has been 'Delivered', in a catastrophic return to a simpler existence after the heady days of expansion into the Solar System. Now the construction of the first space vessel to be built for centuries is under way and Clovis, the chief protagonist, is attempting to work out the future of the ship by studying the half-remembered events of the past. The novel is brilliantly effective in its descriptions of the FAR FUTURE and maintains the speculative political background of Macleod's other books well. It justifiably won the BSFA AWARD for its year, and helped thrust Macleod into the mainstream of the genre.

More recently, Macleod has begun an entirely separate series with the publication of *Cosmonaut Keep* (2000), the first book in his projected *Engines of Light* sequence. Once again, it has its basis in politics, but this time is grander in scale, a SPACE OPERA tale of first contact with ALIENS and the establishment of a colony on a distant PLANET. It remains to be seen where Macleod will take the series next, but it is sure to be an interesting journey.

See Also
ARTIFICIAL INTELLIGENCE; CLONE; CYBERPUNK; DYSTOPIA; NEAR FUTURE; PLANETS; POLITICS; SPACE OPERA

Recommended Further Reading
Nineteen Eighty-Four (1949) by George Orwell; *Hotwire* (1995) by SIMON INGS; *reMix* (1999) by JON COURTENAY GRIMWOOD

Bibliography
The Star Fraction (1995)
The Stone Canal (1996)

The Cassini Division (1998)
Cydonia (juvenile, 1999)
The Sky Road (1999)
Engines of Light: Cosmonaut Keep (2000)

MATHESON, RICHARD (1926–   ), USA

American Richard Matheson is a writer who has always been happy to shift between genres, moving easily from the SF of his early stories into more fantastical realms. The one constant in his work is its pervading sense of HORROR and paranoia – Matheson has always appeared to consider himself as foremost a writer of horrific tales.

His early magazine SF was shot through with this sense of unease, distinguishing it from the work of his peers. At times horrific elements that were quite graphic by the standards of the time would dominate the stories so that the SF content would be overshadowed by the more Grand Guignol aspects of the narrative.

His first novel, however, is an excellent example of Matheson's SF at its best.

I Am Legend (1954) describes a world overrun with a bacterial plague that induces vampirism. Fundamentally a POST-APOCALYPTIC tale, the novel successfully blends Matheson's trade-mark paranoia with a typically SF scenario. The story follows the progress of Robert Neville, the last 'normal' man left alive after everyone else has been infected by the plague; his neighbours bay for his blood nightly and he must fend them off with strings of garlic and with stakes through their hearts. By day he drives around town pulling vampires from their beds and destroying them in the daylight. This is a dark, disturbing novel that describes a form of racial TRANSCENDENCE, as the vampires slowly spread around the globe, eventually to inherit the Earth. What is perhaps most remarkable about the book is Robert Neville's change of perception towards its conclusion, as he comes to realise that it is the vampires who now fear *him* – he has become the misfit, the social outcast who has no place within the new society. In the end Robert Neville demonstrates his redeeming humanity in the face of overwhelming madness.

The book has been filmed twice, first as *The Last Man on Earth* (1964), later as THE OMEGA MAN (1971). The second version is the more satisfactory.

Of Matheson's other work, his most explicitly science fictional is *The Shrinking Man* (1956), although this again draws heavily on the fantastical. It describes the terrifying and exciting adventures of a man who shrinks to microcosmic size. It is perhaps more famous in its movie incarnation, which was scripted by Matheson and appeared in 1957 as THE INCREDIBLE SHRINKING MAN.

Other Matheson stories of SF interest appear in the collections *Born of Man and Woman* (1954) and *The Shores of Space* (1957). After this most of his work is either fantasy or horror.

See Also
GENETICS; HORROR; LITERARY SF; POST-APOCALYPTIC

Recommended Further Reading
The Empire of Fear (1988) by BRIAN STABLEFORD; *Earth Abides* (1949) by GEORGE R. STEWART; *The Death of Grass* (1956) by John Christopher

Bibliography (Selected)
Born of Man and Woman (short stories, 1954)
I Am Legend (1954)
The Shrinking Man (1956)
The Shores of Space (short stories, 1957)
A Stir of Echoes (1958)
Shock (short stories, 1961)
Shock II (short stories, 1964)
Shock III (short stories, 1966)
Shock Waves (short stories, 1970)
Hell House (1971)
Bid Time Return (1975)
What Dreams May Come (1978)
Shock IV (short stories, 1980)
Earthbound (1982)
Collected Stories (short stories, 1989)

MEANEY, JOHN, Great Britain
John Meaney is one of the INTERZONE generation of new British authors, although his output for that particular magazine has not been as prolific as that of some of his peers.

His first novel, *To Hold Infinity* (1998), was published to much acclaim. It depicts a world wired into a vast communications network, much like an evolved version of the Internet. The use of BIOTECHNOLOGY and NANOTECHNOLOGY is rife; Meaney has his characters use implanted secondary 'brains' that are permanently connected to the communications net. They are constantly involved in information exchange, even when their true, biological brains are engaged on other business. The story itself is a post-CYBERPUNK, CRIME thriller, in which a serial killer is stalking the net, assimilating people's minds by introducing viral software into their IMPLANTS. When the killer compromises his position in a very public way, suspicion is aroused and the hunt begins.

Meaney weaves a rich tapestry of a world around his very human characters, whilst at the same time blending Eastern mysticism into the hard- edged technological excesses of his extrapolated Western culture. The result is one of the finest debut novels by a British author in many years.

To Hold Infinity was followed by *Paradox* (2000), which builds on the success of its predecessor and shows signs of Meaney developing his considerable writing skills even further. The setting is Nulapeiron, an impoverished PLANET in which the masses are incarcerated and controlled in vast underground cities by an intellectual yet corrupt elite. The chief protagonist, Tom Corcorigan, has witnessed the death of his parents at the hands of these Overlords; he is impelled to take up arms against them when he is given a data crystal by a mysterious woman in a bazaar. From here on it's adventure all the way: Corcorigan is a master of the martial arts (again we see Meaney injecting aspects of Eastern culture into his otherwise very Western setting), and is sharp enough to work out how to exact his revenge. However, the paradox of the title is this: how can Corcorigan kill one of the Oracles, who has the ability to see into the future and foretell his own death? To do so, he must learn the skills that will enable him to change the already predestined future.

The novel has a well-realized environment, although the characterization is not as well sustained as in the previous novel. *Paradox* is more action-driven than *To Hold Infinity*, and this shows not only in the way in which Meaney portrays his people but in the telling of the story itself; the narrative moves more swiftly than its predecessor. This is not necessarily a bad thing.

Meaney is an author who has yet to make a strong impression on the SF genre. But, given time, he will.

See Also
ARTIFICIAL INTELLIGENCE; BIOTECHNOLOGY; CRIME; CYBERPUNK; NANOTECHNOLOGY

Recommended Further Reading
Red Mars (1993) by PAUL J. McAULEY; *China Mountain Zhang* (1992) by MAUREEN F. McHUGH

Bibliography
To Hold Infinity (1998)
Paradox (2000)
Context (projected)
Resolution (projected)

MILLER, WALTER M. (1922–1996), USA

Born in the American South in 1922, Miller spent most of World War Two as a radio operator and tail gunner in the US Army Air Corps. Among the many combat sorties he flew, the controversial destruction of the Benedictine abbey at Monte Cassino, the oldest monastery in the Western world, had a profound effect. Miller was converted to Catholicism in 1947; 1960 saw publication of his only novel to be published in his lifetime, *A Canticle for Leibowitz*.

This is by common consent one of the best POST-HOLOCAUST novels ever written and is certainly one of only a handful of SF novels, along with JAMES BLISH's *A Case of Conscience* (1958), MICHAEL MOORCOCK's *Behold the Man* (1969) and MARY DORIA RUSSELL's *The Sparrow* (1997), to tackle religion in a thoughtful and honest way. It achieved great success upon publication, winning the 1961 HUGO award. Miller had already written, in his novellas and short stories, some of the most thought-provoking and interesting science fiction to be published during the post-war decades.

However, in 1996, after suffering from nearly thirty years of depression, Miller sadly ended his own life.

For some years before his death, it had been known that Miller was working on a sequel to *Canticle* and that author Terry Bisson was acting as an editorial assistant. The text was duly finished by Bisson and the finished novel, entitled *Saint Leibowitz and the Wild Horse Woman*, was published in 1997. Although not a direct sequel to *Canticle*, the book is a sophisticated and detailed work that tackles many of the same issues.

Miller's best short fiction is collected in *The Best of Walter M. Miller* Jr (2000).

See Also
POST APOCALYPTIC; RELIGION

Recommended Further Reading
Behold the Man (1969) by Michael Moorcock; *A Case of Conscience* (1958) by James Blish; *The Sparrow* (1997) by Mary Doria Russell

Bibliography
A Canticle for Leibowitz (1960)
Conditionally Human (short stories, 1962)
The View from the Stars (short stories, 1965)
The Darfsteller and Other Stories (short stories, 1980)
Saint Leibowitz and the Wild Horse Woman (1997)
The Best of Walter M. Miller Jr (short stories, 2000)

MOON, ELIZABETH (1945–   ), USA

Texan author Elizabeth Moon is well known for her informed and detailed Military Fantasy trilogy, *The Deed of Paksenarrion*. More recently she has produced a sequence of MILITARY SF novels known as *The Serrano Legacy*.

The Serrano Legacy is military SPACE OPERA similar to the work of both DAVID FEINTUCH and DAVID WEBER, although Moon's writing benefits from her spell in the US Marine Corps, grounded as it is in her experiences while on active service. This adds an edge of realism to her stories that is lacking in much military fiction by authors who have not themselves served in the armed forces.

The sequence begins with *Hunting Party* (1994) and continues with *Sporting Chance* (1994), *Winning Colors* (1995), *Once a Hero* (1997), *Rules of Engagement* (1998), *Change of Command* (1999) and *Against the Odds* (2000).

What also sets Moon's writing apart from that of her contemporaries is her use of a female lead protagonist and the way in which it is a family, as distinct from one character, whose progress she charts throughout the series. The sequence is also notably long, but Moon manages to sustain the excitement and tension from one book to the next, developing both her characters and their settings with each new novel. Fiction published in successive instalments like this can be thought of as harking back to the days of pulp fiction, and it is certainly true that Moon's writing captures the same sense of romping adventure and fun that appealed so strongly to readers in those early days of the genre. However, Moon does not over-simplify her work – the books try to tackle serious issues as well as main-tain a feeling of excitement. *The Serrano Legacy* shows no signs of slowing down: new instalments are added to the sequence every year.

Moon has also co-written two SF novels with ANNE McCAFFREY. They are *Sassinak* (1990) and *Generation Warriors* (1992).

The author maintains a website at http://www.sff.net/people/Elizabeth.Moon/

See Also
GENDER; MILITARISTIC SF; SPACE OPERA

Recommended Further Reading
The *Honor Harrington* sequence by DAVID WEBER; the *Seafort Saga* by DAVID FEINTUCH; the *Vorkosigan* sequence by LOIS McMASTER BUJOLD

Bibliography
Sheepfarmer's Daughter (1988)
Divided Allegiance (1988)
Oath of Gold (1989)
Lunar Activity (short stories, 1990)
Surrender None (1990)
Sassinak (1990, with ANNE McCAFFREY)
Generation Warriors (1992, with ANNE McCAFFREY)
Liar's Oath (1992)
Hunting Party (1994)
Sporting Chance (1994)
Winning Colors (1995)
Remnant Population (1996)
Phases (short stories, 1997)
Once a Hero (1997)
Rules of Engagement (1998)
Change of Command (1999)
Against the Odds (projected, 2000)

MOORCOCK, MICHAEL (1939–), Great Britain

To do justice to the literary career of British writer Michael Moorcock is a tough task indeed.

Acclaimed as one of the most adventurous authors (and editors) to adopt the form, it is perhaps surprising to realize that very little of Moorcock's published work is straightforward SF. But, considering his background and the scope of his literary interests, this should not really come as a shock.

Moorcock began his writing career at the tender age of fifteen, went on to publish a number of early fantasy stories under various pseudonyms, and in 1964 accepted the post of editor of the then-flagging NEW WORLDS magazine.

From the pages of this magazine, Moorcock exerted a massive influence on the SF genre, encouraging writers to try their hands at more LITERARY and unconventional SF, to cross-pollinate with the mainstream and to adopt a wider sociological perspective in their writing. He also fostered an emphasis on characterization. This made *New Worlds* the natural home for a number of 1960s genre classics, such as THOMAS M. DISCH's *Camp Concentration* and SAMUEL DELANY's *Time Considered as a Helix of Semi-precious Stones*.

Moorcock's influence extended not only to the writers themselves, but also to the readership of *New Worlds*: his pointed and reflective editorials stimulated discussion and his own fiction began to reflect his vision of the genre's potential.

Some of Moorcock's genre fiction is borderline SF, although most of it is better described as fantasy. One of the most impressive aspects of his achievement is the way in which he has linked much of his fiction together into one monumental sequence, *The Tale of the Eternal Champion*. Central to this ongoing series is Moorcock's concept of the Multiverse.

The Multiverse was introduced in Moorcock's early novel *The Sundered Worlds* (1965) and is an imaginative construct of transitorily intersecting parallel and ALTERNATE WORLDS, an infinite series of concurrent, sometimes intertwined universes between which the Eternal Champion moves. In some of these alternate worlds he is the bizarre and surreal figure of Jerry Cornelius, in others the albino prince Elric of Melniboné, in yet others Prince Corum or a member of the Von Bek dynasty. Some of these tales are SF, some are fantasy, others are simply fiction as only Moorcock could write it. Of them all, perhaps the most 'science fictional' are the tales of Jerry Cornelius.

At the crux of the Cornelius phenomenon is the quartet of novels that starts with *The Final Programme* (1968) and continues with *A Cure for Cancer* (1971), *The English Assassin* (1972) and *The Condition of Muzak* (1977), the last of these winning the prestigious *Guardian* fiction prize upon first publication. Other novels and stories – not all of them by Moorcock – are associated with this main Cornelius sequence or make use of some of its characters.

Jerry Cornelius himself is a 1960s icon, the hip and swinging protagonist of some truly surreal and bizarre adventures. *The Final Programme* sees an almost James Bond-style Cornelius tackling the coolly intelligent Miss Brunner as she plans to run the eponymous 'Final Programme' on her dangerous underground computer. Further books in the sequence develop the character into one of the most enduring literary creations of the period, a multifaceted, androgynous hero who revels in his anarchic humanity as he traverses the various realms of the Multiverse.

An intriguing feature of the stories – echoing one of the central images of world mythology and legend – is the way in which Cornelius is affected by changes in the landscape: if the country becomes sick, so does Cornelius. Like much NEW WAVE fiction of the time, Moorcock's writing displays a powerful sense of social entropy and dissolution.

Moorcock's single most impressive SF achievement, however, remains his bold and beautiful novel of the problems of religious faith. *Behold the Man* (1969) is the tale of Karl Glogauer, a religious obsessive who uses a time machine to travel back to seek the truth behind the crucifixion of Christ. When he arrives in ancient Israel he finds Jesus to be a gibbering idiot, mother Mary a prostitute. Despairing, Glogauer himself adopts the role of MESSIAH and is ultimately put to death in the name of God, thus perpetuating the Christian faith and, on a very personal level, justifying his own existence. Moving and controversial, a book that could not have been published before the effective collapse of fiction censorship in the 1960s, *Behold the Man* holds a place as one of the true classics of SF. A sequel, of sorts, is *Breakfast in the Ruins* (1972), thematically akin to its predecessor but not a direct continuation of the earlier book.

Other important works by Moorcock that are more than worthy of mention include *The Dancers at the End of Time* sequence, which comprises *An Alien Heat* (1972), *The Hollow Lands* (1974) and *The End of All Songs* (1976) and follows an avatar of Jerry Cornelius, Jherek Carnelian, in his journeys through time and space, giving a new twist to the representation of the FAR FUTURE, and the trilogy that comprises *A Nomad of the Time Streams* (beginning with *A Warlord of the Air* (1971) and continuing with *The Land Leviathan* (1974) and *The Steel Tsar* (1981)), which are early examples of STEAMPUNK and alternate-world SF. There is also *Gloriana* (1978), which, although fantasy, is as well a sumptuous example of alternate-world fiction.

Moorcock's Multiverse is diverse and interestingly populated; it is easy to lose oneself entirely within it, and although it is clear that some of the constituent novels were written quickly – as the author himself would cheerfully admit – nearly all of them are first-class pieces of story telling.

More recently, Moorcock has returned to the realms of the Multiverse after an extended break; *Silverheart* (2000, with Storm Constantine) is a fantasy that nevertheless contains echoes of Steampunk and is influenced by Moorcock's abiding interest in imaginative cityscapes, featuring an eclectic mix of ROBOTS, long-defunct AIs and magic.

A website is maintained at www.multiverse.org

See Also
ALTERNATE WORLD SF; LITERARY SF; MESSIAH; NEW WAVE; RELIGION; SCIENCE FANTASY; STEAMPUNK

Recommended Further Reading
A Canticle for Leibowitz (1959) by WALTER MILLER; *The Collapsium* (2000) by WIL McCARTHY; *Barefoot in the Head* (1969) by BRIAN ALDISS; *The Book of the New Sun* by GENE WOLFE; *The Dying Earth* (1950) by JACK VANCE

Bibliography (Selected)
The Stealer of Souls (short stories, 1963)
Stormbringer (1965)
The Sundered Worlds (1965)
The Fireclown (1965)
Warriors of Mars (1965)
Blade of Mars (1965)
Barbarians of Mars (1965)
The Deep Fix (short stories, 1966)
The Twilight Man (1966)
The Jewel in the Skull (1967)
The Final Programme (1968)
Sorcerer's Amulet (1968)
Sword of the Dawn (1968)
The Time Dweller (short stories, 1969)

The Secret of the Runestaff (1969)
The Black Corridor (1969)
The Ice Schooner (1969)
Behold the Man (1969)
The Eternal Champion (1970)
Phoenix in Obsidian (1970)
A Cure for Cancer (1971)
The Knight of the Swords (1971)
The Queen of the Swords (1971)
The King of the Swords (1971)
The Rituals of Infinity (1971)
The Warlord of the Air (1971)
The Sleeping Sorceress (1971)
An Alien Heat (1972)
Breakfast in the Ruins (1972)
The English Assassin (1972)
Elric of Melniboné (1972)
The Bull and the Spear (1973)
The Oak and the Ram (1973)
The Sailor on the Seas of Fate (1973)
Count Brass (1973)
The Champion of Garathorm (1973)
The Sword and the Stallion (1974)
The Land Leviathan (1974)
The Hollow Lands (1974)
The Distant Suns (1975)
The Quest for Tanelorn (1975)
Moorcock's Book of Martyrs (short stories, 1976)
The Lives and Times of Jerry Cornelius (short stories, 1976)
Legends from the End of Time (short stories, 1976)
The End of All Songs (1976)
The Adventures of Una Persson and Catherine Cornelius in the Twentieth Century (1976)
The Sailor on the Seas of Fate (1976)
The Weird of the White Wolf (1976)
Sojan (short stories, 1977)
The Condition of Muzak (1977)
The Transformation of Miss Mavis Ming (1977)
The Bane of the Black Sword (1977)
Gloriana, or the Unfulfill'd Queen (1978)

The Golden Barge (1979)
My Experiences in the Third World War (short stories, 1980)
The Great Rock 'n' Roll Swindle (1980)
The Entropy Tango (1981)
The Steel Tsar (1981)
The War Hound and the World's Pain (1981)
Byzantium Endures (1981)
The Brothel in Rosenstrasse (1982)
The Opium General (short stories, 1984)
The Laughter of Carthage (1984)
The City in the Autumn Stars (1986)
The Dragon in the Sword (1986)
Mother London (1988)
Casablanca (short stories, 1989)
The Fortress of the Pearl (1989)
The Revenge of the Rose (1991)
Jerusalem Commands (1992)
Blood (1994)
Fabulous Harbours (1995)
A War Amongst the Angels (1996)
Tales from the Texas Woods (short stories, 1997)
King of the City (2000)
Silverheart (2000, with Storm Constantine)
The Dreamthief's Daughter (2001)
London Bone (short stories, 2001)

MOORE, CHRIS (1947–   ), Great Britain

Alongside his contemporary JIM BURNS, Chris Moore is one of the most acclaimed visual artists on today's SF scene.

Moore's images are colourful and bold and, importantly, often feature astonishingly well-realized characters in the foreground. It is this juxtaposition of human figures against industrialized or ALIEN landscapes that truly gives Moore's work its character. He shows how the human form relates to its environment, and the ways in which technology will come to affect humanity.

Moore's painting is usually executed in acrylics so that his characters appear more expressive and realistic than if they were generated using computer design technology. Indeed, the usually obvious signs of CGI are often entirely absent from Moore's work.

Moore's work frequently appears on book covers on both sides of the Atlantic. Recently he has become known best for his series of illustrations for the covers of a uniform reprint edition of the works of PHILIP K. DICK. He has also done a large number of wonderful paintings for other classic-reprint novels, including such books as ALFRED BESTER's *The Stars My Destination* (1956) and FREDERIK POHL's *Man Plus* (1976).

Moore's reputation is solidly established and richly deserved. Science fiction titles fortunate enough to bear his cover art enjoy an important sales advantage.

NAGATA, LINDA (1960–   ), USA

Resident for a long time in Hawaii, Linda Nagata, along with a number of other modern SF writers such as KATHLEEN ANN GOONAN, has focused much of her attention on the development of NANOTECH-NOLOGY and the effects that it may have upon the planet and the human race.

Her first novel, *The Bohr Maker* (1995), is a detailed thriller that follows the progress of Phousita, a young woman from the slums who has been infected with a strange nanotech machine known as the Bohr Maker, and Nikko, the man responsible. Nikko himself is dying and needs to recover the Bohr Maker so that he may save his own life: the machine allows the infected to manipulate their biochemical make-up on a molecular scale. This blending of nanotechnology with human BIOLOGY is not new to the genre, but Nagata manages to pull it off with sufficient energy to make it worthwhile.

The second novel in this loose *Nanotechnology* sequence, which also includes Nagata's other books to date, *Deception Well* (1997) and *Vast* (1998), is *Tech-Heaven* (1995).

Tech-Heaven adopts a slightly different approach to the first book. It is set in a NEAR FUTURE in which a woman, shocked by the death of her husband, has him cryogenically frozen (see CRYONICS) in the hope that advancing technology will eventually allow him to be resuscitated. Again, the book does nothing truly new, but nonetheless confirmed Nagata as a writer to be watched.

Nagata's next two novels, *Deception Well* and *Vast*, take the human race into the FAR FUTURE, to a time when war, politics and SPACE divide communities, and ancient ALIEN killing machines stalk and destroy any biological forms of life. *Deception Well* follows a community down to the surface of an alien planet that is suffocating under a blanket of various nanotech viruses, while *Vast* takes four survivors into the heart of the alien territory on board an ancient starship.

Nagata's next novel, *Limit of Vision*, will not have the same setting but is keenly anticipated.

The author maintains a website at http://www.mauri.net/~nagata/

See Also
FAR FUTURE; NANOTECHNOLOGY; PLANET; SPACE OPERA; SPACE TRAVEL; TRANSCENDENCE

Recommended Further Reading
Queen City Jazz (1995) by Kathleen Ann Goonan; *Four Hundred Billion Stars* (1988) by PAUL J. McAULEY; *Bios* (1999) by ROBERT CHARLES WILSON

Bibliography
The Bohr Maker (1995)
Tech-Heaven (1995)
Deception Well (1997)
Vast (1998)
Limit of Vision (projected, 2001)
Skye Object 327OA (projected)

NEWMAN, KIM (1959–   ), Great Britain
Kim Newman is a British author whose work within the genre is more associational than direct. This is not to say that he hasn't written some highly intelligent and literate SF – he has – simply that the bulk of his work would be better classified as Dark Fantasy or HORROR.

Newman's most important work of SF is without doubt the excellent collection of short stories he produced with EUGENE BYRNE, *Back in the USSA* (1997). The book takes a detailed look at an ALTERNATE-WORLD version of America, in which socialism has become the dominant political force and the country is at odds with a capitalist Russia. Many important characters from history make brief and often hilarious appearances – but the novel also has an interesting perspective on democracy and POLITICS as it charts the decline and fall of the American socialist regime.

Alternate History has become a distinguishing feature of much of Newman's work. *The Anno Dracula* sequence, which comprises *Anno*

Dracula (1992), *The Bloody Red Baron* (1995), *Judgement of Tears* (1998) (UK title, *Dracula Cha Cha Cha*) and *Andy Warhol's Dracula* (1999), as well as a number of short stories, takes as its setting an alternate world in which Queen Victoria married Count Dracula. The novels are at once funny and horrific, and Newman shows a flair for deconstructing the standard genre form and rebuilding it into something twisted and different.

Newman has also pseudonymously written a number of novels that tie in with various game worlds created by role-playing-game publishers and manufacturers Games Workshop. A number of these novels, written as by 'Jack Yeovil', blend more standard SF themes with the fantastical settings within which the stories take place. The best of these are without doubt *Demon Download* (1990), *Krokodil Tears* (1991) and *Comeback Tour* (1991). Although they are unavoidably generic (because of the game-world parameters they are written to) they are characteristically high in entertainment value.

Newman is also an important film critic, with columns in various magazines. He has written a number of interesting books of movie criticism, covering a range of cult (including SF) films and series.

The author maintains a website at http://indigo.ie/~imago/newman.html

See Also
ALTERNATE WORLD; HORROR

Recommended Further Reading
The Man in the High Castle (1962) by PHILIP K. DICK; *Finity* (1999) by JOHN BARNES; *The Empire of Fear* (1988) by BRIAN STABLE-FORD; *I Am Legend* (1954) by RICHARD MATHESON

Bibliography (Selected)
The Night Mayor (1989)
Drachenfels (1989, as 'Jack Yeovil')
Bad Dreams (1990)
Demon Download (1990, as 'Jack Yeovil')
Krokodil Tears (1991, as 'Jack Yeovil')
Comeback Tour (1991, as 'Jack Yeovil')
Beasts in Velvet (1991, as 'Jack Yeovil')
Jago (1991)
Anno Dracula (1992)
Genevieve Undead (1993, as 'Jack Yeovil')

The Original Dr Shade, and Other Stories (short stories, 1994)
Quorum (1994)
Bloody Students (1994, as 'Jack Yeovil'*)*
Route 666 (1994, as 'Jack Yeovil')
Famous Monsters (short stories, 1995)
The Bloody Red Baron (1995)
Back in the USSA (short stories, 1997, with EUGENE BYRNE)
Judgement of Tears (1998)
Life's Lottery (1999)
Andy Warhol's Dracula (1999)
Seven Stars (short stories, 2000)
Unforgivable Stories (short stories, 2000)

NEW WORLDS

New Worlds began its life as a British genre magazine in 1946, under the editorship of John Carnell. Carnell had helped to see the magazine through its early days as a fanzine, and when it was picked up for publication as a professional pulp magazine in 1946, he remained editor.

In the early years, and indeed throughout much of its chequered existence, the magazine changed publishers a number of times, although Carnell retained his editorship until issue 141. During this time the magazine was important to the careers of many British SF writers, giving them a stable outlet for much of their work and a forum for their new ideas. (A similar function is now performed by the newer magazine, INTERZONE.) Carnell took a step away from the pulp image of the genre during his editorship of *New Worlds*, encouraging writers such as BRIAN ALDISS and JOHN BRUNNER to produce more intellectually challenging stories.

After passing over the editorship of *New Worlds* to MICHAEL MOORCOCK, at that time a young writer, in 1964, Carnell went on to edit an excellent series of anthologies, *New Writings in SF*, featuring original stories from a variety of genre authors and with very much the same tone and feel to it as earlier issues of *New Worlds*.

Meanwhile, *New Worlds* was undergoing a renaissance. With issue 142 it began publishing as a monthly paperback and editor Moorcock introduced a new policy, encouraging writers to experiment more with their narrative styles and their subject matter. This was the genesis of the British NEW WAVE, a movement that would see SF become more self-consciously LITERARY and character-driven. *New Worlds* stayed at the very forefront of this movement.

Moorcock continued this experimental policy for as long as he edited the magazine, publishing many stories that have since become classics, such as his own *Behold the Man*, THOMAS M. DISCH's *Camp Concentration* and SAMUEL R. DELANY's *Time Considered as a Helix of Semi-precious Stones*. Indeed, when *New Worlds* was dropped by its publishers in 1967, Moorcock, with the help of the British Arts Council, carried on publishing it himself.

For various reasons, chiefly financial, this could not continue, and in April 1970 *New Worlds* published its last issue as a 'proper' magazine. The title was revived in 1971 for a brief (1971–1976) run of ten original paperback anthologies, edited by Moorcock and others.

More recently, after a long hiatus and with the aid of Moorcock as a consulting editor, DAVID GARNETT edited another five issues of the magazine in the anthology format, the first four being published by Gollancz in the UK (1991–1994), the fifth by White Wolf in the USA (1997). It remains to be seen whether any further *New Worlds* anthologies will be issued. Moorcock also briefly stepped back into the editor's role to produce one special, all-star issue (221) in celebration of the magazine's fiftieth anniversary.

Throughout its existence and various formats, *New Worlds* maintained its consecutive numbering, the first issue, although undated, appearing in 1946, the last, numbered 222, appearing in 1997.

New Worlds was for a long time the most important of the British genre magazines, at first giving British writers a regular outlet for their work, and then providing the New Wave movement that would later have such a profound effect on the genre as a whole with a useful launch platform. The legacy of *New Worlds* can be seen in many current publications – early issues of *Interzone* were clearly influenced by it, and the new magazine SPECTRUM SF adopts a similar paperback format and has featured work by a number of its authors.

Years after Moorcock stopped publishing *New Worlds*, its influence can still be felt in SF on both sides of the Atlantic.

NIVEN, LARRY (1938–   ), USA

Larry Niven began his writing career in the 1960s at a time when many younger SF writers were being seduced by the NEW WAVE movement and its emphasis on the SOFT sciences such as psychology and sociology.

But Niven saw from the very beginning that his type of SF just wouldn't fit this mould. His was the new HARD SF, the scientifically based SPACE OPERA that had dominant elements of both solid scientific speculation and high adventure.

Niven published his first novel, *World of Ptavvs*, in 1966. It was to form the beginning of his vast FUTURE HISTORY, which he himself has named the *Tales of Known Space* sequence. This sequence encompassed nearly all of Niven's work for the first decade of his writing career, and describes a galaxy teeming with various forms of advanced ALIEN life, some of whom are at odds with the human race while others go out of their way to protect humanity. Indeed, in the later *Protector* (1973), Niven describes how an alien travels from across the galaxy to protect our race from its own highly evolved species who see us as a form of primitive vermin – in actual fact, a larval form of themselves, as the Pak are a transcendent race derived from the same stock as humanity.

World of Ptavvs itself steps back in time from the events of *Protector* and details the havoc that is set loose when a group of humans release an alien Thrint from its captivity in a stasis field. This Thrint is the last of its kind, the *Thrintun*, a deadly race from the darkest depths of history thought to have been extinct for millennia. The consequences of its release are terrifying.

Other books and short story-collections followed, but the series reaches its peak in the wonderful *Ringworld* (1970), the book for which Niven remains best known.

Ringworld describes in loving detail a vast alien artefact that is found circling a distant star. This artefact represents one segment of a DYSON SPHERE, an ARTIFICIAL ENVIRONMENT built by the ancient Pak to house a variety of people and races. The humans and their dubious alien allies, the Puppeteers, set about exploring.

It is the SENSE OF WONDER that Niven imparts to the reader in *Ringworld* that makes it such a triumph. The novel shows Niven to be a re-inventor of traditional SF and it remains one of the best of its type.

Two direct sequels followed *Ringworld*, *Ringworld Engineers* (1979) and *Ringworld Throne* (1996). Other novels and stories in the sequence followed, but Niven had already branched out into other areas of SF.

The Mote in God's Eye (1974) saw the start of Niven's long series of collaborations with fellow author Jerry Pournelle. It is a true collaborative effort, and describes in big Space Opera terms the first encounter between a human empire and an alien species. The book is massive in every sense and while there are some dubious POLITICS involved and the characterization leaves something to be desired it remains a highly enjoyable read.

Further collaborations with Pournelle and others have made up much of Niven's output since the late 1970s. *The Legacy of Heorot* (1987, with Jerry Pournelle and Steven Barnes) is probably the best of these, a DYSTOPIAN novel set on a hostile alien planet.

Later Niven 'singletons' such as the recent *Rainbow Mars* (1999) have so far failed to recapture the power and complexity of the *Tales of Known Space* sequence which remains one of the most epic, ambitious and adventurous SF series to appear since ROBERT HEINLEIN developed the Future History concept in the 1930s.

See Also
ALIEN; ARTIFICIAL ENVIRONMENT; FUTURE HISTORY; HARD SF; PLANET; SPACE OPERA

Recommended Further Reading
The *Future History* sequence by Robert Heinlein; the *Foundation* sequence by ISAAC ASIMOV; the *Xeelee* sequence by STEPHEN BAXTER; the *Night's Dawn Trilogy* by PETER F. HAMILTON; *Rendezvous with Rama* (1973) by ARTHUR C. CLARKE; *Excession* (1996) by IAIN M. BANKS

Bibliography
World of Ptavvs (1966)
A Gift from Earth (1968)
Neutron Star (short stories, 1968)
The Shape of Space (short stories, 1969)
Ringworld (1970)
All the Myriad Ways (short stories, 1971)
The Flying Sorcerers (1971, with David Gerrold)
The Flight of the Horse (short stories, 1973)
Inconstant Moon (short stories, 1973)
Protector (1973)
A Hole in Space (short stories, 1974)
The Mote in God's Eye (1974, with Jerry Pournelle)
Tales from Known Space (short stories, 1975)
Inferno (1975, with Jerry Pournelle)
The Long ARM of Gil Hamilton (short stories, 1976)
A World Out of Time (1976)

Lucifer's Hammer (1977, with Jerry Pournelle)
The Magic Goes Away (1977)
Convergent Series (short stories, 1979)
The Patchwork Girl (1980)
Ringworld Engineers (1980)
The Magic May Return (anthology, 1981)
Dream Park (1981, with Steven Barnes)
Oath of Fealty (1981, with Jerry Pournelle)
The Descent of Anansi (1982, with Steven Barnes)
More Magic (anthology, 1984)
The Time of the Warlock (short stories, 1984)
The Integral Trees (1984)
Niven's Laws (short stories, 1984)
Limits (short stories, 1985)
Footfall (1985, with Jerry Pournelle)
The Smoke Ring (1987)
The Legacy of Heorot (1987, with Jerry Pournelle and Steven Barnes)
The Barsoom Project (1989, with Steven Barnes)
N-Space (short stories, 1990)
Playgrounds of the Mind (short stories, 1991)
Achilles' Choice (1991, with Steven Barnes)
Dream Park: The Voodoo Game (1991, with Steven Barnes)
Fallen Angels (1991, with Jerry Pournelle and Michael Flynn)
The Gripping Hand (1992, with Jerry Pournelle)
Crashlander (short stories, 1994)
The Dragons of Heorot (1995, with Jerry Pournelle and Steven Barnes)
Ringworld Throne (1996)
Destiny's Road (1997)
Rammer (1997)
Rainbow Mars (1999)
The Burning City (2000, with Jerry Pournelle)
Saturn's Race (2000, with Steven Barnes)

NOON, JEFF (1957–   ), Great Britain

It could never be said that Jeff Noon's first novel, *Vurt* (1994), had quiet beginnings.

Originally published locally in Manchester, England (Noon's home city), it became an instant cult success, going on to win the ARTHUR C. CLARKE AWARD for its year. Literary and daring, *Vurt* is the tale of a young man named Scribble; it is a coming-of-age drama distinguished by its surreal take on the city of Manchester in which it is set. Noon is obsessed by cityscapes and the underbelly of the Mancunian metropolis appears to be his ideal setting for exploring his ideas.

Vurt is a modern classic that explores the boundaries of reality through vividly described drug-induced fantasies. The entire novel is ambiguous about what constitutes reality; the text starts and ends with passages that suggest the whole story is in fact the fantasy of one young man.

Vurt was followed in 1995 by *Pollen*, which draws upon similar imagery and features many of the same themes. As sequels go, it is as surreal and inventive as its predecessor.

Noon's third novel saw him deconstructing Lewis Carroll's *Alice in Wonderland* in the often hilarious *Automated Alice* (1995). Thematically linked to both *Vurt* and *Pollen*, it shows Noon taking a step away from the genre in search of other literary forms.

Nymphomation (1997) returns briefly to SF, serving as a prelude to *Vurt* and its sequel, but *Needle in the Groove* (2000) contains little science fiction, although it still spectacularly showcases Noon's inventiveness and his playfulness with form.

See Also
ALTERNATIVE REALITY; LITERARY SF; SCIENCE FANTASY

Recommended Further Reading
The Three Stigmata of Palmer Eldritch (1964) by PHILIP K. DICK; *Engine Summer* (1979) by JOHN CROWLEY

Bibliography
Vurt (1994)
Pollen (1995)
Automated Alice (1996)
Nymphomation (1997)
Pixel Juice (short stories, 1998)
Needle in the Groove (2000)

ORWELL, GEORGE (1903–1950), Great Britain

Eric Arthur Blair, who wrote under the pseudonym 'George Orwell', was one of the greatest political commentators of the twentieth century. His courageous and passionate works of reportage, such as *Down and Out in*

Paris and London (1933), have guaranteed him a place in the annals of British journalism. His novels have ensured his position in the history of English literature. His most enduring piece of writing, and one of the most important books of the age, is *Nineteen Eighty-Four* (1949).

Nineteen Eighty-Four is Orwell's one contribution to the SF genre, the definitive DYSTOPIA and a blazing, nightmare vision of POLITICS gone mad. It is also a biting satire on the communist Soviet Union of the time when Orwell was writing.

Orwell's dystopia is as bleak as they come. After an atomic war fought to a stalemate during the 1950s, Britain is now known as Airstrip One and is ruled by an all-seeing, all-hearing totalitarian regime. The government imposes its will on the people through means of torture and conditioning. The Thought Police control all public and, increasingly, most private means of expression while portraits of Big Brother, the figurehead who represents the oppressive state, watch from every wall. Two-way television screens – 'telescreens' – monitor every action and movement, books are written by machines and 'history' is altered to suit the prevailing orthodoxy. A new language, Newspeak, is being imposed so that any possible heretical thought will become unthinkable (because impossible to articulate). The population have become slaves of the system, mindless zombies in a society that officially runs as smoothly as a machine but in reality condemns most of its people to lives of drab squalor and deprivation.

The central character, Winston Smith, is aware of the hell of control that surrounds his every thought and action. He falls in love briefly with Julia, a co-worker in the Ministry of Truth. Their passion is, of course, forbidden by the state and hence is doomed. Winston compounds his offence by confiding in the enigmatic Inner Party member O'Brien – who turns out to be a key figure in the state apparatus of mind control. It is he who conducts Winston's 'deconstruction' from ineffectual rebel to totally broken human being. Winston is confronted with his worst nightmare – rats – in Room 101, the ultimate torture chamber, and the last vestige of his defiance collapses. The state's victory over Wionston is complete when Winston's hatred of Big Brother changes to genuine, remorseful love: he is even convinced that, if Big Brother wills it, then two plus two truly equals five.

The vision of *Ninety Eighty-Four* is extreme, deliberately repellent yet at the same time almost unbearably poignant and powerful. As a satire on the state of world politics and the corrupting effects of power it is unmatched by any other novel before or since. It is one of the handful of books by which the twentieth century will be not only remembered but judged.

Also worthy of note is Orwell's other classic dystopia, *Animal Farm* (1945). More allegorical fantasy than SF, it draws its images from the same Soviet Union that inspired *Nineteen Eighty-Four*, but tells its tale through the harsh experiences of a group of farm animals who stage a revolution only to come to the satirical conclusion that 'all animals are equal, but some animals are more equal than others'.

Orwell died in 1950, aged forty-seven.

See Also
DYSTOPIA; POLITICAL SF

Recommended Further Reading
Brave New World (1932) by ALDOUS HUXLEY; *The Star Fraction* (1995) by KEN MACLEOD; *We* (1924) by Yevgeny Zamyatin; *A Clockwork Orange* (1962) by ANTHONY BURGESS

Bibliography (Selected)
Animal Farm (1945)
Nineteen Eighty-Four (1949)

PALMER, STEPHEN (1962–   ), Great Britain

British author Stephen Palmer published his first novel, *Memory Seed*, in 1996. It is an interesting, baroque novel set in a FAR FUTURE in which the Earth, devastated by an ECOLOGICAL disaster, is slowly being covered in a deadly layer of vegetation. The survivors of this plague of greenery live in and around the city of Kray and, as the novel begins, the chief protagonist, Zinina, is attempting to escape the encroaching plant life. The novel has an almost entirely female cast – fertile men are scarce and are kept locked away in breeding farms.

Perhaps one of the most interesting aspects of the novel is the implied concern about BIOTECHNOLOGY and GENETIC engineering: the plague of plants has been brought about by human attempts to modify plant life into biological computers. Although there has been a certain degree of success, with memory modules growing from seed pods, things have gone awry. The novel has the feel of a JOHN WYNDHAM catastrophe about it, but with a modern, post-CYBERPUNK slant.

Memory Seed was followed by *Glass* (1997), a thematic sequel that is also set in a far-future city and describes a different plague, this time of glass. Indeed, the parallels between the two novels are explicit, with the city of the second book being named Cray, after the Kray of the first. However, it is clear that *Glass* is in part a tribute to the work of GENE WOLFE, in the way that it borrows terminology from the fantasy genre as a means of describing its far-future setting. The book also replicates the almost Gothic feel of Wolfe's *Book of the New Sun* and invokes similar imagery in its exploration of the relationship between humanity and its long-forgotten technological past. This is not to say that *Glass* is a mere imitation of Wolfe's classic novel. It is simply that Palmer adopts methods similar to Wolfe's in an attempt to explore the same territory from a different perspective. The result is a well-sustained and detailed work, a worthwhile addition to the milieu.

Palmer has not produced a lot of work in the years since *Glass*. It is hoped that it will not be too long before he returns to writing.

The author maintains a website at http://www.geocities.com/Area51/2162/indexsf/html

See Also
BIOTECHNOLOGY; ECOLOGY; FAR FUTURE; GENETICS; SCIENCE FANTASY

Recommended Further Reading
The Day of the Triffids (1951) by JOHN WYNDHAM; *The Book of the New Sun* (1980–83) by GENE WOLFE

Bibliography
Memory Seed (1996)
Glass (1997)

POE, EDGAR ALLAN (1809–1849), USA
Although perhaps better known as a HORROR and mystery writer, Edgar Allan Poe is one of the early SF innovators. Indeed, some critics, such as THOMAS M. DISCH in his *The Dreams Our Stuff Is Made Of* (1998), have argued that it is was actually Poe who brought about the genre that we know today.

It is certainly fair to say that Poe had an important influence on the works of JULES VERNE, and that Verne in turn influenced. H. G. WELLS. But it seems a little excessive to claim that Poe was the actual originator of the genre, as its development is more sensibly seen as an evolving process to which many authors contributed.

But Poe did to some extent pioneer the use of the short story as a specific narrative form. There are, too, certain qualities to be found in many of his works, as well as some specific concepts, that prefigure aspects of modern SF.

Poe's most obviously science fictional tale is 'Mellonta Tauta' (1849), which opens with a letter dated 1 April 2848 and proceeds to describe a future society, an anti-UTOPIA, that believes itself to be the ideal social form. The future context is used here simply to give Poe the necessary means to produce a social satire, but it works to good effect. Other tales such as 'The Thousand-and-Second Tale of Scheherazade' and 'A Descent into the Maelstrom' make use of similar tricks, and some of his poems describe astronomical events such as the destruction of the Earth or passing asteroids.

However, perhaps the aspect of Poe's thought that is of most interest to SF readers is his fundamental belief in the falsity of perceived reality. In much of his work, particularly in his tales of terror and the 'grotesque', Poe makes use of shifting DIMENSIONS or plays with his characters' perceptions of the world to demonstrate its essentially unknowable nature.

These methods are used to major effect in Poe's longest work, *The Narrative of Arthur Gordon Pym of Nantucket* (1837). The tale begins in typical story-rich Poe fashion with an ill-fated sea voyage, a shipwreck, cannibalism and other untoward goings-on. However, when Pym sets sail on a second vessel for the Antarctic, things become even stranger. He comes across a 'lost world' of the type later used to great effect by EDGAR RICE BURROUGHS, an island inhabited by strange bestial humans who are in effect a direct negative of regular humanity. They are black, even down to their teeth, though this difference in pigmentation is as much a matter of perception as of racial awareness. Pym has encountered the antithetical world whose values are fundamentally opposed to those that he knows – the island's inhabitants slaughter the crew of Pym's vessel because of their own fear of *whiteness*.

Pym himself escapes, and with a half-caste makes his way off the island on a canoe. However, once at sea they experience another of Poe's strange perceptual shifts, and reality fragments further. This time the reader is left without answers – *something* happens, but what? There is no easy answer.

It is this underlying concern with the limitations and unreliability of human perception that truly marks Poe out as a proto-SF writer. Much of his work, even when it is not concerned with any specific scientific concept, shows a man trying to break down the barriers between perceived realities so that he can explore the true nature of the universe. If Poe was writing today, he would be writing about VIRTUAL REALITY and quantum speculation, but during the nineteenth century the scientific 'hoax' or the supernatural tale was the best way in which he could present his notions. Poe will be remembered for many things, not least his vital contribution to the development of mainstream American literature. But his influence on the development of SF is also important. Poe explored in his fiction the structures of differing realities, and this has been a central concern of SF ever since.

Most of the relevant stories are collected in *The Science Fiction of Edgar Allan Poe* (1976).

See Also
ALTERNATIVE REALITY; DYSTOPIA; HORROR; UTOPIA

Recommended Further Reading
The short stories of THEODORE STURGEON; *I Have No Mouth And I Must Scream* (1967) by HARLAN ELLISON; *Vurt* (1993) by JEFF NOON; *Do Androids Dream of Electric Sheep?* (1968) and *The Three Stigmata of Palmer Eldritch* (1964) by PHILIP K. DICK; *The Lathe of Heaven* (1971) by URSULA LE GUIN; the short stories of H. P. Lovecraft

Bibliography (Selected)
The Narrative of Arthur Gordon Pym of Nantucket (1837)
Tales of the Grotesque and Arabesque (short stories, 1840)
Tales of Edgar A. Poe (short stories, 1845)
The Complete Tales and Poems of Edgar Allan Poe (short stories, 1938)
The Science Fiction of Edgar Allan Poe (short stories, 1976)

POHL, FREDERIK (1919–   ), USA
The career of Frederik Pohl has been colourful, varied and distinguished. He began writing short fiction in the 1930s, edited a couple of small SF magazines in the 1940s, turned literary agent during the later part of that same decade, produced some wonderful collaborative novels during the 1950s, went on to edit GALAXY magazine and *If* in the 1960s, and then settled down for a career as a full-time novelist in the 1970s.

Pohl's first stories were written under various pseudonyms, appearing for the most part in *Astonishing Stories* and *Super Science Stories*, the two short-lived magazines he edited during the early 1940s.

His first novel, *The Space Merchants* (1953), co-authored with fellow fan and SF writer C. M. Kornbluth (with whom he had already co-written stories in the late 1930s and early 1940s) is of lasting interest and has come to be recognized as one of the classic genre novels of the period.

The Space Merchants is a social satire set in an America dominated by warring advertising agencies and suffering from OVERPOPULATION and crippling resource shortages. Much of the populace is psychologically battered by the constant onslaught of advertisements, and a weak resistance movement seems tired and ineffective. Even the US government is in thrall to the all-powerful marketing executives.

The Space Merchants describes an archetypal modern DYSTOPIA, an America choked by the waste products of consumerism, and it set a high standard for other satirical works of social extrapolation that were to follow. The future it describes is not the POLITICAL tyranny of GEORGE ORWELL's *Nineteen Eighty-Four* (1949) but the neon-lit, nightmare of cannibal capitalism that would later be so dramatically visualized in Ridley Scott's BLADE RUNNER (1982). Of the two novels, it now seems that *The Space Merchants* was by far the most accurate in its prophecy. A belated sequel by Pohl was *The Merchants' War* (1984).

Pohl and Kornbluth were to produce some of the wittiest and most pointed SF novels of the 1950s. *The Space Merchants* was followed by, among others, *Gladiator-at-Law* (1955), an enjoyable romp through the slums of twenty-first-century capitalist suburbia, and *Wolfbane* (1959), which sees humankind swallowed up by invading ALIENS to become biological parts in their machines.

Sadly, Kornbluth died at the young age of thirty-five in 1958, bringing a premature end to the run of excellent collaborative stories and novels. A few collections and solo works followed, as well as some novels co-written with fellow SF stalwart Jack Williamson. But in 1961 Pohl took the editor's chair at *Galaxy* magazine and his writing output slowed considerably.

The magazine did remarkably well under Pohl, becoming the leading American SF magazine of its time while he stayed at the editorial post. Pohl also did well with *Galaxy*'s then sister magazine, *If*, winning a number of HUGO AWARDS. The better stories from this period of *If* have been anthologized in the two collections *The If Reader* (1966) and *The Second If Reader* (1968).

The 1970s saw yet another shift in Pohl's career, and one that was entirely welcome to SF readers. He left his various editorial positions and began to concentrate for the first time on developing his own fiction. The genre has been reaping the benefits ever since.

Man Plus appeared in 1976, and remains possibly the best treatment of the CYBORG theme to be published to date. The book concerns the process by which a man is adapted to be able to survive the hostile environment on the surface of Mars. But, it is not the physical transformation or accompanying scientific speculation that truly makes *Man Plus* such an important book, it is the psychological impact the process is seen to have on the astronaut. He becomes a victim of science, a latter-day Frankenstein's monster, and suffers a sense of alienation that grows throughout the book as his metamorphosis proceeds. However, although his physical form becomes that of a superman, in essence he remains as vulnerable as the rest of ordinary humanity.

Man Plus won the NEBULA AWARD for its year.

Pohl followed up the success of *Man Plus* with *Gateway* (1977), the book that was to begin his ambitious and lengthy *Heechee* sequence about mankind's expansion into the universe.

It describes the results of a human expedition to an asteroid where the astronauts find a series of working space vessels left behind by an enigmatic alien race, the Heechee. The world governments form a committee, and various people are selected to attempt to make use of the Heechee spaceships. When they do, they are whisked away to mysterious locations across the galaxy. The vessels all travel at speeds faster than light and are programmed to take their passengers to preselected sites, many of which prove inhospitable to human life. Nevertheless, humanity uses the opportunity to spread out across space and later in the sequence they meet up with their mysterious patrons.

Later books in the sequence are *Beyond the Blue Event Horizon* (1980), *Heechee Rendezvous* (1984), *The Annals of the Heechee* (1987) and *The Gateway Trip* (1990). *Gateway* itself won Pohl the Hugo, Nebula and JOHN W. CAMPBELL AWARDS for its year.

Outside of the Heechee sequence there were other fine 'singletons'. *Jem* (1979) is a bleak story of humanity's failure to successfully realize their dream of colonizing another planet to ease the strain of a burgeoning population. *Black Star Rising* (1985) sees an American peasant struggling to break free from a Chinese-dominated NEAR FUTURE. *Mining the*

Oort (1992) tells of a Martian-born colonist training to become a cometary miner in the Oort cloud.

Pohl has certainly had a long career in the genre, with many successes to his credit, but his best work has appeared in the period since the 1970s when he began to focus his efforts on his own writing.

The Space Merchants is undoubtedly a classic dystopian novel, but *Man Plus* and *Gateway* are truly marvellous books, full of depth, insight and adventure. The *Heechee* sequence in particular is the work of a true SF master writing at the height of his mature powers.

See Also
ALIEN; BIOTECHNOLOGY; CYBORG; DYSTOPIA; GENETICS; HARD SF; OVERPOPULATION; PLANET; POLITICS; SPACE; SPACE OPERA; TERRAFORMING

Recommended Further Reading
The *Xeelee* sequence by STEPHEN BAXTER; *The Seedling Stars* (1957) by JAMES BLISH; the *Tales of Known Space* sequence by LARRY NIVEN

Bibliography (Selected)
The Space Merchants (1953, with C. M. Kornbluth)
Search the Sky (1954, with C. M. Kornbluth)
Gladiator-at-Law (1955, with C. M. Kornbluth)
Alternating Currents (short stories, 1956)
The Case Against Tomorrow (short stories, 1957)
Slave Ship (1957)
Tomorrow Times Seven (short stories, 1959)
Wolfbane (1959, with C. M. Kornbluth)
The Man Who Ate the World (short stories, 1960)
Drunkard's Walk (1960)
Turn Left at Thursday (short stories, 1961)
The Abominable Earthman (short stories, 1963)
The Reefs of Space (1964, with Jack Williamson)
Starchild (1965, with Jack Williamson)
A Plague of Pythons (1965)
Digits and Dastards (short stories, 1966)
The Frederik Pohl Omnibus (short stories, 1966)
The Age of the Pussyfoot (1969)
Rogue Star (1969, with Jack Williamson)

Day Million (short stories, 1970)
The Gold at the Starbow's End (short stories, 1972)
The Best of Frederik Pohl (short stories, 1975)
Farthest Star (1975, with Jack Williamson)
The Early Pohl (short stories, 1976)
In the Problem Pit (short stories, 1976)
Man Plus (1976)
Critical Mass (short stories, 1977, with C. M. Kornbluth)
Gateway (1977)
Jem (1979)
Before the Universe and Other Stories (short stories, 1980, with C. M. Kornbluth)
Beyond the Blue Event Horizon (1980)
The Cool War (1981)
Planets Three (short stories, 1982)
Starburst (1982)
Syzygy (1982)
Midas World (short stories, 1983)
Wall Around a Star (1983, with Jack Williamson)
Pohlstars (short stories, 1984)
The Years of the City (1984)
The Merchant's War (1984)
Heechee Rendezvous (1984)
Black Star Rising (1985)
The Coming of the Quantum Cats (1986)
Our Best: The Best of Frederik Pohl and C. M. Kornbluth (short stories, 1987)
BiPohl (short stories, 1987)
Chernobyl (1987)
The Annals of the Heechee (1987)
Land's End (1988, with Jack Williamson)
Narabedla Ltd (1988)
The Day the Martians Came (1988)
Homegoing (1989)
The Gateway Trip (short stories, 1990)
The World at the End of Time (1990)
Outnumbering the Dead (1990)
The Singers of Time (1991, with Jack Williamson)
Stopping at Slowyear (1991)
Mining the Oort (1992)
The Voices of Heaven (1994)

Mars Plus (1994, with Thomas T. Thomas)
The Other End of Time (1996)
The Siege of Eternity (1997)
O Pioneer! (1998)

PRATCHETT, TERRY (1948–   ), Great Britain

The Comedian *Extraordinaire* of the fantasy genre, famous for his long and often hilarious *Discworld* sequence, Terry Pratchett has also produced two fine examples of COMIC SF.

The Dark Side of the Sun (1976) was Pratchett's first adult novel and successfully parodies the pet concepts of SF, featuring ROBOTS, SPACE TRAVEL and interplanetary adventure in a witty send-up of the search for ALIEN life. Full of the sparkling humour that would later become Pratchett's trademark, the book marks the beginning of the road that would lead eventually to his invention of the Discworld and its surreal inhabitants.

Indeed, this sense of humour is even more apparent in *Strata* (1981), the second of Pratchett's humorous SF novels.

Strata follows the adventures of Kin Arad, a PLANET engineer who works for 'The Company' in providing environments suitable for human colonization. Her team go about inserting the appropriate fossils and geology into planetary strata to provide a false sense of ancient history for the new inhabitants. However, when she discovers a strange disc-shaped planet designed and built by aliens (clearly a prototype of the now-famous Discworld), adventure ensues. Although lacking much of the biting satire that was later to make Pratchett so popular, the book does clearly demonstrate his comic skill and literary ability.

Pratchett's *Discworld* sequence now stands at twenty-five novels and its author shows no sign of slowing down. It is doubtful that he will return to writing SF in the future, although many of the *Discworld* books draw upon the genre for comic value.

The *Dark Side of the Sun* and *Strata* may show a writer still developing his craft, but they are both extremely funny and worthy predecessors of the *Discworld* series.

See Also
ALIEN; COMIC SF; PLANET; ROBOT; SPACE TRAVEL

Recommended Further Reading
The Hitch Hiker's Guide to the Galaxy (1979) by DOUGLAS ADAMS; *Untouched by Human Hands* (1954) by ROBERT SHECKLEY; *Bill, the Galactic Hero* (1965) and *The Stainless Steel Rat* (1961) by HARRY HARRISON

Bibliography (Selected)
The Dark Side of the Sun (1976)
Strata (1981)

PRIEST, CHRISTOPHER (1943–), Great Britain

Christopher Priest is a British author whose work has many of the distinguishing features of the fiction of the NEW WAVE even though he was not actively involved in the more public manifestations of the movement. Priest's writing is often concerned with themes of entropy and dissolution, and his narratives tend to be internalized and character-driven.

His first novel, *Indoctrinaire* (1970), is uneven in its depiction of a Brazil two centuries into the future, but his second book, *Fugue for a Darkening Isle* (1972), successfully subverts the typical disaster novel in a NEAR-FUTURE tale that explores a Britain collapsing in on itself under the pressure of civil war and attendant anarchy. A nuclear war in Africa has left thousands of people homeless; they flee to the British Isles in the hope of finding sanctuary, but instead find social unrest and DYSTOPIA. Priest succeeds in his portrayal of a Britain under invasion and there is a clever irony in his vision of invaders who are not necessarily malign.

However, it is Priest's next novel that is his genre masterwork. *Inverted World* (1974) excels in its descriptions of a bizarre and unforgettable environment. The story concerns the progress of a vast wooden city as it is dragged across the surface of a strange PLANET that has apparently infinite boundaries. When the protagonist, Helward Mann, abandons the city for the outside world, elaborate shifts in perception occur, and the planet's very reality is brought into question. The book is undoubtedly Priest's most satisfactory genre work as well as his most explicitly science fictional.

The Space Machine (1976) is also of importance as a genre work. It is a subtle and affectionate pastiche of two of H. G. WELLS's classic early SF novels, *The Time Machine* (1895) and *The War of the Worlds* (1898) and features Wells himself as a protagonist. Inventive and enjoyable, *The Space Machine* is both a homage to and a reassessment of early genre fictions.

It is after *The Space Machine*, however, that we see Priest take a decisive step away from genre SF. *A Dream of Wessex* (1977), although technically a SF novel about a vast network of people wired up to a form of VIRTUAL REALITY, is more concerned with mapping the intricate twists of the human mind. This is an abiding concern of much of Priest's later work. *The Affirmation* (1981) and the collection *The Dream Archipelago* (1999) take place on what is assumed to be a Britain half submerged in the ocean, at some indefinite point in the future. This 'Dream Archipelago' – a series of smaller inhabited islands – becomes the setting for many varied tales of psychological insight and deft explorations of the human condition.

Other later books touch on the genre – *The Quiet Woman* (1990) is a near-future tale of dystopia, and *The Extremes* (1998) explores more of the possible applications of Virtual Reality, chiefly as a tool for coming to terms with loss and need. LITERARY and bold, these later books show Priest to be a writer of great integrity and emotional maturity.

It would be foolish to assume that Priest has altogether abandoned the SF genre, although he personally claims that he will write no more genre fiction. His new work continues to display a clarity of vision and under- standing that allows him to approach topics that others might find diffi- cult or obscure. While Priest may stand today on the sidelines of the genre looking outwards, his fiction has a perspective entirely of its own that remains of interest to all intelligent readers of SF.

Priest's best short fiction is to be found in *An Infinite Summer* (1979), and the linked collection *The Dream Archipelago*.

See Also
ALTERNATIVE REALITY; DYSTOPIA; LITERARY SF; NEAR FUTURE; NEW WAVE; SCIENTIFIC ROMANCE; VIRTUAL REALITY

Recommended Further Reading
The Time Machine (1895) by H. G. Wells; *Vurt* (1993) by JEFF NOON; *Martian Time-Slip* (1964) by PHILIP K. DICK

Bibliography
Indoctrinaire (1970)
Fugue for a Darkening Island (1972)
Real-Time World (short stories, 1974)
Inverted World (1974)
The Space Machine (1976)
A Dream of Wessex (1977)

An Infinite Summer (short stories, 1979)
The Affirmation (1981)
The Glamour (1984)
The Quiet Woman (1990)
The Prestige (1995)
The Extremes (1998)
The Dream Archipelago (short stories, 1999)
Existenz (movie novelization, 1999, as 'John Luther Novak')

REYNOLDS, ALASTAIR (1966–   ), Great Britain

Alastair Reynolds, who has been resident in The Netherlands for a number of years now, is a relatively recent regular contributor to INTER-ZONE magazine. Well respected for such short fiction as 'A Spy in Europa' and 'Stroboscopic', he has already been selected for a number of annual *Best New SF* collections, as well as featuring strongly in *Interzone*'s reader's polls for favourite stories.

His first novel, *Revelation Space*, was published in 2000, and although it 'stutters' in its opening it is well structured and well written. Vast in scope, it is a grandiose SPACE OPERA in the style of PETER F. HAMILTON or IAIN M. BANKS and features the discovery of an important ALIEN artefact as well as using current thought on space travel to good effect within the narrative.

Reynolds, a scientist working for the European Space Agency, manages to inject his space opera with enough added scientific realism to give it the edge of HARD SF while still retaining the exuberance and epic scope of the more adventurous sub-genre.

See Also
ARTIFICIAL INTELLIGENCE; BIOTECHNOLOGY; HARD SF; GENETICS; NANOTECHNOLOGY; SPACE; SPACE TRAVEL

Recommended Further Reading
Engines of God (1994) by JACK McDEVITT; *Four Hundred Billion Stars* (1988) by PAUL J. McAULEY; the *Xeelee* sequence by STEPHEN BAXTER

Bibliography
Revelation Space (2000)

ROBERTS, KEITH (1935–2000), Great Britain

Author and illustrator Keith Roberts came to prominence on the British SF scene during the 1960s. His literate, illuminating stories appeared in magazines such as SCIENCE FANTASY and NEW WORLDS and his expressive illustrations appeared on their covers and, occasionally, in their interiors. He also served as associate editor of *Science Fantasy* from 1965 to 1966 and as editor of its successor, *SF Impulse*, for its entire year-long run.

Roberts's first novel, *The Furies* (1966), is set in a POST APOCALYPTIC England in which GENETIC mutation has spawned a plague of enormous killer wasps. It is rather routine and similar to much of the other SF that was being produced at the time.

However, Roberts's second book, *Pavane* (1968), remains his most impressive achievement, and is surely one of the most outstanding British genre works of the twentieth century. Initially written as a series of linked short stories it describes an ALTERNATE-WORLD England that was conquered by the Spanish Armada and has remained under Papal rule for many hundreds of years. This has stifled scientific and social development with the result that the twentieth century that Roberts describes in the book is technologically retrograde. Steam-powered vehicles traverse the landscape (and are vividly described); castles still darken the horizon, class divisions are almost feudal and rebellion is brewing among the common folk. *Pavane* is realistic, LITERARY SF, and is a book to be cherished. It is one of the finest examples of alternate-world fiction ever written.

A number of short-story collections by Roberts appeared during the 1970s. The best of these is *The Grain Kings* (1976), a collection that features another example of alternate history, 'Weihnachtsabend', about Nazis victorious as well as the innovative title story that concerns vast combine harvesters the size of cities, whose function is to supply grain to the whole OVERPOPULATED planet.

Kiteworld (1985) is the best of Roberts's later work, a disturbing novel about a community of religious fanatics who attach themselves to huge kites as a way of protecting their borders from encroaching 'demons'. The post-holocaust setting is something at which Roberts excels, as is the treatment of RELIGION. *Kiteworld* combines both of these themes into one excellent whole. A sequel, *Drek Yarman*, has recently been serialized in the new Scottish magazine, SPECTRUM SF.

Roberts was one of the most respected twentieth-century British SF writers. Character-driven, literary and HUMANIST, his fiction remains relevant, inspiring and daring.

Sadly, Keith Roberts died in 2000, aged sixty-five.

See Also
ALTERNATE WORLD; HUMANIST SF; LITERARY SF; NEW WAVE; OVERPOPLUATION; RELIGION

Recommended Further Reading
Tunnel Through the Deeps (1972) by HARRY HARRISON; *Back in the USSA* (1997) by KIM NEWMAN and EUGENE BYRNE; *Fatherland* (1992) by Robert Harris; *The Two Georges* (1997) by HARRY TURTLE-DOVE and Richard Dreyfuss

Bibliography
The Furies (1966)
Pavane (1968)
Anita (1970)
The Inner Wheel (1970)
The Boat of Fate (1971)
Machines and Men (short stories, 1973)
The Chalk Giants (1974)
The Grain Kings (short stories, 1976)
Ladies from Hell (short stories, 1979)
Molly Zero (1980)
Kiteworld (1985)
The Lordly Ones (short stories, 1986)
Gráinne (1987)
The Road to Paradise (1989)
Winterwood and Other Hauntings (short stories, 1989)
The Event (1989)

ROBINSON, KIM STANLEY (1952–   ), USA

Kim Stanley Robinson is an American writer whose depth and breadth of vision and excellent grasp of politics and human nature informs much of his writing.

His first novel, *The Wild Shore* (1984) begins his *Orange County Trilogy*, a sequence that presents three different ALTERNATE-WORLD views of the same area of California. *The Wild Shore* depicts a NEAR-FUTURE America devastated after a nuclear bombardment. Survival is a daily struggle for the characters. The story follows the chief protagonist, Henry, as he takes up with a group of people who claim to be the spearhead of the new American resistance. The second book in the sequence,

The Gold Coast (1988), is perhaps the most immediately relevant, describing a DYSTOPIA that is not too far removed from our own society. Technology promises a bright future, but life has become boring and monotonous; the characters struggle to find their identities amongst the multicoloured store façades and video arcades that dominate their existence. *Pacific Edge* (1990) concludes the loose trilogy, describing an America that has fragmented into separate utopian states. The book is one of the first true attempts in modern SF to describe a possible near-future UTOPIA.

As a sequence, the *Orange County* books are remarkable and unusually engaging, so well are the lives of the people who populate Robinson's environments invoked. He has a deft eye for the quirks of human existence, for the little details that define a person, the tiniest of actions or inflections that can give away an underlying thought or insecurity. Robinson was to go on to even better things with the ambitious series of novels that followed, his *Mars* books.

The *Mars* sequence is a triumph of modern HARD SF. Beginning with *Red Mars* (1992), and continuing with *Green Mars* (1993) and *Blue Mars* (1996), it charts the progress of a group of colonists who set off to the PLANET intending to settle and TERRAFORM the harsh environment. Throughout the books we witness their gradual success, and the POLITICAL, economic, technological and emotional trials that they must face along the way. Global corporations on Earth all want a piece of the new planet, whilst on Mars itself rival factions form and attempt to outdo each other with political and military coups. All the while, Earth is reaching a breaking point of OVERPOPULATION and environmental collapse, and to the struggling Terran masses it seems that there is plenty of space available for the taking on Mars.

The *Mars* sequence wonderfully evokes the changing landscapes of the red planet, and is perhaps the most serious attempt yet to envisage the establishment of human life on another planet.

Robinson stresses through his writing the need to work in unison and harmony towards a brighter future, drawing attention to the fact that if humanity is not careful it will take all its political wrangling with it to any new environment.

Red Mars was awarded the NEBULA AWARD and *Green Mars* won the HUGO. The trilogy is one of the most important sequences in modern SF.

Stories and essays associated with the sequence are collected in *The Martians* (1999).

Of Robinson's other work, *Icehenge* (1984) and *Antarctica* (1997) are most worthy of note.

Icehenge concerns the investigation that follows the discovery of a monument at Pluto's north pole, which bears an inscription written in Sanskrit. *Antarctica* is a near-future ECOLOGICAL thriller about a group of activists who attempt to save the frozen continent from corporate interference and asset-stripping conglomerates.

Robinson's best short stories are collected in *Remaking History* (1991).

With each new book Robinson works to refine his vision of the serious choices facing humanity. Everything he writes deserves the attention of thoughtful SF readers.

See Also
ALTERNATE WORLD; DYSTOPIA; ECOLOGY; HARD SF; PLANET; POLITICAL SF; TERRAFORMING

Recommended Further Reading
Red Dust (1993) by PAUL J. McAULEY; *A Fall of Moondust* (1961) by ARTHUR C. CLARKE; *White Mars* (1999) by BRIAN ALDISS and Roger Penrose; *Mars* (1992) by BEN BOVA; *The Martian Race* (1999) by GREGORY BENFORD

Bibliography
The Wild Shore (1984)
Icehenge (1984)
The Memory of Whiteness (1985)
The Planet on the Table (short stories, 1986)
The Gold Coast (1988)
Escape from Kathmandu (1989)
A Short, Sharp Shock (1990)
Pacific Edge (1990)
Remaking History (short stories, 1991)
Red Mars (1992)
Green Mars (1993)
Blue Mars (1996)
Antarctica (1997)
The Martians (short stories, 1999)

ROBSON, JUSTINA, Great Britain

A relatively new genre writer, Justina Robson made her mark in the SF field in 1999 with the publication of her first novel, *Silver Screen*.

The book is an interesting post-CYBERPUNK exploration of ARTIFICIAL INTELLIGENCE and human identity. It tells the story of Anjuli O'Connell, a research scientist who is attempting to uncover the truth behind the mysterious death of one of her colleagues. At the same time, a landmark trial is taking place in an attempt to assess the rights of sentient artificial-intelligence systems that have developed their own personalities. In a cruel twist of fate, Anjuli is the key witness against the AIs, but her only ally in her search for the truth about her colleague is 901, one of the most highly evolved self-aware computer systems in existence.

The novel is a truly innovative examination of racism and technophobia, as well as a startling look at the possible evolution of the human mind into electronic form.

It remains to be seen whether Robson can sustain the success of *Silver Screen* in her next novel, although the smattering of short fiction that has appeared recently has certainly marked her out as a name to be watched.

The author maintains a website at http://www.lula.co.uk

See Also
ARTIFICIAL INTELLIGENCE; CRIME; HARDWARE; TRANSCENDENCE

Recommended Further Reading
Hotwire (1994) by SIMON INGS; the *Greg Mandel Trilogy* by PETER F. HAMILTON; *Neuromancer* (1984) by WILLIAM GIBSON

Bibliography
Silver Screen (1999)
Mappa Mundi (forthcoming, 2001)

RUCKER, RUDY (1946–   ), USA

One of the founding fathers of the CYBERPUNK movement, Rudy Rucker has been writing witty, inventive SF for nearly two decades. But many critics believe the Cyberpunk label is too restrictive to do justice to the sheer range of Rucker's work, much of which is better represented as HARD SF. Still, the *Ware* sequence for which he is best known certainly has recognizable elements of the sub-genre in it.

The *Ware* sequence begins with *Software* (1982) and continues with *Wetware* (1988), *Freeware* (1997) and *Realware* (2000). Humorous, yet with an underlying concern to render coherent the increasingly complex environments that it describes, the sequence begins with the kidnapping of a hippy computer-programmer by ROBOTS who possess ARTI-FICIAL INTELLIGENCE. The series grows ever more bizarre as Rucker first sets up and then satirizes the fundamental concepts of Cyberpunk. The last book in the sequence to date, *Realware*, somewhat loses the comic edge of the previous novels in its attempt to portray characters who have matured and 'grown up'. However, when one considers that some of Rucker's work is reportedly semi-autobiographical, his characters being versions of himself transplanted into various surreal and alien environments, it seems only natural that they should mature alongside their creator.

Rucker himself has a profound knowledge of physics and mathematics, practising both in addition to writing fiction. His love of physics is demonstrated nowhere better than in his various short stories, which are collected in *Gnarl!* (2000). These stories, dissimilar to each other as they are, have one thing in common: they all present the reader with wonderfully intricate and strange landscapes and environments drawn from mathematical and physical theory. This is Hard SF as only Rucker could write it, with credible characters who are obsessed with understanding the world around them, however strange it may seem.

Other important novels by Rucker include *The Hollow Earth* (1990), a STEAMPUNK-influenced ALTERNATE HISTORY in which the Earth is found to contain a strange new world that can be entered via the South Pole, and *White Light* (1980), his first-published novel, which blends fantasy with mathematical theory in an attempt to describe the perceived state of the universe when one is travelling at the speed of light.

Rucker's semi-autobiographical, surrealist SF blends adventure, humour, science and conceptual excess into something unique. Rucker calls it *Transrealist* fiction. Others simply call it bizarre and wonderful.

The author maintains a website at http://www.mathcs.sjsu.edu/faculty/rucker

See Also

ALTERNATE HISTORY; ARTIFICIAL INTELLIGENCE; CYBERPUNK; CYBERSPACE; SCIENCE FANTASY; STEAM-PUNK

Recommended Further Reading

Neuromancer (1984) by William Gibson; *Islands in the Net* (1988) by BRUCE STERLING; *Journey to the Centre of the Earth* (1864) by JULES VERNE; *Vurt* (1993) by JEFF NOON

Bibliography (Selected)

White Light (1980)
Spacetime Donuts (1981)
Software (1982)
The Fifty-Seventh Franz Kafka (short stories, 1983)
The Sex Sphere (1983)
Master of Space and Time (1984)
The Secret of Life (1985)
Wetware (1988)
The Hollow Earth (1990)
The Hacker and the Ants (1994)
Freeware (1997)
Saucer Wisdom (1999)
Gnarl! (short stories, 2000)
Realware (2000)
Spaceland (projected)

RUSSELL, MARY DORIA (1950–   ), USA

A trained paleoanthropologist and author of many scientific articles, American writer Mary Doria Russell published her first novel, *The Sparrow*, to great acclaim in 1996. Concerned primarily with the exploration of RELIGION and the religious impulse, the book thematically resembles the classic *A Case of Conscience* (1958) by JAMES BLISH, although it sets out to discuss slightly different issues.

The novel follows the progress of Jesuit priest Emilio Sandoz and his mission to the distant PLANET Rakhat to make first contact with a race of intelligent ALIENS. These aliens have made their presence known to humanity by transmitting beautiful songs across the void of space.

The Jesuits mount a mission of peace – they wish only to discover the nature of these aliens and their relationship to God. However, things go horrifically wrong: a failure in communication between the two races leads to Sandoz returning to Earth raped and maimed, the only surviving member of his team. Upon his return he is chastised and sidelined by the Church, blamed for the terrible failure of the mission as a whole.

The Sparrow is a powerful and haunting book, a serious exercise in the exploration of self and the deeper questions of faith that sets out to analyse barriers to interracial awareness and understanding.

The book won both the JAMES TIPTREE MEMORIAL AWARD and the ARTHUR C. CLARKE AWARD for its year.

Russell's next novel, *Children of God* (1998), is a direct sequel to *The Sparrow*. It begins with the Jesuits approaching Sandoz to lead a second mission to Rakhat. But, after the distress he suffered during the first mission, he has renounced the priesthood and married. At the same time, the alien inhabitants of Rakhat have thrown themselves into war, a conflict sparked off by the original arrival of the humans. The second mission nevertheless goes ahead, and eventually leads Sandoz to a reconciliation with his God.

Together, the two novels comprise one of the most satisfying literary attempts to reconcile the spirituality of religion with the uncompromising outlook of science. Russell depicts her alien planet and her human characters with skill and sensitivity.

Russell is reportedly working on another novel, mainstream rather than genre. Still, even if she never again turns to SF for a setting, she has enriched it sufficiently with her two novels to date.

A website is maintained at http://www.literati.net/Russell/

See Also
ALIEN; LITERARY SF; PLANET; RELIGION; SPACE TRAVEL

Recommended Further Reading
Behold the Man (1969) by MICHAEL MOORCOCK; *A Case of Conscience* (1958) by JAMES BLISH; *A Canticle for Leibowitz* (1959) by WALTER MILLER

Bibliography
The Sparrow (1996)
Children of God (1998)

RYMAN, GEOFF (1951–   ), Canada

Geoff Ryman's production of genre material over the years has been relatively low in volume but consistently high in quality.

Born in Canada, but for a long time resident in London, Ryman began publishing short fiction during the 1970s in various genre magazines and his first novel, a fantasy entitled *The Warrior Who Carried Life*, appeared in 1985.

However, it was with the magazine publication of his novella *The Unconquered Country* in 1984 that Ryman began to produce the LITERARY, bold and HUMANIST SF that would mark him out as one of the field's most poignant commentators.

The story is set in a ravaged land – clearly a version of Cambodia, although this is never explicitly stated within the text. It follows the progress of a woman who is forced to rent out her womb for the organic growth of weapons so that she may eke out a living. Harrowing and profound, yet written in the most exquisite prose, the novella won the BSFA AWARD and the World Fantasy Award upon publication, and was republished as the title story of a 1986 collection.

Ryman followed *The Unconquered Country* with *The Child Garden* (1988), a novel equally moving in its portrayal of a human life in conflict with a repressive future society.

The setting is essentially that of an ALTERNATE WORLD, a subtropical London where people are educated and controlled by GENETICALLY altered viruses. Thought patterns are interrupted by the introduction of new genes that 'correct' any dysfunctional thoughts and cause every person to behave in the same way. Milena, the chief protagonist, has been brought up in a 'child garden' but is immune to the viruses. She cannot be 'cured' and she is unique among her peers. She is an artist, a homosexual and a natural wonder. Her passions run high, she gets angry, she recognizes the need for love and attachment in a world where human beings have become slaves to their own altered DNA. Milena is humanity's only redemption in this brutal, unforgiving DYSTOPIA. The novel won both the ARTHUR C. CLARKE AWARD and the JOHN W. CAMPBELL MEMORIAL AWARD for its year, and deserves to be far wider read than it is.

A recurring concern in much of Ryman's SF is the loss of pride and sellfhood consequent on the removal of humanity's biological privacy. Several of Ryman's characters become shells that are constantly, horrifically raped – the woman who grows weapons in her womb, a man who stores other people's thoughts in his mind, a child who is forced into bland normality by changes to its own DNA. These characters become symbolic of the isolated people who live outside society in a world rushing headlong into the future.

Ryman's recent novels have tended to move away from the SF genre: *Was* (1992) is a surreal fantasy inspired by *The Wizard of Oz*, whilst *253*

(1998) is set on a Tube train in modern London and was originally published on the Internet.

See Also
DYSTOPIA; ECOLOGY; GENETICS; HUMANIST SF; LITERARY SF

Recommended Further Reading
China Mountain Zhang (1992) by MAUREEN F. McHUGH; *The Left Hand of Darkness* (1972) by URSULA K. LE GUIN

Bibliography
The Warrior Who Carried Life (1985)
The Unconquered Country (1986)
The Child Garden (1988)
Coming of Enkidu (1989)
Was (1992)
253 (1998)
Lust (2001)

SCIENCE FANTASY MAGAZINE

Science Fantasy was a British magazine that began as a companion publication to NEW WORLDS in 1950 and ran until 1966, at which point it changed its name to *Impulse* and ran for a further twelve issues (the last seven appearing as *SF Impulse*) before being terminated.

After *Science Fantasy*'s first two issues, *New Worlds* editor John Carnell edited both magazines, although *Science Fantasy* always had a slightly less reliable publication schedule. It featured an eclectic mix of fantasy and SF, including some of the early *Eternal Champion* stories by MICHAEL MOORCOCK and a large amount of JOHN BRUNNER's early work. It also published the first stories of both BRIAN ALDISS and J. G. BALLARD, although much of their work from that point on tended to be published in *New Worlds*.

Under Carnell, *Science Fantasy* flourished, perhaps more so than *New Worlds*. The magazine certainly looked better, and much of the fiction was of a slightly higher calibre than the stories he was publishing in its sister magazine.

With a change of publishers in 1964 came a change of editors for both magazines. Moorcock took on *New Worlds* while *Science Fantasy* was handed over to Kyril Bonfiglioli.

The frequency and format changed to a more reliable monthly rack-size paperback. In March 1966 *Science Fantasy* changed its name to *Impulse* (and later, in August the same year, to *SF Impulse*). Bonfiglioli stayed on as editor for the first seven issues, after which HARRY HARRISON and KEITH ROBERTS shared the workload. But despite the high quality of the material published in the magazine, adverse market conditions meant that it had to cease publication in 1967, its final issue appearing in February that year.

Over the years of its existence and in its various manifestations *Science Fantasy* was one of the most important British genre magazines. A large number of now-classic stories first appeared in its pages, including Moorcock's early *Elric* stories, Roberts's *Pavane* and Harrison's *Make Room! Make Room!* Many of the authors went on to publish further work in *New Worlds*, with which magazine *Science Fantasy / Impulse* ultimately merged.

SHAW, BOB (1931–1996), Great Britain

Northern Irish writer Bob Shaw was one of the great ideas men of the genre. His imagination knew no bounds, and his enduring creations – 'Slow Glass', 'Orbitsville', the funnel of atmosphere that exists between two planets in his *Ragged Astronauts* sequence – are often recognized as some of the genre's most inventive.

Shaw began his publishing career in the 1950s with a number of short stories for magazines such as *Authentic* and *Nebula*. However, he then stopped writing for nearly a decade before making a well-received return in 1965 with a couple of short stories for ASTOUNDING SCIENCE FICTION. He published his first novel, *Night Walk*, in 1967.

Night Walk concerns the plight of a man called Sam Tallon who has been unjustly imprisoned on a penal PLANET and has had his eyes removed as a punishment for non-cooperation with the authorities. However, he has a secret that he needs to convey to Earth, so he devises an excruciating method of 'seeing', first through the eyes of various animals, then through the eyes of his captors. He uses this ability to assist his escape and, eventually, to get the secret off the planet. The novel is an early indication of Shaw's inventive and powerful imagination.

A series of fairly standard yet enjoyable SPACE OPERAS followed, many tailored towards the American market where they were first published. But with the publication of *Other Days, Other Eyes* (1972), Shaw made a distinct mark on the genre

The book incorporates and revises an earlier (1966) short story, 'Light of Other Days', for which Shaw had been nominated for a NEBULA AWARD and whose premise is simple, yet intriguing. A scientist has developed 'slow glass' – which takes light a number of years to penetrate. This means that the glass can 'record' scenes from the past, as they will not be seen until the light has eventually made its way through to the other side. One of the most poignant scenes in the book comes when a character visits a glass 'farm', where they sell windows with ten years of a beautiful view retained in them, and finds that a woman and child he has seen peering out of a window up at the farmer's house have been dead for six years.

Shaw's next novel, *Orbitsville* (1975), is one of the few attempts in SF to utilize the concept of a DYSON SPHERE, a spherical structure built around a star to make use of its total energy output and with an inner surface that acts as a habitable space.

In *Orbitsville*, a group of astronauts encounters one such sphere, with a surface area vastly greater than that of the Earth and attempts to discover its enigmatic secrets. The structure turns out to be of ALIEN origin, and an odyssey of exploration ensues.

Two sequels followed *Orbitsville*. They were *Orbitsville Departure* (1983) and *Orbitsville Judgement* (1990).

During this period, Shaw was prolific. His next book, *A Wreath of Stars* (1976), describes the disaster caused when an antineutrino star passes through the Solar System and reveals a 'ghost' PLANET hidden within our own. *Medusa's Children* (1977) is a complex yet inviting story of ship-wrecks and the possible transcendent life of the survivors in an under-water environment amongst the stars, while *Vertigo* (1978) examines the impact that personal ANTI-GRAVITY devices have upon a NEAR-FUTURE society.

During the 1980s, however, much of Shaw's work failed to live up to the standards of speculative thought that his previous books had achieved – until publication of *The Ragged Astronauts* (1986), which began his *Ragged Astronauts* sequence and described, ingeniously, the voyage of a manned balloon between two neighbouring planets linked by a column of atmosphere. Two further volumes continued the adventures of the unusual astronauts after they landed on the other world: among other dramatic events, a war breaks about between the two planets. These sequels are *The Wooden Spaceships* (1988) and *The Fugitive Worlds* (1989).

The *Ragged Astronauts* sequence was to be Shaw's last major work: he died in 1996 at the age of sixty-five. His fiction provides many examples of inventive and imaginative SF; he was one of the most distinctively creative writers on the British genre scene during the second half of the twentieth century.

See Also
ALIEN; ARTIFICIAL ENVIRONMENT; DYSON SPHERE; SENSE OF WONDER; SPACE OPERA; TIME

Recommended Further Reading
Ringworld (1970) by LARRY NIVEN; *Rendezvous with Rama* (1973) by ARTHUR C. CLARKE; *Traces* (1998) by STEPHEN BAXTER; *The Light of Other Days* (2000) by Arthur C. Clarke and Stephen Baxter; *The Time-Lapsed Man and Other Stories* (1990) by ERIC BROWN; the *Night's Dawn Trilogy* by PETER F. HAMILTON

Bibliography
Night Walk (1967)
The Two-timers (1968)
Shadow of Heaven (1969)
The Palace of Eternity (1969)
One Million Tomorrows (1970)
Ground Zero Man (1971)
Other Days, Other Eyes (1972)
Tomorrow Lies in Ambush (short stories, 1973)
Orbitsville (1975)
Cosmic Kaleidoscope (short stories, 1976)
A Wreath of Stars (1976)
Who Goes Here? (1977)
Medusa's Children (1977)
Vertigo (1978)
Ship of Strangers (1978)
Dagger of the Mind (1979)
The Ceres Solution (1981)
Galactic Tours (with David Hardy, 1981)
A Better Mantrap (short stories, 1982)
Orbitsville Departure (1983)
Fire Pattern (1984)
Messages Found in an Oxygen Bottle (short stories, 1986)

The Ragged Astronauts (1986)
The Wooden Spaceships (1988)
Dark Night in Toyland (short stories, 1989)
Killer Planet (1989)
The Fugitive Worlds (1989)
Orbitsville Judgement (1990)
Warren Peace (1993)

SHECKLEY, ROBERT (1928–), USA

Robert Sheckley is essentially a satirist, a mordant, witty observer of society's and humanity's foibles and excesses who finds SF an ideal means for the expression of his insights and ideas.

One of Sheckley's best-known books is his first, the short-story collection *Untouched By Human Hands* (1954). It features a number of his best-known stories, such as 'The Cost of Living', 'The Monsters' and 'Specialist', the last being perhaps his most outstanding story to date, describes a galaxy inhabited by various peoples who can TRANSCEND their form, through cooperation, to become space vessels.

Sheckley's first novel, *Immortality Delivered* (1958), is more of a supernatural SCIENCE FANTASY than a straight SF novel, and narrates the exploits of a car-crash victim who is killed in the late 1950s, only to find himself waking up in a strange twenty-second-century America. It was filmed, rather unsuccessfully, as *Freejack* (1992).

This was followed two years later by *The Status Civilization* (1960), perhaps Sheckley's best book-length work. The novel is set on the penal PLANET Omega, where the protagonist is dumped after having his memory blanked out. What he finds, however, is a society where criminal activity has become the social norm. The novel is cutting and effective satire, and remains among Sheckley's most successful work to date.

Sheckley's later career has been more uneven, although both *Mindswap* (1966) and *The Alchemical Marriage of Alastair Crompton* (1978) are good, as are his short-story collections from around the same time.

He has written a *Bill, the Galactic Hero* novel with HARRY HARRISON, as well as a series of routine but effective farces with ROGER ZELAZNY. He has also written his share of media tie-in novels for the mass market.

Sheckley continues to produce his characteristically witty satirical fiction, reminding readers of a tradition of comic and thought-provoking

SF that goes back to a time well before the advent of Discworlds and galactic hitch-hikers.

See Also
COMIC SF; PLANET; SCIENCE FANTASY; SPACE; TIME

Recommended Further Reading
Bill, the Galactic Hero (1965) and *The Stainless Steel Rat* (1961) by Harry Harrison; *The Iron Dream* (1972) by NORMAN SPINRAD; *The Hitch-Hiker's Guide to the Galaxy* (1979) by DOUGLAS ADAMS

Bibliography (Selected)
Untouched by Human Hands (short stories, 1954)
Citizen in Space (short stories, 1955)
Pilgrimage to Earth (short stories, 1957)
Immortality Delivered (1958)
Store of Infinity (short stories, 1960)
Notions: Unlimited (short stories, 1960)
The Status Civilization (1960)
Journey Beyond Tomorrow (1962)
Shards of Space (short stories, 1962)
The Tenth Victim (1966)
Mindswap (1966)
The People Trap (short stories, 1968)
Dimension of Miracles (1968)
Can You Feel Anything When I Do This? (short stories, 1971)
The Robert Sheckley Omnibus (short stories, 1973)
Options (1975)
The Robot Who Looked Like Me (short stories, 1978)
The Alchemical Marriage of Alistair Crompton (1978)
Dramocles (1983)
Is *THAT What People Do?* (short stories, 1984)
Victim Prime (1987)
Hunter/Victim (1988)
Watchbird (1991)
Bill the Galactic Hero on the Planet of Bottled Brains (1990, with HARRY HARRISON)
Minotaur Maze (1991)
Alien: Starswarm (ALIEN novelization, 1991)
Bring Me the Head of Prince Charming (1991, with ROGER ZELAZNY)

If at Faust You Don't Succeed (1993, with ROGER ZELAZNY)
A Farce to be Reckoned With (1995, with ROGER ZELAZNY)
Alien: Harvest (ALIEN novelization, 1995)
The Laertian Gamble (STAR TREK novelization, 1995)
Soma Blues (1997)
A Call to Arms (BABYLON 5 novelization, 1999, with J. Michael Straczynski)
Godshome (1999)

SHELLEY, MARY WOLLSTONECRAFT (1797–1851), Great Britain

Born in 1797, Mary Wollstonecraft Shelley spent her early years in London. Her parents were well known: her mother, who died just ten days after giving birth, was Mary Wollstonecraft, the feminist author of *The Vindication of the Rights of Women* (1792), and her father was William Godwin, political philosopher, novelist and social commentator.

At the relatively young age of seventeen, Mary became involved with the poet Percy Bysshe Shelley, who at the time was a married man, and they eloped to Switzerland. Two years later they married, after Shelley's first wife had committed suicide.

During 1816, the year of their marriage, the Shelleys spent much time with Lord George Byron, the famous poet, at his villa by Lake Geneva. It was during this period that *Frankenstein* (1818) had its genesis.

A challenge was suggested – that each of the small group, which also included John Polidori, Byron's physician, should produce a ghost story. Byron and Shelley wrote nothing of substance in response, Polidori produced his now-classic *The Vampyre* (1819) and Mary began work on *Frankenstein*.

Although technically a Gothic Romance, *Frankenstein* has become one of the most enduring novels to be associated with the SF genre, its images recurring time and again in later works by generation after generation of authors who have fallen under its spell.

It tells the story of Dr Frankenstein, a surgeon who becomes obsessed with the notion that electricity can be used to reanimate the dead. This was indeed a notion that Mary Shelley might have come across when listening to her father hold discussions with other thinkers of the time. In the book, Frankenstein gruesomely pieces together a body from various reclaimed parts and attempts to animate it with an electric shock. He is successful, and the 'monster' comes to life. However, Frankenstein is soon repulsed by his creation and the 'monster' learns bitterness, hate and disgust from its creator: Frankenstein has not only made a living being, he has nurtured a beast. The 'monster' requests that a female companion be made for it so that it may come to know love. When Frankenstein refuses, the 'monster' goes on a murderous rampage that ultimately leads to both its own and Frankenstein's downfall.

In his 1973 study of SF, *Billion Year Spree*, BRIAN ALDISS made a case for *Frankenstein* as the first true SF novel, showing as it does an awareness of current technology and scientific theory and extrapolating it to create a fresh perspective. Indeed, over recent years this line of reasoning has become more and more accepted, although there is still some reason to see *Frankenstein* as more important to the development of Gothic Romance than to science fiction – the next true SF novels were not to appear until nearly fifty years later with the publication of JULES VERNE's *Journey to the Centre of the Earth* (1864) and there was no indication that they had in any way been influenced by Shelley's novel. Nevertheless, the novel does indeed make good use of current scientific thought and poses a moral dilemma whose complexity even rivals those of today's best genre writers; if it was to be published for the first time now it would clearly be marketed as a work of SF.

After *Frankenstein*, Shelley was to produce a number of other books that have no bearing on the genre today, but her *The Last Man* (1826) is certainly of interest. It is set towards the end of the twenty-first century when a plague has drastically reduced humanity's numbers and the protagonist, immune to the disease, wanders the desolate landscapes of Europe in search of survivors. It successfully portrays a bleak and ravaged world and prefigures many POST-APOCALYPTIC novels to come.

Other stories of interest are collected in *Tales and Stories* (1891).

Mary Shelley died in 1851, aged fifty-four.

See Also
The History and Origins of SF; ANDROID; GENETICS; POLITICAL SF; ROBOT

Recommended Further Reading
Frankenstein Unbound (1973) by BRIAN ALDISS; *Do Androids Dream of Electric Sheep?* (1968) by PHILIP K. DICK; the *Robot* sequence by ISAAC ASIMOV

Bibliography (Selected)
Frankenstein (1818)
The Last Man (1826)
Tales and Stories (short stories, 1891)

SHEPARD, LUCIUS (1947–   ), USA

An author proficient in many genres, including SF, fantasy and HORROR, Lucius Shepard has produced a number of works of genre interest.

His first novel, *Green Eyes* (1984), which won the JOHN W. CAMPBELL AWARD, tells the story of a a group of researchers who successfully create zombies by injecting corpses with bacteria recovered from a graveyard. As might be expected, one of the zombies escapes from the laboratory. Although not strictly SF, the novel makes use of the genre for concepts, devices and themes, which together with Shepard's fluid prose makes for a story that *feels* very science fictional in tone and style.

Shepard's second novel, *Life During Wartime* (1987), is more explicitly SF in its elements, although at its heart it is more a study of war and TRANSCENDENCE. It is set in a NEAR-FUTURE Latin American country during a Vietnam-style war. Also of genre interest is the collection *Barnacle Bill the Spacer and Other Stories* (1997) which includes Shepard's NEBULA AWARD-winning title novella.

If he turned his hand to genre SF more often, Shepard would undoubtedly make a much greater impact on the field. As it is, he is a writer ready to make use, from story to story, of whatever category of fiction best suit his considerable narrative talent.

See Also
HORROR; NEAR FUTURE; TRANSCENDENCE

Recommended Further Reading
The Forever War (1974) by JOE HALDEMAN; *Downwards to the Earth* (1970) by ROBERT SILVERBERG

Bibliography
Green Eyes (1984)
The Jaguar Hunter (short stories, 1987)
Life During Wartime (1987)
The Scalehunter's Beautiful Daughter (1988)

Nantucket Slayrides (short stories, 1989, with Robert Frazier)
The Father of Stones (1989)
Kalimantan (1990)
The Ends of the Earth (short stories, 1991)
The Golden (1993)
The Last Time (1995)
Barnacle Bill the Spacer and Other Stories (short stories, 1997)
Beast of the Heartland (short stories, 1999)

SILVERBERG, ROBERT (1935–   ), USA

Robert Silverberg is one of the most prolific authors the SF genre has ever seen. In his early writing days his output of stories for various American magazines under a range of pseudonymns was phenomenal.

His first novel, *Revolt on Alpha C* (1955), was a juvenile, but he followed this with a succession of SPACE OPERAS and straightforward SF adventures, some of them collaborations, others pseudonymous, that saw him through to the beginning of the 1960s.

The later years of the 1960s marked the advent of a steady period of growth for Silverberg, a period that would see him develop into one of the most exceptional SF authors of his era. *Thorns* (1967) and *Hawksbill Station* (1968) are perhaps most representative of this period, the first novel being an interesting and humane tale of a dominating corporate man attempting to affect the lives of two disabled citizens of the future, whilst the second ingeniously explores how a totalitarian regime could use TIME-travel technology to abandon its criminals in the deep and hostile past.

Silverberg has gone on to write many more superb novels. *Nightwings* (1969) sees the Earth ruled by hostile ALIENS, with the human protagonist having to sneak around in disguise to avoid discovery. He eventually succeeds in TRANSCENDING his lowly position. *Tower of Glass* (1970) shows how an egomaniac of a man tyrannizing a group of ANDROIDS eventually leads to his own downfall. It is still, along with PHILIP K. DICK'S *Do Androids Dream of Electric Sheep?* (1968), one of the most satisfactory explorations of the android theme. *Downward to the Earth* (1970) is a study of alien RELIGION and a former planetary colonist's attempts to make amends. *The World Inside* (1971) is set on the crowded world of the twenty-fourth century, where people are holed up in enormous vertical structures or cities. *Dying Inside* (1972), perhaps Silverberg's single most successful novel, is a poignant portrait of a man slowly losing the telepathic powers he has learned to rely on all his life, while *The Book of Skulls* (1972) concerns a search for immortality by a group of students, some of whom must be sacrificed if the others wish to attain their goals.

After 1976, Silverberg stopped writing for four years, claiming disenchantment with the workings of the SF marketplace as his reason. But in 1980 he returned with the first volume of a new, epic and ambitious series.

Lord Valentine's Castle (1980) begins Silverberg's *Majipoor Chronicles*, a vast SCIENCE FANTASY set upon the massive planet Majipoor that is home to masses of alien species who live side by side with sorcery. Further volumes followed – *The Majipoor Chronicles* (1982), *Valentine Pontifex* (1983), *The Mountains of Majipoor* (1995), *Sorcerers of Majipoor* (1997) and *Lord Prestimion* (1998). All develop the original story but the books appear to be written according Silverberg's perception of the commercial requirements of the contemporary marketplace and read as though aimed at readers of epic-fantasy sagas. On this level, though, they work well enough.

However, Silverberg did continue to produce important SF titles alongside the books in the *Majipoor* sequence. *Hot Sky at Midnight* (1994) sees the Earth blighted by an ECOLOGICAL disaster of humanity's own making, and explores the possible routes that the human race may take to survive. It is unerring in its detailed and terrifying portrayal of a planet dominated by mass corporations, with a population reliant on a technocratic elite, but perhaps lets the populace off a little too lightly in its closing chapters. *Starbourne* (1996) sees a desperate group of humans attempting to escape from a dying Earth to find a new Eden in the stars, whilst *The Alien Years* (1997) tackles the alien-invasion theme with a panache and exuberance that harks back to Silverberg's earlier work.

Silverberg remains one of the key American SF writers of our time, and many of his novels from the late 1960s and early 1970s have become recognized as true classics of the genre. His place in the SF hall of fame is already guaranteed, and he continues to produce exciting and innovative stories that appeal to the reader's SENSE OF WONDER and deliver an abundance of exciting, intriguing ideas with an impressive LITERARY flair.

See Also
ALIEN; ANDROID; ECOLOGY; HUMANIST SF; LITERARY SF; MESSIAH; RELIGION; SCIENCE FANTASY; SENSE OF WONDER; SPACE OPERA; TRANSCENDENCE

Recommended Further Reading

Do Androids Dream of Electric Sheep? (1968) by Philip K. Dick; *Stand On Zanzibar* (1968) by JOHN BRUNNER; *The Stars My Destination* (1956) by ALFRED BESTER

Bibliography (Selected)

Revolt on Alpha C (1955)
The Thirteenth Immortal (1957)
Master of Life and Death (1957)
The Shrouded Planet (1957, with Randall Garrett)
Aliens from Space (1958)
Stepsons of Terra (1958)
Invaders from Earth (1958)
Invisible Barriers (1958)
Lest We Forget Thee, Earth (1958)
Starhaven (1958)
The Dawning Light (1958, with Randall Garrett)
The Plot Against Earth (1959)
Starman's Quest (1959)
The Planet Killers (1959)
Lost Race of Mars (1960)
Collision Course (1961)
Recalled to Life (1962)
The Seed of Earth (1962)
The Silent Invaders (1963)
Time of the Great Freeze (1964)
One of Our Asteroids is Missing (1964)
Regan's Planet (1964)
Godling, Go Home! (short stories, 1964)
Conquerors from the Darkness (1965)
To Worlds Beyond (short stories, 1965)
Needle in a Timestack (short stories, 1966)
The Gate of Worlds (1967)
Thorns (1967)
Planet of Death (1967)
Those Who Watch (1967)
The Time-Hoppers (1967)
To Open the Sky (1967)
Hawksbill Station (1968)
The Masks of Time (1968)

Nightwings (1969)

Across a Billion Years (1969)

Dimension Thirteen (short stories, 1969)

The Man in the Maze (1969)

To Live Again (1969)

Up the Line (1969)

Three Survived (1969)

World's Fair 1992 (1970)

The Cube Root of Uncertainty (short stories, 1970)

Downward to the Earth (1970)

Parsecs and Parables (short stories, 1970)

Tower of Glass (1970)

The Book of Skulls (1971)

Son of Man (1971)

A Time of Changes (1971)

The World Inside (1971)

The Reality Trip and Other Implausibilities (short stories, 1972)

The Second Trip (1972)

Dying Inside (1972)

Valley Beyond Time (short stories, 1973)

Unfamiliar Territory (short stories, 1973)

Earth's Other Shadow (short stories, 1973)

Sundance and Other Science Fiction Stories (short stories, 1974)

Born With the Dead (short stories, 1974)

Sunrise on Mercury (short stories, 1975)

The Stochastic Man (1975)

Shadrach in the Furnace (1976)

Capricorn Games (short stories, 1976)

The Shores of Tomorrow (short stories, 1976)

The Songs of Summer and Other Stories (short stories, 1979)

Lord Valentine's Castle (1980)

The Majipoor Chronicles (short stories, 1982)

World of a Thousand Colors (short stories, 1982)

Lord of Darkness (1983)

Valentine Pontifex (1983)

Gilgamesh the King (1984)

The Conglomeroid Cocktail Party (short stories, 1984)

Tom O'Bedlam (1985)

Star of Gypsies (1986)

Project Pendulum (1987)

At Winter's End (1988)
The Mutant Season (1989, with Karen Haber)
The Queen of Springtime (1989)
To the Land of the Living (1989)
Letters from Atlantis (1990)
Nightfall (1990, with ISAAC ASIMOV)
Lion Time in Timbuctoo (1990)
The Face of the Waters (1991)
Thebes of the Hundred Gates (1991)
Child of Time (1991, with ISAAC ASIMOV)
Kingdoms of the Wall (1992)
The Positronic Man (1992, with ISAAC ASIMOV)
Hot Sky at Midnight (1994)
The Mountains of Majipoor (1995)
Starbourne (1996)
The Alien Years (1997)
Sorcerers of Majipoor (1997)
Lord Prestimion (1998)
Sailing to Byzantium (short stories, 2000)

SINCLAIR, ALISON, Great Britain

Born and educated in England, Alison Sinclair has held various posts at sundry institutions around the world. She is currently a resident Anatomic Pathologist at the University of Calgary, as well as a promising SF writer.

Her first novel, *Legacies* (1995), begins on the colony PLANET Burdania. When the inhabitants decide that the colony is failing, they start preparations to move to another world. However, in doing so they activate an experimental star-drive that devastates the surface of the planet. Years later, the colony has settled on a new planet, Taridwyn, and have made contact with the native ALIENS. The story truly begins when a group of the colonists, prompted by the aliens and a man brain-damaged in a childhood accident, decide to return to Burdania and confront their past.

The novel is a good example of LITERARY SF, and successfully blends much-used genre concepts and devices into something that, if not entirely original, is certainly worthy of note.

Sinclair's second novel, *Blueheart* (1996), is again set on a distant colony planet, this time one covered by a world-spanning ocean. Many of the protagonists have been GENETICALLY altered to allow them to survive underwater. However, these adapted humans have begun to form their own subsurface community, entirely separate from the scientists who are confined to an underwater base. This is seen as lawless behaviour by the governing body, and the novel focuses on the relationships between the two groups and the resulting debate over the basic human rights of a genetically altered subspecies.

The next book has an entirely different setting. In *Cavalcade* (1998), aliens arrive on Earth unannounced and invite the human race to join them on a one-way trip to the stars. Various people take up the offer, only to find that, once on board the alien vessel, things are not as they seem and they must find a way to communicate with their captors without the aid of their failing terrestrial technology. Filled with mystery and suspense, *Cavalcade* nevertheless suffers from the lack of a dramatically realized setting such as the colony planets featured in *Legacies* and *Blueheart*. This is not to say that the alien environment is not well portrayed, simply that Sinclair's earlier work was especially notable for its beautifully described landscapes.

More recently, Sinclair has been working in collaboration with Linda Williams on *Throne Price* (2000), the first in the projected *Okal Rel* sequence about two communities descended from human colonists. These communities remember Earth only as a myth: they have forgotten their ancient heritage. Now the two cultures, after being separated for a thousand years, are struggling to coexist.

Sinclair's next solo novel is the projected *Opal*.

The author maintains a website at http://www.sff.net/people/asinclair

See Also
ALIEN; GENETICS; LITERARY SF; PLANET

Recommended Further Reading
Tau Zero (1970) by POUL ANDERSON; *Expatria* (1991) by KEITH BROOKE

Bibliography
Legacies (1995)
Blueheart (1996)
Cavalcade (1998)

Throne Price (projected, 2000, with Linda Williams)
Opal (projected)

SMITH, CORDWAINER (1913–1966), USA

The SF of Cordwainer Smith is not voluminous but what there is of it is LITERARY and evocative. Almost all of it takes place within the framework of a vast and well-realized FUTURE HISTORY, *The Instrumentality of Mankind*.

The stories that comprise this future history are collected in *The Rediscovery of Man* (1988), *The Instrumentality of Mankind* (1979) and the novel *Norstrilia* (1975). All previous collections of Cordwainer Smith stories are reassembled in these later volumes.

Smith led an interesting life and for many years was resident in China, serving there during World War Two with the US Army Intelligence Corps. The name 'Cordwainer Smith' was just one of the several pseudonyms that were adopted by writer Paul Myron Anthony Linebarger during his short lifetime.

In the *Instrumentality* books, humanity has become decadent and effete, ruled by the Instrumentality, a hereditary ruling class founded by a right-wing militant who was awoken from a spell of suspended animation. Initially, SPACE flight is developed and spacecraft are piloted by 'Scanners', men who have had certain areas of their brains manipulated to allow them to control their vessels. Later, advances in technology allow the TERRAFORMING of other planets and new means of spaceflight. The Instrumentality also adopts GENETIC engineering as a way of turning the animal races into a semi-sentient underclass of slaves. The stories in the sequence span many thousands of years and chart the development of the race as it expands across the gulfs of space.

The only full-length novel in the history, *Norstrilia*, focuses on the eponymous colony world, which is ethnically Australian in nature. Upon this planet is found the drug stroon, which confers immortality on its users – thus the Instrumentality becomes ever more powerful. Capitalizing on this drug, a native of Norstrilia, Rod McBan, becomes enormously rich and is able to actually buy Earth.

The novel is witty in tone and lyrical in style, if a little bizarre, and plays an integral part in the overall sequence.

One of the best-realized future histories in the genre, the *Instrumentality of Mankind* sequence has rightly become a classic.

Cordwainer Smith died in 1966, aged fifty-three.

See Also
CRYONICS; GENETICS; LITERARY SF; FUTURE HISTORY; TERRAFORMING; SPACE

Recommended Further Reading
The *Future History* sequence by ROBERT HEINLEIN; the *Technic History* sequence by POUL ANDERSON

Bibliography (Selected)
You Will Never Be the Same (short stories, 1963)
The Planet Buyer (1964)
Space Lords (short stories, 1965)
Quest of the Three Worlds (short stories, 1966)
The Underpeople (1968)
Under Old Earth and Other Explorations (short stories, 1970)
Stardreamer (short stories, 1971)
Norstrilia (1975)
The Instrumentality of Mankind (short stories, 1979)
The Rediscovery of Man (short stories, 1988)

SMITH, E. E. 'DOC' (1890–1965), USA

E. E. Smith is often heralded to be the originator of the SPACE OPERA genre. He was a food chemist who began his writing career with the serialization of his episodic novel *The Skylark of Space* in HUGO GERNSBACK's AMAZING STORIES magazine in the late 1920s.

The story revolves around the discovery of an ANTI-GRAVITY substance by a young scientist who uses it to build a space vessel and go adventuring through the universe. On his travels he meets all manner of strange ALIENS, as well as an enemy scientist. Today, *The Skylark of Space* seems simplistic, with its naive depiction of good and evil as well as its uncritical espousal of American middle-class values. Nevertheless, it was deeply influential, and although it reads like a *Boys' Own* adventure there is an inherent SENSE OF WONDER to it. Smith's was the first real Space Opera, a truly epic romance played out against the backdrop of interstellar space.

The Skylark of Space was first published in book form in 1946, and was followed by three sequels, the first two of which were serialized in genre magazines during the 1930s: *Skylark Three* (1948), *Skylark of Valeron* (1949) and the belated *Skylark DuQuesne* (1966). Although the *Skylark* sequence can be seen as the genre's first attempt at Space Opera, Smith's later *Lensmen* series represents the real flowering of the form.

The *Lensmen* stories saw magazine publication during the GOLDEN AGE of SF, when JOHN W. CAMPBELL was editing ASTOUNDING SCIENCE FICTION. Even as Campbell was shifting the emphasis of his magazine over to serious, thoughtful SF, he continued to publish Smith's steady output of spirited Space Opera. By this time Smith had many fans, and regular publication of his work ensured a continuing wide readership for the magazine.

Essentially, the *Lensmen* stories tell the tale of Kim Kinnison who learns to wield the power of the Lens, a bracelet that bestows on him psychic powers, and eventually comes to realize the part he will play in a vast interstellar struggle. Two opposing races, the Arisians and the Eddorians, have been locked for millions of years in an ongoing struggle. The good Arisians have initiated a selective breeding programme that will, in time, see a race of superhumans born who will be able to confront and defeat the evil Eddorians. However, the children of this breeding programme, the offspring of humanity, must discover for themselves the truth behind their existence, and from then on participate consciously in the fight for universal justice.

The *Lensmen* novels, like their predecessors, the *Skylark* sequence, now appear a little dated. The prose is not of a particularly high standard and the moralizing is naive. Nevertheless, there is a certain quality to Smith's stories, a fundamental narrative zest, that has sustained their popularity over the years. The *Lensmen* series begins with *Triplanetary* (1948) and continues with *First Lensmen* (1950), *Galactic Patrol* (1950), *Gray Lensman* (1951), *Second-Stage Lensman* (1953), *Children of the Lens* (1954) and *The Vortex Blaster* (1960).

Smith wrote a number of 'singletons', none of them as notable as the novels make up his two major series. A later series of novels, the *Lord Tedric* sequence, appeared under Smith's name, but were mostly written by Gordon Eklund.

See Also

ALIENS; SCIENCE FANTASY; SPACE OPERA; SPACE TRAVEL

Recommended Further Reading

The *Gap* sequence by STEPHEN DONALDSON; the *Night's Dawn* Trilogy by PETER F. HAMILTON; the *Culture* sequence by IAIN M. BANKS

Bibliography
The Skylark of Space (1946)
Spacehounds of IPC (1947)
Skylark Three (1948)
Triplanetary (1948)
Skylark of Valeron (1949)
First Lensman (1950)
Galactic Patrol (1950)
Gray Lensman (1951)
Second-Stage Lensmen (1953)
Children of the Lens (1954)
The Vortex Blaster (1960)
The Galaxy Primes (1965)
Subspace Explorers (1965)
Skylark DuQuesne (1966)
The Best of E. E. 'Doc' Smith (1975)
Masters of Space (1976, with E. Everett Evans)
The Imperial Stars (1976, with Stephen Goldin)
Lord Tedric (1978, with Gordon Eklund)
Subspace Encounter (1983, with Lloyd Arthur Eshbach)

SMITH, MICHAEL MARSHALL (1965–   ), Great Britain

Michael Marshall Smith spent much of his youth abroad in the USA, South Africa and Australia. He then returned to England and worked for a time as a comedy writer for the BBC. His first novel, *Only Forward* (1993), draws on this varied experience.

Only Forward is a strange story. Its setting is a place known only as 'The City', a sprawling metropolis divided into separate neighbourhoods, each one self-governing and each with its own bizarre character. First there is the Centre, the hub of The City in which people are driven only to achieve, in whatever they do. Then there is Colour, a neighbourhood in which the surroundings change colour chameleon-like to suit the clothes of its residents. Next is Sound, where everyone is forbidden from making noise of any sort, and Ffnaph, where people are attempting to keep their heads in the clouds, literally. Into this strange environment comes Stark, a man whose job it is to trace and rescue a kidnap victim who is lost somewhere in the labyrinth of The City.

The novel's satirical perspective on the city of London is easy to discern. In many ways, the book could be described as 'Dark Fantasy', a categorization that fits much of Smith's work: he is not an author who shies away from fabulation or the devices of HORROR fiction.

Smith's second novel, *Spares* (1996), is more immediately recognizable as SF. The book is set in a NEAR-FUTURE America and concerns the plight of a group of human CLONES who have been vat-grown as a form of health insurance for rich citizens; their bodies are dissected to be used as 'spare parts' as and when they are needed. But a burnt-out old hero named Jack Randall believes he can help to set the 'Spares' free.

The novel is an interesting exploration of the ethics of the cloning process and the disturbing uses to which human cloning could be put. Technically, it is also very well written. There is a seedy feel to Smith's Virginia, conveyed in dark, brooding prose; the author manages to sustain an atmosphere of terror while still more or less following genre convention. *Spares* is possibly Smith's most effective novel to date.

His next book, *One of Us* (1998), is a near-future detective novel that once again attempts to cross genre boundaries and perhaps suffers a little in the process. The book is well written and interesting – it describes a world in which dreams can be captured and then played back by other people – but feels rather unresolved between its SF and CRIME components. But it is still a satisfying read, showing that Smith is not afraid to try new techniques, including the dismantling of genre barriers.

After *What You Make It* (1999), a short-story collection featuring disturbing LITERARY horror and SF pieces, and *The Vaccinator* (2000), a Dark Fantasy novella, Smith has been at work on a new contemporary novel, *The Straw Men*. It is due for publication sometime in 2001.

A website can be found at http://www.michaelmarshallsmith.com

See Also
ALTERNATIVE REALITY; CLONES; CRIME; GENETICS; HORROR; NEAR FUTURE

Recommended Further Reading
Fairyland (1995) by PAUL J. McAULEY; *How the Other Half Lives* (2000) by JAMES LOVEGROVE

Bibliography
Only Forward (1993)
Spares (1996)
One of Us (1998)

What You Make It (short stories, 1999)
The Vaccinator (2000)
The Straw Men (projected, 2001)

SPECTRUM SF

Editor: Paul Fraser
Founded: 2000
Quarterly
Subscription address: Spectrum Publishing, PO Box 10308, Aberdeen, AB11 6ZR, UK
Website address: http://www.spectrumpublishing.com

Spectrum SF is a recently launched British genre periodical, published as a quarterly paperback book. The issues that have appeared so far have, perhaps inevitably, been compared to the now-defunct NEW WORLDS. Indeed, *Spectrum SF* seems to harbour a certain nostalgia for the 1960s and 1970s when British genre publishing was at its peak, featuring new work from some of the big SF names of that time.

Spectrum SF is a well-produced publication whose quality of content surpasses that of many other semi-professional magazines. One important distinguishing feature is the editor's willingness to commission serials. To date, the magazine has serialized new novels from both KEITH ROBERTS and John Christopher.

Typically, each issue of *Spectrum SF* will feature an episode from an ongoing serial, two novellas, two or three short stories and a selection of reviews. Other authors who have appeared in its pages include ERIC BROWN, Barrington J. Bayley, STEPHEN BAXTER and ALASTAIR REYNOLDS. It is to the editor's credit that he has featured many modern writers of the INTERZONE generation as well as older authors, thus providing readers with a balanced selection of writing.

SPINRAD, NORMAN (1940–   ), USA

During the 1960s and the heyday of the NEW WAVE movement Norman Spinrad became one of the most controversial writers working in the SF field. He wrote several bitingly satirical works that defied the conservative media conventions of the period.

Spinrad began his publishing career with a number of fairly routine SPACE OPERAS such as *The Solarians* (1966) and *Agent of Chaos* (1967), but it was with the publication of his fourth novel, *Bug Jack Barron* (1969), that he truly made his name.

The novel was originally serialized in the British NEW WORLDS magazine, and is essentially the tale of a media star who uses his influence to expose the corruption of a large corporation that is attempting to find the key to immortality. However, the story's explicit sexual scenes and strong language created a minor moral panic that caused the magazine to be withdrawn from sale by a leading news agency chain. This inevitably led to a huge downfall in sales. Today the novel does not seem especially outspoken or bold, and even at the time it was only considered scandalous within the sheltered world of genre SF.

Spinrad followed this up with one of his most inventive works of fiction, *The Iron Dream* (1972), another controversial novel that masquerades as an SF novel from an alternate world written by a Hitler who failed at politics. It pokes fun at both fascism with its corrupted dreams of power and the clichés of right-wing SF with its penchant for militaristic adventure and fetishistic weaponry. The novel is a triumph of deliberate outrageousness and marked Spinrad as a leading SF satirist.

Later novels tend not to have the hard-hitting impact of these earlier books though Spinrad continues to jest with the SF genre, producing fine examples of COMIC SF in many different forms. His most recent offering, *Greenhouse Summer* (1999), concerns an environmentally damaged world dominated by mass corporations.

Spinrad's best short fiction is collected in *The Last Hurrah of the Golden Horde* (1970) and *The Star-Spangled Future* (1979).

See Also
COMIC SF; NEW WAVE; NEW WORLDS

Recommended Further Reading
Untouched by Human Hands (1954) by ROBERT SHECKLEY; *The Man in the High Castle* (1962) by PHILIP K. DICK

Bibliography (Selected)
The Solarians (1966)
Agent of Chaos (1967)
The Men in the Jungle (1967)
Bug Jack Barron (1969)
The Last Hurrah of the Golden Horde (short stories, 1970)
The Iron Dream (1972)

No Direction Home (short stories, 1975)
Passing Through the Flame (1975)
Riding the Torch (1978)
The Star-Spangled Future (short stories, 1979)
A World Between (1979)
The Mind Game (1980)
Songs from the Stars (1980)
The Void Captain's Tale (1983)
Child of Fortune (1985)
Little Heroes (1987)
Other Americas (short stories, 1988)
The Children of Hamelin (1991)
Russian Spring (1991)
Deus X (1993)
Pictures at Eleven (1994)
Vampire Junkies (1994)
Journal of the Plague Years (1995)
Greenhouse Summer (1999)

STABLEFORD, BRIAN (1948–   ), Great Britain

Brian Stableford has worked in several genres, including fantasy and horror, although he seems to be most at home with SF. His early SPACE OPERA owes something to his training as a biologist, with its wonderfully bizarre environments inhabited by even stranger ALIEN life forms.

Stableford began his writing career in the 1960s with a number of short stories for genre magazines. His first novel, *Cradle of the Sun* (1969), is typical of the work that would follow over the intervening years.

Cradle of the Sun concerns a FAR-FUTURE Earth upon which humanity struggles against legions of rodents to remain in control of the planet. It was followed by *The Blind Worm* (1970) and *To Challenge Chaos* (1971), which are of interest partly because of their expert portrayal of exotic ecologies.

It was with the *Hooded Swan* sequence, a fine example of the modern Space Opera sub-genre, that Stableford really began to demonstrate his writing talents. The series comprises six novels – *The Halcyon Drift* (1972), *Rhapsody in Black* (1973), *Promised Land* (1974), *The Paradise Game* (1974), *The Fenris Device* (1974) and *Swan Song* (1975) – and concerns the adventures of space pilot Grainger on various missions to alien PLANETS. Grainger has been infected by a mind-altering parasite that affects both his psychology and his physical abilities.

The Realms of Tartarus (1977) was Stableford's next important book. (It is, in fact, a trilogy of novels published in one volume.) It concerns an ambiguous UTOPIAN state that exists on a vast platform above the surface of the Earth. However, in the shade beneath this platform strange life forms mutate and evolve, eventually coming into conflict with the humans living in their ignorant bliss. Stableford manages here to produce a good story containing a great deal of stimulating biological and EVOLUTIONARY speculation.

A number of similar 'biological' Space Operas followed, although much of Stableford's output during the 1980s consisted of expert non-fiction associated with the SF genre.

Empire of Fear (1988) was without doubt Stableford's most ambitious novel of the 1980s, and is possibly his most successful novel to date. It describes in wholly rational terms an ALTERNATE WORLD in which vampires from the East infiltrated and conquered Western civilization during the seventeenth century. Stableford's vampires are scientifically credible: he describes in sound and ingenious biological terms the way in which their vampiric traits might have evolved. The novel itself is written in a style reminiscent of classic SCIENTIFIC ROMANCE, and benefits greatly from Stableford's acute insights into that particular form. The later novels *The Werewolves of London* (1990), *The Angel of Pain* (1991) and *The Hunger and Ecstasy of Vampires* (1996) are similarly genre-bending.

Perhaps Stableford's best work of the 1990s was his *Genesys* trilogy, comprising *Serpent's Blood* (1995), *Salamander's Fire* (1996) and *Chimera's Cradle* (1997). The novels are set in the far future on a colony planet that has been abandoned by its human occupants. The environment has started to collapse and society has degenerated into a primitive hierarchical feudalism. The story itself is presented as a quest fantasy, in which a band of heroes set out to discover their destiny and heritage, but the novels contain, in customary Stablefordian fashion, some fascinating and serious biological extrapolation.

Stableford continues to produce LITERARY SF of a particularly high standard. Although many of his early novels were published only in America, he has long since established himself as one of Britain's most distinguished SF authors.

See Also
CRIME; ECOLOGICAL SF; EVOLUTION; GENETICS; SCIENCE
FANTASY; SCIENTIFIC ROMANCE; SPACE OPERA; SPACE
TRAVEL

Recommended Further Reading
The Seedling Stars (1957) by JAMES BLISH; the *Confluence Trilogy* and
The Secret of Life (2001) by PAUL J. McAULEY; the *Xeelee* sequence
and *Anti-Ice* (1993) by STEPHEN BAXTER; *The Book of the New Sun*
by GENE WOLFE

Bibliography
Cradle of the Sun (1969)
The Blind Worm (1970)
Day of Wrath (1971)
The Days of Glory (1971)
In the Kingdom of the Beasts (1971)
To Challenge Chaos (1972)
The Halcyon Drift (1972)
Rhapsody in Black (1973)
The Paradise Game (1974)
The Fenris Device (1974)
Promised Land (1974)
Man in a Cage (1975)
Swan Song (1975)
The Face of Heaven (1976)
The Florians (1976)
The Mind-Riders (1976)
Critical Threshold (1977)
Wildeblood's Empire (1977)
The Realms of Tartarus (1977)
The City of the Sun (1978)
The Last Days of the Edge of the World (1978)
Balance of Power (1979)
The Paradox of the Sets (1979)
The Walking Shadow (1979)
Optiman (1980)
The Castaways of Tanagar (1981)
Journey to the Centre (1982)
The Gates of Eden (1983)

The Empire of Fear (1988)
Invaders from the Centre (1990)
The Centre Cannot Hold (1990)
The Werewolves of London (1990)
The Angel of Pain (1991)
Slumming in Voodooland (1991)
The Innsmouth Heritage (1992)
Young Blood (1992)
Sexual Chemistry (short stories, 1993)
The Carnival of Destruction (1994)
Firefly (1995)
Serpent's Blood (1995)
Salamander's Fire (1996)
The Hunger and Ecstasy of Vampires (1996)
Chimera's Cradle (1997)
Inherit the Earth (1998)
Architects of Emortality (1999)
Year Zero (2000)
The Fountains of Youth (2000)
The Cassandra Complex (projected, 2001)

STAPLEDON, OLAF (1886–1950), Great Britain

Olaf Stapledon's key works constitute some of the most important writing of the SF genre, and have had a direct and lasting impact on the development of many of its standard concepts.

Born near Liverpool, England, Stapledon received a first-class education and was fortunate in that his family were moderately rich. He began publishing with a non-fiction book but it was with his first novel, *Last and First Men* (1930), that he truly came into his own.

The book is practically unique in the genre, paying no heed to ordinary characterization or plot development; indeed, the book has no individual protagonist as such. It lays down Stapledon's grand vision of the future of the human race, spanning two billion years and taking us through many varied EVOLUTIONARY stages. The novel is narrated by one of the Eighteenth Men, a variety of human almost unimaginably removed from *Homo sapiens*, who describes the many changes that have occurred over the vast amount of time since the first and most primitive race of Man: us. The scale of the book is quite staggering, and in it Stapledon creates the template for many FUTURE HISTORIES to come, as well as many other genre devices such as TERRAFORMING and the use of GENETIC ENGINEERING. *Last and First Men* reads like a chronicle of the future, a recorded history from the far reaches of time and space.

Last and First Men was followed by *Last Men in London* (1932), in which one of the Last Men has returned to the past and symbiotically bonded with one of the First Men in an attempt to raise the consciousness of the race and speed along the evolution of mankind. He fails, and the First Men are left to wallow in their primitive cities.

The intellectual and conceptual scope of these books would prepare readers for the cosmic vistas of Stapledon's other masterpiece, *Star Maker* (1937). If *Last and First Men* is imagined on a grand scale, the perspective of *Star Maker* is even more vast. The book begins with a man being whisked off a hilltop into space and given a discorporeal, universal perspective of time and space. He witnesses the development of sentient life over billions of years, from humans to symbiotic ALIENS, to Gaia-like planetary organisms, and finally encounters the Star Maker Itself. *Star Maker* remains one of the most important SF novels yet written. There is little else like it and, together with *Last and First Men*, it forms nothing less than a detailed history of the future of the universe.

Of Stapledon's other novels, *Sirius* (1944) and *Odd John* (1935) are of great genre interest. *Sirius* is regarded by many as the finest SF novel to feature a non-human protagonist. It follows the progress of the eponymous dog whose intelligence has been manipulated to raise it to the level of a human's. The dog falls in love with a human girl, and the novel explores the inner turmoil of the animal, as well as examining, through allegory, the role that intelligence plays in the development of consciousness and moral awareness.

Odd John tackles similar themes. The protagonist is a highly evolved human who achieves a superior level of intellect and, together with fellow social outcasts, founds a UTOPIAN society on an island. Eventually they destroy themselves when they find their community threatened by invasion from the outside world.

Although he was not to know it, Olaf Stapledon gave the SF genre a number of its early classics. He quietly produced philosophical, speculative fiction of the highest order that, in addition to its own intrinsic qualities, was to have a profound influence on a significant number of other major authors, including BRIAN ALDISS, JAMES BLISH and ARTHUR C. CLARKE.

See Also
ALIENS; EVOLUTION; FUTURE HISTORY; SCIENTIFIC ROMANCE

Recommended Further Reading
The *Future History* sequence by ROBERT HEINLEIN; the *Xeelee* sequence by STEPHEN BAXTER; *The Time Machine* (1895) by H. G. WELLS; *Dying Inside* (1972) by ROBERT SILVERBERG

Bibliography (Selected)
Last and First Men (1930)
Last Men in London (1932)
Odd John (1935)
Star Maker (1937)
Darkness and the Light (1942)
Old Man in New World (1944)
Sirius (1944)
Death into Life (1946)
The Flames (1947)
A Man Divided (1950)
The Opening of the Eyes (1954)
Nebula Maker (1976)
Four Encounters (short stories, 1976)

STEPHENSON, NEAL (1959–   ), USA

American author Neal Stephenson published his first novel *Snow Crash* (1992), to almost instant cult acclaim. A detailed CYBERPUNK thriller, it portrays a fractured NEAR-FUTURE America that has divided into corporate city states. The internet has developed into a VIRTUAL REALITY universe all of its own, and designer drugs are a growth industry: one such drug, Snow Crash, is causing people accidentally to fry their neural pathways. The story follows the progress of Hiro Protagonist, a pizza-delivery man who leads a double life as a hacker in the virtual-reality 'metaverse' and who must use his skills to combat a new computer virus that is insidiously invading the system.

At times both humorous and moving, *Snow Crash* was perhaps the most satisfying cyberpunk debut novel since WILLIAM GIBSON's classic 1984 novel *Neuromancer*.

Stephenson followed *Snow Crash* with *Zodiac* (1995), an

ECOLOGICAL-disaster novel that finds itself resting rather uneasily between COMIC SF and the technothriller.

The magnificent *The Diamond Age* (1996) saw Stephenson focusing once more on inventive SF. The book depicts a world blighted by an out-of-control NANOTECHNOLOGY revolution. Once again the future landscape has fractured into separate enclaves that have all set about forging their own societies. Much of the story takes place within one such enclave where Victorian values have been reinstated and a hierarchical class system has been reintroduced. The wastelands that exist outside these separated mini-states are populated by airborne nanomachines that are constantly clashing with the machines of other factions – there is a war taking place on the molecular level. In actuality, the novel tells the tale of the education of Nell, a young, underprivileged girl who happens upon a 'book' entitled *A Young Lady's Illustrated Primer*. It is actually a computer that has been forged from nanomachines, and was originally intended for the daughter of a rich Neo-Victorian gentleman. However, it has been stolen, and that crime results in significant changes in the life of Nell.

The Diamond Age is intelligent and touching, an inventive post-cyber-punk novel about humanity's changing environment and how it may evolve.

Cryptonomicon (1999), a book that exists on the periphery of the genre, was Stephenson's next novel. The story takes place in two time frames – the Second World War of the Allied code-breakers and the high-tech 'now' of a nascent data haven in contemporary south-east Asia – and is informed throughout by a keen knowledge of mathematics and cryptology. To this extent it earns its categorization as partly SF, although may perhaps be better described as technologically literate mainstream fiction. Whatever its correct description, it has captured the imagination of many readers and been nominated for various genre awards.

Cryptonomicon is the first novel in a projected sequence.

Stephenson has also written, under the pseudonym 'Stephen Bury', two technothrillers, *Interface* (1994) and *Cobweb* (1996).

See Also
COMIC SF; CYBERPUNK; NANOTECHNOLOGY

Recommended Further Reading
Neuromancer (1984) by WILLIAM GIBSON; *Queen City Jazz* (1995) by KATHLEEN ANN GOONAN; *Fairyland* (1995) by PAUL J. McAULEY

Bibliography
Snow Crash (1992)
Interface (1994, as 'Stephen Bury')
Zodiac (1995)
Cobweb (1996, as 'Stephen Bury')
The Diamond Age (1996)
Cryptonomicon (1999)

STERLING, BRUCE (1954–   ), USA

After WILLIAM GIBSON, Bruce Sterling is perhaps the most important American CYBERPUNK writer. His first novel, *Involution Ocean*
(1978), concerns the lives of a group of people who sail the dust seas on a
desperately parched PLANET, hunting for the creatures that eke out an
existence beneath the arid surface. His second, *The Artificial Kid* (1980),
prefigures certain elements of the then-imminent Cyberpunk sub-genre.

Schismatrix, Sterling's third novel, is set against a backdrop of conflict
between the Mechanists and Shapers, two different factions of humanity
who exist rather precariously in ARTIFICIAL ENVIRONMENTS in
orbit. Associated stories are collected in *Crystal Express* (1989). The
Shapers use GENETIC engineering to manipulate their own form, whilst
the Mechanists are a culture of CYBORGS who augment themselves
with various technological appendages. These two emergent cultures are
struggling for dominance, and in describing the conflict between them
Sterling contributes effectively to the debate about how the human race
will use technology to hasten EVOLUTION, tackling not only the moral
issues raised but the practical aspects also. He sees humanity as eminently
adaptable, master of its own future.

Sterling followed *Schismatrix* with another burst of high-energy
Cyberpunk, *Islands in the Net* (1988). The book is a mature and involving
NEAR-FUTURE thriller in which an apparent UTOPIA is wired
together by a vast communications network (much like an advanced
Internet), within which the heroine discovers pockets of crime and unrest.
The book is startlingly realistic in its portrayal of a post-modern future,
and many of its predictions still look set to come true.

Sterling had by now carved out a niche for himself in the emerging
world of Cyberpunk, a niche in which he could examine the themes of the
emerging genre in his own inventive way.

The Difference Engine (1990) was co-written with WILLIAM
GIBSON, and applies the Cyberpunk template to a novel of nineteenth

century industrial progress that sees Charles Babbage's early mechanical computer not only built but developing sentience.

Later books see Sterling moving more towards the realms of HARD SF, although he takes with him a number of central Cyberpunk concerns and reinvents them to fit within this more scientifically rigorous framework.

Heavy Weather (1994) is once again set in a near-future world and follows the progress of a group of scientists studying tornadoes in the American West. It is set against the backdrop of an ECOLOGICALLY damaged Earth in which global warming has irreparably damaged the weather systems.

More recently, *Distraction* (1998) was awarded the ARTHUR C. CLARKE AWARD. It describes a dislocated future DYSTOPIA where the government has fragmented and citizens lead impoverished, nomadic lives. Sterling successfully satirizes politics, the media and America itself in what is perhaps his most socially engaged novel to date.

Sterling is a visionary. His earlier works will always be associated with the Cyberpunk genre, but he has outgrown that particular label and his later work is among the most imaginative SF of recent years.

See Also
ARTIFICIAL ENVIRONMENT; BIOTECHNOLOGY; CYBER-PUNK; CYBORG; GENETICS; STEAMPUNK; VIRTUAL REALITY

Recommended Further Reading
Neuromancer (1984) by William Gibson; *reMix* (1999) by JON COURTNAY GRIMWOOD; *Hotwire* (1995) by SIMON INGS; *Synners* (1991) by PAT CADIGAN

Bibliography
Involution Ocean (1978)
The Artificial Kid (1980)
Schismatrix (1985)
Islands in the Net (1988)
Crystal Express (short stories, 1989)
The Difference Engine (1990, with WILLIAM GIBSON)
Globalhead (short stories, 1992)
Heavy Weather (1994)
Holy Fire (1997)
Distraction (1998)

A Good Old-Fashioned Future (short stories, 1999)
Hollywood Kremlin (1999)
Zeitgeist (2000)

STEVENSON, ROBERT LOUIS (1850–1894), Great Britain

Born in Scotland and for the last years of his short life resident in Samoa, Robert Louis Stevenson is best known for his works outside the SF genre such as *Treasure Island* (1883) and *Kidnapped* (1886). But it is for the excellent *The Strange Case of Dr Jekyll and Mr Hyde* (1886) that he is included here.

The story is a Victorian mystery, very much in the style of a Gothic romance, yet it prefigures much SOFT SF in its study of the psychology of its chief protagonist. The book can also be seen as a precursor of many later stories that would imitate its use of split personalities or physical transformations.

The Strange Case of Dr Jekyll and Mr Hyde follows the investigations of a Mr Utterson, a London lawyer and executor of the estate of the deceased Dr Jekyll, who becomes suspicious when he finds the benefactor of Jekyll's will to be the mysterious 'Mr Hyde'. Slowly he comes to realize the true circumstances surrounding Jekyll's death and the sinister truth of his violent alter ego.

Jekyll has been experimenting on himself, using drugs as a way of altering his psychological make-up. Things go wrong, and eventually Jekyll's violent, uncivilized self manifests itself in a physical transformation into Mr Hyde. The physical change is a metaphor for the release of Jekyll's repressed desires, represented in the story as violent murder and bitter hatred. Undoubtedly, Stevenson would also have been aware of the sexual implications of this release, although this is not explicitly stated in the book.

A fine example of a Victorian Gothic HORROR story, as well as a precursor of the more psychologically aware SF that would come later, *The Strange Case of Dr Jekyll and Mr Hyde* has ensured Stevenson his place in the history of the genre.

Robert Louis Stevenson died in 1894, aged forty-four.

See Also
HORROR; LITERARY SF; SOFT SF; TRANSCENDENCE

Bibliography
The Strange Case of Dr Jekyll and Mr Hyde (1886)

STEWART, GEORGE R. (1895–1980), USA

A professor of English at the University of California, George R. Stewart published many novels during his lifetime. Only *Earth Abides* (1949) is science fiction. However, with this one magnificent work Stewart created not only his best book but one of the true classics of the genre.

The story follows the life of Isherwood Williams, a naturalist who begins the book on a field trip in the mountains of California. When he returns he finds that a mysterious plague has devastated humanity; he is left to wander the ghost towns and empty roads, watching passively as the unchecked forces of nature begin to return the ECOLOGY to a wild, untamed state. Eventually Williams finds another survivor in San Francisco, a woman who becomes his wife. Over the years they have many children, but they cannot single-handedly maintain civilization and their offspring gradually begin to devolve into hunter-gatherers. The human race has no choice but to return to a gentler, uncomplicated existence, and the Earth abides.

The book is thought-provoking, moving and one of the finest POST-APOCALYPTIC novels of the twentieth century. Reading it now, *Earth Abides* stands as an antidote to the pessimistic, planet-destroying 'disaster' novels of the time. Stewart's ecology is accurate and well realized, and in Isherwood Williams he pays an elegaic tribute to the human condition; 'Ish' is a man who has witnessed spectacular human achievement but he must come to terms with the fact that nature does not recognise civilization and that the planet has its own type of greatness that will always endure, regardless of the doings of humanity.

See Also
ECOLOGY; POST-APOCALYPTIC

Recommended Further Reading
Engine Summer (1979) by JOHN CROWLEY; *The Death of Grass* (1956) by John Christopher

Bibliography (Selected)
Earth Abides (1949)

STURGEON, THEODORE (1918–1985), USA

Known primarily for his vast output of superb short stories, which he began publishing in ASTOUNDING SCIENCE FICTION magazine during the GOLDEN AGE, Theodore Sturgeon was one of the most profound and LITERARY of all American SF writers.

Much of Sturgeon's early work is comparable in its influence to that of contemporaries like ROBERT HEINLEIN and A. E. VAN VOGT, although it often differed markedly in its themes and psychological concerns. It was not until later, during the 1950s and after a number of years away from the field, that his true strengths as a writer became evident.

His stories from this period show a man intrigued by the human condition and perturbed by his alienation from it. Much of his work explores the feeling of being on the outside looking in; Sturgeon has his (often adolescent) characters liberate themselves either sexually or via a form of TRANSCENDENCE that in some cases involves a radical rebellion from the social norm. His best works are characterized by an emotional awareness and sensitivity rare in the genre and examine in close detail the fallibility of society and its tendency to exclude those it sees as abnormal. This is not to say that his work is pessimistic. In fact, it is quite the opposite – Sturgeon's writing is often uplifting when his characters attain their inner goals and desires regardless of their perceived social position.

This is perhaps best exemplified in his classic novel *More Than Human* (1953), in which a number of outcast characters eventually come together to form a complete gestalt entity, achieving a transcendental transformation into something new and bold. This metamorphis, Sturgeon implied, would be the next stage of human EVOLUTION.

In *The Dreaming Jewels* (1950), his first full-length novel, Sturgeon tells the story of 'child', a telepathic shapeshifter who has been 'dreamt' into existence by crystalline ALIENS, who runs away to the carnival where he is accepted by the freaks. (Some commentators believe the novel to be semi-autobiographical in its images of alienation.) The book is beautifully and movingly written and while the mechanics of the story are perhaps more those of SCIENCE FANTASY, Sturgeon was always prepared to break genre convention when he felt such a move would suit the story best.

Sturgeon's production dropped off during his later years, eventually ceasing altogether. *Venus Plus X* (1960) is his last satisfactory novel, although he did carry on producing short fiction for a while longer. The novel is one of the truest attempts to produce a work of American UTOPIAN fiction. The protagonist wakes to find himself in a world populated by beautiful hermaphrodites. At first he is shocked and sickened, but eventually he comes to realize the utopian nature of their existence.

Sturgeon's short fiction has appeared in many collections over the years. A series of uniform, complete editions is currently under way. They are *The Ultimate Egoist* (1994), *The Microcosmic God* (1995), *Killdozer!* (1996), *Thunder and Roses* (1997), *The Perfect Host* (1998), *Baby is Three* (1999) and *A Saucer of Loneliness* (2000).

See Also

ALIEN; EVOLUTION; GOLDEN AGE; HUMANIST SF; LITERARY SF; SCIENCE FANTASY; TRANSCENDENCE; UTOPIA

Recommended Further Reading

I Have No Mouth And I Must Scream (1967) by HARLAN ELLISON; *The Jewels of Aptor* (1962) by SAMUEL R. DELANY; *The Midwich Cuckoos* (1957) by JOHN WYNDHAM

Bibliography (Selected)

Without Sorcery (short stories, 1948)
The Dreaming Jewels (1950)
E Pluribus Unicorn (short stories, 1953)
More Than Human (1953)
Caviar (short stories, 1955)
A Way Home (short stories, 1955)
A Touch of Strange (short stories, 1958)
The Cosmic Rape (1958)
Aliens 4 (short stories, 1959)
Beyond (short stories, 1960)
Venus Plus X (1960)
Some of Your Blood (1961)
Voyage to the Bottom of the Sea (1961)
Sturgeon in Orbit (short stories, 1964)
. . . And My Fear is Great / Baby is Three (short stories, 1965)
Starshine (short stories, 1966)
Sturgeon is Alive and Well . . . (short stories, 1971)
The Worlds of Theodore Sturgeon (short stories, 1972)
Case and the Dreamer (short stories, 1974)
Visions and Venturers (short stories, 1978)
Maturity (short stories, 1979)
The Stars are the Styx (short stories, 1979)
The Golden Helix (short stories, 1979)

Alien Cargo (short stories, 1984)
Godbody (1986)
A Touch of Sturgeon (short stories, 1987)
The Ultimate Egoist (short stories, 1994)
The Microcosmic God (short stories, 1995)
Killdozer! (short stories, 1996)
Thunder and Roses (short stories, 1997)
The Perfect Host (short stories, 1998)
Baby is Three (short stories, 1999)
A Saucer of Loneliness (short stories, 2000)

SULLIVAN, TRICIA (1968–), USA

American high-school teacher Tricia Sullivan published her first novel, *Lethe*, in 1995. A post-CYBERPUNK thriller, it is lyrical in its prose and detailed in its technological extrapolation. The book describes a POST-APOCALYPTIC Earth devastated by the Gene Wars, a biological nightmare that has left the human race mutated and scarred. A recovery effort is run by the Heads – human brains kept alive in suspension tanks – who have created reservations of survivors and are working to restore the environment. At the same time, four supposedly ALIEN stargates have been found on a distant planetoid at the edge of the Solar System. The story follows the progress of Jenae Kim, a mutant who is able to communicate with dolphins. She has discovered some important information about the stargates, as well as an understanding of the origins of the Gene Wars, and now the Heads are seeking to eliminate her in an attempt to keep their secrets buried. The book is a remarkable debut that successfully deconstructs the cyberpunk genre and transplants its themes into something contemporary. Indeed, this can be said of all Sullivan's published SF to date.

Sullivan's second novel, *Someone to Watch Over Me* (1997), is concerned with protagonist Adrien Reyes and his relationship with C, the mysterious person who piggybacks all of his senses and emotions. C is, in fact, a disabled woman who has become disengaged from all five of her senses, and now pays to have someone, in this case Reyes, transmit all of his experiences to her via an implant and a satellite network. The novel successfully explores the seedy, voyeuristic aspects of the technology it is describing.

With her third novel, *Dreaming in Smoke* (1998), Sullivan won the ARTHUR C. CLARKE AWARD. Like its predecessors, the book makes use of many different SF concepts. It describes the lives of a group of human colonists on a distant PLANET, T'nane, who have retreated into small enclosed units on the surface that are maintained by a very powerful ARTIFICIAL INTELLIGENCE. When one of the scientists accidentally causes it to crash, the colonists are forced to attempt to find some way to survive alongside the alien biology that already exists on the planet.

The novel is detailed and LITERARY, drawing on both the cyberpunk and HARD SF genres for inspiration and devices. Although it is perhaps a little thin on background detail, it successfully established Sullivan as one of the genre's major new players.

Sullivan is currently writing a number of fantasy novels under a pseudonym. A website is under construction at http://www.sff.net/people/Sullivan

See Also
ALIEN; ARTIFICIAL INTELLIGENCE; CYBERPUNK; LITERARY SF; NEAR FUTURE; PLANET

Recommended Further Reading
Bios (1999) by ROBERT CHARLES WILSON; *A Million Open Doors* (1992) by JOHN BARNES; *New York Nights* (2000) by ERIC BROWN

Bibliography
Lethe (1995)
Someone to Watch Over Me (1997)
Dreaming in Smoke (1998)

TEPPER, SHERI S. (1929–   ), USA

Sheri Tepper is an American writer who refuses to restrict herself to one genre. She has been prolific in fantasy, HORROR, CRIME and SF for a number of years.

Tepper's first SF novel was *The Awakeners*, which was first published in two volumes, *Northshore* and *Southshore*, in 1987. It is essentially a planetary romance, set on a distant world which is divided by a great river. Many of the narrative trappings are those of SCIENCE FANTASY, but Tepper's ECOLOGICAL notions are of great interest.

However, it was with *The Gate to Women's Country* (1988) that Tepper really showed the SF genre what she could do. The book is set on a POST- APOCALYPTIC Earth where male and female settlements are almost completely separate. The men live a harsh, MILITARY-style life and the women are apparently repressed by them. However, the female protagonist concocts a plan for the women to regain their freedom and it soon becomes clear that the females are far more capable than the men in many respects. The novel is an interesting study of GENDER.

Tepper followed *The Gate to Women's Country* with a loosely linked trilogy of significant novels about human existence on ALIEN worlds. They are *Grass* (1989), *Raising the Stones* (1990) and *Sideshow* (1993). The developments of the sequence are unusually complex, but involve many of the standard genre interests such as aliens, RELIGION and mind control, as well as Tepper's fundamental concern – the role of gender in social structure.

Later books by Tepper tend to blend elements of fantasy and SF. *Gibbon's Decline and Fall* (1997), for example, sees the Earthly goddess Mother Nature reborn in an American classroom. It is deeply feminist and an interesting exploration of the matriarchal impulse. Tepper writes with skill, verve and serious intent and her fiction makes enjoyable reading.

See Also
GENDER; PLANETS; SCIENCE FANTASY; SPACE OPERA

Recommended Further Reading
The Left Hand of Darkness (1969) by URSULA K. LE GUIN; *The Canopus in Argos* sequence by DORIS LESSING; *The Handmaid's Tale* (1985) by MARGARET ATWOOD

Bibliography
King's Blood Four (1983)
Necromancer Nine (1983)
Wizard's Eleven (1984)
The Revenants (1984)
The Song of Mavin Manyshaped (1985)
The Flight of Mavin Manyshaped (1985)
The Search of Mavin Manyshaped (1985)
Jinian Footseer (1985)
Marianne, the Magus and the Manticore (1985)
Dervish Daughter (1986)
Jinian Star-Eye (1986)

Blood Heritage (1986)
The Bones (1987)
Northshore (1987)
Southshore (1987)
The Gate to Woman's Country (1988)
Marianne, the Madame, and the Momentary Gods (1988)
Marianne, the Matchbox, and the Malachite Mouse (1989)
Grass (1989)
Raising the Stones (1990)
Beauty (1991)
Sideshow (1992)
A Plague of Angels (1994)
Shadow's End (1995)
The Family Tree (1997)
Gibbon's Decline and Fall (1997)
Six Moon Dance (1998)
Singer from the Sea (1999)
The Fresco (2000)

THIRD ALTERNATIVE, THE

Editor: Andy Cox
Founded: 1993
TTA Press
Quarterly
Subscription address: TTA Press, 5 St Martins Lane, Witcham, Ely, Cambridgeshire, CB6 2LB, UNITED KINGDOM
Website address: www.tta-press.freewire.co.uk

U.K. magazine of slipstream fiction, science fiction, fantasy and horror.

The Third Alternative is a well-produced glossy A4 magazine. Editor Andy Cox appears to favour the more experimental areas of the genre, and this is reflected in both the artwork and the published fiction. This policy offers publication opportunities for new authors as well as allowing better-established authors to explore new territory.

Each issue typically features five new short stories, an interview, an in-depth study of a movie or director and news from both sides of the Atlantic. Regular contributors include CHRISTOPHER PRIEST, JAMES LOVEGROVE, DAVID LANGFORD and, more recently, Alexander Glass.

The Third Alternative has been publishing for a number of years now, and has so far managed to survive in what is often an extremely difficult market. This is no small achievement.

TURTLEDOVE, HARRY (1949–   ), USA

Harry Turtledove has recently become recognized as the finest contemporary author of ALTERNATE-WORLD SF.

Two of Turtledove's most important sequences, the *Videssos* and *Krispos* novels, concern the adventures of a legion of Roman soldiers slipped into an alternative DIMENSION where magic and sorcery actually work and a Byzantium-like Empire rules. These books are fantasy, but they make good use of alternate-history concepts and, of course, of Turtledove's excellent academic knowledge – he is a highly qualified historian with a doctorate in Byzantine history.

His later series, *Worldwar* and *Colonization*, are more obviously SF, and describe the effects that an ALIEN invasion might have had upon the outcome of the Second World War and on post-war global history. An expert and fascinating blend of military adventure, epic-scale conflict, political intrigue and informed historical speculation, these two linked sequences are the most ambitious, as well as the most entertaining, stories of contact between extraterrestrials and humanity to have appeared during the past decade.

Since so much of human history has involved various kinds of armed conflict, it is hardly surprising that an important alternate-history author such as Turtledove should focus on warfare in many of his novels. In *The Guns of the South* (1992) he skilfully adds an element of time travel to the mix to create an outstandingly successful and thought-provoking variation on the long-established theme of the South winning the American Civil War. His *Great War* series (1998 onwards) – as ambitious in its way as his *Worldwar* sequence, though with not an alien in sight – envisages a First World War, even more devastating than the one that took place in reality, fought largely on the soil of an America still politically divided between North and South.

Harry Turtledove's work, in both the fantasy and SF genres, is consistently exciting and intelligent. In the alternate-history sub-genre to which he has so successfully brought a finely developed expertise he richly deserves his present status as reigning champion.

See Also
ALTERNATE WORLD; SCIENCE FANTASY

Recommended Further Reading
Rebel in Time (1983) by HARRY HARRISON; *Oracle* (1997) by IAN
WATSON; *Pavane* (1968) by KEITH ROBERTS; *The Man in the High
Castle* (1962) by PHILIP K. DICK; *Pasquale's Angel* (1994) by PAUL J.
McAULEY

Bibliography
Wereblood (1979)
Werenight (1979)
Agent of Byzantium (1987)
The Misplaced Legion (1987)
An Emperor for the Legion (1987)
Sword of the Legion (1987)
The Legion of Videssos (1987)
Noninterference (1988)
A Different Flesh (1988)
A World of Difference (1989)
Kaleidoscope (short stories, 1990)
Krispos Rising (1991)
Krispos of Videssos (1991)
Earthgrip (1991)
Krispos the Emperor (1994)
Worldwar: In the Balance (1994)
The Stolen Throne (1995)
Worldwar: Tilting the Balance (1996)
Hammer and Anvil (1996)
Worldwar: Upsetting the Balance (1996)
King of the North (1996)
Thessalonica (1997)
The Thousand Cities (1997)
The Two Georges (1997, with Richard Dreyfuss)
Worldwar: Striking the Balance (1997)
How Few Remain (1997)
Videssos Besieged (1998)
Fox and Empire (1998)
Between the Rivers (1998)
Into the Darkness (1998)

The Great War: American Front (1998)
Colonization: Second Contact (1999)
Down in the Bottomlands and Other Places (short stories, 1999)
The Great War: Walk in Hell (1999)
Darkness Descending (2000)
Colonization: Down to Earth (2000)
Breakthrough (projected, 2000)

VANCE, JACK (1916–   ), USA

Jack Vance is a prolific and imaginative author who is equally at home with fantasy and SF. Indeed, his first novel, *The Dying Earth* (1950) successfully blends the two genres and has influenced the work of many other authors.

The book describes an exotic FAR-FUTURE Earth that is almost unimaginably ancient. The Sun sits red and swollen in the sky, and history itself has become a memory so old that its truth is lost in myth and legend. Magic has become the key to existence, as technology and sorcery have grown irreversibly intertwined and hence indistinguishable from one another. Vance explores this world in loving detail, in bold, LITERARY prose, using superbly vivid imagery.

The Dying Earth was followed by a number of sequels, which together make up one of the most inventive and compelling sequences the genre has known. They are *The Eyes of Overworld* (1966), *Cugel's Saga* (1983) and *Rhialto the Marvellous* (1984). They were collected together in one volume as *Tales of the Dying Earth* (2000).

Vance's most explicitly science-fictional early novel was the excellent *Big Planet* (1957), a planetary romance that realized its environment with a depth of detail rarely seen in the genre at the time, and set the mould for many tales of ALIEN environments to come. Indeed, *Big Planet* and its sequel *Showboat World* (1975) are two of the best explorations of alien landscapes in the genre. The story itself is concerned with a group of human astronauts who find themselves stranded on an enormous PLANET in a distant star system. They must trek for many thousands of miles across the surface of this world to find safety at a distant human settlement.

The Dragon Masters (1963) continues to develop this interest in the development and description of distant landscapes and environments. It won Vance his first HUGO AWARD, and describes life on a human colony planet that has reverted to a feudalistic social structure, and where

GENETIC engineering is used to breed captured aliens for human use. Similarly, the aliens capture and modify humans for use in their own armies. It is an intelligent, witty and pointed, story, told throughout with a detached irony of tone that Vance employs like the master stylist that he is.

Much of Vance's later SF takes the form of various series. The best of these, possibly, is the *Demon Princes* saga, a SPACE OPERA that comprises the novels *The Star King* (1964), *The Killing Machine* (1964), *The Palace of Love* (1967), *The Face* (1979) and *The Book of Dreams* (1981). The novels follow the progress of Kirth Gersen, a protagonist who is seeking to avenge his dead family and seek out those who destroyed them. As always with Vance's work, both style and story offer the reader a satisfaction found all too rarely elsewhere in the genre.

Other sequences that are tenuously linked to the *Demon Princes* titles are the *Gaean Reach* novels and the *Cadwal Chronicles*.

Vance continues to produce wondrous tales of distant lands and exotic locales. As a builder of worlds, he is unsurpassed.

See Also
ALIEN; PLANETS; SCIENCE FANTASY; SPACE OPERA

Recommended Further Reading
The Book of the New Sun by GENE WOLFE; the *Confluence* trilogy by PAUL J. McAULEY; *The Dancers at the End of Time* sequence by MICHAEL MOORCOCK; the *Viriconium* sequence by M. JOHN HARRISON

Bibliography (Selected)
The Dying Earth (1950)
The Space Pirate (1953)
Vandals of the Void (1953)
To Live Forever (1956)
Big Planet (1957)
Slaves of the Klau (1958)
The Languages of Pao (1958)
The Dragon Masters (1963)
Future Tense (short stories, 1964)
The Star King (1964)
The Killing Machine (1964)
Son of the Tree (1964)
The Houses of Iszm (1964)

The World Between (short stories, 1965)
Space Opera (1965)
Monsters in Orbit (1965)
The Many Worlds of Magnus Ridolph (short stories, 1966)
The Brains of Earth (1966)
The Blue World (1966)
The Eyes of the Overworld (1966)
The Palace of Love (1967)
The Last Castle (1967)
City of the Chasch (1968)
Eight Fantasms and Magics (short stories, 1969)
Servants of the Wankh (1969)
Emphyrio (1969)
The Dirdir (1969)
The Pnume (1970)
The Worlds of Jack Vance (short stories, 1973)
The Anome (1973)
The Brave Free Men (1973)
Trullion: Alastor 2262 (1973)
The Asutra (1974)
The Gray Prince (1974)
Marune: Alastor 933 (1975)
Showboat World (1975)
The Best of Jack Vance (short stories, 1976)
Maske: Thaery (1976)
Wyst: Alastor 1716 (1978)
Morreion (1979)
Green Magic (short stories, 1979)
The Seventeen Virgins (1979)
The Face (1979)
Galactic Effectuator (short stories, 1980)
The Book of Dreams (1981)
The Narrow Land (short stories, 1982)
Cugel's Saga (1983)
Lyonesse: Suldren's Garden (1983)
Rhialto the Marvelous (1984)
Light from a Lone Star (short stories, 1985)
Lyonesse: The Green Pearl (1985)
The Augmented Agent (short stories, 1986)
The Dark Side of the Moon: Stories of the Future (short stories, 1986)

VAN VOGT, A. E. (1912–2000), Canada

Canadian by birth, A. E. van Vogt began his SF career in the late 1930s and early 1940s with a number of stories for JOHN W. CAMPBELL and his ASTOUNDING SCIENCE FICTION magazine. It was not long before his prolific output and vaulting imagination established him as one of the key figures of the GOLDEN AGE, and his stories became famous for their high adventure and intricate plots.

Today, many of van Vogt's stories seem, inevitably, outdated. At the time of their original publication, however, his ideas were bold and new, and his importance to the development of the genre at this crucial period in its development should not be underestimated.

Van Vogt's first novel *Slan* (1946) is possibly his most famous work. It tells of a man born into a mutant race whose members have strange paranormal powers. He and his fellow mutants are oppressed by 'normal' society until one day the emergent supermen throw off their social shackles and it is revealed that the dictator of the planetary empire is in fact a mutant 'slan' himself. The story is pure pulp adventure but it is still fondly remembered for the sheer excitement and SENSE OF WONDER that it gave to its readers.

Van Vogt's next important books are the two novels that together comprise the *Weapon Shops* sequence, *The Weapon Shops of Isher* (1951) and *The Weapon Makers* (1946). These novels showcase perfectly van Vogt's style and surrealistic imagery and concern the political wrangling between a totalitarian galactic empire and a libertarian movement over control of the technologically advanced weapon factories built by an immortal.

Other books followed, all in the same style and with similar concerns. *The World of Null-A* (1948) sees its chief protagonist 'reborn' many times because of his profound non-linear mental abilities. *The Voyage of the*

Space Beagle (1950) purports to follow in science fictional terms the voyage of Charles Darwin and his development of EVOLUTIONARY theory, but is actually a SPACE OPERA in which its cast encounters a series of bizarre ALIEN life forms and 'bug-eyed monsters'. Many of Van Vogt's characters are perhaps most usefully seen as wish-fulfilment figures who inevitably TRANSCEND their lowly beginnings, usually out-thinking their enemies to become steadfast representatives of the common good.

It was during this period, as van Vogt's relationship with *Astounding Science Fiction* began to cool, that his passion for alternative modes of thought led him to become involved with L. RON HUBBARD's *Dianetics* and *Scientology* movements. Van Vogt invested much energy in this and when he eventually returned to writing after a decade-long hiatus the NEW WAVE movement was in full swing. Van Vogt's work still had the feel of pulp about it and, although his earlier novels had in their time been at the genre's cutting edge, times – and tastes – had changed.

The writing of A. E. van Vogt occupies an important position in the history of the development of the SF genre. He may not have produced a *Foundation* series or a *Dune* sequence but his novels and stories nonetheless continue to offer readers an intellectual stimulation and narrative excitement that is unique.

A. E. van Vogt died in 2000, aged eighty-eight.

See Also
ASTOUNDING SCIENCE FICTION; JOHN W. CAMPBELL; SPACE OPERA

Recommended Further Reading
The *Lensmen* novels by E. E. 'DOC' SMITH

Bibliography
Slan (1946)
The Weapon Makers (1946)
The Book of Ptath (1947)
Out of the Unknown (short stories, 1948)
The World of Null-A (1948)
The House That Stood Still (1950)
The Voyage of the Space Beagle (1950)
The Weapon Shops of Isher (1951)
Away and Beyond (short stories, 1952)

Destination: Universe (short stories, 1952)
The Mixed Men (1952)
The Universe Maker (1953)
Planets for Sale (1954)
The Pawns of Null-A (1956)
Empire of the Atom (1957)
The Mind Cage (1957)
Siege of the Unseen (1959)
The War Against the Rull (1959)
Earth's Last Fortress (1960)
The Violent Man (1962)
The Wizard of Linn (1962)
The Beast (1963)
Monsters (short stories, 1965)
Rogue Ship (1965)
The Winged Man (1966, with F. Mayne Hull)
The Silkie (1969)
Children of Tomorrow (1970)
Quest for the Future (1970)
More Than Superhuman (short stories, 1971)
M-33 in Andromeda (short stories, 1971)
The Battle of Forever (1971)
The Proxy Intelligence and Other Mind Benders (short stories, 1971)
The Darkness on Diamondia (1972)
Future Glitter (1973)
The Best of A. E. Van Vogt (short stories, 1974)
The Man with a Thousand Names (1974)
The Secret Galactics (1974)
The Anarchistic Colossus (1977)
Supermind (1977)
Pendulum (short stories, 1978)
Cosmic Encounter (1980)
Computerworld (1983)
Null-A 3 (1984)

VARLEY, JOHN (1947–), USA

One of the great white hopes of American SF during the 1970s, Varley first made his mark on the genre with a number of innovative and well-written short stories for various magazines.

His first novel, *The Ophiuchi Hotline* (1977), was to capitalize on this immediate success, and is now considered one of the classics of the decade in which it was first published.

It is the first novel in Varley's FUTURE HISTORY, known as the *Eight Worlds* sequence, and describes a universe in which humanity has been evicted from the Earth by terrifying ALIENS. The race has therefore established itself on various other PLANETS and habitats around the Solar System, including a large network of tunnels within the moon. More importantly, humans have developed a wide-ranging repertoire of BIOTECHNOLOGY, including CLONING, that allows people to modify and repair themselves as they please. The chief protagonist is actually a series of clones of the same person, who is simply regenerated with identical memories every time a 'fatal' incident occurs. Underlying the novel is a bleak message to humanity, a warning that we should look after our planet: Varley implies that the enigmatic aliens view humans as a form of vermin that has been evicted from the Earth as an exercise in cosmic hygiene. Indeed, the 'hotline' of the title is a stream of information that flows through the Solar System, and eventually delivers to the race the message that it must shortly evacuate the system entirely. Humanity is not wanted, and is doomed to wander the stars aimlessly.

Other titles in the *Eight Worlds* sequence include *Steel Beach* (1992), a novel set a number of years before the events of *The Ophiuchi Hotline* and which describes the society created by the remnants of humanity that inhabit the moon, and *The Golden Globe* (1998), which follows the life of conman/actor Sparky Valentine as he makes his way through a NEAR-FUTURE Solar System.

A number of Varley's shorter stories also fit within the future-history framework.

Varley's other sequence, a trilogy that comprises *Titan* (1979), *Wizard* (1980) and *Demon* (1984), describes the results of an exploratory mission to Titan. Once there, the protagonists find that the Saturnian moon is in fact an alien artefact and the domain that exists within it is essentially a vast VIRTUAL REALITY maze. The trilogy features a possibly uneasy blend of fantasy and SF.

See Also

ALIENS; ALTERNATIVE REALITY; BIOTECHNOLOGY; FUTURE HISTORY; NEAR FUTURE; SCIENCE FANTASY; VIRTUAL REALITY

Recommended Further Reading
The *Future History* sequence by ROBERT HEINLEIN; the *Technic History* sequence by POUL ANDERSON; the *Foundation* sequence by ISAAC ASIMOV

Bibliography
The Ophiuchi Hotline (1977)
The Persistence of Vision (short stories, 1978)
Titan (1979)
The Barbie Murders (short stories, 1980)
Wizard (1980)
Millennium (1983)
Demon (1984)
Blue Champagne (short stories, 1986)
Tango Charlie and Foxtrot Romeo (1989)
Press Enter (1990)
Steel Beach (1992)
The Golden Globe (1998)

VERNE, JULES (1828–1905), France

Jules Verne has become recognized as one of the early pioneers of the SF genre and his 'extraordinary voyages' prefigure many of its later concerns.

Verne, the son of a lawyer, was born into a France still recovering from the Napoleonic Wars, and his early writing shows a longing for a brighter future, a world embracing scientific progress and technology to create a more efficient and stable social structure. However, this vision soon became tempered by the realization that progress would inevitably enhance the destructiveness of warfare, and so there was a decided shift in emphasis in Verne's writing: he grew wary of, so to speak, bringing about the future too soon. He nevertheless remained a strong supporter of technology.

Journey to the Centre of the Earth (1864) was the first of Verne's fantastical voyages. It describes the journey of a young man and his scientifically inclined uncle into the mouth of a dormant volcano, which eventually leads them to a hollow Earth containing a variety of prehistoric creatures that have survived for millennia. It is the SENSE OF WONDER that Verne conjures in his readers that is perhaps the most important aspect of the novel – although some contemporary scientific speculation might have endorsed Verne's vision of a lost world preserved deep inside the planet.

His next novel, *From the Earth to the Moon* (1865), is scientifically inaccurate but is perhaps one of the first attempts by an author to present a 'scientific' process by which men might travel to the Moon. (Members of the Baltimore Gun Club build a massive contraption that fires its creators into space.) Again, Verne was breaking new ground, as well as promoting the benefits of modern technological developments.

Twenty Thousand Leagues Under the Sea (1870) and its sequel *Mysterious Island* (1874) see its protagonists kidnapped by the enigmatic Captain Nemo and taken down into the depths of the ocean to witness all manner of strange and wonderful marine life. *The Clipper of the Clouds* (1886) recounts a similar story, but this time from an aerial perspective.

Paris in the Twentieth Century (1994) is a recently discovered early book that has Verne predicting the conditions of Paris life in the 1960s. In many ways, the book is prescient and accurate – Verne depicts fax machines, cars and pneumatic trains – yet the novel was originally rejected by publishers for being too unrealistic.

Jules Verne, along with H. G. Wells, is one of the founding fathers of SF. Indeed, his writing had a profound effect on Wells. Verne took the ideas that had been bubbling away under the surface of popular fiction – the writings of EDGAR ALLAN POE, for example – for a number of years and gave them a new life. His work gave readers a new sense of wonder and, in doing so, helped to establish one of the main aims of the genre.

See Also
The History and Origins of SF; H. G. WELLS; SCIENTIFIC ROMANCE

Recommended Further Reading
The SF stories of Edgar Allan Poe; *The Time Machine* (1895) and *The War of the Worlds* (1898) by H. G. Wells; *The Nomad of the Time Streams* sequence by MICHAEL MOORCOCK; *The Space Machine* (1976) by CHRISTOPHER PRIEST; *Anti Ice* (1993) by STEPHEN BAXTER

Bibliography (Selected)
Journey to the Centre of the Earth (1864)
From the Earth to the Moon (1865)

Around the Moon (1870)
Twenty Thousand Leagues Under the Sea (1870)
Mysterious Island (1874)
The Begum's Fortune (1879)
The Clipper of the Clouds (1886)
Topsy-Turvy (1889)
Paris in the Twentieth Century (1994)

VINGE, VERNOR (1944–   ), USA

A full-time mathematician as well as an author, Vernor Vinge has had a relatively low fiction output, usually with a gap of several years between novels. His work is HARD SF of high quality, although it sometimes features characters with apparently paranormal powers.

His first two novels demonstrate this: *Grimm's World* (1969) concerns the life of a woman on a primitive PLANET who is able to converse with the superior beings that exploit her world and *The Witling* (1976) tells of the arrival of humans on a colony planet where the inhabitants have developed a form of teleportation. Both are good stories but are over-shadowed by the two sequences of books that followed.

The Peace War (1984) and its sequel *Marooned in Realtime* (1986), which were assembled together as *Across Realtime* (1991, with additions), constitute the *Realtime* sequence, and describe a universe filled with fascinating technologies and vivid characters. *The Peace War* deals with a war that breaks out when a new technology is discovered – 'Bobbles', stasis fields within which time comes to a halt. These fields also offer certain possibilities for defence, and so the war of the title begins. The sequel, *Marooned in Realtime*, is the better of the two novels, and follows a group of characters who use the 'bobbles' to travel into the distant FAR FUTURE. Once there, they discover the human race has evolved and abandoned the Earth, but they themselves have no means of returning to the past.

Grand in scale, the *Realtime* sequence is well conceived and tightly plotted, and undoubtedly benefits from the sophisticated scientific aware-ness of its author.

Vinge's next book, *A Fire Upon the Deep* (1992) is a vast SPACE OPERA about the awakening of a truly awe-inspiring ALIEN race that has been dormant for billions of years. The protagonists struggle to find a means to stop the utter destruction that the creatures are leaving in their wake – entire civilizations topple at their whim. The book is set against a wonderfully conceived, galaxy-spanning backdrop – there are zones within our galaxy that affect the level of intelligence of the inhabitants, with 'slower' zones that hold back the EVOLUTION of intelligent species. Some alien races have found ways to move between zones, and humanity can only realize its full potential by leaving the Milky Way and establishing itself on the outer rim of the spiral arm.

The book was awarded the HUGO AWARD for its year. A belated prequel, set many thousands of years before the events that take place in *A Fire Upon the Deep*, is *A Deepness in the Sky* (1999), which narrows the scope of the first book without compromising its vision. Two fleets of human spacecraft have been enticed to a distant planet by mysterious radio signals. There they are effectively stranded, and must wait above the planet until the aliens can develop a level of technology that will allow them to repair their ships and move on. Unlike its predecessor, which looked forward towards a future bright with limitless technology, *A Deepness in the Sky* posits a scenario that may occur if humanity hits a technological plateau. The novel won Vinge another Hugo Award, and along with *A Fire Upon the Deep* constitutes some of the best space opera to be published during the 1990s.

A collection of Vinge's best short fiction can be found in *True Names* (1987).

See Also
ALIEN; FAR FUTURE; HARD SF; PLANET; SPACE OPERA SPACE TRAVEL

Recommended Further Reading
The Bohr Maker (1995) by LINDA NAGATA; the *Galactic Centre* sequence by GREGORY BENFORD; the *Uplift* sequence by DAVID BRIN

Bibliography
Grimm's World (1969)
The Witling (1976)
The Peace War (1984)
Marooned in Realtime (1986)
True Names and Other Dangers (short stories, 1987)
A Fire Upon the Deep (1992)
A Deepness in the Sky (1999)

VONNEGUT, KURT (1922–   ), USA

Kurt Vonnegut was born in Indianapolis in 1922 and served in the US Army during the Second World War. He was captured by the Germans and incarcerated as a prisoner of war in Dresden. Vonnegut survived the saturation bombing of the city and the appalling firestorm that followed, and returned to the USA on his release from captivity. During the 1950s he began his writing career.

As an author, Vonnegut has, perfectly reasonably, distanced himself from categorization as an SF author. His work is undoubtedly LITERARY and often surreal, and it was with a succession of more mainstream-orientated novels that he made his name. Nevertheless, his SF remains important to the genre: it can bask in the reflected glory of the satirical content, dry, humane wit and insightful genius of Vonnegut's work.

Vonnegut's first novel, *Player Piano* (1952) portrays an encroaching DYSTOPIA as the human race hands over first business and manufacture, and then political decision-making to computers, prototypical ARTIFICIAL INTELLIGENCES. As in much of Vonnegut's fiction to come, the novel views the human race with a kind of amused but compassionate disbelief.

His next novel, *The Sirens of Titan* (1959), depicted the human race casually raised from animal ignornaceto sentience by an indifferent ALIEN race that wishes only for humanity to build them a spare part for a probe that has been stuck out on Titan for fifty thousand years. The novel is, among other things, a fine example of COMIC SF.

Slaughterhouse-Five (1969) tackles Vonnegut's personal response to the Dresden firestorm. The novel is simultaneously bitter, hilarious, and harrowing. Its anti-war message is all the more effective for being subtly delivered. The protagonist, Billy Pilgrim, is whisked away to an alien PLANET (which happens to be the home world of the aliens that feature in *The Sirens of Titan*) where he learns that time is not necessarily moving in a linear fashion. He gladly sacrifices his life as a member of the human race, a race of which he is growing tired, to travel through various moments of TIME and SPACE with the aliens. *Slaughterhouse-Five* was the novel with which Vonnegut achieved wide recognition as one of the most important post-war American writers.

Other important Vonnegut titles include *Cat's Cradle* (1963), which describes the creation of Ice-Nine, a chemical construct that ultimately brings about an ECOLOGICAL disaster for the planet, and *Galápagos* (1985), which features, among other delights, a society of devolved seal-like humans.

Many of Vonnegut's other novels exist on the borders of genre fiction, and some of them feature the fictional character Kilgore Trout, a science fiction writer who is said to have been modelled on THEODORE STURGEON.

Vonnegut's best short fiction is collected in *Canary in a Cat House* (1961) and *Welcome to the Monkey House* (1968).

See Also
ALIENS; COMIC SF; ECOLOGY; LITERARY SF; SPACE; TIME

Recommended Further Reading
Empire of the Sun (1984) by J. G. BALLARD; *Camp Concentration* (1968) by THOMAS DISCH

Bibliography (Selected)
Player Piano (1952)
The Sirens of Titan (1959)
Canary in a Cat House (short stories, 1961)
Mother Night (1962)
Cat's Cradle (1963)
God Bless You, Mr Rosewater (1965)
Welcome to the Monkey House (short stories, 1968)
Slaughterhouse-Five (1969)
Breakfast of Champions (1973)
Slapstick (1976)
Jailbird (1979)
Dead-Eye Dick (1982)
Galápagos (1985)
Bluebeard (1987)
Hocus Pocus (1990)
Timequake (1997)
Bagumbo Snuff Box (short stories, 1999)

WATSON, IAN (1943–   ), Great Britain

A British writer who began publishing short fiction in NEW WORLDS magazine during the early 1970s, Ian Watson's, first novel, *The Embedding* (1973) was one of the most important debut novels of its decade.

The book follows three separate plot strands that all concern themselves with experiments in language and perception: Watson explores the notion that language is the key factor in the shaping of our perception of the world. In one of the stories a group of children are taught to speak only in an artificial language, in another a group of ALIENS are attempting to understand and define the human race by studying its words, and in the third a tribe in the Amazon Basin modify their language as their conception of their environment is altered by the use of hallucinogenic drugs. These strands are woven together skilfully at the end of the book.

The Embedding is a fine example of serious SOFT SF, an important exploration of linguistics and its relevance.

Watson's next book, *The Jonah Kit* (1975), is even more complex and rewarding. Again, Watson chooses to adopt a multi-stranded narrative structure, interweaving a number of tales. Foremost among them is an account of a research project exploring the possibility of imprinting human consciousness onto the brains of whales. This eventually leads to scientists at a Russian research facility being able to communicate with modified, programmed whales. There is a salutary sadness in the aquatic mammals' reply.

The book is bursting with additional ideas; Watson also puts forward the theory that our universe is in fact formed out of ANTIMATTER, that it is simply a ghost of the matter universe that constitutes true reality. The novel was awarded the BSFA AWARD for its year.

Of Watson's other early novels, *The Martian Inca* (1977) is also worthy of note. It describes the consequences of the crash of a Soviet probe in the Peruvian Andes. The people living in the immediate environment are infected by a virus that the probe has brought back with it from Mars. This has startling consequences.

During the 1980s Watson published a trilogy of novels whose narrative centred around a vast, sentient river running across the surface of an alien PLANET. The sequence begins with *The Book of the River* (1984), and continues with *The Book of the Stars* (1984) and *The Book of Being* (1985). The eponymous river is a great body of water that cuts across the entire world, separating two very disparate societies by a great, impassable span. The story follows the progress of a young woman who, through joining the boating guild and learning the necessary skills, attempts and succeeds to cross the river. Upon reaching the other side she finds a violent, male-dominated culture, gravely at odds with her own.

The Black Current trilogy, as an evocation of a strange and surreal environment, is a very worthwhile read.

More recently, Watson has produced the two-book *Mana* sequence, *Lucky's Harvest* (1993) and *Fallen Moon* (1994), which draw upon world myth to replay a great epic in terms of SF, and are set on a multiracial colony planet known as Kalera.

Nearly all of Watson's short-story collections are good. For depth and range, the best of them are *The Very Slow Time Machine* (1979) and *Stalin's Teardrops* (1991).

A website is maintained at http://kdsi.com/~dmackey/watson.html

See Also
ALIEN; ANTIMATTER; ARTIFICIAL INTELLIGENCE; HARD SF; LITERARY SF; SCIENCE FANTASY

Recommended Further Reading
The *Videssos* and *Krispos* sequences by HARRY TURTLEDOVE; *Sirius* (1944) by OLAF STAPLEDON; the *Riverworld* sequence by PHILIP JOSÉ FARMER

Bibliography (Selected)
The Embedding (1973)
The Jonah Kit (1975)
Alien Embassy (1977)
The Martian Inca (1977)
Miracle Visitors (1978)
The Very Slow Time Machine (short stories, 1979)
God's World (1979)
The Gardens of Delight (1980)
Deathhunter (1981)
Under Heaven's Bridge (1981, with MICHAEL BISHOP)
Sunstroke (short stories, 1982)
Chekhov's Journey (1983)
Converts (1984)
The Book of the River (1984)
The Book of the Stars (1984)
The Book of Ian Watson (short stories, 1985)
Slow Birds and Other Stories (short stories, 1985)
The Book of Being (1985)
Queenmagic, Kingmagic (1986)
Evil Water (short stories, 1987)
The Power (1987)
The Fire Worm (1988)
Whores of Babylon (1988)

Meat (1988)
Salvage Rites (short stories, 1989)
The Flies of Memory (1990)
Inquisitor (1990)
Stalin's Teardrops (short stories, 1991)
Nanoware Time (1991)
Space Marine (1993)
Lucky's Harvest (1993)
The Coming of Vertumnus and Other Stories (short stories, 1994)
Harlequin (1994)
The Fallen Moon (1994)
Chaos Child (1995)
Hard Questions (1996)
Oracle (1997)
Mockymen (2000)

WEBER, DAVID (1952–   ), USA

In a similar way to both DAVID FEINTUCH and ELIZABETH MOON, American writer David Weber has, over the last decade, produced a series of episodic SF novel that are reminiscent of both the *Hornblower* books of C. S. Forrester and the *Sharpe* novels of Bernard Cornwell.

The *Honor Harrington* sequence charts the progress of the eponymous heroine as she battles her way up through the ranks of the Royal Navy of the PLANET Manticore in a vast MILITARISTIC SPACE OPERA. The sequence is bursting with high adventure and entertainment, in effect the print counterpart of wide-screen, special-effects-laden cinema.

What sets the *Honor Harrington* books apart from their generic counterparts is Weber's use of a female protagonist. This is E. E. 'DOC' SMITH updated for the new millennium, with an advocacy of equal opportunities.

The sequence begins with *On Basilisk Station* (1993), and continues with *The Honor of the Queen* (1993), *The Short Victorious War* (1994), *Field of Dishonor* (1994), *Flag in Exile* (1995), *Honor Among Enemies* (1996), *In Enemy Hands* (1997), *Echoes of Honor* (1998), *Ashes of Victory* (2000) and the short-story collections *More Than Honor* (1998) and *Worlds of Honor* (1999). It looks set to continue over the next few years.

See Also
GENDER; MILITARISTIC SF; SPACE OPERA

Recommended Further Reading
The *Serrano Legacy* by ELIZABETH MOON; the *Seafort Saga* by
DAVID FEINTUCH; The *Vorkosigan* sequence by LOIS McMASTER
BUJOLD

Bibliography
Insurrection (1990, with Steve White)
Mutineer's Moon (1991, with Steve White)
Crusade (1992, with Steve White)
Path of the Fury (1992)
On Basilisk Station (1993)
The Honor of the Queen (1993)
A Short Victorious War (1994)
The Armageddon Inheritance (1994)
Field of Dishonor (1994)
Flag in Exile (1995)
Oath of Swords (1995)
Heirs of the Empire (1996)
Honor Among Enemies (1996)
In Death Ground (1997, with Steve White)
In Enemy Hands (1997)
More Than Honor (short stories, 1998)
Echoes of Honor (1998)
The War God's Own (1998)
Worlds of Honor (short stories, 1999)
The Apocalypse Troll (1999)
Ashes of Victory (2000)

WELLS, H. G. (1866–1946), Great Britain

Herbert George Wells can certainly be considered one of the founding
fathers of SF as a genre distinct from the literary mainstream. Indeed, it
has been argued that without the wonderful SCIENTIFIC
ROMANCES of this supremely intelligent man the genre would not exist
in the form that it does today.

Originally apprenticed as a draper but then 'reinventing' himself as a
teacher and lecturer, Wells began his writing career with a series of
popular-science articles and essays for various journals.

Wells's first novel is of great importance to the genre, and stands as one
of the most respected and influential debuts in modern literature. *The*

Time Machine (1895) takes its Victorian protagonist into a future when Natural Selection has divided the human species into two distinct races, the Eloi and the Morlocks. The Eloi at first appear to have created a UTOPIAN society, whilst the Morlocks have made a DYSTOPIA. However, upon more detailed inspection things are shown to be far more complex than this: the Eloi are gentle but naive and docile, the Morlocks brutal but intelligent and successful. After various escapades, including a wonderfully evocative scene where he witnesses the end of the Earth, the Time Traveller returns to his Victorian epoch to tell his confederates about his adventures.

Aside from the sheer originality and the exhuberant SENSE OF WONDER of Wells's novel, perhaps its most significant feature is its author's use of contemporary scientific thought to provide him with the basis of his imagined future. Wells studied EVOLUTION under T. H. Huxley, a great supporter of Darwin, and this obviously played a part in Wells's vision of his future, in which he saw the human race dividing into two independent subspecies over a vast period of time. The novel also uses technology to transport its hero to and from the future – until this point authors had usually used magic or hibernatory slumber to move their protagonists forward through time. Wells changed this.

The Time Machine is the epitome of an SF novel: it extrapolates its futue from current scientific thought, it provides a thought-provoking perspective on contemporary society, it explores how humanity will come to use technology to manipulate its own existence, and, perhaps most importantly, it is compellingly readable and full of adventure. The novel has spawned several imitations over the years, none quite as good as STEPHEN BAXTER's authorized sequel *The Time Ships* (1995), published to celebrate the centenary of Wells's original.

Alongside *The Time Machine*, Wells's best-known scientific romance is *The War of the Worlds* (1898), a dark and disturbing novel of ALIEN invasion.

The War of the Worlds begins with a strange cylinder crash-landing in a field in England. Soon other craft are landing and disgorging their Martian passengers. These aliens come armed with three-legged fighting machines and deadly heat rays. Eventually, they are overcome but, tellingly, Wells does not allow his human protagonists the privilege of success – the Martians succumb to a strain of the common cold that mercilessly destroys them all.

The War of the Worlds remains one of the greatest-ever works of SF and its conclusion is one of the most thoughtful and satisfactory in the history

of the genre. When Wells sat down to write this story of malign, technologically superior aliens invading from another planet, humans had not
yet mastered powered flight. Wells was both prescient and daring in his
speculations.

Many of Well's notions and ideas were adopted by early genre writers
who were eager to develop them in different directions. Themes and
devices that have now become clichés in the genre were innovative and
exciting in the time when Wells wrote – indeed, he pioneered many of
them in his own writing.

In *The Island of Dr. Moreau* (1896), Wells again explores ideas of
evolution, but this time he explores how the process might be hastened by
the adoption of dubious surgical techniques. He describes an island where
the eponymous doctor has used surgery to alter the bodies and cosncious-
nesses of a number of animal species, raising them to a semblance of
sentience. However, when the animals begin to revert to their former
nature and chaos breaks out on the island, Moreau is made to realize the
error of his ways.

There are many other important SF books by Wells: *When the Sleeper
Wakes* (1899) tells the story of a man who wakes from a spell of suspended
animation to find himself in the middle of a twenty-second-century revolution; *The War in the Air* (1908) matter-of-factly predicts the development of aerial combat; *The First Men in the Moon* (1901) has its characters
use an ANTI-GRAVITY device to propel them to the Moon; *The Shape
of Things To Come* (1933) is a detailed attempt at FUTURE HISTORY
and an excellent example of POLITICAL SF.

Wells's short fiction is collected in *The Complete Short Stories of H. G.
Wells* (1998), and includes such classics as *The Country of the Blind* and
The Stolen Bacillus.

In his later life Wells became increasingly involved in politics and this
interest informs much of his later writing, some of which is SF, much of
which is not. The fact remains that H. G. Wells has had the most
profound influence of any author upon the SF genre. There were big
ideas to be thought in those early days of the genre – and no one thought
them like Wells did.

See Also

The History and Origins of SF; ALIEN; DYSTOPIA; EUGENICS;
EVOLUTION; FAR FUTURE; GENETICS; PLANET; SCIEN-
TIFIC ROMANCE; SENSE OF WONDER; SPACE TRAVEL;
TIME

Recommended Further Reading

Journey to the Centre of the Earth (1864) by JULES VERNE; *The Time Ships* (1995) and *Anti Ice* (1993) by STEPHEN BAXTER; *The Space Machine* (1976) by CHRISTOPHER PRIEST; *Last and First Men* (1930) and *Star Maker* (1937) by OLAF STAPLEDON

Bibliography (Selected)

The Time Machine (1895)
The Stolen Bacillus and Other Incidents (short stories, 1895)
The Wonderful Visit (1895)
The Island of Dr Moreau (1896)
The Invisible Man (1897)
The Plattner Story, and Others (short stories, 1897)
The War of the Worlds (1898)
When the Sleeper Wakes (1899)
Tales of Time and Space (short stories, 1899)
The First Men in the Moon (1901)
The Sea Lady (1902)
Twelve Stories and a Dream (short stories, 1903)
The Food of the Gods, and How It Came to Earth (1904)
A Modern Utopia (1905)
In the Days of the Comet (1906)
The War in the Air (1908)
The Country of the Blind and Other Stories (short stories, 1911)
The World Set Free (1914)
Men Like Gods (1923)
The Dream (1924)
The Shape of Things to Come (1933)
The Camford Visitation (1937)
Star Begotten: A Biological Fantasia (1937)
The Holy Terror (1939)
All Aboard for Ararat (1940)
The Man with the Nose and Other Uncollected Stories (short stories, 1984)
The Complete Short Stories of H. G. Wells (short stories, 1987)
The Complete Short Stories of H. G. Wells (short stories, 1998)

WHELAN, MICHAEL (1950–   ), USA

Michael Whelan is at present the most acclaimed professional artist working in SF. He has been awarded numerous HUGO AWARDS for his book illustrations and is generally considered to be America's best living visualizer of the fantastic.

Whelan's work is reminiscent of that of his British contemporaries JIM BURNS and CHRIS MOORE, and aims for realistic and accurate portrayals of humanity in alien and futuristic contexts. It is also evident in many of Whelan's paintings that he clearly understands the stories he is illustrating and has chosen something central to the narrative to depict. Like Burns, he does this with style and precision.

Whelan frequently produces jackets for some of the genre's biggest names. He is a formidable artist whose genre repuation is richly deserved.

WILLIAMS, TAD (1957–), USA

Tad Williams is perhaps better known for his vast, mature fantasy sequence *Memory, Sorrow and Thorn*. However, Williams's most recent series, *Otherland*, blends SF concepts with fantasy in what has proven to be an interesting mix.

The *Otherland* sequence begins with *City of Golden Shadows* (1996) and continues with *River of Blue Flame* (1998), *Mountain of Black Glass* (1999) and *Sea of Silver Light* (2001), and describes an enormous VIRTUAL-REALITY construct in which human beings are losing their minds; children are being found either comatose or dead, their minds adrift in the mysterious golden realm of Otherland. This Otherland is an artificial reality that has been created by a sinister organization, the Grail Brotherhood, that is attempting to find a form of virtual immortality. Various characters become embroiled in the plot, at first to discover what has happened to these children and then to find Otherland and blow open the portals to let everyone in. There are many well-developed characters in its pages – a First World War veteran, a serial killer, an aborigine, for example.

The real-world setting, a NEAR-FUTURE America, draws for its images on CYBERPUNK to depict the ways in which human beings have learned to interface with their technology.

Otherland itself, where the normal laws of physics do not apply and dreams can become reality, operates on terms that are more akin to fantasy than SF. However, everything is fundamentally explained as a virtual-reality construct and so is, to some extent, SF.

There are also hints throughout the books that one of the mysterious characters may in fact be an avatar of Otherland's sentient operating system or ARTIFICIAL INTELLIGENCE.

The *Otherland* sequence represents world-building on a truly magnificent scale, and the story is a once satirical and exciting, tense and bold.

See Also
ALTERNATIVE REALITY; ARTIFICIAL INTELLIGENCE; NEAR FUTURE; SCIENCE FANTASY; VIRTUAL REALITY

Recommended Further Reading
Neuromancer (1984) by WILLIAM GIBSON; *Islands in the Net* (1988) by BRUCE STERLING; *The Book of the New Sun* by GENE WOLFE

Bibliography
Tailchaser's Song (1985)
The Dragonbone Chair (1988)
Stone of Farewell (1990)
Child of an Ancient City (1992, with Nina Kiriki Hoffman)
To Green Angel Tower (1993)
Caliban's Hour (1994)
Otherland: City of Golden Shadows (1996)
Otherland: River of Blue Flame (1998)
Otherland: Mountain of Black Glass (1999)
Otherland: Sea of Silver Light (2001)

WILSON, ROBERT CHARLES (1953 –), USA

Born in America but for a long time resident in Canada, Robert Charles Wilson has for a number of years been quietly producing literate, character-based, HUMANIST SF. Often the human characters are defined by their juxtaposition with an ALIEN or an alien situation; their simple humanity is thrown into relief by being set against something entirely *not* human.

Wilson's first novel, *A Hidden Place* (1986) concerns an alien intrusion into a small town in Western America.

His next novel was *Memory Wire* (1987), which is set against a CYBER-PUNK background with a protagonist who is 'wired' to record everything he sees.

Other novels followed, including *Gypsies* (1989), which tells of a family who have the ability to step between ALTERNATE WORLDS or parallel realities, and *The Harvest* (1993), which describes what happens when an enormous alien vessel enters the Solar System and infects humanity with a plague of nano-machines that provide longevity and increased intelligence.

Mysterium (1994) was to win the PHILIP K. DICK MEMORIAL AWARD for Wilson. It tells the story of a group of scientists experimenting on an alien artefact, who find themselves transported to an ALTERNATIVE REALITY.

Wilson's next novel, *Darwinia* (1998), takes place in the year 1912 and describes a world in which one day, inexplicably, Europe disappears and is replaced by a strange continent covered in alien vegetation and bizarre animals.

Darwinia was followed by *Bios* (1999), an EVOLUTIONARY tale that follows a group of scientists and explorers at an outpost on an extremely toxic colony world. Here Wilson enters into the territory of HARD SF, as he describes the ECOLOGY of the planet and the fascinating alien intelligence inherent in its biology.

Wilson has also published a number of shorter pieces, which are collected together in *The Perseids and Other Stories* (2000).

See Also
ALIENS; ALTERNATIVE REALITY; BIOTECHNOLOGY; GENETICS; HARD SF; PLANETS; SPACE TRAVEL; VIRTUAL REALITY

Recommended Further Reading
Queen City Jazz (1995) by KATHLEEN ANN GOONAN; *Deathworld* (1960) by HARRY HARRISON

Bibliography
A Hidden Place (1986)
Memory Wire (1987)
Gypsies (1989)
The Divide (1990)
A Bridge of Years (1991)
The Harvest (1993)
Mysterium (1994)
Darwinia (1998)
Bios (1999)
The Perseids and Other Stories (short stories, 2000)

WOLFE, GENE (1931–   ), USA

Gene Wolfe is one of the finest writers in or out of the SF genre. Born in New York but for a number of years now resident in Illinois, he took a long time to break into print. His first novel, *Operation ARES* (1970) is a rather straightforward story of a Martian colony that, when abandoned by a repressive government on Earth, decides to invade the mother planet. However, Wolfe's second novel, *The Fifth Head of Cerberus* (1972) shows him coming truly into his own.

A fixup collection of three linked tales, *The Fifth Head of Cerberus* is and obviously science fictional work, as well as a complex and LITERARY exploration of identity. The action takes place on the twin PLANETS Sainte Anne and Sainte Croix, former French colonies that have long since diverged. Tradition states that the ancient shapeshifting ALIENS that once inhabited Sainte Anne have long been extinct, but some believe that the aliens survive and have actually killed off the colonists and taken their place.

The book is dark and intriguing, a masterpiece of the genre surpassed only by Wolfe's next major work, *The Book of the New Sun*.

The Book of the New Sun is a four-volume work that comprises The *Shadow of the Torturer* (1980), *The Claw of the Conciliator* (1981), *The Sword of the Lictor* (1982) and *The Citadel of the Autarch* (1983). There is also a later sequel, *The Urth of The New Sun* (1987).

Sometimes labelled a SCIENCE FANTASY, this multi-volume epic is in fact a rich and expressive work of FAR–FUTURE science fiction. It follows the progress of Severian, a trained torturer who is cast out from his home and is left to wander the degraded environment of his world. It is a startling evocation of an Earth past its zenith: the Sun is dying and the human race has relapsed into a state of ignorance – enormous spaceships stand proud against the horizon but have been converted into blocks of buildings, and the relics of centuries lie scattered about for all to see and none to comprehend. Wolfe succeeds brilliantly in utilizing the images of fantasy and sword-and-sorcery to portray this world – technological items are 'magical' and the text has a deliberately archaic flavour. However, everything is eventually explained in logical terms and the sequel novel is explicitly SF.

Severian is a MESSIAH figure who, as the story proceeds, grows increasingly aware of his role as the person intended to save the planet and bring about the New Sun of the title, a white hole. He grows in stature as his story progresses, eventually becoming Autarch of the now-ancient 'Urth' and setting off on a starship to bring home the New Sun.

The sequence is perhaps the finest treatment of the far-future theme ever written.

Thematic sequels to *The Book of the New Sun* are *The Book of the Long Sun* and *The Book of the Short Sun*, two further sequences that, together with the *The Book of the New Sun*, comprise one long connected novel.

The Book of the Long Sun is, once again, a four-volume work, beginning with *Nightside the Long Sun* (1993) and set aboard a vast GENERATION STARSHIP known as the 'Whorl'. The theme is one already tackled by ROBERT HEINLEIN in *Universe* (1951) and BRIAN ALDISS in *Non-Stop* (1958). A colony of humans aboard this starship have, over successive generations, 'forgotten' that they are on board a starship at all. When religious leader Patera Silk finds that his institution is about to be closed down, he sets off a chain of events that eventually leads to his realization of the true nature of their surroundings. He must also cope with a massive memory store that has been downloaded into his brain by one of the Gods – descendants of one of the ancient Autarchs of old 'Urth' who rule over the starship enigmatically from behind the scenes. Like its predecessor, *The Book of the Long Sun* borrows images from fantasy, and it continues to explore the ramifications of the story's RELIGIOUS myths.

The Book of the Short Sun continues the story of *The Book of the Long Sun*, picking up the narrative a number of years after the generation starship has reached its destination – a distant star system that contains the twin planets Blue and Green. The first book in the sequence is *On Blue's Waters* (1999). Horn, one of the young protagonists from the 'Whorl', is now an adult and takes over the role of narrator as the colony attempts to survive and establish itself.

Together, the twelve *Sun* books form one of the grandest sequences ever produced by a genre author. So intricately linked are the various volumes that they are perhaps best read as one single novel of exceptional length and quality.

Wolfe is also renowned for his shorter fiction and essays, the best of which are collected in *Endangered Species* (1989), *Castle of Days* (1992), *The Island of Doctor Death and Other Stories and Other Stories* (1980) and, more recently, *Strange Travellers* (2000).

Many of Wolfe's other novels, such as *Peace* (1975) and *Castleview* (1990), are fantasies, but are worth noting here as nearly all of Wolfe's books are of such a high quality that they deserve (and will reward) the attention of any reader with a claim to a brain..

To know the work of Gene Wolfe is to know *literature*, not merely genre fiction, at its best. His genius is apparent on nearly every page.

See Also
ALIEN; CLONING; FAR FUTURE; GENERATION STARSHIP; LITERARY SF; PLANET; SCIENCE FANTASY

Recommended Further Reading
The Dying Earth (1950) by JACK VANCE; the *Confluence Trilogy* by PAUL J. McAULEY; the *Viriconium* sequence by M. JOHN HARRISON

Bibliography
Operation ARES (1970)
The Fifth Head of Cerberus (1972)
Peace (1975)
The Devil in a Forest (1976)
The Island of Doctor Death and Other Stories and Other Stories (short stories, 1980)
The Shadow of the Torturer (1980)
Gene Wolfe's Book of Days (short stories, 1981)
The Claw of the Conciliator (1981)
The Sword of the Lictor (1982)
The Wolfe Archipelago (short stories, 1983)
The Castle of the Otter (short stories and essays, 1983)
The Citadel of the Autarch (1983)
Bibliomen (short stories, 1984)
Plan[e]t Engineering (short stories, 1984)
Free Live Free (1984)
The Boy Who Hooked the Sun (1985)
Soldier of the Mist (1986)
Empires of Foliage and Flower (1987)
The Urth of the New Sun (1987)
Storeys from the Old Hotel (short stories, 1988)
There Are Doors (1988)
Endangered Species (short stories, 1989)
Soldier of Arete (1989)
Castleview (1990)
Pandora by Holly Hollander (1990)
Castle of Days (short stories and essays, 1992)
Nightside the Long Sun (1993)
Lake of the Long Sun (1994)
Caldé of the Long Sun (1994)

Exodus of the Long Sun (1996)
On Blue's Waters (1999)
Strange Travellers (short stories, 2000)
In Green's Jungles (2000)
Return to the Whorl (2001)

WYNDHAM, JOHN (1903–1969), Great Britain

It is all too easy to look at the work of John Wyndham and see only a succession of 'comfortable' disaster novels aimed astutely at a market of middle-class readers still getting over the effects of the Second World War. But to do so is to miss the point.

It may be true that much of Wyndham's early magazine work was unspectacular, even run-of-the-mill. Indeed, some critics tend to divide his career into two distinct periods: pre- and post-Second World War. Present in his later work is a prevailing sense of unease that is only partly masked by the pragmatic stoicism that his protagonists usually adopt in extreme situations.

His best-known book is undoubtedly *The Day of the Triffids* (1951), which was the first of his 'cosy catastrophes'. It describes the living nightmare that ensues when mysterious orbital flares cause the majority of the human race to go blind. Deadly bioengineered plant life – 'Triffids' – begins to take over the planet and the hero, who has not been blinded, attempts to retreat with his newly acquired family to a haven where they hope to establish some sort of stability. Middle-class values adapt to drastically changed circumstances.

The Kraken Wakes (1953) was to follow next, and confirmed Wyndham's abilities as a writer in tune with his readers' preferences.

Reminiscent of the previous novel, it details the panic that follows the awakening of dangerous ALIENS that have taken up residence at the bottom of our oceans and are intent on melting the polar ice caps. A rising water level threatens civilization, floods and storms devastate the landscape, and icebergs float through the English Channel. However, the human race endures.

Parallels can be drawn here to the war that had recently taken place: the whole world is thrown into turmoil, but sense and valour prevail. It could be said that Wyndham's writing reflects the desire of an exhausted nation for restored order and sanity after the chaos and destruction of total war.

But with his next novel, *The Chrysalids* (1955), Wyndham created a POST-APOCALYPTIC vision that explored the horrific consequences of a darker and more immediately threatening disaster, one brought about by all-too-human actions.

The world has been devastated by nuclear war and its population blighted by GENETIC mutation caused by fallout. Any deviation from normality is hunted down and burnt out with cold and heartless precision. The story follows the life of David Storm, a creature of this horrific society who has developed a limited form of telepathy. He lives in fear of discovery – which inevitably comes.

The novel marked, for Wyndham, a move away from the 'comfortable' threat of an outside force such as the Triffids or the Kraken, which his characters might be able to learn to overcome, to the bleaker and more intractable threat posed by humanity to itself.

The Midwich Cuckoos (1957) remains one of Wyndham's most memorable novels. In what is perhaps one of his most disturbing scenarios, Wyndham describes the events that take place following a myserious daylong lapse into unconsciousness of the already sleepy English village of Midwich. The next morning the entire female population of the village has become pregnant. After a tense gestation period, these women give birth to their strange, hybrid children, the 'cuckoos' of the title, who come to dominate the village – they are, disturbingly, born with a frighteningly high level of intelligence.

Wyndham's best short fiction is collected in *The Seeds of Time* (1956) and *Consider Her Ways* (1961); *The Trouble With Lichen* (1960) and *Chocky* (1968) are also worth seeking out.

See Also
ALIENS; POST APOCALYPTIC; SCIENCE FANTASY

Recommended Further Reading
The Body Snatchers (1955) by JACK FINNEY; *The Puppet Masters* (1951) by ROBERT HEINLEIN; *Memory Seed* (1996) by STEPHEN PALMER

Bibliography
The Secret People (1935, as 'John Beynon')
Stowaway to Mars (1935, as 'John Beynon')
The Day of the Triffids (1951)
The Kraken Wakes (1953)
Jizzle (short stories, 1954)
The Chrysalids (1955)

ZELAZNY, ROGER (1937–1995), USA

The death of Roger Zelazny in 1995 at the age of fifty-seven marked the passing of one of the genre's most interesting writers.

Zelazny first made his mark during the 1960s, and was soon to become associated with the American NEW WAVE. His first novel, *This Immortal* (1966), tells of a POST-APOCALYPTIC Earth where the immortal protagonist, Conrad Nomikos, is employed as a guide to an ALIEN official. Indeed, the wastelands of Earth have become a place of entertainment for these aliens, the Vegans. Nomikos, however, has other ideas, and becomes a type of curator for the planet, helping to preserve the remnants of humanity. The novel won the HUGO AWARD in 1966, and deservedly so – it is a genuinely impressive achievement.

His next novel, *The Dream Master* (1966), tells the salutary story of a top psychiatrist who is able to enter and affect his clients' dreams through electronic means. It was expanded from an earlier NEBULA AWARD-winning novella.

However, it was with *Lord of Light* (1967) that Zelazny produced his single most successful novel. Human colonists have settled a distant PLANET, but have developed a technology that allows them to don godlike personas taken from various Eastern RELIGIONS such as Hinduism and Buddhism. So it is that they re-enact the ancient myths of these religions, battling for power on the distant colony world. *Lord of Light* won Zelazny another Hugo award for its year.

Outside of the SF field Zelazny is best known for his *Chronicles of Amber*, a long ten-book fantasy sequence that takes place on a plane of reality different to the known. The writing of this vast series took up much of his later life. The first five novels were collected together as *The Chronicles of Amber* (2000).

Zelazny's bibliography features a number of collaborations, the most interesting being *Deus Irae* (1976) with PHILIP K. DICK and *Psychoshop* (1998) with ALFRED BESTER. In both cases Zelazny finished the novels from uncompleted manuscripts: Dick's because for various reasons he could not finish the novel himself, Bester's because he had, sadly, died before completing it.

Of Zelazny's short fiction, the best can be found in the early collections, *Four for Tomorrow* (1967) and *The Doors of His Face, the Lamps of His Mouth* (1971).

Zelazny's writing won numerous awards, and established him as one of the most successful authors to come out of the American New Wave movement.

See Also
ALIEN; NEW WAVE; POST APOCALYPTIC; RELIGION

Recommended Further Reading
Shiva 3000 (2000) by JAN LARS JENSEN; *Valis* (1981) by PHILIP K. DICK

Bibliography
This Immortal (1966)
The Dream Master (1966)
Four for Tomorrow (short stories, 1967)
Lord of Light (1967)
Isle of the Dead (1969)
Creatures of Light and Darkness (1969)
Damnation Alley (1969)
The Doors of His Face, The Lamps of His Mouth, and Other Stories (short stories, 1971)
Jack of Shadows (1971)
Nine Princes of Amber (1970)
The Guns of Avalon (1972)
Today We Choose Faces (1973)
To Die in Italbar (1973)
Sign of the Unicorn (1975)
The Hand of Oberon (1976)
Bridge of Ashes (1976)

Doorways in the Sand (1976)
Deus Irae (1976, with PHILIP K. DICK)
My Name is Legion (1976)
The Courts of Chaos (1978)
Roadmarks (1979)
The Bells of Shoredan (1979)
The Last Defender of Camelot (short stories, 1980)
Changeling (1980)
Madwand (1981)
The Changing Land (1981)
Dilvish, the Damned (1982)
Coils (1982, with Fred Saberhagen)
Eye of Cat (1982)
Unicorn Variations (short stories, 1983)
Trumps of Doom (1985)
Blood of Amber (1986)
Sign of Chaos (1987)
Frost and Fire (short stories, 1989)
Knight of Shadows (1989)
The Black Throne (1990, with Fred Saberhagen)
The Mask of Loki (1990, with Thomas T. Thomas)
Prince of Chaos (1991)
Bring Me the Head of Prince Charming (1991, with ROBERT SHECKLEY)
Flare (1992, with Thomas T. Thomas)
Gone to Earth (short stories, 1992)
If at Faust You Don't Succeed (1993, with ROBERT SHECKLEY)
A Night in the Lonesome October (1993)
Wilderness (1994)
A Farce to be Reckoned With (1995, with ROBERT SHECKLEY)
Home is the Hangman (1996)
Donnerjack (1997, with Jane M. Lindskold)
Psychoshop (1998, with ALFRED BESTER)
The Chronicles of Amber (2000)

Science Fiction on the Screen

ABYSS, THE (1989, 146 minutes)

Director: James Cameron
Producer: Gale Anne Hurd
Screenplay: James Cameron
Starring: Ed Harris, Mary Elizabeth Mastrantonio, Michael Biehn, Leo Burmeister, Todd Graf, John Bedford Lloyd

Following his success with two of SF cinema's most important and enduring movies, THE TERMINATOR (1984) and ALIENS (1986), director James Cameron wrote and shot *The Abyss*.

A nuclear submarine has become stranded on a ledge deep in the ocean, and Harris and Mastrantonio are brought in to go down and save its crew. Along for the ride is a small team of US Navy SEALS led by the distinctly neurotic Biehn.

What follows is an underwater adventure, full of technological gadgetry and inspired special effects, unlike anything ever before seen on the screen. The atmosphere is suitably oppressive, and the characters react to the mounting tension with increasing alarm. When a powerful storm starts to rage on the surface, the rescue team too are stranded below. Oxygen levels drop at a frightening rate and soon the rescuers are wondering whether they are going to survive. It is then that they encounter the strange phosphorescent creatures that have been lurking outside the submarine. These ALIENS eventually make themselves known to the crew in a memorable scene that includes one of the first major examples of CGI in the movies: an entity sculpted from animated water enters the submarine and introduces itself to the astounded humans.

There are other memorable scenes: Harris must watch his wife 'drown' before she is resuscitated so that he can save her life. Later, he too must drown himself in oxygenated fluorocarbons so that he can breathe underwater for an extended period.

Biehn gives an excellent performance as a man driven to breaking point by the escalating suspense. He becomes obsessed with the notion that the aliens are a Russian secret weapon and he plans to detonate a nuclear warhead to destroy them. Harris must attempt to defuse the situation as well as get his team through the crisis alive.

The climax sees Harris descending into the depths of the ocean to stop the warhead going off, from where he goes on, in a scene of impressive TRANSCENDENCE, to discover the alien habitat. But at the last moment Cameron gives in to mainstream Hollywood commercial pressures and the aliens not only show Harris the right way to live but his stormy relationship with his wife is resolved in a sentimental happy ending. In previous Cameron movies, any closing reconciliation was tentative and ambiguous. In *The Abyss*, he ends his otherwise tense, exciting and atmospheric film not with a bang but a whimper.

That said, *The Abyss* is by genre standards a mature, involving work that makes a genuine effort to combine real scientific ideas with a big-budget, action-laden plot. The result is a well-crafted piece of cinema that stands as one of the better SF movies of the 1980s.

ALIEN (1979, 112 minutes)
Director: Ridley Scott
Producers: Gordon Carroll, David Giles, Walter Hill
Screenplay: Dan O'Bannon
Starring: Sigourney Weaver, John Hurt, Ian Holm, Veronica Cartwright, Harry Dean Stanton, Yaphet Kotto

Alien is one of the most unsettling SF movies to be produced during the latter half of the twentieth century.

An enormous mining vessel, *Nostromo*, answers what the crew perceives to be a distress call to a large, abandoned spacecraft. The signal turns out to be a warning – inside they find large pods containing strange, ALIEN creatures. One of these creatures attaches itself to the face of a member of the *Nostromo*'s crew and impregnates him with the seed of an alien being which later bursts out of his chest cavity in spectacular fashion and escapes into the disused corridors of the ship. What follows is an exercise in survival, as this dark and brutal killing machine picks off the crew members one by one. The alien is horrific and utterly unforgiving.

Ian Holm plays the role of an ANDROID who knows more about the aliens than he originally lets on, whilst Sigourney Weaver plays Ellen

Ripley, who is not the bitter, battle-scarred women she will later become in the various sequels, but a scientist who is thrust into a sinister and horrific situation and must attempt to survive. The movie becomes a battle of wits between her and the ferocious alien monster, which she eventually defeats by blowing it out of an airlock.

The movie is a classic, not for its plot, which harks back to the early days of 1950s alien invasion stories, but for its style and sinister edginess. It is shot with a real attention to detail, and it is a measure of Scott's directorial skill that the film continues to terrify its viewers. Its success lies in the stylish and claustrophobic atmosphere created by the director to increase the horrific nature of the alien beast, which is rarely seen on camera but stalks the crew members from just out of sight.

The creature itself was designed by artist H. R. GIGER, and he also designed many of the sets, giving them a wholly alien feel.

Alien is one of the most important SF HORROR movies.

There are three sequels – ALIENS (1986), Alien 3 (1992) and Alien: Resurrection (1997).

ALIEN NATION
Starring: Gary Graham (Sykes), Eric Pierpoint (Francisco)

This short-lived television series was derived from a 1988 movie, *Alien Nation*, and combined elements of police drama with an interesting take on the ALIEN invasion theme.

It is the NEAR FUTURE, and Los Angeles is home to quarter of a million dispossessed aliens, the Newcomers, whose space vessel crash-landed in the desert three years before the start of the series. These Newcomers are members of a slave race who were GENETICALLY designed to be compatible with any given environment. Now stranded on Earth, they attempt to settle in and integrate themselves into modern American society.

The chief protagonists of the series are detective Matt Sykes and his Newcomer partner George Francisco. Francisco is the first alien to make it to the rank of detective in the LAPD, and initially he must fight to overcome the xenophobia of his new partner. Gradually, however, as the series progresses, they begin to develop a strong friendship as they work together to solve each new crime.

This premise is no different from a handful of other cop shows, with the exception that the detailed alien background allows for a lot of moral philosophising about racism and the oppression of minority groups. Indeed, these themes are thoughtfully explored in many of the episodes, with Sykes eventually taking a Newcomer girlfriend and Francisco moving into a new neighbourhood where his family are the only aliens in the area.

Sadly, due to a lack of strong public support, *Alien Nation* was cancelled after just one season. It ran for twenty-one fifty-minute episodes between 1989 and 1990, with a feature-length pilot proceeding the series. There were also four follow-up television movies, *Dark Horizon*, *Body and Soul*, *Millennium* and *The Enemy Within*. All attempted to inject rather too much excitement and drama into their plots at the expense of further characterization.

ALIENS (1986, 137 minutes)
Director: James Cameron
Producer: Gale Ann Hurd
Screenplay: James Cameron, Walter Hill, David Giler
Starring: Sigourney Weaver, Michael Biehn, Paul Reiser, Carrie Henn

It is unusual for a sequel to have a real impact in its own right, and to be considered by a number of critics better than the original. However, James Cameron's *Aliens* was such a sequel.

It is a brave and creative film that subverts its subject matter and in doing so produces not a second SF HORROR movie, but a militaristic action thriller that draws heavily on images of World War Two and Vietnam.

Ellen Ripley (Weaver) is found drifting through space in suspended animation, the lone survivor of the *Nostromo*. She is revived and, to her dismay, discovers that nearly sixty years have passed since she went into hibernation. After a brief period of recovery in which she attempts to convince the big corporate chiefs of her experiences, which they seem all too keen to dismiss, she is recruited into a MILITARY mission which entails returning to a colony PLANET that has been overrun with ALIENS. It is thought her experiences with the creatures will provide the marines with first-hand expertise. A scout party sets out to locate and attempt to quarantine the danger. However, in typical Cameron style, everything does not go according to plan.

On one level the movie becomes a battle of muscle and will between the aliens and the marines, who, inevitably, cannot win against such a ferocious foe. It is not now the deadly hunter of the first film that the humans fear, but the overwhelming power of their hive. The colony is teeming with the creatures.

On another level, it becomes an exploration of the ineffectiveness of war to resolve any crisis, as well as taking a look at the role of the soldiers who are sent, perhaps knowingly, to their deaths.

Yet at its most primal level, *Aliens* is a movie about motherhood and the impulse to protect one's offspring for the perpetuation of the race. During the movie, Ripley comes across a scared little girl who, like Ripley herself at the end of the first movie, is the sole survivor of the alien invasion. Ripley takes this young girl under her wing, and at the end of the film, when the humans are retreating from the horrors of the alien hive, it becomes a matriarchal battle between Ripley and the alien queen.

The special effects are wonderfully done, and Cameron is true to Scott's original movie in the manner that the aliens are envisaged. The scenery is also important to the overall atmosphere of the movie, as the aliens have redesigned the human colony, metamorphosing it into an neo-Gothic, organic structure in which their biology plays a fundamental part. Indeed, Cameron draws a lot on the CYBERPUNK genre, fleshing out the details of the alien technology to illustrate their fundamental superiority over us – they have learned to manipulate biology for their own ends. However, the movie is laden with human gadgets and inventive military hardware, as if Cameron is trying to make the point that humanity is great at making war, but still has more fundamental skills to learn. What comes across though is an impression of Cameron's fetish for big guns and lots of action.

The actors themselves do their duty without question – the initial gung-ho of the marines is soon transformed into terror when they come face to face with their deadly foes, and Ripley wears a knowing 'told you so' expression throughout.

With *Aliens*, Cameron proved that sequels could be inventive and expressive in a way that does not simply retread old ground. He developed Scott's initial concept without at all detracting from the earlier film, at the same time reinventing the idea and transposing it into an altogether different type of movie. Aliens is SPACE OPERA with big guns and scary monsters.

Two further sequels followed *Aliens*. *Alien 3* (1992) sees a return to the format of the first movie, as Ripley heads to a penal colony in which a lone alien wreaks terror and death, whilst *Alien: Resurrection* (1997), the weakest of the films to date, sees her CLONED many years into the future, her genes irrevocably intertwined with that of the alien creatures. Ripley becomes a hybrid, much in the same way that the earlier films blend the SF element of their concept with something darker and more sinister. The *Alien* franchise continues to appeal.

ANDROMEDA STRAIN, THE (1971, 131 minutes)

Director: Robert Wise
Producer: Robert Wise
Screenplay: Nelson Gidding
Starring: Arthur Hill, David Wayne, James Olson, Kate Reid, Paula Kelly

Appearing twenty years after his seminal THE DAY THE EARTH STOOD STILL (1951), *The Andromeda Strain* is Robert Wise's subtle translation of MICHAEL CRICHTON'S novel, *The Andromeda Strain* (1969) to the screen.

A probe returns from space carrying an extraterrestrial virus. It crash-lands in a small town in New Mexico and, soon enough, all but two of the population are dead. A team of scientists is called in to quarantine and study the virus. However, it shows resilience and begins to mutate, eventually learning how to penetrate the seals of the scientists' protective garments. It becomes a race against time to learn how to defeat and contain the deadly virus that is threatening to kill not only the scientists working on it, and the population of the immediate area, but the majority of the human race. The film attempts to portray accurately and intelligently a group of scientists working together in a crisis situation.

However, there is more to this movie than a simple biological thriller. There are undercurrents of scientific POLITICS.

The ALIEN invaders in this movie are not intelligent or malicious, they are simply indiscriminate and merciless. But this is not really a film about an alien virus, more a cautionary tale of the failures of science, a story of the fallibility of our modern religion. Crichton has always questioned the morals and application of science, to the extent that on occasion his work has appeared decidedly antiscientific. *The Andromeda Strain* is a more subtle than this. The performances of the actors are quietly understated and emphasize the pre-eminence of the machines, which are seen to be the dominant force in the laboratory setting of much of the movie. Man has created a monster – a mechanical Frankenstein which is taking the place of humanity. It was the machine that brought back the virus from space and, although it devastated the human population where it landed, the probe itself is unharmed. Humanity is slowly becoming obsolete as a stronger, more resilient form of engineering takes over. This seems a little reactionary, and probably is, but the excellent manner in which it is portrayed on screen almost makes it a worthwhile argument. *The Andromeda Strain*, unlike later films such as THE TERMINATOR (1984) and THE MATRIX (1999) is not explicit in its exploration of the war against technology, but displays a more insidious and dangerous invasion – one which we are encouraging ourselves. In *The Andromeda Strain*, it is not the alien virus which is the true danger to the Earth, but humanity's reliance on machines.

BABYLON 5
Starring: Michael O'Hare (Sinclair), Jerry Doyle (Garibaldi), Bruce Boxleitner (Sheridan), Claudia Christian (Ivanova), Mira Furlan (Delenn), Peter Jurasik (Londo), Andreas Katsulas (G'Kar), Bill Mumy (Lennier), Andreas Thompson (Kosh)

Unique in genre television, Michael Straczinski's *Babylon 5* set out to provide a long and complex narrative that saw the development of a large cast of characters and took place over five distinct and complete seasons. From the very beginning, Straczinski had an ending in mind, and never intended the series to last any longer than was necessary to put the entire story across to the viewer. Essentially, *Babylon 5* is a television series with the structure of a novel.

Perhaps the most important thing about *Babylon 5* is that it was not like STAR TREK, but something new, breaking the mould that had become an integral part of SF television. For once, a story did not have to be resolved at the end of each episode, but could breathe and expand over the length of the entire series. Indeed, no episode was a complete adventure in itself, but built on the events of those that has already gone to work towards a stunning and revelatory climax.

This break from tradition had the obvious effect of alienating a number of viewers who would otherwise have watched the series on an occasional basis, but for those who invested in it from the start, it became a tale of truly epic proportions, a myth for a modern generation.

The events are centred around the human outpost, Babylon 5, which plays host not only to a small community of human beings but an array of representatives from various ALIEN species. The aim of the station and its commander, Jeffrey Sinclair, is to hold peaceful negotiations between warring alien factions in an attempt to bring about an era of galactic peace.

The plot itself is complex, and follows the lives of a group of characters – Sinclair, Sheridan, Garibaldi, Ivanova, Delenn, Londo, G'Kar – who all have different alliances but are brought together by a common need for peace. However, Straczinski's is a dark vision, and his future is marred by war and unrest. Indeed, many of the characters begin the story as enemies, and it is not for a long time that they begin to trust each other enough to form fresh alliances.

It is difficult even to begin to discuss the complexities of *Babylon 5* and its intricate plotting. It has its roots in the battle between good and evil, or between chaos and order. Suffice to say, it is one of the best SPACE OPERA television shows yet to be made, and benefits from being complete unto itself. Although occasionally a little melodramatic or camp, the actors play their parts well and develop their characters over the span of the series. The special effects are all computer generated, but are of a consistently high standard that compares well to the show's contemporaries. In the end, *Babylon 5* is a visual triumph.

In total, the series ran for one hundred and nine episodes (with an initial pilot) between 1994 and 1998.

Four television movies were also made. They are *In the Beginning*, *Thirdspace*, *River of Souls* and *A Call to Arms*. A short-lived spin-off series was *Crusade*.

BACK TO THE FUTURE (1985, 116 minutes)

Director: Robert Zemeckis
Producers: Steven Spielberg, Bob Gale, Neil Canton
Screenplay: Robert Zemeckis, Bob Gale
Starring: Michael J. Fox, Christopher Lloyd, Crispen Glover, Lea Thompson

Back to the Future is a well-constructed, humorous movie. It doesn't stand up to a great deal of analysis but it remains an engaging piece of entertainment.

The movie opens with a young, exuberant Marty McFly (Fox) visiting his friend, the archetypal mad professor (Lloyd), who has been at work converting a Delorean into a TIME machine. However, this time machine is powered by plutonium, and the terrorists from whom he stole it turn up to seek their revenge. Within ten minutes of the movie opening, the 'Doc' is shot dead. Marty escapes the terrorists in the Delorean, only to find that the time machine actually works and he is stranded in the 1950s. What follows is a fantastical romp in which multiplying time paradoxes threaten to deconstruct Marty's existence, unless he can bring his mother and father together in an unlikely union that will eventually lead to his birth. One of the most enduring images of the film is the photograph that Marty carries in his pocket, from which people keep disappearing as they cease to exist.

There are, however, issues that Zemeckis deals with in a subtle but affecting way.

The 1980s that he portrays, although far from being the DYSTOPIC nightmare of GEORGE ORWELL, is still brutal and unwelcoming. Marty's parents are ineffectual – one is a drunk, the other a deferential geek. His family is the epitome of modern existence, the nuclear family grown stale. The time machine is fuelled by terrorist plutonium, and the 'Doc' has been shot dead where he stands (although it later turns out that he was wearing a bulletproof vest and is fine). Indeed, Marty is at once comfortable and distressed in his own world, though his sensibilities seem more in keeping with the 1950s America in which he finds himself stranded. At least there he is recognized for what he is – a teenager with a bright future. *Back to the Future* is a nostalgic call to arms for a return to the heady days of the American dream.

Back to the Future is an excellent SCIENCE FANTASY, a well-scripted piece of COMIC SF that is bursting with charisma. Michael J. Fox puts in a good performance, and Christopher Lloyd becomes the quintessential nutty professor, defining the role for many future films to come. The supporting actors are also well cast, and the effects live up to all expectations.

The two other instalments in the trilogy are as deftly put together as the first, and continue the story of Marty and the 'Doc' as they attempt to unravel the time streams and return to their previous lives. *Back to the Future II* (1989) sees a trip forward in time, where Marty must save both himself and his future son from becoming too like his father, whilst *Back to the Future III* (1990) returns to the Wild West where the 'Doc' has been stranded and cannot find the necessary equipment to get him back to the 1980s.

BARBARELLA (1967, 98 minutes)
Director: Roger Vadim
Producer: Dino de Laurentiis
Screenplay: Terry Southern, Roger Vadim, Claude Brule, Vittorio Bonicelli, Clement Biddle Wood, Brian Degas, Tudor Gates
Starring: Jane Fonda, John Phillip Law, Anita Pallenberg, Milo O'Shea, David Hemmings, Marcel Marceau

Barbarella is a psychedelic fantasia of pop-art sensibilities and adult fairy tales, interwoven with all the genre clichés of SPACE OPERA, and with a chief protagonist who is a sex kitten to die for. If that all sounds confusing – it is.

Based on a comic strip from the 1960s, which was originally intended as an antidote to the rather brash adventures of FLASH GORDON, *Barbarella* is a blend of genres, from soft pornography to high space adventure.

The plot of the movie, such as it is, follows the eponymous heroine (Fonda) of the fortieth century as she journeys to Tau Ceti in search of the mad scientist Duran Duran (O'Shea) and his deadly 'positronic ray'. Much of what takes place is an exercise in displaying the scantily clad Fonda.

It took seven people, including Terry Southern, to construct the screenplay for the film, and the result is a cornucopia of different ideas and notions. We see a community of feral children with malicious dolls, we see a blind angel (Law), we see bizarre sex in a variety of different positions and techniques, and we see gadgets such as lurid spacecraft, deadly ray guns and a rather exciting 'excessive pleasure machine'. Indeed, Barbarella's quest is as much about her search for the ultimate orgasm as it is about Duran Duran.

The film is good to look at, and Fonda is suitably camp and sensuous in the lead role. The supporting cast do what they have to, but this is really about making Fonda into a star.

Barbarella is surreal and bizarre, and very much a product of its time. Its vision of a decadent future, full of free love and high adventure stems directly from the optimism of the decade in which it was written and filmed. *Barbarella* should perhaps be more properly considered a fantasy, but its enduring appeal and sheer unconventionality make it worthy of repeated viewing.

BATMAN (1989, 126 minutes)

Director: Tim Burton
Producers: Jon Peters, Peter Grober
Screenplay: Sam Hamm, Warren Skaaren
Starring: Michael Keaton, Jack Nicholson, Kim Basinger, Robert Wuhl, Pat Hingle, Billy Dee Williams

A dark and Gothic rendering of the caped crusader that is consistent with director Tim Burton's dark, surrealist vision.

Batman saw the first reinvention of the hero on screen since the heady, camp days of Adam West and his grey tights, and completely reassessed the character and his world in a more mature light. Gotham City becomes a sprawling, seedy metropolis, with sinister shadows around every corner and ornate, decadent architecture that is reminiscent of a scene from a particularly nasty fairy tale. Batman himself becomes a neurotic vigilante clad in semi-erotic black rubber, whilst his nemesis, The Joker, is a psychologically battered mugger. There is not a great deal of plot aside from the cool and often humorous interplay of the characters as they attempt to stalk, kill, or make love to each other. This doesn't matter; the movie is stylish and inventive, and perhaps the most worthy representation of the comic book hero yet to appear.

Burton's Gotham City and its inhabitants represent a fine piece of SF *noir*, and the controversial casting of Keaton as Batman pays off in the manner in which he portrays the character's psychologically inept, duel personality. Batman is not the generous saviour of the streets that he has been before, but a schizoid vigilante out for his own ends, wanted as much by the police as the criminals. Nicholson is remarkable as The Joker. Indeed, Keaton's Batman and Nicholson's Joker are from the same mould, and the beauty of Burton's vision is this ambivalence. Who is the hero and who is the villain? The reason that Batman becomes so intent upon defeating The Joker is that his enemy represents a manifestation of his own dark psyche which he is driven to conquer and destroy.

Batman spawned three sequels. *Batman Returns* (1992), also by Burton, was another triumph, and worked on developing the character even further, this time pitting him against both The Penguin (played by Danny DeVito) and Catwoman (played by Michelle Pfeiffer). *Batman Forever* (1995) and *Batman and Robin* (1997) are both weaker and return the character to his comic book roots, and are more reminiscent of the Adam West television series of the 1960s and 1970s.

BLADE RUNNER (1982, 117 minutes)

Director: Ridley Scott
Producer: Michael Deeley
Screenplay: Hampton Fancher, David Peoples
Starring: Harrison Ford, Rutger Hauer, Sean Young, Edward James Olmos, M. Emmet Walsh, Daryl Hannah

Based upon the novel, *Do Androids Dream of Electric Sheep?* (1968) by PHILIP K. DICK, *Blade Runner* had an enormous impact and is a much discussed and analysed film.

It is not so much in the telling of the story that the film excels, but more in the clarity of vision and the stylish *noir* settings that decorate the screen throughout.

The first theatrical release of the film failed in a number of respects, not least due to Ford's bland voice-over and the addition of a rather trite happy ending. These were removed, and additional footage was restored, for a far superior *Director's Cut* in 1992.

Set in a dank, dark and rain-soaked NEAR FUTURE America, an environmental DYSTOPIA that draws heavily on the emerging CYBER-PUNK genre, the movie follows the progress of bounty hunter Rick Deckard as he stalks the streets (and skies) of future Manhattan in search of a group of dissident ANDROIDS, or 'replicants'. The world has been blighted by ECOLOGICAL disaster, and much of the populace has moved off planet. The Tyrell Corporation develops the short-lived human replicants for use on the distant colony worlds. However, four have escaped from their oppressive bondage, and Deckard is employed to hunt them down and destroy them. This he does with an air of confused necessity – Deckard is an experienced 'blade runner', but his character appears forever unsure of his grimy surroundings, depressed and unable to escape the inevitable encroachment of death.

Whilst in pursuit of the androids, who ultimately want only to be free to live out their own short existence, Deckard falls in love with Rachel, who, it turns out, is also a replicant. The psychology of the situation is both painful and acute – Deckard shares no empathy with the androids he must execute, but at the same time, if he is to truly love Rachel, must come to realise their inherent humanity. In many ways, they are more alive than he, as Deckard is a hollow man, devoid of any recognisable morality. And this brings us to the crux of the movie, the debate as to whether Deckard himself is a replicant. It is certainly apparent in the *Director's Cut* that there is a level of ambiguity about Deckard's authenticity as a 'real' human being – it is suggested that one of the police chiefs is aware of the contents of Deckard's dreams, in turn implying that they may not be real.

Whatever the case, what is so important about *Blade Runner*, is the manner in which it is all put together; the magnificent set designs and the extraordinary lighting are what stick in the mind above all else. The movie is an example of style over substance. *Blade Runner* clicks into place, and each and every one of the actors provides a performance that is entirely in keeping with their character's surroundings. Scott reinvents not only the plot of the novel but the whole genre itself – SF movies would never look the same again. His streets are dirty and filled with drizzly pollution, his skies blaze with advertising and immense buildings – this is recognizable as the America of the future. The old has infected the new, and the urban squalor permeates everything. This is not an optimistic movie.

In the end, *Blade Runner* remains a very stylish, innovative and influential SF film of enormous importance to the genre.

BLAKE'S SEVEN
Starring: Gareth Thomas (Blake), Paul Darrow (Avon), Michael Keating (Vila), Jan Chapell (Cally), Jacqueline Pierce (Servalan), Stephen Grief (Travis), Peter Tuddenham (Zen, Orac, Slave)

Developed and written by Terry Nation, the man who had created the Daleks for DOCTOR WHO, *Blake's Seven* is a decidedly dark and pessimistic SPACE OPERA, with POLITICAL overtones.

Blake's Seven is set within a galactic DYSTOPIA in which 'The Federation' rules over the human race with a heavy hand, and any dissenters are swiftly executed or despatched to a distant penal colony. We follow the progress of Blake, a dissident who begins the series brainwashed and wrongly framed for child molestation, en route to the edge of the galaxy for incarceration.

However, it is not long before Blake defeats the psychologists and becomes aware of his real nature. Fortune has it that the penal ship comes across an abandoned ALIEN spacecraft, and the commanders decide to send six expendable prisoners over to see if it is safe. These prisoners, which include Blake, manage to hijack the vessel, and escape. They name their new ship *The Liberator*.

What follows is a four-season series that sees Blake and his gang pursued by the evil Federation representative Servalan and her obsessive sidekick Travis, while they attempt to give the Federation as much trouble as they can.

The special effects are decidedly wonky, but the scripts are intelligent and driven, and the emphasis of the series is more on the development of the characters than the adventures that they become involved in on their travels. In a similar way to the later BABYLON 5, *Blake's Seven*'s cast develop from episode to episode, eventually becoming fully rounded characters as opposed to the stereotypes that fill many of the roles in other SF shows. Essentially, the crew of *The Liberator* are criminals, and although they are doing battle against an oppressive regime, they remain of dubious morality. It is this equivocal approach to good and evil that defines *Blake's Seven*. It is fundamentally pessimistic about humanity but at the same time attempts to show that people who do wrong by their society are not necessarily evil.

The series culminates at the end of the fourth season with the death of the entire crew of *The Liberator* at the hands of the Federation.

Another interesting aspect of *Blake's Seven* is the nature of one of the characters. Zen was an ARTIFICIAL INTELLIGENCE that inhabited the computer systems on board *The Liberator*. This was most original at the time, and it is of great interest to see how the human characters interact with this machine, apparently viewing it as 'almost a human'. Far from being a tool for human or alien use, Zen was a character in his own right and formed one of the initial seven characters when the series began.

Blake's Seven remains one of the darkest SPACE OPERAS to be shown as a television series, and has attracted a massive cult following over the years. For those who found *Doctor Who* too juvenile or STAR TREK too righteous, *Blake's Seven* was the show to be watched.

Blake's Seven ran for a total of fifty-two episodes between 1978 and 1981. There is now a series of radio plays in production which reprises the roles of many of the cast.

BLOB, THE (1958, 85 minutes)

Director: Irvin S. Yeaworth Jr
Producer: Jack H. Harris
Screenplay: Theodore Simonson, Kate Phillips
Starring: Steve McQueen, Aneta Corseaut, Earl Rowe, Olin Howlin

Appearing the same year as the original version of THE FLY (1958), *The Blob* is fondly remembered for its shaky special effects and camp performances from the actors.

A gelatinous substance from outer space is brought to the Earth on the back of a meteor, which crashes into the area surrounding a small town in America. The Blob begins to grow larger and larger, until, after absorbing a number of townsfolk, it is spotted by a young Steve McQueen. He quickly goes to the authorities, but he is not believed and The Blob continues to devour the people of the town, and McQueen, getting desperate, rallies a group of troublesome teenagers to aid him in his quest. The authorities refuse to listen to the hero until the Blob gets so big that it cannot be ignored and they are forced to rely on his help in bringing it under control. They eventually destroy it by freezing it to death in the Antarctic.

The film is really nothing more than a glorified B-movie, but it makes good use of the few effects it has, and is original in its portrayal of teenagers as helpful citizens as opposed to delinquents. When compared to some of the other movies of the same period, such as *The Fly* and the earlier FORBIDDEN PLANET (1956), *The Blob* seems sadly lacking in content and structure, but nevertheless makes enjoyable and humorous viewing.

A direct, yet silly sequel followed in *Beware! The Blob* (1971). It is of no particular interest or ability. *The Blob* (1988) is a straight remake of the original and although it has much better special effects, it suffers from lack of originality, as well as an inferior cast.

BRAZIL (1985, 142 minutes)
Director: Terry Gilliam
Producer: Arnon Milchan
Screenplay: Terry Gilliam, Tom Stoppard, Charles McKeown
Starring: Jonathan Pryce, Robert DeNiro, Michael Palin, Kim Greist, Katherine Helmond, Ian Holm

Brazil is Terry Gilliam's homage to GEORGE ORWELL's *Nineteen Eighty-Four* (1949), but it is also more than that. It is a profound DYSTOPIAN fantasy and presents a painfully humorous critique of modern existence.

In a bizarre, regimented world, in which the majority of society lives in a vast network of subterranean tunnels around the bowels of an enormous machine, we follow the progress of investigator Sam Lowry (Pryce) as he attempts to reconcile a piece of erroneous data for the Ministry of Information. This mistake has come about because a bug in the computer system has altered the name of a known terrorist, and Lowry is charged with discovering the 'truth'. However, during the course of his investigation he meets and falls in love with Jill Layton (Greist), his version of Orwell's Julia. This causes the state to investigate him.

Gilliam's nightmare world is both oppressive and bleak. The pipes and ducts that run vein-like through the characters' world represent the cranky, decrepit body of the state upon which they rely without question – it brings them warmth and sustenance, but at a price. They must work to maintain it, to subscribe to its terrible and exacting regime, to help perpetuate it so that it grows stronger and does not fail. The people of *Brazil*, although Gilliam is at times sympathetic, have brought about their own problems. Like many Gilliam movies, *Brazil* is dark and unforgiving, lyrical and breathtaking.

CAPRICORN ONE (1978, 128 minutes)
Director: Peter Hyams
Producer: Paul N. Lazarus III
Screenplay: Peter Hyams
Starring: Elliott Gould, James Brolin, Brenda Vaccaro, Sam Waterson, O. J. Simpson

A cynical movie which capitalized on the paranoia prevalent after the uncovering of the Watergate conspiracy in the 1970s.

A group of three astronauts who are taking part on the first manned mission to Mars, are suddenly removed from their spacecraft at the last minute due to technical failures in the life-support systems. NASA, fearing repercussions for this failure, blackmails the astronauts into staging the Mars landing in a secret studio. The rocket is sent to Mars unmanned, and the landing is broadcast as if all had gone according to plan. However, when the rocket is destroyed upon returning to Earth, the astronauts are officially pronounced dead and begin to fear for their lives. Sure enough, the conspiracy darkens, and NASA assassins are despatched to 'remove' the last pieces of evidence in the conspiracy.

With a premise that sets out to provoke intelligent debate about

NASA and the openness of the US Space Program to the average citizen, *Capricorn One* is both worthwhile and of interest. Unfortunately, the latter part of the film descends into a series of run-of-the-mill action sequences as the astronauts attempt to escape from the NASA assassins. Indeed, a sequence straight out of a James Bond movie sees the astronauts rescued from their would-be killers. The movie is certainly not without merit and, although it eventually fails as a consistently good movie, *Capricorn One* explores the public perception of state institutions, and, perhaps more importantly, considers their duties to the public.

CHARLY (1968, 106 minutes)

Director: Ralph Nelson
Producer: Ralph Nelson
Screenplay: Stirling Silliphant
Starring: Cliff Robertson, Claire Bloom, Leon Janney, Lilia Skala, Dick Van Patten, William Dweyer

Based on the novel *Flowers for Algernon* (1966) by DANIEL KEYES, *Charly* is in many ways superior to the later THE LAWNMOWER MAN (1992) which attempts to tackle similar issues. However, it is over-sentimental and does get bogged down in a rather zealous attempt to point out the faults of contemporary society.

The story adheres closely to that of the novel. Charly (Robertson), a mentally retarded young man, becomes the object of an experiment in surgery and psychology, which aims to improve the level of his intelligence. Initially, the process is a success, and Charly is elevated to the level of a genius, growing into emotional maturity and becoming aware of the social stigma associated with his previous condition. However, when Algernon, the mouse who preceded Charly in the experimental process, begins to fade, Charly can only sit back and wait as his newfound intelligence seeps away and he returns to his previous moronic state.

Emotive and moving, the movie does get a little clichéd in places, particularly during the central part of the story when Charly begins to spout an ill-considered diatribe against the world.

However, it is a worthy interpretation of Keyes's novel.

CLOCKWORK ORANGE, A (1971, 136 minutes)

Director: Stanley Kubrick
Producers: Stanley Kubrick, Bernard Williams
Screenplay: Stanley Kubrick
Starring: Malcolm McDowell, Patrick Magee, Michael Bates, Adrienne Corri

A disturbing and controversial film which has its basis in ANTHONY BURGESS's classic novel, *A Clockwork Orange* (1962).

After its original release, Kubrick himself, in a reaction to an alleged spate of violent copycat episodes throughout the country, removed the movie from the British market. It was again released after Kubrick's death in 1999.

It is a startling film, a creative extravaganza which, although notorious for its portrayal of 'ultra violence', isn't actually about violence at all. *A Clockwork Orange* draws on the great tradition of British DYSTOPIAN writing and, in a manner reminiscent of GEORGE ORWELL's *Nineteen Eighty-Four* (1949), has more to do with state repression and the search for individual freedom than the gang violence it is purported to champion. It is a brave and unwavering study of humanism.

Alex (McDowell) and his gang of 'Droogs' set out on an orgy of drugs, violence and rape. Alex is a highly intelligent man with a penchant for Beethoven, yet his immoral approach to life is manifested in the most horrific ways. Kubrick does not approve of Alex's antics – far from it – but the film is a statement about freedom of choice and the right to break away from the mechanics of the state. It does not make easy viewing, but that is the point of *A Clockwork Orange* – there are no easy ways to live a human life.

In the end, Alex is betrayed by his associates and, having been arrested, is institutionalized for psychological 'treatment'. In their attempts to eradicate Alex's unacceptable behaviour, the authorities remove his very humanity. One of the most effective moments in the film is when Alex, having been 'cured' and released, finds himself unable to listen to Beethoven any longer. Not only has his penchant for violence gone, but so has his appreciation of the finer arts.

The language that permeates the movie, 'Nadsat', is derived directly from Burgess's novel and is a clever hybrid of English and Russian. Into this heady mix of linguistics is thrown a smattering of slang that gives the characters an opportunity to express themselves in a various manner of ways, and adds a quality of realism that is lacking in so much SF.

McDowell is wonderful in the role of Alex, and Kubrick fulfils all of the potential of Burgess's novel. *A Clockwork Orange* is an intelligent, harrowing movie that, like Alex, can be read on two very different levels. As a piece of political, dystopian SF, it remains a valid study of humanity.

CLOSE ENCOUNTERS OF THE THIRD KIND (1977, 135 minutes)

Director: Steven Spielberg
Producers: Julia Phillips, Michael Phillips
Screenplay: Steven Spielberg
Starring: Richard Dreyfuss, François Truffaut, Teri Garr, Melinda Dillon

Close Encounters of the Third Kind is perhaps the most optimistic and profound ALIEN contact movie. Far superior to the later Spielberg *E. T.* (1982), which descends into heavy-handed sentimentality, and more mature than STAR WARS which appeared the same year, *Close Encounters* explores the spiritual and pseudo-RELIGIOUS aspects of extraterrestrial intelligence, and prefigures many alien movies to come.

An electrical engineer, Roy Neary (Dreyfuss), is witness to a series of bright lights in the sky. Afterwards, he finds inexplicable images imprinted on his mind, and becomes obsessed with a spiritual quest to seek out the aliens he believes he has witnessed. His family life is devastated, but as he draws nearer to his goal it becomes clear that he is fated to make a pilgrimage to Devil's Tower, an enormous geographical structure in Wyoming. Once there, he is witness to one of the most dazzling and effective scenes in cinematic history – the arrival of a vessel from the stars.

The human welcoming party communicates with the alien spacecraft through sequences of music and flashing lights and then, in a moment of religious fervour, Neary goes on to TRANSCEND his human identity and leaves with the aliens to explore the stars.

There is nothing frightening about the aliens in *Close Encounters*; they are harmless creatures who have come to teach us about the universe. It is clear from Spielberg's direction that he is optimistic about the future of the human race. He sees us as children, vulnerable and naive, but, because of this, more open to wonder and new modes of thought. It is Neary's innocence and wide-eyed faith in the intentions of the visitors that cause him to be selected by them to visit the stars.

In his portrayal of humanity as a young race, ignorant of the wider canvas of the universe, Spielberg redeems us, allows for our mistakes and suggests that we are only just learning how to live. It will be years before, as a race, we reach maturity, but the aliens will help us along the way.

In a similar way to CONTACT (1997), but with a much earlier perspective, *Close Encounters* is a movie about faith, both in the inherent goodness of the human race and in the existence of extraterrestrial life.

Dreyfuss is cast well in the role of Neary, and plays his child-like fascination with the aliens well. But it is the special effects that truly lift *Close Encounters* above the other movies of its time. The arrival of the alien vessel is one of the most enduring scenes in SF cinema, and one which had an amazing effect on the genre as a whole.

Close Encounters of the Third Kind is a movie which has not aged. As relevant today as it was when it was first released, it succeeds in exploring the religious impulse in an utterly fresh way, as well as offering a vision of alien contact that has inspired and affected the genre for many years. It is Spielberg's best foray into the genre, and one of the better SF movies to come out of the 1970s.

CONTACT (1997, 144 minutes)

Director: Robert Zemeckis
Producers: Robert Zemeckis, Steve Starkey
Screenplay: James V. Hart, Michael Goldenberg
Starring: Jodie Foster, Matthew McConaughey, James Woods, John Hurt, Tom Skerritt, Angela Bassett

Based on the novel *Contact* (1985) by renowned physicist Carl Sagan, *Contact* is a thoughtful, provocative film that discusses the differences between science and RELIGION and the tension that may exist between them upon FIRST CONTACT with an ALIEN species. What the movie does, and the book does not, is strike a balance between the human interest of the story and the scientific wonder at the discovery of extra-terrestrial life.

Ellie Arroway (Foster) is an obsessive research scientist at work on the SETI project (the Search for Extraterrestrial Intelligence), who deciphers a stream of data that is received at a South American satellite base. This data turns out to be a message from an alien intelligence which provides a blueprint for a spacecraft and the coordinates to where they can be found. The debate begins as to whether to build this vessel, and who should sit at the helm.

At this point the movie almost descends into a complex science vs RELIGION debate, as Arroway comes up against the will of poet turned evangelist, and former lover, Palmer Joss (McConaughey). However, Arroway finally comes through, winning the opportunity to man the one-person craft and, to the relief of the viewers, the plot moves on. Yet religion remains an integral part of the movie. Arroway's trip in the space vessel becomes almost metaphysical, as, through a TIME dilation effect, she appears to the monitoring scientists to have been out of reach for only seconds. The ship does not appear to leave Earth, and it is thought that the mission has been a failure. However, in a beautiful and enigmatic moment of TRANSCENDENCE, Arroway is provided with a vision of the extraterrestrial, who she encounters on a moonlit beach in the form of her father. It is suggested that the creatures have provided this manifestation as a means of allowing Arroway to comprehend their otherwise impenetrable form. It also allows for a rather trite moment as she is able to reconcile the loss of her father and, in a rather oversentimentalized scene, come to understand the extraterrestrials.

In the end, the movie appears to make the point that science itself is a form of religion. Arroway is disbelieved by the other scientists, who claim that she could not possibly have witnessed the events that she claims in the time that she was out of communication with them. She maintains that she did, and her experience amounts to a pseudo-religious vision within which she comes face to face with her deepest desire – an encounter with an alien race. The viewer is left to ponder whether this has been inspired by her personal need to believe in life outside of Earth. This ambiguity is the key to the success of *Contact* as a piece of film. It is intelligent, thought provoking and satisfying.

CUBE (1998, 87 minutes)

Director: Vincenzo Natali
Producer: Mehra Meh, Betty Orr
Screenplay: Vincenzo Natali, Andre Bijelic, Graeme Manson
Starring: Nicole DeBoer, Nicky Guadagni, David Hewlitt, Andrew Miller

An independent SF HORROR movie that seemed to come from nowhere in 1998, but which nevertheless everyone was talking about, *Cube* is, perhaps, a little overrated.

The premise is an interesting one – a small group of people wake up to find themselves inside an enormous cubic structure, which is divided into a number of linked and booby-trapped chambers. These chambers are all numbered, and shift about on a vast mechanical axis. The protagonists have no idea why they are inside this contraption, and attempt to work together to free themselves from its constraints. Many of them fall prey to the grisly booby traps along the way.

Cube attempts to offer a psychological insight into the mind of a group of people who have been trapped and cornered like animals. As they search for the elusive exit and begin to solve the puzzles that will enable them to locate it, tensions build and fragile relationships break down. However, the action all takes place on one set (which does change colour to indicate various different chambers), and the movie lacks characterization and pace.

It does have some redeeming features – the unpredictable outcome of the plot, the psychological tension that builds as the protagonists near their destination, the sense of mystery inherent to their surroundings (it is left unclear who has constructed this massive mantrap, and why).

The result is a prosaic and unsatisfactory movie that remains an interesting attempt to inject an intelligent freshness into a cinematic genre that can all too often become stale and self-referential. For that it should be applauded. It is just a shame that it does not quite succeed as planned.

DARK CITY (1997, 97 minutes)
Director: Alex Proyas
Producers: Andrew Mason, Alex Proyas
Screenplay: Alex Proyas, Lem Dobbs, David S. Goyer
Starring: Rufus Sewell, Kiefer Sutherland, Jennifer Connelly, Richard O'Brien, Ian Richardson, William Hurt

Dark City is a bleak, paranoiac movie about ALIEN abduction and one of the forms it could take.

John Murdoch (Sewell) awakens to find that his life has been irrevocably changed. He can't quite remember what it was supposed to be like, but is sure that the dark, Gothic streets of the city don't quite look like they used to. He soon realises that he is trapped in the city, and that he can never seem to get to the beach for which he is always seeing signs. The sun never comes out, and every day people awaken with a sense of amnesia. Murdoch begins the search for his missing past, and in doing so unravels a plot that sees reality itself deconstructed before his eyes and the life of everyone he knows in ruins.

It transpires that sinister aliens have been abducting human beings and transporting them to a vast ARTIFICIAL ENVIRONMENT in space, which is shaped and formed into a twisted version of Manhattan. These aliens, who have inherent telekinetic powers, are intent upon researching the human race and are trying to find out what constitutes a soul. Every night they steal the memories of those abducted, so that, upon waking, they go about their business with only a mild sense of dislocation. To them, life has always been this way. However, the enigmatic Dr Schreber (Sutherland), who is supposedly in league with the aliens, has other plans, and concocts a plot that will allow him to create a superhuman out of Murdoch and bring the reign of the aliens to an end. This he does, in a rather trite action sequence which eventually results in Murdoch remodelling the city to his own ends and bringing about a dawn by giving birth to a star.

The movie ultimately fails because of an over-reliance on a big finale which is not in keeping with the tone of the rest of the movie. The premise itself is of great interest, and the images of a vast city floating through uncharted space, carrying its unwitting citizens into the perpetual abyss, are both moving and inspiring. It is also interesting to see the aliens portrayed as not necessarily malicious, but simply questing to attain a level of knowledge that will allow them to better understand the universe. However, the point at which Murdoch inherits the telekinetic powers that will allow him to destroy the entire alien population, as well as destroying the machines which they use to shackle humanity, is both overplayed and ill advised. The movie descends into an action adventure that destroys all of the carefully developed tensions and ideas that had carried it through to this point.

The performances throughout the movie vary, but Sewell, Sutherland and Hurt put in good performances, in keeping with the *noirish* feel of the movie. The aliens themselves are little more than discoloured human beings with strange powers, but O'Brien is satisfactory as one of their agents, obsessed himself with knowing the secrets of human existence.

In the end, *Dark City* does not live up to the expectations which are created from the outset of the film, but it does make use of some interesting themes.

DARK STAR (1974, 83 minutes)

Director: John Carpenter
Producer: John Carpenter
Screenplay: John Carpenter, Dan O'Bannon
Starring: Brian Narelle, Dre Pahich, Cal Kuniholm, Dan O'Bannon

The first movie to be made by director John Carpenter, who would later go on to shoot, among others, ESCAPE FROM NEW YORK (1981) and the remake of THE THING (1982), *Dark Star* was originally shot by a group of students at film college, but was later picked up by a studio who provided funding for further footage.

The movie successfully satirises the other SF movies of the time, and offers a view of life in space that is far removed from the bright, clean, optimistic pretences of its contemporaries; the ship is dirty and malfunctioning, the crew bored and alone.

The plot is simple. The crew of the space vessel, upon which the entirety of the film is shot, are charged with wandering the stars in search of unstable PLANETS which they destroy with their armoury of nuclear weapons. However, the captain is 'dead' and stored CRYO-GENICALLY on the ship, woken only when the crew is in need of advice, an ALIEN mascot which is kept on board has gone on the rampage and is chasing crew members around the ship, and one of the ARTIFICIALLY INTELLIGENT bombs has to be talked out of prematurely detonating itself. This often hilarious combination results in one of the freshest and most satisfactory pieces of SF cinema to appear before STAR WARS (1977) and CLOSE ENCOUNTERS OF THE THIRD KIND (1977).

Eventually, everything is resolved in the only possible way – the bomb decides to explode. The human characters, who are all lost in various states of psychotic surreality, accept this with an almost calm inevitability, going on to act out their fantasies in their final moments – one goes surfing on the nuclear wave whilst another dreams only of becoming one with an asteroid belt. Ironically, in the entire movie, the only thing to fulfil its potential is the intelligent, man-made bomb.

Dark Star is an important film, as it was shot on such a small budget and became an antidote to the blandly optimistic movies about space travel that were beginning to appear. It parodies 2001: A SPACE ODYSSEY (1968) with an intelligent clarity and happily mocks the serene sterility of ship life that the other film portrays, instead preferring to liken prolonged periods in space to spending time in a kind of Alcatraz in the sky. When the bomb decides to explode the characters are almost thankful that something exciting is happening.

Dark Star is a wonder, a fine example of COMIC SF and SPACE OPERA, and a testament to its director's skill.

DAY THE EARTH CAUGHT FIRE, THE
(1961, 99 minutes)
Director: Val Guest
Producer: Val Guest
Screenplay: Val Guest, Wolf Mankowitz
Starring: Edward Judd, Janet Munro, Leo McKern, Michael Goodliffe, Bernard Braden, Reginald Beckwith

A wonderfully conceived movie that examines, in a fresh and thoroughly inventive manner, the threat of atomic weapons and the effect that their testing may have upon the planet.

Russian and American explosions at the North and South Poles knock Earth out of its usual orbit and send it careering towards the sun. Disruption follows, as the planet looks increasingly doomed and the temperature begins to rise. In the offices of the *Daily Express*, London, a small group of journalists attempts to keep the populace informed. The reactions of these reporters represent a microcosm of the reactions of the world's populace – fascination, horror and ultimately relief. They report on the changing climate – the River Thames dries up – and the attempts by each of the world's powers to avert the crisis.

Ironically, it is only with the detonation of four other atomic bombs that Earth is saved from burning up and is knocked back into its own, original orbit. This represents the ambiguity that is *The Day the Earth Caught Fire*; atomic weapons may have won World War Two for the Allies, but their use has become a dangerous double-edged sword. This is best exemplified by the famous scene in which two newspaper headlines are pictured side by side, one reading 'World Doomed', the other 'World Saved'.

The movie does not rely on amazing special effects, but rather on a well-crafted script and a an increasing sense of tension as the catastrophe nears its conclusion. It is bleak but also cautionary and of importance. In keeping with the rest of the movie, the performances of the actors are both engrossing and memorable.

DAY THE EARTH STOOD STILL, THE (1951, 89 minutes)
Director: Robert Wise
Producer: Julian Blaustein
Screenplay: Edmund H. North
Starring: Michael Rennie, Patricia Neal, Hugh Marlowe, Billy Gray, Sam Jaffe, Lock Martin

The Day the Earth Stood Still is a landmark genre movie that changed the face of SF cinema and injected a certain degree of intelligence and dignity into what was then considered to be only a pulp field. The movie did much to reinvent the genre and present it as serious and rational.

The plot is a simple one. An ALIEN, Klaatu (Rennie), and his disturbingly powerful and enigmatic ROBOT bodyguard Gort visit the Earth in an attempt to inform the human race of the dangerous nature of their ways. From the very first scenes, when the arrival of a speeding spacecraft in an unknown area of America sparks off a mass deployment of military force, *The Day the Earth Stood Still* speaks volumes.

Klaatu and Gort disembark from their vessel, speaking the words 'We have come to visit you in peace and with goodwill', only to be shot at by a nervous army sniper. The gift of extraterrestrial technology that they have brought with them is swiftly destroyed. And so the film continues. Klaatu attempts to bring his news to the attention of various authorities, but to no avail. He eventually befriends a small boy, Bobby, who leads him to a powerful scientist, and together they hatch an ingenious plot that will enable Klaatu to deliver his message to a world shocked into silent attention – they plan to cause a power cut that will affect the entire planet. However, Klaatu finds himself betrayed to the army and is executed upon returning to his vessel. Gort retaliates with his devastating laser, but Bobby's mother (Neal), whom Klaatu had earlier confided in, commands Gort to stop short of destroying Earth. Instead, he resurrects Klaatu, and they activate the power cut, bringing the world to a total standstill. He delivers his message – that various alien races are disgruntled at the human use of atomic weapons, and that if we do not stop our planet will be obliterated – and then, after depositing Gort as a guardian of the planet, leaves in his spacecraft.

The RELIGIOUS analogies of the movie are clear. Klaatu arrives in a bright chariot from the stars and attempts to inform humanity of the means of their redemption. His words at first fall on deaf ears, so he assembles a small group of confederates to aid him in his quest. However, one of them betrays him, and he is executed by the authorities, only to rise again to deliver his message to a race now stunned by his dignity and power. He then disappears into the ether to leave humanity to ponder his words without question. Klaatu is an alien reinvention of the MESSIAH, a Christ arrived from the stars to teach us how to live.

The performances are superb. Neal, unusually for a film of the 1950s, is a strong, active woman who is never fazed by her experiences, but ultimately confronts the danger and saves the planet from utter destruction. Rennie is the quintessential alien – smart, serious and patient.

The Day the Earth Stood Still is seminal and, with its acute, intelligent approach to its subject matter, as well as its inimitable style, it remains a benchmark by which all other alien movies are judged.

DELICATESSEN (1990, 90 minutes)
Directors: Jean-Pierre Jeunet and Marc Caro
Producer: Claudie Ossard
Screenplay: Gilles Adrien, Marc Caro, Jean-Pierre Jeunet
Starring: Marie-Laure Dougnac, Jean-Claude Dreyfuss, Dominique Pinon
French with English subtitles.

Set against the backdrop of a POST APOCALYPTIC world, *Delicatessen* is a darkly comic SCIENCE FANTASY.

It is sometime in the indefinite future and the inhabitants of a dilapidated block of flats above a butcher's shop survive by encouraging their landlord's cannibalistic tendencies. This equilibrium is soon destroyed when a charming circus clown accepts a position as odd-job man in the building (unwittingly stepping into line as the butcher's next victim) and finds himself falling in love with the butcher's daughter. Chaos ensues when she enlists the aid of the Troglodistes, an underground vegetarian movement, to help her protect her beloved from her meat-cleaver-wielding father.

Containing elements of fantasy alongside more traditional SF themes (the dying, DYSTOPIAN landscape, the forced continuation of a 'civilized' lifestyle, the formation of an extremist underclass), *Delicatessen* is a highly original and entertaining piece of film that explores not only the slow dissolution of a society struggling to survive after a holocaust, but the darker recesses of the human condition.

DESTINATION MOON (1950, 91 minutes)
Director: Byron Haskin
Producer: George Pal
Screenplay: Rip Van Ronkel, ROBERT HEINLEIN, James O'Hanlon
Starring: Warner Anderson, John Archer, Tom Powers, Dick Wesson

Based on the novel *Rocketship Galileo* (1947) by Robert Heinlein, and co-scripted by the writer, *Destination Moon* is one of the first SF movies to attempt to inject some realism into its portrayal of space flight and lunar exploration.

The film itself is relatively unspectacular. It describes in great detail the first ascent of mankind to the Moon. Once there, they discover that they have not saved enough fuel for the return journey, and so must attempt to work out a way in which they can jettison the excess weight and take off for home. This they do, in a rather ingenious and inventive way.

The movie itself is dry and uninvolving. The narrative is structured in a documentary style which, at the time, was almost revolutionary, but now appears a little tired and weak. The performances are satisfactory but plodding, and the sets, although excellently realized, are put to little dramatic use.

However, in this instance it is not the movie itself that is important, but the effect that it had upon the industry of the time. *Destination Moon* showed that SF could be serious as well as fun, and gave the genre an entirely new lease of life.

The film is prescient and almost accurate in the way it portrays the journey of the astronauts and their descent to the surface of the Moon. Indeed, the director and producers enlisted the aid of top physicists to ensure that what they finally committed to film was as authentic as possible.

It also carried an urgent message to the American people – get into space now before anyone else does. It is almost as if the writers were predicting the space race that would later take place between America and Russia, and were attempting to give the Americans a head start.

Destination Moon is the first attempt at HARD SF to be seen in the cinematic genre, and it opened up the floodgates that allowed many other important SF movies of the 1950s to be made. In a similar way to the British THE QUATERMASS XPERIMENT (1955), the success of *Destination Moon* paved the way for many fine pictures.

DOCTOR STRANGELOVE, OR HOW I LEARNED TO STOP WORRYING AND LOVE THE BOMB (1964, 94 minutes)

Director: Stanley Kubrick
Producers: Stanley Kubrick, Victor Lyndon
Screenplay: Stanley Kubrick, Terry Southern, Peter George
Starring: Peter Sellers, George C. Scott, Peter Bull, Sterling Hayden

Yet another triumph from Stanley Kubrick, *Doctor Strangelove* is a dark and biting satire on the relationship between humans and their doomsday technology. Featuring a marvellous script and perhaps Seller's best ever performance, the movie is both a serious exploration of human POLITICS and a hysterical romp through the darker side of lunacy.

An American general (Hayden), obsessed with conspiracy, believes the Russians to be plotting the theft of our bodily fluids, and so, disregarding all safety protocols, orders a nuclear bomb to be dropped on the USSR. Suddenly, all hell is let loose.

Sellers takes three disparate roles – a very English RAF officer held captive by the American general, an ex–Nazi scientist with a mechanical arm and a balding, ineffectual president of the USA.

A meeting is quickly convened in the War Room, but attempts to contact the B–52 with the bomb on board fail as communications go down. The President is left to explain to the Russian ambassador, in his most disarming manner, that a trifling mistake has been made and a nuclear warhead is about to fall on his country.

It seems inevitable that there will be a retaliation from the Russian army, and instead of attempting to avert the crisis, the powers that be sit back and wait for the end of the world. It is a poignant moment – the knowledge that one man with the wrong idea could bring about the end of civilization. This is the crux of *Doctor Strangelove*, the irony that although it has taken some of the most intelligent people in the world to devise and develop a doomsday weapon, it only takes one madman to use it.

The film is irreverent and bold, and looks at the ludicrous nature of nuclear weapons and the inevitable results if they ever come to be used. Before its time, it heralds the advent of the true nuclear movie, taking a decidedly political stance and displaying a distinct lack of respect for authority. However, perhaps even more relevant than that, it is an important marker in the exploration of the relationship between humanity and their machines, a sideways swipe at the technologists who have focused their attentions on devising ever more powerful weapons rather than working towards a unifying, peace-giving goal. Kubrick's sentiment is very clear – if we are not careful, our own technology will herald our downfall as a species.

Of the various films that Kubrick produced for the genre, *Doctor Strangelove* has to be his most poignant and pointed. It is not in the telling that the film excels, but more in the way it causes one to laugh at the fallibility of our own race. For, although the movie is exceptionally funny, it has a pressing and deadly message to us all. When it comes to nuclear weapons, we really shouldn't be laughing.

DOCTOR WHO
Starring: William Hartnell, Patrick Troughton, Jon Pertwee, Tom Baker, Peter Davidson, Colin Baker, Sylvester McCoy, Paul McGann

Doctor Who is the quintessential British SF television show. It is also the longest consecutively running genre series in the world. This is partly due to the flexibility of its format, allowing almost any plot to be slotted easily into the adventures of the eponymous Timelord, and for any number of leading actors to be able to adopt the role.

The premise is simple. A rebellious ALIEN Timelord – the Doctor – sick of the bureaucracy of his home PLANET Gallifrey, steals a TARDIS and sets off adventuring through time and space.

The TARDIS was an ingenious invention, a space-time vessel that, because its interior existed outside reality, was far bigger inside than it appeared from without. It also had a chameleon circuit that would allow it to camouflage itself to blend in with the local scenery wherever it came to rest. However, the Doctor's TARDIS was an old, malfunctioning model that would frequently displace him and his various human companions to random sites across the universe, where they would always attempt to avert whatever crisis they found themselves in the middle of before moving on to their next stop. The chameleon circuit on the Doctor's TARDIS was also stuck in the form of a 1960s British Police telephone box, meaning that the Doctor could never make his appearances as incongruously as he would have liked. Indeed, it is this ironic humour that characterises *Doctor Who* above anything else, and gives it a kind of self-deprecating eccentricity that is at once both charming and hilarious.

The actual plots of the stories, which ran to anything from four to fourteen episodes, are derived from classic pulp SF, although the series often gave them an unusual and intelligent spin. Often there would be a monster of some sort involved, none so terrifying as the Daleks developed by Terry Nation, a race of CYBORG killing machines hell bent on universal domination.

Many later episodes also featured the Doctor's nemesis, the Master, an evil Timelord whose terrible plans the Doctor was always keen to foil, but who nevertheless seemed to be able to get away in his own TARDIS just in time to escape.

Doctor Who's stories were in many ways true to the SF genre from which they came. Although the concepts were rarely based on real scientific theory, attempts to rationalise the plots were always in good faith, and at least a good number of the intelligent alien species the Doctor encountered were more than simple 'bad guys', but had their own intentions and desires. Indeed, many writers who cut their teeth writing episodes of *Doctor Who*, such as DOUGLAS ADAMS, later went on to do other things in the genre.

The series itself was sustained for so long by the fact that the Doctor, being an alien, had any number of different incarnations. This entailed a succession of actors adopting the role as each of the incarnations of the Timelord was killed off in some way or other. This in turn led to a welcome diversity, as each of the actors brought with him a new personality and an entirely different take on the Doctor. Some were camp, some eccentric, some miserable and some adventurous. All were a joy to watch.

The most famous incarnation of the Doctor was played by Tom Baker during the 1970s, and for many people he remains the epitome of what the Timelord represents.

Doctor Who, like STAR TREK in America, is a national institution, the most important British SF series ever created. Although there are regular rumours of it resurfacing, this looks unlikely. Given that the sets were always wobbly and the tone of the series as a whole was decidedly pulp in nature, it would perhaps be a little out of place in today's modern special- effects climate. Indeed, an attempt to resurrect the series did come in 1996 with the production of a television movie set in the USA, starring Paul McGann as the Doctor. Ultimately, it failed to satisfy fans and failed to capture any new audiences, and so the project was indefinitely suspended. Only time will tell if it ever will make a proper comeback.

The series comprised a total of six hundred and ninety-four episodes between 1963 and 1989, most of which were twenty-five minutes in length. Unfortunately, many of the earlier episodes have been lost or degraded in the BBC archives and are unavailable for viewing.

The Doctor also had two brief flirtations with the big screen. Peter Cushing starred in *Dr Who and the Daleks* (1965) and *Daleks: Invasion Earth* (1966), although both failed miserably to capture the inherent fun that made the series so good.

There is a whole industry of spin-off books and radio plays that has sprung up in the intervening years, and continue the adventures of the various Doctors. Most, but not all, are produced in cooperation with the BBC.

DUNE (1984, 136 minutes)
Director: David Lynch
Producer: Raffaella de Laurentiis
Screenplay: David Lynch
Starring: Kyle MacLachlan, Sting, Max Von Sydow, Patrick Stewart, Linda Hunt

A sadly disappointing adaptation of FRANK HERBERT's classic novel *Dune* (1965).

The movie is a vast, sprawling SCIENCE FANTASY, that tries, perhaps too closely, to follow the plot of the novel. This results in a fractured, fragmentary film that looks good but suffers from internal inconsistencies.

The story is that of the Atreides family, who inherit the PLANET Arrakis, or Dune, from the galactic emperor, and with it all the inherent strife and conspiracy that plagues such an important constituency. For Arrakis is the only known planet to produce the immortality drug, Melange, the spice that keeps the emperor on his throne and the upper classes in power.

Interwoven into this tale is the climate of infighting and back stabbing that exists between the almost medieval élite classes, in particular the feud between House Atreides and House Harkonnen. Paul Atreides, heir to the Dukedom of the Atreides, sets out to avenge the murder of his father at the hands of the Harkonnens, and almost unwittingly steps into the role of MESSIAH, eventually becoming the saviour of Arrakis. He leads the nomadic Fremen people into a rebellion against the empire and is hailed as their religious leader, Muad'Dib.

The movie maintains the intense study of RELIGION that was so important to the feel of the novel. Indeed, Lynch manages to create the right atmosphere, with beautiful, intense imagery and the roles that are well played by the cast. It is simply that the film is too short to tell the whole tale of *Dune*, so that, by the end, the viewer is left confused and many of the story lines are unresolved.

EMPIRE STRIKES BACK, THE (1980, 124 minutes)
Director: Irvin Kershner
Producer: Gary Kurtz
Screenplay: Leigh Brackett, Lawrence Kasdan
Starring: Mark Hamill, Harrison Ford, Carrie Fisher, Billy Dee Williams, David Prowse

By far the best STAR WARS movie to appear to date, *The Empire Strikes Back* benefits greatly from its dark atmosphere. The story continues the events that began in *Star Wars* (1977), developing the myth and the characters.

The movie itself feels a little episodic, but charts the individual progress of Luke Skywalker and his colleagues as they part and go their separate ways in an attempt to aid the growing resistance movement. Luke himself journeys to a backwater PLANET to seek out Yoda, the mystical alien sage who teaches him to better control the Force and to realize the moral responsibility he must shoulder in adopting the messianic role.

The story culminates in a betrayal which sees the mercenary Han Solo in suspended animation, and a battle between Luke and Darth Vader, in which Vader reveals his true identity to Luke – that he is his father. This revelation adds to Luke's character, and shows a possible dark side that does much to bring down the stereotypical polarization that the first movie set up between the sides of good and evil. The sequence as a whole benefits greatly from this added complexity.

The special effects far surpass those of *Star Wars*, as the budget was effectively trebled, but the characters remain a little wooden and ineffective.

Nevertheless, *The Empire Strikes Back*, because of its added moral complexity and moody atmospherics, as well as its lighter moments, is superior to the rest of the Star Wars SCIENCE FANTASY sequence.

ESCAPE FROM NEW YORK (1981, 99 minutes)

Director: John Carpenter
Producers: Denra Hill, Larry Franco
Screenplay: John Carpenter, Nick Castle
Starring: Kurt Russell, Ernest Borgnine, Lee Van Cleef, Donald Pleasance, Isaac Hayes, Harry Dean Stanton

A NEAR FUTURE tale in which Manhattan Island has been fenced off as a penal colony, inhabited by all manner of violent criminals and gangs. When the president's plane crashes on the island and he is taken hostage by one such gang (led by Hayes), Snake Plisskin (Russell), an ex-soldier turned lawbreaker is offered an opportunity to earn his freedom. He is freed from a penitentiary and implanted with timed explosives that ensure his return in twenty-four hours if he is not dead. His mission is to rescue the president and bring him to safety on the other side of Manhattan.

What follows, unfortunately, is a rather mediocre affair which sees both director and protagonist running through some fairly routine action sequences with various criminal elements. Indeed, everything about *Escape from New York* seems contrived once Plisskin arrives in Manhattan, and amounts to no more than a typical action adventure. It is a shame as the premise is superb and the special effects are put to good use, but the plot peters out as Plisskin literally fights his way in only to fight his way out.

Russell's performance is adequate yet forced, and the supporting cast are given only stereotypical roles to play. They do this well enough.

Escape from New York is obviously Carpenter's attempt at straight action adventure, and falls into all of the pitfalls typical of its generic format. As a result, its thoughtful and provoking premise seems wasted.

A sequel, *Escape from LA*, followed in 1996 and saw Russell reprise his role as Plisskin. It covers much the same ground, seeing Russell this time enter a penal colony in Los Angeles to attempt to assassinate the president's daughter.

E.T., THE EXTRATERRESTRIAL (1982, 115 minutes)

Director: Steven Spielberg
Producers: Steven Spielberg, Kathleen Kennedy
Screenplay: Melissa Mathison
Starring: Henry Thomas, Dee Wallace, Peter Coyote, Robert MacNaughton, Drew Barrymore

A rather oversentimental movie from the director of the classic CLOSE ENCOUNTERS OF THE THIRD KIND (1977).

A young boy, Elliott (Thomas), discovers an abandoned ALIEN in the woods near his home and takes him under his wing. They foster a relationship which develops into a mutual need – the alien is in need of an accomplice to help it get home, Elliott is in need of a father figure as his own father is absent from his family unit. This need is manifested physically in one of the most affecting scenes in the movie, when ET grows sick and declines into a near death state, so does Elliott.

Essentially, the movie deals with the inherent vulnerability of a fatherless child, but also of an alien left stranded by its companions on a world unknown to it. Elliott and the alien are attracted to each other as they each recognise the inherent loneliness within the other.

Eventually, Elliott matures and ET is released to his own kind, but not before a ritual has taken place which ensures that Elliott will recognise the good nature of his race and come to be happy with his lot. He learns to trust the adult world again, and is reconciled to the absence of his father. In essence, he no longer has a need for the alien.

The movie draws on the same themes as *Close Encounters*, seeing children, or the innocent, as the most worthy members of our race, before they become tainted by the world. This is not to say that Spielberg views adults with disdain, simply that he sees them as fundamentally unreceptive to the world and its experiences.

There is also the very obvious RELIGIOUS analogy to consider. ET is delivered to the world, attempts to teach us a harmonious way of life, performs miracles, dies, and then, like the MESSIAH, ascends into the sky, his work on Earth done – Elliott has come to trust humanity again. All of this is perhaps a little overdone, at times giving the movie a romantic tone that does not seem to gel with its subject matter.

Nevertheless, *ET* remains a good film, if not as great as *Close Encounters*. The movie works best as a study of child/adult relationships, and an exercise in viewing the world through the eyes of the young. As an exploration of the alien theme it is decidedly flat and fails to offer the SENSE OF WONDER that was so important to *Close Encounters*. Perhaps this is partly due to the manner in which the alien becomes explicitly known to us as a character, rather than remaining enigmatic and mysterious. In defining ET, Spielberg took a step too far towards humanising the inhuman, and that is where the movie stumbles.

EVENT HORIZON (1997, 92 minutes)

Director: Paul Anderson
Producers: Lawrence Gordon, Lloyd Levin, Jeremy Bolt
Screenplay: Philip Eisner
Starring: Laurence Fishburne, Sam Neill, Kathleen Quinlan, Joely Richardson

Dark, dismal and gory, *Event Horizon* is a powerful SF HORROR movie that borders on the hysterical.

An experimental ship, *The Event Horizon*, which contains an interstellar drive created by harnessing the power of a BLACK HOLE, has mysteriously returned to the Solar System, but lays dormant, and a salvage crew must attempt to find out what has happened in the intervening years. What they find when they arrive is a ship alive with a DIMENSIONAL terror, an ALIEN hell haunted by the remains of the original crew, and the worst fears of those who step foot on board. The ship has not only traversed interstellar space, but realities too.

The movie is stylish and dark, and draws heavily on the Russian movie SOLARIS (1971). In *Event Horizon*, the sentient entity is represented as being a manifestation of pure evil, but it is perhaps better to view it as an incomprehensible intelligence which is too profound for humans to even begin to understand. Instead, they fear it and what it represents. As one of the characters is drawn into this fundamental insanity, he becomes aware of a greater intelligence, a broader base of experience which can be found on the other side. He loses his eyes, yet he is able to 'see' more without them.

There is also a pseudo–RELIGIOUS aspect to *Event Horizon*, in that the entity that Neill's character becomes is almost the antithesis of Christ: he commands miraculous powers and is intent on converting the remaining crew members to his mystically inspired cause. He is the Antichrist manifested by his desire for knowledge and experience, and because of this his body is inflicted with its own form of the Stigmata.

Fishburne maintains his role with his usual panache, and the supporting cast are strong and capable. Neill appears to revel in the sheer surreality of the tale, and it shows in the manner in which he portrays his character. The sets are first rate and claustrophobic.

Like so many important SF films of the last century, *Event Horizon* rewards attentive viewing. There are layers of meaning which can be easily lost in the multiplying horrors that engulf the crew. In the end, *Event Horizon* is a horror movie, yet its intelligent use of SF concepts adds a dimension of speculation that is undeniably worthwhile.

EXISTENZ (1999, 93 minutes)

Director: David Cronenberg
Producers: David Cronenberg, Andras Hamori, Robert Lantos
Screenplay: David Cronenberg
Starring: Jude Law, Jennifer Jason Leigh, Ian Holm, Don McKellar, Callum Keith Rennie, Sarah Polley, Christopher Eccleston, Willem Dafoe

Existenz is a disturbing examination of the nature of reality, and the methods that the human race may use to construct various realities of their own. Tackling similar issues to THE MATRIX (1999), but with a darker and more mature tone, *Existenz* adopts a NEAR FUTURE setting based upon a modern USA.

The movie begins with the testing of a new, experimental VIRTUAL REALITY game known as Existenz. A gunman bursts in just as the players are about to begin – they scatter and the movie becomes a hunt for understanding and the gradual uncovering of a conspiracy. What remains ambiguous throughout the film, however, is whether or not the characters are actually still playing the 'game'. Subtle clues are provided by Cronenberg, such as barely noticeable changes to clothing and characters who appear under compulsion to act in ways which seem obscure, surreal or disgusting.

What follows is a descent into multiplying layers of reality, a black and disturbing look at the true nature of existence, and how, ultimately, it remains an enigma to us.

The movie makes interesting use of SF genre concepts. Aside from the obvious virtual reality aspects of the film, the portrayal of the near future is a post-modern take on the seedy landscapes of CYBERPUNK. This is apparent in the biological interfaces that are used by the characters to engage with the virtual reality machine, and the very machine itself: fashioned by GENETIC engineering, it is a living, semi-sentient entity. When the machine is infected by a programmed virus, it shows itself as a physical illness and the entire 'game' grows sick.

America itself is portrayed as a country rushing headlong into a DYSTOPIA, or certainly a country divided by technological class; those not involved in the development or application of new technology have become an underclass destined to work out their lives in factories or other service industries.

Existenz provides a commentary on the future of the human race and its evolving relationship with machines. If not as pessimistic as *The Matrix*, which sees machines as our ultimate enemies, it does issue a sobering warning of the moral and psychological aspects of our headlong race into the future and suggests that every step we take should be considered with our eyes fully open. When games become reality, what does reality become?

Both Jude Law and Jennifer Jason Leigh provide excellent performances, with Willem Dafoe and Ian Holm supporting well. The result is a movie which asks more questions than it answers. Reality is left as an ambiguous state, and the viewer is left debating whether the characters are still wallowing in the 'game'. Like many Cronenberg movies, *Existenz* replaces reality with a twisted, original surreality that is unlike anything else in the genre.

FAHRENHEIT 451 (1966, 112 minutes)
Director: François Truffaut
Producer: Lewis M. Allen
Screenplay: François Truffaut, Jean-Louis Richard
Starring: Julie Christie, Oskar Werner, Cyril Cusack, Anton Diffring

Fahrenheit 451 is based on the DYSTOPIC novel, *Fahrenheit 451* (1953) by RAY BRADBURY. It is perhaps Bradbury's most important foray into the SF genre, and the main impetus of the book – that literature is an important, almost sacred part of our civilized world – is unfortunately lost in the translation to the screen.

The story is that of a fireman (Werner) – not a proud public servant who puts out fires, but an employee of a fascist regime who burns books – and his gradual realization of the error of his ways. The setting is a dystopic USA which has outlawed all reading and literature. However, an underclass of outlaws has developed, within which people memorize books as a means of perpetuating art and education. Werner's character becomes involved in this underworld group and, casting aside his role, sets about aiding them in their plight.

However, the movie fails to capture the most important aspect of the novel – the sanctity of literature – and instead portrays the rebels as a group of mindless outcasts who memorize the words of the books but fail to understand their meaning. Instead of keeping literature alive for further generations, they have killed it by failing to grasp its complexities.

In some respects the movie is worth watching; its images of burning books are still haunting and eerily beautiful. Within the boundaries defined by the director, the actors perform well, and the sets, if a little dated, are still worthy of note.

It is a shame that *Fahrenheit 451* fails to live up to expectations. Nevertheless, in its own way it has become a genre classic, and a remake is currently being considered for production in 2001.

FANTASTIC VOYAGE (1966, 100 minutes)
Director: Richard Fleischer
Producer: Saul David
Screenplay: Harry Kleiner
Starring: Stephen Boyd, Raquel Welch, Edmund O'Brien, Donald Pleasance, Arthur Kennedy, Arthur O'Connell

Fantastic Voyage is a romping SCIENCE FANTASY that is remembered more as a kitsch classic than a serious piece of SF film.

A small contingent of doctors are miniaturized along with their submarine, *Proteus*, and injected into the blood stream of a Czech scientist so that they may operate on an otherwise inoperable clot in his brain. Along the way they must negotiate such obstacles as the heart and lungs, fight off attacks from white blood cells, as well as deal with a member of their own crew who turns out to be a double agent. Ultimately, they must attempt to complete their task and make an exit from the scientist's body before they are returned spontaneously to their normal size.

The special effects of the movie are true to the title – fantastic and innovative – and whilst there is no real depth to the plot, as an episode of scientific adventure it does succeed. The internal workings of the scientist's body are all rendered accurately, to the extent that enormous models of each organ were made specifically for the film.

The performances of the actors, if a little melodramatic, are satisfactory, and in the end the movie makes consistent and enjoyable viewing.

A similar theme was not quite so successfully explored in *Innerspace* (1987), a spoof of *Fantastic Voyage* that leans too heavily on slapstick humour and absurdity to be of real interest.

FIFTH ELEMENT, THE (1997, 127 minutes)
Director: Luc Besson
Producer: Patrice Ledoux
Screenplay: Luc Besson, Robert Kamen

Starring: Bruce Willis, Milla Jovovich, Ian Holm, Gary Oldman, Chris Tucker, Luke Perry, Lee Evans, Julie Wallace

The Fifth Element is a fantasia of comic book imagery and style, an over-sentimental romp through a wholly unconvincing future time. It is nevertheless a SPACE OPERA of the highest order.

Although he draws much of his early imagery from the seminal BLADE-RUNNER, Besson's portrayal of an ECOLOGICAL DYSTOPIA is light-hearted in comparison, without the sinister, dreary backdrops and rain-soaked streets. Indeed, Besson's future is gaudy and full of colour and comedy.

The plot is simple – members of an ALIEN race have been acting out the role of guardians to the human race for many thousands of years, holding the key to an ancient device that represents the inherent goodness of humanity. This device will save the planet from utter destruction at the hands of a recursive entity of pure evil, which returns to the Solar System every ten thousand years to wreak havoc and death. This key to this arte-fact is the 'fifth element', a being of purity and naiveté that must learn the ways of humanity and then judge whether we are worth saving. However, this key has been lost, and it falls into the hands of a down-and-out taxi driver played by Willis.

With costume designs by Jean Paul Gaultier, the movie looks exquisite, if a little eccentric. The cast all put in worthwhile performances, with the annoying exception of Chris Tucker as an irrelevant DJ who is deeply irritating. In the End, *The Fifth Element* is rather too sentimental and comical – it sets off as an interesting space opera and descends into absurdity. However, the movie does have some redeeming features and is enjoyable as a piece of COMIC SF, with set pieces that are beautifully realized and developed.

FIRST MEN IN THE MOON, THE (1964, 103 minutes)
Director: Nathan Juran
Producer: Charles H. Schneer
Screenplay: Nigel Kneale, Jan Read
Starring: Lionel Jeffries, Edward Judd, Martha Hyer

Based on the novel, *The First Men in the Moon* (1901) by H. G. WELLS, with a script co-written by SF veteran Nigel Kneale and effects by Ray Harryhausen, it was thought that *First Men in the Moon* could be nothing but a triumph. A triumph it is not, but it does make an interesting and enjoyable piece of entertainment.

The movie sees a rather eccentric Victorian inventor discover a substance with the properties of ANTI-GRAVITY. He uses this to construct a spherical space vessel within which he propels himself and two companions to the Moon. Once there, they attempt to claim the PLANET for Great Britain, but are captured by a strange race of insectoid ALIENS that lives in a series of caverns beneath the surface. After an agonizing spell of captivity, they manage to escape, slaughtering a large number of aliens along the way and eventually returning to their vessel.

The movie is mostly faithful to Wells's plot, and describes in fascinating detail the principles behind the flight of the spacecraft – that flaps covered in a form of anti-gravity 'paint' are manipulated to create energy fields which are then used to direct the vessel. The ascent of the three characters to the Moon is an exciting and interesting piece of film.

The astronauts are portrayed with verve and style by Jeffries, Judd and Hyer, and the special effects are delivered with typical Harryhausen panache.

The film itself defies detailed analysis, not from any level of inherent complexity, but simply because it is best considered as a quality B-movie. The movie is enjoyable and fun, and whilst the story is that of Wells, it doesn't have the subtlety that makes the novel such a classic.

FLASH GORDON (1980, 115 minutes)
Director: Michael Hodges
Producer: Dino de Laurentiis
Screenplay: Lorenzo Semple Jr
Starring: Sam J. Jones, Melody Anderson, Topol, Max Von Sydow, Brian Blessed, Timothy Dalton

Flash Gordon is a camp, pulp-orientated remake of the classic black and white serial starring Buster Crabbe and, although it makes good use of a large budget and excellent special effects, it eventually fails to recapture the essence of the original.

The plot remains relatively faithful to the earlier sequence, having Gordon (Jones), a famous American football hero, and his two companions stranded on the PLANET Mongo after an accident with a scientist's space vessel. There they are captured by the evil troops of Emperor Ming

(Sydow), who, in a wonderfully melodramatic fit of pique, declares he is going to marry Gordon's lady friend Dale (Anderson) and destroy Earth. What follows is a high adventure in which Gordon fights for the freedom of himself and his companions, eventually managing to enlist the aid of various disgruntled characters and spark a revolution which sees Ming dead and both Mongo and Earth free from any further threat.

There are RELIGIOUS analogies to be made. Gordon becomes the saviour of both Earth and Mongo, bringing an end to the terrible reign of Emperor Ming. He dies and is brought back from the brink by the love, or in this case lust, of a (beautiful) woman, and goes on to bring about a new era of peace and happiness. Brian Blessed's troupe of winged humanoids can also be seen to represent a flock of angels that come to Gordon's aid at the crucial moment, shunning their impartiality and getting thoroughly stuck in with the revolution. If director Hodges does attempt to create a religious metaphor in *Flash Gordon*, it is with his tongue firmly in his cheek.

Fundamentally, *Flash Gordon* remains a highly sexed romp, overflowing with handsome people and flashy action sequences. The performances of the actors are hammed up to say the least, but oddly it all seems in keeping with the grand operatic plot and the colourful set pieces. It can be said of *Flash Gordon* that it sets out to entertain, and it succeeds.

Flash Gordon remains, even after repeated viewing, a particularly enjoyable piece of SCIENCE FANTASY film.

A musical score was provided by rock band Queen, who went on to have a hit song off the back of the movie's success.

FLY, THE (1958, 94 minutes)

Director: Kurt Neumann
Producer: Kurt Neumann
Screenplay: James Clavell
Starring: David Hedison, Vincent Price, Patricia Owens, Herbert Marshall, Charles Herbert

The original version of *The Fly* – it was later remade by David Cronenberg as THE FLY (1986) – sees experimental scientist (Hedison) construct a matter transmitter (teleportation machine) within which he inadvertently becomes mixed up with a fly.

The human and insect swap body parts – the scientist is left with the fly's head and wing whilst the fly obtains Hedison's head and arm. The idea is utterly preposterous, but on screen it becomes an effective piece of SF HORROR.

Eventually, after a number of failed attempts to separate himself from the insect, as well as succumbing to a rapidly encroaching psychosis, the scientist coaxes his wife (Owens) to end his life. The fly, on the other hand, finds itself caught in a spider's web and poignantly screams for help as the arachnid slowly makes its move in for the kill.

The movie successfully explores the evolving relationship between man and machine and, if a little sensationally, it offers a clear pointer to the films that would come later, discussing the advent of nuclear weapons and their possible use. *The Fly* is utterly unforgiving – if humanity wishes to build machines capable of deconstructing its very biology, the race must be prepared to suffer the consequences. This the scientist does in spectacular fashion; indeed, the particularly morose ending of the movie is far from typical of genre cinema of the time. It is also important in that it discusses the repercussions of our actions on the innocent bystanders – in this instance the fly – who naively get caught up in our technological games. The fly does not have the necessary intelligence to act upon its new state, and so therefore the burden remains ours. We become responsible not only for ourselves, but those around us who do not know better.

The movie is an impressive attempt to do something original in 1950s SF cinema, and succeeds. The script, which was written by novelist James Clavell, is sharp and realistic, and so are the performances. Hedison is wonderfully creative in his role as the blighted scientist, whilst Price offers excellent support from the sidelines, as the scientist's brother. The effects are not terribly outstanding, but they do what they need to in order to make the movie work.

The Fly is a classic movie that has shocked and inspired viewers ever since its initial release. Scientifically implausible, yet still profound in its exploration of the human/machine relationship, as well as the effects that it may have upon any innocent parties in the near vicinity, it is an evocative and understated achievement.

The success of *The Fly* inspired two direct sequels. *Return of the Fly* appeared in 1959 and is rather episodic, re-treading the same ground as its predecessor. *Curse of the Fly* came another six years later and did develop the idea, seeing various people transmitted to London where they suffer from bizarre mutations caused by the machine. Although good, neither of the movies could compare to the sheer originality of the first film in the sequence.

FLY, THE (1986, 96 minutes)

Director: David Cronenberg
Producer: Stuart Cornfield
Screenplay: Charles Edward Pogue, David Cronenberg
Starring: Jeff Goldblum, Geena Davis, John Getz, Joy Boushel

More of a reinvention than a remake of the classic 1958 movie THE FLY, David Cronenberg's *The Fly* is an intelligent and worthwhile study.

In a similar manner to the earlier film, a cranky scientist, Seth Brundle (Goldblum), develops a matter transmission machine that enables him to teleport living entities from one unit to another. He tests this on himself, only to find that he has accidentally combined his DNA with that of a fly. However, unlike the original movie, Brundle does not emerge from the pod bearing any visible signs of the amalgamation, but later finds himself developing superhuman powers, particularly in the areas of stamina and sexual prowess. So begins an odyssey of transformation that eventually leads to a complete restructuring of Brundle, a metamorphosis that sees him become a giant insectoid that is neither human nor fly, but a twisted, horrific abomination. Ultimately he loses his humanity in the depths of the encroaching mutation.

In typical Cronenberg fashion Brundle takes a philosophical approach to his slow metamorphosis into 'Brundlefly', watching with interest as his limbs fall away, and offering a counterpoint to the sheer horror evident in his girlfriend (Davis). However, far from being the TRANSCEN-DENCE into something bold and new that Brundle obviously believes it is, his transformation becomes a metaphor for human mortality and the perishable nature of our form.

It is not long before Brundle descends even deeper into the bizarre, and begins digesting his food before he eats it, in the process losing all dignity as a human being. He becomes totally 'other', an ALIEN created entirely by his own technological ineptitude. In a final, climactic scene, Brundle is fused with one of the matter transmission pods, and begs his girlfriend to kill him. This she does out of both pity and love. The creature he has become is no longer Brundle, but some horrible monster transplanted directly from a terrible nightmare.

The Fly at first sets out to provide some scientific rationale for the transformation of Brundle into a monster, with mutterings about new combinations of DNA and strange GENETIC sequences. However, it seems to eventually give up on this in favour of a more detailed exploration of Brundle's psychology as we follow his changes throughout the film. It does not, unlike the previous film, seem to comment so much on the relationship between Brundle and his machine, but more upon Brundle and his awareness of his approaching death. It seems inevitable that he will eventually perish as a result of his failed experiment.

The Fly is a deeply intelligent SF HORROR movie that studies the psychology of a dying man in terms that are utterly at odds with what we know. Cronenberg excels in detailing the more surreal realms of human existence, the fringes of reality on which some of us exist. Goldblum is perfectly cast as the eccentric Brundle, and Davis balances his quirky behaviour with a fine performance. In the end, unusually for a remake, the movie surpasses its predecessor on many levels.

An inferior sequel, *The Fly II*, appeared in 1988 and followed the progress of Brundle's son as he begins to metamorphose in a similar manner to his father.

FORBIDDEN PLANET (1956, 98 minutes)

Director: Fred M. Wilcox
Producer: Nicholas Nayfack
Screenplay: Cyril Hume
Starring: Walter Pidgeon, Anne Francis, Leslie Nielsen, Warren Stevens, Jack Kelly, Richard Anderson

Forbidden Planet is an intellectual, thought-provoking SPACE OPERA that has its basis in William Shakespeare's *The Tempest*. At the same time it provides a cautionary tale about the horrors of technology, very much in the same way as its contemporaries THE DAY THE EARTH STOOD STILL (1951) and THE FLY (1958).

Originally written as a wholesome family drama in which an optimistic and all-powerful America has conquered the stars, director Wilcox turned the script on its head and presented a subversive, intelligent film about the possible hazards of technology and space travel.

Commander Adams (Nielsen) and his crew set off on a rescue mission to the distant PLANET Altair-IV, upon which a previous vessel had landed, but then vanished without explanation. Upon arriving at Altair-IV, the team discovers a survivor, the sinister Dr Morbius (Pidgeon) and his beautiful daughter, Altaria (Francis). Morbius has in tow one of the most enduring and impressive creations of 1950s SF – Robby the Robot, the prototype for all screen ROBOTS to come. Robby is an intelligent machine who maintains Morbius's home and is, in many ways, his personal servant. Adams and his crew proceed to set up a base.

What follows is a descent into the Freudian wilderness of the mind, as a strange monster begins stalking the crew and sabotages their spacecraft. It transpires that an ALIEN race, the Krel, once inhabited the planet, but developed the ability to manifest their inner psyches in physical form and this eventually led to the devastation of their race. Morbius has inherited not only the Krel's high technology – thus Robby the Robot – but their extrasensory powers, and now his Id is roaming the planet destroying all in its wake. The previous mission to the planet saw the crew destroyed by their own psyches – but this is left ambiguous, and it is almost implied that this too could be down to Morbius.

In a wonderfully climactic scene that sees the sinister doctor make a move towards redemption, he throws himself into the arms of his own manifested unconscious, and the crew of the space vessel are able to escape to safety with Altaria and Robby behind them. They bomb the planet from orbit and begin the long journey home.

What is so important and refreshing about *Forbidden Planet*, aside from the splendid special effects and inspiring sets, is the underlying levels of complexity and meaning. The movie is resonant with ideas and references that defy easy interpretation. On one level, *Forbidden Planet* is a superb action adventure in which the American ideal triumphs over the alien intelligence, and in this respect Wilcox gave the studio exactly what they were looking for. However, this is oversimplistic and misses the point of the movie. It is not actually the aliens who are stalking the intrepid human adventures, but aspects of themselves. Wilcox is making the fundamental point that we do not need aliens to bring danger to our fragile lives. We can do that quite easily ourselves. *Forbidden Planet* rails against the optimistic technological future that it purports to uphold, instead showing how humanity is basically at odds with technology. Before we can begin to understand its application we should learn to understand ourselves. Wilcox's astronauts set off with all the confidence of an America which believed itself to be master of the world, but when they leave the orbit around Altair-IV, it is with a slow limp that they make their way home. It is also of importance that the astronauts themselves do not defeat the 'monster', but instead, in true *War of the Worlds* style, it is left to someone with powers beyond their control to save the day. If Morbius had not redeemed himself by sacrificing himself to the phantasm of his mind, the astronauts would not have survived the encounter.

Forbidden Planet is a movie to be cherished. It does everything it sets out to do, and more. The movie subverts the genre and in doing so creates one of the finest criticisms of modern society to be filmed to date. It also had an enormous budget, and so the full scale of the director's vision is able to shine through in glorious Technicolor. *Forbidden Planet* is a seminal film that made so many others possible. Not only does it stand repeated viewing itself, it inspired a rash of imitators and television series, some of which have become classics in their own right.

After *The Day the Earth Stood Still*, *Forbidden Planet* is perhaps the most important prototype for modern SF cinema, a milestone by which all other movies are compared.

GATTACA (1998, 102 minutes)
Director: Andrew Niccol
Producers: Danny DeVito, Michael Shamberg, Stacey Sher
Screenplay: Andrew Niccol
Starring: Ethan Hawke, Jude Law, Uma Thurman

With themes reminiscent of ALDOUS HUXLEY's *Brave New World* (1932), *Gattaca* is a stylish, intelligent piece of HUMANIST SF.

In a society where the aristocracy or 'valids' are created in test tubes via GENETIC engineering, we follow the progress of Vincent, a 'non-valid' who has been conceived and born through entirely natural means.

Throughout the course of the film Vincent undergoes excruciating surgery and painstaking daily preparation in a ploy to adopt the role of an 'elite', trading places with Jerome, a paralysed professional swimmer. It is the story of the underling made good, the outwitting of the aristocracy by a proletarian as he installs himself into one of their most highly regarded institutions – Gattaca, home of the space mission.

Claims that this is an anti-science film are ill founded – the chief protagonist dreams of being part of a mission to Titan, third moon of Saturn and eventually realises that dream. In this respect he betters all preconceived expectations, unlike, ironically, his 'valid' sibling who fails to achieve his full potential as a police inspector by not managing to solve a murder case.

This is the crux of *Gattaca*, a moralistic warning of EUGENICS, a reminder that, although genetics may be used to enhance our bodies, they may not necessarily improve our minds. The film is stylish and retro-futuristic; the technology is evident yet understated. The characters are portrayed well, and the plot is well realized and developed.

Gattaca is perhaps one of the most emotionally driven science fiction movies to appear in recent years, and although it reveals nothing truly new it does succeed in undermining the UTOPIAN myth that has sprung up around the science of genetic engineering over recent years.

INCREDIBLE SHRINKING MAN, THE
(1957, 81 minutes)
Director: Jack Arnold
Producer: Albert Zugsmith
Screenplay: RICHARD MATHESON
Starring: Grant Williams, Randy Stuart, April Kent, Paul Langton, Raymond Bailey, William Schallert

Scripted by author Richard Matheson after his own novel, *The Shrinking Man* (1956), *The Incredible Shrinking Man* is one of the classics of genre cinema.

The film is typically paranoiac and of its time, but its themes have not dated and it remains of profound interest. When a man (Williams) inadvertently passes through a cloud of radiation, he begins to shrink at an ever-increasing rate. At first, the main object of concern becomes his wife (Stuart), who pesters him with patronising comments and soon towers well above him, but soon all that is familiar about his home is lost, and his surroundings become sinister and overwhelming. He struggles to survive in the face of ever-increasing threat – first he has to fight off the family cat, then as he gets even smaller he must tackle a spider if he wishes to survive. As he proceeds to shrink in size, the world becomes ever more deadly, and all of his humanity is lost.

It is not long before his relationship with his wife breaks down, and he is unable to take part in society as he knows it. Soon he is forgotten by the world and life becomes a single-minded exercise in survival.

Eventually, in the most poignant and moving episode of the movie, the character escapes into the garden just as he disappears into nothingness. The message is this – without civilization, we become nothing.

However, it is the loss of the comforting surroundings of middle America that is the most disturbing factor in *The Incredible Shrinking Man*, the realization that our grip on the familiar is tentative at best and could be whipped away from us at any moment, leaving us stranded in an environment both terrifying and strange. The world is a dangerous place, and our complacency could bring about our downfall.

The Incredible Shrinking Man is a profound and pessimistic exploration of society and the perceived safety of our world. The performances are excellent, particularly Williams, and the script is polished and well constructed. The effects are decidedly low budget, but they are pulled off with great style and skill.

The Incredible Shrinking Man is one of the better movies to come out of the Cold War era, and its themes of unfamiliarity and lost identity are terrifying and bold.

INDEPENDENCE DAY (1996, 139 minutes)
Director: Roland Emmerich
Producer: Dean Devlin
Screenplay: Roland Emmerich, Dean Devlin
Starring: Will Smith, Jeff Goldblum, Bill Pullman

Independence Day hit cinema screens in 1996 with a bang. It is a genre pastiche, a dismal rendering of all things that have gone before, hurriedly packed into one effects-fuelled movie. It is also a clichéd reinvention of H. G. WELLS's classic novel, *The War of the Worlds* (1898), updated for the 1990s but failing to capture any of the original style or depth. Nevertheless, it was popular at the time.

The story is derived directly from *The War of the Worlds*. One morning the human race awakens to find enormous alien spacecraft stationed over the major cities of the world. At first they are enigmatic, but after various attempts to break the stand-off on the part of humanity, the aliens set about destroying the world. There is no explanation for their hostility; they are simply hellbent on committing genocide. A group of unlikely American heroes eventually saves the day by fixing a dilapidated spacecraft that was found at Roswell and flying into orbit to dock with the alien mothership. From here they upload a computer virus from a laptop, and bring about the destruction of the alien legion. And with that we see the fundamental difference between *Independence Day* and *The War of the Worlds* – Wells's story was inherently pessimistic about his contemporary society, with his human characters floundering about helplessly and the aliens finally being defeated by means beyond human control. *Independence Day* instead revels in the belief that America can and will save the world, no matter what the threat or how ferocious the enemy. It is a dangerous and ultimately naive perspective.

Independence Day pays homage to many classic SF movies, as well as giving a nod to the epic disaster films that were prevalent during the 1970s. The actors try their best to pull a performance from the script, but terribly clichéd lines mean that the roles they play lack any real depth. They fit more snugly into stereotypical roles, as either hero, hero's love interest, military hard man or cannon fodder.

The film's B-movie sensibilities win through, and although brimming with magnificent special effects, the movie ultimately fails to satisfy. As a piece of SF entertainment, or perhaps an exercise in 'spot the homage', it is fun, but there is nothing more to be gleaned from this movie. The 1953 adaptation of THE WAR OF THE WORLDS is a superior film in almost every respect.

INVASION OF THE BODY SNATCHERS (1956, 80 minutes)

Director: Don Siegel
Producer: Walter Wanger
Screenplay: Daniel Mainwaring
Starring: Kevin McCarthy, Dana Wynter, Larry Gates, King Donovan, Carolyn Jones

The first of two movies based upon the classic novel, *The Body Snatchers* (1955) by JACK FINNEY, *Invasion of the Body Snatchers* is one of the best known SF movies of all time. It is a horrifying and detailed study of humanity and what makes us human.

The plot is similar to that of the book. A doctor (McCarthy) returns to his home town in California to find everything is mysteriously different. At first, he can't quite put his finger on it, but he soon comes to realize that ALIENS have taken over the town, replacing each member of society with a simulacrum devoid of a soul. It is not long before he encounters the mysterious pods that the aliens use to grow replica bodies of the townsfolk when they are asleep. To his horror, he finds a pod that, if at any time he lapses into unconsciousness, will become 'him'. He is terrified, but can't do anything about it, when the members of the town begin despatching pods to all ports of America. He realizes that, soon, the entire planet will be taken over by the alien invaders and that humanity will be lost in all but form.

One of the most memorable scenes of the film is towards its conclusion, when McCarthy stands in the road shouting at the passing cars. Nobody will stop and listen. Nobody believes that their very existence is threatened, especially from the inside, from a threat grown in their very own homes.

Whatever the political standpoint, and this has been much debated, the movie amounts to an unsettling study of the loss of individuality and personality in modern society. Its ideas were fresh, its commentary biting, its visuals carefully put together and well crafted. McCarthy portrays with real depth the frustrations of a man being slowly driven insane by the realization that as soon as he closes his eyes he will die. Yet, every moment he grows more and more tired, and people refuse to listen to him. His performance is an achievement to be proud of.

Indeed, the movie itself is an achievement to be proud of, a groundbreaking film that encapsulates all the hopes and fears of a nation in the throes of the Cold War. *Invasion of the Body Snatchers* is a film about America in the 1950s – the aliens are not dangerous mutants from outer space, or blobs of gelatinous soup that arrived on a meteor, but ourselves and our neighbours. That is indeed a disturbing thought.

INVASION OF THE BODY SNATCHERS (1978, 115 minutes)
Director: Philip Kaufman
Producer: Robert H. Solo
Screenplay: W. D. Richter
Starring: Donald Sutherland, Brooke Adams, Leonard Nimoy, Veronica Cartwright, Jeff Goldblum

An inventive and worthwhile reinterpretation of the earlier *Invasion of the Body Snatchers* (1956).

The themes of the movie are similar, but updated to consider the more extreme consumer-based society of the 1970s. Indeed, where the previous movie explored a number of different notions about the loss of identity and the terrible wrong that the ALIENS were inflicting on the human race, this later version of *Invasion of the Body Snatchers* focuses chiefly on the notion that the aliens are inflicting upon us nothing that were are not doing to ourselves, that a shift into the bland, soulless existence of a society of simulacra is already underway, and that all that the aliens are doing is speeding the process up a little.

The plot is very similar to the original. Donald Sutherland plays a public health inspector who begins to notice a change in his home suburb of San Francisco. Surely enough, he comes to discover the truth – that mysterious plant-like entities from space have invaded and are replacing the human population of the world one by one, growing duplicate bodies and turning the original people to dust. These simulacra are conformist and without soul – they lack the necessary emotions to make them human. Sutherland's character attempts to rebel, but to no avail. The aliens are too powerful and all pervading, and in the end the paranoiacs worst nightmare comes true – we are all assimilated.

In a light-hearted moment, Kevin McCarthy makes a cameo appearance in which he reprises his role from the previous film, attempting to convince people of the existence of the extraterrestrial threat.

The images of *Invasion of the Body Snatchers*, have, like the insidious aliens themselves, pervaded our consciousness. Particularly moving is the scene in which Sutherland finally succumbs to his fate, and we are casually informed that all resistance will fail. These creatures will not be fended off by human hands, nor by any saviour or handy common cold – they are us, our alter egos, and for that reason will not rest until we are subjugated.

The most frightening image of the whole film comes in its closing seconds, when the last 'real' person left alive in San Francisco wanders a city where everyone is going about their business in a cool and eerily subdued manner, and 'life' continues in almost exactly the same way that it did before the invasion. With only one difference – humanity is nowhere to be seen.

Invasion of the Body Snatchers is an important film, a diatribe against the loss of humanity and the encroaching oblivion that could face us all. Unlike many attempts to reinvent older pictures, this movie succeeds because it doesn't attempt to retread the same ground in the same way, but updates the idea to make it more applicable to its time. It is a film that should be watched again and again, and then watched some more. It reminds us what it is to be human, and that is all that good SF has to do.

A further adaptation of the movie appeared in 1993 as *Body Snatchers*, and, although good, transplanting the action this time to a US Army base, it failed to have such a profound effect as the previous two versions.

INVISIBLE MAN, THE (1933, 71 minutes)
Director: James Whale
Producer: Carl Laemmle Jr
Screenplay: R. C. Sherriff, Philip Wylie

Starring: Claude Rains, Gloria Stewart, Henry Travers, William Harrigan, Uno O'Connor

Directed by the irrepressible James Whale, fresh from his success filming *Frankenstein* (1931) with Boris Karloff, *The Invisible Man* is a fine adaptation of H. G. WELLS's novel *The Invisible Man* (1897).

A scientist, Jack Griffin (Rains), develops a drug that induces invisibility. He takes it himself and, having become totally transparent, is driven utterly mad. He begins entertaining himself with a series of pranks, but as his psychosis develops, he sets his sights on greater things, eventually taking the first steps on a spiralling pathway of crime that first sees him robbing a bank, but later descends into murder. The authorities are turned on to Griffin's condition by one of his old friends and, as he becomes more and more confident, he gives himself away and the police are able to track him down. He slips away from their grasp, but is wounded, and the bobbies are able to track his trail of blood and locate his hideout on a farm. He is quickly admitted to the nearest hospital, but dies there, and in his final moment his body returns to visibility.

Fundamentally a SCIENTIFIC ROMANCE, *The Invisible Man* is one of the finest early attempts to bring the genre to the screen. It explores nothing so much as the psychology of a man driven mad by his own experiments, and is intended as a cautionary tale which, at its most basic level, represents a great fear of technology and progress. The movie is cynical about the uses to which man will put his scientific knowledge, and it warns us not to meddle with nature.

Rains provides a fantastic performance as the scientist descending into madness, and the script, as well as the direction, is funny and black. The early invisibility effects pioneered by John Fulton for the film soon became used widely throughout the industry, but their appearance here marks the advent of a dazzling, ingenious technique.

The Invisible Man is an important marker on the road to intelligent, moralistic SF film. It is certainly the best treatment of the invisibility theme, even though it inspired a whole subgenre of sequels and spin-offs. Both the performance of Rains and the special effects remain very effective.

JURASSIC PARK (1993, 121 minutes)
Director: Steven Spielberg
Producers: Kathleen Kennedy, Gerald R. Molen

Screenplay: MICHAEL CRICHTON, David Koepp
Starring: Sam Neill, Laura Dern, Richard Attenborough, Jeff Goldblum, Bob Peck, Martin Ferrero, B. D. Wong, Samuel R. Jackson, Wayne Knight

Based on the best-selling novel *Jurassic Park* (1990) by Michael Crichton, who also co-wrote the screenplay, *Jurassic Park* is a monster of a film.

Seminal in its use of modern special effects technology, and topical in that it perfectly captured the public unease regarding CLONING and GENETIC engineering that was prevalent at the time, the film has a plot reminiscent of Crichton's earlier WESTWORLD (1973) but with an undeniable SENSE OF WONDER that harks back to the animatronic movies of Ray Harryhausen.

A wealthy entrepreneur has developed a theme park on a Costa Rican island, featuring live dinosaurs that have been genetically bred from scraps of ancient DNA. A preliminary party of experts from various fields – palaeontology, palaeobotany and mathematics – are invited to experience the park, along with a couple of children, before it is officially opened to the public. However, once there, havoc ensues when a saboteur switches off the power and the dinosaurs break loose. The various carnivores begin hunting the scared and unprotected human beings.

The film is a triumph of special effects, with dinosaurs that both look and sound realistic. However, the sentiment of the movie is very much anti-science or, at the very least, an oversimplistic interpretation of the dangers of science. Where the book attempts to portray a scenario in which science has been put into the wrong hands, without any attempt at moderation or control, the movie considerably dumbs down the moral issues and becomes a scarifying, anti-scientific diatribe.

That said, if viewed as a simple action-adventure movie of the type popular in the 1950s and 1960s, where cowboys fought giant lizards and enormous apes would steal our women, then there is much to be said for *Jurassic Park*. Partly because of the fun in watching dinosaurs rampage across the screen, partly because of the amazing special effects, *Jurassic Park* broke all box office records and became one of the most popular films in history. It also went on to win an Oscar for best sound.

A sequel, *The Lost World*, followed in 1997 and was also directed by Spielberg. It picks up the story a number of years later when it is found that, although the initial island was bombed by the military, a number of dinosaurs still exist on a neighbouring land mass that had been used as a breeding ground during the development of the original theme park. They have been left to grow wild in the intervening years. An expedition is sent out to attempt to study the creatures in their 'natural' habitat. Of course, things go wrong and a band of hunters also arrive on the island, intent on capturing a T. Rex. This they do, and having shipped it over to the American mainland, allow it to escape. The result is a farcical, weak attempt at what, in the end, amounts to a Godzilla clone. Although it begins well, the movie ultimately fails to live up to its predecessor.

A third sequel is projected, and is due to be released in 2001.

LAND THAT TIME FORGOT, THE (1974, 91 minutes)

Director: Kevin Connor
Producer: John Dark
Screenplay: James Cawthorne, MICHAEL MOORCOCK
Starring: Doug McClure, John McEnery, Susan Penhaligon, Keith Barron, Anthony Ainley

The Land That Time Forgot is sheer confection and is based on the 1924 novel of the same name by EDGAR RICE BURROUGHS. More truly a fantasy movie, it prefigures a number of other 'lost world' films based on the works of Burroughs, but is nonetheless of interest here.

A German submarine picks up the survivors of a wrecked cargo vessel and unwittingly takes them to a nearby island in the Arctic which turns out to contain a variety of dinosaurs and cavemen who have survived there since the mists of time. High adventure follows as the various monsters and prehistoric humans attempt to kill, capture or simply provoke the heroes, who themselves are desperately trying to find a means of escape. It is not to be – a volcanic eruption eventually saves the day, but maroons two of the heroes on the island.

The performances are camp and hammed up, and the special effects leave something to be desired, but the movie is nevertheless a delight of escapist SCIENCE FANTASY. What is perhaps most interesting is the fact the script was written by Michael Moorcock and James Cawthorne, two friends who were heavily involved in the BRITISH science fiction NEW WAVE movement (particularly Moorcock, who edited the pioneering magazine NEW WORLDS). Here they are true to Burroughs's novel, but the movie is glossy and superficial.

Two further films based on Burroughs's work, and developed by the same production company are *At the Earth's Core* (1976), the first in his Pellucidar sequence, and *The People That Time Forgot_*(1977), a pseudo-sequel to *The Land That Time Forgot*.

LAWNMOWER MAN, THE (1992, 108 minutes)
Director: Brett Leonard
Producers: Gimel Everett, Milton Subotsky
Screenplay: Brett Leonard, Gimel Everett
Starring: Pierce Brosnan, Jeff Fahey, Jenny Wright, Geoffrey Lewis, Jeremy Slate

Allegedly based on a short story by Stephen King, (although he went to great lengths to have his name removed from the title credits), *The Lawnmower Man* is an effects-laden CYBERPUNK thriller about the possible uses of VIRTUAL REALITY.

With a plot that is reminiscent of DANIEL KEYES's classic novel, *Flowers for Algernon* (1966), which was also filmed as CHARLY (1968), it describes the intellectual growth of a mentally retarded gardener (Fahey), who becomes the guinea pig in an experiment in human intelligence staged by a crazed scientist (Brosnan). These experiments involve long periods immersed in virtual reality, and it eventually becomes clear that Fahey's character, Jobe, has been raised to the level of a genius. However, he also becomes malign and sets about destroying various people who had treated him badly throughout his life, before going on to undergo a kind of electronic TRANSCENDENCE which sees him metamorphosed into a being of pure electricity who exists only in the virtual realm. This powerful position allows him, miraculously, to change the fabric of reality in the real world.

The special effects and action sequences are carried out with some flair, but Brosnan and Fahey struggle to perform well with unoriginal material that had been examined before in a superior and more intelligent way. *The Lawnmower Man* is not without merit, but it fails to explore the more psychological aspects of Jobe's condition, instead choosing to descend into the realms of an improbable action adventure.

The Lawnmower Man also inspired a direct sequel, The *Lawnmower Man II: Beyond Cyberspace* (1995). The movie failed, however, even to capture the few worthwhile aspects of the original.

LOGAN'S RUN (1976, 118 minutes)

Director: Michael Anderson
Producer: Saul David
Screenplay: David Zelag Goodman
Starring: Michael York, Jenny Agutter, Richard Jordan, Roscoe Lee Browne, Farrah Fawcett-Majors, Peter Ustinov, Michael Anderson Jr

Based on the novel *Logan's Run* (1967) by William F. Nolan and George Clayton Johnson, *Logan's Run* is a rather simplistic exploration of the themes of OVERPOPULATION and UTOPIA. It describes a society in which people are required to commit ritual suicide at the age of thirty, or are gunned down by 'Sandmen' who maintain peace and order. This has resulted in an inexperienced society of the perpetually young, in which no one questions the social order and those that do are terminated without thought. It has become a totalitarian regime which is presided over by a decrepit ARTIFICIAL INTELLIGENCE.

The story follows the progress of Logan (York), a renegade Sandman and his girlfriend (Agutter) as they flee the city in search of the mythic Sanctuary within which they will be saved from their ritual termination. However, once outside the great city they find the crumbling remains of Washington DC, complete with rundown old monuments and moss-covered walkways. They also find and converse with an old man (Ustinov), who embodies the living proof that society does not have to dispose of its members at the age of thirty. It transpires that the technique was originally a method of population control, but has taken on a RELIGIOUS meaning – Logan heads back to the city and, after confusing the AI to the extent that it self-destructs, adopts the role of saviour and becomes the people's new religious leader.

The story itself is interesting and original, but director Anderson fails to translate the tension and excitement of the original novel to the screen, resulting in a movie that sags in the middle, with Logan leaving the city to wander around a bit, before returning and sparking a revolution.

The effects are adequate, but not necessarily in keeping with the mood of the film; the cityscape represents a rather naively realized future, which, far from looking like the ambiguous utopia it purports to portray, resembles nothing so much as a vast theme park. Moreover, York and Agutter provide dull performances which do not capitalise on the situations their characters find themselves in. As a result, the movie is a failure.

That said, it does have some redeeming features, especially in the way it undermines the typical utopian dream without resorting to the bland and overused dystopia that has become typical of the genre.

It is a shame that *Logan's Run* does not live up to the vision of the original novel; Nolan and Johnson would not write anything as worthwhile again, although there was a number of lesser sequels to *Logan's Run*.

The movie was a box office success upon initial release, and spawned a short-lived television series. Logan ran on in *Logan's Run* for thirteen episodes before being cancelled after receiving poor ratings. This cancellation was entirely justified.

LOST IN SPACE
Starring: Guy Williams (John Robinson), June Lockhart (Maureen Robinson), Bill Mumy (Will Robinson), Marta Kristen (Judy Robinson), Angela Cartwright (Penney Robinson), Mark Goddard (West), Jonathan Harris (Smith), Bob May (as the Robot)

Lost in Space became one the best-loved and most watched American SPACE OPERAS during the 1960s, with ratings second only to STAR TREK. Basically a pulp series, it nevertheless moralized on the benefits of the family unit and attempted to perpetuate the old American values.

The space family Robinson began the series by being selected to pioneer a mission to a distant PLANET in order to set about colonizing it for the benefit of humanity. They board the interstellar vessel, *Jupiter 2* and, along with geologist West and a rather kooky ROBOT, set off on their long voyage to the stars. However, their plans are foiled by a saboteur, Dr Smith, who has stowed away on board and reprogrammed the robot to destroy the ship. The Robinsons discover Smith and manage to avert the crisis, but find that they are thousands of light years off course. The series then continues to chart the progress of the Robinsons as they attempt to find their way back home, often stopping off on various planets *en route*. Inevitably, these planets are inhabited by various monsters, who they must confront before returning to their spacecraft and blasting off back into the depths of space.

The series is camp and fun, and utterly devoid of literary or scientific content. Nonetheless, it remains entertaining, especially in the witty banter between Dr Smith and the Robot, who against all odds became the true heroes of the show.

In a wave of nostalgia, a movie adaptation of *Lost in Space* was produced in 1999, but, like the series it was based on, remained hollow and without substance.

Lost in Space originally ran for eighty-three fifty-minute episodes between 1965 and 1968.

MAD MAX (1979, 100 minutes)

Director: George Miller
Producer: Byron Kennedy
Screenplay: James McCausland, George Miller
Starring: Mel Gibson, Joanne Samuel, Hugh Keays-Byrne, Steve Bisley

A POST APOCALYPTIC tale set in Australia, exploring the descent into barbarism as civilization slowly collapses.

World War Three has blighted the world, and petrol has become a rare, finite resource. An obsession with machines has arisen amongst the savage nomads who exist out on the barren plains of Australia, and they terrorize the surviving populace as a means of obtaining petrol to fuel their elaborate bikes and cars.

Max (Gibson) is a bitter, violent cop who turns vigilante and sets off on a crusade of revenge when his wife and child die at the hands of one such tribe of barbarians. What follows is an odyssey of violence and death as Max's more primal instincts take over. Eventually, his dead family is avenged but Max is tainted by violence and has learned a dubious lesson – that the best way to live in such a simple world is by the sword.

Mad Max is an important film, not because of its content, but more because of its style. Miller's post-holocaust landscape is realistic and bleak, and he succeeds in producing a powerful effect by revealing only what is necessary to the viewer. For the most part, we remain in the dark, creating an air of mystery about the war and the consequences it has had on the world. All the viewer is shown is the effect it has had on Max and his immediate environment, a microcosm of the whole world picture.

Gibson's is an excellent, taut performance, and the technical excellence of the movie seems not in keeping with its strictly low budget. *Mad Max* rightly made Gibson a star and Miller a name in directing. It is one of the best visions of a post-apocalyptic world to make it to the screen, due in part to its simplicity and desolation. *Mad Max* does not need amazing special effects – it has power enough of its own.

Mad Max was followed by the excellent *Mad Max II* (1981), which continued to develop both the character of Max and the desolate world in which he ekes out an existence. He is recruited by a small township to drive the last petrol tanker out of the stronghold and past the hordes of barbarian bikers, in the process redeeming himself and helping to maintain a small pocket of civilization. With a bigger budget, the movie made better use of special effects and well-choreographed action scenes, and is as good as its predecessor. The same cannot be said of *Mad Max: Beyond Thunderdome* (1985), which is the third and final instalment in the sequence and details Max's attempts to save a group of feral desert children by flying them to safety. With a guest appearance by singer Tina Turner, the movie certainly looks good, but retreads old ground and in the end is unsatisfactory.

MAN WHO FELL TO EARTH, THE (1976, 138 minutes)
Director: Nicolas Roeg
Producers: Michael Deeley, Barry Spikings
Screenplay: Paul Mayersburg
Starring: David Bowie, Candy Clark, Rip Torn, Buck Henry, Bernie Casey, Jackson D. Kane

Intellectual, brave and surreal, *The Man Who Fell to Earth*, based on the novel by Walter Tevis, is one of the classics of genre film.

It details the progress of an ALIEN (Bowie) who comes to Earth and adopts human form, in the hope that he may be able to find a way to save his dying race. He constructs a massive industrial empire, with which he plans to build a starship capable of rescuing his people from their home world, which is suffering from a devastating drought. However, the alien becomes corrupted by humanity and, upon revealing his true nature to the authorities, is blinded and mistreated. He becomes an alcoholic and is cursed to wander the streets of America whilst his home world dies somewhere far away in space.

The movie is poignant and visually bold. Bowie puts in a strong performance as the alien perverted by the decadence of humanity, and the supporting cast is also strong.

The movie succeeds on a number of different levels, not least in its study of alienation and the trauma felt by the people who are doomed to live their lives on the fringes of 'normal' society. It is also an intense study of race and the conflict that exists between social groups.

The Man Who Fell to Earth is a film that demands to be watched. It is artful and strong, a stunning comment on modern society and the excesses of human existence.

MANGA

A Japanese animation genre that has an intelligent, adult style derived from the superior Eastern comic books of the 1980s and 1990s.

Manga is a term that refers to the whole range of Japanese art of this type, but the English-speaking world tends to see it as representing the SF, fantasy and horror comic books and the animated feature films into which they are adapted. Most Manga on screen represents, in effect, serious movies made without live action actors.

Many of the more SF-orientated Manga draws on standard genre concepts, but when mixed with the stylistic inventiveness of the Japanese animators they become more original and fresh. Therefore it is not uncommon to come across future societies in which BIOTECH-NOLOGY is rife and the cities have become overpopulated and DYSTOPIC in nature. Indeed, in many respects Japanese scriptwriters have drawn heavily on CYBERPUNK for inspiration, yet portray its ideas in a manner which is totally at odds to our own. The mythic or RELIGIOUS often blends seamlessly with the technological and futuristic, resulting in detailed, complex plots that need careful attention if they are to be understood.

There are many fine examples of Manga from the previous two decades, but there are two major movies that have become popular in the Western world – *Akira* (1987) and *Ghost in the Shell* (1995).

Akira sees a put-upon teenage gang member develop psychic powers, and, after discovering the eponymous superhuman character CRYO-GENICALLY frozen underneath a vast sports arena, metamorphoses into a higher being who will bring about a new world order. The movie draws on many classic SF themes. In describing the weakling character who rises from his lowly beginnings to go on to become a psychic superhuman, *Akira* defines a new myth. However, the complex intonations of the plot are almost an aside to the power that is *Akira*. It is a profound and adult animation and, although it cycles uneasily through episodes of violence and moments of POLITICAL commentary, it remains a fine piece of film.

The Ghost in the Shell is an exploration of identity in NEAR FUTURE Tokyo, when the majority of humans live out their existence on a network of VIRTUAL REALITY scenarios. Electronic beings, representing ARTIFICIAL INTELLIGENCE, also roam these digital pathways, and it has become difficult to tell people from programs.

A young policewoman, who has been augmented to the point that she is more CYBORG than human, is investigating a criminal who is hacking his way into people's minds and reprogramming them to commit crimes.

It transpires that the entity is a state-controlled AI who is searching for a means to become human.

Ghost in the Shell, like *Akira* before it, is complex and at times confusing, but stylistically bold and intelligent. It tackles issues close to the heart of the SF genre, while at the same time demonstrating a profound insight into the human condition.

MARS ATTACKS! (1996, 106 minutes)

Director: Tim Burton
Producers: Tim Burton, Lerry Franco
Screenplay: Jonathan Gems
Starring: Jack Nicholson, Glenn Close, Annette Benning, Pierce Brosnan, Danny DeVito, Tom Jones, Lukas Haas, Martin Short, Michael J. Fox, Sarah Jessica Parker

Mars Attacks! is an hilarious romp which pays affectionate tribute to the classic ALIEN invasion movies of the 1950s whilst parodying the genre for all it is worth. Based on the infamous Topps Trading Cards of the 1960s, which were banned due to excessive use of violence and gore, *Mars Attacks!* details the invasion of small, chattering Martians and their hostile takeover plans for the Earth.

A message is received from the Martian ambassador, which is interpreted by the US Government as representing a peaceful attempt at first contact between the two races. They provide a welcoming committee for the Martian envoy, only to find the creatures open fire on the crowd with their ray guns. The Martians then perform a similar feat in Congress and begin their takeover of the planet.

However, a small group of unlikely heroes forms, including Tom Jones, a hippie, an alienated teenager and an ex-boxer, and it sets about saving Earth from the Martian invaders.

Mars Attacks! is a fun movie. It is all gloss with no real content, but at the same time its satirising of genre cliché is witty and well realized. The special effects are superb – the funny, noisy little Martians are superbly crafted with computer effects and the spacecraft are descended directly from a 1950s B-movie. The all-star cast is perhaps a little wasted – there are a number of walk-on cameos – but Nicholson is his usual charming self and actors seem simply to be enjoying themselves. This is what *Mars Attacks!* is all about. Watch it and you are almost guaranteed a laugh.

MARY SHELLEY'S FRANKENSTEIN
(1995, 123 minutes)

Director: Kenneth Branagh
Producers: Francis Ford Coppola, James V. Hart, John Veitch
Screenplay: Steph Lady, Frank Darabont
Starring: Kenneth Branagh, Robert DeNiro, Helena Bonham-Carter, Tom Hulce, Aiden Quinn, Richard Briers, John Cleese, Ian Holm, Robert Hardy, Cherie Lunghi, Celia Imrie, Trevyn McDowell

There are many differing adaptations of MARY SHELLEY's classic novel, *Frankenstein* (1818), not least the wonderful 1931 movie starring Boris Karloff as the monster. That particular film, although seminal, is perhaps more important to the development of Gothic HORROR movies and monster films than science fiction, and for that reason this volume will focus on the later 1995 movie by Kenneth Branagh which is truer to the original book.

Mary Shelley's Frankenstein boasts an enormous budget and a star-studded cast, headed by Branagh who plays Frankenstein and Robert DeNiro who plays the monster. As suggested by the title, the movie attempts to provide a faithful adaptation of Shelley's book.

Frankenstein is a young doctor, who, driven to create life in his laboratory by the death of his mother in childbirth, patches together a being out of various body parts and uses electricity to reanimate it. He is successful, and the 'monster' is born.

However, starved of love and affection, the monster suffers at the hands of society and, being refused a mate, seeks its revenge by murdering Frankenstein's lover. In a move away from the original novel, Frankenstein attempts to reanimate his Elizabeth (Bonham-Carter), but she memorably dies in a self-inflicted blaze. Frankenstein then pursues his creation to the Arctic, where they both perish in the frozen wastes, but not before the doctor has time to relate his story to the captain of a nearby fishing vessel.

Ultimately, sadly, the movie fails, becoming overmelodramatic and overemphasising the relationship between Frankenstein and Elizabeth, whilst underplaying that of Frankenstein and the monster.

The film is certainly sumptuous and brimming with marvellous costumes and set pieces, but it fails on the intellectual and emotional levels. When DeNiro describes his anguish, it is without real passion and fails to move the viewer.

Many critics condemned the movie for not living up to its Gothic heritage – this is unfair, and it is more likely that these reviewers were confusing a Gothic climate with that of modern horror, in the sense that modern horror movies attempt to scare their viewers. Scenically, *Mary Shelley's Frankenstein* is beautifully Gothic and entirely apt – what it misses is the sense of impending dread that made the 1931 adaptation such a seminal film.

However, as a piece of SF, *Mary Shelley's Frankenstein* is the closest that genre cinema has come to a faithful version of the classic book, and for that it remains of interest.

MATRIX, THE (1999, 131 minutes)
Directors: Andy Wachowski, Larry Wachowski
Producer: Joel Silver
Screenplay: Andy Wachowski, Larry Wachowski
Starring: Keanu Reeves, Laurence Fishburne, Carrie-Anne Moss, Hugo Weaving, Joe Pantoliano

One of the most stylish and extravagant SF thrillers of recent years, *The Matrix* is a post-CYBERPUNK study of the nature of reality and our human perception of it.

Advanced VIRTUAL REALITY systems hide a bleak DYSTOPIC world in which humanity has become enslaved by malign ARTIFICIAL INTELLIGENCE units, with which we are at war. The majority of the human race is unknowingly held prisoner within tanks of amniotic fluid and wired up to a vast computer network, the eponymous Matrix, which inspires the collective belief that we are living in a late twentieth-century America but in fact the world has been blighted by war and reality is a POST APOCALYPTIC nightmare landscape of terror.

The movie follows the progress of Neo (Reeves), a computer hacker who finds himself inadvertently drawn into the conspiracy that is the Matrix. He meets up with Morpheus (Fishburne) and his unlikely band of followers, and eventually finds himself ejected from the Matrix and resuscitated in the 'real world'. He joins Morpheus in his crusade for freedom, and in doing so comes to adopt the role of MESSIAH. Indeed, on one of its many levels, *The Matrix* becomes a retelling of the Christian fable. Neo learns to enact miracles, is betrayed by his very own Judas, and then dies, only to be reborn into something greater, an entity so powerful that he is able to bring about the end of the Matrix and free humanity from the shackles of the machines.

The Matrix is a modern classic. The special effects are impeccable and truly outstanding, with action sequences derived from the popular kung fu movies of the 1970s. New techniques were developed especially for the film, including a wonderful stop motion cinematography effect that allowed the directors to 'pause' live action sequences on the screen. The new techniques will go on to revolutionise action of the future.

The plight of the characters is both harrowing and exciting, and the viewer comes to believe, as does Neo himself, in the spiritual nature of his character. Aside from anything else, *The Matrix* underscores the search for personal identity in the modern world, as Neo tries to establish himself as an individual being, an entity separate from the vast system into which he was born.

Fishburne gives a strong performance in the role of Morpheus, first disciple of Neo and unwavering believer in the cause. Weaving, as the villain, is the archetypal Man in Black, the manifestation of the computer program that exists solely to seek and destroy any unauthorized entrants into the Matrix. Reeves is perfect in the role of Neo; mysterious, quiet and sultry, yet capable of passion and action when the role requires it.

The Matrix is SF *noir* at its best, blending the paranoia and seediness of Cyberpunk with the excesses of action kung fu, all the while maintaining a comic book morality that leaves just enough room for adventure and fun. Unlike the similar movie EXISTENZ (1999), *The Matrix* leaves nothing ambiguous about its world, and in the end everything becomes clear. This is a double-edged sword, but there is enough subtext within the film to allow plenty of analysis.

MEN IN BLACK (1997, 98 minutes)
Director: Barry Sonnenfeld
Producer: Walter F. Parkes
Screenplay: Ed Solomon
Starring: Tommy Lee Jones, Will Smith, Linda Fiorentino, Vincent D'Onofrio, Rip Torn, Tony Shalhoub, Siobhan Fallon

Men in Black is a fine example of a COMIC SF movie, as well as one of the better translations of a comic book to the big screen. The movie successfully parodies the X-FILES and the many UFO conspiracy theories which have developed a following over the last fifty years.

ALIENS are among us. They are friendly and most have adopted human guise to remain anonymous amongst the masses of people who inhabit New York City. An élite group – the Men in Black – maintain control of this alien influx, issuing passports and regularizing immigration. However, when a psychopathic insectile alien descends on the planet with the intention of sparking off an interstellar war, Agent K (Jones) and fresh-faced recruit Agent J (Smith), set out to save the day. What follows is an often hilarious romp which sees the two agents pitted against all manner of weird and wonderfully realized extraterrestrials.

The movie is perhaps best considered a humorous SCIENCE FANTASY, as it makes no attempt to consider traditional genre conventions, except when it chooses to satirise them for its own ends. However, what this does show is an excellent grasp of the SF genre on the part of the writer, as he is able to pepper the film with jokes derived from all aspects of the field. The result is a very funny and enjoyable movie with an intelligent script.

Both Jones and Smith come across well in their respective roles, Jones the established straight man and Smith the wide-eyed newcomer. The supporting actors are similarly effective.

METROPOLIS (1926, 180 minutes)
Director: Fritz Lang
Producer: Erich Pommer
Screenplay: Fritz Lang, Thea von Harbou
Starring: Brigitte Helm, Alfred Abel, Gustav Froehlich, Rudolf Klein-Rogge, Fritz Rasp, Theodor Loos, Olaf Storm, Heinrich George, Grete Berger, Helene Weignel

There are many different cuts of the early German classic *Metropolis*, each with its own differing soundtrack. Some are silent (as was the original release which is sadly no longer in existence), one has had a classical sequence imposed upon it, another modern pop. All have their own strengths and weaknesses. What these different versions of the movie do not do is remove its sheer cinematic power and appeal; *Metropolis* was the first big budget SF movie ever to be made, and it has stood the test of time well.

It is somewhere near the year 2000 and in a thriving German city an underclass of workers slave away at enormous, brutal machines that maintain the city itself. (Indeed, one of the most enduring images of this film is its opening sequence in which a team of machine operators work in perfect synchronicity with the vast engine they control). All the while a rich élite reap the benefits of the workers' efforts.

It falls to the beautiful Maria (Helm) to maintain the peace, coercing the workers back to their tasks with inspiring speeches and calm words, and convincing them not to revolt against their masters.

However, the industrialist leader (Abel) kidnaps Maria and has his scientist Rothwang (Klein-Rogge) – the archetypal mad professor – develop a ROBOTIC duplicate of her with which to sublimate the workers. Meanwhile, the industrialist's son (Froelich) has fallen in love with Maria and searches for her among the underground caverns of the workers.

After a truly triumphant scene in which Rothwang's robot is transformed into an evil replica of Maria, the good Maria escapes and is chased around the city by the scientist.

The robot (also Helm, now looking rather wild eyed and dishevelled) sets off, against its master's intentions, inciting the workers to rebel. They promptly destroy the city, flooding the underground network of buildings and caverns in which they live and bring the industrialists' machines, as well as the decadent city, to a standstill.

Whilst this has been going on, Froelich has rescued his love and together they set about saving the work force from obliterating themselves. Eventually, all is put right, and in keeping with all happy endings, Froelich gets the girl and the leader of the workers shakes hands with the rich industrialist, sealing a pact of mutual respect between them.

If the plot, which is rather contrived, were all that there was of *Metropolis*, then it would not be the classic that it is today. However, Lang was a director never truly concerned with the machinations of plot, but more with the general cinematic appeal of the film. It is true that the final scenes are weak and sentimental, and that the overall script is unworthy of the cinematography of the picture, but Lang manages to make it all fit together.

His camerawork is truly inspiring. The initial view of the cityscape is modern and accurate, and correctly anticipates the arrival of massive skyscrapers and tower blocks full of offices. The scene in which Maria is transformed into an evil doppelgänger of herself would be replicated many times in *Frankenstein* movies to come, but remains the original and most effective. Perhaps the best scene in the movie comes when Rothwang searches for Maria in the dark. His torch beam arcs across the screen like a fork of lightning, occasionally catching glimpses of the terrified Maria. It is one of the most tense and truly frightening moments in cinematic history.

Metropolis is also a POLITICAL film, an early attempt to discuss the oppression of the masses and the incorrect use of technology. It is also an unsuccessful attempt to understand the origins of myth. Fundamentally, though, it is a celebration of humanity and a call for respect from the authorities, a request that the barriers between class should become less stringent so that information can pass more freely between them. It is ironic that, at the beginning of the film, the workers are more mechanistic than Helm's robot.

The actors' performances vary, but Helm is a marvel and she plays both the wholesome, saintly Maria and her beautiful, dishevelled doppel-gänger admirably. Indeed, it is not just her manner that changes, but her whole appearance – Maria's replacement is a vampiric seductress that represents the antithesis of Maria. Klein-Rogge is wonderfully hammy as Rothwang, a neurotic genius at odds with his own abilities. His appearance would become the stereotypical mad scientist, imitated in later movies such as BACK TO THE FUTURE (1985) and the many versions of *Frankenstein*. Froelich is rather too camp to be a genuine hero, and Abel is satisfactory in his role as the industrialist who learns his lesson and begins to make amends.

Metropolis is a genre-defining movie, a wonder of cinematography that remains as relevant today as it was when it was first released. It heralded the beginning of big budget SF cinema, and has had a direct and lasting impact on the genre as a whole.

MORK AND MINDY
Starring: Robin Williams (Mork), Pam Dawber (Mindy)

Mork and Mindy was a strange spin-off show from the non-genre series *Happy Days*, and featured the exploits of an ALIEN, Mork, who was sent to Earth by his own people to study the customs of humanity.

Mork is adopted by Mindy and her father, and they attempt to teach him the means to get by in society. Mork, as expected, cannot quite grasp the complexities of modern human life, and constantly fumbles to get things right. With Williams in the lead role, this often led to all manner of bizarre and surreal hilarity.

The show was a vehicle for Williams and his wonderful comic activities, which frequently saw him standing on his head, wearing his clothes backwards or generally not getting on very well with American society. Indeed, this portrayal of society through the eyes of an outsider allowed for a wide range of moralizing and philosophizing to take place, the lessons of which were regularly summed up by Mork at the end of each episode when he made his report to back to his superiors on his home PLANET of Ork.

There is not a lot of depth to *Mork and Mindy* and, as it progressed, the series got ever more tiresome, as the same gags were repeated over again and it became clear that Mindy did not really have a proper role to play. In a rather bizarre move the writers married her off to Mork, and they proceeded to have an alien 'child' – actually a middle-aged man, as Orkians grow younger rather than older as the years go by. This was entirely detrimental to the humour of the series, and eventually the show lost its viewers and was cancelled.

Mork and Mindy remains, however, one of the most popular series of its day, and its satirical approach to the portrayal of modern life is entirely in keeping with the exploration of the alien theme. The earlier episodes are a fine example of COMIC SF making it to the small screen, although the later episodes descend into absurdity.

NINETEEN EIGHTY-FOUR (1984, 110 minutes)

Director: Michael Radford
Producer: Simon Perry
Screenplay: Michael Radford
Starring: John Hurt, Richard Burton, Suzanna Hamilton, Cyril Cusack, James Walker

Based on the classic novel of DYSTOPIA, *Nineteen Eighty-Four* (1949), by GEORGE ORWELL.

This, the second big screen adaptation of Orwell's novel (the first was the unsatisfactory *1984* in 1955), was filmed and released in 1984 to capitalize on the publicity surrounding the book at that time. The movie owes much to the book in terms of plot, but unfortunately trivializes the POLITICAL nature of Orwell's vision in favour of an overemphasis on the tragic love affair between Smith (Hurt) and Julia (Hamilton).

It is set within the totalitarian state of Oceania (formerly Great Britain), within which the infamous eyes of Big Brother watch from every corner. Anyone stepping out of line is swiftly removed and psychologically 'reconditioned'.

Winston Smith is a state worker who begins to question his environment and the effectiveness of the regime. He rebels on a very personal level – he begins writing a diary which discloses his misgivings, and seeks an affair with a co-worker, Julia. They soon fall in love, and together realize that the state controls are both demeaning and dehumanising. However, Smith becomes too trusting and discloses his personal beliefs to the wrong man (Burton), who admits him to the horrifying Room 101 for a bout of vicious psychological torture in which he succumbs to his worst nightmare and is reprogrammed into seeing the 'truth' – he comes to believe that two plus two equals five, illustrating how utterly his position has been compromised.

However, where the book is a startling, unsettling vision of state control and conformity, the movie becomes bogged down in detailing the relationship between Smith and Julia and the realization that their love can only end in failure. There is some excellent acting, but the plot becomes too slow moving and melodramatic, and eventually it becomes all too clear that the movie has failed to capture the true essence of the book.

It is a shame that *Nineteen Eighty-Four* does not succeed – the excellent cast and consistent art direction should have amounted to more. Orwell's future is a bleak one, a true Dystopia for our times. Compared to the novel, *Nineteen Eighty-Four* becomes ineffectual.

The best screen adaptation of Orwell's novel remains the first, the 1954 television play scripted by Nigel Kneale (of QUATERMASS fame) for the BBC, and starring Peter Cushing as Winston Smith.

OMEGA MAN, THE (1971, 98 minutes)
Director: Boris Sagal
Producer: Walter Seltzer
Screenplay: John William Corrington, Joyce M. Corrington
Starring: Charlton Heston, Rosalind Cash, Anthony Zerbe, Paul Koslo

Charlton Heston is Robert Neville, the last man left alive after a viral plague has turned the rest of the species into vampires, in this adaptation of RICHARD MATHESON's important novel, *I Am Legend* (1954). The film is only a partial success.

A biological war with the Russians has caused much of humanity to be destroyed, and those left alive have mutated into bloodsucking vampires. Robert Neville is a doctor who, having been working on immunity serums during the war, has found himself immune to the virus. By day he roams the empty streets of Los Angeles, living the life of a lonely king, drinking fine wines and doing whatever he chooses. By night, he locks himself up in his house and attempts to ward off the vampires as they bay for his blood.

However, the plot deviates greatly from that of the book. Where Neville is portrayed as a disenchanted, pessimistic man in the book, Heston's character is a gung-ho hero who appears to view the death of humanity as a great chance to get down and do all the things he'd always wanted to.

Eventually, Neville comes across a small enclave of other survivors who are struggling to eke out a living in the green belt outside of the city. He develops a love interest (Cash), and eventually begins work on an immunization serum that will protect the remainder of humanity from the virus, and allow them to propagate the species.

Ultimately, Neville fails in his battle against the vampires, and in a climactic moment is murdered with a spear. However he leaves behind enough serum to protect the human race and their children from the evils to come. Unusually for this type of movie, however, the vampires are left to walk free at the end.

The movie lacks the power of the novel to terrify, in that it offers a cosy solution to the problem of the virus and the continuation of the human race. The book offers us no such comfort.

Nonetheless, the film is satisfactory and, misgivings aside, succeeds in portraying an America brought to its knees by foreign weapons. This is unusual in itself, but then the movie goes on to offer us an image of science as both a harbinger and a redeemer – biological weapons have devastated the race, but it is only scientific endeavour that will save us from extinction.

It is this ambiguity that finally saves *The Omega Man*, providing it with a layer of added depth, that, although distinctly more upbeat than the novel, is thought-provoking.

OUTER LIMITS, THE

The Outer Limits was one of the better television pulp shows of the 1960s, an anthology sequence that, rather than having a cast of characters who went from one episode to the next, took the different approach of producing a series of unconnected, one-off dramas, all with a similar theme: the monster.

The Outer Limits was a series intended to scare its viewers. The monsters, which were frequently more fantastical or supernatural than science fictional, were never intended to represent anything more than beasts derived from nightmares, or the manifestation of the ghouls that live under the bed. The monsters were intended to represent the 'outer limits' of human imagination and terror.

The original manifestation of *The Outer Limits* drew most of its plots and ideas from the earlier pulp magazine and stories. Occasionally, one of the stories would hit upon a true SF idea or notion, but it was never really explored in full.

However, the series was revived in 1995 and, retaining the same title and format, was reinvented for a modern audience. The monsters did not disappear, but neither did they remain the focus of the series. Indeed, many of the newer episodes do not even feature monsters at all.

The new series, which is still running and being produced in the USA, takes its ideas from more recent SF, and has a tendency to explore these ideas better and tease out their full potential. It is also to the credit of the individual directors that they have managed to obtain guest appearances from a number of celebrated genre figures such as Mark Hamill (Luke Skywalker from STAR WARS), Leonard Nimoy (Spock from the original STAR TREK) and Michael Dorn (the Klingon Worf from *Star Trek: The Next Generation*). The special effects have also improved accordingly.

In effect, with the new series, *The Outer Limits* has become the visual representation of an SF short-story anthology. Each new story tackles different ideas, and explores in terms of SF the impact that new technologies and innovations may have upon the social structure. And every now and then, just for laughs, a monster is thrown in for good luck . . .

The original series of *The Outer Limits* ran for forty-nine hour-long episodes between 1963 and 1965.

The later series began in 1995 and has recently finished its sixth season.

OUTLAND (1981, 109 minutes)
Director: Peter Hyams
Producer: Richard A. Roth
Screenplay: Peter Hyams
Starring: Sean Connery, Peter Boyle, Frances Sterhagen, Kika Markham, Clarke Peters, Steven Berkoff

Outland is a movie which takes all the trappings of a Western and transplants them into space.

The action takes place aboard a mining station on Jupiter's desolate moon, Io. A rash of suicides in which people are stepping out of airlocks leads the marshal (Connery) to begin an impromptu investigation. Strange occurrences follow, and the investigation is blocked at every turn. It eventually transpires that the manager of the station has concocted an elicit drugs ring which increases the production of the workers but, as an unfortunate side-effect, induces spells of insanity. As in all classic Westerns, the marshall eventually manages to bring the perpetrators to justice.

Outland is not an original movie, yet it is entertaining. The special effects are satisfactory and Connery gives an excellent performance as the lawbringer. It is perhaps true that the SF setting becomes almost superfluous to the plot, but as an update of *High Noon* the movie does succeed.

Outland has also given its name to a national SF and Fantasy newsletter.

PHANTOM MENACE, THE (1999, 127 minutes)
Director: George Lucas
Producer: Rick McCallum
Screenplay: George Lucas
Starring: Liam Neeson, Ewan McGregor, Natalie Portman, Jake Lloyd, Ian McDiarmid, Anthony Williams, Kenny Baker

A prequel to STAR WARS (1977) and the first in a projected trilogy of movies intended to provide the story that leads up to the events that take place in the earlier films. *The Phantom Menace* lacks the narrative appeal and mythical qualities of the earlier Star Wars movies. It is dry and less than adventurous, and the token ALIEN sidekick of the main protagonists is a truly annoying distraction.

The movie follows the progress of a young Obi Wan Kenobi and his Jedi Master, played by Liam Neeson, as they set about attempting to divert a POLITICAL crisis that is brewing amongst various trading groups. However, events conspire against them and they end up joining the battle to save the PLANET Naboo from hostile invasion, in the process adopting a young Anakin Skywalker (who will later become Darth Vader) and rescuing Naboo's princess regent.

The special effects are unsurpassed in genre cinema, but the movie feels like a collection of unrelated episodes strung together to form a makeshift story. Indeed, at times it as if the plot is a rather weak excuse for a number of admittedly impressive action sequences involving huge armies of ROBOTS or evil Sith warriors.

The actors appear to struggle with a bland script, and in the end the movie ultimately fails to satisfy. Nevertheless, it proved hugely popular amongst Star Wars fans and, when considered in the context of the earlier movies, can be seen to add a historical dimension to the Star Wars myth. Many of the individual scenes in *The Phantom Menace* are accomplished and well realized, but as a coherent movie it lacks structure and form.

PLANET OF THE APES (1968, 119 minutes)
Director: Frank J. Schaffner
Producer: Mort Abrahams
Screenplay: Michael Wilson, Rod Serling
Starring: Charlton Heston, Roddy McDowall, Kim Hunter, Maurice Evans, James Whitmore, Linda Harrison

Based on the novel *Monkey Planet* (1963) by PIERRE BOULLE. *Planet of the Apes* has to be one of the single most effective SF movies of all time. Its images are haunting and enduring, and while it was not the first movie to posit the eventual collapse of human civilization, it was certainly one of the most original.

A team of astronauts, headed by Charlton Heston, sets out on a mission to visit and explore a distant PLANET. After being brought around after a spell in CRYOGENIC suspension, they fail to regain control of the ship and crash-land in a lake in the middle of a blighted desert. They manage to escape with a small amount of provisions and, after setting out to explore, they soon discover signs of life.

Eventually, the three surviving astronauts stumble across a tribe of nomadic humans who appear to have slipped into a primitive state and exist in the simple form of hunter-gatherers. They attempt to make contact, but in doing so inadvertantly become embroiled in a terrifying occurrence – a band of intelligent primates riding horses arrives on the scene. The humans attempt to flee, but a number of them are shot dead and many are captured by the talking monkeys. Two of the astronauts are killed, and Heston is first wounded in the throat and then captured and taken back to the ape city and slavery.

He finds that monkeys and gorillas have evolved to such a point that they have formed their own civilization, and that humanity is considered to be a dirty, primitive slave race. Whilst the primates struggle to achieve scientific knowledge and high art, the human beings are left to scrabble around in the dirt.

What follows is an odyssey towards revelation as Heston attempts to escape from the apparent lunacy of his environment and the shackles it entails. He enlists the aid of two rebellious ape scientists and eventually manages to demonstrate to them that he is an intelligent being who deserves his freedom. After a showdown at an archaeological excavation, where Heston unwittingly proves that humanity used to have an intelligent civilization of its own, he is set free and, with one of the tribal women from the ape city, he sets out on horseback into the desolate landscape. However, the final and most powerful revelation is left until the end. Heston rounds a rocky bend in the road to come face to face with one of the most affecting symbols of human civilization, half submerged in the sand – the Statue of Liberty. The movie ends in a dramatic moment of silence, as Heston finally comes to realize the true fate of the human race. He has not been visiting some strange, exotic world, but the future of Earth. Through time dilation and relativity, his spacecraft had actually travelled into the future and returned to Earth at some distant point in the future, when mankind has devolved into animals and apes have inherited the planet.

Planet of the Apes is one of the best explorations of the POST APOCA-LYPTIC theme yet to be filmed, and Heston's performance as the stranded astronaut who must learn to cope with a society utterly at odds with his own, is strong and emotive. Roddy McDowell and Kim Hunter are also superb as the baffled ape scientists who find an intelligent, talking human a complete enigma, an ALIEN fallen from the stars.

There are many ways the movie can be viewed. The moral complexities of the situation dictate that, although our allegiance remains entirely with Heston, the apes too garner sympathy and support. Their society has become infiltrated by this noisy intruder, and all they wish to do is preserve their own civilization and prevent the human beings from creating another world-changing catastrophe. Indeed, one of the most effective moments is the recognition that the chief apes know the truth about the rise and fall of the human species, and that they are attempting to protect their people from a reccurrence of the same events. That is why they maintain such an oppressive control over the surviving human population.

Heston's plight can also be seen as a reversal of the typical alien contact scenario, in that the human becomes the outsider who is branded as an animal and given no opportunity to prove himself to his captors.

Planet of the Apes begins with an excellent premise, and tackles each and every one of the issues it raises, while providing the viewer with a great adventure story.

Planet of the Apes spawned four sequels, which saw the story come full circle and explain how the apes eventually came to dominate the world. In doing so, they lose a little bit of the mystery inherent in the first film, and shrinking budgets meant that the films got progressively worse. They are *Beneath the Planet of the Apes* (1969), *Escape from the Planet of the Apes* (1971), *Conquest of the Planet of the Apes* (1972) and *Battle for the Planet of the Apes* (1973). There was also a spin-off television show, that lasted one season and ran for fourteen fifty-minute episodes in 1974.

It is rumoured that director Tim Burton is currently engaged in a remake of the original film.

POSTMAN, THE (1997, 170 minutes)
Director: Kevin Costner
Producers: Jim Wilson, Steve Tisch, Kevin Costner
Screenplay: Eric Roth, Brian Helgeland
Starring: Kevin Costner, Will Patton, Larenz Tate, Olivia Williams, James Russo, Tom Petty

The Postman is based on the novel, *The Postman* (1985) by DAVID BRIN, and was produced and directed by actor Kevin Costner, who also starred.

Set in a POST-APOCALYPTIC America which is struggling to rebuild itself after a nuclear war, the movie follows the progress of one man who adopts the role of 'postman' and, in restoring communications between isolated pockets of survivors, brings about the slow recovery of civilisation. However, working against this 'postman' is a warrior army known as the Holnists, who are attempting to keep people out of communication with each other so that they may maintain their reign of terror.

Brin's original novel received mixed reviews upon first publication, but went on to win him the John W. Campbell Memorial Award. However, the movie shifts the focus away from the emphasis on social rehabilitation that was so predominant in the book, to the conflict between Costner's 'postman' and the Holnists. This results in an action-fuelled thriller that ultimately fails to capture the subtleties of the novel, and sentimentalises Costner's character.

This is a shame because the movie looks good and has the right feel about it, but is too long and too opaque.

PREDATOR (1987, 107 minutes)

Director: John McTiernan
Producers: Lawrence Gordon, Joel Silver, John Davis
Screenplay: Jim Thomas, John Thomas
Starring: Arnold Schwarzenegger, Carl Weathers, Bill Duke, Elpidia Carrillo, Jesse Ventura

An ALIEN visitation movie that begins with an interesting premise and then descends into predictable action adventure, *Predator* was nevertheless the first movie to blend a typical Vietnam scenario with an SF idea.

A MILITARY squad is despatched to South America on a dangerous rescue mission, but the people it has been sent to save have been savagely butchered. The soldiers engage in combat with some *thing*, which appears to have the power to camouflage itself. As they attempt to withdraw from the jungle, the creature begins picking them off one by one.

It transpires that an alien (referred to only as Predator) is visiting Earth so that it may hunt humans for sport. After killing and skinning all the members of a previous expedition to the area, the creature is now attempting to take out the remaining members of the second special forces squad. In the end the movie is reduced to a sequence of one-on-one combat scenes between Schwarzenegger and the alien. Schwarzenegger finally wins through, blowing the creature apart with a hand grenade after he has trapped it under a tree trunk.

The special effects are of a particularly high standard, and the alien itself is realized with real panache and care. The sequences from the Predator's point of view are shot through a heat-detecting camera, offering a different visual spectrum.

The tension is built up well, and it is clear that the alien and the marine played by Schwarzenegger have a mutual respect for one another – the alien views humanity as a vermin race, but in Schwarzenegger meets a worthy adversary.

As action entertainment the movie works well enough, but it does not follow through any of its ideas.

Predator was followed by the unusually good *Predator II* (1990), which this time sees an alien stalking the streets of America, seeking human trophies to display alongside its hoard of other winnings. Danny Glover is the cop who investigates, and eventually comes to realize that an extraterrestrial is responsible for the spate of murders. It becomes a battle of wits between him and the alien, until, in much the same way as in the first film, he unrealistically manages to defeat the monster. What sets *Predator II* apart from its predecessor is the fact that the director takes time out from the action to allow some parody of the American media.

PRISONER, THE
Starring: Patrick McGoohan

Devised and partly-written by the show's star, *The Prisoner* has become one of the most memorable and enigmatic television series of all time.

It starts with a government official resigning from his top secret job, only to be abducted and sped away to be incarcerated in the Village, a sleepy British township of unknown location.

Upon waking he finds himself unable to leave, and is expected to answer to Number Six; he soon discovers everyone in the village is known by a number, and that Number Two is the leader of the community. The all powerful Number One remains constantly absent from the proceedings.

What follows is a quest for understanding, as McGoohan attempts to discover the reasons for his imprisonment, and to escape. Meanwhile, a succession of Number Twos (they are never the same person twice) attempt to extract from him the reasons why he resigned from his job as a British spy.

In a final, climactic scene in the last episode, McGoohan manages to achieve his freedom from the Village, but remains imprisoned inside his own mind; Number One is eventually revealed to be himself, and the cryptic message is that free will is a state of mind, not a state of being.

There are many, many interpretations of *The Prisoner*, and that has become one of the chief reasons for its success – it defies casual viewing and encourages deeper analysis. At times the series deals with psychology, the misuse of psychotropic drugs, the right to democracy and the abuse of power and violence. It is a subtle exploration of the human mind as well as a study of the controlled environment, a theme that would later come to be used to great effect in THE TRUMAN SHOW (1998).

The show was without doubt before its time and really does repay careful attention. It was filmed in the small picturesque town of Portmeirion in Wales.

QUANTUM LEAP
Starring: Scott Bakula (Beckett), Dean Stockwell (Al)

Quantum Leap is, in essence, a timeslip fantasy that attempts to rationalize the constant temporal shifts of scientist Sam Beckett in terms of quantum theory.

Beckett is a quantum physicist who, in experimenting with a machine he calls the 'quantum accelerator', finds himself slipped back in time and housed in the body of another person. To the viewer, Beckett is clearly visible, but to the other characters in each episode he is the person whose body he has 'fallen into'. Aided only by his associate Al, who projects a hologram of himself into the past to accompany Sam and offer him advice about the best course of action, Beckett must attempt to make sense of his surroundings and adopt the role of the person whose body he has borrowed.

It transpires that if he ever wants to get home, Beckett must attempt to rectify some mistake or unfortunate occurrence in the person's life before he is able to 'leap' on to the next adventure. Therefore, each episode takes the form of Bakula leaping into a different person's body and helping them to solve their life's problems before leaping out again. This allows some interesting character exploration, as Beckett does not always like the person whose life he temporarily hijacks, even at times finding himself in the body of a murderer.

The SF aspects of the plotting are relatively non-existent, and the premise is simply an attempt to rationalise a device that, on the face of it, is more fantastical than scientific. Nevertheless, *Quantum Leap* proved popular amongst fans, who followed Beckett's exploits for nearly one hundred different episodes or 'leaps'.

The programme is also pseudo-RELIGIOUS, in that Beckett and Al become increasingly convinced that God is behind the leaping and that Beckett is now acting under the watchful eye of the Supreme Being. Indeed, this theory is compounded in an episode in which Bakula encounters a terrifying entity he interprets to be the Devil, and in the final episode in which Bakula has a discussion with a barman who he believes to be God.

It is interesting that Beckett never made it home again to his friends and family, suggesting, in keeping with the religious tone of the series, he must sacrifice his own life to improve the nature of the race as a whole. In effect, Beckett becomes an unseen MESSIAH

Quantum Leap, remains a popular show, being rerun on television frequently and developing its own cult following. Some spin-off books were published when the show was at its peak but they didn't really work.

QUATERMASS XPERIMENT, THE (1955, 82 minutes)
Director: Val Guest
Producer: Anthony Hinds
Screenplay: Val Guest, Richard Landau
Starring: Brian Donlevy, Margia Dean, Jack Warner, Richard Wordsworth, David King Wood, Harold Lang, Lionel Jeffries

The first of three Hammer movies to be based on Nigel Kneale's seminal television serials, *The Quatermass Xperiment* was to become the film that sparked off a whole movement in British genre cinema. Without the success of this movie, Hammer would not have had the impetus to go on to develop the many *Frankenstein* and *Dracula* movies for which they are best remembered. It is now regarded as a classic.

The Quatermass Xperiment begins with a space rocket returning to Earth from a mission in space. It crashes, and the one survivor (Wordsworth) is found to have brought back strange ALIEN spores which attach themselves to him and begin to grow. He escapes from hospital to find that the growth is taking over his body. It is not long before he changes into a strange blob (similar to that seen later in THE BLOB (1958)) and goes on a rampage around London, murdering helpless citizens. Eventually the creature is cornered in Westminister Abbey by investigative scientist Dr Quatermass (Donlevy), who proceeds to electrocute it to death.

The Quatermass Xperiment and especially its later sequels, *Quatermass II* (1957) and *Quatermass and the Pit* (1967), show a witty and inventive intelligence that was lacking in much pulp SF of the time. Wordsworth is genuinely touching as a scared and confused astronaut who is slowly being eaten alive by an alien terror. Donlevy is superb in the role of Dr Quatermass, a proud proponent of science who is unafraid to tackle whatever terrors outer space may throw at him.

The *Quatermass* sequence is optimistic about the future and the inherent ability of the human race to overcome any hardships, and perhaps this gives some indication as to why it was such a startling success.

The *Quatermass* films, along with DR WHO, remain a British SF institution.

RED DWARF
Starring: Craig Charles (Lister), Chris Barrie (Rimmer), Danny John-Jules (Cat), Robert Llewellyn (Kryten)

A spoof British comedy that is suitably irreverent about the SF genre whilst still making use of some its best themes and clichés.

The mining vessel *Red Dwarf* succumbs to a radiation leak, in which all but one of the human crew perish. Dave Lister is passing the time in suspended animation as punishment for smuggling his pet cat aboard the spacecraft.

After three million years have passed and the radiation levels have returned to normal, Lister is released from his CRYOGENIC sleep. He is dismayed to find that his only companions are the ship's ARTIFICIAL INTELLIGENCE, a hologram of his former boss, and a humanoid evolved from his pet cat in the intervening years. When Lister attempts to turn the ship about and head for home, he discovers not only is he millions of light years away from the Solar System, but the entirety of the human race has been destroyed. He is the last remaining specimen of his species.

Eventually, as the series progresses, the crew is joined by a neurotic ROBOT, Kryten. They also lose the main ship and find themselves stranded on a tiny, claustrophobic runabout named *Starbug*. They spend the next few series attempting to catch up with *Red Dwarf*.

Essentially, *Red Dwarf* began as a sitcom set aboard an abandoned space vessel, but developed into an SF comedy classic. The gags are laden with parodies of typical genre notions and devices, such as ALIENS, TIME TRAVEL, CYBORGS and NANOTECHNOLOGY. Indeed, underneath the witty hilarity are some genuinely interesting explorations of SF ideas.

To date, there have been eight seasons of *Red Dwarf*, which debuted in 1988, totalling thirty-six half-hour episodes. A movie is rumoured to be in production.

RETURN OF THE JEDI, THE (1983, 132 minutes)
Director: Richard Marquand
Producer: Howard Kazanjian
Screenplay: Lawrence Kasdan, George Lucas
Starring: Mark Hamill, Harrison Ford, Carrie Fisher, Billy Dee Williams, Anthony Daniels, Peter Mayhew, Ian McDiarmid

Return of the Jedi, the third of the STAR WARS movies to appear, is entertaining but unfortunately descends into juvenile episodes.

It opens well. Han Solo, frozen alive in carbonite, is rescued by Princess Leia from the clutches of the giant ALIEN mollusc, Jabba the Hutt. However, she is caught in the process, and it falls to Luke Skywalker to come to their aid. He too is captured and imprisoned, but it is not long before his ROBOTS aid his escape and all of the good guys are set free. They escape to the PLANET Endor, which is populated by trite little teddy bear creatures known as Ewoks. Many battles ensue, and Luke steals away to confront the evil emperor and his father Darth Vader aboard a newly constructed Death Star (a space station the size of a small moon which is capable of destroying whole worlds). After refusing to cross over to the Dark Side of the Force, Luke is nearly killed by the emperor, but Vader redeems himself and reverts to the Light, rescuing his son and sacrificing himself to destroy the emperor.

Eventually all of the battles are won and, after Luke has been reconciled with his father, the rebels rejoice in bringing about the end of the totalitarian regime. Skywalker and Leia also discover they are siblings.

Return of the Jedi neatly puts a cap on the trilogy of original Star Wars movies, and does much to develop the modern myth that Lucas was aiming to create. Unfortunately, it shies away from the maturity shown in its predecessor, THE EMPIRE STRIKES BACK (1980) and instead reverts to the simplistic formula of the first film. Nevertheless, as entertainment it succeeds, although it does remain the poorest of the original movies.

ROBINSON CRUSOE ON MARS (1964, 112 minutes)

Director: Byron Haskin
Producer: Aubrey Schenck
Screenplay: Ib Melchior, John C. Higgins
Starring: Paul Mantee, Adam West, Vic Lundin

From the director of 1950s classics DESTINATION MOON (1950) and WAR OF THE WORLDS (1953), *Robinson Crusoe on Mars* was, obviously, inspired by Daniel Defoe's classic novel *Robinson Crusoe* (1719), and is in the grand tradition of SPACE OPERA.

A rocket ship crash-lands on the barren surface of Mars. One of the two co-pilots is killed, but the other (Mantee) survives, along with his pet monkey. He manages to salvage some provisions, and retreats to a nearby cave. Through sheer strength of mind and ingenuity, he manages to eke out an existence, melting rocks to replenish his oxygen supply and living off the salvaged rations. Naturally enough, it is not long before the loneliness begins to affect his mind, and he is becomes plagued by visions of his dead friend. The character witnesses the arrival of ALIEN spacecraft which have abducted a number of human slaves. He rescues one (Lundin), who goes on to adopt the role of his Man Friday.

The movie is intelligent and interesting, although the arrival of the Martians heralds a change of pace.

It is a superior study of human survival against the odds. The title is ridiculous, but the movie itself is surprisingly good.

ROBOCOP (1987, 98 minutes)
Director: Paul Verhoeven
Producer: Arne Schmidt
Screenplay: Edward Neumier, Michael Miner
Starring: Peter Weller, Nancy Allen, Dan O'Herlihy, Kurtwood Smith, Miguel Ferrer, Robert Do Qui, Ray Wise

RoboCop is set in the NEAR FUTURE DYSTOPIA of Detroit, a rank network of mean streets and dirty suburbs in which corporate corruption and criminal activity thrives.

The OCP Corporation owns not only most of the city's business enterprises, but the corrupt and privatized police force. Alex Murphy (Weller) is a cop killed in action, his body fragmented in a moment of horrific violence in which his partner manages to escape. However, the OCP Corporation has uses for Murphy's remains, and develops a CYBORG police officer, RoboCop, who will become the saviour of the city. He is given a set of Prime Directives (much in line with ISAAC ASIMOV'S Three Laws of Robotics) to ensure that he stays in line, and turned out on to the street to uphold the law. However, the cyborg begins to suffer from agonizing flashbacks to his previous existence as a human being – which provides Verhoeven with an opportunity to offer an intense study of the psychology of the man/machine hybrid – and sets out to avenge his 'death'. This eventually leads him into a web of corruption which involves many of his superior officers. With his increasingly returning humanity RoboCop manages to override his Prime Directives and exact his revenge.

RoboCop is a biting satire of the fascist run totalitarianism that plagued the early part of the twentieth century. It also aims a blow at the mass media and the corporate-dominated society that is more prevalent today. This is exemplified in the television adverts that punctuate the movie, hammering home Verhoeven's message that there is something twisted and perverted about the direction in which modern society is headed.

The action sequences and special effects are superb, if a little gory, and there are many enduring images. It has been pointed out many times that *RoboCop* is a filmed comic book. If this is the case then it is a particularly thoughtful example.

For a further exploration of a similar theme, FREDERIK POHL'S extraordinary novel *Man Plus* (1976) is well worth seeking out.

RoboCop inspired two direct sequels, as well as a later television series. *RoboCop 2* (1990) was scripted by comic book writer Frank Miller and, although fairly stylish, retreads the same ground as the original. *RoboCop 3* (1993) descends into absurdity, whilst the television series, which ran for twenty episodes between 1994 and 1995, has little to redeem it. It is rumoured to be making a return in the near future.

ROLLERBALL (1975, 118 minutes)

Director: Norman Jewison
Producer: Norman Jewison
Screenplay: William Harrison
Starring: James Caan, John Houseman, Ralph Richardson, Maud Adams, John Beck, Moses Gunn

Rollerball is a look into the NEAR FUTURE, to a time when the world is run by mass corporations and an anti-UTOPIA is in place in America.

The movie tackles similar themes to THE RUNNING MAN (1987), in that it portrays a violent, gory game show that is broadcast around America to satisfy the people's sadistic impulses and so quash any thoughts of rebellion against the corporate state.

The game itself takes the form of a bastardized hockey match, with its contestants riding motorbikes or roller skates, armed with vicious spikes. The death count is high and the survival rate is low.

Jonathan E, the game's greatest player, is becoming too popular, and so the powers that be request that he officially retire from the game, fearful that his continued success will inspire the populace with dreams of empowerment. He rebels, however, and takes his team of Rollerball players through to the grand finals of the game, spattering everything with blood, fending off murder attempts from all angles, and eventually bringing down the corrupt system almost single-handedly.

Rollerball is rather too pedestrian to become the cult classic that it set out to be. Its notion of one man succeeding against the might of the state is both naive and unbelievable. Some of the action sequences that take place in the Rollerball arena are well choreographed, but in the end the movie is simply too unrealistic and pompous to satisfy.

RUNNING MAN, THE (1987, 101 minutes)
Director: Paul Michael Glaser
Producers: Tim Zinnemann, George Linder
Screenplay: Steven E. de Souza
Starring: Arnold Schwarzenegger, Maria Conchita Alonso, Yaphet Kotto, Jim Brown, Jesse Ventura, Richard Dawson

Based on the novel *The Running Man* (1982) by Richard Bachman (Stephen King), the movie tackles a similar subject to the earlier ROLLERBALL (1975), but in a far superior manner and with a much better script.

Arnold Schwarzenegger plays a cop who is framed for committing mass murder when he fails to carry out the orders of his superiors, which would amount to, well, mass murder. He is offered a choice – he can either be executed, or entered into a game show which entails battling his way through the remains of an underground city whilst being filmed and broadcast around the country. If he succeeds, he will be able to reclaim his freedom. He chooses the latter option.

What follows is a sequence of highly effective, yet bloody action sequences in which Schwarzenegger gets the better of a variety of gaudily costumed gladiators. During his way around the old city he picks up another contestant (Alonso), who also becomes a love interest.

However, his continued success wins the affections of the show's vast audience, and the producers fake his death and attempt to murder him outright. It transpires that no one has ever succeeded in defeating the system, and that the corrupt governors have set the show up as a way of maintaining public support and instilling conformity into the masses. Those who are entered into the game are first exploited, and then summarily executed anyway.

However, Schwarzenegger and Alonso escape from the various assassins despatched to execute them, discover an underground network which is plotting to overthrow the game show and demonstrate to the public the corrupt nature of their political system. The rebels interrupt the live broadcast to inform the viewers of Schwarzenegger's innocence, and then he leads them in the overthrow of the government.

The Running Man succeeds on a number of different levels. Firstly it is an entertainment, which, ironically, highlights the exploitation which it seeks to satirise. However, it is also a biting comment on the mass media and the voyeurism which plays an inherent part in our lives (even more relevant today than it was at the time, given the recent spate of fly-on-the-wall television shows). *The Running Man* shows how the media can manipulate the fate of not only the innocent victims of conspiracy, but of every person who relies on it for information.

Schwarzenegger is typically stiff in his role as the framed action hero, whilst Alonso is rather over the top. If anything, the movie fails to capture quite the same grimy, insipid tone of the novel, but this is a trifle compared to the message that it gets across.

The Running Man remains a greatly enjoyable movie, and it shows how the truth will eventually out, and that people working together can ensure that both the media and the government will remain representative of their people.

SCANNERS (1980, 102 minutes)

Director: David Cronenberg
Producer: Claude Heroux
Screenplay: David Cronenberg
Starring: Stephen Lack, Jennifer O'Neill, Patrick McGoohan, Lawrence Dane, Michael Ironside, Robert Silverman

Since its release in 1980, *Scanners* has become known as the definitive movie about telepaths.

It is also a cult favourite, due in no small part to the infamous exploding-head scene. Like many Cronenberg projects, the film is an example of SF HORROR, and charts the progress of one bewildered telepath (Lack) who eventually comes to understand both his history and his strange ability.

In the 1940s a drug, Ephemerol, was given to pregnant women. This caused an unexpected side-effect in both the women and their offspring – the spontaneous development of telepathic powers. For years these confused people, or 'scanners', have been left to get on with their lives without interference, but now two opposing corporations are attempting to round them up. Dr Ruth (McGoohan), the head of one such organization, kidnaps Lack and gives him medication that allows him to bring his telepathic abilities under control. He informs him that a ruthless scanner (Ironside) has been organizing a force of evil telepaths and is hellbent on world domination. McGoohan and his cronies are the last line of defence against this madman. Lack joins McGoohan, and they set off to stop Ironside.

The plot is no more than an excuse for lots of startling telepathic battles and psionic drama. However, the movie is stylish and artfully shot, and confirmed Cronenberg as one of the most able directors of his generation. The set pieces alone make the movie worth watching. Lack is a little too melodramatic in his role as the lonely, confused telepath, but Ironside more than makes up for it as the criminally insane Revok.

Scanners is a good example of SF Horror and, though Cronenberg was to go on to do better with THE FLY (1986) and EXISTENZ (1999), it remains worthy of note.

The movie inspired various cheap sequels which went straight to video.

SILENT RUNNING (1971, 90 minutes)
Director: Douglas Trumball
Producer: Michael Gruskoff
Screenplay: Deric Washburn, Michael Cimino, Stephen Bocho
Starring: Bruce Dern, Cliff Potts, Ron Rifkin, Jesse Vint

A touching and poignant movie of ECOLOGICAL disaster that, although unrealistic in many ways, remains of interest.

Earth is in the throes of a POST-APOCALYPTIC nightmare, in which nuclear explosions have killed all plant life except for a number of small hydroponic gardens which are left circling in orbit.

When the authoritarian government of Earth orders the gardens destroyed, one of the gardeners, Freeman Lowell (Dern), strikes out and murders his three colleagues, before jettisoning his garden into space as a means of ensuring the potential for life still exists somewhere in the universe. It is suggested that, with Lowell's eventual passing, his ROBOT assistants will continue to tend his garden.

Silent Running is very much of its time. It deals with many of the concerns of 1970s SF (impending disaster and the fear that advancing technology will be misused), and although the special effects are wonderfully timeless, much of the film, including the soundtrack, shows its age. Nevertheless, there are complexities underneath the surface of the movie that deserve further consideration.

The overall message of the film remains genuinely ambiguous. On first appearance it is fair to assume that *Silent Running* carries an anti-nuclear, conservationist message. However, the apparently remorseless murders seem at odds with this analysis. Lowell himself is highly neurotic, if not psychotic, and the murders seem to be an inevitable step forward in his descent into madness. At times it seems that Lowell's only intention is to preserve the garden for himself, as a refuge from insanity.

Dern gives an excellent performance as Freeman Lowell, and Trumball demonstrates considerable ability in his first film as director. *Silent Running* remains an interesting, yet disturbing film.

SIX MILLION DOLLAR MAN, THE
Starring: Lee Majors (Austin), Richard Anderson (Goldman)

The Six Million Dollar Man began life as a one-off television movie in the USA, but it proved very popular and was turned into a weekly series.

It charts the adventures of Steve Austin, an astronaut who is almost killed in a horrific plane crash, but is rescued by the government and secretly rebuilt as a powerful CYBORG. Austin, now equipped with an armoury of BIONIC prosthetics, is then conscripted into a secret government agency run by Oscar Goldman, who dishes out missions that only Austin and his cybernetic body could complete.

From here the story develops into a rather typical super-spy series, although there are some interesting episodes which predict the advent of series such as THE X-FILES, in that they make use of high-technology conspiracy theories, and, at one point, ALIEN visitation.

The Six Million Dollar Man ran for five successful seasons between 1973 and 1978, and totalling one hundred and two episodes of varying length. There was also a successful spin-off show, *The Bionic Woman*, with which there was considerable cross-over in later episodes.

The initial premise was very loosely based on the novel *Cyborg* (1972) by Martin Caiden.

SLEEPER (1973, 88 minutes)
Director: Woody Allen
Producer: Jack Grossberg
Screenplay: Woody Allen, Marshall Brickman
Starring: Woody Allen, Diane Keaton, John Beck, Mary Gregory

Sleeper is a farce from the pen of one of America's greatest comic writers, Woody Allen.

The movie draws on the images of many genre favourites, and thankfully doesn't restrict itself by relying simply on SF movies for material. It is clear that when Allen and his co-writer Brickman sat down to script the movie, they also had an understanding of SF literature.

The film follows the progress of Miles Monroe (Allen), a health food obsessive who is CRYOGENICALLY frozen when an operation on a peptic ulcer goes wrong. He is awoken two hundred years later to find a decadent society. However, a revolution is underway, and Allen is enlisted to help the movement overthrow the dictator who is currently holding America in his iron grasp. It later turns out that all that is left of this dictator is his nose (a very Freudian comment in keeping with much of Allen's work), from which a group of scientists hope to CLONE a replacement.

Some wonderfully comic scenes follow: Allen's character attempts to disguise himself as a ROBOT and ends up getting inadvertently stoned on twenty-second century drugs, and he peels a GENETICALLY modified banana as big as himself, and then proceeds to slip up on the skin.

Sleeper is a slapstick triumph, an intelligent and effective parody of the SF genre. It makes use of the works of H. G. WELLS and ALDOUS HUXLEY, as well as borrowing from previous movies. While making us laugh, Allen manages to provide some cutting remarks about the America of the time, even going on to predict the advent of GM foods. There is also plenty of room left for Allen's usual preoccupation with sex and psychology, and Allen himself carries his gags off with his usual aplomb. The set pieces are remarkable given the film's relatively small budget, and Allen gets as much out of them as he can.

Of the many films to parody the SF genre over the years, *Sleeper* has to be one of the best. Witty, intelligent and hysterically funny, *Sleeper* is a movie to be applauded.

SLIDERS

Starring: Jerry O'Connell (Mallory), John Rhys-Davies (Arturo), Sabina Lloyd (Wells), Cleavant Derricks (Brown), Charlie O'Connell (Mallory)

Similar in many respects to QUANTUM LEAP, the more speculative and enjoyable cult series *Sliders* details the exploits of a group of people who inadvertently tumble into a WORMHOLE and 'slide' into an ever-increasing series of parallel universes.

Quinn Mallory is the young physics prodigy who manages to open up a wormhole in his San Francisco basement into which he and his four companions are drawn. They find themselves slipping between ALTER-NATE WORLD realities in which the San Francisco they know does not exist and their parallel selves lead very different lives. Unfortunately for them, they are lost in the ether world between universes and cannot consciously make their way home.

The premise is the only thing that is similar to *Quantum Leap*. The individual episodes tend to deal with more obvious SF ideas, and there are some wonderful alternate history episodes in which America does not exist, or Elvis is still alive. Indeed, *Sliders* is one of the more inventive television series to become popular over recent years, blending the idea of *Quantum Leap* with the format of THE OUTER LIMITS, providing a succession of tentatively linked episodes in which the characters must deal with a series of scientifically based problems.

The tone of *Sliders* is also much darker than *Quantum Leap*, and thankfully it lacks the RELIGIOUS angle that ultimately caused the former series to fail.

There is a bitter humour running through *Sliders* that reveals a deeper side to the series – the universe is fundamentally unforgiving and we should be careful when we tamper with it. The alternate worlds that the sliders visit are often in danger of self destructing, and it becomes clear that it has been luck as much as human endeavour that has got us where we are today. Reality is a cold place, and humanity is devoid of friends. This is exemplified in the final episode where the sliders remain stranded, without rhyme or reason. Unlike *Quantum Leap*'s Bakula, they are not on a mission from God, but are simply stranded a long, long way from home.

Sliders ran for eighty-seven episodes of various length between 1995 and 2000.

SOLARIS (1971, 165 minutes)

Director: Andrei Tarkovsky
Producer: Mosfilm
Screenplay: Andrei Tarkovsky, Friedrich Gorenstein
Starring: Natalya Bondarchuk, Donatas Banionis, Yuri Jarvet, Nikolai Grinko

Tarkovsky's adaptation of STANISLAW LEM'S *Solaris* (1961) has to be one of the darkest and most affecting SF movies ever to be made.

A psychologist (Banionis) is sent from Earth to the space station orbiting the distant PLANET Solaris, chiefly to investigate the strange goings on amongst the crew. He finds a station falling into disrepair and a broken and disconcerted set of people unable to describe their experiences. Soon he finds himself haunted by a manifestation of his dead wife, who appears in a disturbing physical form. He destroys her, but she returns, and in turn the psychologist comes to understand the circumstances behind the mysterious events at the station, as well as questioning the validity of his own sanity.

Solaris is covered by a vast, sentient ocean, and the manifestations are an attempt by the entity to communicate with the station crew. However, this ALIEN (although it could be a RELIGIOUS analogy for God), remains utterly incomprehensible; there is no level upon which the human beings may come to understand it.

In a scene towards the end of the movie, Solaris replicates a small portion of Earth upon its surface, the family home of one of the characters. This differs from Lem's novel, and suggests two possible interpretations.

Firstly, that if Solaris is not God, then it may in fact represent the human psyche and be, a tangible manifestation of the unconscious, fulfilling our unrequited dreams. Secondly, it shows the character's inability to comprehend the entity that is Solaris. At a moment when he is offered the key to unlocking the nature of the enigmatic alien, he can only realize the human desire for comfort and familiarity.

This is the crux of *Solaris*. Humanity just doesn't have the necessary level of perception and insight to be able to comprehend the scale of the universe. The entity Solaris remains enigmatic and we can do nothing but long for the comfort of Earth.

Solaris remains one of the most thoughtful of SF movies.

SOYLENT GREEN (1973, 97 minutes)
Director: Richard Fleischer
Producers: Walter Seltzer, Russell Thatcher
Screenplay: Stanley R. Greenberg
Starring: Charlton Heston, Edward G. Robinson, Leigh Taylor-Young, Chuck Connors, Joseph Cotten, Brock Peters

Charlton Heston stars in the only partially successful adaptation of HARRY HARRISON's classic novel of OVERPOPULATION, *Make Room! Make Room!* (1966).

The film is set amongst the teeming streets of a DYSTOPIC, NEAR FUTURE America, in which the population relies on a synthetic food produced by the Soylent Corporation to subsist. Older members of society are persuaded to commit euthanasia as a means of population control, and the social structure in general is teetering on the brink of collapse. Charlton Heston is a solitary cop assigned to a murder case, who in the process of his investigations discovers the sinister truth about 'Soylent Green', the synthetic food which keeps the nation from starving – it is formed from the remains of human corpses.

This rather indigestible revelation works well enough in the context of the movie, but is utterly at odds with the themes of the original novel. In the book, Harrison discusses the issues of contraception and its beneficial effect on population, and his society was vegetarian.

Nevertheless, *Soylent Green* achieves what it sets out to do. It provides commentary on the population crisis (a theme that was recurrent throughout the 1970s), and adds a little shock value to make people sit up and pay attention. As a movie it fails to offer a consistent narrative or inspiring art direction, although there are a number of scenes that do make it worthwhile.

Soylent Green won a NEBULA AWARD for the Best Dramatic Presentation.

STAR TREK
Originally a television series developed by Gene Roddenberry in the 1960s, *Star Trek* has become nothing short of a phenomenon.

The series originally ran for three seasons between 1966 and 1969, and upon initial release was deemed something of a failure. However, during a series of reruns on US terrestrial television, it developed a dedicated following of fans.

Star Trek was something new to American television. It was a bright and optimistic vision of the twenty-third century in which Captain James T. Kirk went off exploring the universe with his multiethnic crew, had daring adventures in outer space, but nevertheless always managed to extract himself from danger just in time.

However, perhaps the most important aspect of *Star Trek* was the manner in which Roddenberry and his writers fleshed out the background details of the series. These characters were not simply wandering around in space without aim (although it sometimes appears that way in some of the more off-the-mark episodes), but they were part of a huge interstellar Federation, a human organization that incorporated friendly ALIEN life forms and was structured in the form of a MILITARY hierarchy. Thus Kirk was the captain of his vessel, *The Enterprise*, and he had a whole naval command structure operating beneath him. What is even more impressive is the fact that many of Kirk's junior officers were either women or representatives from minority groups, offering a vision of the future in which humanity had become more tolerant and united.

William Shatner was rather melodramatic as Kirk, but also full of charm and charisma, while Leonard Nimoy was excellent as the logical Vulcan, Spock, and DeForest Kelley suitably exasperated as 'Bones', the doctor. Indeed, the majority of the cast performed surprisingly well, and although the constant moralizing was a little tiresome, and the plot structure of many of the episodes was repetitive – *The Enterprise* encounters an alien race, defeats it or bargains with it and then moves on – it remained compulsive viewing.

It took a decade in which nothing new appeared before *Star Trek* was finally resurrected for the big screen. *Star Trek: The Motion Picture* appeared in 1979, and reinvented the old series, bringing a new dimension of philosophy and maturity to the format. The movie pits the reunited crew of *The Enterprise* against an immensely powerful alien who is threatening to destroy Earth. It transpires that the entity had at one time devoured a human space probe and, learning of the existence of human life, attempted to communicate with us in a search for universal companionship. In our ignorance we never replied, and now the entity is planning to destroy Earth and all of humanity along with it. Kirk and his fellow crew must attempt to avert the crisis and turn the alien's intentions away from the destruction of the planet.

However, rather than adopting the bland approach of many of the episodes, the story interestingly moves towards a wonderful climax which sees the being united with a human in a mystical scene of TRANSCENDENCE in which it manages to achieve the desired companionship in a pseudo-sexual way.

Unfortunately, the movie, although it was a box office success, failed to satisfy many *Star Trek* fans, and later movies adopted the approach of glorifying small-screen episodes by reworking their themes into movie-length plots. *Star Trek: The Motion Picture* was followed by *Star Trek II: The Wrath of Khan* (1982), *Star Trek III: The Search for Spock* (1984), *Star Trek IV: The Voyage Home* (1986), *Star Trek V: The Final Frontier* (1989) and *Star Trek VI: The Undiscovered Country* (1991), all of which failed to do anything new, yet proved popular amongst fans.

However, this was not to be the end. The success of the Star Trek movies prompted television chiefs to reinvent the series for the small screen and in 1987 a new spin-off series, *Star Trek: The Next Generation* debuted on American television.

The new show, at first, stuck to the format of the original *Star Trek*, but with an all new cast and a far bigger budget. The series was also set a further century into the future, offering writers the opportunity to develop the background that was created for the original series. The new *Enterprise* was bigger and better – a GENERATION STARSHIP – and the Federation had now allied itself to the Klingons, the alien enemy from the first series of the show. New adventures ensued, but it took the series a couple of seasons to really establish itself. Eventually, the format was slightly changed, and the emphasis was shifted to that of character development and longer story arcs with more appeal.

After this, the new series was a startling success, and many excellent episodes followed, tackling more true science fictional ideas whilst still maintaining the air of philosophical moralising and sentimentality that had made the original so popular.

The series ended in 1994, but continues in the form of big screen movies. Of these, there have been three to date. They are *Star Trek: Generations* (1994), *Star Trek: First Contact* (1996) and *Star Trek: Insurrection* (1998).

Two further spin-off television series continued. *Star Trek: Deep Space Nine* ran from 1993 to 1999 and, like the similar BABYLON 5, was set almost entirely on and around a space station orbiting a distant planet. It was much darker in tone and atmosphere than the previous incarnations of the show, and more mature and sophisticated because of it. The series culminated in a very bloody battle when a war broke out between the Federation and the denizens of another part of the universe over the control of a natural WORMHOLE that existed in neutral space nearby to the station.

Star Trek: Voyager, meanwhile, began in 1995 and is still running. It follows the progress of a small starship which has been stranded somewhere in another galaxy and is attempting to make its way home to Federation space. It returns to a similar format to the original show, with one major exception – it has a woman playing the role of captain.

Star Trek continues to be the most popular television show in existence, and rumour has it that it is constantly playing on some channel somewhere around the world. Perhaps it is the optimistic appeal of the show that provides it with continued appeal, but more than likely it is the inherent SENSE OF WONDER that it brings to the screen, as well as its constant reinvention, that has made it the most successful television franchise ever.

STAR WARS (1977, 121 minutes)

Director: George Lucas
Producer: Gary Kurtz
Screenplay: George Lucas
Starring: Mark Hamill, Harrison Ford, Carrie Fisher, Alec Guinness, Anthony Daniels, Peter Cushing, Kenny Baker

Of all the SF movies ever produced, *Star Wars* has had the biggest impact upon the public consciousness. This pseudo-mythical tale has become a fable of our times, and the massive marketing hype that followed in the wake of the movie saw it become the most recognized SF franchise in the world.

Essentially, the movie is a SCIENCE FANTASY that borrows devices and ideas from numerous other movies and genres, and yet manages, with the aid of startling special effects, to succeed. There is nothing deep about *Star Wars* – it is a fairy tale retold in science fictional terms, the pitting of good against evil, with a moralistic structure that is naive and a little too innocent to ring true. Yet, the sheer sense of excitement and adventure is enough to carry the movie on its own, and when fitted into the framework of the other Star Wars movies, it becomes far more significant as a piece of film.

Luke Skywalker, an orphan adopted by his aunt and uncle, finds himself thrust into an adventure when he attempts to locate a missing ROBOT in the desert. Fate has him meet with Obi Wan Kenobi, the mystical Jedi Knight who, over the course of the movie, trains him to wield the power of the Force (a form of magic), and eventually sees him embroiled in a plot to aid the resistance movement that is preparing to take up arms against the evil, oppressive empire. Luke succeeds in rallying the rebellion, rescuing the damsel in distress, redeeming the mercenary and defeating his evil nemesis Darth Vader. In the process he becomes the new mythic hero, and adopts the role of MESSIAH.

The story has its roots in mythology and, although it is a little simplistic in its telling of the chivalrous knight defeating the terrible overlords, it keeps the viewer enthralled. Indeed, perhaps it is this reminder of ancient childhood stories that enables us to suspend our disbelief and enjoy the movie for what it is.

At the time the movie was released, the special effects were unprecedented. There are walking, talking robots, vast spacecraft making their way between star systems, ALIENS and action sequences still unparalleled in SF cinema.

On one level, *Star Wars* fails to capture the essence of the SF genre, and damages the good reputation the genre had built up as a thoughtful, artistic medium. However, on another, it is a thrilling action adventure that reminds the viewers of their childhood innocence and the days of pulp SF when excitement and SENSE OF WONDER were the key elements in any story. On this level it succeeds. *Star Wars* remains a joy.

The movie has seen three sequels to date – *The Empire Strikes Back* (1980), *The Return of the Jedi* (1983) and *The Phantom Menace* (1999). There has also been an entire industry of spin-off merchandise, including books, magazines and toys.

STARGATE (1994, 121 minutes)
Director: Roland Emmerich
Producers: Joel B. Michaels, Oliver Eberle, Dean Devlin
Screenplay: Roland Emmerich, Dean Devlin
Starring: Kurt Russell, James Spader, Jaye Davidson, Viveca Lindfors, Alexis Cruz, Mili Auital

An interesting blend of SF and Ancient Egyptian mythology, *Stargate* harks back to the action adventure pulps of EDGAR RICE BURROUGHS and other 'lost world' tales.

A strange, ring-shaped artefact has been found and excavated in the Egyptian desert, and a young hotshot archaeologist (Spader) decrypts its prosaic hieroglyphs, only to find that the object is in fact a gateway to another PLANET. The US military is called in, and an expedition is mounted.

After passing through the 'Stargate', Spader and Russell (playing the captain of the marine squad) find themselves on a desert world halfway across the universe. This planet appears to be inhabited by Ancient Egyptians, but it transpires that a malign ALIEN (Davidson) has been presiding over them for thousands of years. The original populace was transported from Earth via the stargate during Earth's ancient history, and the Egyptian civilization was founded on the worship of Davidson's alien race.

Spader and Russell, after both embarking on rather trite personal relationships with two of the natives, spark a revolution and bring down the reign of the powerful alien. Russell returns through the stargate, whilst Spader stays behind with his new love.

The special effects are magnificently done, and the plot is absolutely peppered with gadgets (including a restorative coffin and a pyramidal space vessel). The acting is all rather melodramatic, but fitting for the SCIENCE FANTASY style of the movie. Russell is unexceptional as the psychologically scarred warrior, Spader is too kooky as the unconventional Egyptologist and Davidson is too petite and androgynous to be convincing as a supremely powerful alien overlord. Nevertheless, it all hangs together nicely and the good guys go on to save the day.

In the sense of the old lost world adventures, such as THE LAND THAT TIME FORGOT (1974), *Stargate* is a joy to watch. Suspend your disbelief and revisit the days of classic pulp.

Stargate inspired a television series, *Stargate SG1*, which is still currently running in America.

The same writing and directing team would later provide us with the rather less successful INDEPENDENCE DAY (1996).

STARSHIP TROOPERS (1998, 124 minutes)

Director: Paul Verhoeven
Producers: Jon Davison, Alan Marshall
Screenplay: Ed Neumeier
Starring: Casper Van Dien, Dina Meyer, Denise Richards, Jake Busey, Neil Patrick Harris, Patrick Muldoon, Michael Ironside

Starship Troopers is based upon the novel *Starship Troopers* (1959) by ROBERT HEINLEIN and succeeds on a number of different levels.

The movie was released in 1998 to great controversy for its light-hearted portrayal of violence and military endeavour. Nevertheless, it managed to pull in large audiences and became a huge box office hit. It is a fine example of MILITARY SF which follows the progress of a group of high-school graduates in NEAR FUTURE America who join the services in an attempt to gain citizenship within the planetary federation. This eventually leads to a number of them, and particularly chief protagonist Johnny Rico, taking part in the invasion of a nearby PLANET which is inhabited by hostile insectile ALIENS. Johnny Rico eventually goes on to become the hero of the war effort, and comes face to face with the intelligent alien who appears to be behind the alien's hostile activities.

The movie successfully parodies the right-wing, fascist future that it purports to describe, and in this respect moves away from Heinlein's original novel which many consider to actively promote the causes it describes. However, at its most simple level the movie can be enjoyed as a piece of COMIC, well structured SF that is perhaps a little naive in its polarization of 'good against evil'.

Starship Troopers has a comic, mischievous tone that is missing from the novel, and is the better for it. The special effects sit neatly within the plot, although the 'power armour' that played such an important role in the book is a distinct loss. The insectlike aliens are well portrayed and the acting, if a little hammed up, is satisfactory.

Starship Troopers is a valiant attempt to bring a classic novel to the screen, and succeeds in parodying the rather ambiguous message of the original book without ruining its appeal.

STRANGE DAYS (1995, 139 minutes)

Director: Kathryn Bigelow
Producers: James Cameron, Steven-Charles Jaffe
Screenplay: James Cameron, Jay Cocks
Starring: Ralph Fiennes, Angela Bassett, Juliette Lewis, Tom Sizemore, Michael Wincott, Vincent D'Onofrio

Strange Days is a millennial CYBERPUNK thriller that, although good, ultimately feels like it arrived too late. The plot and tone of the movie hark back to the early cyberpunk novels of the 1980s, like WILLIAM GIBSON'S *Neuromancer* (1984) and BRUCE STERLING'S *Islands in the Net* (1988).

The plot follows the progress of Lenny Nero (Fiennes), an ex-cop who now ekes out a living in a NEAR FUTURE metropolis selling data discs containing people's recorded experiences. These experiences can be relived through a neural interface that fits over the head like a set of headphones. However, when one of Lenny's friends is killed and he gets hold of a decidedly 'hot' data disc, he finds himself drawn into an increasingly sleazy underworld of murder and corruption.

Strange Days does nothing new. The seedy, technological underworld has been seen before in countless novels, and although it is perhaps one of the best renderings of the cyberpunk subgenre on the screen, it arrived on the scene well after the movement had diversified and reinvented itself as something fresher and new. Fiennes does a good job as the unlikely anti-hero, and his profound lust for his ex-girfriend (Lewis) is both sickening and refreshing, in that his desires are unrequited and his passion for her remains unfulfilled. Bassett is steadfast yet rather predictable in her role as a personal security expert, and Lewis is rather too girlish and immature as the love interest. That said, the movie does successfully capture the spirit of cyberpunk.

SUPERMAN (1978, 142 minutes)

Director: Richard Donner
Producer: Pierre Spengler
Screenplay: Mario Puzo, Robert Benton, Leslie Newman
Starring: Christopher Reeve, Marlon Brando, Gene Hackman, Margot Kidder, Jackie Cooper, Ned Beatty, Susannah York, Glenn Ford

Superman resurrected the flagging comic book hero from the 1930s and gave him a big screen makeover.

The story is well known. The parents of a young ALIEN boy from the PLANET Krypton save their child from the destruction that is befalling their home world by sending him to Earth. He lands, meteor-like, in the wheat fields of a farm in Midwest America, where he is found and adopted by two kind hearted locals. He grows up with great powers – he is incredibly strong, he can fly, and his eyes emit laser beams when he is angry. He steals away and builds his headquarters in the Antarctic ice fields, and adopts a duel identity. In one life he is Clark Kent, college graduate and reporter for the *Daily Planet*, in the other he is Superman, saviour of mankind.

What follows is a series of extraordinary adventures in which Superman saves American citizens from all types of danger, such as car crashes, earthquakes and collapsing dams – Superman is the MESSIAH of the comic book world, able to perform miracles and protect humanity from the evils of the greater universe.

This big screen adaptation sees Christopher Reeve don the Superman tights and provide an excellent performance as the Man of Steel. He battles arch criminal Lex Luthor (Hackman), whilst at the same time attempting to win the love of Lois Lane (Kidder), fellow reporter at the *Daily Planet*. The effects are suitably grand – especially the flying sequences – and the movie shows a real nostalgia for the old American values of peace, love and righteousness. At the same time, the script is both jocular and dramatic, and the performances from the other actors are camp and in keeping with tone of the whole production.

Reeve's alienation from normal society is carefully and tastefully portrayed, and his bumbling alter ego Kent represents Superman's own fragility and dubious confidence; indeed, Superman is pictured as being just as 'human' as the rest of us, with his own misgivings about the hope that his presence affords the American people. Indeed, the Christ analogy is very thoughtfully examined, in that Superman adopts the human race with an almost paternal instinct, attempting to teach us a moral framework from which to draw inspiration. Superman puts himself at risk to protect the American people, and in the later sequel, sacrifices his powers for the love of a woman. It is not clear whether Superman was ever intended to adopt the Messianic role, but to the people of Metropolis, the imaginary city which he inhabits, he is indeed a saviour figure.

The SF elements of the movie are really only superficial, an attempt to rationalize the superhero's abilities in terms acceptable to a modern audience. In many ways this succeeds, and the film transcends its pulp origins, becoming a well crafted, intelligent piece of SCIENCE FANTASY.

The success of *Superman* led to various sequels. They are *Superman II* (1980), *Superman III* (1983) and *Superman IV: The Quest for Peace* (1987). They go progressively downhill as the series continues, although Reeve did reprise his role for each new instalment. There was also the spin-off, *Supergirl* (1984), a rather trite imitation with a young female in the lead role.

A recent television series, *The New Adventures of Superman* (known latterly as *Lois and Clark*), returned the superhero to the small screen, but tended to be rather too immature and ill considered.

SURVIVORS, THE

Starring: Carolyn Seymour (Grant), Lucy Fleming (Richards), Ian McCulloch (Preston), Talfryn Thomas (Price)

A British disaster series in the tradition of JOHN WYNDHAM, *The Survivors* describes a POST-APOCALYPTIC world in which ninety-five per cent of the population has been wiped out by a new Oriental virus. Those that found themselves immune, or managed to avoid being infected by the deadly disease, are now attempting to eke out a living amongst the devastated ruins of civilization.

The series follows the progress of four, decidedly middle class, people who are trying to deal with the aftermath of the devastation and discover what has happened to their families. They come across other people on their travels, and realize that the remnants of the race are living in small communities. Gradually, these enclaves begin to develop the skills necessary to survive in a world without power or manufacturing technology. These pockets of people slowly evolve into townships and, as the series ends, the initial group of survivors sets out to make contact with other small communities and so begin the slow process of putting civilization back together again.

The Survivors was devised by Terry Nation, the man who designed the Daleks for DOCTOR WHO, and although initially pessimistic about humanity's ability to deal with a crisis of this scale, the survivors eventually win through. Society begins its reconstruction.

The series is an interesting take on the post-apocalyptic theme and, given its length (three seasons), works much better than many movies in illustrating the gradual process by which humanity could take stock and start to recover. It is evident throughout the series that Nation believes that humanity has come to rely too heavily on technology and science, as his characters attempt to make do with what they have, and fundamental items such as soap, matches and transport become sorely missed.

However, the final message of *The Survivors* is in the title – people will survive, no matter what is thrown at them – and in the end it is optimistic about the future and the progress of the human race.

The Survivors ran for three seasons between 1975 and 1977, for a total of thirty-eight fifty-minute episodes.

Science Fiction on the Screen

TERMINAL MAN, THE (1974, 107 minutes)
Director: Mike Hodges
Producer: Mike Hodges
Screenplay: Mike Hodges
Starring: George Segal, Joan Hackett, Richard A. Dysart, Jill Clayburgh, Donald Moffat, Matt Clarke, Michael Gwynne, James Sikking

Based on the novel *The Terminal Man* (1972) by MICHAEL CRICHTON, this is a competent thriller which discusses the failure of the human condition, and the failure of technology to prevent it.

A serial killer (Segal) is operated on by a group of scientists who IMPLANT a tiny computer into a brain in an attempt to control his violent temperament. The device stimulates the relevant centres of his brain when he feels the urge to kill, providing a calming effect. However, he becomes addicted to the calming effect and goes on a murder spree simply to undergo the physiological change which he so much enjoys. Indeed, he is worse after the treatment than he was before it was implanted; he cannot stop himself from ending the life of his former girl-friend, simply to get a hit.

Eventually, the movie ends with the murderer being shot dead.

The movie is stylish, with superb cinematography: the doctors are filmed in black and white but the rest of the movie is in colour; the music of Bach can be heard accompanying scenes; famous poetry is quoted. It is also true to Crichton's novel, dealing with the relationship between man and machine and the ultimate failings of technology.

The Terminal Man is an incisive and impressive film. Its characters are portrayed with vitality and depth, and the script and direction are perfectly balanced and of merit.

TERMINATOR, THE (1984, 108 minutes)
Director: James Cameron
Producer: Gale Ann Hurd
Screenplay: James Cameron, Gale Ann Hurd
Starring: Arnold Schwarzenegger, Michael Biehn, Linda Hamilton, Paul Winfield, Lance Henriksen

The Terminator is a gruesome, yet utterly enthralling, action-adventure movie with a well realized plot that sees a deadly ROBOT from the NEAR FUTURE travelling back in TIME to change the course of the future.

In 2029 Earth has been devastated by a nuclear war with intelligent machines. Killer robots, or 'terminators', seek out enclaves of survivors and mercilessly execute them. Humanity stands only a handful of people away from extinction, and the machines have inherited the world. However, into this devastated environment steps John Connor, the saviour of mankind, who will lead a resistance movement against the machines that may lead to the continued existence of the human race and a brighter future in general.

To combat this threat, the machines develop a time-travel device and send one of their terminators (Schwarzenegger) back to 1984 in an attempt to murder Connor's mother before she has conceived and thus change the course of human history. Connor's right-hand man (Biehn) also travels back to seek her out and protect her.

What follows is an intelligent, carefully constructed movie in which Sarah Connor and her marine friend from the future battle against the constant attentions of Schwarzenegger's killing machine.

The Terminator has everything that is expected from a modern SF movie. The plot is thoughtful and complex, and draws heavily on genre literature for inspiration (particularly HARLAN ELLISON), and at the same time offers fast, effects–laden action sequences and enough gore to appeal to a wider audience.

The actors all provide excellent performances, and Schwarzenegger is well cast as the heartless villain who relentlessly stalks Connor across America.

However, it is the special effects that really lift *The Terminator* above its contemporaries, with scenes in which Schwarzenegger loses half of his 'face' to reveal the metal superstructure underneath, or tampers with his own inner workings inside a motel room. Better still is the sequence towards the end in which, having been through a massive explosion and roaring flame, Schwarzenegger's exoskeleton rises from the ashes to continue in its task. Although the effects are not on par with the earlier STAR WARS, they are of a quality rarely seen in cinema of the time, and added a sense of extra 'realism' and shock value to the movie.

There is, of course, in *The Terminator* an inherent fear of technology and the EVOLUTION of ARTIFICIAL INTELLIGENCE.

The Terminator is one of the better examples of an SF HORROR movie from the 1980s and, alongside its sequel, TERMINATOR II: JUDGEMENT DAY (1991), it is a tribute to its director's clarity of vision.

TERMINATOR II: JUDGEMENT DAY
(1991, 136 minutes)

Director: James Cameron
Producer: James Cameron
Screenplay: James Cameron, William Wisher
Starring: Arnold Schwarzenegger, Linda Hamilton, Edward Furlong, Robert Patrick, Earl Boen, Joe Morton

Terminator II: Judgement Day sees Cameron continuing, with even more aplomb and style, the tale that he began in THE TERMINATOR (1984).

Having had a child by the now deceased marine from the first film (played by Michael Biehn), Sarah Connor (Hamilton) has been committed to a mental institution where she is preparing herself physically for what she sees as the coming onslaught. She is patronised and studied by the doctors who believe her rants about the nightmare future to be nothing more than a figment of her imagination. Meanwhile, her son, John Connor, who we were told in the first film would go on to become the saviour of mankind, has reached the age of ten and lives an unhappy existence as a foster child.

However, the machines of the future, having been thwarted in their previous attempt to eliminate the Connors, have devised a new class of terminator, the T-1000, an entity formed out of liquid metal. It can change shape to represent any person or object, and is able to reform itself after being blown apart or otherwise destroyed. One such deadly machine (Patrick) is sent back to track down and eliminate the young John Connor. In response, the resistance movement has captured and reprogrammed one of the old model terminators (Schwarzenegger) to protect him. The movie becomes first a race against time to get to John and his mother, and then a battle of wits as the two terminators attempt to outdo each other and gain control of the child.

There are some excellent scenes including the storming of a microcomputer company which, in a cruel twist of fate, has rescued the damaged remains of the terminator from the first movie and will, unknowingly, use it to bring about Armageddon. Other well-realized sequences include a tanker chase down an American highway, a frantic rescue mission to get Hamilton out of the mental institute, and the tense ending that takes place in a metal works.

The special effects at the time surpassed anything that had gone before – indeed, the movie had a budget of over a hundred million dollars – and are still impeccable today.

Many of the issues of the movie are the same as those of the previous film, although there is the rather contrived relationship between the boy and Schwarzenegger. Schwarzenegger's protective attitude towards John Connor is somewhat paternal, and in this respect it is difficult to see him as the remorseless killing machine that he is supposed to be. Patrick is far more convincing as a model of calm, calculated menace. That aside, the performances are satisfactory. Hamilton builds on her character and does a good job of playing the neurotic mother of Connor who has come to doubt her own sanity.

Terminator II is not a straight rerun of the first movie and succeeds because of its own plot and fine special effects. It is for this reason that it has received an entry of its own; the impact that it had on the SF genre was as important as that of the original.

This is not to say that it is better than the first film. Although its effects and action sequences certainly outdo those of *The Terminator*, it lacks some of the originality that made the previous movie so enjoyable. But, as sequels go, *Terminator II* is one of the best.

THING, THE (1982, 109 minutes)

Director: John Carpenter
Producers: Lawrence Turman, David Foster
Screenplay: Bill Lancaster
Starring: Kurt Russell, A. Wilford Brimley, T. K. Carter, David Clennon, Richard Dysart, Richard Masur

Not so much a remake of the classic B-movie, THE THING FROM ANOTHER WORLD (1951), as a return to the original short story, *Who Goes There?* by JOHN W. CAMPBELL.

A group of scientists at an isolated research station in the Antarctic discover a strange body frozen in the tundra. They excavate and examine it, and in doing so inadvertently wake it. It transpires that the creature is in fact an ALIEN entity with the ability to shapeshift and imitate the form of its victims. True to Campbell's original story, it is not long before the alien is toying with the human inhabitants of the station, who appear ineffectual and terrified in the face of the unseen danger. Paranoia makes the tension mount, as everybody begins to doubt each other and nobody knows which one of them the alien will take next.

The Thing is a dark and haunting movie, even though it is often criticized for being a simple showcase of special effects. The awakening of the carnivorous alien catalyses the breakdown of the community at the research post and poses questions about the susceptibility of the human form and the irrational manner in which we view each other in a crisis. The movie is as much a study of human behaviour as it is an action SF HORROR movie and, while it lacks some of the subtleties and the Cold War POLITICS of the 1951 adaptation, it still succeeds. Of particular note is the ambiguity and the lack of a conclusion at the end of the movie, as either of the two men left standing (from an original community of twelve) could be the alien.

The Thing is certainly better than Carpenter's ESCAPE FROM NEW YORK (1981), and features a more powerful and resonant performance from Russell. The special effects are extravagant, although perfectly in keeping with the theme and plot of the movie, and it succeeds in being both a strong horror movie and an excellent psychological thriller.

THING (FROM ANOTHER WORLD), THE
(1951, 87 minutes)

Director: Christian Nyby
Producer: Howard Hawks
Screenplay: Charles Lederer
Starring: Robert Cornthwaite, Kenneth Tobey, Margaret Sheridan, Bill Self, Dewey Martin, James Arness

A superior adaptation of JOHN W. CAMPBELL'S famous short story, *Who Goes There?*, *The Thing* is one of the best SF HORROR or monster movies to come out of the 1950s and the Cold War.

A group of researchers at a remote Antarctic science base discover the remains of a space vessel buried in the ice. They recover and thaw it, only to find it contains an inhabitant; a vegetable-based ALIEN who proceeds to lay siege to the research station in search of human blood. The team fractures as the tension mounts and each individual has different ideas about the course of action to take. The scientist wishes to communicate with the alien and, finding it is vegetative, attempts to grow more; the soldier is the one who actually unfreezes the creature in the first place; the journalist can do nothing but provide ill-thought-out commentary on the situation. Indeed, it is not until the end when they unite and electrocute the 'monster' that some form of organization appears amongst their ranks.

The message is clear, and is exemplified nowhere better than in the immortal words that are spoken in the closing scenes of the movie – 'Watch the skies!' Unite against a common threat or risk being destroyed, a common theme in the days of the Cold War.

The movie simplifies Campbell's story, removing the shapeshifting ability of the alien to create, instead, an entity akin to that seen later in Ridley Scott's ALIEN (1979), a creature that wants only to survive and attempts to do so in the only way it knows. Initially, the characters appear rather stereotypical in their representation of a cross-section of society, but it soon becomes clear that Hawks (who in reality was the main force behind the creation of the film) demanded a fully rounded performance from each and every member of the cast; they are all superb and very human, with as much in the way of failings as heroic capabilities.

Where the later John Carpenter adaptation of the movie has a monster created from special effects, this original film boasts Arness in the role of the Thing. Unfortunately, the effects of the time meant that the alien looked just like what it was – a man in a suit. Nyby and Hawks wisely keep the majority of the action off screen.

The movie is dark and paranoid, reflecting the Cold War mentality of the time. It led the way for other movies to deal with the Cold War, and SF became the most obvious source of allegory and metaphor for invasion and the insidious, sinister work of other races. Aliens became representative of the threat much closer to home.

The Thing is a classic movie that deserves its reputation as one of the most important SF movies of the 1950s. Its impact is comparable to that of INVASION OF THE BODY SNATCHERS (1956) or *Alien*, and it remains essential viewing for any SF cinema fan today.

THINGS TO COME (1936, 113 minutes)

Director: William Cameron Menzies
Producer: Alexander Korda
Screenplay: H. G. WELLS
Starring: Raymond Massey, Ralph Richardson, Edward Chapman, Margaretta Scott, Cedric Hardwicke, Sophie Stewart

Based on H. G. Wells's late SF novel *The Shape of Things to Come* (1933) and with a screenplay written by Wells himself, it is a shame that *Things to Come* ultimately fails to satisfy. Nevertheless it remains one of the most important SF movies ever, in that it set the mould for much to come and, with its beautiful art direction, gave the future an image that has been hard to shake off.

The movie begins in the 1940s, and accurately predicts the development of a world war which sees devastation across much of the globe. The scene then shifts to the 1970s when, in the shattered remains of the cities left over from the decades-long war, a new society is forming. This emerging society is ruled over by a dictator played by Richardson, but when the technologically aided Cabal (Massey) arrives, everything changes. He uses his 'Peace Gas' to bring the unruly citizens under control and sets about building an ideological society of the future. The story then takes a further shift forward in time to the early twenty-first century, where an elitist UTOPIAN state has formed on the ruins of the old world. The new world order is decidedly undemocratic, and a technological upper class makes all the important decisions. However, there is hope for the future, as this peaceful society sends a man and a woman to the stars in search of possible TRANSCENDENCE. If there is one good thing about Wells's script, it is a positive and confident vision of a technological future.

The movie is, in essence, a vehicle for Wells's outdated philosophizing, and with little plot or narrative to keep it going, it ends up as a showcase for Menzies wonderful directing abilities and some marvellous set pieces. Nevertheless, *Things to Come* had a profound impact on the history of genre cinema, in that it illustrated how good SF movies could look. There is also a confidence about the movie's predictions that, has an inspiring effect on the viewer.

Things to Come is a movie worth watching for the window it provides into the future of the cinematic genre. For drama, and humanity, THE INVISIBLE MAN (1933) remains unbeatable.

3RD ROCK FROM THE SUN

Starring: John Lithgow (Dick Solomon), Kristen Johnston (Sally Solomon), French Stewart (Harry Solomon), Joseph Gordon-Levitt (Tommy Solomon), Jane Curtin (Albright)

A spoof COMIC SF series in the vein of MORK AND MINDY.

A small group of ALIENS is sent to Earth on a mission to uncover the mysteries of humanity's foibles. They pose as a typical American family. What follows is a series of slapstick episodes filled with cheap gags and one liners, yet somehow it all manages to work. There is nothing outstanding about *3rd Rock from the Sun*, but it is enjoyable and manages to raise a laugh.

The format is very similar to that of *Mork and Mindy*, with the added dimension that the aliens' frequent social *faux pas* threaten to reveal their secret to the humans they encounter. The gags are witty and often visual as well as verbal, and Lithgow is excellent in the lead role of Dick Solomon – he seems utterly confused by human beings and the manner in which they go about their business.

3rd Rock from the Sun is perhaps the best SF sitcom to come out of the USA since *Mork and Mindy* and, although not always tastefully done, the observations about American society are charming and pointed.

3rd Rock from the Sun has been running since 1996 and has four seasons to its credit to date.

THIS ISLAND EARTH (1955, 86 minutes)
Director: Joseph Newman
Producer: William Alland
Screenplay: Franklin Coen, Edward G. O'Callaghan
Starring: Jeff Morrow, Rex Reason, Faith Domergue, Lance Fuller, Russell Johnson, Eddie Parker, Karl Lindt, Douglas Spencer

This Island Earth is perhaps the best of the 1950s pulp SF movies, in that it embraces wholeheartedly the essence of the SF of the time, attempting to convey a real sense of speculation and demonstrating a level of intelligence far beyond that of the other pulp movies of its time. Unusually for 1950s SF, it is consciously optimistic about the uses of science and does not see humanity as a race threatened by its own creations.

It is based on the 1952 novel of the same name by Raymond F. Jones, and details the kidnapping of a group of scientists by an ALIEN race, the Metalunians. However, far from being the malign monsters that aliens tended to be at the time, the Metalunians are fundamentally friendly, and plea with the human scientists to help them save their PLANET from destruction.

It transpires that another, hostile, alien race, known as the Zahgons, is bombarding Metaluna with meteoric debris that is wearing away the planet's cosmic shield. The scientists are enlisted to aid the repair and maintenance of the shield, but arrive too late and witness the planet destroyed in a spectacular sequence of special effects. The Metalunian who kidnapped the humans in the first place (Morrow) then proceeds to ensure their safe return home.

On the surface the movie is a grand SPACE OPERA about the war between two alien species and the human beings who become unwilling spectators, but underneath this there are more detailed issues to consider.

Firstly, the movie ignores the Cold War mentality that was informing so much SF at the time, including such classics as THE THING (FROM ANOTHER WORLD) (1951) and INVASION OF THE BODY SNATCHERS (1956), instead preferring to show our first contact with an alien race as amicable. The Metalunians are not a race of bug-eyed monsters or cretins from Outer Space, but a mature and friendly people who require our assistance to help them protect their world from outside threat. That brings us on to the second point, that the movie sees science and technology as a possible salvation for the future, that the atomic age could bring about a new era of scientific endeavour that would see the human race become powerful masters of their own destiny. It is through no fault of the scientists that they arrive at Metaluna too late for their work to be effective, although there is irony in the fact that a space-faring race would need to come to us for help with their technology. *This Island Earth* is optimistic about our future.

However, there is also the interesting conflict between the Metalunians and the Zahgons. Perhaps a hint of Cold War paranoia has sneaked in after all, with the friendly Metalunians representing the Americans, and the Zahgons the Russians. If that is the case, then it is worth to noting that the 'good guys' don't win the war and are decimated by the marauding 'baddies'.

The performances are a little stiff, with the exception of Eddie Parker, but the script is good and the fabulous sets more than make up for this. *This Island Earth* is a true science fiction film, an intelligent study of the world that is also entertaining and exciting.

THUNDERBIRDS

The most famous of Gerry Anderson's puppet series, *Thunderbirds* is periodically revived. It had a big impact upon the viewers of SF television, particularly for a show that only ran for two seasons.

Thunderbirds details the adventures of International Rescue, a family-run organization formed by the rich Jeff Tracy and staffed by his five sons, who set about rescuing people in distress. The Tracy brothers are aided by Brains, the scientist who designed and built all of their high-tech gadgets and vessels, including the all–important Thunderbirds 1, 2, 3, 4 and 5 (a mobile command base, a heavy transport, a spacecraft, a submarine and an orbital station respectively), as well as Lady Penelope and her manservant Parker (who drives a wonderful pink Rolls Royce with a full armoury of weapons).

Plotting against them is the Hood, a mysterious master criminal intent on stealing the Tracy's technology, and his assistant Kyrano, a double agent who works for one of the Tracy brothers.

Thunderbirds is a dynamic and entertaining SF serial partly due to the flexibility offered by the form – there is much that can be done by puppets that can't be done by stunt persons – and partly due to the splendid scripts and sheer sense of adventure. It has rightly earned a cult following across the globe.

Thunderbirds was first shown over the years 1965 and 1966. There were thirty-two fifty-minute episodes made in total, although two feature length films were made for America, *Thunderbirds Are Go* (1966) and *Thunderbird 6* (1968). It has recently been remastered for digital television and shown again to the delight of a new audience.

THX 1138 (1970, 95 minutes)
Director: George Lucas
Producer: Lawrence Sturhahn
Screenplay: George Lucas, Walter Murch
Starring: Robert Duvall, Donald Pleasance, Don Pedro Colley, Maggie McOmie, Ian Wolfe

Although it is probably controversial to say it, given the incredible success of STAR WARS (1977), *THX 1138* is probably George Lucas's best foray into the SF genre. It was his first professional movie, and details a bleak DYSTOPIA in the mould of GEORGE ORWELL'S *Nineteen Eight-Four* (1949) or ALDOUS HUXLEY's *Brave New World* (1932).

It is set in a world in which alpha–numerics have replaced names and a repressive state governs without mercy. The majority of the human race lives in bland underground cells where they are conditioned to stay in line with the law.

We follow the progress of THX 1138 (Duvall), a young man who experiments with sex even though he is aware that it is outlawed. After his cell mate (McOmie) becomes pregnant and is executed, he is sent away for detention. After a period of terrible incarceration, he escapes, and eventually makes it to the outside world, where he will learn to live by free will again and be able to revel in his humanity.

The film is stylistically adept. Lucas maintains a distance with his camera at all times. The sets are bland and white; the people are forced to wear identical clothing and shave their heads, and the ROBOTIC police carry out their instructions in a remorseless, mechanical way. Indeed, in contrast to this, when THX 1138 eventually makes it to the outside world, his life becomes flooded with colour.

THX 1138 is a critique of the totalitarian state and a brave and interesting piece of film. It works on both an intellectual and artistic level, and is far removed from the SCIENCE FANTASY that is Star Wars. Indeed, it sometimes seems surprising that the same director and writer was involved in the two very different projects.

The ideas that the movie present are not new to SF, but do represent one of the most important movements in the genre (the dystopic theme). The film was cut by the production company and was not a mainstream success but it did eventually become a cult classic.

TIME BANDITS, THE (1981, 113 minutes)
Director: Terry Gilliam
Producer: Terry Gilliam
Screenplay: Terry Gilliam, Michael Palin
Starring: David Rappaport, Kenny Baker, Ian Holm, John Cleese, Ralph Richardson, David Warner, Sean Connery, Shelley Duvall, Michael Palin

A Pythonesque romp through director Terry Gilliam's very individual interpretation of history and mythology.

The Time Bandits sees a group of six dwarves travelling through ruptures in the space-time continuum with a young English schoolboy, Kevin. The dwarves have stolen a map of time from the Supreme Being, and are using it to visit numerous past eras and steal for themselves a vast horde of treasure. What follows is a fantastical odyssey in which Kevin discovers the fundamental ambivalence of the universe and God, and witnesses the violence inherent in human nature. The dwarves are conscripted by the Supreme Being to locate and undo any pockets of evil that have been left lying around in the depths of time by their adventures, and it transpires that he had intended that events occur in the manner they did all the while. There is a bitter irony in this, especially as Kevin loses both of his parents to their curiosity and is left without a family or a home.

Gilliam's universe is violent and unforgiving. There are intense moments of hilarity in the film, especially at the beginning, but there are also moments of despair.

The movie itself is a satirical romp which gets increasingly bizarre and surreal with every passing moment. However, Gilliam never lets the viewer feel safe or comfortable. Just as events seem to be heading in one direction, they double back on themselves and go somewhere else entirely.

Ultimately, the movie is a fantasy, although Gilliam makes free use of concepts from both genres, at one time portraying the future as a technological nightmare. He also rationalizes the more fantastical aspects of the movie in terms of RELIGION.

TIME TUNNEL, THE
Starring: James Darren (Newman), Robert Colbert (Phillips), Lee Meriwether (MacGregor), John Zaremba (Swain), Whit Bissell (Heywood) .

After a number of other classic television series such as LOST IN SPACE, producer Irwin Allen turned his attentions to *The Time Tunnel*, a decidedly more scientifically based television series that saw its two protagonists journeying back through TIME to various important events in history.

A government-funded project to build a time machine has apparently succeeded as the series opens, having generated a swirling 'time tunnel' (the best effect of the entire series), and one of the scientists, James Darren, agrees to test it out. He steps into the tunnel and is whisked back in time to land on the deck of the *Titanic*, only hours before it hits the iceberg and sinks. The other scientists monitor his progress from a screen in mission control, and send another of their number back to help him out. Together the two scientists attempt to convince the *Titanic*'s captain to change course, and history, but to no avail, and they are zapped back to mission control just in the nick of time.

The series followed this grand opening episode by sending Darren and Colbert back to other various points in history, such as the D-Day landings and the eruption of Krakatoa. They never managed to change history, however, and after a shaky period in which the writers seemed to become stuck for fresh ideas, the series was cancelled after just thirty episodes. Nevertheless, it remains one of Allen's better productions, and it did manage to tackle a few interesting questions about changing history. There was also a number of later, decidedly weaker episodes, which featured supernatural occurrences and appearances by fellow time travellers.

The Time Tunnel ran for two seasons between 1966 and 1967, for a total of thirty fifty-minute episodes.

TOTAL RECALL (1990, 109 minutes)
Director: Paul Verhoeven
Producers: Buzz Feitshans, Ronald Shusett
Screenplay: Ronald Shusett, Dan O'Bannon, Gary Goldman
Starring: Arnold Schwarzenegger, Rachel Ticstin, Sharon Stone, Ronny Cox, Michael Ironside, Marshall Bell, Mel Johnson

Total Recall is based on the short story by PHILIP K. DICK, *We Can Remember It For You Wholesale*.

A building constructor (Schwarzenegger) in the future is haunted by images of Mars every night as he sleeps. He has never visited the colony PLANET and, as his wife (Stone) refuses to holiday there, he visits a memory clinic to have a sequence of false memories of Mars implanted. However, before the memories are implanted he suffers a near breakdown and, rushing home to discuss it with his wife, he finds she turns on him and attempts to stab him to death. He flees and the conspiracy deepens.

It eventually turns out that Schwarzenegger is not a building constructor at all, but a secret agent who has information stored in his head that is vital to the resistance movement on Mars, but has had his memory wiped by the cronies of the Martian dictator and a false life set up to provide him with an illusion of normality. He flees to Mars, where he encounters his former life and love, aids the resistance, turns out to be one of the bad guys all along, redeems himself and, after killing and maiming lots of people, activates an ancient ALIEN air device that floods the planet with breathable atmosphere and ends the dictatorship of his former employer. There are plot twists aplenty, and true to Dick's spirit every one of them remains questionable.

In the end, *Total Recall* is a successful movie. There is a little too much gore, and some of the Martian scenes are risible, but the ambiguity is absolutely delicious. Are all the images of Mars just the product of implanted memories? It is tempting to believe that, in true Dickian style, Schwarzenegger has been living out his Martian fantasies in his head.

Schwarzenegger himself puts in a strong performance and his obligatory silly remarks during action sequences do not really detract from the overall tone of the movie. If Schwarzenegger seems confused, it is only because his character is struggling to maintain some form of identity whilst the reality around him keeps being changed. The supporting actors are efficient, and the effects are generally OK, although some of the Martian mutants are a little too obviously the result of makeup.

The movie was a box office success, but was lambasted by SF fans as a preposterous and rather silly excuse for an action-adventure movie. This is a little unfair as it can also be read as a complex and entertaining examination of the multiple layers of reality. The latter reading is certainly more in keeping with the original Dick.

TRIP TO THE MOON, A (1902, 21 minutes)

Director: Georges Melies
Producer: Georges Melies
Screenplay: Georges Melies
Starring: Georges Melies, Victor Andre, Bleutte Bernon

This masterwork of early SF cinema, by the French inventor of the cinematic special effect Georges Melies, is more properly known under its original title, *Le voyage dans la lune*. It was distributed in America, illegally, as *A Trip to Mars*. The movie was the first real attempt to tell a proper SF story on screen, and upon release was the longest piece of continuous film ever produced. It made cinematic history.

The story itself is now a familiar one, and has its basis in the SCIENTIFIC ROMANCES of JULES VERNE and H. G. WELLS. Indeed, when *Le voyage dans la lune* was actually made, the SF genre as we know it did not yet exist.

A professor and a group of colleagues build an enormous gun that will propel them to the Moon. They cast a vessel within which they can travel, and fire themselves into the sky, eventually coming down to land, memorably, in the left eye of the Man in the Moon. They take shelter from a storm in a crater, which they find leads down into a network of underground caverns and tunnels. They go on to encounter a race of Selenites, based on those that appear in H. G. Wells's *The First Men in the Moon* (1901), are captured but escape. Finding their way back to the vessel, they set off for home, pulled back to Earth by the force of gravity. They splash down in the ocean and are pulled to safety, only to find that a statue has been erected in their honour.

The film was innovative, and can be considered as the first real SF film. The special effects are obviously of their time, but are amusing and enjoyable and, given that this was the first time some of the techniques had ever been used to full effect, are worthy of applause.

If Verne and Wells can be seen as the founding fathers of the SF genre, then Melies should be seen as their cinematic counterpart.

TRUMAN SHOW, THE (1998, 99 minutes)

Director: Peter Weir
Producers: Scott Rudin, Andrew Niccol, Edward S. Feldman, Adam Schroeder
Screenplay: Andrew Niccol
Starring: Jim Carrey, Laura Linney, Noah Emmerich, Natascha McElore, Holland Taylor, Ed Harris

The Truman Show is a movie with a wonderful premise and, although it has no real plot, it is completely successful.

Truman Burbank (Carrey) lives out his life in Seahaven, an idyllic small town in America where everybody is friendly and where the old American ideals of family and righteousness are upheld. However, he has grown to suspect that there is something going on just out of sight, some conspiracy on the periphery of his sphere of experience which he just can't explain. He confides in his best friend, who reassures him that he is mistaken, but he still can't shake the feeling that something is wrong.

He is right and, shockingly, it transpires that Burbank is living his life in the confines of an enormous film set, and that he is the subject of a twenty-four-hours-a-day television programme. The entire world watches his every moment, and he, quietly unaware, goes about his business as usual.

That is, until he takes the first steps on the road to truth, and discovers that his entire life is a fiction, and all of his friends and family are actors. This is a breathtaking revelation and Burbank finds his identity taken away. Nevertheless, he continues in his search for truth, which culminates in a heart-wrenching sequence which sees him sailing a boat out to the edge of the ocean only to find a wall. In a beautiful scene of TRAN-SCENDENCE at the end of the movie, Burbank confronts the man who has orchestrated his life, the man who considers himself Burbank's 'father' (Harris), and finds him wanting.

Every scene in the movie is well thought out and choreographed with expertise. The sets – an entire town and surrounding scenery – are imaginative and detailed, and each of the actors performs well. Carrey's initial paranoia appears real and his later disbelief at the turn of events in his life is almost palpable. He gives the best performance of his career, using his expressive face not for the slapstick appeal for which he is famed, but to put across a broad range of confused emotions.

The SF premise here is in the controlled environment, the psychological experiment. Obviously, the situation is utterly abhorrent, but the movie tackles the idea with real style, and does not shy away from confronting the issues it raises about control and free will. The father figure appears genuinely proud of the way in which Burbank has captured the imagination of millions of viewers but, at the same time, he almost approves of Burbank's move towards normality. The plot and its message are ambiguous.

The Truman Show is a wonderful film, a movie that gets ever more relevant as time goes by. Only time will tell how far we are from Burbank's story becoming a reality,

TWELVE MONKEYS (1995, 124 minutes)
Director: Terry Gilliam
Producer: Charles Roven
Screenplay: David Peoples, Janet Peoples
Starring: Bruce Willis, Madeline Stowe, Brad Pitt

Inspired by the 1963 French film, *La jetée*, which tells a similar tale in a series of lush black and white stills, *Twelve Monkeys* remains very much the product of director Terry Gilliam's profound and bizarre imagination.

The story is that of James Cole, a resident of a DYSTOPIAN future in which an ECOLOGICAL disaster has driven the human race underground. Cole is selected by a committee of scientists to take part in an experimental process which will send him back in TIME to the mid 1990s where he will set about tracking down the leader of the mysterious Army of the Twelve Monkeys, who the scientists believe to be responsible for bringing about the biological disaster. Cole accepts the role and is sent back into the past. Once there, he comes across both psychologist Kathryn Railly (Stowe) and a deranged lunatic (Pitt), and sets about attempting to locate the source of the viral plague, as well as defining his own sanity.

The film is a disturbing study of how psychologically fragile the human mind can become – Cole is haunted by a prophecy of his own death, which eventually becomes a recursive reality. Pitt puts in a strong performance as a mentally unstable animal rights activist, and Stowe is successful in her portrayal of a psychologist who begins to doubt the nature of her reality. Willis is a pleasure to watch.

As in many Gilliam movies, including BRAZIL (1985) and THE TIME BANDITS (1981), *Twelve Monkeys* is at once profound and surreal. The scenery is fantastically realized and imparts the atmosphere of an encroaching dystopia all too well, with criminals living in an abandoned cinema, and animals let loose to roam the streets of New York.

Ultimately, almost inevitably, the biological disaster turns out to have nothing to do with the Army of the Twelve Monkeys, and Cole's search has been almost in vain. His death provides the key to unlocking the future, but on a personal level, for both Cole and Railly, it is a hollow victory.

Twelve Monkeys is a challenging, provocative movie that repays careful attention. Psychologically insightful, it has all the hallmarks of a Gilliam classic.

TWILIGHT ZONE, THE

An anthology series in the same vein as the original THE OUTER LIMITS, but far, far superior in both content and direction, *The Twilight Zone* was the creation of Rod Serling, and was much influenced by the SF that had appeared in ASTOUNDING SCIENCE FICTION magazine during Campbell's GOLDEN AGE era. Indeed, a number of the scripts even see favourite short stories translated to the screen.

The Twilight Zone is the true SF fan's series – each episode was an entirely new story, and toyed with notions and ideas that appeared in the magazines and paperbacks of the time. Some of the stories are decidedly pulp, others are more supernatural, but there are plenty of good examples of real scientific speculation.

The calibre of actors the show attracted was outstanding. There were guest appearances by William Shatner, Robert Redford, Lee Marvin, Burt Reynolds and Dennis Hopper.

The Twilight Zone was revived in the 1980s for a series of new episodes. Many of these were written by excellent contemporary SF writers and, true to the original series, these episodes once again featured guest appearances from well-known American actors. This second series was not as successful as its predecessor, chiefly because it lacked the dulcet tones of Serling as narrator. Nevertheless, it was bursting with good ideas and many of the short films were of a quality rarely seen on modern television.

The original series of *The Twilight Zone* ran between 1959 and 1964, and consisted of one hundred and fifty-six episodes of various length (usually twenty-five minutes). The later series ran between 1985 and 1986 and consisted of twenty-four hour-long episodes and forty-nine twenty-five minute episodes.

2001: A SPACE ODYSSEY (1968, 141 minutes)

Director: Stanley Kubrick
Producer: Stanley Kubrick
Screenplay: Stanley Kubrick, ARTHUR C. CLARKE
Starring: Keir Dullea, Gary Lockwood, William Sylvester, Leonard Rossiter, Daniel Richter, Douglas Rain, Robert Beatty

Based on the short story 'The Sentinel' (1951) by ARTHUR C. CLARKE, and co-scripted by Clarke and Kubrick, *2001: A Space Odyssey* is one of the most influential movies of all time. It is a visual triumph, a masterwork of style and design, and full of ideas. The movie is a piece of speculative SF and it sparked a revolution in the way that SF movies would come to be made in the future.

The story begins in prehistory, with the arrival of a strange black monolith amongst a tribe of primitive primates. The apes develop weapons and begin to slaughter each other. Man has been born.

The scene then passes into the future, to a time when mankind has developed a superior technology. Space stations and rockets dot the sky.

However, the discovery by archaeologists of a strange monolith buried on the Moon begins the story proper. They excavate, and in uncovering the ALIEN artefact inadvertently set off a transmission that beams out into space in the direction of Jupiter. They mount an expedition, and a crew of astronauts head out to the PLANET on board the space vessel

Discovery, on a mission to locate and investigate the destination of the mysterious alien message.

However, en route everything seems to go wrong. The ARTIFICIAL INTELLIGENCE, Hal 9000, is driven insane by conflicting imperatives and decides that the best course of action would be to terminate the human crew. This results in only one astronaut surviving till the closing stages of the mission, as the *Discovery* approaches orbit around Jupiter. Once there, he discovers yet another monolith but, in a beautiful moment in cinema, passes through it. The astronaut witnesses his own death, but then is reborn as some greater, spiritual being, and becomes as much an enigma to the viewer as the magnificent monoliths themselves.

2001: A Space Odyssey is ultimately a pessimistic movie. It sees humanity as 'belonging' to a superior alien race, as a species of evolved primate helped along by elusive alien beings whose intentions remain unknown. However, the movie is visually magnificent. Kubrick portrays life in space as a mundane and sterile activity, a boring regime of routine that leaves no time for human expression or identity. Indeed, the astronauts become the machines, and Hal 9000 becomes the complex human, with the most developed and interesting personality of all the crew. The ship itself is a marvel of special effects, and the long, panning shots of its exterior have since become a cliché in the genre, replicated many times in classic movies such as STAR WARS.

The actors all perform well in their roles and although they seem wooden at times, this is intentional. Kubrick is informing us of the blandness of space travel and the monotony of his version of the future. Douglas Rain is terrifying as the voice of Hal 9000.

2001: A Space Odyssey remains one of the most important movies of the 1960s, and changed the face of SF cinema for ever. From 1968 onwards, spacecraft looked realistic and functional, and directors strived to portray life in space as it was likely to be – full of monotonous routine. Special effects became an ever-more important feature of the SF movie, as attempts were made to recapture the sheer SENSE OF WONDER that *2001* had created. It is a movie that should be watched, and it marks a turning point in the history of genre film.

It was followed in 1984 by a weaker sequel, *2010: Odyssey Two*, which sees a return mission to Jupiter and the eventual ignition of the planet into a second star for the Solar System.

V

Starring: Jane Badler (Diana), Marc Singer (Donovan), Faye Grant (Julie), Michael Durrell (Maxwell), Peter Nelson (Brian), Blair Tefkin (Robin), David Packer (Daniel), Michael Wright (Elias), Robert Englund (Willy), Michael Ironside (Tyler)

V was one of the most effective and extravagant SF mini-series ever to be produced. It was essentially an allegorical tale that railed against oppression and totalitarian regimes, and parodied the Nazi movement from World War Two to great effect.

Pleasant, humanoid ALIENS arrive upon Earth in their flying saucers and are welcomed by humanity. They bring us gifts of high technology, and solve many of the world's crises. Then, as suddenly as they arrived, the aliens begin their hostile takeover of the planet. Human scientists are marched off to concentration camps, and the human youth are enlisted in 'training programmes' that see them becoming subservient to the regime. The aliens are decked out in Nazi regalia, with costumes and uniforms to match. However, it is not long before the visitors reveal their true nature – sickly reptilians with a penchant for live flesh.

Meanwhile, a resistance movement has started up, headed by a news reporter, a mercenary and a couple of renegade scientists, as well as a smattering a dissident lizards sympathetic to the human cause. Eventually, after many exciting and well-choreographed action sequences, the resistance prevails and the lizards are finally and triumphantly defeated.

V was a triumph of POLITICAL SF, and successfully satirized the German Fascist movement of the 1930s and 1940s. It did not shy away from tackling the issues it raised. Although the aliens eventually turned out to be monsters, this did not detract from the message of the series. Indeed, the use of 'masks' to hide their true nature from the American populace was an important metaphor in itself.

V was followed by a full television serial that, although many of the actors reprised their roles, did nothing to add to the original story, and even abandoned the political allegory in favour of straight action adventure.

VILLAGE OF THE DAMNED (1960, 78 minutes)
Director: Wolf Rilla
Producer: Ronald Kinnoch
Screenplay: Stirling Silliphant, Wolf Rilla, Geoffrey Barclay

Starring: George Sanders, Barbara Shelley, Michael Gwynn, Martin Stephens, Laurence Naismith, Peter Vaughan

Village of the Damned is based on JOHN WYNDHAM'S classic novel of the 1950s, *The Midwich Cuckoos* (1957), and is often unfairly underrated as a rather cold and heartless movie.

The residents of an English village fall under a mysterious sleeping spell which lasts for exactly twenty-four hours; they wake to slowly discover that the entire female population of the village is pregnant.

What follows is a spooky, insidious invasion of the village, as the women all give birth, only to find that their offspring are not 'normal' – they have an eerie telepathic ability and a 'group mind' (much like that also seen in THEODORE STURGEON'S contemporary *More Than Human* (1953)). The children develop at an unnatural pace, and it soon becomes clear to one of the villagers (Sanders) that these 'cuckoos' are in fact ALIENS and they have begun the slow process of taking over Earth. His suspicions are confirmed and he comes to realize that the aliens are indeed malevolent.

He decides that they must be destroyed and, arming himself with a bomb, heads to the school to confront them. There is a marvellous scene where the group mind literally assaults Sander's mind and tears down his psychological defences bit by bit. Nevertheless, he manages to activate the bomb and the alien children are all destroyed.

The movie, like the novel before it, tackles themes of 'cosy catastrophe'. Although a disaster befalls the village of Midwich, it is contained and inevitably dealt with, restoring normality and middle-class virtues. However, in keeping with the Cold War period of the movie, the invasion, although ultimately of alien origin, comes from within our very selves. It is the villagers' loved ones who give birth to the monsters, and the paranoia that this revelation inspires in the viewers is perfectly intentional. The most deadly threats come from within.

Village of the Damned is extraordinarily faithful to Wyndham's original novel, and features one of the best performances by a child actor in the whole genre. Stephens, who plays Sanders' child, is decidedly unnerving as the spokesperson for the group mind. His cool and calculating expression smacks of an intelligence disconcerting in a boy of his age. Sanders himself is excellent as the suspicious villager, and the supporting cast, although at times a little stiff, suffice.

Village of the Damned deserves a better reputation than it has. It is scary and engaging, and although the movie itself is very British, the themes it tackles are universal.

A remake/sequel appeared in 1963 under the title *Children of the Damned*. It moves the action to an urban setting and adopts more of an international approach to the handling of the alien children.

WAR OF THE WORLDS (1953, 82 minutes)
Director: Byron Haskin
Producer: George Pal
Screenplay: Barre Lyndon
Starring: Gene Barry, Anne Robinson, Less Tremayne

Based on the pioneering novel, *The War of the Worlds* (1898) by H. G. WELLS, but with the action transplanted from the Victorian Home Counties to 1950s America, *The War of the Worlds* is an excellent piece of SF cinema.

A meteor crash-lands in California and, in much the same way as in the novel, an ALIEN vessel emerges. Soon further meteors are landing all over the world, and the Martian invasion begins in earnest.

The tripod machines of Wells's book have been put aside for a more up-to-date flying saucer, which is highly stylized, but classic heat ray weapon of the original is retained. Soon fleets of these flying saucers are laying waste to the cities, and the chief protagonist attempts to find a way to protect himself and his loved one from the Martians. True to Wells's novel, the aliens are eventually defeated by a strain of the common cold.

The War of the Worlds is one of the classic SF films of the 1950s, and successfully brought Wells's vision to the screen. The addition of a lacklustre love affair does nothing to help the plot move along, but it hums with a resonance drawn from the pages of the novel. It is not humanity which brings about the end of the invaders, as even their atom bombs fail to do that, but a simple biological incompatibility.

At the time of filming the special effects were amazing moments of camera trickery. They remain of a high quality today, even though, on more than one occasion, the strings that support the Martian vessels can be seen in the background.

There was also a diabolical television series which retained the same title and premiered in 1988, running for forty-three episodes. A pseudo-sequel to the 1953 movie, the action takes place in a contemporary America and details the adventures of an underground resistance movement which is battling to fight off the resurrected remains of the

Martian invaders. The series was occasionally thoughtful and very downbeat, but failed to achieve the impact of either the film or the original novel.

WATERWORLD (1995, 135 minutes)
Director: Kevin Reynolds
Producers: Charles Gordon, John Davis, Kevin Costner
Screenplay: Peter Rader, David Twohy
Starring: Kevin Costner, Dennis Hopper, Jeanne Tripplehorn, Tina Majorina, Michael Jeter, Zakes Mokae, Chaim Jeraffi, Ric Aviles

Waterworld is an ECOLOGICAL disaster movie that ultimately wastes its time staging too many spectacular special effects and fails to achieve a narrative or story of any real substance.

With a similar premise to that of MAD MAX (1979), the movie charts the progress of a lone traveller in the aftermath of an apocalypse that saw the polar ice caps melt and flood the entire planet.

Costner plays Mariner, a man who travels across the endless ocean searching for the mythical Dryland. He is at odds with a band of pirates led by Deacon (Hopper), who continue to pollute the atmosphere and are wasting the last of Earth's natural resources. Costner, however, lives by entirely natural means, being at peace with the world around him.

Plenty of posing and some excellent action sequences follow, and Costner promises to help a woman and her adopted daughter to find Dryland. This he does, after defeating the bad guys with even more flashy special effects and attempting to teach everyone about the error of their ways.

The movie does make some attempt to put across an environmental message, but founders on its lack of substance and becomes preachy. Costner is surprisingly good in the role of the action hero, although he is let down by too many scenes in which he is portrayed as the righteous good guy.

Waterworld was one of the most expensive movies ever made and it does little for the theory that money makes good movies. The effects are certainly spectacular, but the entire film seems to consist of Costner jumping about on rafts and encountering pirates.

WESTWORLD (1973, 89 minutes)
Director: MICHAEL CRICHTON
Producer: Paul N. Lazarus III
Screenplay: Michael Crichton
Starring: Yul Brynner, Richard Benjamin, James Brolin, Norman Bartold, Alan Oppenheimer

Written and directed by MICHAEL CRICHTON, *Westworld* is a classic of SF cinema. This is not down to Crichton's rather stilted directing, or indeed the virtues of his script, but has more to do with the inventive premise of the movie and the performance of its key protagonist, Yul Brynner.

Two holidaymakers visit a theme park which claims to fulfil a person's wildest fantasies. Once there, they find a town decked out like a scene from a Wild West movie, inhabited by ROBOTS, and free for them to enjoy. They are told that they can do whatever they like – shoot the mechanical residents of the town, sleep with them, or otherwise interact with them in anyway they please. So begins a period of debauchery, in which the two humans act out their dreams of whoring and killing in the American West.

However, it is not long before things go wrong, and one of the robot gunmen (Brynner) malfunctions and begins killing any humans it finds. One of the two human protagonists is shot dead, and the movie becomes a race against time for the other to escape from Brynner's psychopathic machine, which is stalking him through the tunnels underneath the theme park. After a tense and exciting finale, the robot is cornered and incinerated, but it is a hollow victory as people lie dead in the streets.

Brynner is superb in the role of the heartless killer robot, who will carry on searching out and executing the human holidaymakers until it ceases to exist.

Indeed, *Westworld* prefigures THE TERMINATOR (1984) in its portrayal of a ruthless killing machine with no emotion or conscience. Crichton makes repeated use of the 'Man Vs Machine' scenario throughout much of his work, with the topic resurfacing in a number of his classic novels such as *Jurassic Park* (1990) and *The Andromeda Strain* (1969). It is this inherent technophobia that is the crux of *Westworld*, the belief that mankind will overstep the boundaries of science and create a monster that will eventually see us all defeated. Crichton is at heart a pessimist. He sees humanity as failing our creations, as we are too decadent and ill equipped to handle the power that science puts in our hands.

The machines themselves are totally devoid of morality or intent, it is the uses to which they are put that Crichton questions.

Westworld was innovative and original when it was first released and was very influential. As a movie it is not entirely satisfactory, but the chase sequence towards the end is unparalleled in the genre for tension and excitement.

An inferior sequel, *Futureworld*, followed in 1976.

WHEN WORLDS COLLIDE (1951, 83 minutes)
Director: Rudolph Mate
Producer: George Pal
Screenplay: Sydney Boehm
Starring: Richard Derr, Barbara Rush, Peter Hanson, John Hoyt, Larry Keating

An enjoyable 1950s disaster movie that has its basis in the pulps of the 1930s and a premise that today appears rather scientifically naive.

The PLANET Zyra is heading for the Solar System and looks set to cross paths with Earth. Scientists predict the ensuing damage will be catastrophic, but we remain helpless in the face of such an immense adversary. The human race sits and awaits its fate at the hands of the universe.

However, a rich industrialist (Derr) manufactures a rocket that will save forty people by carrying them over to Zyra as it passes Earth. He holds a lottery to select the people he will take with him, and they plan their eventual escape.

As expected, Zyra enters the Solar System and begins to disrupt the natural order of Earth. Huge tidal waves wreak devastation across the landscape and earthquakes rock the foundations of society. In a now classic scene, Times Square is destroyed when the Atlantic Ocean shifts in accordance with the gravitational forces being inflicted upon the planet from above.

Earth is finally wrenched out of its orbit around the Sun by the colossal forces exerted upon it by Zyra, and is sent careening into a nearby star. Humanity perishes by a simple twist of fate.

Meanwhile, however, the rocket abandons Earth just in time to make a landing on Zyra and avoid the fate of its mother world. Zyra turns out to be a lush and verdant paradise, much like Earth in a past era of human history.

However, the closing shots leave us with an ambiguous feeling. Earth has been catastrophically destroyed, and the surviving humans who have made it to Zyra happen across the view of a futuristic city rising up above the distant horizon. There are no explanations, and for the first time in a movie of this sort the viewer is left wondering what is going to happen to the human explorers next.

When Worlds Collide is a tense and exciting piece of pulp SF, with a premise that now seems rather outdated. It seems all too obvious today that a planet such as Zyra would need a stable orbit around a star if was going to support life of the kind found there by the visiting humans. It also seems rather unlikely that any planet of that size would not already have been captured by the gravitational pull of a star or BLACK HOLE.

Nevertheless, the special effects are memorable for their period, and the actors keep the story moving throughout. There is an inherent SENSE OF WONDER to *When Worlds Collide*. After THIS ISLAND EARTH (1955), it remains one of the best pulp movies of its era.

X-FILES, THE
Starring: David Duchovny (Mulder), Gillian Anderson (Scully), Mitch Pileggi (Skinner), William B. Davis (Cigarette Smoking Man)

The X-Files is a phenomenon, or, at least, a series about phenomena. The inception of *The X-Files* in 1993 caused a big stir, and generated a wave of publicity that was positively unprecedented in genre television. For a while, it seemed that *everyone* was watching the show. It didn't take long before this initial wave of hysteria died away, but in its place formed a hard core of dedicated *X-Files* fans that have seen the series progress through seven seasons, several new characters and a fully fledged feature film.

The series itself follows the investigations of FBI agent Fox Mulder and his partner Dana Scully. Mulder is in charge of the X-Files, the strange and unexplained phenomena that are reported to the police every day, whilst Scully is the sceptical forensic pathologist assigned to assist him.

Over the course of the seven seasons, they encounter all manner of strange goings-on, including ALIEN contact, GENETICALLY engineered mutants, psychotic telepaths and shapeshifting serial killers. In many ways the show takes a more supernatural approach than a scientific one, but there is a definite and irresistible speculative edge that asks the right questions and provides just enough information to keep the viewer engrossed. This is compounded by Scully's hard-edged rationality and her attempts to explain all of the strange occurrences she encounters in terms of her scientific training.

Perhaps the most important aspect of *The X-Files*, however, the fundamental difference that gives the series an edge over its contemporaries, is the story arc that deals with Mulder's search for his missing sister (who he believes has been abducted by aliens), and the inevitable government conspiracy which he uncovers during the course of his investigations. This conspiracy involves a number of high-ranking officials, a handful of whom are willing to leak titbits of information to Mulder in exchange for his continued assistance in their plotting. It never becomes entirely clear what the conspiracy is hiding, but Mulder, and the viewer, is led to believe that the government has been in contact with an alien species for a number of years, and is quietly helping them to invade America.

The X-Files has a continued appeal. Not only are the stories well scripted and of a consistent quality, but Duchovny and Anderson have an undeniable on-screen chemistry that provides an almost tangible atmosphere of tension and excitement. Many of the stories are thought provoking and different, and some are genuinely scary. Others are self-parodies that have more in common with the pulp monster movies of the 1950s than the exploration of the unexplained, but this is often a welcome reprise.

With the advent of the seventh season, however, the impetus behind *The X-Files* appeared to be flagging. Indeed, the two investigators were beginning to run out of stories and the show was constantly re-treading much of the same ground. Duchovny quit, and has now been replaced by Robert Patrick (who played the T-1000 in TERMINATOR II: JUDGEMENT DAY), who will appear in the eighth season as a new, sceptical FBI agent assigned to locating the supposedly 'abducted' Mulder. Only time will tell if this fresh blood will reinvigorate the series and provide a new batch of exciting stories for its fans.

The X-Files, for a while, was one of the most important genre series to appear on television. That it is still running is tribute to its ingenuity and the subversive storytelling ability of its writers. After STAR TREK, it is the American series that has had the biggest impact on popular culture, and it will be a long time before its legion of fans stop believing that 'the truth is out there'.

Terms, Themes and Devices in Science Fiction

ALIEN

An alien is a non-human entity from somewhere other than Earth. While no alien life forms have yet been detected by human scientists anywhere in the universe, there is still speculation that out in the far reaches of SPACE other sentient beings may have evolved on some distant PLANET(S).

Before the twentieth century it was believed that life might exist on the other planets of the Solar System. Early astronomers believed they could see networks of canals upon the surface of Mars, and some people thought that this was evidence enough of the existence of intelligent life. In *The War of the Worlds* (1898), H. G. WELLS pondered this phenomenon and asked what would happen if the aliens that existed on the Red Planet were hostile and decided to colonize the Earth. It is a wonderful novel, full of suspense and ingenuity, and blazed the trail for many more alien-invasion stories to come. Indeed, the alien-invasion story became one of the most popular and overused devices in the genre.

Other classic invasion stories include JACK FINNEY's *The Body Snatchers* (1955), ROBERT HEINLEIN's *The Puppet Masters* (1951) and JOHN WYNDHAM'S *The Midwich Cuckoos* (1957).

However, as SF became more sophisticated, authors began to question the wisdom of attempting to represent superior alien intelligences in their work. After all, considered logically such beings could well be completely beyond our comprehension. STANISLAW LEM wrote the classic novel *Solaris* (1961) in which an interstellar expedition encounters on a distant planet what appears to be a sentient ocean. It attempts to communicate with the human scientists, but in doing so drives them utterly mad while still remaining impenetrable and enigmatic.

Other authors felt that it would be more appropriate to include alien artefacts in their work, objects that would be evidence of the existence of alien species but that would not involve the authors in detailed descriptions of alien anatomy and appearance. This was the case in ARTHUR C. CLARKE's classic *2001: A Space Odyssey* (1968), as well as in his later

Rendezvous with Rama (1973) which explores the mystery of a huge mysterious object entering the Solar System with no visible beings at the controls. FREDERIK POHL also used this concept to great effect in *Gateway* (1977), which sees a group of humans discovering an asteroid that contains dozens of still-functional alien spacecraft.

The manner in which humanity may encounter alien races has also been a matter of great speculation. If these beings are not hostile invaders or aloof superbeings who have abandoned the physical universe, then by what means will mankind make first contact with them?

Both physicist Carl Sagan in his novel *Contact* (1985) and SAMUEL R. DELANY in *Babel-17* (1966) envisage aliens eventually contacting us through radio transmissions or interstellar signals. Other writers maintain that our first true contact with alien species will be when our attempts to colonize the Galaxy brings us to their home worlds. GENE WOLFE explores in *The Fifth Head of Cerberus* (1972) the sinister possibility of shapeshifting aliens who may adapt to kill and take the place of human colonists. JAMES BLISH, in his *A Case of Conscience* (1958), explores the ethical dilemma of a Jesuit priest who encounters an alien race on a distant world and must attempt to come to terms with the fact that they have no concept of God.

Robert Heinlein rings interesting changes on the alien-contact theme in his bizarre *Stranger in a Strange Land* (1961), in which a human being who has been adopted by an alien race returns to Earth, in effect becoming a visiting alien himself.

Alien species and humanity's encounters with them have been a staple feature of SF ever since the very early days of the genre. Their presence in a story allows the writer to better examine the potential and the limitations of our own race, either through the eyes of an outsider or through the mindset of a human being struggling to come to terms with aliens' existence. Readers can relate to the sense of awe or dread that the human characters may feel upon encountering these strange beings, and although many of the aliens described in SF are unfeasible or even downright ridiculous, many of them are carefully, scientifically conceived and portrayed.

For as long as SF exists, alien races will populate its pages.

ALTERNATE WORLD

Alternate world SF is that which describes a version of Earth where history took a different turn. This device has provided authors with numerous possibilities for exploring extrapolated events and speculated futures that may have come about had something different happened at some important turning point in history. One of the most obvious subjects for this type of treatment is the outcome of (the Second World War) and the world that may have come about had Hitler and the Nazis won the war.

This has been explored by PHILIP K. DICK in his seminal *The Man in the High Castle* (1962), as well as by a number of more recent authors such as Robert Harris in *Fatherland* (1992) and JOHN BARNES in *Finity* (2000).

HARRY TURTLEDOVE, an author whose main output consists of various alternate world stories, has also suggests in his Worldwar sequence what would have happened if ALIENS had invaded at the time of the war and joined in the battles that were happening in Europe. They are decidedly tongue in cheek.

Other famous alternate world scenarios include postulation about the state of America if Britain had won the War of Independence – Turtledove's *The Two Georges* (1997) and HARRY HARRISON's *The Tunnel Through the Deeps* (1972): how England would have coped with the early death of Queen Elizabeth I and the continued rule of the Catholic Church – KEITH ROBERT's wonderful *Pavane* (1968): and the effect on the development of the Italian Renaissance if Leonardo da Vinci's various designs had been manufactured – PAUL J. McAULEY'S *Pasquale's Angel* (1994).

History provides easy and fruitful pickings for the authors of SF, and offers a wealth of different scenarios and ideas. SF is a speculative literature, and the alternate world device has proved a popular method of processing this speculation.

ALTERNATIVE REALITY

An alternative reality is one that is different from the perceived natural order of the world, a universe that is not our own, or not considered to be the natural norm, that the characters of any given story may inhabit.

Many alternative realities come about through the deconstruction of a character's perception. This can be through mind-altering drugs, dream states, alternate DIMENSIONS or the use of VIRTUAL REALITY. Alternative realities are often found in fantastical literature, in which characters either fall asleep or receive a blow to the head before proceeding to fantasize the existence of an entirely separate reality to their own. However, the device has also been much used in SF.

Both PHILIP K. DICK and JEFF NOON have become famed for their use of drug-induced fantasies to construct alternative internal realities. In *The Three Stigmata of Palmer Eldritch* (1964), Dick has the eponymous anti-hero deliver a new drug to a group of human colonists who use it to escape the monotony of existence on the colony PLANET. However, Eldritch is versed in the ways of the drug and is able to enter these individual realities and manipulate them to his own ends. Noon creates a similar effect in *Vurt* (1993), which sees its characters imbibing 'Vurt feathers' so that they may slip into dream-inspired game worlds where reality becomes just one of many different options.

GREG EGAN has his character construct an entire virtual reality universe in *Permutation City* (1994), into which he escapes with his associates in a search for immortality. TAD WILLIAMS has his characters devise a monumental digital city in his Otherland sequence to similar effect.

Dimensional rifts have also been used as a means of moving characters between realities. In *Raft* (1991), STEPHEN BAXTER has his protagonists slip into a tiny parallel universe within which the conditions and laws of physics are far more intense than they are used to, whilst EDWIN ABBOTT uses alternate dimensions as a means of exploring mathematical theory in *Flatland* (1884).

Alternative realities are a useful device in SF, as they allow the author to rationalize otherwise fantastical events or experiences, whilst still maintaining a level of normality in the 'real' world. Indeed, virtual reality in particular enables the writer to have their characters 'switch off' from the strange environments they have been exploring and step back into normality.

ANDROID

A synthetically created human, usually of organic or biological origin. The term was not generally adopted until sometime in the early-to-mid 1940s.

These artificially created 'people' are often developed for the purposes of slavery or forced labour, and in this respect are thematically akin to ROBOTS. Indeed, at times the terms appear to be interchangeable, especially when considering the work of PHILIP K. DICK.

An example of a proto-android in SF is the monster created by the eponymous doctor in MARY SHELLEY'S *Frankenstein* (1818). In it, the character of Frankenstein uses surgery and electricity to construct and eventually reanimate a human being. This 'monster', assembled out of various exhumed body parts, is cast out by society and eventually confronts its maker. It is a superb study of the morality of using science as a means of controlling the processes of life.

In modern SF, however, one of the most startling treatments of androids can be found in Philip K. Dick's *Do Androids Dream of Electric Sheep?* (1968). The androids are here portrayed as a victimised minority who are attempting to escape the shackles of human oppression. By finding their way back to Earth from colony planet Mars and assuming their independence, they make themselves targets for termination; society at large views the androids as a group of malfunctioning machines. In a similar way to Shelley in *Frankenstein*, Dick illustrates the repulsiveness, yet inevitability of such a response. Indeed, one need only look at the public reaction to genetically modified foods towards the end of the 1990s as a measure of how society at large reacts to this type of scientific alteration of nature.

ROBERT SILVERBERG, in his *Tower of Glass* (1970), describes how a man asserts power over a group of androids by assuming the role of MESSIAH. However, the androids become wise to his ploy, and his pretence becomes the grounds of his downfall.

Scepticism and a criticism of the blind assumption that through science mankind can become masters of life and death pervades much of the writing about androids.

ANTI-GRAVITY

Anti-gravity is a device infrequently used in modern SF, chiefly due to the unlikeness of it ever becoming a reality. It is defined as a force that opposes gravity, and therefore allows objects or people to hover, float or be propelled. Antigravity does not feature in any known science and has been portrayed in many different ways.

H. G. WELLS, in his *First Men in the Moon* (1901), describes ingeniously how anti-gravity could be used to send rockets to the Moon. JAMES BLISH, in *Cities in Flight* (1970) uses anti-gravity as a means of lifting flying cities, or 'spindizzies', away from the planet.

However, Einstein's general theory of relativity states that the curvature of space would have to be modified to effect such an anti-gravitational force, therefore necessitating a complete restructuring of the universe. The chance of this ever happening is not great. For this reason the use of anti-gravity as a device in SF has waned, and is now associated with the early pulp SF of the GOLDEN AGE, and, more recently, with SPACE OPERA that does not adhere to strict scientific principles.

ANTIMATTER

A postulated substance which consists of 'anti-particles'.

Anti-particles appear not to be naturally occurring, although they have been created in laboratories on a very small scale. An example of an anti-particle is a positron, which has a positive charge equal to that of the negative charge of an electron. This suggests that contact between the two particles would cause a mutually exclusive reaction.

For this reason, antimatter is usually described as a highly volatile substance, as its physical properties dictate that huge amounts of energy would be released upon contact with matter, as the two substances react to cancel each other out.

This has led to many authors of SPACE OPERA finding a use for antimatter as either a weapon or a fuel supply for faster-than-light spacecraft. This has been seen recently in PETER F. HAMILTON's Night's Dawn Trilogy, as well as many episodes of STAR TREK.

IAN WATSON discusses the possibilities of an antimatter universe in *The Jonah Kit* (1975). In it, an observational scientist named Paul Hammond discovers that the universe is actually formed out of antimatter, and that the matter universe that we know is only a 'ghost' of the real structure that will eventually coalesce and collapse.

There are many possibilities for the use of antimatter, and it featured in much early GOLDEN AGE SF.

However, as theoretical physics has suggested better methods of traversing the universe, and with the problems of containment and availability raising doubts, it has begun to feature less frequently in the pages of modern SF. There are also fears that the creation and use of large amounts of antimatter could be damaging to the fabric of space.

ARTIFICIAL ENVIRONMENT

An environment that has been created for a specific purpose, usually to make a previously inhospitable place habitable. This has been ingeniously described in a number of different ways in SF.

Before the advent of the TERRAFORMING notion, it was suggested that vast domes could be erected on the surface of other planets or underwater. These domes would create a habitable space, a self-contained environment in which plant life would provide a natural source of food and oxygen. Indeed, this notion has led to experiments involving hermetically sealed rooms and biologically altered plants. It has also been speculated that such technology could be developed for use aboard space stations or vessels.

This idea was developed in SF to include not only space stations but ringworlds and habitats – vast human constructs that would eventually become their own planetary bodies and generate gravity by spinning about on an axis. This idea is best examined by LARRY NIVEN in his classic *Ringworld* (1970), in which he describes a partial DYSON SPHERE which circles a star. Light and energy are provided by the star, and gravity is maintained by keeping the construct in constant motion.

This concept has been adapted by IAIN M. BANKS for use in his Culture novels. He describes a vast semi-UTOPIA in which billions of humans and aliens live aboard self-contained Orbitals, which are similar in nature to Niven's Ringworld. Banks paints a vivid portrait of these artificial worlds, describing vast tundra, teeming jungles and thriving oceans. The ARTIFICIAL INTELLIGENCES that keep a watchful eye over the Orbitals are often as eccentric as the human characters. Banks takes a very detailed look at one such environment in *Look to Windward* (2000).

Another notion that has found much use in SF is the mining of asteroids to create habitable spaces. Asteroids, rich in ore and minerals, would be hollowed out, providing not only a huge source of raw materials, but also a vast network of tunnels and caverns that could be adapted for habitation.

The advent of GENETIC engineering has also suggested a wealth of possibilities for the development of artificial environments. PETER F. HAMILTON, in *The Reality Dysfunction* (1996), describes organic habitats which are generated from genetic seeds. These habitats use photosynthesis to retrieve energy from stars, and excrete oxygen as a waste product into their interiors. These interiors can be moulded and 'grown' to accommodate a very large and demanding population.

Terraforming is the suggested means by which humans could adapt another planetary surface for colonization. It refers to the process which could be used to 'force' a planet to conform to an environment suitable to support life as it is found on Earth. KIM STANLEY ROBINSON has explored the possibilities of this concept in great detail in his Mars trilogy, beginning with *Red Mars* (1992). It is still current thought that if humans are eventually to colonize another planet, then some degree of terraforming will be necessary. However, there are obvious moral considerations involved in destroying any existing environment that may already be in place on a planetary body. It would also involve enormous spans of time and vast investment to make such a theory become a reality.

ALTERNATIVE REALITIES such as VIRTUAL REALITY and drug–induced fantasies can also be viewed as forms of artificial environment. A good example of this is the quantum computer universe created in GREG EGAN's *Permutation City* (1994).

ARTIFICIAL INTELLIGENCE

The creation of sentient life that is not human, usually described in terms of computer systems, programs or ROBOTS (although the term can also refer to genetically manipulated intelligences such as ANDROIDS).

This often takes the form of an advanced computer program or neural net that learns from its environment in much the same way as a child, eventually developing into a self–aware system.

The AI is a motif explored in all types of SF. SPACE OPERA usually takes a certain level of artificial intelligence for granted, featuring characters that are often as intelligent or more intelligent than their human counterparts. HARD SF tends to look into the actual possibilities of AI, whilst LITERARY SF considers the more moralistic and psychological considerations.

Classic examples include the ROBOT stories of ISAAC ASIMOV, the Culture Minds of IAIN M. BANKS and the novels *Dreaming in Smoke* (1998) by TRICIA SULLIVAN and *The Moon is a Harsh Mistress* (1966) by ROBERT HEINLEIN.

Computers that have developed intelligence, either purposefully or spontaneously, have also been seen as menacing and dangerous in SF. An example of this is the character Hal in 2001: A SPACE ODYSSEY, based on the short story, 'The Sentinel' (1951) by ARTHUR C. CLARKE, who, through a conflicting set of directives and logical imperatives, comes to the conclusion that it needs to terminate its crew.

Another aspect of artificial intelligence is the postulated notion that human beings could eventually download or copy themselves into a computer. This creates an interesting debate into identity and intellectual ownership, as the copies immediately begin to distance themselves from the original person. GREG EGAN explores these themes in *Permutation City* (1994), in which a lonely computer programmer creates a VIRTUAL REALITY universe as a haven for digital immortality. WILLIAM GIBSON discusses the possibilities of memory backup and transfer in his novella, *Johnny Mnemonic* (1981), which was filmed in 1995 and retained the same title.

A similar process has also been used by a number of authors as a way of describing an alternative to the afterlife, usually by somehow recording the synaptic structures of the brain. The Noonsphere in CHRISTOPHER EVAN's *Mortal Remains* (1995), as well as the Edenist society in PETER F. HAMILTON's Night's Dawn Trilogy are good examples of this. Both see characters 'downloading' themselves into computer processors as a means of existing after their bodies have perished. This creates a symbiotic society in which the living can easily consult the 'dead' and vice versa. In a sense, this type of virtual representation of the human mind can be seen as a practical solution to the type of TRANCENDANCE described by many earlier authors, and offers a scientific method of representing the supernatural.

The process of downloading human intelligence into machines is now widely used in many different subgenres of science fiction.

Other forms of artificial intelligence see humans or animals tampered with (either through GENETICS or augmentation), to create beings with enhanced levels of intelligence. A moving example of this is DANIEL KEYES' *Flowers for Algernon* (1966), in which an unintelligent floor-sweeper named Charlie is boosted to the level of a genius. However, his triumph is short lived, as the increased capacity of his mind leads to a shortening of his life span.

DAVID BRIN has also described the possibilities of adapting animals in his Uplift novels. He describes how various races could be 'uplifted' to increase their IQs, which eventually leads to dolphins acting as the engineers and navigators of starships.

BIONIC

The term bionic is a contraction of the phrase 'biological electronics'. It is an early term used to describe humans or animals augmented with machine technology. This can take the form of an artificial limb or organ, as well as a complete structural rebuild, sometimes only retaining the original brain.

This type of modified being is usually referred to as a CYBORG.

BIOTECHNOLOGY

A general term which is used to describe the technological applications of biological research.

In science fiction this takes many forms, including biological warfare, GENETIC engineering, CLONING and body augmentation. More recently, with the development of the concept of NANOTECH-NOLOGY, authors have begun to discuss the possibilities of biological manipulation on an atomic scale. This was explored in depth in the award-winning *Fairyland* (1995) by PAUL J. McAULEY.

Many authors see biotechnology as the next progressive step in human EVOLUTION, as we learn to adapt to our changing environment at a rate far exceeding that of natural selection. This view is symptomatic of the widely shared vision of a future controlled by science and technology.

Early SF novels which deal with genetics include H.G. WELLS's *The Island of Dr Moreau* (1896) and ALDOUS HUXLEY's *Brave New World* (1932), and FREDRICK POHL's *Man Plus* (1976) and RUDY RUCKER's *Wetware* (1988) both consider the possibilities of human augmentation.

GREG EGAN has also explored many of the applications of biotechnology in his short fiction, collected in *Axiomatic* (1995) and *Luminous* (1999).

BLACK HOLE

A region of space, theoretically formed by the collapse of a star, in which gravity is so strong that even light cannot escape its pull.

The boundary of a black hole, the point at which gravity becomes too strong for light or radiation to escape, is known as the event horizon. It is not known what becomes of matter that passes within the event horizon, but it is suspected that the standard laws of physics break down and no longer apply. A number of theorists have suggested that the presence of such an enormous amount of gravity concentrated in one place may cause a curvature or hole in space-time (see DIMENSIONS). This hole could represent the opening or mouth of a WORMHOLE, and has led to speculation that the black hole itself could be used as a portal or gateway for faster-than-light SPACE TRAVEL. It is also theorized that a singularity, a point where the density of the collapsed star becomes infinite, exists within each black hole.

In science fiction, black holes have become a standard method of portraying faster-than-light space travel. This is chiefly due to the theoretical possibilities that still exist; until more is known about the nature of black holes and singularities, travel though this type of spacial flaw can still be viably speculated. Good examples can be found in JOE HALDEMAN's *The Forever War* (1974) and FREDRICK POHL's *Gateway* (1977).

There also exists the possibility that humans could eventually harness the immense power of a black hole. This has been used recently by WIL McCARTHY in *The Collapsium* (2000), in which a crystal substance formed from miniature black holes is the basis of long-distance communication and travel, as well as the movie EVENT HORIZON which envisages a star drive that derives its power from a hermetically contained black hole.

GREGORY BENFORD broke new ground with the publication of *Eater* (2000), in which he describes a black hole that is sentient. It arrives at the edge of the galaxy, wishing to 'swallow' the solar system in an attempt to assimilate our knowledge and experience. Although the possible sentience of a black hole may appear to be fanciful, nothing is known about the structures contained within them. Benford does a good job of making his 'character' believable.

CLONING

A highly speculative science that found itself at the forefront of popular debate towards the end of the last century, chiefly due to the limited success of experiments involving sheep and pigs. It refers to the manipulation of DNA and the reproductive system that is used to create an exact biological replica of a living organism. Twins are naturally occurring clones as they share identical genetic makeup.

Many SF stories, until recently, saw clones as an ideal dopplegänger device – an evil twin or body double who in some way could affect the actions of the chief protagonist.

However, since the advent of cloning as a real scientific process, authors have begun to examine the more realistic, moral and psychological implications of its use. The first novel to popularise the notion was MICHAEL CRICHTON's *Jurrasic Park* (1990). In it, he describes a theoretical process by which dinosaurs could be recreated from samples of their DNA recovered from fossilized amber. Gaps in their genetic code are replaced with amphibian DNA, and the completed sequence is implanted in various embryos. After incubation, the eggs are hatched to reveal juvenile dinosaurs. However, Crichton's is a cautionary tale – the dinosaurs are put on show in an amusement park, but go on the rampage and wreak havoc. In this respect it deals with similar themes to H. G. WELLS's earlier *The Island of Dr Moreau* (1896).

Other, more considered, approaches to the topic include *The Fifth Head of Cerberus* (1972) by GENE WOLFE, *Where Late the Sweet Birds*

Sang (1975) by KATE WILHELM and *The Ophiuchi Hotline* (1977) by JOHN VARLEY.

Wolfe's classic novella, which was later expanded, tells the tale of a young boy who is constantly subjected to humiliating tests and conditioning by his father. His only refuge is a massive library near to his home; he dreads the evenings when he knows his father will come to take him away. However, it transpires towards the end of the narrative that the child is actually the latest in a long chain of clones, and that his 'father' is a previous clone of the same man.

Wilhelm's book deals with a POST-APOCALYPTIC world in which sterility has afflicted the human race. An enclave of people begin to propagate clones of themselves as a means of survival, and the novel focuses on the reactions of the clones to the 'real' people, and vice versa.

There are, however, philosophical problems with the cloning process that still need to be answered. Top of this list is the age debate – the question of whether a cloned being will age at a normal rate from the point of its 'birth', or whether, genetically speaking, it will be as old as the being that provided the original cells. Recent research has shown that the latter may in fact be true – previously cloned animals have deteriorated at a rate more consistent with the age of the original cell donor.

Whatever the case, cloning has provided a wealth of ideas for writers of SF, and in much the same way as ARTIFICIAL INTELLIGENCE and human electronic 'backup' has pervaded SF over recent years, cloning has now become an accepted notion.

COMIC SF

A subgenre of SF that often finds itself closer to the realms of SCIENCE FANTASY than those of science fiction. This is chiefly due to the comical devices employed; it is difficult to reconcile the absurd with serious scientific extrapolation. That is not to say, however, that all comic SF follows the same pattern.

Perhaps the best-known writer of comic SF is HARRY HARRISON, whose *Bill, the Galactic Hero* (1965) and *The Stainless Steel Rat* (1961) are two of the most humorous novels in the genre. *The Stainless Steel Rat* follows the progress of space adventurer Jim diGriz through his many strange encounters. Both books have spawned a number of sequels, with none living up to the promise of the originals.

British writer DOUGLAS ADAMS was also well known for his comic SF. His radio series and novel, *The Hitchhiker's Guide to the Galaxy*

(1979) takes as its starting point the destruction of Earth by ALIENS to make way for an interstellar bypass. Happily for Arthur Dent, who is having a pretty miserable day, his best friend turns out to be an alien and whisks him off to safety aboard one of the demolition craft. The rest of the book, along with four sequels, tells the tales of their adventures together as they traverse the universe.

Popular author TERRY PRATCHETT, who is world renowned for his series of Discworld comic fantasies, has also written two comic SF novels. *The Dark Side of the Sun* (1976) and *Strata* (1981) are very much in the same mould as his fantasies, but take place on various planets around the universe.

At the more literary end of the scale, MICHAEL MOORCOCK's Dancers at the End of Time trilogy and *Jerry Cornelius* stories make good satirical use of comedy. This is another aspect of comic SF. Satire underpins much of this subgenre, offering authors the opportunity to lighten the mood of their writing without compromising their opinions. KURT VONNEGUT is perhaps the master of satirical SF; his many works inside the genre are both biting and self deprecating, with *Cat's Cradle* (1963) being an excellent example.

On the screen, shows such as RED DWARF, MORK AND MINDY and 3RD ROCK FROM THE SUN have helped raise the profile of comic SF. In these shows, it is often the alien perspective on our human foibles that raises the laugh, as opposed to any true aspect of science fiction.

As a literary device, comedy has been used to good effect within SF, parodying itself and plundering the genre's stock of ideas to humorous effect. It is refreshing in a genre that often takes itself a little too seriously.

CRIME

As a separate genre, crime writing is one of the most popular mediums in modern fiction. Crime, like SF, has its dedicated followers and its own subgenres, but is more flexible. Whereas SF has become an exclusive genre with its own ground rules and definitions, crime is more inclusive, in that, all a story has to do to constitute a crime novel is have a crime enacted that then becomes the main focus of the novel, regardless of the background environment. This has meant that crime and SF, although not perhaps easily compatible, can work together, and on a number of occasions have done so to great effect.

In his ROBOT sequence, ISAAC ASIMOV produced two short novels about investigator Elijah Bayley and his robotic sidekick Daneel. *The Caves of Steel* (1954) sees the two partners tracking a killer and saboteur through an underground labyrinth, and *The Naked Sun* (1956) follows them as they leave the safety of Earth to go investigating the outer PLANETS of the human empire.

Perhaps the most important SF novel to make use of the crime genre, however, is ALFRED BESTER's classic *The Demolished Man* (1953), which sees a businessman attempting to plot the murder of a competitor in a world dominated by mind-reading telepaths. To avoid discovery he must learn to hide his thoughts. The novel is highly original and proposes new ways to commit and investigate crimes. Indeed, one of the most important aspects of SF is the consideration of the sociological and psychological impact of any new ideas or developments on the society around them.

BRIAN STABLEFORD uses the hard-boiled narrative to good effect in his Hooded Swan sequence (1972–5) of SPACE OPERAS, which sees the pilot of a faster-than-light spacecraft sent to various ALIEN PLANETS to investigate biological mysteries.

Other recent examples of standard crime themes crossing over into SF include GREG EGAN's *Quarantine* (1992) and ERIC BROWN's *New York Nights* (2000).

CRYONICS

The term cryonics refers to the preservation of human bodies through freezing, often in liquid nitrogen. This is usually for the purposes of later reanimation.

It has long been postulated that corpses frozen and preserved at the point of death could be resuscitated and regenerated at a point in the future when the appropriate level of technology would allow it. This has led in recent years to a spate of rich business executives taking out policies to ensure that they, or at least their heads and brains, are cryonically stored after their deaths. Some also believe that terminal diseases and cancers will be curable in the future, so have had themselves stored in the hope that they could later be reanimated and cured.

Many SF stories have made use of this notion of SUSPENDED ANIMATION. However, before the process of cryonic freezing became generally adopted, many authors made use of a deep sleep or hibernatory period as a means of projecting their protagonists through to some future time. An early example of this is H. G. WELLS's *When the Sleeper Wakes* (1899), in which the chief protagonist awakens to find a society that has changed beyond all recognition.

CYBERPUNK

Cyberpunk, as a subgenre, is very much a product of the 1980s. Major advances were being made in technology and there was a strong faith in a technological future. Developments in VIRTUAL REALITY had also opened up the possibilities of alternative digital realities – computer-generated environments linked together via CYBERSPACE.

In literature this translated into the predominately American movement of cyberpunk, which was full of gritty, seedy high-tech NEAR FUTURES in which people could plug themselves directly into their home computers and hold discussions with their guns, where biological humans could interface seamlessly with electronic computers.

The term itself was first used by BRUCE BETHKE in his story, 'Cyberpunk' (1983), but is perhaps best defined as a subgenre by WILLIAM GIBSON's novel *Neuromancer* (1984). The book follows the progress of Case, a data thief who finds his wares among the many hidden niches of cyberspace. It goes on to discuss ARTIFICIAL INTELLI-GENCE and the bid for freedom by a powerful electronic entity. Gibson also made an impact with *Johnny Mnemonic* (1981), a novella in which the main character is a data trafficker who stores other people's information in his head. To do this, he must download the information directly from the web to his brain.

Another author very closely associated with the cyberpunk movement is BRUCE STERLING, whose *Islands in the Net* (1988) successfully posits a post-industrial world in which everyone is connected via a world-wide network of data. This almost seems to predict the huge internet boom that was to happen just a few years later.

More recently, authors such as JON COURTENAY GRIMWOOD have married many of the stylistic aspects of the movement with the more desolate and pessimistic landscapes of late 1990s SF. In these works there appears to be a heightened awareness of the possible dangers of tech-nology as a whole, leading to decreased optimism and a more cautious approach to change. This is epitomized in Grimwood's loose sequence of novels, *NeoAddix* (1997), *Lucifer's Dragon* (1998), *reMix* (1999) and *redRobe* (2000).

CYBERSPACE

A word coined by WILLIAM GIBSON in his classic novel *Neuromancer* (1984), but since adopted by many other writers and, more recently, by the English language as a whole.

Generally, it refers to a network of computer-generated VIRTUAL REALITIES, into which human beings can enter via a virtual interface. These environments are perceived as an artificial or ALTERNATIVE REALITY in which human minds and artificial constructs such as intelligent programs (ARTIFICIAL INTELLIGENCE) can coexist.

With the advent of the internet, a world-wide digital network, this concept has found much footing, with the term itself beginning to permeate the language as a means of referring to the internet as a whole.

Developments of the notion have seen protagonists using cyberspace to control military vehicles and weapons over great distances – JOE HALDEMAN's *Forever Peace* (1997); or to spread information or misinformation – KEN MACLEOD's *The Star Fraction* (1995). Some authors have even represented cyberspace as a place of transcendence or retreat; the characters in GREG EGAN's *Permutation City* (1994) create a virtual universe into which they download copies of their personalities. This becomes a non-physical life, of sorts – the virtual copies have their own, independent experiences and point of reference.

Cyberspace has also been the birthplace of many self-aware computer systems over the years, or the home of malignant artificial intelligences.

However it is represented or adapted, the notion of cyberspace has found much support in SF and can be found in most modern novels. It has become more and more difficult to imagine the internet not evolving into the primary means of communication over the next few years, and cyberspace is simply the next step on the ladder.

CYBORG

Cyborg is a shortening of the phrase cybernetic organism. It refers to the augmentation of a biological entity, usually a human being, with machine components. In reality this could be anything from a prosthetic limb to a microchip IMPLANT, but in SF it is usually a little more spectacular.

Perhaps the best novel to deal with the creation of a cyborg is FREDERIK POHL's *Man Plus* (1976), in which the protagonist, Roger Torraway, is deliberately modified to enable him to survive on Mars. The book successfully deals not only with the technological aspects of such a procedure, but with the underlying emotional distress and trauma that Torraway suffers at the hands of his 'creators' as well.

This type of augmentation technology has since become a staple of CYBERPUNK, with many characters enhancing their natural functions and senses, as well as developing ports and interfaces that allow them to plug themselves directly into their computers.

Cyborgs have also translated well to the screen, with television series such as THE SIX MILLION DOLLAR MAN and THE BIONIC WOMAN popularizing the idea. On screen, however, cyborgs are more often than not represented as indestructible killing machines, in movies such as TERMINATOR and *Universal Soldier*.

It is generally believed that at some point in the future, most humans will have at least a small amount of augmentation, whether for medical or some other purpose.

DIMENSIONS

A term used in mathematics to describe spacial perception. Human beings can see in three different dimensions; it has long been suggested that there could be many more.

Indeed, Einstein's general theory of relativity suggests that a combination of space and time, space-time, as it is generally known, can be classified as a fourth dimension. This has found much support in SF, with authors such as ISAAC ASIMOV, who saw the penetration of space-time, or hyperspace, as the key to faster-than-light travel. This is a notion much adopted by SF writers today, although they have inherited a more developed concept of space-time that suggests that BLACK HOLES and WORMHOLES, if stabilized, would provide a far superior method of faster-than-light travel.

An early attempt to discuss dimensions was EDWIN ABBOTT's *Flatland: A Romance of Many Dimensions* (1884), in which Mr A. Square, an inhabitant of a two-dimensional world, is transported into a three-dimensional environment. We follow his progress as he attempts to come to terms with the catastrophic change in his surroundings.

Developments in theoretical mathematics and physics have allowed authors to capitalize on new aspects of dimensional theory. In *Raft* (1991), STEPHEN BAXTER sends his characters into a parallel universe where gravity is amplified many times over; theory suggests that such parallel universes could exist concurrent with our own. The protagonists in GREGORY BENFORD's *Cosm* (1998) accidentally create a tiny alternative universe which is in itself an entirely separate dimension. The mathematical possibilities are great, and therefore create endless opportunities for SF writers to create new environments.

DNA

DNA is the popular expression for Deoxyribo Nucleic Acid. It is a biological term referring to the genetic material that constitutes all living organisms.

DNA is an acid composed of various linked substances which together form a ladder shaped molecule called a double helix. DNA molecules describe a genetic code from which the biological structure of an organism is 'built'. Therefore, hereditary characteristics and diseases are usually transferred via the DNA. The enormous amount of coding that describes an entire species is usually referred to as a genome.

In SF the manipulation of DNA has taken many forms; the creation of ANDROIDS or CLONES, the forensic identification of a person or animal (as in modern forensic science), the development of biological weapons or drugs, the design of entirely new species from scratch, the curing of disease or disorder, and the fashioning of biological computers or ARTIFICIAL INTELLIGENCE. The possibilities are endless.

At present, the reprogramming of DNA is a highly controversial subject, yet it refuses to go away. The first draft of the human genome has already been mapped, and speculation is high as to what its first application may be. A very basic calculator has already been engineered from cells taken from a leech, and research into the topic looks set to continue.

It was perhaps MICHAEL CRICHTON's famous novel, *Jurassic Park* (1990) that really brought the possibilities of DNA restructuring to the forefront of modern debate. In it he describes how recovered scraps of dinosaur DNA could be used in a bastardization of the cloning process to recreate living dinosaurs. However, it seems unlikely that enough intact dinosaur DNA will ever be found to enable such a process to become a reality.

DYING WORLD
See FAR FUTURE

DYSON SPHERE

A term named after physicist Freeman Dyson and his notion that any advanced extraterrestrial species would be likely to have engineered a shell around their star to make maximum use of its energy output. This shell would create a multitude of possibilities for energy retention and use, as well as offering an enormous inner surface which could eventually be inhabited. Inside the habitable area of the sphere would be constant sunlight, and by ensuring that the sphere was set at the optimum distance from the star, a consistent, favourable environment could be created.

SF writers have used the concept, most notably BOB SHAW in *Orbitsville* (1975), in which the protagonist, searching for signs of another habitable planet in deep space, encounters a Dyson Sphere with a surface area six hundred and twenty-five million times that of Earth.

LARRY NIVEN's *Ringworld* (1970) also draws its main concept from that of the Dyson Sphere, but on a smaller, more manageable scale. Niven creates a single ring around the Sun, as opposed to an immense sphere. This would still be, nevertheless, an epic task to undertake.

It is now generally accepted that a Dyson Sphere would be impractical, if not impossible, to build. Its appearances in fiction have been thought-provoking and intelligent studies of an interesting, if implausible, concept.

DYSTOPIA

A dystopia, a community or society gone wrong, is the opposite of a UTOPIA. Dystopias are often portrayed as social structures that have collapsed under an environmental burden or political regime. Due to their very nature they are often set at some indefinite point in the future; societies do not decay over years but over decades.

The most famous of literary dystopias is that inhabited by Winston Smith in GEORGE ORWELL's *Nineteen Eighty-Four* (1949). It is a political nightmare, where 'Big Brother' is always watching and people are defined by their thoughts not their actions. The book deals with the private rebellion of Smith and his unapproved love affair with Julia. The superpowers are at war, and an unforgiving dictatorial regime governs the country. Anyone who is considered an enemy of the state is removed and conditioned, brainwashed, in an attempt to make them comply. Television screens and microphones monitor every moment of every person's life. *Nineteen Eight-Four* is a dark and bleak vision, yet its images have pervaded the public consciousness and its terminology has become synonymous with a fear of the state.

RAY BRADBURY, in perhaps his best work, *Fahrenheit 451* (1953), tells of a dystopia in which books and written materials are outlawed and hunted out. The chief protagonist, a 'fireman' who is employed to destroy these books, is redeemed by his realization of the error of his ways. However, this is a small triumph, as a single man is powerless against an oppressive state.

JOHN BRUNNER's *The Sheep Look Up* (1972) and *Stand on Zanzibar* (1968) take a detailed, unforgiving look at environmental damage and collapse, and PHILIP K. DICK's *Do Androids Dream of Electric Sheep?* (1968) describes an Earth blasted by world war, in which animals are moving toward extinction and most people who can afford it have moved off planet.

ALDOUS HUXLEY explores a dystopia in *Brave New World* (1932). He describes a disturbing society in which everyone is manufactured in a test tube and grows up addicted to the pacifying 'Soma'. It is a bleak examination of EUGENICS and BIOTECHNOLOGY.

Other excellent novels to feature dystopias include *The Handmaid's Tale* (1985) by MARGARET ATWOOD and *A Clockwork Orange* (1962) by ANTHONY BURGESS.

It can be argued that much SF takes place in either a utopia or a dystopia; they are the obvious choices for science fiction as they instantly communicate an alternate situation or environment. Dystopias particularly give characters reason to act, as there is a very definite need to create a better society.

ECOLOGY

Ecology has played a large part in SF, examining not only the future of our own planet, but also the adaption of other planets for possible human colonization.

Other world ecology has been successfully explored by both FRANK HERBERT and KIM STANLEY ROBINSON, the former in his epic Dune sequence, the latter in his Mars trilogy.

In *Dune* (1965), Frank Herbert describes an arid desert world, 'Arrakis' on which human colonizers are struggling to carve out an existence. There is a distinct lack of water and the nomad 'Fremen' are forced to wear 'stilsuits', tight-fitting body suits that recycle their body moisture. It is this battle against the environment, as well as the harvesting of a rare drug, 'Melange', that forms the crux of *Dune*. Herbert's book succeeds because of his attention to detail. Later books in the series, although less successful than the first, see the planet undergoing a metamorphosis as it is slowly adapted by the Fremen in a TERRAFORMING project.

Terraforming is also the key to Kim Stanley Robinson's Mars saga, beginning with *Red Mars* (1992). It follows the gradual adaptation and habitation of the Red Planet, over the course of three books. Vast in scope, it details not only the changing ecology of the planet, but the politics and economics involved in the creation of a new planetary home for the race. In a sense, Robinson attempts to describe his own particular brand of UTOPIA, and his Mars trilogy has become one of the standard texts in the ongoing debate as to whether we should attempt to colonize Mars.

Ecological stories that examine the future prospects of the Earth, however, tend to present it in a rather more pessimistic light. Novels such as J. G. BALLARD's *The Drowned World* (1962), John Christopher's *The Death of Grass* (1956) and JOHN BRUNNER's *The Sheep Look Up* (1972) all take place in environmental DYSTOPIAS, where the ecology is so severely damaged it is beyond easy repair.

GEORGE R. STEWART takes a slightly different approach in *Earth Abides* (1949), describing the changing ecology of the planet after a mysterious plague has all but wiped out humanity. Gradually, the remnants of the human race return to the status of hunter-gatherers, and the planet once again runs wild and flourishes.

Another use of ecology in SF is in the description of ALIEN habitats and worlds. PETER F. HAMILTON touches on this briefly in his Night's Dawn trilogy, as do many other modern SF authors who wish to describe alien landscapes with at least some degree of credibility. An excellent example of this is HAL CLEMENT's *Mission of Gravity* (1954), in which the human protagonists visit the alien planet of Mesklin where the gravity reaches up to seven hundred times that of Earth. All life on this planet has therefore evolved to be peculiarly flat. ROBERT CHARLES WILSON also very successfully describes a highly toxic alien ecology in *Bios* (1999). In that book, interstellar travel is slow and expensive, so the human colonists are attempting to settle the nearest planet they can find that has life. Unfortunately, that life is proving to be lethal to humans and animals introduced from Earth.

The reasoning behind this, that for alien life to survive it must exist in some form of viable ecology, is perhaps best credited to Stanley G. Weinbaum, an American writer who broke new ground with his early descriptions of alien life on Mars. Until this point, many of the pulp SF writers of the GOLDEN AGE featured fantastical monsters or strange humanoid people in their descriptions of extraterrestrial life.

EUGENICS

A highly controversial subject that refers to the 'improvement' of the human race through various means of unnatural selection.

This can be effected in three ways: through ethnic or age-related culling, through biological selection or through GENETIC manipulation. Many people find these concepts morally repugnant. Nevertheless, they have all been represented in SF, almost exclusively as anti-eugenic warnings or statements.

Perhaps the best known of these is ALDOUS HUXLEY's *Brave New World* (1932), a dark DYSTOPIAN novel in which humans are artificially manufactured and conditioned, in a so-called 'improvement' of the natural conception process. Similar themes were explored in the movie GATTACA, which describes the development of an élite class.

Logan's Run (1967) by William Nolan and George Clayton Johnson, as well as the later movie and television series of the same name, describes a society in which people are ritually terminated before the age of thirty. This has led to a juvenile society whose members believe it to be a UTOPIA ruled by a vast computer; in actuality it is quite the opposite.

Indeed, the politics of eugenics follow a similar pattern; the purveyors have all believed they were striving towards a utopia, whilst the oppressed minority have suffered without a voice.

EVOLUTION

Evolutionary theory was developed and popularized by scientist Charles Darwin to explain how the current diversity of life and species could have developed from early primitive organisms. The key to this theory is the concept of natural selection, in which beneficial characteristics are passed on to offspring in a constant process that allows a species to better adapt to its environment.

The evolutionary notion is of great use to SF writers as it allows them to propose how a species or environment may appear in the future. For this reason, FAR FUTURE SF often involves highly evolved characters, plant life or species.

An early example of this is in H. G. WELLS's *The Time Machine* (1895), in which the human race has split into two subspecies over many thousands of years, developing into the peaceful and docile Eloi and the base, yet more recognizably human, Morlocks.

OLAF STAPLEDON also used his FUTURE HISTORIES, *The Last and First Men* (1930) and *Starmaker* (1937), to discuss the evolution of Earth and the human race, taking a godlike perspective and detailing almost unimaginable periods of time.

Evolution has also been used to discuss the possibilities of TRAN-SCENDENCE, most famously in ARTHUR C. CLARKE's *Childhood's End* (1953), in which strange ALIEN beings arrive on Earth to help guide the race into the next stage of its existence. This form of evolutionary transcendence has also been discussed by THEODORE STURGEON in *More Than Human* (1953), GREG BEAR in *Darwin's Children* (1999) and GREG EGAN in *Terenesia* (1999).

Many authors have also speculated that human beings will actually take themselves to the next stage of evolution via BIOTECHNOLOGY and augmentation, adapting their bodies to suit the changing environment around them.

FREDERIK POHL discusses this type of forced evolution in *Man Plus* (1976) when he has his characters create a CYBORG that will withstand the harsh Martian environment. ALDOUS HUXLEY also reinvents the conception process in his famous DYSTOPIAN novel *Brave New World* (1932), detailing a system of EUGENICS which specifies that human children should all be grown in laboratories.

However, this type of GENETIC or biological interference would not necessarily be restricted to the human species. H. G. Wells examined proto-genetic manipulation of animals in *The Island of Dr Moreau* (1896), and DAVID BRIN illustrates how other species, such as dolphins and primates, could be 'uplifted' to superior intelligence via similar means.

Evolutionary theory has also been applied to ALIEN and computer life forms (ARTIFICIAL INTELLIGENCE), such as the Lithians who appear in *A Case of Conscience* (1958) by JAMES BLISH and the Mesklinites in *Mission of Gravity* (1954) by HAL CLEMENT.

FAR FUTURE

A particular subgenre of SF that concerns itself with the distant, often almost unimaginably so, future.

Due to the difficulty in speculating so many thousands of years ahead, as well as the problems in representing the sheer strangeness of a distant future, many authors have made use of fantastical imagery to describe 'dying Earth' scenarios. This SCIENCE FANTASY, as it is sometimes known, is often allegorical in nature. JACK VANCE's *The Dying Earth* (1950), as well as its many sequels, is an excellent example of this. Although it is true to say that the book is more fantasy than SF, it has had an enormous impact on the genre as a whole, inspiring many authors to adopt their own far-future settings.

One such is GENE WOLFE's classic sequence The Book of the New Sun, beginning with *The Shadow of the Torturer* (1980), which is one of the bravest and most successful attempts by an author to tackle a far-future setting.

It is a wonderful evocation of a future time in which, the remnants of an advanced technological civilization lies scattered about; enormous rocket ships, now dormant and transformed into buildings, stand proud against the horizon. We see this ancient 'Urth' through the eyes of Severian, a torturer who is banished from his home, yet goes on to adopt the role of MESSIAH and eventually replaces the dying Sun with a white hole, restoring light and life to the planet. It is a masterful work that explores, through fantastical and quasi-religious imagery, the perpetuation of the human race into a strange and unknown future.

Another aspect of far-future SF is a consideration of the EVOLU-TIONARY process, as authors speculate what may become of our race and others over great spans of time. H. G. WELLS touches on this briefly in *The Time Machine* (1895) when he discusses the division of the human race into two subspecies, the Eloi and the Morlocks. OLAF STAPLEDON also discusses the implications of the evolutionary theory in his sweeping FUTURE HISTORY of mankind, *The Last and First Men* (1930). More recently, authors have begun to consider the possibilities of machine and ARTIFICIAL INTELLIGENCE, and the roles they may play in our distant future. POUL ANDERSON sets out a vision of a time when machine intelligence has entirely superseded biological life in his startling book, *Genesis* (1999).

STEPHEN BAXTER describes the eventual destruction of our universe at the hands of elusive ALIENS in *Ring* (1994), and PAUL J. McAULEY sets his Confluence trilogy, beginning with *Child of the River* (1997), on an artificial planet long abandoned by its human manufacturers.

MICHAEL MOORCOCK also makes good use of a far future setting in his Dancers at the End of Time sequence. Here he describes a decadent society populated by bored pseudo-immortals who occupy their days with constant parties and holidays back in time.

Images of entropy and dissolution persist in most far-future SF, as authors describe the final stages of the Solar System and the end of human experience. It is difficult to imagine a far-future setting without any point of reference to the modern day, but those authors that have tried have produced many excellent allegorical or moral tales.

FIRST CONTACT
See ALIEN

FUTURE HISTORY
A term used to describe a framework of future events constructed by an author to offer a detailed background of 'history' to their own particular vision of the future. Usually, a series of plots will be interwoven within this framework to create a loose sequence, and to provide some frame of human reference, although this is not always the case.

In his *The Last and First Men* (1930) and *Star Maker* (1937), OLAF STAPLEDON takes us on two sweeping journeys – the former through the two-billion-year EVOLUTION of mankind, marking all of our triumphs and tragedies along the way, the latter through the history of all intelligent life in the universe. They are classics of the genre, proto-future histories that offer us a perspective on our lives within the immensity of the universe.

After Stapledon, it is generally accepted that the first structured future history to form the backdrop to a number of stories and novels was created by ROBERT HEINLEIN in the 1940s. It is perhaps still the best-known sequence of linked stories of this type. The best books in the series include *Sixth Column* (1949), *Methuselah's Children* (1958) and *Time Enough For Love* (1973).

STEPHEN BAXTER, over recent years, has built an epic future history around his Xeelee sequence, a series of novels and stories that tell of human encounters with ALIENS, the ensuing wars and the eventual destruction of our universe by the elusive Xeelee themselves. The series comprises *Raft* (1991), *Timelike Infinity* (1992), *Flux* (1993), *Ring* (1994), *Vacuum Diagrams* (1997) and *Reality Dust* (2000).

Another classic future history is POUL ANDERSON's Technic History, which follows two threads; the stories of Nicholas Van Rijn, a merchant prince, and those of Dominic Flandry, a soldier.

ISAAC ASIMOV could also be said to have proposed a future history with his descriptions of the rise and fall of interstellar empires in the Foundation books, as could URSULA K. LE GUIN with her Hainish books.

Indeed, the future history has become a popular method of adding depth and detail to an environment, or creating a framework against which to set a series of linked stories and novels.

GENDER

Gender issues in SF are not frequently raised but are of great importance.

The 1970s saw a number of female SF writers coming to prominence, including such important novelists as URSULA K. LE GUIN and OCTAVIA BUTLER. A number of these writers used SF as a means of describing the plight of an oppressed gender, or the means by which they may be redeemed.

Le Guin's classic *The Left Hand of Darkness* (1969) is perhaps the most important of these novels and highlights the lack of understanding that exists between genders and the barriers that must be destroyed if we are ever to become united as a race. The novel follows the progress of a human anthropologist who accepts a mission to an ALIEN PLANET whose people are entirely androgynous and only develop a sexual identity during certain periods in their bodily cycle. Throughout the course of the novel, the protagonist believes himself to be talking with a man, but he comes to discover his error and eventually falls in love with his companion. In essence, Le Guin was pointing out that gender is no longer an issue when two people come to love each other.

Another important study of the role of women can be found in MARGARET ATWOOD's *The Handmaid's Tale* (1985), which charts the progress of a female 'breeding machine' as she breaks loose from the constraints of her environment and TRANSCENDS her situation, either by beginning a new life or by dying. It is a poignant study of human morality and the ambiguous ending makes it all the more impressive.

It was not long before female characters were taking the lead role in SF stories. A number of authors pioneered this, including DORIS LESSING and Octavia Butler, who are both strong supporters of women's rights.

In the movies, films such as ALIEN (1979) aided the work of women in this redressing of the balance by portraying strong women taking control of their own destinies.

More recently, ELIZABETH MOON has produced a series of MILITARISTIC SPACE OPERAS which feature a strong and intelligent female as the chief protagonist.

SF is perhaps one of the better genres for the successful exploration of gender issues, as it allows writers to develop allegorical scenarios or subverted environments that enable them to explore the issues in a more explicit and pointed way than other genres will allow. It is to the benefit of the SF field that so many gifted women now add to the body of work.

GENERATION STARSHIP

The generation starship concept came about chiefly in reaction to Einstein's claim that nothing will ever travel faster than light. If this is indeed true, then mankind will need an alternative method of reaching the stars, as many hundreds or thousands of years may be involved in travel to other planets and systems.

Therefore, it has been suggested that an enormous starship could be built to house an entirely self-sufficient society; that people would live, die and procreate on board, and that the original crew members would perish well before the ship ever reached its final destination. This is perhaps a slightly romantic notion but, given a large enough population, it is thought that a closed society such as this could prosper.

In SF, the notion was being explored as early as 1951 in ROBERT HEINLEIN's 'Universe', which was later fixed up with another story, 'Common Sense' and published as *Orphans of the Sky* (1963). In it he describes a devolved society which has forgotten it is resident on a starship. Revelation comes when they discover the true nature of their surroundings.

Unhappy with Heinlein's treatment of the concept, BRIAN ALDISS set about tackling the issue in *Non-Stop* (1958), which successfully draws on a similar plot device but to greater effect; the novel remains one of Aldiss's best to date.

Perhaps the most intriguing examination of the generation starship concept, however, is GENE WOLFE's Book of the Long Sun, beginning with *Nightside the Long Sun* (1993) and extending to a further three volumes. The series is related to Wolfe's previous sequence, Book of the New Sun, and again draws on much of the same fantastic imagery. In a similar way to both the books by Heinlein and Aldiss, the protagonists have forgotten they are on board an interstellar starship. The Long Sun of the title is an enormous artificial light strip that provides the interior with daylight. Society has returned to a pseudo-medieval stage, and we follow the progress of Patera Silk, a religious leader who is trying to come to terms with a vast memory download from a 'god'. At the same time he is attempting to save his religious establishment from being closed down.

A later pendant to the series, the three-volume Book of the Short Sun, which begins with *On Blue's Waters* (1999), sees the starship arrive on an inhabitable world.

A further representation of the generation starship concept is the *Enterprise* in the television series STAR TREK: THE NEXT

GENERATION. The ship is portrayed as a self-sufficient, contained society, but curiously it has the capability to travel faster than light and regularly returns to the Solar System.

GENETICS

The study and manipulation of genes and the genetic code.

This can take many forms – anything from the adaptation of plants and crops to create a more successful harvest (currently a very controversial topic), to the complete rewriting of a species genetic code or DNA to allow it to survive in a hostile environment.

H. G. WELLS was one of the earliest authors to dabble in the field, when he described a society of animals that had been surgically altered in an attempt to raise their intelligence. *The Island of Dr Moreau* (1896), although not strictly about genetics, deals with many of the same themes and in many ways set the moral standard for many works on genetics yet to come. When everything goes terribly wrong and the animals begin reverting to primitive behaviour, Wells is very quick to point out that there are still many lessons to be learned.

ALDOUS HUXLEY, in his *Brave New World* (1932), bleakly predicts the advent of a culture which will begin growing its children in test tubes in a dangerous step towards EUGENICS.

However, it was with the cracking of the genetic code by scientists in the 1950s that the full potential, as well as the implications, of genetic manipulation was realized.

Some authors began discussing the possibilities of CLONING, the creation of exact genetic replicas of a living organism, in such novels as *The Fifth Head of Cerberus* (1972) by GENE WOLFE. Others, such as JAMES BLISH in his *The Seedling Stars* (1957), saw that genetic adaptation could provide a means of colonizing otherwise hostile environments. The ability to modify ourselves fundamentally could indeed become one of the key elements involved in our quest to inhabit other worlds. Some believe that genetic engineering of the human form will become the next stage of human EVOLUTION, and with the first draft of the human genome being completed in 2000, it looks ever more likely.

More recently, with developments in biological research leading the way, authors have begun to examine the possibilities of adapting bacteria or viruses for beneficial use, as well as using NANOTECHNOLOGY as a means of bringing this about. A good example of this is *Blood Music*

(1985) by GREG BEAR, in which nanotechnology is used to create microscopic biological computers.

In *Fairyland* (1995), PAUL J. McAULEY has his chief protagonist engineer bacteria for use as recreational drugs. He also goes on to develop the blood supply of the 'fairies', a form of artificially created ANDROID.

Authors such as MICHAEL CRICHTON have also discussed the possibilities of using genetics to rebuild previously extinct species, such as dinosaurs or mammoths, from recovered scraps of their ancient DNA. However, although theoretically sound, it is unlikely that enough intact DNA will ever be found to enable to process to be developed.

GOLDEN AGE

There is a long standing joke between science-fiction authors that the Golden Age of SF is between thirteen and fourteen – the age when most people discover SF for the first time and are captivated by a SENSE OF WONDER at the big ideas inherent in much of its best writing.

In fact, it is the label given to the period of SF history between the late 1930s and early-to-mid 1940s when editor JOHN W. CAMPBELL was publishing stories by many important genre figures in ASTOUNDING SCIENCE FICTION MAGAZINE. Therefore, Golden Age SF is predominately American.

Headway was being made in the genre at this time. Although the magazine was still considered a pulp that was aimed at the teenage mass market, Campbell was encouraging authors such as ROBERT HEINLEIN, ISAAC ASIMOV, A. E. VAN VOGT, CLIFFORD SIMAK and LESTER DEL REY to consider the implications and scientific plausibility of their ideas. As BRIAN ALDISS puts it in his excellent history of the genre, *Billion Year Spree* (1973), 'Campbell shunned the "bug-eyed monster" format of pulp science fiction for more elaborate and realistic notions.'

Many motifs and themes of the modern genre were laid down in the pages of *Astounding*. They later went on to become clichés as they were emulated time and again because of their success. Nevertheless, it is fair to say that the genre of today was shaped during these formative years, when many of the giants of science fiction cut their teeth on shorter fiction.

HABITAT
See ARTIFICIAL ENVIRONMENT

HARD SF

A term used to define a particular subgenre of SF that has its basis in real scientific fact and extrapolation.

The phrase was originally coined by P. Schuyler Miller in 1957 to distinguish between SF that was actually dealing with scientific issues and more mainstream fiction that was adopting many of the typical devices of SF.

However, hard SF quickly developed into a subgenre of its own, as more and more writers found themselves under that label. It is now generally accepted that SF that adopts the scientific spirit and looks for a natural, rather than supernatural, solution to a problem can be classified as hard SF. This is not to say that devices such as TELEPORTATION and TIME TRAVEL will not feature in works of hard SF, it is simply that all scientific pathways will be explored to find an explanation, and that extrapolated concepts will be based in real theory.

The term can also be used to differentiate between SF that adopts the 'hard' sciences such as physics, biology and chemistry from SF that tends to have its basis in the 'softer' sciences such as psychology and sociology.

The hard SF form was pioneered in the 1950s by authors such as ARTHUR C. CLARKE and HAL CLEMENT, the latter's *Mission of Gravity* (1954) being typical of the subgenre.

It is concerned with a disc-shaped ALIEN planet, Mesklin, which, due to its peculiar shape, has a particularly varied range of surface gravity. A human probe has crashed near one of the poles and the human protagonists must enlist the aid of the strange Mesklinites in order to retrieve it.

The book is fascinating, if a little dry, and it opened up the way for more authors who wished to use true scientific theory in their fiction.

Other authors who find their work classified as hard SF include STEPHEN BAXTER, GREGORY BENFORD, GREG BEAR, GREG EGAN, PAUL J. McAULEY and KIM STANLEY ROBINSON.

A fine anthology that charts the development of hard SF is *The Ascent of Wonder: The Evolution of Hard Science Fiction* (1994), edited by David Hartwell and Kathryn Cramer.

HARDWARE

In computer terminology, hardware refers to a machine (electronic or otherwise) on which a program or piece of SOFTWARE operates.

In SF this can also refer to ROBOTS and ARTIFICIAL INTELLIGENCE, or even advanced weaponry and IMPLANTS which may have programmable components.

In CYBERPUNK, biological entities, including human beings, are often augmented with pieces of hardware such as computer ports or prosthetic limbs. These people are usually known as CYBORGS.

HORROR

As a genre, horror works well with SF, chiefly because it operates on the fear of the unknown.

The SF repertoire, by definition, contains many unknown aspects, such as ALIEN life forms, ARTIFICIAL INTELLIGENCE and ALTERNATIVE REALITIES, which all marry well with a sense of unease. Indeed, the horrific aspect of most horror stories only comes across in the manner of the telling. With the lights on, everything seems quite normal.

Frankenstein (1818) by MARY SHELLEY, proposed by BRIAN ALDISS as the first true SF novel, also has its basis in Gothic romance. Indeed, this is quite true of much proto-SF – *The Strange Case of Dr Jekyll and Mr Hyde* (1886) by ROBERT LOUIS STEVENSON and much of the writing of EDGAR ALLEN POE, for example. It was not a reaction to the scientific process itself that prompted these authors to write in the vein that they did, but more a fear of the application of science. It is what is done with the knowledge that matters, not the obtaining of the knowledge itself.

As science has grown and become more accepted over the last century, these initial fears have subsided.

However, the motifs of the horror genre at times appear to be interchangeable with those of SF. In *I am Legend* (1954), RICHARD MATHESON describes a world overrun with a disease that induces vampirism. The novel follows the progress of Robert Neville, the last man alive who has not been infected by the plague. Every night he barricades his doors and windows to keep the creatures out.

PETER F. HAMILTON offers a more recent example of horror motifs crossing into SF when a DIMENSIONAL portal is opened up by an ALIEN, allowing the dead to return to possess the living in his Night's Dawn Trilogy.

The combination of horror and SF has also proved fruitful in film. Movies such as Ridley Scott's ALIEN (1979) and John Carpenter's THE THING (1989) both portray encounters with hostile, horrific aliens. *Alien* particularly plays on our fear of being stalked by an unknown and terrifying assailant.

Other classic movies that cross the genre boundaries include the QUATERMASS films, EVENT HORIZON (1997) and SOLARIS (1971).

HUMANIST SF

Humanist SF is a general term which applies to SF that is akin to both LITERARY SF and SOFT SF in that it concentrates on the psychological, emotional and sociological implications of any given situation or action.

Most humanist SF will focus less on the scientific aspects of a story and more on the personal or interpersonal conflicts which arise from events that take place during the course of the plot. Therefore, it can be seen as quite the opposite to HARD SF, although the two are by no means mutually exclusive. It is also fair to say that a fair amount literary SF is at the same time humanist in nature, as it tends to examine in detail the progress of one particular protagonist or character.

A good example is URSULA K. LE GUIN's classic *The Left Hand of Darkness* (1969), in which a delegate from Earth is at first baffled by the hermaphroditic nature of the society he is visiting, before going on to fall in love with one of its members.

The movie GATTACA, in a similar way, is a moving evocation of the personal implications of GENETIC engineering.

This is not to say that humanist SF should be considered anti-science in nature – the protagonist in *The Left Hand of Darkness* learns to adapt along with his changing emotions, whilst Vincent, the 'Non-valid' conspiricist of *Gattaca*, realizes his dream to take part in a mission to Titan.

IMPLANTS

In SF, an implant is a biological, mechanical or electrical component which is fitted into a biological entity (usually human) to replace or improve a bodily function. This can be anything from a pacemaker to a neurological upgrade.

Generally speaking, if a person is greatly modified with a large number of implants, they become known as a CYBORG. However, most implants in SF are on a smaller scale, often involving a replacement eye or a neural socket or interface to allow the recipient to communicate directly with a piece of computer HARDWARE.

Implants are most often found in CYBERPUNK novels, exemplified by characters such as Molly in *Neuromancer* (1984) by WILLIAM GIBSON. She is a dangerous assassin and her implants, such as enhanced artificial eyes and razor blades underneath her fingernails, become the tools of her trade.

On a small scale, implants are already being used for a number of medical purposes. It cannot be long before it becomes morally acceptable for people to begin modifying themselves for professional or recreational purposes.

LITERARY SF

A general term that refers to SF that focuses more on style and character than scientific content. The sciences that do appear in its pages are often the SOFT sciences of psychology and sociology.

Literary SF will usually follow the progress of one particular character or protagonist, developing their emotional involvement with the plot and examining the implications of their, or other people's, actions on a very personal level. This is not to say that writers of literary SF are not concerned with the bigger picture, simply that this form of writing lends itself better to representation on a personal level; the character's situation is probably representative of a greater issue.

A good example of literary SF is M. JOHN HARRISON's *Signs of Life* (1997). The events which take place are viewed through the confused eyes of narrator Mick Rose as he tries to make sense of his lover's desire to fly. Perhaps the dream itself is allegorical, but the GENETIC manipulation involved in her metamorphosis is not; she visits a clinic where they attempt to turn her into a human-bird hybrid. However, this is chiefly the story of Rose and his failure to interface with the reality of the world around him.

GENE WOLFE is also a highly skilled literary craftsman, as his *The Fifth Head of Cerberus* (1972) clearly illustrates. The setting is a colony planet in a distant system where the shape-shifting native ALIENS may or may not have exterminated the colonists and taken their form. The most startling section of the book (it is a fix up of three linked stories) is narrated by one of the colonists who begins to doubt, along with the reader, whether he is actually a colonist at all.

There are many examples of literary SF which also belong to other subgenres. It is not an exclusive subgenre in its own right but, like HUMANIST SF, more of a general tone and style.

MESSIAH
See RELIGION

MILITARISTIC SF

Military forces are often represented in SF, although there are few novels that can actually be labelled 'militaristic'. Perhaps the most obvious of these is ROBERT HEINLEIN's *Starship Troopers* (1959), in which the young protagonists, in an attempt to earn citizenship in a planetary federation, become involved in a war against a hostile insectile species of ALIEN. The book is seen by many to positively sing the praises of a military existence, and it is therefore argued that it betrays Heinlein's rightwing inclinations. Whatever the case, the novel is one of the key books of the militaristic subgenre, and was the inspiration of many other books to come.

More recently, a number of American authors have produced long-running series of novels which follow the progress of characters through the military hierarchy, detailing their exploits along the way. The Seafort Saga by DAVID FEINTUCH, beginning with *Midshipman's Hope* (1994), is a good example of this, and has been described as an SF version of C. S. Forrester's Hornblower books. ELIZABETH MOON has also produced The Serrano Legacy, a long sequence of novels based around a female soldier. They are very similar in nature to The Seafort Saga, and begin with *Hunting Party* (1994).

Other authors to produce militaristic series in much the same way are LOIS MCMASTER BUJOLD and DAVID WEBER.

On the other side of the debate is PETER F. HAMILTON's Night's Dawn trilogy – *The Reality Dysfunction* (1996), *The Neutronium Alchemist* (1997) and *The Naked God* (1999) – which, through a clever plot device, illustrates the inevitability, yet ineffectuality, of war. A freak occurrence means that the dead are returning to possess the living, and a way must be found to control the situation, because the more deaths that occur, the more souls there are to return. Nevertheless, against all common sense, a military campaign is still staged.

Other worthwhile explorations of war include *The Forever War* (1974) by JOE HALDEMAN, *Final Blackout* (1948) by L. RON HUBBARD and *The War of the Worlds* (1898) by H. G. WELLS.

NANOTECHNOLOGY

A hypothetical technology that has also been called 'nanonics'. The term refers to tiny self-replicating machines engineered on an atomic scale, which would be able to work with materials at a molecular level. This provides endless possibilities, the most obvious being the medical applications. The machines would be able to enter a human or animal body to perform delicate microsurgery or repairs. It has also been suggested that eventually they may even be able to slow or even halt the ageing process. This would be effected by having nanomachines in every part of the body, working constantly to keep the body at an optimum.

However, there are many other possibilities: matter could 'easily' be rearranged to create food from discarded substances, ending the world's food shortage; volatile waste products could be safely disposed of; enormous engineering programmes could be tackled in a matter of days; new, deadly weapons could be developed. Many of these possibilities have already been explored in the pages of SF.

IAN MCDONALD describes how nanotechnology could be used to turn people into mindless zombies in *Necroville* (1994), GREG BEAR has a scientist create intelligent cells which he proceeds to inject into himself in *Blood Music* (1985) and PAUL J. McAULEY discusses the biological implications in great depth in *Fairyland* (1995).

Perhaps the most extravagant examination of nanotechnology, however, can be found in *The Diamond Age* (1995) by NEAL STEPHENSON. Here he examines the changes in society in the wake of developing nanotechnology. An élitist class of neo-Victorians have taken charge of Shanghai, and deadly nanomachines fill the air of the wastelands between cities. Against this background, a young girl takes her education from an underground book created by a brilliant nanotechnologist. It is a startlingly imaginative book, and Stephenson manages to maintain the realism throughout.

Nanotechnology already exists in some forms; enzymes are pre-existing, biological nanomachines. However, from a mechanical point of view, scientists have already developed an engine the size of a grain of sand, that can pull a bag of sugar across a table.

NEAR FUTURE

SF that takes as its setting the near or not-too-distant future. This is distinguishable from mainstream fiction by the thematic terms and devices employed. Near future SF creates a world only one step removed from our own; it is credible and plausible and we can see our children inhabiting it. Often the stories can be all the more poignant because of this.

Where FAR FUTURE SF will usually detail an entropic, alien time, near future SF attempts to bring science fiction closer to home and shows us an imminent, fundamental change to our lifestyles, which could be anything from a new technological gadget to an incredible realization of our place in the changing universe.

It is not a new subgenre. Indeed, many of the SCIENTIFIC ROMANCES of H. G. WELLS and JULES VERNE took the near future as a setting, Wells in such books as *The War in the Air* (1908) and *The War of the Worlds* (1898), Verne in *Journey to the Centre of the Earth* (1863) and *Paris in the Twentieth Century* (1994). In this latter book, Verne showed astonishing prescience, predicting the advent of fax machines, cars and pneumatic trains.

However, during the latter half of the twentieth century, the near future became bleaker, more unfriendly. Authors took a more pessimistic stance; these futures were not places we would like to inhabit. This can be traced back to fears of OVERPOPULATION and ECOLOGICAL disaster. Books such as JOHN BRUNNER's *Stand on Zanzibar* (1968) and J. G. BALLARD's *The Drowned World* (1962) are representative of this, as is the rather murky future portrayed in RIDLEY SCOTT's adaptation of PHILP K. DICK's *Do Androids Dream of Electric Sheep?* (1968), BLADE RUNNER. Other near futures were subject to harsh political regimes; FREDERIK POHL and C. M. Kornbluth's *The Space Merchants* (1953) and KEN MACLEOD's *The Star Fraction* (1995) both see their protagonists struggling against oppressive situations (see POLITICAL SF).

Authors such as GREG EGAN and PAUL J. McAULEY envisage a biological revolution just around the corner. Egan examines this best in *Terenesia* (1999) and his many short stories, McAuley in *Fairyland* (1995).

Near future settings have also been used to highlight the strangeness of a particular change the author wishes to make use of. In *The Demolished Man* (1953) by ALFRED BESTER, telepaths and mind readers play an important role in society. Setting this against the backdrop of a near future setting, Bester picks out this anomaly and helps the reader identify with the protagonist, who is not a telepath.

NEW WAVE

The term used to describe a loose movement in SF that promoted experimental fiction during the 1960s. In the United Kingdom this centred around NEW WORLDS magazine under the editorship of MICHAEL MOORCOCK.

New Worlds was already the premier British magazine of speculative fiction when Moorcock took over, focusing on serious SF from the likes of BRIAN ALDISS and J. G. BALLARD; Moorcock instigated a more experimental policy. This experimental fiction shied away from the established themes of pulp SF, instead concerning itself more with mainstream issues such as narrative and character development. Later, a preoccupation with entropy and dissolution evolved, demonstrating a pessimistic streak that did much to counter the blind optimism that had arisen around the technological myth during the GOLDEN AGE.

Moorcock himself published many of his best work in *New Worlds*, including the classic *Behold the Man* (expanded 1969) and his many Jerry Cornelius stories, the latter also being adopted as the basis of a number of SHARED WORLD stories by other contributors.

Writers such as M. JOHN HARRISON and JOHN BRUNNER developed much of their style during the New Wave period, and CHRISTOPHER PRIEST was another British author to become associated with the movement.

Aside from Moorcock's Jerry Cornelius stories, perhaps Aldiss's *Barefoot in the Head* (1969) is the most representative British book of this period.

American contributors to the New Wave included THOMAS DISCH, John Sladek and SAMUEL R. DELANY, with both Disch's *Camp Concentration* (1968) and Delany's 'Time Considered as a Helix of Semi-Precious Stones' (1969) first appearing in the pages of *New Worlds*.

HARLAN ELLISON also picked up on the sensibilities of the New Wave, editing a series of anthologies in the States entitled *Dangerous Visions*, which represented similar concerns to those being discussed in the UK. After the work that appeared in the pages of *New Worlds*, *Dangerous Visions* represented some of the most important writing to come out of the movement.

However, the New Wave was a movement that defies true definition. It has more to do with the shedding of the pulp image and attempting a cross-fertilization with the mainstream than anything truly new. The very nature of this type of experimental fiction demanded a more LITERARY approach, which inevitably led to the more scientific themes falling by the way to make room for the softer sciences such as psychology and sociology.

By the 1970s the movement had more or less been subsumed by genre SF, although many of the lessons and themes were carried forward for later development and the genre as a whole can be seen to have benefited greatly from the movement.

OVERPOPULATION

The late 1960s saw fears about overpopulation come to prominence, both in SF and in society. This was chiefly due to alarmist works of non-fiction such as Paul Ehrlich's *The Population Bomb* (1968).

Fears were founded on an earlier notion that the growth rate of the human race would increase exponentially to the point that all resources would be expended and an ECOLOGICAL catastrophe would occur. This led to speculation about possible methods of population control and resource management.

An early examination of these issues in SF is ROBERT SILVER-BERG'S *Master of Life and Death* (1957), but it was not until a decade later that the theme would be truly explored in great depth.

Make Room! Make Room! (1966) by HARRY HARRISON is one of the finest treatments of the overpopulation theme. It follows the progress of a murder enquiry, set against the seething backdrop of a New York struggling with overcrowding and a lack of resources. It was filmed in 1973 as *Soylent Green*, with Charlton Heston, although the screen version fails to live up to the promise of the book.

A Torrent of Faces (1967) by JAMES BLISH and Norman L. Knight deals with similar themes, although set further into the future at a point where society, still suffering from terrible overcrowding, has managed to stabilise itself.

Logan's Run (1967) by William F. Nolan and George Clayton Johnson is a disturbing projection of the future, to a time in which EUGENICS are used as a means of keeping the population at an optimum.

Perhaps the most satisfactory treatment of the overpopulation issue, however, can be found in JOHN BRUNNER'S *Stand On Zanzibar* (1969), which describes a world overrun with people and on the brink of hysteria. The title is drawn from Brunner's notion that, if stood side-by-side, the human population of the twenty-first century would fill Zanzibar. It is a harsh, DYSTOPIC work, an unforgiving vision of where the human race could be heading, as well as a warning that we must step back and consider the implications of our actions with regard to the planet. Brunner went on to discuss ecological catastrophe in his seminal *The Sheep Look Up* (1972).

Indeed, more authors went on to stress the further implications of an overcrowded planet, the chief concern being that of pollution. Worthy explorations of this can be found in *Earth* (1990) by DAVID BRIN and *Hot Sky at Midnight* (1994) by Robert Silverberg.

More recently, concerns over population control have retreated from the pages of SF, as authors have begun to explore the possibilities of TERRAFORMING other PLANETS, or creating ARTIFICIAL ENVIRONMENTS as a means of containing the human race. It remains to be seen whether any of these theoretical methods will develop sufficiently before the overpopulation issue re-emerges and comes to a head.

PLANETS

Many SF novels take as their setting some alternate world or TERRAFORMED planet – this is often incidental to the actual plot and is done to create a sense of distance or strangeness. This is the case with much early pulp SF or SPACE OPERA; it is not until the advent of real manned space missions to the Moon that planets truly began to feature realistically in SF.

With the Moon being our next nearest galactic body, it is often seen as the first destination for human colonists; current technology would allow us to ship provisions without excessive expense and permanent radio contact could be maintained with the colony. Recently, the discovery of ice on the Moon has done much to fuel speculation that a Moon base could realistically be established in the not-too-distant future.

A Fall of Moondust (1961) by ARTHUR C. CLARKE still remains one of the most successful treatments of the theme. It successfully blends 'disaster' fiction with speculation about human life existing on another planet. The story follows the progress of a group of tourists whose 'boat', the *Selene*, sinks without trace in the dusty Sea of Thirst. The passengers struggle to find ways to survive while the rescue party searches frantically to locate them. It is not one of Clarke's best books, but it does much in describing the conditions on the surface of the Moon.

However, it has been known for some time that the Moon is a 'dead' planet, having long ceased activity, so minds have turned to our next nearest planet, Mars.

For many years it was speculated that life may exist on the Red Planet; it was supposed that the vast tracks that were visible from Earth were in fact canals, that there was frozen water on the surface of the planet, and that arable lands existed between the enormous red deserts.

In *The War of the Worlds* (1898), H. G. WELLS described strange ALIEN invaders who had come from Mars in a ploy to steal Earth from the humans. Wells's novel was all the more plausible as popular belief at the time supported the notion that intelligent life could survive on the planet.

EDGAR RICE BURROUGHS also made Mars the home of his vast SCIENCE FANTASY, the Barsoom sequence.

However, with the landing of the Mariner probes in the 1970s, it became clear that, even if water had at one time run naturally across the surface of Mars, it was now a dry, arid and uninhabited desert. This realization was furthered in the late 1990s with the NASA Pathfinder missions, which succeeded in landing a remotely controlled rover on the Martian soil and gave scientists the opportunity to explore the landing site in great detail. The chances of finding anything actually alive on Mars seem increasing unlikely.

Mars, however, still holds a certain fascination for writers of SF, as it now appears to be the most likely target for any TERRAFORMING project that might take place.

PHILIP K. DICK imagined an early colony on the planet in *Martian Time-Slip* (1964), and PAUL J. McAULEY suggested a means of adapting Mars to our needs in *Red Dust* (1993). It is with KIM STANLEY ROBINSON, however, that we see the first fully worked out HARD SF examination of the terraforming concept. In his Mars trilogy, comprising *Red Mars* (1992), *Green Mars* (1993) and *Blue Mars* (1996), Robinson imagines a gradual process that could lead to Mars becoming a hospitable environment for human beings. Although sometimes held back by heavy prose, the novels succeed in portraying a realistic attempt to colonize the Red Planet, and the scientific, political and emotional considerations that would be involved.

FREDERIK POHL, in *Man Plus* (1976), describes in detail the consequences of taking the alternative approach to terraforming: adapting the human form through augmentation to make it suitable for the hostile environment of Mars.

STEPHEN BAXTER also illustrates how a manned mission to Mars could be carried out using existing NASA equipment and technology in *Voyage* (1996).

Baxter also helped to popularize the notion that there may be other inhabitable planets further out in the Solar System. In *Titan* (1997) he explores the possibilities of finding traces of life on the moon of Saturn. Other authors, such as Arthur C. Clarke, have suggested that other moons such as Jupiter's Europa may hold the key to finding evidence of alien life. This is due to the supposed warm core of the planet that keeps an internal ocean in its fluid state.

Many other planets have been inhabited in the pages of SF. Venus, before it was found to be a hostile, toxic inferno, was imagined to be a lush, verdant paradise.

PETER F. HAMILTON has seen Jupiter mined for precious gases, and Arthur C. Clarke suggested in *2010: Odyssey Two* (1982) that it would be productive to ignite Jupiter in order to create a second Sun for the Solar System.

Of course, the exploration and colonization of other planets in SF has not been restricted to the Solar System; often we see authors inventing entire worlds for their characters to make use of and inhabit.

A classic example of this is FRANK HERBERT'S *Dune* (1965), in which he realizes a full and detailed ECOLOGY for the desert planet, Arrakis. HAL CLEMENT also describes a startling alien environment in *Mission of Gravity* (1954), a hard SF tale that examines the effect of gravity on the EVOLUTION of life when it reaches up to seven hundred times the strength of that on Earth.

BRIAN ALDISS evocatively describes an alien planet in his Helliconia trilogy, beginning with *Helliconia Spring* (1982), whilst ROBERT CHARLES WILSON attempts to colonize an extremely toxic ecosystem in *Bios* (1999).

We also find vast Science Fantasies, such as JACK VANCE'S *The Dying Earth* (1950) and GENE WOLFE's The Book of the New Sun, which, although set on Earth, are vastly alien to us because of the immense stretches of time that have passed. These 'planetary romances', as they are sometimes known, cleverly make use of Earth in an attempt to offer us a glimpse of the distant future.

Indeed, other worlds are the staple of much SF. Through examining the possibilities of life existing on other planets, be it human or alien, it is possible to discuss our place in the universe and to search for solutions to problems such as OVERPOPULATION and pollution, providing us with an allegorical window with which to view ourselves.

POLITICAL SF

As in much mainstream literature, politics can be seen to play a varied role in SF.

As early as 1752, French satirist Voltaire was using ALIENS as a device to comment on Parisian culture and expound his philosophical theory in *Micromegas*. However, it is with H. G. WELLS, pioneer of the SCIENTIFIC ROMANCE, that politics and social commentary truly begin to feature in the pages of science fiction.

Wells was a confirmed libertarian who despised the excesses of Victorian culture. This is reflected in much of his work, particularly in such pieces as *When the Sleeper Wakes* (1899), which has its protagonist wake, after a long period of suspended animation, in the midst of social revolution. He goes on to play a decisive role in the uprising happening around him.

Wells also described his vision of UTOPIA in *The Shape of Things to Come* (1933), although it is not his strongest book and tends to be bogged down with both Wells's agenda and some rather weighty prose. His classic *The War of the Worlds* (1898), however, is a fine example of how Wells made use of his own particular brand of pessimistic commentary. In it, it is not the invaded Victorian society that eventually manages to overcome the Martians, but a simple strain of the common cold; the human beings survive by default. This is still one of the most original and thought-provoking endings in the genre.

As with all literature, SF is often representative of its time. This becomes particularly clear when examining the fiction of the NEW WAVE, which concerns itself with entropy and dissolution and takes as its reference points the defining aspects of 1960s culture.

The feminist movement also made its presence felt in SF, in such tales as *The Female Man* (1975) by Joanna Russ and *The Handmaid's Tale* (1985) by MARGARET ATWOOD. The feminist ideals are well represented by the adoption of SF themes such as GENETICS and EUGENICS, which allow the exploration of GENDER identity to be amplified beyond its usual realms.

However, GEORGE ORWELL's masterful *Nineteen-Eighty-Four* (1949) is without doubt the most outstanding piece of political SF to be written to date. In it, Orwell paints images of a dark, brutal DYSTOPIA. We follow the progress of Winston Smith as he attempts to liberate himself from the system and indulge in an illicit affair with Julia, a co-worker. He is, however, coaxed into giving himself away; he is then subjected to a horrifying and demeaning regime of torture and psychological conditioning. This is Orwell's final blow – the future system has become infallible and the individual becomes meaningless amongst the masses. Similar themes are explored in *We* (1924) by Yevgeny Zamyatin, a book from which it is claimed Orwell drew his ideas. *Animal Farm* (1945), Orwell's earlier political fantasy, is also worthy of mention.

RAY BRADBURY also takes a step towards portraying a political dystopia in *Fahrenheit 451* (1953), a bleak novel which describes a society in which books and written materials have been unconditionally banned. The protagonist works as a 'fireman' – a force employed to seize and destroy all books – who learns to appreciate the beauty and value of the written word.

More recently, a number of authors have attempted to address the political implications of possible future societies, such as those that may exist on TERRAFORMED PLANETS and devolved states.

KIM STANLEY ROBINSON takes great pains to describe the political institutions that evolve during the gradual colonization of Mars in his Mars trilogy. He suggests that many of the age-old political crises that have affected the evolution of civilization on Earth will simply be recreated on any colony planet unless careful measures are taken to avoid them.

KEN MACLEOD uses *The Star Fraction* (1995) to realize his notion of an anarchic state that has nevertheless found a certain degree of stability. He imagines groups of political crusaders forming to help instil their ideals into the society at large.

Politics also plays a role in ALTERNATE WORLD SF. This can be seen in novels such as PHILIP K. DICK'S *The Man in the High Castle* (1962), in which Germany and Japan were successful in conquering America during World War Two. Other examples include the many alternate world settings of HARRY TURTLEDOVE, *Back in the USSA* (1998) by KIM NEWMAN and EUGENE BYRNE and the 'Napoleonic' future which appears in the novels of JON COURTENAY GRIMWOOD.

POST-APOCALYPTIC SF

The post-apocalyptic theme can be found to recur in much SF, be it ECOLOGICAL catastrophe, natural disaster or human-induced holocaust.

As early as 1826, MARY SHELLEY described a world blighted by plague in *The Last Man*, which has her lonely protagonist (very clearly a recasting of her then dead husband, Percy Bysshe Shelley) wander the desolate landscapes of Europe in search of survivors.

Along similar themes is RICHARD MATHESON's *I Am Legend* (1954), a more modern novel in which a disease has swept across the world inducing vampirism throughout the population. We follow the story of the last 'normal' human being left alive as he is hounded nightly by neighbours hungry for his blood.

Taking a slightly less pessimistic approach to the same topic, GEORGE R. STEWART's *Earth Abides* (1949) is an allegorical tale which details the gradual return of nature as Earth's presiding power as humanity is decimated by a deadly plague.

However, although these tales can be said to have been born from a certain degree of paranoia, it was not until the advent of the atomic age and the devastating effects it had during World War Two that the post-apocalyptic theme really began to develop.

WALTER MILLER's *A Canticle for Leibowitz* (1959), arguably the most outstanding of all post-war SF novels, describes the gradual reformation of civilization after a nuclear holocaust. An order of monks discovers and preserves some relics from the pre-holocaust age; this sets off a chain of events that leads to a cyclical repetition of history.

DAVID BRIN's *The Postman* (1985) is a later exploration of the same theme, in which one character adopts the role of 'postman', spreading information and communications between separated enclaves of survivors after a nuclear war. He eventually aids in the slow rebuilding of civilization.

This type of human-induced holocaust tale is often based on an almost contradictory set of morals; the initial warning is of man's foolishness and ignorance in the face of nuclear technology, but the novels also champion the human spirit and show how humanity will win through and survive the disaster brought about by an ignorant minority.

Other catastrophes come in the form of ecological disasters.

J. G. BALLARD's loose quartet of novels, *The Drowned World* (1962), *The Burning World* (1964), *The Crystal World* (1966) and *The Wind From Nowhere* (1962), all take as their setting some form of elemental disaster that has left the world blighted; they do much to confirm Ballard's reputation as a pessimist, but also as a novelist of remarkable integrity. The best of these, *The Drowned World*, describes a London submerged by tropical swamps in which the plant life is reverting to a pre-ice-age state.

The Death of Grass (1956) by John Christopher is another intelligent take on the natural catastrophe; it follows the struggle of humanity to survive after the world's grass and cereal crops have been rendered extinct.

POST HOLOCAUST
See POST–APOCALYPTIC SF

RELIGION

There are those who believe that science, by its very nature, refutes religion. There are others who believe it does not. Others still take a more philosophical point of view, arguing that both science and religion are valid occupations in the search for universal meaning.

Whatever the case, religion has been expressed in SF in many different ways, including exploration of the religious experience, the study of the MESSIAH complex and the use of religion as a sociological framework.

In his 1937 novel *Starmaker*, OLAF STAPLEDON provides his narrator with a universal perspective which encompasses the progress of sentient life over billions of years. During this epic visualization we are witness to all manner of human and ALIEN life, but it is with his depiction of the 'Starmaker' himself, a scientifically inclined God figure who is constantly toying with the universe, that Stapledon truly breaks new ground. It is more often the case that SF mirrors life in the portrayal of God; He is absent, leaving the human or alien protagonists to ponder their religious inclinations without answer.

JAMES BLISH, in his classic *A Case of Conscience* (1958), describes the conflict of a Jesuit priest who is confronted with sentient life on an alien planet. When faced with the realization that these aliens have no concept of God, he is drawn to the conclusion that they must be creations of the Devil.

Adopting similar themes is MARY DORIA RUSSELL's *The Sparrow* (1997), which describes tentative first contact with an alien species. The Jesuit scientist who is sent to the alien world learns more about himself and his humanity than he does about the souls of his alien counterparts. Again, God remains aloof.

The depiction of God Himself may be rare in the pages of SF, but there are those who have attempted to portray the religious experience.

PHILIP K. DICK, towards the end of his life, believed himself to have been party to a pseudo–religious experience. He recorded his thoughts in the autobiographical novel *Valis* (1981) – the Vast Active Living Intelligence System. In it, Dick portrays a remarkable evocation of a man struggling to come to terms with a new perspective of the world.

Cult religion plays a large part in some of Dick's best work, including *The Three Stigmata of Palmer Eldritch* (1964) and the famous, *Do*

Androids Dream of Electric Sheep? (1968), in which a new cult has been adopted by much of the world's remaining populace. Towards the end of the novel, the protagonist, Deckard, comes to realize that the figurehead of this new cult may in fact be an impostor. There is also a strain of interpretation which suggests that, ambiguously, Deckard comes to view himself as his own MESSIAH. This exploration of religion is secondary only to Dick's fundamental discussion of ANDROIDS and ARTIFICIAL INTELLIGENCE.

Indeed, the messianic impulse is well represented in SF.

Perhaps the most startling study of this can be found in MICHAEL MOORCOCK's *Behold the Man* (1969). It follows the progress of social misfit Karl Glogauer as he travels backwards in an experimental TIME machine to the epoch of Christ. However, once there he discovers a mentally retarded Jesus and, finding no one else to fulfil the legend, adopts the messianic role himself. Glogauer is horrifically crucified to ensure the perpetuation of the Christian faith.

ROBERT HEINLEIN also explored the messianic impulse in his *Stranger in a Strange Land* (1961), in which the chief protagonist, Valentine Michael Smith, returns to Earth from his adoptive Mars equipped with supernatural powers. He goes on to become a pseudo-messianic figure.

FRANK HERBERT, in his seminal SPACE OPERA *Dune* (1965) detailed the process by which a child could be elevated to the position of messianic saviour of a culture by virtue of his mystical and spiritual insight into the plight of the people. It is a bold and important study of religion and the way in which it can shape the entire progress and development of a culture by way of its belief structure.

English theologian C. S. LEWIS, most famous for his children's fantasy The Chronicles of Narnia, also wrote a trilogy of SF novels. The Cosmic Trilogy, beginning with *Out of the Silent Planet* (1938), is an allegorical tale that begins well but unfortunately descends into rather heavy-handed Christian apologetics.

A Canticle for Leibowitz (1959) by WALTER MILLER takes an interesting look at the religious institution, as well as seeing the monastic orders as protectorates of the human race. The novel begins in a POST-APOCALYPTIC setting in which a nuclear war has taken place. An order of monks studies and preserves any and all remaining scientific knowledge. This eventually leads to a recurrence of the fateful events that led to the original downfall.

ROGER ZELAZNY has also expertly explored Eastern religion and mysticism in his *Lord of Light* (1967). The colonization of a distant PLANET becomes a re-enactment of the Indian myths. Another, more recent, attempt to discuss the same themes is *Shiva 3000* (2000) by JAN LARS JENSEN.

It should also be noted that GOLDEN AGE author L. RON HUBBARD went on to found his own, highly controversial religion known as Scientology. This has been adopted by a number of high-profile personalities, including fellow SF writer A. E. VAN VOGT and actor JOHN TRAVOLTA.

ROBOT

The term Robot usually refers to a machine created by human beings to perform some specific task or function. Usually this will involve some form of manual labour or monotonous assembly-line work in a factory. In SF, the term also has close affiliations with the terms ANDROID and ARTIFICIAL INTELLIGENCE.

The word robot was first used in this context to describe a series of organically created workers who had been developed to carry out forced labour in Karel Capek's play *R. U. R.* (1922). These beings, in reality, are more akin to androids than the robots of SF.

However, it is the image of the humanoid machine in Fritz Lang's seminal movie METROPOLIS (1926) which persists in the genre today, as most writers accept the difference between a biological android and a mechanical or electrical robot.

For many years after *Metropolis*, authors portrayed their robots as either artificial men or women created specifically for the purposes of evil tasks, or as marauding household appliances that would turn on their human masters without question.

It was not until ISAAC ASIMOV began his sequence of Robot stories, and developed the three laws of robotics, that robots were imbued with real artificial intelligence and became proper characters struggling to find an identity.

However, it was not long before writers saw these intelligent robots turning on their masters as well, only this time for different reasons – they wished to break away from their lives as oppressed slaves and be free to develop and evolve as they pleased. This led a number of writers to suggest that, eventually, the human form may be superseded by that of the robot. GREGORY BENFORD, in his Galactic Centre sequence, sees a future in which humans are at war with the highly evolved flesh-hating machines that they have created. Similar themes are still tackled in both literature and film. THE MATRIX (1999), one of the hit films of recent years, portrays robots as dangerous Frankenstein-like creations that will eventually eliminate the human spirit.

Society's technophobia can be measured by looking at how the opinions of robots have changed in SF over the years. New developments occur every day in the real world, but as yet we cannot create walking, talking, self-aware machines. Some authors would have us believe that we never should, whilst others believe it will be the next step forward in evolution. Only time will tell.

SCIENCE FANTASY

A term used to describe a subgenre of SF that makes use of fantastical imagery and tends not to have its basis in real scientific theory. However, science fantasy is a term that has never been truly defined. As a genre it does not necessarily adopt all the characteristics of either science fiction or fantasy, and rather sits somewhere between the two.

JACK VANCE's *The Dying Earth* (1950) is a classic example of this, although it does tend to sit more comfortably with the fantasy genre than with SF. It describes an Earth grown inextricably ancient, in which magic has replaced science. In it, Vance set the tone for many FAR FUTURE novels to come; the fragmentary, crumbling landscape, the Sun swollen and red, the image of a planet on the verge of death.

The Dying Earth was to having a major and lasting influence on GENE WOLFE's The Book of the New Sun, an epic four-volume sequence that adopts a similar setting and is perhaps the best work to be associated with the science fantasy genre. However, although Wolfe does make use of the fantastical in his portrayal of the far future, everything is eventually explained in terms of scientific logic and the novel is more truly defined as science fiction.

M. JOHN HARRISON deconstructs the sword and sorcery genre in his Viriconium sequence, collected as *Viriconium* (2000), when he uses its classic imagery as a literary device to describe a POST-APOCALYPTIC future.

At least part of the success of FRANK HERBERT's *Dune* (1965) can be put down to his ability to blend the feel of a fantasy saga with what is, upon further examination, an explicit SPACE OPERA. Herbert describes a pseudo-medieval empire, composed of barons and dukes, which nevertheless spans galaxies and is technologically advanced. This defunct hierarchical structure becomes instrumental in the development of the plot.

MICHAEL MOORCOCK's Dancers at the End of Time trilogy is fundamentally a satirical fantasy, but also plunders science fiction, being partly set in a distant far future and making use of devices such as TIME TRAVEL.

The movie STAR WARS and its sequels can also be viewed as science fantasy; the images employed are those of warrior monks (Jedi) who battle against evil with the aid of magic (the Force). However, magic and technology are not mutually exclusive – the Jedi use light sabres and laser guns to aid them in their plight. It is this cross-pollination that perhaps best defines science fantasy as a subgenre. A willingness to employ devices and images taken from a combined pool of resources, creates a hybrid that is neither standard fantasy nor standard science fiction.

SCIENTIFIC ROMANCE

The scientific romance was a form of early SF that was pioneered by writers such as JULES VERNE and H. G. WELLS during the latter part of the nineteenth century.

The term itself is a misnomer, as there is little in the way of romance involved in the tales themselves. Nevertheless, it is perhaps the first incarnation of SF as self-aware genre, as opposed to the Gothic romance of such novels as MARY SHELLEY's *Frankenstein* (1818).

Verne's early scientific romances, or 'Fantastic Voyages' mark the real beginning of SF, with such novels as *Journey to the Centre of the Earth* (1863) and *From the Earth to the Moon* (1865). However, it is with Wells that we truly see the genre come into its own.

Wells published *The Time Machine* in 1895, and *The War of the Worlds* in 1898, and this was to bring about a new era in the development of the SF genre. His works inspired many other authors to adopt similar devices and eventually led HUGO GERNSBACK to produce AMAZING STORIES magazine, giving birth to the SF field that we know today.

As pulp SF began to take root in America, British writers continued to produce SF that was akin to scientific romance right up until the 1960s and the advent of the NEW WAVE movement. Indeed, some nostalgic examples of the medium are still produced today, examples including STEPHEN BAXTER's *Anti-Ice* (1993) and CHRISTOPHER PRIEST's *The Space Machine* (1976).

Scientific romance was, in many ways, SF under an earlier name. Wells made use of scientific devices and speculation to produce his tales, at the same time going on to examine the consequences of his ideas and the effect that they would have upon the society of the time.

SENSE OF WONDER

A term usually associated with the GOLDEN AGE of SF and the pulp magazines prevalent at that time.

It refers to the sense of inspired awe that is aroused in a reader when the full implications of an event or action become realized, or when the immensity of a plot or idea first becomes known.

Many critics believe the term to be outdated and with no frame of reference, arguing that most, if not all, of the 'Big Ideas' of SF have already been explored. (Thus the association of the term with Golden Age SF, a period when many of the genre's themes were first explored). However, it is also fair to say that new and developing technologies allow for new notions and revelations, which can in turn lead to their own 'Big Ideas'. This is often the case with much modern HARD SF, which brings cutting-edge science into the realm of science fiction.

The term has been used by a number of modern reviewers when describing particularly innovative or outstanding new works such as PETER F. HAMILTON's Night's Dawn Trilogy, beginning with *The Reality Dysfunction* (1995).

Other authors associated with this type of awe inspiring SF also tend to be associated with SPACE OPERA or the early SF of the 1930s, 1940s and 1950s, and include A. E. VAN VOGT, EDGAR RICE BURROUGHS, E. E. 'DOC' SMITH, as well as more literary authors such as ROBERT HEINLEIN and OLAF STAPLEDON.

SHARED WORLD

A shared world is an environment or set of characters created by an author with the specific intention of letting other writers produce work within its framework. This work will often vary in quality and style, but will always be associated with the original scenario or characters in some way.

Fine examples of shared world SF include MICHAEL MOORCOCK's Jerry Cornelius sequence, which features stories by a number of popular NEW WAVE writers, and LARRY NIVEN's Man-Kzin Wars sequence, which although set within his famous Tales of Known Space framework is comprised of short stories by other hands.

SOFT SF

Soft SF is a very ambiguous term, which is generally accepted to refer to SF that makes use of the 'softer' sciences such as psychology and sociology. It was coined chiefly to complement and clarify the phrase HARD SF, which is used to describe SF that focuses in great detail on the traditional sciences such as physics, chemistry and biology. Soft and hard SF should not, however, be considered polar opposites.

Soft SF usually entails a more LITERARY or character-driven approach; the scientific aspects of the story may not be fully worked out. Perhaps this is part of the influence of the NEW WAVE movement which took place during the 1960s, in which a cross-fertilization with the mainstream led to the adoption in SF of many of the more mainstream concerns.

ALFRED BESTER's *The Demolished Man* (1953) is a fine example of a soft SF novel, examining as it does the sociological implications of a world saturated by telepathy and mind reading. In it, non-telepathic protagonist Ben Reich attempts to plot and execute a murder, at the same time trying to avoid discovery by the telepathic community. The novel is stylish and rich in characterization, but the mechanics of the mental powers are not explored, the author preferring to concentrate on the emotional aspects of his story.

Much of the work of PHILIP K. DICK also explores the softer sciences, or rather brushes over the more detailed scientific aspects of his plots or environments.

Other authors who could be considered to have written soft SF novels include THOMAS M. DISCH, Michael Bishop and J. G. BALLARD.

SOFTWARE

The term used to describe, in computer technology, the program that runs or operates on a machine or piece of HARDWARE. It is usually developed by a software programmer or engineer and tends to be created for a specific purpose.

In SF the term can also refer to the neural net or digital coding that constitutes an AI, or ARTIFICIAL INTELLIGENCE. This has led to speculation by some psychologists that the human mind may in fact be an incredibly complex piece of software which operates within the confines of the brain, a unit of biological hardware. Artificial intelligence is wonderfully explored in the novel *Dreaming in Smoke* (1998) by TRICIA SULLIVAN.

Interesting examinations of software include MICHAEL MOORCOCK's *The Final Programme* (1968), which tells of a power-crazed woman who is attempting to run 'the final programme' on her enormous underground computer, and KEN MACLEOD's *The Star Fraction* (1995), which charts the EVOLUTION of a self-aware program called the Watchmaker.

SPACE

The vacuum that exists outside Earth's protective atmosphere.

Space is peppered with planetary bodies and clouds of various gases, some of which have ignited to bring about STARS. It is thought that the universe is the result of an explosion, the Big Bang, which is still taking place, and that it consists of a single-sided object that is in the process of expanding in every direction at once.

What exists outside the vacuum we call space is still unknown.

SPACE TRAVEL between planetary bodies has already taken place but, for prolonged periods of flight, new forms of STARSHIP will have to be designed to allow enough food and oxygen to be taken with the astronauts.

SPACE OPERA

A subgenre of SF that has its roots in the pulp origins of SF, and derives its name from the term soap opera.

In many ways, early space opera was very much the soap opera of the genre, with an emphasis on adventure and narrative drive over any attempt at realism or the exploration of issues. Indeed, the space opera of writers such as E. E. 'DOC' SMITH, who made his name writing gung-ho space adventures in the 1930s, is perhaps more akin to fantasy than true SF. Nevertheless, it helped bring about the genre that we know today, and added a welcome dimension of fun to what at times appeared to be rather dry examples of early science fiction.

Latterly, space opera has been going through a revival of sorts, but it has been totally reinvented for the modern day, developing a strategy for dealing with real issues and making use of scientific speculation as a way of adding a touch of realism to the adventures it describes. Good modern examples of the genre include PETER F. HAMILTON's Night's Dawn Trilogy, IAIN M. BANK's Culture sequence and DAVID FEINTUCH's Seafort Saga.

SPACE TRAVEL

The navigation of SPACE is a theme that is explored in the vast majority of SF novels and stories. From the use of modern technology to get us to the Moon and Mars, to vast interstellar GENERATION STARSHIPS, to quick and nimble faster-than-light vessels, to wormhole and space-time manipulation, SF authors have seen travel through space as a fundamental stepping stone on the road into the future.

Many early pulp and SPACE OPERA stories made light of the comings and goings of interstellar craft, and it is not until the almost banal functionality of ROBERT HEINLEIN's *Rocket Ship Galileo* (1947) and ARTHUR C. CLARKE's *Prelude to Space* (1951) that we see a true attempt to describe the boundaries that had to be crossed before mankind would ever make it into space.

With the Apollo space programme in the 1960s, and the eventual landing of man on the Moon, there was a change in the way that SF began to look at travel through space. A realistic attempt to describe the monotony and routine of space travel became the norm, and voyages within the Solar System began to be described in terms of real, modern technology. This is exemplified nowhere better than in Stanley Kubrick's seminal movie, 2001: A SPACE ODYSSEY (1968).

Nevertheless, with the understanding of Einstein's general theory of relativity, there was a distinct shift in the way in which authors saw space travel unfolding in the future. If it was going to be impossible to surpass the speed of light, then other ways had to be found to get humanity to the stars.

Generation starships were filled with astronauts and their families and sent off to distant star systems where they would eventually be able to settle and colonize. Invariably, however, the descendants of the original crew would 'forget' they were on a starship altogether, and have to pass through a revelation to allow them to finally achieve the aims of the mission.

Other ingenious ways of traversing the void were suggested. In *Tau Zero* (1970), POUL ANDERSON describes how a spacecraft may latch on to a passing asteroid which it will then use to power it for the rest of its long journey. Other authors skipped over the problem entirely, having their vessels pass through hyperspace with little or no explanation as to how.

More recently, however, authors have looked to quantum physics as a means of supplying the necessary theory by which their space vessels can pass amongst the stars. Wormhole manipulation – the use of 'holes' through space–time – would allow them to travel across vast distances in a matter of minutes. The interface into such a network of tunnels and pathways is usually thought of as being the event horizon of a BLACK HOLE.

Still other authors, such as ALASTAIR REYNOLDS in his *Revelation Space* (2000), maintain that Einstein's laws cannot be broken and that space travel will be bound by the rules of relativity for ever.

Whatever the case, it seems sure that for as long as SF exists, its characters will be travelling through space, encountering all manner of strange and outlandish phenomenon and meeting a variety of bizarre ALIEN life forms. For as long as SF has existed, humanity has desired to reach out into space. In SF it can do so, and one of the most optimistic aspects of the genre is the manner in which it envisages a human future amongst the stars. Indeed, it seems ever more possible that scientists will eventually begin to look to SF as a provider of notions and ideas that may aid the future development of interstellar vessels.

STARS

A star is a gaseous body consisting chiefly of hydrogen and helium in a state of fusion.

The stars appear in the night sky as distant points of light because they are so far away from the Earth. Our own Sun is the most readily recognizable star in the sky.

Stars, although there is a certain poetical reference to them in much science fiction, do not actually feature in much depth in most SF stories. There are a couple of notable exceptions.

ISAAC ASIMOV, in his classic short story 'Nightfall', describes the catastrophic effects upon society that the sudden appearance of stars in the sky could bring about. In the story, scientists studying the cyclical collapse of civilization on a PLANET with a binary star system which maintains a perpetual daylight become aware that they are nearing the end of the most recent cycle. The planet is due to pass through a period of total eclipse, and darkness will descend on the landscape for the first time in two thousand years. It causes devastation, but not because of the darkness, but because of the realization that there are millions of other suns out there in the night sky.

ARTHUR C. CLARKE produced a similar story of revelation, 'The Star', in which space travellers discover that the Star of Bethlehem was in fact a distant supernova, and in the process refute the claims of RELIGION.

STEPHEN BAXTER, in his two novels *Flux* (1993) and *Ring* (1994), describes in exquisite detail the interior of a star and the possible future colonization of some its outer layers by engineered organisms.

GENE WOLFE in *The Urth of the New Sun* (1987) describes the process by which a dying FAR FUTURE Earth could be resuscitated by the introduction of a white hole to the Solar System.

However, in the main, the stars themselves remain relatively untouched in the pages of SF, and exist simply as a means of providing light and warmth to planets they we may wish to visit or colonize.

STARSHIP
See SPACE TRAVEL and GENERATION STARSHIP

STEAMPUNK
A bastardization of the term CYBERPUNK, used to describe a modern subgenre of SF that places technological developments within an historical framework and attempts to assess their impact on the progress of past events.

MICHAEL MOORCOCK is one of the early proponents of this type of story, as his Oswald Bastable Trilogy, collected as *A Nomad of the Time Streams*, sees its chief protagonist thrust into an Edwardian future dominated by enormous airships and republican terrorists.

The Difference Engine (1990) by WILLIAM GIBSON and BRUCE STERLING, however, is perhaps the most important steampunk novel yet to be produced, and sees a nineteenth-century London pulled kicking and screaming into an industrial future when Charles Babbage's early mechanical computer is successfully built.

PAUL J. McAULEY has also gone further back in time to describe an industrial Renaissance period brought about by the successful manufacturing of Leonardo da Vinci's devices in *Pasquale's Angel* (1994).

TELEPORTATION
A term used to describe the instantaneous transference of matter from one place to another. In SF this usually entails breaking down the matter to its constituent components and then rebuilding it at some other, predestined, point.

However, the theory behind this concept raises some interesting questions: once living matter has been transported and rebuilt, will life processes continue, and if the mind is separate from the brain, will it be transferred as well?

Many examples of teleportation in SF skirt around these questions, and it becomes a simple device for just moving characters from one place to another. It is unlikely that teleportation will ever become a reality and for this reason it does not frequently appear in the pages of modern SF. There are, however, some very interesting examinations of the subject.

In *The Stars My Destination* (1956), ALFRED BESTER describes how a character left to die in space by his employers learns the ability to 'jaunt', and uses it to his advantage to seek revenge on those who left him for dead.

JOHN BARNES, in his *A Million Open Doors* (1992), posits a society in which teleportation has opened up the barriers between civilized worlds, and his leading protagonist must journey to a distant colony PLANET to help them cope with the new changes to their culture.

In visual SF there has been a tendency to make use of teleportation as a convenient narrative device as well as an impressive special effect. This is particularly true of STAR TREK, in which the method of matter transference is highly implausible but continues to appear in nearly every episode. It was originally included in the series because it was too expensive to keep producing sequences in which spacecraft shuttle people from orbit to the PLANET they are visiting.

Matter transference was slightly more realistically explored in David Cronenberg's remake of the 1950s movie, THE FLY (1986), in which the protagonist accidentally combines his GENETIC material with that of a fly.

TERRAFORMING

To terraform a PLANET is to make it like Earth (Terra). The term refers to the scientific speculation that human beings could adapt another planetary surface to create a habitable space that would be acceptable to the Earth's life forms.

Many planets have been suggested in SF, but Mars is the most frequently cited example, as it is relatively near to Earth and would still benefit from the warming effects of the Sun. The process by which Mars could be adapted to suit human and plant life was classically explored by KIM STANLEY ROBINSON in his Mars trilogy, beginning with *Red Mars* (1992) and continuing with *Green Mars* (1993) and *Blue Mars* (1996). The titles of the series refer to the gradual changes which will take place on the surface of the planet as it comes to develop into a living biosphere.

Other writers have suggested that planets such as Venus, or the outer moons of Jupiter and Saturn would also be good contenders for a terraforming project.

TIME

Time is the linear process by which human beings perceive a sequence of events.

It is thought that the process of time is somehow connected to SPACE and that together they form a negotiable DIMENSION known as space-time. To be able to breach or manipulate this dimension would allow a person to revisit a previous event in the course of history, or else, perhaps more unlikely, visit the events of the future. On occasions such as these the course of events could be altered, and whilst some physicists see space-time as a resilient construct, others see it as ultimately fragile, and that any interference with events already passed would create a fundamental failure in the nature of the universe and a breakdown of reality as we know it.

Early fantasy and pulp stories often had their characters fall into a deep, centuries-long slumber that would see them awaken a number of years in the future. This form of 'hibernation', aside from the fantastical 'time-slip', was the only way in which protagonists could be moved through time to a future event.

However, in modern SF, space-time is frequently manipulated by adventurers who have developed time machines that allow them to inhabit the time streams that exist between realities.

The most famous use of a time machine in SF has to be H. G. WELLS's seminal novel, *The Time Machine* (1895), which sees its Victorian protagonist move forward in time to a point when the human race has evolved into two distinct subspecies. He then carries on forward in time to witness the death of the Solar System before returning to his own time to recite his tale to his fellows. The book was imaginatively followed by a sequel, *The Time Ships* (1995) by STEPHEN BAXTER, who used complex quantum physics to explain the shifting, multiplying paradoxes that follow the time traveller as he navigates through time.

This idea has found much use in SF – ROBERT HEINLEIN comically showed how a time traveller could travel backwards in time to become his own father in *Time Enough for Love* (1973), whilst KURT

VONNEGUT, in *Slaughterhouse Five* (1969), illustrated how ALIENS might consider time in a non-linear fashion, so that death does not become the end of existence, but simply another event in the journey of a person's life.

The television series DOCTOR WHO is also founded on the premise that space-time is a negotiable dimension that can be traversed at one's leisure.

Recognizing the implications of Einstein's general theory of relativity, it came to be considered that SPACE TRAVEL itself would effectively become a method of travelling into the future, as travelling at speeds near the speed of light would mean that the time which passes on board the space vessel would be greatly amplified on any PLANETS. Therefore, a round trip of the Solar System at light speed would mean that everyone the astronauts ever knew would be long dead before they arrived home. Without the aid of a time machine there would theoretically be no means by which the astronauts could travel back to their own time. These themes were explored in excellent detail in *The Forever War* (1974) by JOE HALDEMAN, in which a group of soldiers travelling out to the distant war return home to find the human race changed beyond recognition.

TRANSCENDENCE

A means by which humanity could eventually achieve enlightenment and surpass their current restrictions to become something greater. Usually this entails leaving behind the flesh to become some form of spiritual entity, but it can also be seen as the means by which a person may break out of an oppressive political or social regime.

Perhaps the best example of transcendence in SF can be seen in ARTHUR C. CLARKE's *Childhood's End* (1953), which describes how ALIEN visitors arrive on Earth to help guide the human race through the next stage of EVOLUTION and on to the next plane of existence. The moment in which the last human beings watch the final stages of the racial transformation is both beautiful and emotive.

The movie 2001: A SPACE ODYSSEY (1968), based on a Clarke short story, also sees its chief protagonist transcend his biological roots when he passes through the stargate and is reborn as something different and new.

Other authors have seen human transcendence in a different light. GREG BEAR in his recent *Darwin's Radio* (1999) envisages how the human race will painfully give literal birth to a new GENETIC species, whilst GREG EGAN in *Permutation City* (1994) sees humanity abandoning the physical form and adopting a form of electronic immortality in VIRTUAL REALITY. IAIN M. BANKS in various novels in his Culture sequence also alludes to how a number of his alien races have 'sublimed' and abandoned this universe to become demigods.

A different form of transcendence can be seen, however, in MARGARET ATWOOD's *The Handmaid's Tale* (1985), in which the oppressed female character revolts against the totalitarian regime and brings about her own freedom. Whether this is through escape or death is never made clear.

UTOPIA

The hypothetical POLITICAL state first ironically described by Thomas Moore in his classic *Utopia* (1516).

Utopia is an ideal state of civilization and society that exists in perfect harmony with itself. It is thought to be purely theoretical as human nature would never allow for such a transcendental state to exist. Most utopian fiction is in actual fact anti-utopian or DYSTOPIAN, in that it stresses how the utopian state is a fundamentally unsound ideal, and that even when it is thought to have been achieved, the members of the society who believe they are living in the utopian state are not, and it is only their ignorance that blinkers their perception of reality. It is difficult to imagine a society in which everyone is satisfied and fulfils their human potential. Indeed, Moore himself was satirizing his contemporary political systems when he developed the notion, which in reality has more in common with concepts of Heaven and RELIGIOUS states than it does with real politics.

There are many examples in SF of utopias that have failed, or are indeed political states that are masquerading as utopias, some of them being *The Dispossessed* (1974) by URSULA K. LE GUIN, *Jem* (1979) by FREDERIK POHL and *Island* (1962) by ALDOUS HUXLEY. This latter books attempts wholeheartedly to portray a real utopia, but fails to convince even the most optimistic reader of the reality of its notions and ideas.

The phrase dystopia was coined to provide a direct opposite to utopia, to describe societies that have disintegrated to a state which is far worse than our own.

VIRTUAL REALITY

Virtual reality has become one of the staple tools of the CYBERPUNK genre. It describes a form of digitally constructed ALTERNATIVE REALITY which usually exists in the realms of CYBERSPACE and can be interfaced through a computer.

Often, as in WILLIAM GIBSON's *Neuromancer* (1984), the protagonists can plug their nervous system directly into the virtual domain, allowing them to experience every sensation as if the virtual world was another version of reality. Indeed, many stories sees characters completely lose themselves in the virtual realms, some even 'forgetting' that an entirely separate version of reality exists on the outside. The protagonist in *Neuromancer* uses virtual reality as a tool to commit information crimes, but he is also addicted to its shifting sense of reality. In some ways, the virtual world he prefers to inhabit is more satisfactory than the corporate DYSTOPIA that the real world has become.

In *Permutation City* (1994), GREG EGAN suggests an alternative use for virtual reality technology, and the means by which it may be used to construct an entirely new and exotic universe. His character first downloads a copy of himself into this digital reality, and then commits suicide in the real world as he feels he has achieved his aim and the 'real' him now exists in the electronic framework.

TAD WILLIAMS uses virtual reality in his Otherland sequence to rationalize the use of a fantasy world. His characters are left to explore this fantastical realm, but the premise remains science fictional – they are stuck within a complex computer-generated reality.

Some authors also see virtual reality as the means by which we will eventually communicate with our own ARTIFICIAL INTELLIGENCE creations, a common ground within which both the human and the computer can manifest themselves as they please. This was exemplified recently in the excellent *New York Nights* (2000) by ERIC BROWN.

Like many alternative reality stories, virtual reality provides authors with a means of enabling the more fantastical elements of their stories to become rationalized in terms of science fiction. This in turn allows the SF subtext to be maintained whilst the characters make use of virtual worlds both fantastic and strange.

WORMHOLE

See SPACE TRAVEL

Societies and Awards

ARTHUR C. CLARKE AWARD

An award set up by ARTHUR C. CLARKE to celebrate the best SF novel published in its British first edition the previous year.

The award is administered jointly by the SCIENCE FICTION FOUNDATION and the BRITISH SCIENCE FICTION ASSOCIATION, and a panel of six judges decide first a six-book short list, then a winner. The winner is awarded with a plaque and a cheque. The award began in 1987.

The previous ten years winners are listed below.

1990 *The Child Garden* by GEOFF RYMAN
1991 *Take Back Plenty* by COLIN GREENLAND
1992 *Synners* by PAT CADIGAN
1993 *Body of Glass* by Marge Piercy
1994 *Vurt* by JEFF NOON
1995 *Fools* by PAT CADIGAN
1996 *Fairyland* by PAUL J. McAULEY
1997 *The Calcutta Chromosome* by Amitav Ghosh
1998 *The Sparrow* by MARY DORIA RUSSELL
1999 *Dreaming in Smoke* by TRICIA SULLIVAN
2000 *Distraction* by BRUCE STERLING

The Arthur C. Clarke Award is Britain's most prestigious genre award.

BRITISH SCIENCE FICTION ASSOCIATION

The *British Science Fiction Association* is a national organization which aims to provide both writers and fans with a suitable outlet for their musings, as well as providing support to local fan groups and initiatives for bigger genre projects.

The association was formed in the late 1950s, and ever since has continued to produce an invaluable quarterly journal, *Vector*, as well as various other minor publications such as *Matrix* and *Focus*. This latter aims to encourage new genre writers and provide them with a support structure upon which they can test their ideas.

Since the 1970s the association has been primarily concerned with the running of the BRITISH SCIENCE FICTION AWARDS which it instigated after the success of the earlier *British Fantasy Awards*. This is an annual democratic award that is voted for by members of the society.

The *British Science Fiction Association* is an important aspect of UK fandom, and as such benefits from a thriving membership. Its quarterly journal is full of worthwhile articles and book reviews, and its various other projects, such as the British Science Fiction Awards, help to enrich the genre and provide readers and fans with a means of making their voices heard.

The association maintains a website at http://www.members.aol.com/tamaranth/

Membership enquires can also be made to Membership Secretary, 1 Long Row Close, Everdon, Daventry, Northamptonshire NN11 3BE, UNITED KINGDOM

BRITISH SCIENCE FICTION AWARD

An annual award administered by the BRITISH SCIENCE FICTION ASSOCIATION and voted for by its members. The award was originally given in four categories – Novel, Short Story, Media and Artist – and, like the NEBULA AWARDS, maintains the date of first publication (i.e.: the awards given in 2000 are classified as the 1999 awards, as this is the year that the winning entrants first appeared). However, in 1992 the media category was dropped in favour of making the award a more literary based exercise.

The winners from the previous ten years are listed below.

1990
Novel *Take Back Plenty* by COLIN GREENLAND
Short Story 'The Original Doctor Shade' by KIM NEWMAN
Media *Twin Peaks*
Artist Ian Miller

1991
Novel *The Fall of Hyperion* by Dan Simmons
Short Story 'Bad Timing' by Molly Brown

Media TERMINATOR 2: JUDGEMENT DAY
Artist Mark Harrison

1992
Novel *Red Mars* by KIM STANLEY ROBINSON
Short Story 'The Innocents' by Ian McDonald
Artist JIM BURNS

1993
Novel *Aztec Century* by Christopher Evans
Short Story 'The Ragthorn' by Robert Holdstock and Garry Kilworth
Artist JIM BURNS
Special Award *The Encyclopedia of Science Fiction* (edited by JOHN CLUTE and Peter Nicholls)

1994
Novel *Feersum Endjinn* by IAIN M. BANKS
Short Story 'The Double Felix' by PAUL DI FILIPPO
Artist JIM BURNS

1995
Novel *The Time Ships* by STEPHEN BAXTER
Short Story 'The Hunger and Ecstasy of Vampires' by BRIAN STABLEFORD
Artist JIM BURNS

1996
Novel *Excession* by IAIN M. BANKS
Short Story 'A Crab Must Try' by Barrington J. Bayley
Artist JIM BURNS

1997
Novel *The Sparrow* by MARY DORIA RUSSELL
Short Story 'War Birds' by STEPHEN BAXTER
Artist SMS

1998
Novel *The Extremes* by CHRISTOPHER PRIEST
Short Story 'La Cenerentola' by Gwyneth Jones
Artist JIM BURNS

1999
Novel *The Sky Road* by KEN MACLEOD
Short Story 'Hunting the Slarque' by ERIC BROWN
Artist JIM BURNS

HUGO AWARD

The most renowned of all genre awards, the Hugo Award, or Science Fiction Achievement Award, was founded in 1953 and has been given annually since 1955.

Named after editor HUGO GERNSBACK who founded AMAZING STORIES magazine in 1926 and is affectionately known as 'the father of the science fiction magazine', the award is maintained by the WORLD SCIENCE FICTION SOCIETY and voted for by members of their annual Worldcon convention.

The very first Hugo was awarded to ALFRED BESTER in 1953 for his now classic, *The Demolished Man* (1953), and there have been many important winners since, including JOHN BRUNNER, ARTHUR C. CLARKE, WILLIAM GIBSON, WALTER MILLER, LARRY NIVEN and KIM STANLEY ROBINSON.

The Hugo's are separated into various categories which have changed over the years, but presently are: Novel, Novella, Novelette, Short Story, Non-Fiction or Related Book, Dramatic Presentation (Film or Television), Professional Editor, Professional Artist, Semiprozine (a magazine somewhere between a fanzine and a professional publication), Fanzine, Fan Writer and Fan Artist.

Undoubtedly, to win a Hugo Award is an enormous boost to an author/editor/artist's career.

The winners for the previous ten years are listed below.

1990
Novel *Hyperion* by Dan Simmons
Novella 'The Mountains of Mourning' by LOIS McMASTER BUJOLD
Novelette 'Enter a Soldier. Later: Enter Another' by ROBERT SILVERBERG
Short Story 'Boobs' by Suzy McKee Charnas
Non-Fiction Book *The World Beyond the Hill* by Alexei Panshin and Cory Panshin

Dramatic Presentation *Indiana Jones and the Last Crusade*
Professional Editor Gardner Dozois
Professional Artist Don Maitz
Semiprozine LOCUS
Fanzine *The Mad 3 Party*
Fan Writer DAVID LANGFORD
Fan Artist Stu Shiffman

1991
Novel *The Vor Game* by LOIS McMASTER BUJOLD
Novella 'The Hemingway Hoax' by JOE HALDEMAN
Novelette 'The Manamouki' by Mike Resnick
Short Story 'Bear Discovers Fire' by Terry Bisson
Non-Fiction Book *How to Write Science Fiction and Fantasy* by ORSON
SCOTT CARD
Dramatic Presentation *Edward Scissorhands*
Professional Editor Gardner Dozois
Professional Artist MICHAEL WHELAN
Semiprozine LOCUS
Fanzine *Lan's Lantern*
Fan Writer DAVID LANGFORD
Fan Artist Teddy Harvia

1992
Novel *Barrayar* by LOIS McMASTER BUJOLD
Novella 'Beggars in Spain' by Nancy Kress
Novelette 'Gold' by ISAAC ASIMOV
Short Story 'A Walk in the Sun' by Geoffrey A. Landis
Non-Fiction Book *The World of Charles Addams* by Charles Addams
Dramatic Presentation TERMINATOR 2: JUDGEMENT DAY
Professional Editor Gardner Dozois
Professional Artist MICHAEL WHELAN
Semiprozine LOCUS
Fanzine *Mimosa*
Fan Writer DAVID LANGFORD
Fan Artist Brad W. Foster

1993
Novel *A Fire Upon the Deep* by VERNOR VINGE
Novella 'Barnacle Bill the Spacer' by LUCIUS SHEPARD

Novelette 'The Nutcracker Coup' by Janet Kagan
Short Story 'Even the Queen' by Connie Willis
Non-Fiction Book *A Wealth of Fable* by Harry Warner Jr
Dramatic Presentation *The Inner Light* (STAR TREK)
Professional Editor Gardner Dozois
Professional Artist Don Maitz
Semiprozine *Science Fiction Chronicle*
Fanzine *Mimosa*
Fan Writer DAVID LANGFORD
Fan Artist Peggy Ranson

1994
Novel *Green Mars* by KIM STANLEY ROBINSON
Novella 'Down in the Bottomlands' by HARRY TURTLEDOVE
Novelette 'Georgia On My Mind' by Charles Sheffield
Short Story 'Death on the Nile' by Connie Willis
Non-Fiction Book *The Encyclopedia of Science Fiction* edited by JOHN CLUTE and Peter Nicholls
Dramatic Presentation JURASSIC PARK
Professional Editor Kristine Kathryn Rusch
Professional Artist Bob Eggleton
Semiprozine *Science Fiction Chronicle*
Fanzine *Mimosa*
Fan Writer DAVID LANGFORD
Fan Artist Brad W. Foster

1995
Novel *Mirror Dance* by LOIS McMASTER BUJOLD
Novella 'Seven Views of Olduvai Gorge' by Mike Resnick
Novelette 'The Martian Child' by David Gerrold
Short Story 'None So Blind' By JOE HALDEMAN
Non-Fiction Book *I, Asimov: A Memoir* by ISAAC ASIMOV
Dramatic Presentation *All Good Things* (STAR TREK)
Professional Editor Gardner Dozois
Professional Artist JIM BURNS
Semiprozine INTERZONE
Fanzine ANSIBLE
Fan Writer DAVID LANGFORD
Fan Artist Teddy Havia

1996
Novel *The Diamond Age* by NEAL STEPHENSON
Novella 'The Death of Captain Future' by Allen Steele
Novelette 'Think Like a Dinosaur' by James Patrick Kelly
Short Story 'The Lincoln Train' by MAUREEN F. McHUGH
Non-Fiction Book *Science Fiction: The Illustrated Encyclopedia* by JOHN CLUTE
Dramatic Presentation *The Coming of Shadows* (BABYLON 5)
Professional Editor Gardner Dozois
Professional Artist Bob Eggleton
Semiprozine LOCUS
Fanzine ANSIBLE
Fan Writer DAVID LANGFORD
Fan Artist William Rotsler

1997
Novel *Blue Mars* by KIM STANLEY ROBINSON
Novella 'Blood of the Dragon' by George R. R. Martin
Novelette 'Bicycle Repairman' by BRUCE STERLING
Short Story 'The Soul Selects Her Own Society . . .' by Connie Willis
Non-Fiction Book *Time and Chance* by L. Sprague de Camp
Dramatic Presentation *Severed Dreams* (BABYLON 5)
Professional Editor Gardner Dozois
Professional Artist Bob Eggleton
Semiprozine LOCUS
Fanzine *Mimosa*
Fan Writer DAVID LANGFORD
Fan Artist William Rotsler

1998
Novel *Forever Peace* by JOE HALDEMAN
Novella '. . . Where Angels Fear To Tread' by Allen Steele
Novelette 'We Will Drink A Fish Together' by Bill Johnson
Short Story 'The 43 Antarean Dynasties' by Mike Resnick
Non-Fiction Book *The Encyclopedia of Fantasy* edited by JOHN CLUTE and John Grant
Dramatic Presentation CONTACT
Professional Editor Gardner Dozois
Professional Artist Bob Eggleton
Semiprozine LOCUS

Fanzine *Mimosa*
Fan Writer DAVID LANGFORD
Fan Artist Joe Mayhew

1999
Novel *To Say Nothing of the Dog* by Connie Willis
Novella 'Oceanic' by GREG EGAN
Novelette 'Taklamakan' by BRUCE STERLING
Short Story 'The Very Pulse of the Machine' by Michael Swanwick
Non-Fiction Book *The Dreams Our Stuff is Made Of* by THOMAS M. DISCH
Dramatic Presentation THE TRUMAN SHOW
Professional Editor Gardner Dozois
Professional Artist Bob Eggleton
Semiprozine LOCUS
Fanzine ANSIBLE
Fan Writer DAVID LANGFORD
Fan Artist Ian Gunn

2000
Novel *A Deepness in the Sky* by VERNOR VINGE
Novella 'The Winds of Marble Arch' by Connie Willis
Novelette '10 16 to 1' by James Patrick Kelly
Short Story 'Scherzo With Tyrannosaur' by Michael Swanwick
Non-Fiction Book *Science Fiction of the 20th Century* by Frank M. Robinson
Dramatic Presentation *Galaxy Quest*
Professional Editor Gardner Dozois
Professional Artist MICHAEL WHELAN
Semiprozine LOCUS
Fanzine *File 770*
Fan Writer DAVID LANGFORD
Fan Artist Joe Mayhew

JOHN W. CAMPBELL MEMORIAL AWARD

A prestigious award which is named after late editor JOHN W. CAMPBELL and has been operating since 1972.

John W. Campbell was for many years editor of ASTOUNDING SCIENCE FICTION magazine (now ANALOG), and pioneered the

GOLDEN AGE of American SF during the late 1930s and early 1940s. Campbell encouraged writers to consider the broader implications of their ideas, to explore the psychological and scientific repercussions of their stories and to treat both their characters and, more importantly, their readers, in a mature and intelligent manner. This manifested itself in a maturing of the genre as a whole, and a period of bold activity in which many of the classics of the genre appeared, setting precedence for the years to come.

The John W. Campbell Memorial Award is given to the best newcomer to the genre and is awarded annually at Worldcon, the convention held by the WORLD SCIENCE FICTION SOCIETY (WSFS). The WSFS is also responsible for operating the award, which coincides with the HUGO AWARDS.

The winners for the last ten years are listed below.

1990 Kristine Kathryn Rusch
1991 Julia Ecklar
1992 Ted Chiang
1993 Laura Resnick
1994 Amy Thomson
1995 JEFF NOON
1996 DAVID FEINTUCH
1997 Michael A. Burstein
1998 MARY DORIA RUSSELL
1999 Nalo Hopkinson
2000 Cory Doctorow

Other important winners of the award are ORSON SCOTT CARD (1978), STEPHEN DONALDSON (1979) and LUCIUS SHEPARD (1985).

MADE IN CANADA
Made in Canada is a website that can be found at http://www. geocities.com/canadian_sf

The site bills itself as the homepage of Canadian SF, and rightly so – it is comprehensive and well maintained, with monthly news updates and constant revisions.

The main body of the site is comprised of the *Made in Canada*

Newsletter, which features information about the comings and goings of Canadian genre authors, listings of forthcoming Canadian publications and in-depth book and film critiques. Also useful is the recently added listing of all published Canadian SF anthologies to date.

The site also hosts a number of author home pages, including that of ROBERT CHARLES WILSON.

Made in Canada is a specialist site with a very specific goal in mind – the promotion of Canadian speculative fiction. Although it lacks the general appeal of internationally minded sites such as SFF.NET and SFSITE, for fans of Canadian literature it is well worth a visit.

NEBULA AWARD

The Nebula Award is given by the SCIENCE FICTION WRITERS OF AMERICA, and is voted for by members of that organization. The Nebula is presented annually in four categories – Novel, Novella, Novelette and Short Story. After the HUGO AWARD, it is considered the most prestigious of SF honours as the winners are selected by their peers.

The winning shorter pieces are collected, along with a number of the short-listed entries, in an annual anthology *Nebula Award Stories*, the royalties of which help maintain the award itself.

The winners from the last ten years are listed below.

1990
Novel *Tehanu: The Last Book of Earthsea* by URSULA K. LE GUIN
Novella 'The Hemingway Hoax' by JOE HALDEMAN
Novelette 'Tower of Babylon' by Ted Chiang
Short Story 'Bears Discover Fire' by Terry Bisson

1991
Novel *Stations of the Tide* by Michael Swanwick
Novella 'Beggars in Spain' by Nancy Kress
Novelette 'Guide Dog' by Mike Conner
Short Story 'Ma Qui' by Alan Brennert

1992
Novel *Doomsday Book* by Connie Willis
Novella 'City of Truth' by James Morrow

Novelette 'Danny Goes to Mars' by Pamela Sargent
Short Story 'Even the Queen' by Connie Willis

1993
Novel *Red Mars* by KIM STANLEY ROBINSON
Novella 'The Night We Buried the Road Dog' by Jack Cady
Novelette 'Georgia on My Mind' by Charles Sheffield
Short Story 'Graves' by JOE HALDEMAN

1994
Novel *Moving Mars* by GREG BEAR
Novella 'Seven Views of Olduvai Gorge' by Michael Resnick
Novelette 'The Martian Child' by David Gerrold
Short Story 'A Defence of the Social Contracts' by Martha Soukup

1995
Novel *The Terminal Experiment* by Robert J. Sawyer
Novella 'Last Summer at Mars Hill' by ELIZABETH HAND
Novelette 'Solitude' by URSULA K. LE GUIN
Short Story 'Death and the Librarian' by Esther M. Friesner

1996
Novel *Slow River* by Nicola Griffith
Novella 'Da Vinci Rising' by Jack Dann
Novelette 'Lifeboat on a Burning Sea' by Bruce Holland Rogers
Short Story 'A Birthday' by Esther M. Friesner

1997
Novel *The Moon and the Sun* by Vonda N. McIntyre
Novella 'Abandon in Place' by Jerry Oltion
Novelette 'Flowers of Aulit Prison' by Nancy Kress
Short Story 'Sister Emily's Lightship' by Jane Yolen

1998
Novel *Forever Peace* by JOE HALDEMAN
Novella 'Reading the Bones' by Sheila Finch
Novelette 'Lost Girls' by Jane Yolen
Short Story 'Thirteen Ways to Water' by Bruce Holland Rogers

1999
Novel *Parable of the Talents* by OCTAVIA BUTLER
Novella 'Story of Your Life' by Ted Chiang
Novelette 'Mars is No Place for Children' by Mary A. Turzillo
Short Story 'The Cost of Doing Business' by M. Night Shyamalan

PHILIP K. DICK AWARD

The Philip K. Dick Award was set up in 1983 in memory of the late writer. It is awarded annually by a small panel of judges comprised of writers, editors and previous winners. Like the NEBULA AWARDS it is dated by the year of publication as opposed to the year of award. The prize goes to the best novel to be published as a paperback original in America during the previous year. A monetary prize is provided by the administrators, whilst a plaque is provided by the estate of Philip K. Dick.

The winners from the last ten years are listed below.

1990 *Points of Departure* by Pat Murphy
1991 *King of Morning, Queen of Day* by Ian McDonald
1992 *Through the Heart* by Richard Grant
1993 *Growing up Weightless* by John M. Ford and *Elvissey* by Jack Womack
1994 *Mysterium* by ROBERT CHARLES WILSON
1995 *Headcrash* by BRUCE BETHKE
1996 *The Time Ships* by STEPHEN BAXTER
1997 *The Troika* by Stepan Chapman
1998 *253* by GEOFF RYMAN
1999 *Vacuum Diagrams* by STEPHEN BAXTER

SCIENCE FICTION FOUNDATION

The Science Fiction Foundation is an organization based at the University of Liverpool, England, which sees its aim as the promotion of the study of science fiction as a serious form of literature.

Its sets out to do this in two ways. Firstly, and perhaps most importantly, the Foundation manages and maintains an impressive collection of SF, fantasy and horror, which takes many forms and includes books, magazines and articles on microfilm. This impressive library is made available upon request, both to those studying at the university and those who simply have an academic interest in the genre. Secondly, the Foundation supports the publication of *Foundation*, a triannual magazine devoted to the academic study of the genre and featuring an impressive array of book reviews and articles.

The SF Foundation was founded in 1970 by writer George Hay, and its patrons are ARTHUR C. CLARKE and URSULA K. LE GUIN. Members of the organization are also involved in the annual judging of the ARTHUR C. CLARKE AWARD.

To become a member of the SF Foundation and to receive copies of *Foundation*, visit the official website at http://www.liv.ac.uk/~asawyer/fof.html

SCIENCE FICTION WRITERS OF AMERICA

Science Fiction Writers of America (SFWA) is the world's premier non-profit organization of SF and fantasy authors and aims to provide a supporting network of like-minded people who will inform each other of important genre news and help each other to deal with the publishing environment. To qualify as a member, the applicant must have at least three professional short story sales or one full-length novel to their name.

SFWA was formed in 1965 by writer Damon Knight, who believed that the genre was in need of a identifiable body or organization to support SF writers. There has since been a succession of important writers holding the chairperson's seat, including ROBERT SILVERBERG, FREDERIK POHL, GREG BEAR and BEN BOVA.

SFWA produces two publications – the *SFWA Bulletin*, which is available to the public at large, and the *SFWA Forum*, which is restricted to members only. They also maintain a website at http://www.sfwa.org

Perhaps most importantly, SFWA administrates the NEBULA AWARDS each year, a prize that was set up by SFWA in 1966.

SCIFI.COM

A website that can be found at www.scifi.com

Scifi.com is a spectacular-looking site that focuses its attentions more on SF television series and movies than on literature. However, although it is true that the site may foster a bias towards the visual side of the genre, careful exploration will yield high rewards.

There is a lot going on at Scifi.com – an online store, a news room, message boards for online chat, reviews of computer games, movies and TV series, interviews with genre characters. Nearly all are worth a look, but the true strength of the site lies in the affiliated weekly webzine, *Science Fiction Weekly* (www.scifi.com/sfw).

This sub-site is updated very frequently and has been established for a number years. It features regular book reviews and film critiques, non-fiction popular science articles, in-depth author interviews, and perhaps best of all, an irregular review column, 'Excessive Candour', by JOHN CLUTE.

All of the worthwhile articles are archived, and 'back issues' of the webzine are available for access. This has led to an invaluable online library of interviews and reviews that are as essential to any SF reader as the back issues of any genre magazine. Clute's column in particular makes engaging reading.

All in all, a worthwhile site once the initial media-orientated blizzard has been navigated and the layers of quality reading have been found.

SF CROWSNEST

A website that can be found at http://www.sfcrowsnest.com

SF Crowsnest is a media-orientated website that nevertheless manages to maintain a high standard of content. It features one of the best SF search engines on the web, as well as a small selection of short fiction, news reviews and a comprehensive website directory. There are also chat rooms where users can interact with other SF fans, as well as the option to develop and post an original website which the administrators of SF Crowsnest will kindly host.

The media news is up to the standard of other websites and while the literary SF content is not high, the search engine is well worth seeking out.

SF SITE

A website that can be found at http://www.sfsite.com

SF Site is perhaps the best unaffiliated website to cover the world of SF and fantasy literature. It is updated monthly, and provides an excellent review service, of both new titles and classic reprints. There are selected lists of forthcoming titles, regular in-depth interviews with genre authors, television and movie critiques and convention listings.

One of the other important aspects of SF Site is the fact that it hosts pages for many of the important genre magazines, including ANALOG, ASIMOV'S SCIENCE FICTION and INTERZONE. This enables the user to use the site as a stop-off point on the way to other sites that belong to their favourite magazines. A number of authors also maintain pages within its framework.

For its review services and its excellent network of further links, SF Site has become one of the most visited SF sites on the web. It serves as a hub for the online SF field and helps points users to the sites that will be most useful to them, as well as providing an excellent array of services itself.

WORLD SCIENCE FICTION SOCIETY

The World Science Fiction Society is an organization which co-ordinates a massive annual convention and administrate both the HUGO AWARDS and the JOHN W. CAMPBELL AWARDS.

The conventions usually take place in the USA, and are announced on the organization's website, http://www.wsfs.org

Members of the public can pay to join a particular convention, but there are no further services available and after each convention the membership expires. Nevertheless, the conventions are well worth attending, and feature the final award ceremonies for the Hugo and the John W. Campbell Awards.

Appendix

Beasts in Velvet	NEWMAN, KIM
Beasts of Tarzan, The	BURROUGHS, EDGAR RICE
Beauty	TEPPER, SHERI S.
Bedlam Planet	BRUNNER, JOHN
Before the Universe and Other Stories	POHL, FREDERIK
Begum's Fortune, The	VERNE, JULES
Behold the Man	MOORCOCK, MICHAEL
Bells of Shoredan	ZELAZNY, ROGER
Ben, in the World	LESSING, DORIS
Berserker	LOVEGROVE, JAMES
Betrayal, The	CHERRYH, C. J.
Better Mantrap, A	SHAW, BOB
Between Planets	HEINLEIN, ROBERT A.
Between the Rivers	TURTLEDOVE, HARRY
Beyond	STURGEON, THEODORE
Beyond Heaven's Mirror	BEAR, GREG
Beyond Lies the Wub	DICK, PHILIP K.
Beyond the Beyond	ANDERSON, POUL
Beyond the Blue Event Horizon	POHL, FREDERIK
Beyond the Fall of Night	BENFORD, GREGORY
Beyond the Farthest Star	BURROUGHS, EDGAR RICE
Beyond This Horizon	HEINLEIN, ROBERT A.
Bibliomen	WOLFE, GENE
Bicentennial Man, The	ASIMOV, ISAAC
Bid Time Return	MATHESON, RICHARD
Big Planet	VANCE, JACK
Big Time, The	LEIBER, FRITZ
Bikini Planet	GARNETT, DAVID
Bill, the Galactic Hero	HARRISON, HARRY
Billenium	BALLARD, J. G.
Bios	WILSON, ROBERT CHARLES
Bipohl	POHL, FREDERIK
Black Alice	DISCH, THOMAS M./
	SLADEK, JOHN
Black Corridor, The	MOORCOCK, MICHAEL
Black Easter	BLISH, JAMES
Black Genesis	HUBBARD, L. RON
Black Horses for the King	McCAFFREY, ANNE
Black Light	HAND, ELIZABETH
Black Star Passes, The	CAMPBELL, JOHN W.

Black Star Rising	POHL, FREDERIK
Black Throne, The	ZELAZNY, ROGER
Blade of Mars	MOORCOCK, MICHAEL
Blind Worm, The	STABLEFORD, BRIAN
Blindfold	ANDERSON, KEVIN J.
Blood	MOORCOCK, MICHAEL
Blood Heritage	TEPPER, SHERI S.
Blood Music	BEAR, GREG
Blood of Amber	ZELAZNY, ROGER
Bloody Red Baron, The	NEWMAN, KIM
Bloody Students	NEWMAN, KIM
Bloom	McCARTHY, WIL
Blown	FARMER, PHILIP JOSÉ
Blue Champagne	VARLEY, JOHN
Blue Mars	ROBINSON, KIM STANLEY
Blue Shifting	BROWN, ERIC
Blue World, The	VANCE, JACK
Bluebeard	VONNEGUT, KURT
Blueheart	SINCLAIR, ALISON
Boat of a Million Years, The	ANDERSON, POUL
Boat of Fate, The	ROBERTS, KEITH
Bodily Functions	ALDISS, BRIAN
Body Snatchers, The	FINNEY, JACK
Bohr Maker, The	NAGATA, LINDA
Bones of Time, The	GOONAN, KATHLEEN ANN
Bones, The	TEPPER, SHERI S.
Book of Being, The	WATSON, IAN
Book of Days	WOLFE, GENE
Book of Dreams, The	VANCE, JACK
Book of Ptath, The	VAN VOGT, A. E.
Book of Skulls, The	SILVERBERG, ROBERT
Book of the River, The	WATSON, IAN
Book of the Stars, The	WATSON, IAN
Borders of Infinity	BUJOLD, LOIS McMASTER
Born of Elven Blood	ANDERSON, KEVIN J.
Born of Man and Woman	MATHESON, RICHARD
Born Under Mars	BRUNNER, JOHN
Bow Down to Nul	ALDISS, BRIAN
Boy Who Hooked the Earth, The	WOLFE, GENE
Brain Wave	ANDERSON, POUL

Chain of Chance, The	LEM, STANISLAW
Chalk Giants, The	ROBERTS, KEITH
Challenge Chaos, The	STABLEFORD, BRIAN
Challenger's Hope	FEINTUCH, DAVID
Challenges	BOVA, BEN
Champion of Garathorm	MOORCOCK, MICHAEL
Champions of the Force: Star Wars	ANDERSON, KEVIN J.
Change of Command	MOON, ELIZABETH
Change War, The	LEIBER, FRITZ
Changed Man, The	CARD, ORSON SCOTT
Changeling	ZELAZNY, ROGER
Changing Land, The	ZELAZNY, ROGER
Chanur's Homecoming	CHERRYH, C. J.
Chanur's Legacy	CHERRYH, C. J.
Chanur's Venture	CHERRYH, C. J.
Chaos and Order	DONALDSON, STEPHEN R.
Chaos Child	WATSON, IAN
Chapter House Dune	HERBERT, FRANK
Chateau d'If	VANCE, JACK
Chekhov's Journey	WATSON, IAN
Chernobyl	POHL, FREDERIK
Chessmen of Mars, The	BURROUGHS, EDGAR RICE
Chi	BESHER, ALEXANDER
Child Garden, The	RYMAN, GEOFF
Child of an Ancient City, The	WILLIAMS, TAD
Child of Fortune	SPINRAD, NORMAN
Child of the River	McAULEY, PAUL J.
Childhood's End	CLARKE, ARTHUR C.
Children of Dune	HERBERT, FRANK
Children of God	RUSSELL, MARY DORIA
Children of Hamelin, The	SPINRAD, NORMAN
Children of the Lens	SMITH, E. E.
Children of the Mind	CARD, ORSON SCOTT
Children of the Thunder	BRUNNER, JOHN
Children of Tomorrow	VAN VOGT, A. E.
Chimera's Cradle	STABLEFORD BRIAN
China Mountain Zhang	McHUGH, MAUREEN F.
Chocky	WYNDHAM, JOHN
Chronicles of Amber, The	ZELAZNY, ROGER
Chronicles of Pern	McCAFFREY, ANNE

Count Brass	MOORCOCK, MICHAEL
Count Zero	GIBSON, WILLIAM
Counter-Clock World	DICK, PHILIP K.
Country of the Blind and Other Stories, The	WELLS, H. G.
Course of the Heart, The	HARRISON, M. JOHN
Courts of Chaos, The	ZELAZNY, ROGER
Crack in Space, The	DICK, PHILIP K.
Cradle	CLARKE, ARTHUR C.
Cradle of Splendor	ANTHONY, PATRICIA
Cradle of the Sun	STABLEFORD, BRIAN
Crash	BALLARD, J. G.
Crashlander	NIVEN, LARRY
Creatures of Light and Darkness	ZELAZNY, ROGER
Crescent City Rhapsody	GOONAN, KATHLEEN ANN
Critical Mass	POHL, FREDERIK
Critical Threshold	STABLEFORD, BRIAN
Crucible of Time, The	BRUNNER, JOHN
Cruel Miracles	CARD, ORSON SCOTT
Crusade	WEBER, DAVID
Crutch of Memory, The	BRUNNER, JOHN
Cryptonomicon	STEPHENSON, NEAL
Crystal Express	STERLING, BRUCE
Crystal Line, The	McCAFFREY, ANNE
Crystal Singer, The	McCAFFREY, ANNE
Crystal World, The	BALLARD, J. G.
Cuckoo's Egg	CHERRYH, C. J.
Cugel's Saga	VANCE, JACK
Cure for Cancer, A	MOORCOCK, MICHAEL
Currents of Space, The	ASIMOV, ISAAC
Cyberbooks	BOVA, BEN
Cyberiad, The	LEM, STANISLAW
Cyberpunk	BETHKE, BRUCE
Cycle of Fire	CLEMENT, HAL
Cydonia	MACLEOD, KEN
Cyteen	CHERRY, C. J.
Cythera	CALDER, RICHARD
Daemonomania	CROWLEY, JOHN
Dagger of the Mind	SHAW, BOB
Damia	McCAFFREY, ANNE

Damia's Children	McCAFFREY, ANNE
Damnation Alley	ZELAZNY, ROGER
Dancer from Atlantis, The	ANDERSON, POUL
Dandelion Wine	BRADBURY, RAY
Dangerous Visions	ELLISON, HARLAN
Dare	FARMER, PHILIP JOSÉ
Darfsteller and Other Stories, The	MILLER, WALTER
Dark and Hungry God Arises, A	DONALDSON, STEPHEN R.
Dark Apprentice: Star Wars	ANDERSON, KEVIN J.
Dark Carnival	BRADBURY, RAY
Dark Design, The	FARMER, PHILIP JOSÉ
Dark Heart of Time, The	FARMER, PHILIP JOSÉ
Dark is the Sun	FARMER, PHILIP JOSÉ
Dark Light Years, The	ALDISS, BRIAN
Dark Night in Toyland	SHAW, BOB
Dark Side of the Earth, The	BESTER, ALFRED
Dark Side of the Sun, The	PRATCHETT, TERRY
Darkness and the Light	STAPLEDON, OLAF
Darkness Descending	TURTLEDOVE, HARRY
Darkness on Diamondia, The	VAN VOGT, A. E.
Darksaber: Star Wars	ANDERSON, KEVIN J.
Darwinia	WILSON, ROBERT CHARLES
Darwin's Radio	BEAR, GREG
Daughter of Regals and Other Stories	DONALDSON, STEPHEN R.
David Starr, Space Ranger	ASIMOV, ISAAC
Dawn	BUTLER, OCTAVIA, E.
Dawning Light, The	SILVERBERG, ROBERT
Day After Judgement, The	BLISH, JAMES
Day it Rained Forever, The	BRADBURY, RAY
Day Million	POHL, FREDERIK
Day of Creation, The	BALLARD, J. G.
Day of Forever, The	BALLARD, J. G.
Day of the Star Cities	BRUNNER, JOHN
Day of the Triffids, The	WYNDHAM, JOHN
Day of Their Return	ANDERSON, POUL
Day of Wrath	STABLEFORD, BRIAN
Day the Martians Came, The	POHL, FREDERIK
Daybreak on a Different Mountain	GOONAN, KATHLEEN ANN
Days	LOVEGROVE, JAMES
Days of Cain	DUNN, J. R.

Earthman, Come Home	BLISH, JAMES
Earthman, Go Home!	ANDERSON, POUL
Earth's Last Fortress	VAN VOGT, A. E.
Earthworks	ALDISS, BRIAN
Eater	BENFORD, GREGORY
Eating Memories	ANTHONY, PATRICIA
Ecce and Old Earth	VANCE, JACK
Echo in the Skull	BRUNNER, JOHN
Echo Round His Bones	DISCH, THOMAS M.
Echoes of Honor	WEBER, DAVID
Eden	LEM, STANISLAW
Eight Fantasms and Magics	VANCE, JACK
Eighty-Minute Hour, The	ALDISS, BRIAN
Einstein Intersection, The	DELANY, SAMUEL R.
Ellison Wonderland	ELLISON, HARLAN
Elric of Melniboné	MOORCOCK, MICHAEL
Embedding, The	WATSON, IAN
Emperor for the Legion, An	TURTLEDOVE, HARRY
Emphyrio	VANCE, JACK
Empire Builders	BOVA, BEN
Empire of Fear, The	STABLEFORD, BRIAN
Empire of the Atom	VAN VOGT, A. E.
Empire of the Sun	BALLARD, J. G.
Empire Star	DELANY, SAMUEL R.
Empires of Foliage and Flower	WOLFE, GENE
Enchantment	CARD, ORSON SCOTT
Encounter with Tiber	BARNES, JOHN/Aldrin, Buzz
End of All Songs, The	MOORCOCK, MICHAEL
End of Eternity, The	ASIMOV, ISAAC
End of Exile	BOVA, BEN
End of the World News, The	BURGESS, ANTHONY
Endangered Species	WOLFE, GENE
Ender's Game	CARD, ORSON SCOTT
Ender's Shadow	CARD, ORSON SCOTT
Endless Shadow	BRUNNER, JOHN
Ends of the Earth, The	SHEPARD, LUCIUS
Enemies of the System	ALDISS, BRIAN
Enemy Stars, The	ANDERSON, POUL
Enemy Within, The	HUBBARD, L. RON
Engine Summer	CROWLEY, JOHN

Engineman	BROWN, ERIC
Engines of God	McDEVITT, JACK
English Assassin, The	MOORCOCK, MICHAEL
Enigma from Tantalus	BRUNNER, JOHN
Ensign Flandry	ANDERSON, POUL
Entropy Tango, The	MOORCOCK, MICHAEL
Eon	BEAR, GREG
Equinox	DELANY, SAMUEL R.
Escape!	BOVA, BEN
Escape from Kathmandu	ROBINSON, KIM STANLEY
Escape on Venus	BURROUGHS, EDGAR RICE
Escape Plus	BOVA, BEN
Escardy Gap	LOVEGROVE, JAMES
Eternal Champion, The	MOORCOCK, MICHAEL
Eternal Light	McAULEY, PAUL J.
Eternal Lover, The	BURROUGHS, EDGAR RICE
Eternity	BEAR, GREG
Eternity Road	McDEVITT, JACK
Ethan of Athos	BUJOLD, LOIS McMASTER
Event, The	ROBERTS, KEITH
Evil Water	WATSON, IAN
Excession	BANKS, IAIN M.
Exiled from Earth	BOVA, BEN
Exiles Gate	CHERRYH, C. J.
Exiles on Asperus	WYNDHAM, JOHN
Existenz	PRIEST, CHRISTOPHER
Exodus from the Long Sun	WOLFE, GENE
Expanded Universe	HEINLEIN, ROBERT A.
Expatria	BROOKE, KEITH
Expatria Incorporated	BROOKE, KEITH
Expedition to Earth	CLARKE, ARTHUR C.
Explorations	ANDERSON, POUL
Extremes, The	PRIEST, CHRISTOPHER
Eye	HERBERT, FRANK
Eye in the Sky	DICK, PHILIP K.
Eye of the Cat	ZELAZNY, ROGER
Eye of the Heron, The	LE GUIN, URSULA K.
Eyes of Heisenberg, The	HERBERT, FRANK
Eyes of the Overworld, The	VANCE, JACK
Fabulous Harbours	MOORCOCK, MICHAEL

Flow My Tears, the Policeman Said	DICK, PHILIP K.
Flowers for Algernon	KEYES, DANIEL
Flux	BAXTER, STEPHEN
Flux	CARD, ORSON SCOTT
Flying Sorcerers, The	NIVEN, LARRY/Gerrold, David
Folk of the Fringe, The	CARD, ORSON SCOTT
Food of the Gods, The	WELLS, H. G.
Fools	CADIGAN, PAT
Footfall	NIVEN, LARRY
Forbidden Knowledge	DONALDSON, STEPHEN R.
Foreign Bodies	ALDISS, BRIAN
Foreign Constellations	BRUNNER, JOHN
Foreigner	CHERRYH, C. J.
Foreigners, The	LOVEGROVE, JAMES
Forever Free	HALDEMAN, JOE
Forever Peace	HALDEMAN, JOE
Forever War, The	HALDEMAN, JOE
Forge of God, The	BEAR, GREG
Forgotten Dimension, The	GARNETT, DAVID
Forgotten Life	ALDISS, BRIAN
Fortress in the Eye of Time	CHERRYH, C. J.
Fortress of Dragons	CHERRYH, C. J.
Fortress of Eagles	CHERRYH, C. J.
Fortress of Owls	CHERRYH, C. J.
Fortress of the Pearl, The	MOORCOCK, MICHAEL
Fortune of Fear	HUBBARD, L. RON
Forty Thousand in Gehenna	CHERRYH, C. J.
Forward in Time	BOVA, BEN
Forward the Foundation	ASIMOV, ISAAC
Foundation	ASIMOV, ISAAC
Foundation and Chaos	BEAR, GREG
Foundation and Earth	ASIMOV, ISAAC
Foundation and Empire	ASIMOV, ISAAC
Foundation's Edge	ASIMOV, ISAAC
Foundation's Fear	BENFORD, GREGORY
Foundation's Triumph	BRIN, DAVID
Fountains of Paradise, The	CLARKE, ARTHUR C.
Fountains of Youth, The	STABLEFORD, BRIAN
Four Encounters	STAPLEDON, OLAF
Four for Tomorrow	ZELAZNY, ROGER

Four Hundred Billion Stars	McAULEY, PAUL J.
Four Ways to Forgiveness	LE GUIN, URSULA K.
Fox and Empire	TURTLEDOVE, HARRY
Fox, the Dog and the Griffin, The	ANDERSON, POUL
Fractal Paisleys	DI FILIPPO, PAUL
Frankenstein	SHELLEY, MARY WOLLSTONECRAFT
Frankenstein Unbound	ALDISS, BRIAN
Free Live Free	WOLFE, GENE
Freedom's Challenge	McCAFFREY, ANNE
Freedom's Choice	McCAFFREY, ANNE
Freeware	RUCKER, RUDY
Frenzetta	CALDER, RICHARD
Fresco, The	TEPPER, SHERI S.
Friday	HEINLEIN, ROBERT A.
From the Earth to the Moon	VERNE, JULES
From the Land of Fear	ELLISON, HARLAN
From This Day Forward	BRUNNER, JOHN
From Time to Time	FINNEY, JACK
Frost and Fire	ZELAZNY, ROGER
Fugitive Worlds, The	SHAW, BOB
Fugue for a Darkening Island	PRIEST, CHRISTOPHER
Full Tide of Night	DUNN, J. R.
Furies, The	ROBERTS, KEITH
Furious Gulf	BENFORD, GREGORY
Future Crime	BOVA, BEN
Future Glitter	VAN VOGT, A. E.
Future Tense	VANCE, JACK
Futurological Congress, The	LEM, STANISLAW
Galactic Cluster	BLISH, JAMES
Galactic Dreams	HARRISON, HARRY
Galactic Effectuator	VANCE, JACK
Galactic Patrol	SMITH, E. E.
Galactic Pot-Healer	DICK, PHILIP K.
Galactic Storm	BRUNNER, JOHN
Galactic Tours	SHAW, BOB
Galápagos	VONNEGUT, KURT
Galaxy Primes, The	SMITH, E. E.
Game of Empire	ANDERSON, POUL
Gamearth	ANDERSON, KEVIN J.

Hollywood Kremlin	STERLING, BRUCE
Holy Fire	STERLING, BRUCE
Holy Terror, The	WELLS, H. G.
Home is the Hangman	ZELAZNY, ROGER
Homebody	CARD, ORSON SCOTT
Homegoing	POHL, FREDERIK
Homeworld	HARRISON, HARRY
Homeworld and Beyond	ANDERSON, POHL
Honor Among Enemies	WEBER, DAVID
Honor of the Queen, The	WEBER, DAVID
Hope, The	LOVEGROVE, JAMES
Hopscotch	ANDERSON, KEVIN J.
Hot Sky at Midnight	SILVERBERG, ROBERT
Hot Sleep	CARD, ORSON SCOTT
Hothead	INGS, SIMON
Hothouse	ALDISS, BRIAN
Hotwire	INGS, SIMON
Hour of the Thin Ox, The	GOONAN, KATHLEEN ANN
House Atreides: Prelude to Dune	ANDERSON, KEVIN J./
	HERBERT, BRIAN
House Corrino: Prelude to Dune	ANDERSON, KEVIN J./
	HERBERT, BRIAN
House Harkonnen: Prelude to Dune	ANDERSON, KEVIN J./
	HERBERT, BRIAN
House of Numbers, The	FINNEY, JACK
House That Fear Built, The	DISCH, THOMAS M.
House That Stood Still, The	VAN VOGT, A. E.
Houses of Iszm, The	VANCE, JACK
How Few Remain	TURTLEDOVE, HARRY
How the Other Half Lives	LOVEGROVE, JAMES
Hrolf Kraki's Saga	ANDERSON, POUL
Humpty Dumpty in Oakland	DICK, PHILIP K.
Hundredth Millennium, The	BRUNNER, JOHN
Hunger and Ecstasy of Vampires, The	STABLEFORD, BRIAN
Hunter of Worlds	CHERRYH, C. J.
Hunter / Victim	SHECKLEY, ROBERT
Hunting Party	MOON, ELIZABETH
I Am Legend	MATHESON, RICHARD
I Have No Mouth, And I Must Scream	ELLISON, HARLAN

Lost Pages	DI FILIPPO, PAUL
Lost Race on Mars	SILVERBERG, ROBERT
Lost World, The	CRICHTON, MICHAEL
Lost World, The	DOYLE, ARTHUR CONAN
Love Ain't Nothing But Sex Misspelled	ELLISON, HARLAN
Love and Sleep	CROWLEY, JOHN
Love Song	FARMER, PHILIP JOSÉ
Lovelock	CARD, ORSON SCOTT
Lovers, The	FARMER, PHILIP JOSÉ
Low-Flying Aircraft and Other Stories	BALLARD, J. G.
Lucifer's Dragon	GRIMWOOD, JON COURTENAY
Lucifer's Hammer	NIVEN, LARRY
Lucky Starr and the Big Sun of Mercury	ASIMOV, ISAAC
Lucky Starr and the Moons of Jupiter	ASIMOV, ISAAC
Lucky Starr and the Oceans of Venus	ASIMOV, ISAAC
Lucky Starr and the Rings of Saturn	ASIMOV, ISAAC
Lucky's Harvest	WATSON, IAN
Luminous	EGAN, GREG
Lunar Activity	MOON, ELIZABETH
Lust	RYMAN, GEOFF
Lyonesse	VANCE, JACK
Lyonesse: Madouc	VANCE, JACK
Lyonesse: The Green Pearl	VANCE, JACK
Lyon's Pride	McCAFFREY, ANNE
M.D., The	DISCH, THOMAS M.
Machine in Shaft Ten, The	HARRISON, M. JOHN
Machineries of Joy, The	BRADBURY, RAY
Machines and Men	ROBERTS, KEITH
Mad Goblin, The	FARMER, PHILIP JOSÉ
Mad God's Amulet, The	MOORCOCK, MICHAEL
Mad Man, The	DELANY, SAMUEL R.
Madwand	ZELAZNY, ROGER
Magic	ASIMOV, ISAAC
Magic Goes Away, The	NIVEN, LARRY
Magic Labyrinth, The	FARMER, PHILIP JOSÉ

Mission Child	McHUGH, MAUREEN F.
Mission of Gravity	CLEMENT, HAL
Mississippi Blues	GOONAN, KATHLEEN ANN
Mixed Men, The	VAN VOGT, A. E.
Modern Utopia, A	WELLS, H. G.
Molly Zero	ROBERTS, KEITH
Moment of Eclipse, The	ALDISS, BRIAN
Mona Lisa Overdrive	GIBSON, WILLIAM
Monkey Planet	BOULLE, PIERRE
Monkey Sonatas	CARD, ORSON SCOTT
Monster Men, The	BURROUGHS, EDGAR RICE
Monsters	VAN VOGT, A. E.
Moon is a Harsh Mistress, The	HEINLEIN, ROBERT A.
Moon is Hell, The	CAMPBELL, JOHN W.
Moon Men, The	BURROUGHS, EDGAR RICE
Moonfall	McDEVITT, JACK
Moonrise	BOVA, BEN
Moonseed	BAXTER, STEPHEN
Moonwar	BOVA, BEN
More Magic	NIVEN, LARRY
More than Honor	WEBER, DAVID
More Than Human	STURGEON, THEODORE
More Than Human	VAN VOGT, A. E.
Moreau's Other Island	ALDISS, BRIAN
Moreta: Dragonlady of Pern	McCAFFREY, ANNE
Morreion	VANCE, JACK
Mostly Harmless	ADAMS, DOUGLAS
Mote in God's Eye, The	NIVEN, LARRY/Pournelle, Jerry
Mother London	MOORCOCK, MICHAEL
Mother Night	VONNEGUT, KURT
Mother of Plenty	GREENLAND, COLIN
Mother of Storms	BARNES, JOHN
Mountain of Black Glass	WILLIAMS, TAD
Mountains of Majipoor	SILVERBERG, ROBERT
Moving Mars	BEAR, GREG
Multiple Man, The	BOVA, BEN
Murder in Black Letter	ANDERSON, POHL
Murder in the Solid State	McCARTHY, WIL
Mutant Season, The	SILVERBERG, ROBERT
Mutineer's Moon	WEBER, DAVID

Options	SHECKLEY, ROBERT
Oracle	WATSON, IAN
Orbit Unlimited	ANDERSON, POUL
Orbital Resonance	BARNES, JOHN
Orbitsville	SHAW, BOB
Orbitsville Departure	SHAW, BOB
Orbitsville Judgement	SHAW, BOB
Origin	BAXTER, STEPHEN
Original Dr Shade, The	NEWMAN, KIM
Orion	BOVA, BEN
Orion Among the Stars	BOVA, BEN
Orion and the Conqueror	BOVA, BEN
Orion in the Dying Time	BOVA, BEN
Orion Shall Rise	ANDERSON, POUL
Orsinian Tales	LE GUIN, URSULA K.
Other Americas	SPINRAD, NORMAN
Other Days, Other Eyes	SHAW, BOB
Other End of Time, The	POHL, FREDERIK
Other Log of Phileas Fogg, The	FARMER, PHILIP JOSÉ
Other Side of the Sky, The	CLARKE, ARTHUR C.
Other Voices	GOONAN, KATHLEEN ANN
Otherness	BRIN, DAVID
Our Friends from Frolix 8	DICK, PHILIP K.
Our Lady of Chernobyl	EGAN, GREG
Our Lady of Darkness	LEIBER, FRITZ
Out of My Mind	BRUNNER, JOHN
Out of the Silent Planet	LEWIS, C. S.
Out of the Sun	BOVA, BEN
Out of the Unknown	VAN VOGT, A. E.
Outnumbering the Dead	POHL, FREDERIK
Outward Urge, The	WYNDHAM, JOHN
Over the Edge	ELLISON, HARLAN
Overloaded Man, The	BALLARD, J. G.
Pacific Edge	ROBINSON, KIM STANLEY
Pail of Air, A	LEIBER, FRITZ
Paingod and Other Delusions	ELLISON, HARLAN
Painkillers	INGS, SIMON
Palace of Eternity, The	SHAW, BOB
Palace of Love, The	VANCE, JACK
Paladin, The	CHERRYH, C. J.

Pandora by Holly Hollander	WOLFE, GENE
Parable of the Sower	BUTLER, OCTAVIA E.
Parable of the Talents	BUTLER, OCTAVIA E.
Paradise Game, The	STABLEFORD, BRIAN
Paradox	MEANEY, JOHN
Paradox of the Sets, The	STABLEFORD, BRIAN
Parallax View	BROWN, ERIC/ BROOKE, KEITH
Paris in the Twentieth Century	VERNE, JULES
Partnership	McCAFFREY, ANNE
Pashazade	GRIMWOOD, JON COURTENAY
Pasquale's Angel	McAULEY, PAUL J.
Passing Through Flame	SPINRAD, NORMAN
Passion of New Eve, The	CARTER, ANGELA
Past Times	ANDERSON, POUL
Pastel City, The	HARRISON, M. JOHN
Patchwork Girl, The	NIVEN, LARRY
Path of the Fury	WEBER, DAVID
Patriarch's Hope	FEINTUCH, DAVID
Patternmaster	BUTLER, OCTAVIA E.
Patterns	CADIGAN, PAT
Patton's Spaceship	BARNES, JOHN
Pavane	ROBERTS, KEITH
Pawns of Null-A, The	VAN VOGT, A. E.
Peace	WOLFE, GENE
Peace War, The	VINGE, VERNOR
Peacekeepers	BOVA, BEN
Pebble in the Sky	ASIMOV, ISAAC
Pegasus in Flight	McCAFFREY, ANNE
Pegasus in Space	McCAFFREY, ANNE
Pellucidar	BURROUGHS, EDGAR RICE
Pendulum	VAN VOGT, A. E.
Penultimate Truth, The	DICK, PHILIP K.
Penumbra	BROWN, ERIC
People of the Wind, The	ANDERSON, POUL
People Trap, The	SHECKLEY, ROBERT
Perelandra	LEWIS, C. S.
Perfect Host, The	STURGEON, THEODORE
Perfect Vacuum, A	LEM, STANISLAW

Perish by the Sword	ANDERSON, POUL
Permutation City	EGAN, GREG
Perseids and Other Stories, The	WILSON, ROBERT CHARLES
Persistence of Vision, The	VARLEY, JOHN
Phantom Universe	GARNETT, DAVID
Phases	MOON, ELIZABETH
Phoenix in Obsidian	MOORCOCK, MICHAEL
Phoenix Without Ashes	ELLISON, HARLAN Bryant, Edward
Pictures at Eleven	SPINRAD, NORMAN
Pilgrimage to Earth	SHECKLEY, ROBERT
Pirates of Venus	BURROUGHS, EDGAR RICE
Pixel Juice	NOON, JEFF
Plague from Space	HARRISON, HARRY
Plague of Angels, A	TEPPER, SHERI S.
Plague of Pythons, A	POHL, FREDERIK
Plan[e]t Engineering	WOLFE, GENE
Planet Called Treason, A	CARD, ORSON SCOTT
Planet Killers, The	SILVERBERG, ROBERT
Planet of Bottled Brains, The	HARRISON, HARRY / SHECKLEY, ROBERT
Planet of Death	SILVERBERG, ROBERT
Planet of Exile	LE GUIN, URSULA K.
Planet of No Return	ANDERSON, POUL
Planet of No Return	HARRISON, HARRY
Planet of Robot Slaves, The	HARRISON, HARRY
Planet of Tasteless Pleasure, The	HARRISON, HARRY / Bischoff, David F.
Planet of Ten Thousand Bars, The	HARRISON, HARRY / Bischoff, David F.
Planet of the Damned	HARRISON, HARRY
Planet of the Zombie Vampires, The	HARRISON, HARRY / Haldeman II, Jack C.
Planet of Your Own, A	BRUNNER, JOHN
Planet on the Table, The	ROBINSON, KIM STANLEY
Planet Story	HARRISON, HARRY
Planets for Sale	VAN VOGT, A. E.
Planets Three	POHL, FREDERIK
Plattner Story, The	WELLS, H. G.

Robots and Empire	ASIMOV, ISAAC
Robots of Dawn, The	ASIMOV, ISAAC
Rocannon's World	LE GUIN, URSULA K.
Rocket Ship Galileo	HEINLEIN, ROBERT A.
Rogue Planet	BEAR, GREG
Rogue Ship	VAN VOGT, A. E.
Rogue Star	POHL, FREDERIK/ Williamson, Jack
Rogue Sword	ANDERSON, POUL
Rolling Stones, The	HEINLEIN, ROBERT A.
Romance of the Equator	ALDISS, BRIAN
Route 666	NEWMAN, KIM
Rude Awakening, A	ALDISS, BRIAN
Ruins	ALDISS, BRIAN
Ruins: X-Files	ANDERSON, KEVIN J.
Rules of Engagement	MOON, ELIZABETH
Runestaff, The	MOORCOCK, MICHAEL
Running Wild	BALLARD, J. G.
Rusalka	CHERRYH, C. J.
Rushing to Paradise	BALLARD, J. G.
Russian Spring	SPINRAD, NORMAN
S is for Space	BRADBURY, RAY
Sailing Bright Eternity	BENFORD, GREGORY
Sailing to Byzantium	SILVERBERG, ROBERT
Saint Leibowitz and the Wild Horse Woman	MILLER, WALTER/ Bisson, Terry
Salamander's Fire	STABLEFORD, BRIAN
Sailor on the Seas of Fate, The	MOORCOCK, MICHAEL
Saliva Tree and Other Strange Growths, The	ALDISS, BRIAN
Salvage Rites	WATSON, IAN
Sam Gunn Forever	BOVA, BEN
Sam Gunn, Unlimited	BOVA, BEN
Sanctuary in the Sky	BRUNNER, JOHN
Sands of Mars	CLARKE, ARTHUR C.
Santaroga Barrier, The	HERBERT, FRANK
Sassinak	McCAFFREY, ANNE/ MOON, ELIZABETH
Satan's World	ANDERSON, POUL

Seventh Son	CARD, ORSON SCOTT
Sex Sphere, The	RUCKER, RUDY
Sexual Chemistry	STABLEFORD, BRIAN
Shadow of Heaven	SHAW, BOB
Shadow of the Hegemon	CARD, ORSON SCOTT
Shadow of the Torturer, The	WOLFE, GENE
Shadow's End	TEPPER, SHERI S.
Shadows With Eyes	LEIBER, FRITZ
Shadrach in the Furnace	SILVERBERG, ROBERT
Shape of Space, The	NIVEN, LARRY
Shape of Things to Come, The	WELLS, H. G.
Shards of Honor	BUJOLD, LOIS McMASTER
Shards of Space	SHECKLEY, ROBERT
Shatterday	ELLISON, HARLAN
Sheep Look Up, The	BRUNNER, JOHN
Sheepfarmer's Daughter, The	MOON, ELIZABETH
Shield	ANDERSON, POUL
Shift Key, The	BRUNNER, JOHN
Ship of Shadows	LEIBER, FRITZ
Ship of Strangers	SHAW, BOB
Ship Who Sang, The	McCAFFREY, ANNE
Ship Who Searched, The	McCAFFREY, ANNE
Ship Who Won, The	McCAFFREY, ANNE
Ships of Earth, The	CARD, ORSON SCOTT
Ships to the Stars	LEIBER, FRITZ
Shiva 3000	JENSEN, JAN LARS
Shiva Descending	BENFORD, GREGORY/
	Rotsler, William
Shock	MATHESON, RICHARD
Shock II	MATHESON, RICHARD
Shock III	MATHESON, RICHARD
Shock IV	MATHESON, RICHARD
Shock Waves	MATHESON, RICHARD
Shockwave Rider, The	BRUNNER, JOHN
Shores of Space, The	MATHESON, RICHARD
Short Victorious War, The	WEBER, DAVID
Short, Sharp Shock, A	ROBINSON, KIM STANLEY
Showboat World	VANCE, JACK
Shrine of Stars	McAULEY, PAUL J.
Shrinking Man, The	MATHESON, RICHARD

Strength of Stones	BEAR, GREG
Subspace Encounter	SMITH, E. E.
Subspace Explorers	SMITH, E. E.
Sudanna, Sudanna	HERBERT, BRIAN
Summer Before the Dark, The	LESSING, DORIS
Sundered Worlds, The	MOORCOCK, MICHAEL
Sundiver	BRIN, DAVID
Sunfall	CHERRYH, C. J.
Sunstroke	WATSON, IAN
Super Barbarians, The	BRUNNER, JOHN
Super-Cannes	BALLARD, J. G.
Supermind	VAN VOGT, A. E.
Surrender None	MOON, ELIZABETH
Survivor	BUTLER, OCTAVIA E.
Swan Song	STABLEFORD, BRIAN
Sword and the Stallion, The	MOORCOCK, MICHAEL
Sword of the Dawn	MOORCOCK, MICHAEL
Sword of the Lictor, The	WOLFE, GENE
Swords Against Death	LEIBER, FRITZ
Swords Against Wizardry	LEIBER, FRITZ
Swords and Deviltry	LEIBER, FRITZ
Swords and Ice Magic	LEIBER, FRITZ
Swords for the Legion	TURTLEDOVE, HARRY
Swords in the Mist	LEIBER, FRITZ
Swords of Lankhmar	LEIBER, FRITZ
Swords of Mars	BURROUGHS, EDGAR RICE
Synners	CADIGAN, PAT
Synthetic Men of Mars, The	BURROUGHS, EDGAR RICE
Syzygy	POHL, FREDERIK
Tailchaser's Song	WILLIAMS, TAD
Take Back Plenty	GREENLAND, COLIN
Talent for War, A	McDEVITT, JACK
Tales from Earthsea	LE GUIN, URSULA K.
Tales from Known Space	NIVEN, LARRY
Tales from the Texas Woods	MOORCOCK, MICHAEL
Tales from the White Hart	CLARKE, ARTHUR C.
Tales of Nevèrÿon	DELANY, SAMUEL R.
Tales of Pirx the Pilot	LEM, STANISLAW
Tales of Ten Worlds	CLARKE, ARTHUR C.
Tales of the Flying Mountains	ANDERSON, POUL

Tales of the Grotesque and Arabesque	POE, EDGAR ALLAN
Tales of Time and Space	WELLS H. G.
Tanar of Pellucidar	BURROUGHS, EDGAR RICE
Tangents	BEAR, GREG
Tango Charlie and Foxtrot Romeo	VARLEY, JOHN
Tarzan Alive	FARMER, PHILIP JOSÉ
Tarzan and the Ant Men	BURROUGHS, EDGAR RICE
Tarzan and the Castaways	BURROUGHS, EDGAR RICE
Tarzan and the City of Gold	BURROUGHS, EDGAR RICE
Tarzan and the Forbidden City	BURROUGHS, EDGAR RICE
Tarzan and the Foreign Legion	BURROUGHS, EDGAR RICE
Tarzan and the Golden Lion	BURROUGHS, EDGAR RICE
Tarzan and the Jewels of Opar	BURROUGHS, EDGAR RICE
Tarzan and the Leopard Man	BURROUGHS, EDGAR RICE
Tarzan and the Lion Man	BURROUGHS, EDGAR RICE
Tarzan and the Lost Empire	BURROUGHS, EDGAR RICE
Tarzan and the Madman	BURROUGHS, EDGAR RICE
Tarzan and the Tarzan Twins	BURROUGHS, EDGAR RICE
Tarzan and the Valley of Gold	LEIBER, FRITZ
Tarzan at the Earth's Core	BURROUGHS, EDGAR RICE
Tarzan, Lord of the Jungle	BURROUGHS, EDGAR RICE
Tarzan of the Apes	BURROUGHS, EDGAR RICE
Tarzan the Invincible	BURROUGHS, EDGAR RICE
Tarzan the Magnificent	BURROUGHS, EDGAR RICE
Tarzan the Terrible	BURROUGHS, EDGAR RICE
Tarzan the Untamed	BURROUGHS, EDGAR RICE
Tarzan Triumphant	BURROUGHS, EDGAR RICE
Tau Zero	ANDERSON, POUL
Tea from an Empty Cup	CADIGAN, PAT
Tech-Heaven	NAGATA, LINDA
Technicolor Time Machine, The	HARRISON, HARRY
Tehanu: The Last Book of Earthsea	LE GUIN, URSULA K.
Telepathist	BRUNNER, JOHN
Telling, The	LE GUIN, URSULA K.
Tender Loving Rage	BESTER, ALFRED
Tenth Victim, The	SHECKLEY, ROBERT
Terenesia	EGAN, GREG
Terminal Beach, The	BALLARD, J. G.
Terminal Man, The	CRICHTON, MICHAEL
Test of Fire	BOVA, BEN

That Hideous Strength	LEWIS, C. S.
Thebes of the Hundred Gates	SILVERBERG, ROBERT
There Are Doors	WOLFE, GENE
There Will Be Time	ANDERSON, POUL
Thessalonica	TURTLEDOVE, HARRY
They Fly at Ciron	DELANY, SAMUEL R.
They Shall Have Stars	BLISH, JAMES
ThigMOO	BYRNE, EUGENE
Things Unborn	BYRNE, EUGENE
Third Level, The	FINNEY, JACK
Thirteenth Immortal, The	SILVERBERG, ROBERT
This Day All Gods Die	DONALDSON, STEPHEN R.
This Immortal	ZELAZNY, ROGER
This Side of Judgement	DUNN, J. R.
Thorns	SILVERBERG, ROBERT
Those Who Watch	SILVERBERG, ROBERT
Thousand Cities, The	TURTLEDOVE, HARRY
Three Stigmata of Palmer Eldritch, The	DICK, PHILIP K.
Three Worlds to Conquer	ANDERSON, POUL
Threshold of Eternity	BRUNNER, JOHN
Throne Price	SINCLAIR, ALISON
Through the Eye of a Needle	CLEMENT, HAL
Throy	VANCE, JACK
Thunder and Roses	STURGEON, THEODORE
Thuvia, Maid of Mars	BURROUGHS, EDGAR RICE
THX 1138	BOVA, BEN
Tides of Light	BENFORD, GREGORY
Tides of Time, The	BRUNNER, JOHN
Time	BAXTER, STEPHEN
Time and Again	FINNEY, JACK
Time and Stars	ANDERSON, POUL
Time Dweller, The	MOORCOCK, MICHAEL
Time Enough for Love	HEINLEIN, ROBERT A.
Time in Eclipse	GARNETT, DAVID
Time Jump	BRUNNER, JOHN
Time Machine, The	WELLS, H. G.
Time Must Have a Stop	HUXLEY, ALDOUS
Time of Changes, A	SILVERBERG, ROBERT
Time of the Great Freeze	SILVERBERG, ROBERT

Vacuum Diagrams	BAXTER, STEPHEN
Valentine Pontifex	SILVERBERG, ROBERT
Valis	DICK, PHILIP K.
Vampire Junkies	SPINRAD, NORMAN
Vandals of the Void	VANCE, JACK
Vanguard from Alpha	ALDISS, BRIAN
Variable Man, The	DICK, PHILIP K.
Vast	NAGATA, LINDA
Vengeance of Orion	BOVA, BEN
Venus	BOVA, BEN
Venus Hunters, The	BALLARD, J. G.
Venus Plus X	STURGEON, THEODORE
Vermilion Sands	BALLARD, J. G.
Vertigo	SHAW, BOB
Very Slow Time Machine, The	WATSON, IAN
Victim Prime	SHECKLEY, ROBERT
Videssos Besieged	TURTLEDOVE, HARRY
View from the Stars, The	MILLER, WALTER
Viewpoint	BOVA, BEN
Villainy Victorious	HUBBARD, L. RON
Vindication, The	CHERRYH, C. J.
Violent Man, The	VAN VOGT, A. E.
Virgin Planet	ANDERSON, POUL
Viriconium	HARRISON, M. JOHN
Viriconium Nights	HARRISON, M. JOHN
Virtual Destruction	ANDERSON, KEVIN J.
Virtual Light	GIBSON, WILLIAM
Virtual Unrealities	BESTER, ALFRED
Visible Light	CHERRYH, C. J.
Visions and Venturers	STURGEON, THEODORE
Voices of Heaven, The	POHL, FREDERIK
Voices of Hope	FEINTUCH, DAVID
Voices of Time, The	BALLARD, J. G.
Void Captain's Tale, The	SPINRAD, NORMAN
Vor	BLISH, JAMES
Vor Game, The	BUJOLD, LOIS McMASTER
Vortex Blaster, The	SMITH, E. E.
Voyage	BAXTER, STEPHEN
Voyage of the Space Beagle, The	VAN VOGT, A. E.
Voyage of Vengeance	HUBBARD, L. RON

Voyage to the Bottom of the Sea	STURGEON, THEODORE
Voyager in Night	CHERRYH, C. J.
Voyagers	BOVA, BEN
Voyagers II: The Alien Within	BOVA, BEN
Voyagers III: Star Brothers	BOVA, BEN
Vulcan's Hammer	DICK, PHILIP K.
Vurt	NOON, JEFF
Waking the Moon	HAND, ELIZABETH
Waldo and Magic Inc.	HEINLEIN, ROBERT A.
Walkabout	BROWN, ERIC
Walking Shadow, The	STABLEFORD, BRIAN
Wall Around a Star	POHL, FREDERIK/
	Williamson, Jack
Wanderer, The	LEIBER, FRITZ
Wanderers of Time	WYNDHAM, JOHN
Wanting Seed, The	BURGESS, ANTHONY
War Against the Rull, The	VAN VOGT, A. E.
War Amongst the Angels, A	MOORCOCK, MICHAEL
War Fever	BALLARD, J. G.
War God's Own, The	WEBER, DAVID
War Hound and the World's Pain, The	MOORCOCK, MICHAEL
War in the Air, The	WELLS, H. G.
War of the Wing-Men	ANDERSON, POUL
War of the Worlds, The	WELLS, H. G.
War of Two Worlds	ANDERSON, POUL
War with the Robots	HARRISON, HARRY
War Year	HALDEMAN, JOE
Warlord of Mars, The	BURROUGHS, EDGAR RICE
Warlord of the Air, The	MOORCOCK, MICHAEL
Warren Peace	SHAW, BOB
Warrior Who Carried Life, The	RYMAN, GEOFF
Warrior's Apprentice, The	BUJOLD, LOIS McMASTER
Warriors of Day, The	BLISH, JAMES
Warriors of Mars	MOORCOCK, MICHAEL
Was	RYMAN, GEOFF
Washington's Dirigible	BARNES, JOHN
Watchbird	SHECKLEY, ROBERT
Watching Trees Grow	HAMILTON, PETER F.
Watchmen, The	BOVA, BEN

Appendix

Index

Index